PRAISE FOR RAFIK SCHAMI'S
The Dark Side of Love

"A masterpiece! A marvel of prose that mixes myths, tales, legends, and a wonderful love story..."

Die Zeit

"A superb novel... Rafik Schami is one of the best German-language storytellers..."

Brigitte magazine

"An Arab retelling of Romeo and Juliet with a happy ending... An immense declaration of love to Damascus..."

Neue Zürcher Zeitung

"A superb book—one of the richest, most fruitful, and most beautiful attempts to capture the world in recent years."

Deutschlandradio

"An opulent mosaic of stories..."

Die Welt

"Rafik Schami tells a wonderful story about forbidden love..."

Sächsische Zeitung

"Rafik Schami's novel is a festival for the imagination..."

Süddeutsche Zeitung

"This Arab version of Romeo and Juliet paints a unique picture of the historic and social panorama of Syria."

Deutschlandradio Kultur

The Dark Side of Love

Rafik Schami

Translated from the German by Anthea Bell

Interlink Books

An imprint of Interlink Publishing Group, Inc.
Northampton, Massachusetts

First American edition published in 2009 by

INTERLINK BOOKS
An imprint of Interlink Publishing Group, Inc.
46 Crosby Street, Northampton, MA 01060
www.interlinkbooks.com

First published in German in 2004 as
Die dunkle Seite der Liebe by Carl Hanser Verlag München

Library of Congress Cataloging-in-Publication Data

Schami, Rafik, 1946-
[Dunkle Seite der Liebe. English]
The dark side of love / by Rafik Schami ; translated from the German by
Anthea Bell. -- 1st American ed.
p. cm.
ISBN 978-1-56656-780-0 (pbk.)
1. Murder--Investigation--Fiction. 2. Vendetta--Fiction. 3.
Clans--Syria--Fiction. 4. Religion and politics--Syria--Fiction. 5.
Persecution--Syria--Fiction. 6. Damascus (Syria)--Fiction. 7. Political
fiction. I. Bell, Anthea. II. Title.
PT2680.A448D8613 2009
833'.914--dc22
                                    2008054192

Printed in Great Britain
by J. H. Haynes & Co. Ltd., Sparkford

To request our complete 40 page full color catalog,
please call us toll free at 1-800-238-LINK, visit our
website at www.interlinkbooks.com, or write to
Interlink Publishing
46 Crosby Street, Northampton, MA 01060
email: info@interlinkbooks.com

For two great women,
Hanne Joakim and Root Leeb

FAMILY TREE OF THE SHAHIN CLAN

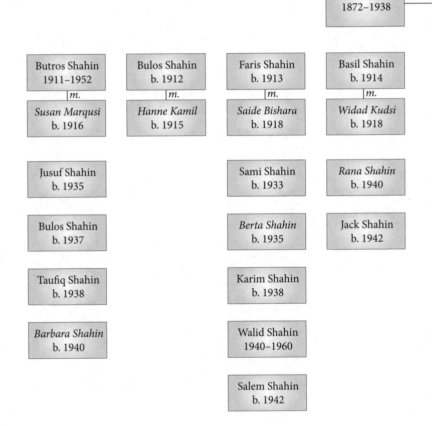

Jusuf Shahin
1872–1938   *m.*

Butros Shahin 1911–1952	Bulos Shahin b. 1912	Faris Shahin b. 1913	Basil Shahin b. 1914
m.	*m.*	*m.*	*m.*
Susan Marqusi b. 1916	*Hanne Kamil* b. 1915	*Saide Bishara* b. 1918	*Widad Kudsi* b. 1918

Jusuf Shahin b. 1935		Sami Shahin b. 1933	*Rana Shahin* b. 1940
Bulos Shahin b. 1937		*Berta Shahin* b. 1935	Jack Shahin b. 1942
Taufiq Shahin b. 1938		Karim Shahin b. 1938	
Barbara Shahin b. 1940		Walid Shahin 1940–1960	
		Salem Shahin b. 1942	

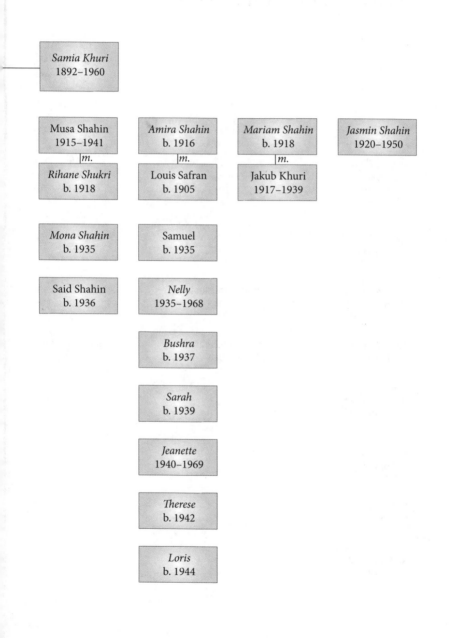

FAMILY TREE OF THE MUSHTAK CLAN

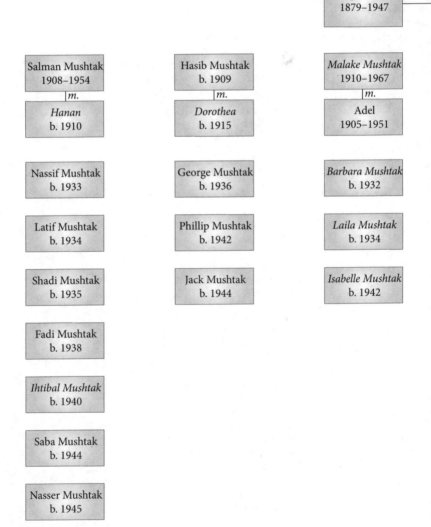

George Mushtak *m.*
1879–1947

Salman Mushtak	Hasib Mushtak	*Malake Mushtak*
1908–1954	b. 1909	1910–1967
m.	*m.*	*m.*
Hanan	*Dorothea*	Adel
b. 1910	b. 1915	1905–1951

| Nassif Mushtak | George Mushtak | *Barbara Mushtak* |
| b. 1933 | b. 1936 | b. 1932 |

| Latif Mushtak | Phillip Mushtak | *Laila Mushtak* |
| b. 1934 | b. 1942 | b. 1934 |

| Shadi Mushtak | Jack Mushtak | *Isabelle Mushtak* |
| b. 1935 | b. 1944 | b. 1942 |

Fadi Mushtak
b. 1938

Ihtibal Mushtak
b. 1940

Saba Mushtak
b. 1944

Nasser Mushtak
b. 1945

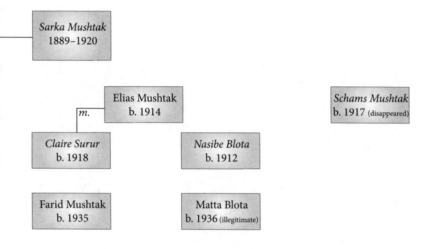

Sarka Mushtak
1889–1920

m. Elias Mushtak
b. 1914

Schams Mushtak
b. 1917 (disappeared)

Claire Surur
b. 1918

Nasibe Blota
b. 1912

Farid Mushtak
b. 1935

Matta Blota
b. 1936 (illegitimate)

BOOK OF LOVE I

Olive trees and answers both need time.

ঌ

1. The Question

"Do you really think our love stands any chance?"

Farid asked this question not to remind Rana of the blood feud between their families, but because he was feeling wretched and could see no hope.

Three days ago his friend Amin had been picked up as he left home and taken away by the secret police. Witch-hunts against communists had been in progress ever since the union of Syria and Egypt in the spring of 1958, and 1959 was a particularly bad year. President Satlan had made irate and inflammatory speeches denouncing communists and the Iraqi dictator Damian's regime. There was no let-up as the year drew to its close; jeeps raced down the streets of the capital even by night carrying victims of the secret service. Their families were left weeping with fear. Tales were told of the bloodshed on New Year's Eve. Rumours went from mouth to mouth, creating even more fear of the secret service, which seemed to have its informers in every home.

Love seemed to Farid a luxury that day. He had spent a few hours with Rana in his dead grandmother's house, undisturbed. Here in Damascus, every meeting with her was an oasis in the desert of his loneliness. Very different from those weeks in Beirut, where they had hidden eight years ago. There, every day began and ended in Rana's arms. There, love had been a wide and gentle river landscape.

His grandmother's house hadn't been sold yet. Claire, his mother, had given him the key that morning. "But your underpants had better stay on," she laughed.

The sun was shining, but it was a bitterly cold day. Musty damp met him as he entered the house. He opened the windows, letting fresh air in, and finally lit the stoves in the kitchen and bedroom. Farid hated nothing more than the smell of damp, cold stagnation.

When Rana arrived just before twelve, the stoves were already red-hot. "Was it at your grandmother's house we were going to meet, or in the hammam?" she joked.

As always, she was enchantingly beautiful, but he couldn't shake off a sense of impending danger. While he kissed her, he thought of the Indian who sought safety from a flood on a rooftop and slowly sank to a watery death. Farid clung to his lover like a drowning man. Her heart beat against his chest.

In spite of the heat he was freezing, and her laughter – the wild laughter that kept breaking out of her and leaping his way – released him from his fear only for seconds at a time.

"What a model of proper behaviour you are today," she teased him as they left the house again a few hours later. "Anyone might think my mother had told you to keep an eye on me. You didn't even take off your..." And she uttered a peal of laughter.

"It's nothing to do with your mother," he said, wanting to explain it all to her, but he couldn't find the right words. He walked along the narrow streets to Sufaniye Park near Bab Tuma beside her. Every jeep made him jump in alarm.

The President's words boomed out from café radios, declaring implacable war on the enemies of the Republic. Satlan had a fine, virile voice. He intoxicated the Arabs when he spoke. The radio was his box of magic tricks. With a population that was over eighty percent illiterate, the opposition had no chance. Whoever controlled the radio station had the people on his side.

And the people loved Satlan. Only a tiny, desperate opposition feared him, and after that pitiless wave of arrests a strange anxiety held the city in its grip. But the Damascenes will soon forget it all and go about their business again smiling, thought Farid as they reached the park.

His fear was a beast of prey gnawing at his peace of mind. He kept thinking of Amin the tiler, who must now be suffering torture. Amin wasn't just his friend. He was also the contact man between the communist youth group that Farid had been running for the last few months and the Party in Damascus. Only a few days ago he had assured Farid that he had gone to ground, cutting all the links leading to him. Amin was an experienced underground fighter.

A few weeks ago, Farid's mother had suddenly said over her morning coffee that the death of her parents, aunts, and uncles made her feel both sad and naked, for when the defensive wall of the older generation was gone, you came closer to the abyss yourself. Now he was naked too and looking down into the abyss. The ground beneath his feet was giving way. His friend Josef, a fervent supporter of Satlan, railed against the "agents of Moscow", as the President called communists. Farid was on the wrong side, said Josef, he was the only real human being among a bunch of totally heartless people, it was high time he left the Party. How could Josef say such things?

Rana was Farid's great good fortune. He loved her so much that he almost wished them to part so that she would be in no danger of persecution. He looked at her ear. He had to love her if only for that innocent ear.

Rana was silent for a long time. She seemed to be watching the children playing in the park, but in fact only one girl attracted her attention, a child staging a performance on her own, a little way from a group. Dancing, she twirled in a circle, then suddenly stopped and sank to the ground as if hit by a bullet. A few moments later she rose again and went on dancing, only to drop to the ground again quite soon.

It was a long time since Damascus had seen such weather: all the good work of the winter rains was undone by this springtime cold. Flowers and buds froze.

This was the first sunny day after a damp eternity. Pale and coughing, the inhabitants of the Old Town streamed out of their mud-brick houses, which weren't built for cold weather, and went to the parks and gardens outside the city walls. The adults held barbecues, drank tea, played cards, told stories, or smoked their water-pipes and stared quietly into space. Their children played noisily, boys with balls, girls with the hula hoops that had just arrived from America, instantly taking Damascus by storm. Hips swaying, the girls tried to keep the plastic hoops in motion around them. Most of them were still bad at it, but a few could already keep the hoops circling for minutes on end.

The girl dancing alone didn't seem to mind the cold. Her movements had a strange, summery composure. Rana looked at the child's neck and wondered, if a bullet really did hit the little girl, what sign her blood would paint in the air. When her aunt Jasmin died, the jet of blood on the wall had traced a number eight lying on its side, the symbol of infinity. That was ten years ago. Jasmin, Rana's father's youngest sister, had come back from Beirut, where she and her Muslim husband had been hiding from her family's wrath for a long time. But she was homesick for her native city of Damascus and her mother. A smile appeared on Rana's lips for a few fleeting seconds, only to vanish again instantly. It must be in the family, she thought, we all elope to Beirut when we're in love.

One summer day Aunt Jasmin had invited her to the famous Bakdash ice cream parlour in the Suq al Hamidiye. Sitting there, she had said in a perfectly matter-of-fact and cheerful tone, "Time out of mind, life in Arabia has moved between two sworn enemies, love and death, and I've decided in favour of love." But death did not accept her decision.

Jasmin's nephew Samuel shot her outside a cinema. Her companion fled, uninjured. Samuel didn't fire after him, but stood over his aunt as she bled, calling out to the passers by, almost shrieking it, "I've saved my Christian family's honour after my aunt dragged it through the dirt by marrying a Muslim." And many of the passers by applauded.

Samuel, Aunt Amira's spoilt son, had been sixteen at the time and still a minor. He was released after a year in custody, and his relations, their voices raised in song, carried him home on their shoulders in triumph to his parents' house, where more than a hundred guests celebrated his heroic deed until dawn. Rana's father Basil was alone in staying away from the festivities. They were too primitive for his liking, but even he could understand the shooting of his own sister. He thought she had brought shame on the family.

Only Samuel's grandmother, Samia, made it clear to the boy and his mother that she would curse him every day when she rose in the morning, and every night before she went to bed. Jasmin had been her favourite daughter, which was probably the reason behind the rumours that, never mind exactly who commissioned Samuel to kill his aunt, the act was fuelled by his mother's resentment. She had always felt slighted.

After that Rana never spoke to her cousin again. Whenever he came to see her brother Jack, she stayed in her own room. Nor did she ever set foot in her Aunt Amira's house. But she hung Aunt Jasmin's photograph in her little room, next to the picture of the Virgin Mary.

Rana was silent for a long time that cold March day, holding Farid's warm hands tight.

The little girl dropped to the ground once more, very elegantly this time, and lay there for a while before her hands began to flutter like a butterfly, showing that life had come back into her prostrate body.

In the distance, someone happily sang lines steeped in melancholy and despair: "I forced myself to part with you / So that I might forget you." They were from the Egyptian singer Umm Kulthum's latest song. Ahmad Rami, the shy, sensitive author of those verses, had written over three hundred songs for Umm Kulthum in his fifty years of unrequited love for her.

"I need time," said Rana, "to find an answer to that question."

BOOK OF DEATH I

Questions are the children of freedom.

ჯი

2. A Body in the Basket

A warm wind swept down Ibn Assaker Street from the south. Day had not yet shed her grey mask. Behind the walls of the Old Town, Damascus woke from sleep as unwillingly as a much-indulged girl.

The first buses and vans were clattering noisily as they drove down the long street, taking labourers from the surrounding villages to the many building sites in the new quarter of the city. One of the construction workers, a short little man, was walking up and down beside the road, going a few steps from Bab Kisan, near the doors of the Bulos Chapel, towards the eastern gate and back again. He was waiting for his bus. Like all labourers from the country around Damascus, he carried a bundle of provisions wrapped in faded blue cloth in his left hand. With his right hand, he was gesticulating vigorously as if engaged in earnest conversation with some invisible partner. The loop he traced as he walked grew longer and longer, as if he were willing the bus to appear when he next turned around.

Just as the sun began shedding golden light on the top of the old city wall, he turned once more. As he did so, he looked briefly southward. His glance fell on the large basket hanging over the entrance to the Bulos Chapel, where according to legend Bulos himself, the

6

sainted founder of the Church, had escaped from his pursuers over the wall in a basket after his revelation on the Damascus road.

A hand that might have been a drowning man's hung out of the basket, which was still in the shadows. The construction worker immediately knew that the man attached to the hand must be dead. Suddenly he was indifferent to all else: the bus, the tiles he had to carry up three sets of steps on his back, even his quarrel with his skinflint of a boss.

"There's a body in the basket!" he shouted excitedly, and when a policeman finally came along, cycling sleepily towards the police station by the eastern gate, he accosted him so vigorously that the stout officer only just managed to keep his balance. An expression of alarm came over the policeman's face as the little man shook his handlebars like one demented, shouting over and over again, "A body! A body!"

"What do you mean, a body? Are you crazy? Let go of my bike!" In his thirty years of service he had seen dead bodies everywhere: in bed, in the canal, even hanging in toilets, but never in a basket on top of the city wall. "Calm down!" he tried telling the man. "That's not a body. The Christians are celebrating the memory of their apostle Bulos. He escaped over the wall right here, that's all there is to it." And he glanced once more at the basket, which had been hanging over the gateway for weeks.

But instead of boarding the bus when it finally arrived, the construction worker went on shouting excitedly. He clung to the policeman's bicycle. "And I'm telling you there's a body in that basket," he bellowed hoarsely.

The bus driver, his curiosity aroused, switched off the engine and climbed out of his vehicle. Several passengers followed him. They all surrounded the policeman, backing up their colleague and his suspicions.

At last the police officer gave in and promised to notify the Criminal Investigation Department, but he also insisted on naming as a witness the man who had ruined his morning. He wrote down the construction worker's details, and told him to be ready to make himself available at any time. Then he cycled off again. The bus driver continued his journey north.

3. Police Commissioner Barudi

The CID specialists found a man with a broken neck in the basket. A folded piece of greyish paper was stuck into the breast pocket of his pyjama jacket. It said: *Bulos betrayed our secret society.*

Young Commissioner Barudi looked at this note. The writing was a scrawl, but legible if you made an effort. The paper had been torn from a large sheet of the kind used in the Old Town's many souvenir shops to wrap glass vases or expensive, delicately inlaid wooden boxes. The writer had tried to neaten up the torn edges.

Around ten o'clock a policeman drove the old and visibly alarmed janitor of the Bulos Chapel to the gateway. The basket hadn't been his idea, the man explained, it was young Father Michael who had thought of it, keen as he was to remind passers by how the founder of the Church had fled. He added, despairingly, that every day for the last two weeks he himself had had to clear away the rubbish that young people threw into it: bottles, dead rats and cats.

The corpse, a man in his late thirties, was wearing pale blue pyjamas. The medical examiners established that death had occurred around midnight, and the body's hair and clothing contained large numbers of fibres from a jute sack, in which it had probably been transported to the place where it was found.

Three days later the corpse was identified, thus raising the next question: the man was Major Mahdi Said, so who was the Bulos mentioned in the note?

Commissioner Barudi conducted an initial interview with the man's beautiful young widow. She was composed, cool, and monosyllabic. Either she really knew nothing about her husband, or she knew too much. Asked if she hadn't noticed his absence, she responded with chilly irony. "It was normal for him to be away for days or weeks on end. His profession was his mistress. I was only his wife."

The commissioner felt sure that the dead man's wife had constructed a defensive wall of cold indifference to conceal either pain or burning hatred. He found her erotically arousing, and would have liked to catch a glimpse of whatever lay behind her façade. After all, he was a bachelor, and lonely.

He told his scene-of-crime team to search the attic storey above the apartment, where the major had been murdered in his bed. He must have struggled with his killer or killers, but it seemed that the widow had heard nothing because she slept one floor lower down, and at the other end of the apartment. Her husband sometimes used to make a lot of noise right into the small hours in the attic above the marital bedroom, playing music, telephoning, pushing his chair back and forth. This had been a trial to her for a long time, because the slightest little noise woke her, so about a year earlier she had been forced to exchange the brightly lit bedroom with its balcony for a dark but quiet one at the back of the apartment.

Her husband's attic had its own entrance. A small flight of steps led from the big second-floor balcony to the top storey under the roof. Here the major's domain consisted of two sparsely furnished rooms and a modest bathroom. He slept in one of the rooms and used the other, smaller room as an office, with a desk and a metal filing cabinet in it.

"The murderer must have come up from the street," said First Lieutenant Ismail, leading the scene-of-crime team, when the commissioner asked for his first impressions. Barudi and Ismail got on well. They were both new to Damascus, and quite often went out late in the evening to eat together.

They were standing on the balcony in front of the steps leading up to the attic. "We found obvious marks left on the old ivy. The murderer climbed up it to the balcony, then just went upstairs to the top floor," explained Ismail, his right hand pointing. "And then," he continued, leaning on the balustrade, "he must have taken the body through the balcony room and out of the front door of the apartment. We found fibres from the sack on the sharp metal edge of the safety lock. He went down the main staircase and into the street."

"Why do you say *he*? Are you sure it was a man? And are you certain he was acting on his own?" asked Barudi, his eyes tracing the way from the street back up to the balcony.

"That broken neck is clearly a man's work, no woman did it, but of course there could have been several men," replied Ismail.

"So why not a man and a woman?"

The expert smiled. "That may sound likely, but if the murderer had the wife helping him, he was a fool. Far too risky to climb the ivy into the apartment if you can just walk through the front door unnoticed." He paused briefly. "No, I have a feeling that the murderer didn't care about anything, even being arrested himself, so long as he killed the major. There's a whiff of bitter vengeance about this, not cold-blooded murder by the wife's lover."

"And suppose the whole thing was planned well in advance? It seems our man had a sensitive position in the secret service. I don't know details yet, but he was a major, after all, and such men live dangerously," said Barudi.

"We can't rule that out. The climb itself wouldn't take a real pro more than two or three minutes," replied Ismail, going thoughtfully up the steps to the top floor, just as the widow came to tell the commissioner that his adjutant Mansur wanted him on the phone.

It was after eleven by the time he left the widow's apartment. He couldn't help thinking of her. "Major Mahdi, my husband, had many enemies," she had said straight out, only quarter of an hour into the interview. And Barudi had the impression that she herself didn't much like her husband either. She didn't even bother to pretend she did. Instead, she always called him Major Mahdi, like a stranger, and then, quietly and almost as if ashamed of it, added the explanatory "my husband."

What was the woman's secret? How dead inside must a man be, the commissioner kept wondering, to sleep alone in a rundown attic instead of in the soft arms of this beauty? He could find no answer.

A ravenous hunger for bread was gripping his guts. The widow had served him coffee and sweetmeats five times. He drove his beat-up Ford to Iskander's delicatessen shop in Straight Street, near Abbara Alley and, as usual, ordered a flatbread filled with thinly sliced pasturma. Iskander knew this delicious air-dried beef with its piquant crust of sharp spices was his favourite food, but nonetheless, every day he asked politely, "The usual?" And as usual the commissioner had a flatbread sandwich and a glass of cold water. Together they cost a lira, and while the commissioner ate his sandwich Iskander quickly made two coffees, hoping to hear some tale or other about the depravity of human nature. His wish was quite often granted. Commissioner

Barudi liked talking to the little man, although on condition that he never asked for names.

Today the commissioner said, "No coffee, thank you. I've drunk five already and I feel quite dizzy."

The man could tell that the commissioner didn't plan to tell him anything, so he kept quiet and hoped the net of his silence would soon catch a bigger fish.

Omar the ironer had stepped out of his little shop opposite Iskander's for a moment, to get a breath of fresh air. On seeing him, Barudi remembered that he wanted to bring the ironer his own laundry. What a terrible job Omar's was! He seemed to be nothing but skin and bone. His shop was small and stuffy, and he stood at his ironing board all day, emaciated and sweating, pressing other people's laundry with his hot, heavy iron. And all for a few paltry piastres.

Commissioner Barudi paid, finished drinking his water, and hurried back to his small apartment. On days like this he despaired. He felt he was doing everything wrong. Moving to the capital without a wife had been a mistake, and he blamed himself for it every morning. There was no one here to look after him. He even had to do his own laundry, and now he must take it to the ironer instead of sitting in the office thinking about this murder case. Every morning he made his own coffee and drank it alone in the kitchen, with a view of an ancient, yellowed calendar on the wall. What was he to do? Nadia had chosen the village schoolteacher instead. "He won't rise far, but he won't fall far either," she had said, when Barudi threw his future as a high-ranking police officer into the balance against the poor elementary schoolteacher's expectations. But the prospect of the good life hadn't weighed with her. Barudi could offer no more. The teacher was a handsome man with a captivating voice.

At this point in his morning lamentations he always looked at his face in an old mirror hanging on the wall above the table. It was half blank where the silvering had flaked away. He had never admired his own looks. His Creator, he thought every day, must have been drunk or short-sighted, and he smiled.

He had spent four years with the Criminal Investigation Department in the big northern city of Aleppo. His boss had liked him, and

11

when the job with the homicide squad in Damascus fell vacant he pulled strings. Barudi had been in the post for a year now. He found his task in the capital demanding, sometimes too demanding for a young commissioner. However, he tried hard to learn, and he was industrious. His working day was twelve hours, sometimes fourteen, but he didn't complain. In general he was glad to be at police head-quarters doing something. The mountains of files familiarized him with a city that still puzzled him, a farmer's son from the south. The one fly in the ointment at work was his boss, Colonel Kuga, a vain, chilly diplomat. "Things are different in the capital," his kindly boss in Aleppo had told him when he left, "but you're a hard worker, you'll soon show them."

Barudi felt as if Kuga ignored his achievements on purpose, so he was hoping for a difficult case to come his way at long last. Then he might be able to shine by solving it.

The front door of the building was left unlocked, as usual. In the Christian quarter of Damascus, people lived as serenely as if their alleys still had gates that were locked at night in the fashion of the last century. From a modern criminologist's viewpoint, leaving the door of a building unlocked was pure carelessness.

He was his old landlady's only tenant. Two small rooms and a kitchen on the first floor, not a bad place. However, he had to share the toilet and bathroom with her. He knew he could live a bachelor life here, and out of the kindness of her heart the old widow cleaned his apartment for him. She regarded him as a good, well-brought-up boy from a Christian village, who never had visitors, paid his rent in advance, and neither smoked nor drank. He wasn't interested in women, and no woman seemed to be interested in him. He was short, wore thick glasses, and had gone prematurely grey, all three of them factors likely to put off the girls of Damascus.

His landlady had only one fault to find with him. Like her, he had been baptized a Catholic, but he never showed his face in church. When she reproved him, he had replied that he didn't commit any sins. And then he had laughed, adding that he had no spare time for sinning.

Today he gave her a hasty greeting. She looked up briefly from the old dress she was mending. Soon he was on his way out of the apartment again with his laundered shirts and trousers stuffed into a big bag.

"But you've only this moment come home," said the widow.

"I just dropped in for my laundry. There's a lot going on right now. You'll have heard about the murder in the Bulos Chapel," he replied, secure in the knowledge that nothing, absolutely nothing that happened within a radius of two kilometres escaped the old lady. Her house in Ananias Alley wasn't far from the entrance to the Bulos Chapel.

"People don't fear God at all these days. A murder in church! Whoever would think of doing such a thing?"

"I only wish I knew," sighed the commissioner.

4. In the Jungle

As Commissioner Barudi sat down at his desk, he remembered the note found on the body. He took it out of its folder, examined the words, absorbed them, closed his eyes and repeated them. Then he said, quietly, "It's as if the murderer wanted to leave a clue." He recollected a case discussed as part of the syllabus while he was studying at police academy: a murderer who kept returning to the scene of the crime and even offered to help the police. They kicked him out because he was hampering their investigations. Until one clever commissioner took notice. He accepted the man's offer of assistance, and very soon the murderer had his statements all tangled up and gave himself away. He wasn't even upset when he was arrested, he was finished with life, all he wanted was peace.

Barudi's friend First Lieutenant Ismail had said jokingly, as they parted, "*Cherchez la femme*." Absently, the commissioner sniffed the paper. The smell was faint, but reminded him slightly of furniture polish. Or was it perfume after all?

'This piece of paper could well put us on the right track,' he said to himself, but loud enough for it to seem as if he wanted to communicate his confidence to Adjutant Mansur.

However, Mansur rolled his eyes. "There's something weird about the case. A Muslim, and what's more a Muslim major in state security or whatever it is, hanging in a basket over the Bulos Chapel with a note giving a false name in his pocket? My nose tells me it stinks to high heaven. Don't get too excited. Hang around a while, or you could burn your fingers on this case."

After a year of Mansur, Barudi was sick and tired of his adjutant's scepticism and caution. He was just waiting for a good moment to remove the old nuisance from his office and appoint a young policeman with a more optimistic cast of mind. Mansur didn't merely irritate Barudi, he turned his stomach. His heart was as rotten as his teeth. The man was obsessed with the notion of destroying all the mice in the world. On Commissioner Barudi's very first day at work, Mansur had told him all his mouse-catching theories, and showed him the infernal devices he himself had developed over the years and set every evening. Barudi had to be careful not to trip over one of those cruel traps himself.

He felt he was in a madhouse. Everyone else seemed keen on Mansur's machines. Even the boss Colonel Kuga, from whom the recent solving of an almost perfect murder by a prosperous widow hadn't drawn so much as a weary smile, whinnied with delight when he saw the executed mice.

Commissioner Barudi had already tried all sorts of ways of getting rid of Mansur. But the old wretch had over thirty years of service behind him, and knew all the tricks of the trade. He never laid himself open to attack, for he carried out every task stolidly but strictly to rule.

At five in the afternoon – eight hours after the corpse had been identified – the commissioner was facing Colonel Badran. Badran, President Amran's youngest brother and head of security, cancelled Barudi's authority to continue investigating the case of Major Mahdi Said. It was a political murder, he said, and as such not within the remit of the CID. He spoke quietly and unemotionally, as if discussing no more than a sip of water. Major Mahdi Said, he added, had been his best man, and he was going to track down and eliminate the murderer. Colonel Kuga kept nodding like a wound-up clockwork doll. Barudi was surprised not just by the security chief's rigour and his vanity but also by his high rank, for he had learned to be wary of all who were too young for their rank in the services. They usually belonged to the inner circle of power, men who had carried out a coup or the sons of such men, the kind ready to stake everything on a single throw of the dice, and at the age of thirty they ended either on the gallows or in top government posts. In the last five years alone there had been eleven uprisings, four successful and seven failures, there had been coups, men who rose to power and men who fell from power, there had been victors, and young officers executed in a hurry.

But the hierarchy of the authorities forced the young commissioner to keep his mouth shut. The secret service was at the very top of the pyramid of power, just below the President, and many even whispered in private that the President himself ruled only by permission of the secret service. The CID occupied a very lowly position in the hierarchy. It was authorized to deal with criminals so long as they didn't belong to the upper crust of society, or the military caste, or the ruling Ba'ath Party.

"Only night watchmen have less power," said Mansur the cynic.

Barudi was forced not just to call his men off, but to assure the colonel meekly that so far as he was concerned the dead man no longer existed. And within twenty-four hours Barudi was told to bring Colonel Badran, head of the secret service, all the results of his investigations *in person*. There was no mistaking the threat contained in that emphasis.

5. Mansur

"Knowledge," stated Adjutant Mansur, "is a lock, and the key to it is a question, but we're not allowed to ask questions in this country. And that, my dear Barudi," he added portentously, "is why there isn't a single good crime novel in Syria. Crime novels feed on questions." And he grinned. "Remember the anti-corruption campaign announced by President Amran in spring 1969? He set up a committee of eminent scholars and judges to ask everyone the standard question, 'Where did you get that?' Still laughing, the President told the committee right there, in front of the TV cameras, 'And gentlemen, do by all means start with me.' But the committee decided to start with the most corrupt Syrian of all time: the President's brother Shaftan. They sought him out and politely asked him their question. 'Where did you get that?' Shaftan was the second most important man in the state, commander of the dreaded special task force units. He immediately threw all the committee members into jail and kept them there until they publicly stated: 'Allah gives boundless wealth to those he loves.' Only then were the men set free."

The commissioner had indeed heard of the President's corrupt brother, but he didn't see what this had to do with the present murder case. He glared angrily at his subordinate.

"One more word and you'll be up in court for slandering the President. And in future I'm not your dear Barudi, I'm First Lieutenant Barudi. Do you have that straight, Adjutant Mansur?'

The adjutant nodded in silence. He knew these young fellows only too well. A few months at police academy and they strutted like generals. He would have liked to tell this greenhorn that his information about the local lack of crime novels and the questions that were never asked came from no less than Agatha Christie, whom he had once accompanied through Syria. Her archaeologist husband Max Mallowan had been travelling in the northeast of the country during the early 1940s, carrying out excavations.

At the time Mansur was almost dying of starvation. Drought and a plague of mice such as had never been seen before had destroyed all his village's stocks of provisions. Agatha Christie took a fancy to the lad, and in spite of her husband's dislike of him employed him. Later he became their head boy, and Agatha Christie called him "our Number One boy" in her memoir *Come Tell Me How You Live*. He looked after them, he fixed their accommodation and catering. She was a refreshing character, fourteen years older than her husband, but with a much better sense of humour, she'd laugh at everyone, most of all herself. Mansur often had to translate her comical remarks. "My dear," she had told his sister Nahla, when Nahla invited the English couple to a meal, "I advise you to marry an archaeologist. Then the older you get, the more interesting he'll think you."

Shortly before the couple left, Mansur had found a post in the police force, which was just being built up at the time. When the Mallowans said goodbye he was already in uniform.

That had been thirty-one years ago.

For safety's sake, however, Mansur said no more about his knowledge of crime fiction, which had been his second passion in life since his encounter with Agatha Christie. Here, in this very room, he had worked for sixteen officers who passed by leaving no more trace than summer clouds, and in the process he had learned when to keep his mouth shut. He still had three years to go before he drew his pension, and getting transferred to some lousy village in the south would be a catastrophe. That fate was the usual penalty for quarrelling with a senior officer.

For the first time in years he suddenly felt afraid. When he cracked a joke, no superior had ever before threatened to inflate it into an insult to the President. That could easily earn him a prison sentence, might even cost him his pension. From the start, however, he had thought this first lieutenant too ambitious, and thus dangerous.

6. Colonel Badran and the Course of Events

As Colonel Badran saw it, the case was clear. The murder of Major Mahdi Said had a political background. He thought the note was proof that the major had to die because he knew too much about some conspiracy, the work of a secret society whose members either feared betrayal, or had already condemned Mahdi as a traitor. The colonel assumed that the name Bulos on the note was a cover name. Probably because the major used to be a Christian and had lived in the Christian quarter until his death. Badran knew that the murdered man's original name was Said Bustani, but as he had been so badly treated by his stepfather as a child he didn't want to be known by the same surname in his new life as a Muslim. Consequently, when he converted to Islam, he had called himself Mahdi Said, *the happy follower of the right way.*

As the dead major's immediate superior, Badran's first reaction on hearing of his best officer's violent death was horror. Mahdi Said had been ambitious, reliable, and tough as steel. He had been the only friend on whom Badran could count in a fix.

When the horror died down, a suspicion surfaced that made the colonel uneasy. Suppose the ambitious Mahdi Said had betrayed *him*, making contact with plotters behind his back? The idea kept Badran awake at night. He was so obsessed by it that two days later he dispatched a whole troop of his best men to collect all the information they could about Mahdi Said. He himself led the small special unit that examined the dead man's home in microscopic detail.

Day after day he sat in the young widow's drawing room, let her serve him lemonade, coffee, and sweetmeats, and turned on the charm, trying get past the veil of indifference surrounding the woman by dint of clever questions. His men took the attic storey apart, searching the major's little upstairs apartment inch by inch.

Soon Colonel Badran's suspicions seemed to be confirmed: an inconspicuous little notebook in the dead man's safe contained names in code. They were deciphered by methods taught to the Syrian secret service on certain courses given by East German and Russian officers. The six people whose names were decoded were in the highest ranks of the army and the secret service. Mahdi had entered himself under the name of Bulos. Badran was triumphant: his presentiment had been correct.

After interrogation and torture, one general confessed that he and five other officers had founded a "Secret Society of Free Officers" to fight for the Fatherland.

"You mean you were planning a coup, you bastard!" the colonel shouted at the general, who whispered despondently and in terror, "Anything you say, my lord."

Knowing he faced execution, the general pinned his tiny remaining scrap of hope on that obsolete honorific. Perhaps the colonel would feel royally flattered, perhaps he would magnanimously overlook the torture victim's little lapse, which hadn't affected the state adversely in any way at all.

However, the only effect his servile "my lord" had on Badran, whose rank was far lower than the general's, was to convince him that the man was a slimy hypocrite.

They had contacted Mahdi Said a year ago, the general continued in a low voice, because he himself and the other officers thought there were too many Russians and too many German communists around in their proud land of Syria. They'd wanted to save the Fatherland, and what they admired about Mahdi Said was his implacable hatred for communism as well as his brains and his tough stance. At first the major had not disliked the idea of saving the country, but three months ago he had suddenly backed out, and would have no more to do with the officers and their secret society.

"And for that you broke his neck!" said the colonel rather more calmly, almost quietly, because now he knew he was on the right track. At the same time he felt a malicious satisfaction when he thought of the dead man. For at this same moment Badran realized that Major Mahdi Said had indeed been a traitor. He should never have kept such a conspiracy secret from the colonel. He could have been sure of a decoration for revealing it, a golden order, whereas now his reward was a broken neck. The colonel smiled at this reflection, and thought of the widow's soft knees. Like all modern women, she was wearing miniskirts that year.

The general began weeping pitifully. Never in their lives, he pleaded, had they dreamed of hurting so much as a hair of the major's head, for he and the others had soon realized that the whole idea of the coup was absurd, and the new government under the brothers Amran and Badran was as patriotic as it could possibly be. At the very latest when he, Colonel Badran, had sent the Russians and East Germans packing, they had all agreed that when Mahdi Said backed out he had opened their eyes and liberated them from the clutches of the devil. As a result...

The colonel rose to his feet and left. He paid no attention either to this eulogy or to anything else the general went on to say. Outside, he gave the man on duty orders to torture the high-ranking officers until they all confessed to Mahdi's murder and signed their confessions.

"And how far may I go?" asked the man on duty, holding the car door open for his master.

"As far as death," replied the colonel, and he got into his limousine and drove away to visit Major Said's widow.

A week later the six high-ranking officers went on trial. They were found guilty of planning a coup against the government and murdering, with malice aforethought, a former fellow conspirator whose remorse and love for the Fatherland had caused him to withdraw his support for them. The trial was held in secret in an empty barracks in Damascus. The condemned men were shot the same day.

Badran made this conspiracy an excuse to purge and reorganize the secret service. A wave of arrests rolled over the entire network, and men who had been powerful only a day before suddenly found themselves interned with their enemies in dreary prison camps. All secret service contacts were closely checked. From now on, absolute obedience was required throughout the whole system.

Under Colonel Badran, the East German and Russian advisers on military matters, torture, and the running of a secret service also had to accept drastic cuts in their authority. He expressly banned the arrogant tone that these experts had allowed themselves in their dealings with Syrian officers since the devastating defeat of the Arabs in the Six Days' War with Israel. The Russians had treated Syrian army officers like stupid schoolboys.

The colonel also forbade them to intervene directly in the affairs of the army and the secret service. His declared aim was to preserve state secrets. His arguments were logical, and convinced the political leadership. The experts, Badran argued, had come to Damascus to answer questions about technical matters, not to ask questions of their own, and definitely not to express political opinions. It wasn't easy to keep a close eye on their informal, politically wide-ranging involvement, so there was a danger of information trickling through to Israel at some point. The colonel was standing in front of a blackboard in a small room as he made these points. Three men sat around a table listening to him: his eldest brother President Amran; his cousin General

Sadan, the Minister of Information; and Sadan's son-in-law Colonel Hardan, the Interior Minister. Soon after he had spoken to them, the three most powerful men in the country gave Badran the go-ahead for any measures he thought necessary.

The Russian experts, who had patronized him as a man over-eager for advancement when, in a memo of the previous year, he had politely asked them to adopt a friendly tone with Syrian army officers, now had to stand by and see one of their generals taken by night from his villa in the upper-class quarter of Abu Rummanah and humiliatingly flown home to Moscow in his pyjamas, because an hour earlier, while drunk, he had insulted a young Syrian officer. And once the Russians knuckled under, the East German, Bulgarian, and Romanian experts crawled to the resolute colonel too. He himself reacted to these concessions not with satisfaction but with even greater suspicion. That day, however, the officers of the Syrian army and secret service had found a hero who restored to them the honour they had lost in the war against Israel.

In the Christian quarter, on the other hand, it was whispered in private that the widow and Colonel Badran themselves were behind the murder. The rumour was that one day Mahdi Said had discovered the relationship between his wife and his superior officer. In revulsion, said the neighbours, he had separated from his wife, preferring to sleep alone in the attic storey. He had not raged and ranted, nor had he beaten his wife, as most men would, but in secret he had plotted to murder Badran. Only then would he revenge himself on her. In the process, however, he had made a fatal mistake. His wife, according to this version of events, had found a note in the waste bin listing all the stages of his plan in detail and even giving the date. She alerted her lover, whereupon the colonel had hidden with her. That night the two of them had gone up to the attic, and together they strangled her husband in his bed. A neighbour, the goldsmith Butros Asmi, claimed to have seen a short, sturdy figure with a sack over his shoulders going downstairs. He couldn't identify the man, he said, because it had been dark, but after all, Badran himself was short and of athletic and muscular build.

As evidence for this macabre theory the neighbours adduced the

fact that, only a week after the major's death, Colonel Badran was brazenly spending nights with the widow. His bodyguard stood outside
the building, searching everyone who went in or out of the place,
which had a number of tenants.

However, when the sole witness, that same goldsmith Butros Asmi,
died in a strange accident, the building where the murdered major
had lived in Marcel Karameh Street, in the middle of the Christian
quarter, suddenly became a desert island cut off from the rest of the
world by an ocean of fear.

The case of Mahdi Said's murder was officially closed on 19 March
1970, and the three fat files containing the records of the investigation,
the evidence, and the witness statements, as well as the indictment of
the high-ranking officers and the court's verdict on them, found their
way into the secret service archives. The little note with the handwritten scrawl lay neglected inside transparent film in the first file.

Commissioner Barudi learned about the murdered major's Christian past from his contacts. Now he was sure that the name Bulos and
the note were the compass he must use to give him his bearings as he
followed the trail leading to the murderer. Before handing over his
own thin file on the case to the colonel, he had photocopied all the
results of his investigations, and cut a strip about twenty centimetres
long and a finger's breadth wide from the note found with the body.
He stored all these things carefully away in a secret compartment that
he built into his desk one night.

Barudi believed that the murder victim's childhood would lead
him to the murderer. He felt certain of solving the case if he set about
it carefully.

And he did set about it carefully. The trail he was following would
finally prove to be the right one, but he had no idea where his curiosity would lead him just six months later.

BOOK OF LOVE II

Love is poverty that makes you rich.

૩ઙ

DAMASCUS, MALA, SPRING 1953

7. The Fire

Claire woke him. There was alarm in her voice. When Farid sat up in bed he heard screams in the village. He ran out on the balcony, with his mother following him barefoot in her nightdress.

He guessed at once that his father was already among the crowd by the village well, and he knew inside him why. Astonished, he looked at the burning elm tree on the distant hill.

The icy wind made him shiver, and only slowly did he realize that he himself was responsible for the fire. Its distant flames shone like a mighty torch, bathing the village in an infernal light.

Some of the peasants hurried across the village square and past the Mushtak house. One young man stopped opposite the balcony and stood there for a moment staring up at him, then shook his head angrily, spat on the ground, and hurried on. The inhabitants of Mala were well known for their gloomy reticence. Farid knew the spitting was meant for him.

His mother's cold hand made him jump. All her life Claire was a chilly mortal, just like his girlfriend Rana. He led his mother back to bed and lay down beside her. She fell asleep at once, and soon he heard her rhythmic breathing. Her features were finely drawn: she

23

had smooth black hair, a delicate little nose, almond-shaped eyes under those closed lids, and skin as white as snow. Farid stroked his mother's face.

He lay awake, looking up at the ceiling.

8. Strangers

The Mushtaks were a powerful clan, but they were still strangers in Mala. George, the founder of the family, had taken refuge in this Christian mountain village forty-five years ago. Farid and his many cousins were only the third generation. You didn't really belong in the village until the seventh generation. That was the time it was supposed to take before you could speak the village dialect without any accent, and feel the characteristic pride deeply embedded in the hearts of even the poorest of the poor in Mala.

Farid had grown up in Damascus, and since his mother was a Damascene he had always spoken Arabic rather than the harsh dialect of Mala, which he understood without any difficulty but could never speak faultlessly. Nor was he for a moment proud of the village. Why would he be proud? Just because the ancestors of its modern inhabitants were said to have known Jesus in person, having fled from Galilee after his crucifixion? After that, as if obsessed by a secret mission, the peasants of Mala had defended their religion with their lives. You might have thought the fate of world Christianity depended on this one little village's readiness to fight for it.

Farid felt something of a stranger in the village church. And the gruff, silent villagers were strange to him too; they seemed to be in perpetual mourning in their black peasant garments, they smiled only rarely, but could always find an excuse for drinking and brawling. Even less did he understand the fanatical mutual hatred of the Mushtaks and Shahins, the two most powerful families in the village. And least of all could he see why deep-rooted hostility existed between the Orthodox Church and the Catholic Church in Mala. It was not uncommon for Muslims to mediate between quarrelling Christians.

One incident in particular had shaken Farid badly. A retired teacher and ten or twelve young people had renovated a dilapidated but attractive stable, put in new windows, doors and bookshelves, and wired it for electric light. The stable belonged to the Orthodox convent of St. Thecla, and the abbess had let the man have it free. The teacher, who had no children of his own, was a great booklover. He installed a village library in the renovated stable, donated all of his own seven thousand volumes as its basic stock, and then, over a period of months, went begging more from publishers and booksellers in Damascus. He finally came back with a truckload of books. By the time the library opened in the summer of 1950, he had accumulated twenty thousand volumes.

But the library was closed down again a month later, for the teacher had forgotten two things. He was related by marriage to the Shahin family, and in addition he was Orthodox. The Mushtaks and their Catholic supporters moved quickly. The teacher had been a communist in his youth, they claimed, he used to give the children candy and whisper that it came from Uncle Stalin. It was also said that he would take pretty children on his lap and indecently assault them.

None of this was true except that the teacher really had been a member of the Communist Party for three years. The rest of the claims were all malicious lies, but they spread like wildfire, because they had half the village behind them. After a short talk with Lieutenant Marwan, the new police chief, the abbess dropped her support for the teacher. The Mushtaks, and many other Catholics with them, celebrated the closing of the library with dancing, music, and wine.

The last remnants of any sympathy for the dusty village died in Farid that day.

Embittered, the old teacher withdrew to his little house, to come out of it again for the first and last time six years later – in a coffin. No one but his wife followed it, by her husband's express wish. He did not want either friends or relations at his funeral.

˜

Farid's family didn't visit Mala only in summer, to escape the sultry air of the capital city of Damascus so that they could sleep at night in the mountains; year after year they also came for a whole week at Easter to commemorate the founder of the family. Friends and relations prayed with them for the soul of that first Mushtak, not just in church on Easter Sunday but for all the seven days of Easter, hoping that in God's bosom he would find the peace he had never known in life. Most important of all, however, the guests, friends and strangers alike, were royally entertained for an entire week. Life in the village seemed to be one long orgy of guzzling. Columns of peasants converged on Mala from the countryside all around. Beggars and tricksters, gypsies and craftsmen, everyone came to join in the week of celebrations.

Easter week was very much the Mushtak family's affair. Christmas, however, was firmly in the hands of the Shahin clan, which was involved in a blood feud with the Mushtaks. The village was split: half its inhabitants followed the Greek Orthodox rite and with it the rich Shahin family, while the other half belonged to the Roman Catholic Church. In Mala, the Roman Catholic Church was almost entirely financed by the Mushtaks.

Since the two churches celebrated their festivals according to different calendars, Easter often presented an extremely macabre spectacle. No soon had Jesus risen from the tomb and ascended into heaven by the Western, Gregorian calendar of the Catholics than the Orthodox Christians were having him arrested, tried, and crucified on Good Friday by the Eastern, Julian calendar. The Muslims had cause for mirth every year.

At Christmas, however, the windows and the church in the Orthodox quarter were brightly illuminated, and the Shahins celebrated all week until the second of January. Family members even came all the way from America just to be at the party. The Mushtaks' houses, on the other hand, remained dark at Christmas, and the Catholic church celebrated the day as modestly as if Jesus were only some third-rate saint.

Farid's mother, a typical city dweller, regarded the whole thing, her husband's behaviour included, with some amusement as earthy peasant folklore. In all these years, she had never found her way to anywhere near the true soul of Mala. Nor did she want to. Instead, she made the villagers respect her for her generosity, and she also distanced herself from the Mushtaks. She was the only woman in the clan known everywhere by her first name, as "Madame Claire".

The local dishes of Mala, which always smelled of sheep or goat urine, were not to her taste, nor were the cakes baked there, and certainly not the dried fruits that the village people offered visitors. She amused herself by watching the comings and goings in the streets and the village square from her balcony as if she were in a theatre. Claire loved vaudeville drama.

Together with autumn, Easter was the best season in Mala. There was summer sunshine, but without the disadvantage of summer heat. A fresh breeze blew from the mountains of Lebanon, still snow-covered at this time of year. Nature was already in full bloom, and the picturesque rocks on the outskirts of the village were surrounded by young green shoots.

But Farid felt ashamed of his father, who underwent a metamorphosis every Easter. The man who played the part of distinguished and elegant city gentleman in town, larding his Arabic with French words, changed on arrival in Mala and became a grunting, bawling, quarrelsome peasant who staggered home night after night on the verge of alcohol poisoning. At home he seldom laughed; in the village street he was a clown and a tiresome, sentimental groper of women.

Farid was embarrassed when he was with the villagers because, particularly when drunk, they were free with their comments and gibes, always on the same subject: his father's affairs with women and the outsize thing that Elias had between his legs. The assembled men of the village often laughed at Elias's shy son. Only Sadik the village miller, who was hard of hearing, never bothered him with sly digs – but talking to Sadik was hard work. You had to shout the whole time. Sadik was funny when he was telling secrets. He acted like a man whispering, but in fact he broadcast his allegedly confidential news at such loud volume that even the dead in the distant cemetery must have heard it.

"The ones who laugh loudest are the men whose wives your father's already screwed," Sadik had shouted in his ear at the barber's last year. Farid had gone red in the face, and hated the village, where life seemed to consist solely of working in the fields, guzzling, drinking, and crapping everywhere. The villagers were also puffed up with pride because Jesus Christ had, allegedly, saved them from ruin.

"If I were Jesus," Farid had said to his mother when he was only ten, "I'd appear above the altar on Sunday – even if it was only for a minute – and shout in their hypocritical faces: 'You can all kiss my arse, you and your horrible Christianity.'"

9. Rapprochement

Farid could always find interesting children to play with in Mala in summer. They came to spend the vacation here with their parents, prosperous city dwellers. In the company of those children, he could feel that the village was a place for adventure after all. They turned the rocky landscape into the film set of a Western, and played cowboys and Indians or cops and robbers all day, quite often riding real horses and donkeys.

But at Easter he thought Mala a dreary place. He was just nine when his mother saw him hanging around the apartment one day, counting the hours until they went back to Damascus. She suggested taking a nice picnic and going for a long walk with some of the village children, saying they could show him the local countryside and the trail of his forebears.

At first he didn't want to, but then he joined the other children after all, and soon they were out and about in the mountains every day. The village boys hadn't the faintest notion of his forebears or the history of the place, but Farid, whose physical speed and stamina were considered outstanding back in Damascus, had to admit that hard as he might try, he couldn't compete out here in the wilderness. In the village square these boys looked slow and ponderous, but out in the open country they suddenly became lithe and fast. They ran like young gazelles, scrambled up smooth, erect tree trunks like lizards, chased hares and rock partridges like hounds. Thirteen-year-old

Abdullah could kill any living creature, however swift, with a pebble from his sling. His first catch when Farid went out with them was a rock partridge. Soon after that he brought down a hare. The boys fell on his prey, and within a very short time the partridge and the hare had been plucked, skinned, neatly gutted, and washed. They broiled the meat over a fire near the old elm tree, throwing thyme and other herbs into the flames, and a pleasant aroma rose into the air. Farid had never tasted such deliciously seasoned meat before.

Matta, a notably taciturn and simple soul, was as strong as an ox. He could tackle all the other four boys on his own, throwing them over on their backs and pinning them down on the ground. He also picked up rocks weighing over fifty kilos and held them above his head without visible effort. But the really amazing thing was the ease with which he could climb trees just like a bear. As if his hands and feet had made all the trunks, branches and twigs their own, they fitted every tree. He seemed to glide upward, and then he swung from branch to branch and tree to tree like a monkey.

Matta idolized Farid and was glad to call the pale-skinned city boy his friend. He never guessed that Farid admired him too, as if he were some strange and wonderful creature.

Claire gave her son's friends lavish presents. Year after year, each of them received an Easter gift: expensive penknives, ingenious little tools, picnic sets for their expeditions, and large quantities of chocolate. Soon they were looking forward eagerly to Farid's arrival at Easter and in the summer. They felt strangely attracted to the pale city boy, who might not be able to aim a stone accurately enough even to hit a mountain, but was never at a loss for words. His gift of the gab seemed to them positively miraculous. Not only did amusing remarks just bubble out of him, he could harness his tongue and ride it away in a style that left the others breathless. Farid told a story so well that you could see it all before your eyes. That was the miraculous part, for the boys weren't used to such stories. They were told hardly any stories at home, and those they did get to hear were steeped in morality and soon bored them. Farid's words, however, were colourful, fast-moving and intriguing.

He carried them away with those words to a strange world, a world of beautiful women where mere daily survival wasn't the only thing that mattered, where the year consisted not just of sowing and harvest, but of three hundred and sixty-five days and nights when something exciting was always going on.

Oddly enough, however strange the stories he told them, they trusted him implicitly and believed every word he said. And the provisions that Madame Claire gave them for their picnics were even more like something out of a fairy tale. They enjoyed the good food as they listened to Farid, and soon they didn't know whether the storytelling or the picnic was the greater attraction.

They had never really been children themselves, had never owned a toy, hadn't eaten the brightly coloured sweetmeats of the city. They couldn't build and fly kites, or make little paper boats and sail them on the water. Farid could do all those things with magical dexterity. The village boys, on the other hand, had learned at the age of four to tell weeds from blades of wheat and pull them up with their little hands. They could say what creature lived in every nest and every hole in the ground, and they knew a great many secret hiding places among the rocks.

At first they brought their own picnics with them, if only out of pride. On their walks they would always kill a hare or several rock partridges along the way. Then they would go off to the ancient elm, broil the meat, and brew strong black tea over the embers of the fire. After that they listened, spellbound, to the enchanting tales from the city.

In time, however, the boys overcame their inhibitions and left their dry bread, salty sheep's milk cheese, and wrinkled black olives at home. They still hunted hares and partridges, but only because that was a short cut to broiling the meat, drinking their tea, and hearing Farid's stories. All the months he was away, they kept looking forward to the hours they would spend with him under the ancient elm tree next time he came to Mala.

The narrow path wound its way through a dry, hilly landscape, only sparsely planted with vines. Here and there you saw old almond trees, elms and wild brambles; apart from that there were just stones, thistles, and more thistles. The village of Mala was no more than three hours' walk from the Lebanese border. Many of the farmers earned more money from smuggling than agriculture.

The mighty elm, which was surrounded by legends, stood on top of the highest hill. Not far from it there was a small spring famous for its fresh water. As well as the refreshing spring, another reward awaited you when you reached the tree, for a dreamlike panorama spread out before the beholder's eyes. The view extended over several gently rolling hills to the village square of Mala down in the valley, and on clear days all the way into the Syrian steppes. Like an eagle, you could see the smallest movement on the plain below from that hill. It was even better after Claire gave Farid an expensive pair of German binoculars, so that he could watch birds and animals in their natural habitat.

After that the boys derived mischievous glee from spotting the bare backside of every peasant woman squatting somewhere because she couldn't put off doing her business any longer. Once they turned the binoculars on a newly married farmer who interrupted his work in the fields three times to mount his wife quickly, and then went back to work. His wife stayed put, lying under the walnut tree. After each time, she adjusted her dress and then seemed to go to sleep.

10. The End of Childhood

Later, wondering when his childhood had ended, Farid thought it must have been in the spring of 1953. That was when he learned that love in Arabia depends more on what your identity card says than the feelings of your heart. Only adults know that.

The cause of this discovery of his lay a little further back in the past. Two months before going to Mala for Easter he had visited his school friend Kamal Sabuni, a rich but ingenuous Muslim student. Kamal's family owned not only extensive landed estates but also large financial interests in the modern textiles industry near Damascus. In addition, his father was the king of Saudi Arabia's chief economic adviser, a rather unusual and entirely mysterious profession at the time, and it made him millions. His family, however, wouldn't for the world have exchanged Damascus for the hot desert sands, so Kamal and his sisters stayed on in the Syrian capital with their mother, while his father shared a house in Saudi Arabia with two slave-girls. The boy often laughed at his father, who was such an old goat himself but wrote him pompous letters preaching morality. And although his father always waxed enthusiastic about Damascus, he never came home except for weddings and funerals.

It was at Kamal's house that Farid first saw the girl called Rana. He had often visited the wealthy Muslim family before. A year ago, his school friend had invited him and a few of their fellow pupils to hear the new gramophone records he had just been sent from Paris.

Farid had felt very curious about the family. When he rang the bell, a black maid opened the door. He asked to see Kamal, and was amazed by the respect in the elderly woman's voice when she spoke of "the young master". Then she went quietly away. Soon after that, he heard his friend calling, "Come on in – what are you doing standing there in the doorway?"

As a Christian, Farid had learned not to enter Muslim houses without his host's permission, and not to let his eyes wander but keep them on the person he was talking to. When you passed open doors it was forbidden to look at the rooms inside them; you had to cast your eyes down as you followed your host. And you must call out, "Ya Allah!" at frequent intervals as you went along, giving any careless women around the place a last chance to hide from a guest's eyes.

The Sabuni house in Baghdad Street was not so very far from the street where Farid lived, but once inside it he entered a completely different, foreign world. At the age of eight he had realized that his Christian quarter was only a tiny part of a great Muslim city. Up till then he had believed what their neighbour Nassif so often said when he was drunk. "The world isn't America, the world isn't Africa, it's this quarter, and even if it has just ten inhabitants, then eight will be Christians, one a Jew and one a Muslim, and out of those eight Christians you'll find just one decent man to talk to."

The Jews lived in a nearby alley, so Farid had thought that somewhere in the city there must be another little alley for Muslims. In time, however, he discovered that Nassif wasn't to be relied on, for arrack had eaten the man's brain away. None the less, it was years before he first set foot in a Muslim home. That was at a party given by Ali the master baker, who had worked for his father for many years.

Farid had suddenly felt something unusual. Ali's modest house was an entirely different world. People's voices were louder there, they wore brighter clothes, and they ate much heartier food than his mother ever cooked. Even Muslim tea was stronger and sweeter than in the Christian quarter. And if anyone at home had ever slurped it as noisily as the Muslims did at Ali's party, Claire would have fainted away with shame.

An odd feeling came over Farid. It was a mingled sensation of fear, curiosity, closeness and distance. He felt attracted to it, as if part of his soul were at home in these surroundings. He had never known such closeness in any Christian house. After that his fascination led him to accept any invitation from a Muslim fellow pupil, in the hope of discovering the secret of that mysterious attraction.

Kamal Sabuni didn't really stand out at school, where he was considered rich but dim. For that very reason, his mother and siblings were glad to meet the pale boy Farid who, so Kamal had told them, was top of the class. They wanted him to come back often, and visit by visit he learned to know more about the differences between the lives of Christians and Muslims. The Sabunis had been textile merchants since the Middle Ages, so they were seriously rich. They dressed like Europeans, but still seemed a hundred times more Arab than his own parents. Strange how near and yet how far they often appeared to him. It wasn't like visiting his friend Josef, whose home lost all interest for him as time went by; when Farid stood at Kamal's door it was always like visiting for the first time. The maid knew him well, but every time she impersonally asked what he wanted.

Here, as in no other Muslim house, all rooms were open to him, even the most private, and in no other family was he so confused by the switch from Islamic to European ways and back again. The same family that strictly segregated the sexes in public enjoyed sensuous physical contact within their own four walls. Once Kamal's eldest sister Dalal even became so aroused by flirting with her husband during a meal that she had to leave the room with him. When they had been away for some time Farid guessed what was going on. To make sure, he asked to go to the bathroom, and on the way heard Kamal's sister moaning in orgasm. The bed creaked, and his heart raced. He felt guilty, like a child who has stolen something entrusted to him. In the bathroom he calmed down, and finally went back, hoping to hear more, but this time all was quiet. The couple took their time, and no one else at table paid any attention to their absence. They didn't return until the dessert course, and although their hair was combed and they were freshly perfumed, they looked a little drowsy.

Baker Sahed, a well-known painter who was President of the Damascus Academy of Art, had spend months portraying members of the family. He sat at his easel in the drawing room and painted and painted; his work never came to an end. Farid had a feeling that the artist was going slow on purpose to keep up his intimate association with the family and their rich friends, and in fact many commissions were said to have come his way through the Sabunis.

Kamal couldn't stand the painter. The man was a closet gay, he told Farid, and kept pawing him "down there" as if by accident. There was something feminine about the artist's movements, his voice was high as a eunuch's, and the look in his eyes betrayed his desire for young men. As for his elaborately phrased request – how would the young gentleman like to pose naked in his studio, as model for the statue of *Youth* that he was planning? – Kamal could only laugh nastily. Strangely, his mother had no objection to the idea at all. Somehow, thought Farid, Muslims have a healthier attitude to their bodies than we Christians do, they enjoy them more. They wash themselves before cleansing their souls, evidence in itself of their high regard for the body.

After that first visit when Kamal proudly played his latest records, Farid went to see him almost every week, and his family made it very obvious that they approved of his friendship with their son. For one thing was clear to them: Kamal didn't take school seriously, or his teachers either, men whose salaries were less than his own pocket money. His mother, however, realized that his classmate was ambitious and her son respected him. Farid enjoyed the affection of the

Sabuni family. Soon they wanted him to stay for a while when he called, even if Kamal had forgotten that they were to meet and was out somewhere in Damascus. One of his three sisters Dalal, Latifa and Dunia, or their mother would insist on his coming in to drink lemonade or tea before he left again, and they kept him company meanwhile. Sometimes this was rather too much of a good thing for Farid, because he could see how agitated the family usually became when a man visited. With him, however, the sisters would begin to wander around casually after a while, often clad only in a thin negligée or a see-through house dress, which always made him leave in a hurry, to avoid feeling that he was sexless and they didn't need any protection from him.

One day in January 1953 Farid went to help Kamal with an essay. The black maid, indifferent to him as usual, took him to the drawing room. This time Dunia, the youngest of the three sisters, was sitting for the painter. A group of four or five young people were fooling around and making faces to tease her. The artist despairingly appealed for peace and quiet. Kamal was leader of the gang. Suddenly, Farid saw Rana. He later found out that this was her first visit to her friend Dunia's home.

Curiously enough, he took her for a Muslim girl at first, and she too took him for a Muslim. Unlike purely Muslim names such as Muhammad, Ali, Ayesha, and Fatima, or the typically European names like George, Michael, and Therese that were given to Christians, the names Farid and Rana said nothing definite about anyone's religious affiliations. Farid means *unique, valuable*, and Rana means *the beauty who attracts the gaze*.

She thought he was related to the Sabuni family. She was particularly fascinated by his voice and his hands, but then she felt sudden alarm, painfully aware that she was stumbling into something for which her aunt Jasmin had paid the bitter price of death. Jasmin too had first fallen in love with her Jalal's voice and hands. When he spoke, so she had told Rana just before she was murdered, she felt weak, and when he touched her with his finely shaped fingers she was lost.

Rana tried to ignore Farid. Ever since her arrival she had been busy keeping Kamal at arm's length anyway, while he made eyes at her and indulged in suggestive remarks. He claimed boldly that if a Christian like Rana loved him, he'd convert to Christianity at once even if it cost him his life. And he laughed brazenly and said then at least he'd be a true martyr to love. Rana didn't like such jokes. She took very little notice of Kamal, but did not answer back sharply either, not wishing to risk her friendship with his sister. For secretly Dunia was opposed to her family's Westernization. Following the Islamic tradition, she wanted to marry a powerful Muslim and look up to him. "Everything passes – love, virility, beauty. What matters to me is feeling deep respect for a fine man," she had told Rana even before she was fourteen. She was one of those people who know, by the time they are ten, exactly what they want and who they will be.

But unlike Kamal, this other boy couldn't simply be overlooked. Soon the essay was finished, and the two of them came back to the drawing room. Farid was preceded by his laugh, infectious laughter that almost pushed the windows open. The whole room suddenly seemed full of fresh air. Even years later Rana often remembered that moment, and how ever since then she had thought of her love for Farid as opening a window to let in fresh air. He surrounded her with his laughter, beguiled her with his attentions, bewitched her with his brilliant talk. It was strange, but she felt both restless and at rest when he was there, and after her first two meetings with him she caught her heart racing whenever she was visiting the Sabunis and the doorbell rang. And if Farid really did come through the door she felt the blood shoot into her face, and didn't know where to look.

As either chance or her friend Dunia would have it, Rana and he sat beside each other at one of these encounters, when everyone was drinking tea.

"Where are you from?" asked Farid circumspectly, for whatever part of town she named could be a clue to her religion. Something Kamal had said made him wonder whether Rana was a Muslim after all.

"We live in the Salihiye quarter," she replied. It was a high-class district where both Christians and Muslims lived. "What about you?"

"In Bab Tuma, not far from the gate," said Farid. His answer was not strictly accurate, for the Bab Tuma gate was over fifteen hundred metres from his house. He should really have named the eastern gate, Bab Sharqi, less than a hundred metres from the entrance to their alley. But saying "Bab Sharqi" told no one anything. All religious communities lived together in that part of town, whereas Bab Tuma was the quintessentially Christian quarter. The reply did not fail to take effect. Rana pricked up her ears.

"Oh, so you live among Christians?" she asked, smiling.

"What do you mean, among them? I *am* a Christian," he replied. Rana's heart was racing. She began to laugh.

"What's so funny?" he asked, surprised.

"Nothing. I'm laughing because I thought you were a Muslim. I'm a Christian too," she said quietly, so that only he could hear her. She blushed.

"I'm glad, although religion doesn't really make any difference to me," Farid replied. His relief made his assumed indifference less than plausible.

"I feel the same, although it makes a difference to the rest of the world," said Rana, and grief immediately came into her face. Farid looked at her, and at that moment he was lost. He had to take a deep breath in case his heart stopped beating.

He sought her hand under the table, and when he touched her Rana jumped, just for a moment, but then placed her hand firmly in his. And for a minute the earth stood still and the world became a place of infinite peace. At that moment there were only two people in all Damascus, sitting there holding hands. A deep calm hovered almost audibly above their heads. Then the normal world came back, with its noise and the tea-drinking and Rana's friend's laughter.

"The rest of us are still here too," whispered Dunia with a meaning look as she handed the two of them their tea. Rana and Farid woke up, quite shocked to find that the world was still in full swing. Even before leaving the Sabuni house, they had arranged to meet again in Sufaniye Park near Bab Tuma.

He had picked up the information that her father was a lawyer and her surname was Shahin. As Shahin is a common name in all Middle Eastern countries, it told him nothing at first, but later that night he was overcome by anxiety: could Rana be a daughter of the Shahin clan of Mala, his family's arch-enemies? The forty-year-old feud between them had only recently flared up again. Since January, in fact, all hell had been let loose, and his father was now triumphantly celebrating some severe setback or other suffered by the Shahins.

Farid tossed and turned uneasily in bed. He woke early next day. His mother was surprised by his grave face, and even more by his first remark to her.

"Do you know which of the Shahins are on bad terms with our family? Is one of them a lawyer?" he asked even before taking his first sip of tea.

Claire stroked her son's head. "If you've lived with a Mushtak for as many years as I have, you know about their enemies the Shahins from great-grandson to great-great-grandfather. Why?"

"Oh, nothing. I was only asking. I met someone whose surname is Shahin," he said, glossing over the facts. She smiled at his poor attempt at camouflage.

"There are Shahins everywhere, but it's only the Mala family that the Mushtaks hate. Let me think," said Claire. "Yes, I believe one of them *is* a lawyer or a judge. I don't know for sure, but I could soon find out. A friend of mine knows him. Shall I ask her?"

"No, no, never mind," replied Farid. He had made up his mind to ask Rana himself.

He was absent-minded all day. His chemistry teacher was the first to notice. "Our promising chemist has gone missing today," he said, when he had asked the class a question and Farid just went on staring into space. This remark too passed him by. Only the laughter of the class roused him.

"What? Why?" he stammered.

"I was asking about the difference between olefins and paraffins," said the teacher patiently, without a trace of sarcasm.

"Paraffins are saturated hydrocarbons and olefins are unsaturated."

"Correct," said the teacher, admiring Farid's ability to come up with the right answer even when his mind was on something else, while the rest of the class were concentrating hard and still couldn't reply. That boy will be a chemist some day, he thought to himself, smiling with satisfaction.

11. An Obstacle

He couldn't eat lunch. Claire had laid the table for him and then went to her neighbour's, to help prepare the house for the arrival of a hundred mourners in a few hours' time. Faris, the neighbour's husband, had been fifty-nine and sound as a bell when his head suddenly dropped on his chest as he drank his morning coffee. "Faris! Oh God, Faris!" his wife cried out, full of foreboding. But her husband had taken her cry away with him into eternity.

Many of the neighbouring women were hurrying to the house to help. Some cooked food, others brewed huge quantities of coffee. Claire and her friend Madeleine were busy arranging borrowed chairs in the inner courtyard, with a sofa and an armchair for the bishop and the priest. The late Faris had been an important man in the Catholic community of Damascus, sitting on almost all the church committees.

Farid smartened himself up and finally rubbed his face with some of his father's eau de toilette. It had a pleasantly fresh orange-blossom scent. When his mother came home in the afternoon, she found his lunch untouched.

Sufaniye Park is next to the Christian Bab Tuma quarter. Farid gave himself plenty of time to get there, and still it took him only ten minutes. He was sweating. It was March, but almost as hot as summer. There was no sign of Rana anywhere.

After a while she came walking through the park, and saw him sitting lost in thought on one of the benches. She thought he looked wonderful in his white shirt, white trousers and beige leather shoes. His brown skin gleamed in the sunlight. Tall and thin as he was, he looked almost like an Italian, as if he might be a foreigner among the other rather stout figures out in the park on this warm day.

Suddenly Farid looked up. He saw her, and they both laughed. He kissed her for the first time, though only on the cheek, but his lips briefly brushed her mouth.

"Ooh, look, he kissed her," a boy told his mother, who was playing cards with him on a brightly coloured quilt spread on the grass.

"They're brother and sister. Anyone can see that. Your turn to play a card," she reproved him.

Farid was slightly disappointed when he told Rana how his thoughts had kept him awake last night, and heard that she herself had slept better than ever before. Obviously the question of his own surname hadn't yet occurred to her. Damascenes were not particularly interested in surnames. He asked what her father's first name was.

"Basil. Why are you interested?"

"Because I want to know which Shahins you are," he replied. And he felt even more vexed with himself as he mentioned his suspicion that she might be one of the Shahin clan from Mala, his own family's enemies.

"So you come from Mala? And you're one of those Mushtaks?" asked Rana in surprise.

He nodded.

"I thought you were half-European. So my feet haven't carried me very far from that dunghill of a place," she said, with disappointment in her voice.

"You're from Mala too?" asked Farid, barely audibly, because he already knew the answer.

She nodded in silence. Her laughter was gone.

He took her hand. It was cold, and he felt that Rana was trembling.

"He's not her brother," Farid heard the boy on the quilt tell his mother.

"Play your cards," she crossly told her son. "It's none of our business! Are you playing cards or setting up as a marriage broker?"

Rana looked at Farid. She saw longing and sorrow in his eyes, and although she was very much afraid, she knew for certain at that moment that she wanted to live with him. But next minute she remembered her mother's words: "A Muslim is still a human being, but the Mushtaks are rats! Rats! Rats!" The voice echoed through her head.

"Did you hear about my family's latest catastrophe?" she asked.

He nodded, and he realized she knew that the Mushtaks were held to blame for the arrest of Rana's uncle and the financial ruin of the entire Shahin family.

She didn't know much about the feud between the two clans, she was just aware that there was one name her parents always repeated when they wanted to suggest something ugly, malicious, contemptible and hateful, and that name was Mushtak.

"Why does life have to be so complicated?" asked Rana.

"Because I'm a walking disaster area," he replied. There were tears in his eyes, for at that moment he saw the mighty wall that was rising in front of him, and he was in despair because he couldn't get over it.

She kissed him, and he didn't know what to do. Her lips were cold; it was a strange feeling. He wasn't carried away as much as he had expected; instead, he saw himself like an actor on screen and tried to embrace Rana as an actor would. She laughed. He kissed her on the mouth.

"That's not the way a brother kisses his sister," said the boy. His mother took no notice. She was dealing the cards again.

12. In Love

That spring of 1953 Farid didn't want to go to Mala for Easter, not at any price. He claimed that he wasn't well and wanted to rest. Couldn't his father, he asked, make an exception just for once?

Elias Mushtak wouldn't hear of any exceptions or compromises. The entire family must go to the village and publicly commemorate his father. They would also celebrate the latest ignominious defeat inflicted on his enemies of the Shahin clan.

"You can wear the city around your neck like a jewel the rest of the year, but we all belong in Mala for this one week," he said calmly but implacably. Any further argument, as usual, was futile. What Elias said was law. Even Claire seldom protested.

So Farid obeyed, and went up into the mountains with the others in a very bad temper. That year he noticed for the first time how dangerously his father drove along the winding road. Three times, he almost crashed into vehicles coming the other way. Farid pictured himself falling into the abyss. It was always his father's fault, but Elias Mushtak cursed the other drivers at the top of his voice.

The higher up the mountain road the car made its way, the bleaker and more unattractive the boy found the landscape. And it seemed to be reflected in his face. A moment came when his mother noticed the grief in it as he stared at their surroundings. It was very unusual for him to look like that. He's in love, she thought, unhappily in love. And Claire was not wrong.

13. Scruples

All the Mushtaks arrived in Mala on Good Friday, in relays, and light and music filled their long-deserted houses again.

As if they had been waiting all winter for this solemn moment, the five village boys came to the Mushtak villa in their best clothes next morning, making a rather shy and restrained noise under the big balcony until Farid heard them and asked them in for a lemonade, as he did every year. They liked it very much, particularly with ice cubes from the only electric refrigerator in the village at that time, which of course belonged to the Mushtaks. Sticking to their usual custom of the last few years, as they drank their lemonade on the balcony they decided to go for a picnic under the huge old elm tree on the hill after church on Easter Sunday. From that vantage point, you could think of the village as charmingly small and insignificant, the way the boys liked it. Furthermore, no one could catch them smoking up on the hill. They kept watch through the binoculars on anyone and anything moving further down. They didn't really have anything to fear during Easter week, for no one else felt like going up to the distant elm tree when festivities were in full swing in the middle of the village.

So next day, soon after church, Farid and his five friends set off uphill to the elm tree. His mother had packed as much food as if he and all the others were emigrating to America. The contents were pure delight for the Mala boys, who these days brought nothing with them but their appetite for any number of strange delicacies.

When they reached the elm they lit a small fire on the spot where shepherds, stopping to rest on the hill, had lit their fires for decades.

Farid wasn't hungry, and gave the other his sandwiches. But he drank the strong, smoky tea and enthusiastically described the beautiful women of the capital city to his friends. The farmers' sons relished his exciting descriptions, and couldn't get enough of them.

They sat there for hours, feeding the fire with stout branches and thistles, and warming themselves even more on the women's bodies delivered up by Farid to their wild imaginations.

But suddenly the usually silent Matta said this was the last time he'd be with them. Hesitating slightly, he poked the embers of the fire with a twig. "My father's a distant cousin of the new abbot of some monastery in the north. I have to go into it. They need novices, and there are hardly enough priests these days for all the Christian villages. But I don't want to go." And then he fell silent again.

"Oh, come on, what's the matter with that? It's better than this dump. All you can do here when you finish school is feed goats, grow wheat, and have children. It's worth leaving Mala for the good life in the monastery. I've heard everyone has a bed to himself there," said Simeon the beekeeper Isaak's son, trying to encourage his friend.

"That's true, it's something to look forward to." Butros, son of the shepherd Fadlu, joined in the conversation. "It'll be worth going into the monastery just to get away from your brothers and sisters farting at night."

But Matta shook his head.

"No, really," Butros persisted, "you ought to be glad. You'll get clean clothes and enough to eat. And you'll learn a lot more than in our lousy school here. What else do you want?"

Simeon went on cheering him up. "Yes, and these days priests live like millionaires."

"But what's he going to do with the prick between his legs? Those monks in black aren't allowed to marry," pointed out Ghassan, the vegetable dealer Tanius's son. Matta smiled grimly.

"Oh, he can put it in olive oil to keep it fresh and crisp," joked Butros, "until one of those randy women comes along confessing that she needs three men a day plus her own husband or she can't sleep at night." He turned to Matta himself. "And then she asks you, 'What am I to do?' And you say, like the man of God you are, 'My daughter, consider your husband and the other three your main course, and have me for dessert.'"

Butros laughed a lot at what he considered his own excellent joke. The other boys laughed too, and even Matta smiled faintly. Only Farid was quiet.

"What's the place called?" he asked.

"The monastery of St. Sebastian."

Farid knew that it was on the Mediterranean coast. "It's a good one," he said, pretending enthusiasm out of sympathy. But Matta's face remained unmoved. He looked as if he were desperately trying to find a way out of an invisible maze.

When the sun set they rose to go home. Instead of fetching water from the nearby spring to put out the embers, the five others lazily pissed on the ashes. Only Farid refrained.

The boys laughed at him. He didn't dare piss just because he was superstitious, they said. For in the village it was thought that if you pissed on a hearth your pee would hit the Devil, who likes to swelter in any fire, and he'd be so angry that he'd strike men impotent and light an inextinguishable fire in their wives' cunts, forcing the women to cuckold their husbands. The goatherd Habib, who used to screw not only his wife and his maidservant every week but his forty goats too, had been impotent, so rumour had it, ever since he drank too much tea one night and was too lazy to move a few steps away from the fire on the hearth. Then the Devil hissed with anger, and his hairy hand shot out of the embers and scratched Habib's glans. The poor man jumped and felt a strange chill in his limbs, like a snowstorm sweeping through his bones.

Next day, so the story continued, he felt unwell and went to Damascus to be examined and cured. In vain. A week later his prick was dried up, wrinkled, and dark brown. It looked like an old fig. Ten days later it simply fell off. Habib didn't even feel any pain. He saw his prick lying in bed beside him early in the morning. At first he thought it was a black olive, but then he wondered how an olive could have come into his bed. All he had left was a hole above his testicles. And after that, so the tale went, his wife went flitting about like a fairy every night – in search of a man.

Later, a distant aunt told Claire the true story of the goatherd. Farid pretended to be asleep on the sofa, and heard that the wily man had served up this tall story about pissing on the fire to his simple-minded wife so that she wouldn't discover the truth.

"And what was that?" asked Claire, amused.

"The fact was that the goatherd was insatiable and visited the whores in Damascus every month. There he met the famous Nariman. All the citizens of Damascus are in awe of her, and it's not for nothing they call her She Who Sucks You Dry. And it was Nariman, of all people, whom the miserly goatherd refused to pay one day, saying she hadn't given him a good time. So she sucked his penis away to punish him, and sent him off with nothing but the husk of it," said the aunt, laughing. "Now he has only a limp rag between his legs – you could dry your hands on it, but there's no pleasure to be had from it any more."

Up on the hill under the elm, however, superstition was not Farid's reason for holding back. He was violently lovesick for the first time in his life. His lovesickness not only took away his appetite and left him sleepless at night, it even made him unable to pass water that day. But he couldn't and wouldn't tell the village boys about his love. They were between fourteen and sixteen, they'd have laughed at him and insulted Rana with their coarse remarks. Love doesn't tolerate coarse tongues, and the tongues of the village boys were coarser than a rasp.

However, there was another reason for him not to breathe a word about his love. Rana had sworn him to silence, for if the secret of their love came to light she feared for her life. And Farid knew from the evidence of his own eyes that her fears were not exaggerated. The previous summer young Ayesha had indeed paid with her life for love. She was a butcher's daughter, and the whole village was talking about her relationship with the bus driver Bassam, whose family were at daggers drawn with Ayesha's parents. Both families were Muslims, part of a small minority in the otherwise Christian village of Mala. Their dispute, which began over a large consignment of smuggled cigarettes, had led to three dead and over ten injured on both sides within the space of five years. The original cause of it, the cigarettes, retreated entirely into the background. The blood that had been shed now lay between the two families.

Ayesha's parents, relations, and friends urged her to leave Bassam, but he was the only man she wanted. In the end they wrote a letter to her brother, who was earning his living as a labourer in Saudi Arabia, and he came back in a hurry. He offered her immediate marriage to his school friend Hassan, who was in the police, but Ayesha wouldn't hear of it, and met Bassam secretly to tell him about her brother's threats. She hoped they would induce her lover to flee abroad with her until tempers had calmed down again, but she didn't guess that her brother was in the barber's on the village square at that very moment, keeping watch on her. Bassam drove out of the village with his lover. It was afternoon, and he had an hour's break before the next journey to Damascus. Where he took Ayesha no one knew, but an hour later they came back in the bus.

Farid was standing on the balcony drinking tea when Ayesha climbed out of the bus in the village square. Her brother marched out of the barber's shop opposite the bus stop, crying, "Treacherous woman, you have let an enemy of our family defile you!"

He fired three shots. Farid's glass fell from his hand. The bus driver, realizing his danger, stepped on the gas and saved his own life. Ayesha uttered a loud and terrified scream. "Mother, help me!" Then she died, there in the middle of the square.

14. Atonement

The fire wasn't extinguished until midday. Then the crowd came home exhausted and dirty. Many of them, without naming names, were cursing "the boys", meaning Farid and his friends.

Farid's father wouldn't say a word to him for two hours. Elias showered, dressed, and then went to the café in the village square, where the men discussed the matter until early evening. It was more the shock than any material loss that upset most of the farmers. Some of them were merely amused to think that one of the Mushtaks' own offspring had spoiled their Easter for them, others thought none of it worth mentioning. But the Shahins were triumphant.

Elias Mushtak didn't come back from the café until it was time for the evening meal. His face was grey and set. He muttered something to Claire, and she guessed that he had already come to a decision.

"After the summer vacation you're going into the monastery of St. Sebastian," he shouted at his son. "And you can be glad I don't murder you on the spot. You're the first Mushtak ever to burn down a sacred tree. You've dragged the name of the Mushtaks through the mud, and you must atone for it. And when you're a priest later, saying your prayers, I hope you'll remember that you owe the village something."

"But I don't want to go into a monastery," said Farid, looking his father straight in the eye. Elias slapped his face. He fell over on his back, hitting his head on the floor.

"Stop it!" cried the horrified Claire. She began crying, ran to her son and helped him up.

"I didn't do anything!" he told his father, with tears in his eyes. The second slap hit him. Farid stumbled.

"If I say you're going into a monastery then you're going into a monastery, and you don't say another word, not even 'yes'. Understand?"

"It's all right," wailed Claire, "he'll do it, but don't kill him."

Farid wanted to shout that he wasn't going to leave Damascus and Rana for a single second, but fear of his father paralysed his tongue.

His mother gently pushed Elias into the bedroom, where she talked to him for a long time. But Farid just heard his father repeating, over and over, that the monastery would do him good. Claire wept again. For a moment he was furious, and it occurred to him for the first time that he'd have to murder his father some day.

15. Suspicion

Next day, from the balcony, he saw his friends outside the house. They were playing marbles in the village square. He quickly dressed, but when he went to join them, they froze and avoided his eyes. Finally they quietly went away without a word. Only Matta stayed, smiling at him.

"What's the matter with them?"

"They're afraid."

"Afraid? Why?"

"Because they're cowards. They don't want to be seen with you any more and be thought of as fire-raisers," replied Matta.

"What about you?"

"To hell with the village. You're my brother," said the boy quietly, almost indifferently.

"I want to go up to where the fire was again. Coming?" asked Farid.

"Of course," said Matta, almost cheerfully.

Two hours later they were at the top of the hill, where a great surprise awaited them. The elm had been growing as two different halves for a long time. One half was fresh and strong, the other old and dried up. Now Farid and Matta saw that only the dried-up part of the tree had burned. The other part was intact, slightly blackened with soot, yes, but otherwise not even singed. The really surprising thing was that the unharmed part of the tree was the one right next to the site of their fire.

"That's odd, don't you think? The spark must have flown past this half of the tree in a semicircle and then set the other half on fire. That's practically a miracle," said Matta, staring into space.

"Yes, it really is funny," Farid agreed. His thoughts were with Rana again. Where are you? he whispered deep inside himself. I need you.

❧

At that moment she was talking to her best friend Dunia Sabuni, because otherwise her thoughts would have choked her. She was telling Dunia about the feud between the two families, but she was disappointed by her friend's down-to-earth approach.

"That's all very well in a movie, but it doesn't work in real life. The family is stronger, it will crush you both. And then I'm afraid it's not as good as the stories of Madjnun Leila or Romeo and Juliet. You'd better steer clear of that boy and find a steady respectable man, one your parents will admire, and then they'll leave you alone and no one can stop you warming yourself on the memory of this romance of yours," she said, with a sudden clear peal of laughter. "But only in your thoughts," she was quick to add. "Everything else will be your husband's, understand?" And she laughed again, but this time with much meaning.

At that moment Rana heard Farid's voice, and she cried almost indignantly, "But he needs me, and you can't just run away and let someone down."

"What poet said that? Tell me his name and I'll show you how he let those fine sayings loose on the world, and then stayed with his wife like a good boy. No, my dear, you're a dreamer, and it's my thankless task to wake you up."

※

Farid heard a voice inside his head, saying: I'm here with you.

"And where's the shame that Ghassan was talking about just now?" Matta brought him back to the hilltop and the elm. "This dry half belonged to the Mushtaks anyway. The other half, the living one, belongs to the church of St. Giorgios. But never mind, the main thing is no one was hurt and no fields were damaged either."

At these simple words, Farid himself suddenly couldn't understand why his father had been talking about a sin. Surely not just for a chunk of rotten wood, he said to himself.

When word went around in Mala that the fire had spared St. Giorgios's half of the tree, many people took it as a kind of final proof from heaven. It was the work of Providence that a descendant of old George Mushtak, of all people, had burned his part of the tree.

A week after the fire, Farid's father spoke normally to his son again. At lunch he suddenly asked in a perfectly friendly tone, "Pass the water jug, would you?"

Claire had insisted that Elias must be reconciled with Farid, and then she herself would back the idea of sending the boy to the monastery, although only to ensure that he had a good education. She had agreed when she learned that the monastery of St. Sebastian was run by Jesuits. But her mind was firmly made up on one point: her son was not going to become a priest.

Encouraged by his father's friendliness, Farid told him what he had seen on the site of the fire.

"That doesn't mean anything. There was a strong wind, it could have blown a spark on to a dry thistle, and then the thistle started the fire that burned everything around the tree, but fire doesn't have much chance with green wood. A rotten part is different," replied Elias calmly.

"Saliha the dairywoman thinks one of the Shahins was behind the fire. She says they wanted to spoil our Easter," Claire told him.

Elias dismissed the idea. "We mustn't look for Shahins behind every silly trick. What your son and his friends did was ..." Elias hesitated as she cast him a warning glance, "... was a stupid, childish prank," he finished, toning down what he had been about to say.

This conversation didn't help matters. Apparently his father had had the monastery plan in his head for a long time, and was just waiting for an opportunity to carry it out. And when the fire burned the elm tree, that opportunity seemed, in a strange way, to have fallen right into his hands.

BOOK OF LOVE III

Women are like elm trees, beating them does no good.

৵৹

16. Sarka's Laughter

At noon on a clear, cold spring day, two strangers came riding down the dusty road to Mala in great haste. Even before they reached the mill on the way into the village, most of the villagers could see that the couple needed help.

The riders stopped outside the church of St. Giorgios. The barber came out of his shop and offered them fresh water.

"What's the name of this church?" asked the elder of the two.

"The church of St. Giorgios," said a young shepherd who happened to be in the square outside it.

The barber thought the stranger on his fine white mount must be about fifty. A woman dressed in man's clothing was sitting on the vigorous black horse. She had blue eyes, so blue that you couldn't look at them for long without smiling in confusion. She was very young, and the villagers took her for the man's daughter.

He asked to see the village elder. There was no pleading note in his voice. The man he wanted, Mobate, lived in the big house opposite the mill on the way into Mala. For generations, village elders had been drawn from the Mobate clan. They were good at dealing with friend and foe alike, and had shrewdly found out how to settle quarrels between the other clans and avert the despotism of the Ottoman authorities while always staying on top themselves.

Old Daud Mobate had died a year before. A week later, the most powerful men in the village elected his forty-year-old son Habib to succeed him. He was even wilier and a smoother operator than his father, who had been jokingly nicknamed "The Eel" in his lifetime.

At that time, as prescribed by the Arab law of hospitality, a stranger could stay in the village as the elder's guest for three days without a word to explain why he was on the road.

"George Mushtak," replied Mobate's guest when an old farmer civilly asked his name. "And this is my wife Sarka," he added. The woman laughed, a clear sound, and laid her head against her husband's arm. He was sitting beside her on the rug, like everyone else present. Her new name amused her. Every time they met anyone her lover invented two new names, one for himself and one for her. But she particularly liked the sound of Sarka, *the blue woman.*

Jusuf Shahin, the richest man in the village, cast a disapproving glance at the woman. He thought her laughter unseemly. Later he used to say he had known at that moment that the devil was in her.

On the other hand, he liked the man. He seemed mature and courageous, and said little, but what he did say came swift as an arrow from his mouth and hit its mark.

George Mushtak told them straight out that he had fled here because of the woman at his side. He and she were Christians, he said, but a rich Muslim farmer was determined to marry Sarka by force. He, Mushtak, had chosen to come to Mala because even as a child he had heard of the chivalry and hospitality of the village.

Mobate sat up and took notice. He knew that his grandfather had once found himself in considerable difficulties when he granted the protection of the village to a fugitive. Soon after that, Mala had been surrounded. Its attackers wanted the villagers to surrender the man they were after. Their leader hated him so much that he didn't even respect the sacred Arab custom which obliges a host to deliver himself up to death sooner than his guest.

The village held out against the attackers for weeks, until their leader and his exhausted warriors finally withdrew. After that, however, the men of Mala had urged their village elder to look twice at the next stranger before giving his word and plunging them all into misfortune again.

"You may have your three days, but do your pursuers know you rode to Mala?"

"No," replied George Mushtak grimly, "or I wouldn't have come. I went a long way round, and there's been no one on my trail for days. I give you my word."

"Good," said Mobate, "then in three days' time I'll tell you whether you can stay here. Now let us eat and make you welcome." He clapped his hands, and the meal was immediately carried in, as if the women had been just waiting on the other side of the door. Sarka laughed.

While the guests enjoyed the stranger's stories and admired his wife's beauty, the village elder sent three reliable young men to the lookout posts on the mountains, where they could see down into the plain leading to Mala.

When there was still no sign of pursuers three days later, he felt reassured. His guest did indeed seem to have been cautious. They granted him the right to stay in Mala. Only then did the man ride away once more, leading his wife's horse behind him. Sarka stayed in the Mobates' house.

The women there liked the beautiful girl, but they were surprised to see that she never prayed. She didn't say grace with them before or after meals, just sat there smiling. One of the women, feeling suspicious, asked Sarka if she was a Christian. "No," she said. Nor was she Jewish.

"A Muslim?" asked another woman. Sarka cheerfully shook her head.

"Then what in the world are you?" cried Mobate's sister Badia.

"Love, love is my religion," replied Sarka with her clear laugh. And the women were charmed by her sense of humour, never guessing that she spoke the truth.

It was almost a day before George Mushtak came back and carried two heavy saddlebags into the house. They were full of gold coins.

Mobate was very pleased, since a rich man was a godsend for both the village and himself. Soon George Mushtak bought four old houses on the village square, had them pulled down, and instead built a large new property with a grand house, a garden and outhouses. Mobate helped him to acquire fields, barns and threshing floors, and before two years were up George Mushtak could compete with Jusuf Shahin, until now the richest man in the village. But it wasn't long before the original friendship between the two men turned to enmity. There was much speculation about the reason.

The Catholics in particular were delighted to have the newcomer there. Not only did he get the Catholic church renovated at his own expense, he also backed the Catholics against the hitherto dominant Orthodox Christians. But their delight was premature.

17. Laila's Decision

In her later years, when Sarka was alone in the house feeling sad, or wandering around at night in the dark, she always remembered herself as a little girl running through the orchard and splashing about in the brook near her parents' home. She had been called Laila then, the world had been a game, her heart was free and unscarred. It hadn't yet suffered the wounds of love or worn the chains of fear.

But her memory of the hammam warmed her more than anything else. The details of visits to that splendid bathhouse had remained more vivid in her mind than all the weddings, circumcisions and religious festivals of which she retained only a vague idea. Going to the hammam in Damascus with her mother had been a great event for her, one that came only two or three times a year. Over ten women and twenty girls from the neighbourhood travelled in the big cart driven by a bearded old man. Laila had felt excited anticipation whenever she saw her mother packing everything up: food, sweetmeats, tobacco secretly abstracted from her husband's supplies, combs, soap, henna and bath towels, although they never used the towels because there were much better ones in the hammam.

Laila could still see it before her eyes: those beautiful rooms, the dome, the tiny windows letting coloured light shine in, and then all the fun of sliding around on the soapy marble floors with the other girls. And the women sitting together, and their stories, the laughter and all that food. Laila was scared the first time she saw the fat lady who was always putting leeches on her breasts, belly, and legs. For a moment she thought they were worms growing out of the woman's body.

Only later, when Laila noticed her breasts beginning to swell, did she suddenly notice the glint in men's eyes out in the street, and the women's whispers in the hammam intensified and became a definite plan. Her mother was the first to say anything to her straight out. Hassan, son of the big farmer Mahmud Kashat, had his eye on her. The old midwife Fatima had told her so. He'd met Laila and liked her. Now he was going to indulge himself by taking her as his fifth wife.

"How many hearts does this man have?" Laila had asked, out of sheer curiosity.

"He's rich enough to keep ten wives, child, just like his father. With him you'll be able to fill your belly, wash in clean water every week, lie down in a bed without bugs and lice, and sleep easily. That's not bad payment for the bit of pleasure you give a man. Look at me. I have to bear that burden by myself, and slave for your father at home and in the fields as well. But you'll be sharing Hassan Kashat with four other women. His slaves will feed you and pamper you like a princess. And all that for a little carrying on every fifth night," said her mother, who had lived through years of famine and bloodsucking insects.

The old midwife Kadriye, who was visiting that day, drew on the water pipe that Laila's mother had prepared for her. Water gurgled in the belly of the pipe. "And his thing isn't as big as all that. There's nothing for you to fear. Besides, he'll go far in the world. A famous soothsayer has prophesied a great future for Hassan. When she saw him," said the midwife, suddenly waxing enthusiastic, "she seized his hand and kissed it. Alarmed and nauseated, the young gentleman pushed the woman away from him, but she clung to his cloak saying she must do it, she wanted to be the first to kiss the hand of a future king of the Arabs. The young gentleman, oh, wasn't he just astonished! He gave her a lira and thought she would run off with the reward for her flattery, but the woman looked him straight in the eye and said she didn't want his money, but he was not to forget her when he became king, as he would one day. Now she was holding both his hands. He would have to climb over a thousand dead bodies to reach his throne, she said, but he was to marry a fifth wife whose sign was the moon and whose name was the night, and that's you, my child," the midwife ended her eloquent speech in a kindly tone of voice. She knew that Laila had a birthmark shaped like a crescent moon above her heart.

Laila knew the rich farmer Kashat's son. He was short, and had a long, dark beard and big ears which didn't seem to fit his almost dwarfish face at all. His eyebrows were comically crooked. He had an ugly mouth, with the huge lower lip split like a camel's. Although he was always elegantly dressed, as if he were going to a party, he never laughed, and always walked with a stoop, as if he had all the cares of the world on his shoulders.

And that dwarf wants me as his fifth wife, thought Laila, fretting. "But I want to be the first," she said, and didn't understand why her mother was horrified.

"For God's sake, my child!" replied that gentle and devout woman.

Laila hardly knew her father. She addressed him as "sir", and knew that his name was Muhammad Khairi. He was hardly ever there, and when he did come home he didn't want to see his children. He ate alone, slept alone, and talked to no one. Laila's mother, on the other hand, slept in a small room with the children. Sometimes she slipped into her husband's room in the night, and then her daughter heard the wooden bedstead creaking while her mother groaned in pain. Laila had hated her father for that.

He dealt in spices and dried fruits, and often had to make long journeys to see his suppliers. Their large orchard and vegetable patch, however, was left to the care of Laila's mother and the children. Although Laila had never known the real hunger that plagued many families, they had sometimes been forced to live on meagre rations.

When she told her father that she wanted to be a first wife he didn't answer at all. But her mother told her that he had already given Hassan Kashat his word. That night Laila was so scared that, for the first time, she found it difficult to breathe. You're going to die, an inner voice had whispered to her. I must run away, Laila told herself. At that moment her mother came over to her to pick bloodsucking bugs out of the bed. She was holding a small oil lamp in one hand, and she plunged the plump bugs in a bowl of water.

"Oh, child, you're awake," she had said in surprise. In the darkness Laila's eyes looked to her larger, unfathomable.

"Tell me, Mother, how many hearts does Kashat have?"

Her mother did not reply.

જી

Laila could no longer remember when she had first seen Nassif Jasegi, but oddly enough, on the day he spoke to her she immediately saw that this was the only man who could save her. He was the son of a rich Christian who was not particularly good at managing his fortune. The peasants cracked jokes about the "unbeliever" who had served the Sultan so long, and in return was given landed property but didn't know what to do with it. His farm lay only a few hundred paces from Laila's home, but her family kept its distance from the "impure" Christians.

Laila heard that these Christians prayed to blocks of wood, ate pigs and drank wine. Their shameless women sat unveiled in the company of men, and they never let their husbands take a second wife.

"Mother," Laila had said, "those unbelieving men have only one heart, just like Muslim women."

Her mother was scared almost to death. Her husband was asleep in the next room. She took the girl by the ear and hauled her outside. "Child, you're out of your mind. It's better if you marry soon. I'm dying of fear for you," she whispered.

When Laila, undeterred, told her father for the second time that she wanted to be a first wife, he slapped her face. After that her brothers Mustafa and Yunus beat her, although they were younger than she was. Their blows came thick and fast as mosquitoes on the humid summer nights of Damascus, and as they increased and multiplied so did Laila's questions. Her mother wept. "Child, you're playing games with your life. We can't break the word your father has given."

57

And the midwife, seductively, told her, "Once you have a husband, you know, you'll have his fortune, and you can send your mother lovely things every day."

Ganging up together, they told Laila that what little prosperity her grandfather Mustafa Khairi had achieved came only because he kept his word and gave the governor of Damascus the hand in marriage of Laila's beautiful Aunt Balkis, her father's sister. She was the governor's twelfth wife, but then she had turned the old man's head with her charms and her skill in the art of love, and in less than a year he had promoted her to be his first wife.

A voice inside Laila, cold as night, told her that this story was a lie. If Balkis had been the governor's first wife, then why did she kill herself at the age of twenty-five? Laila's cousin Fatmeh didn't believe Balkis had been happy either. Her grave was quite close, and Fatmeh's family often made a pilgrimage to her resting place.

I want to come first and I want to be happy, Laila kept telling herself, and she swore not to marry Hassan Kashat.

18. Laila and the Madman

"What's your name, lovely one?" were the first words she had heard Nassif Jasegi say. He came riding along beside the stream. She hadn't noticed him at all, being far away in her thoughts again while her hands pulled weeds out of the radish bed. She started, and turned around. A window opened in her heart. She took a deep breath, and felt the relief of fresh air blowing in.

"Laila," she replied. "And yours? What do they call you?"

"They call me Nassif, the Righteous Man, but I'm not righteous at all," he replied, smiling.

"What are you, then?" she asked.

"I," said the man, "am Madjnun Laila."

Like all Arabs, she knew the legend of the unrequited love of her namesake Laila and the poet who went mad for love of her, singing his beloved's praise until the day he died. His poems made the woman immortal. Very few knew his real name, and he was known simply as Laila's madman, *Madjnun Laila*.

"And are you really mad?" she asked.

"Only for you," said the man.

"You don't look like a lunatic," she said, examining him from his shining shoes to his clean white headcloth. Hamdi, her crazy cousin, screamed like an animal in his room with its barred window, threw his filth at everyone, and kept banging his head against the wall.

What happened next opened three more windows in her heart. Nassif Jasegi, so elegantly mounted on a noble Arab horse, said softly, "I'd run mad three hundred times over to hear you laugh." And he jumped off his horse, stood on his head in the brook, leaped to his feet again, made faces like a monkey, climbed a tree like a cat, and from there jumped back on to his horse which, apparently used to such extraordinary behaviour, hadn't moved from the spot.

Laila laughed out loud, and when Nassif stood on his saddle, flapped his arms and cried, "Look, I'm a little sparrow," she could no longer keep on her feet. With a single leap he was down beside her. He squatted on the ground and looked into her eyes. He was a playmate, even though he looked like a man of mature years.

"And how many hearts do you have?" she asked quietly, and he touched her lips.

"Only one, and you have filled it entirely," he replied.

"Nassif," said Laila, in an almost pleading tone, and he immediately understood everything.

Years later the wild joy of those days was still fresh in her mind. Even when her brain was almost entirely eaten away she remembered the happiness of that time, an eternity ago. But when Laila met her madman and the world seemed to shake beneath her feet, what she didn't know is that joy is very treacherous.

Her brother Mustafa was the first to see her happiness in her face. Clumsily, like a careless puppy, it gave everything away. He faced Laila, and his knife flashed. But although death was staring at her from that knife she wouldn't deign to give it so much as a glance. Nassif alone lived in her eyes.

"You marry Hassan or you die," said Mustafa. He was not fifteen yet, but as the firstborn son he bore his grandfather's name and acted like a pasha. He had spoken to Hassan, said bandy-legged, snot-nosed little Mustafa, and he acted as if Kashat were a friend of his. Mustafa's face, so like Laila's own, was suddenly as grave as if the "jug-eared dwarf", as Laila called Hassan Kashat to herself, had unloaded on her brother some of the grief that kept his back bent all the time. The boy had learned the words he spoke to her by heart, the way he could chant the words of the Koran sura by sura, without understanding them.

"Love or death! One is in my hand, the other in yours," she whispered softly. Their mother, coming back from a neighbour's at that moment, threw herself on her son, and pleaded with him until he gave her the knife.

Nassif just nodded when Laila told him all this.

Three days later a horseman muffled in a heavy cloak attacked Hassan Kashat on his way home from hunting gazelles. He struck both Hassan's hands with a stick for so long that one of them, the left hand, was permanently crippled.

An extensive search for the man who had done it came to nothing. Only Laila knew who he was, and she smiled, but this time secretly under the covers, for she was afraid that her delight would give her away again.

The wedding was to be in March, when the almonds were in blossom. But one cold morning in February Laila, disguised as a man, mounted the black horse that Nassif was holding for her not far from her house. They rode south for two weeks, and Nassif intentionally left a trail leading to Jerusalem. Then they crossed the Holy Land going north, and continued their journey in Lebanon, but now without leaving any trail at all. Arabia was an Ottoman province at the time, and Sultan Abdulhamid had ruled with an iron hand until he was deposed in 1909, but the French had exerted pressure and Lebanon eluded his grasp. Nassif knew that, but he didn't guess that his rival had seen through his clever idea. Kashat's men went on hunting Nassif in Lebanon. Their master wanted him alive. By now he had found out that the horseman muffled in the cloak was none other than that Christian man from his own neighbourhood.

Laila and Nassif only just escaped a trap set for them by a monk whom Kashat had bribed. But they got away. They rode through the mountains by a circuitous route in order to reach Mala.

Only years later did Nassif discover that on one of those nights when he desired his lover, and was embracing her tenderly in their warm bed of furs, his entire family had been butchered. His two younger brothers Butros and Fuad were killed in a shoot-out, his mother and his sister Miriam were brutally murdered. The family's possessions were robbed, and their farm burned down to its foundations. The slaughter had been carried out by Laila's brothers and Kashat's men. Laila's family had thereby saved its honour in the eyes of its neighbours, and atoned for its guilt to the powerful Kashat.

Later, when Kashat mustered a whole army to try bringing as many villages as possible under his control, the girl's brothers Mustafa and Yunus were his lieutenants and marched at the head of the troop.

And on one of the nights that Laila and Nassif spent under assumed names in inns, with Bedouin, in caves, or with village elders, she suddenly sensed something inside her. It began to throb. She took Nassif in her arms and kissed his eyes. "What will we call our son?" she asked, as if she were sure it would be a boy.

"Salman," replied Nassif, with tears in his eyes. "The name of my father, who died far too young. I will conquer death with my son's birth."

On the rest of their journey Laila laughed a great deal with the man who always had death riding hard on his heels, but still thought up countless crazy ideas for his lover's delight. He claimed that her laughter sounded like the gurgling water of a brook, and whenever he heard it he was thirsty for her. She once said, later, that during those months before they arrived in Mala, she had used up all the laughter that was meant to last her life.

19. Hyenas

Wherever they rode they met with misery and starvation. The tax collectors of the Sultan in Istanbul drained the last coins from the people's purses, for Sultan Abdulhamid was deep in debt to the West. But a pitiless drought had descended on many parts of his Ottoman Empire, and there was nothing to be harvested but dust. Epidemics had spread, tuberculosis, plague and cholera were raging, and whole areas of the country were already depopulated. No talisman offered any hope of an end to these hardships. People were dying like flies.

Laila and Nassif had not known such wretchedness in the lush countryside south of Damascus, which was like a garden. But on their flight north, the roads were full of people who didn't know where to go to escape the cholera. Malaria drained the light from children's eyes.

A few young men were making their way fast in the direction of Damascus, hoping that salvation might yet be found there. It was winter. In spite of the cold weather, they walked barefoot, carrying their shoes on a string tied around their necks to save the leather. When they came close to the city they were going to wash their feet and then put their clean shoes on again. They firmly believed that they would attract more attention with a good pair of shoes.

Laila and Nassif turned away from the main roads. Their journey to Mala took them over high mountains, down through deep ravines again, and from there along winding paths up to the top of the next mountain. The winter landscape made nature harsh and forbidding. The cold was unbearable. Laila had never known anything like it. The further they wound their way into the mountains, the more she froze, yet they had only reached a thousand metres, and they would have to climb almost as high again. Laila's heart failed her at the thought of it.

Nassif joked with her, saying that there were wolves and bears in the mountains, creatures who would eat a human being up within seconds. She begged him to stop, but he went on teasing her until the day the hyenas appeared. They were on a mountain ridge, letting the horses follow the path slowly. In many places it wasn't even a metre wide, and the ever-hungry maw of the abyss gaped to their left. Nassif was riding a little way in front of Laila, singing softly and gazing into the distance.

The morning light had banished enough of the darkness of night for them to be able to see across the valley to the top of the next height. Suddenly Laila saw the hyenas on the other side of the abyss. They had attacked a woman walking to the nearby village with a bundle of firewood on her head. To the eye, the rising ground lay so close that not only could Laila count the hyenas, she could also see the woman's face clearly.

"Nassif," she screamed in horror. Startled out of his thoughts, he stopped his horse, but could not turn it. He carefully dismounted and turned to Laila, and at that moment he too saw the hyenas.

The woman was trying to drive the beasts off with a stick. They retreated briefly, then attacked again, and through their greedy howls, which sounded like laughter, the two travellers heard cries for help.

Nassif shouted and cursed, but only a single hyena looked back at him in surprise, while the others attacked the woman yet more fiercely, and no one came to her aid. Laila had no strength left. She slipped from her saddle. Nassif tied his horse to a bush, went to her and held her tight.

"I love you, Laila," he said, and kissed her. His kiss made her frozen blood flow again.

"Can you go on?" he asked. She nodded. He helped her back into the saddle, then remounted his own horse, and sent it trotting slowly down the narrow, dangerous path. She followed him. It was the last time he ever called her Laila.

Three hours later they reached Mala. Later she said that the hyenas had been the warning sign that her days in Mala would begin with misfortune and end in misfortune too, but she ignored the sign.

20. Sarka's Fever

After her early death in 1920, the villagers spoke ill of Sarka. Years before her death, they said, she had betrayed George Mushtak and

THE DARK SIDE OF LOVE

Mala by encouraging the reapers to revolt. But Sofia the midwife defended her, saying it was her husband's fault. A week before the birth of her first child, Sarka had fallen sick with a strange fever. It lasted two days, and she had talked nonsense. Then, soon after the delivery of the baby, she fainted and lay unconscious for hours. That had been with Salman, and later it was the same with her second child Hasib. And at Hasib's birth, said Sofia, when the young woman came back to her senses after several hours, she herself had heard her making sounds like a wounded animal for half a day. No one could understand her. With her third child, her daughter Malake, Sarka fell into a dreadful state of derangement for a while. She screamed that her husband would hate the girl and kill her because she had the mark of a crescent moon just below her left breast, like her mother. As an experienced midwife, Sofia told George Mushtak that he should either stop getting his wife pregnant or take her to doctors in the city, but he just said angrily, "Women's foolishness!" Sarka, he said, had nine lives, like a cat, and could bear twenty children. At the birth of their fourth child Elias, however, she fainted away again, and when she regained consciousness she didn't recognise anyone for a while. After that she was afraid of the baby, and cried out that he was an elephant. At this point Sofia guessed that the woman had lost her wits, but George Mushtak still wouldn't hear of it.

"The fever's eaten her brain away," said the midwife, and she thought that was the only reason why Sarka's husband was able to forgive her everything later. "When she came back she was out of her mind, just a miserable creature deserving not punishment but pity."

21. The Elm Tree

The great elm tree, with the rotten half that burned down at Easter in 1953, had a story that had imprinted itself like no other on the collective memory of the village.

Sarka had felt unwell in Mala from the first. The climate was too harsh for her, the peasants too crude, and George Mushtak didn't love her any more now that hatred of his rivals increasingly filled his heart, leaving no room for his wife any more. Obsessed by that hatred as he was, he was no longer the Nassif who loved her laughter and understood every stirring of her emotions. Instead, he followed his instinct, which no longer saw the difference between his beloved Laila and any other woman. Hatred also left its mark on his pride, for he realized that the more women he took, the more virile he would seem to the men of the village.

A year after Salman's birth, chance or the devil took her to the granary where George was making love to Saliha, the barber's wife.

Sofia the midwife told anyone who would listen that she didn't understand the man, whoring around like that but still consumed by jealousy. He ought to have been a Muslim, she said, then he would have hidden Sarka from all eyes behind a veil. He felt wretched when other men looked at his beautiful wife and she let them share in her clear laughter. But Sarka loved him alone, and as long as she could still put two and two together she was faithful to him. She had a heart as pure and transparent as glass. When her lover betrayed her, however, that glass was left with a crack the size of a star in it. She wept for four days. "You don't love me, you don't love me," she repeated countless times, long after he had left the room, and she flung her head back and forth and took no notice of anything going on around her.

But George Mushtak realized that his love for her crippled him. She wasn't well, she complained and wept all the time, as if Laila had died and Sarka was only her wretched husk. He didn't know what to do. When he was with her, she begged him not to go away. But life outside wouldn't wait. He couldn't sit at her bedside for ever, holding her hand, while that bastard Jusuf Shahin was trying to destroy him.

Jusuf had married a clever woman from Aleppo. She was his closest confidante, and the secret leader of the anti-Mushtak campaign. Her name was Samia. She was a witch, but she lent her husband wings, whereas Sarka had been like a leaden weight clinging to George's feet ever since their arrival in Mala. When little Salman began crying at night, he had another room prepared for her, on the first floor at the other end of the house, and from then on he slept more peacefully.

One night soon after the birth of her second son Hasib she felt that she couldn't breathe. She rose from her bed and quietly went out. The wind refreshed her face. She took deep breaths of night air. The moon was shining brightly; you could almost hear the silver silence. Suddenly the yard gate sprang open, and she felt a strange current drawing her away. Like a feather with no will of its own, she flitted through the gateway and on past the church of St. Giorgios to the terraced fields. Only when she reached the distant threshing floor did she realize that she was barefoot. She turned and went back to bed, and next day she would have thought the whole thing was only a dream, but for the thistles still clinging to her dress.

A little while after that, people began whispering about a ghost that haunted the fields on nights of full moon, softly singing nursery rhymes. Those who heard that song, they said, fell victim to a spell that turned them too into children and led them to their ruin.

Sarka was indeed always out and about now when the moon was full. One night she was walking over the hill near the graveyard when she noticed a man following her. She stopped and turned to face him. He stood rooted to the spot in the moonlight. He was slender, and as beautiful as a youth. Sarka went on singing, and he listened to her song like a child.

"What do you want?" she asked. He trembled with fear, and stammered as he said he had never touched a woman yet, he would like to lay his head in her lap just once. She laughed and reached her hands out to him, but then he ran away.

He came back every night when the moon was full, but he never ventured to touch her. Instead, he always whispered, "Holy Virgin, stand by me."

After that the villagers of Mala spoke of two ghosts. At first they laughed at the strange couple, but when the shepherd Ismail was found hanged close to the graveyard one morning the peasants were afraid. Three days before, Ismail had been saying that he was going to listen to the nocturnal singing. The ghost was a friendly one, he said, and surely they could see that nothing had happened to him yet.

The shepherd died a month after the birth of Malake, Sarka's third baby. George Mushtak took a dislike to the child from the first, and his arch-enemy Jusuf Shahin knew why and was happy to tell other people what he thought. The baby's father, he said, wasn't Sarka's husband but the handsome shepherd Ismail, who had hanged himself for love.

But many in the village believed that the ghost who wandered the fields had turned the shepherd's wits, and they felt fear weighing them down. For it was at this of all times that they *had* to go out at night, because the water from the spring was running short, and was shared out between families according to a precise timetable. That way, every farmer could irrigate his field at an allotted time, and those times alternated between day and night.

So after the shepherd's tragic death they stopped up their ears with wax by night, and if they heard a sound all the same they exclaimed, "Holy Virgin, stand by me!" As they couldn't hear how loud they were speaking, their cries rang out from the terraced fields and echoed all the way down into the valley.

After the difficult birth of her fourth child Elias, Sarka was unwell for a long time. The midwife Sofia had to spend the night with her, in case she was needed. George Mushtak paid her generously, but he refused to listen when Sofia said it would soon be impossible for his wife to be left alone. And when the catastrophe happened, it was too late.

One hot June day in 1916, Sarka suddenly appeared in the large field. Itinerant reapers always came to Mala for the wheat harvest at the end of June, and found plenty of work for two weeks. They were badly paid, but poor pay was still better than starvation. This was the middle of the First World War, and poverty and misery reigned in the Ottoman Empire.

George Mushtak was a harsh taskmaster. Not only did he pay badly, he didn't hesitate to whip his reapers if he caught them idling – or what he took for idling. On the other hand, he gave them employment from the first to the last day of the harvest, and he paid money, which was better for many of the reapers than the usual payment in kind. These itinerant workers went from village to village with their womenfolk, offering their services. There were many tales about the women reapers who earned five piastres for ten hours' work by day, but three times as much by night. In Mala, harvest was also the fornication season, and for many young men it was the one chance they had in the year to satisfy their sexual urges. They saved up their piastres for those last two weeks in June.

So on that hot June day Sarka came to the field where the reapers were at work. She looked with feverish eyes at the men bending, sickle in hand, to cut the blades of wheat and lay them on the ground in bundles. Younger men then gathered them into larger sheaves, and finally carried them to the threshing floor on the backs of donkeys.

Suddenly Sarka crouched down, and to the horror of the reapers raised her dress, bared her buttocks, laughed out loud and pissed. The men looked away. One of the shocked women asked, "Aren't you ashamed to bare your backside in front of men, mistress?" Sarka laughed and cried, "I'm never ashamed in front of cockroaches. What does it matter if they see my backside?"

"Cockroaches?" cried several of the reapers. "Cockroaches?"

"Yes, what else are you? They whip you, they screw your women, and as for you, you twirl your moustaches with pride in the evenings, thinking of the money your wives will bring home!" cried Sarka in a hoarse voice.

At that the men suddenly all shouted at once. They felt that they and their wives had been mortally insulted. A little later they killed two of George Mushtak's men in their rage, and set his fields and some others on fire. That was the beginning of the biggest riot in the history of the village.

The reapers went through Mala, looting and murdering, setting fire to houses and to the church of St. Giorgios. The blaze quickly ate its way through the dry wood of the buildings. The villagers had difficulty keeping the flames in check and saving any neighbouring houses. As if by a miracle, however, the church survived, and only the porch and a part of the east wing burned down. The fire went out in front of the altar of its own accord.

There was fighting everywhere, and crowds of reapers from nearby villages hurried in to help their comrades. On the third day, they were clearly in the majority as they faced the men of Mala. Mushtak only just escaped an attempt on his life.

Infuriated, he gathered his loyal supporters together, and with the help of Mobate's men he attacked the reapers. Jusuf Shahin and other rich farmers now joined the fray too. The fighting went on for days, and over seventy of the itinerant workers were killed.

There was no police station in Mala at the time, and the Ottoman governor of Damascus refused to send reinforcements. He was afraid of being thought a traitor if his troops defended a Christian village against Muslim workers.

The reapers took plenty of loot. They went off with horses, jewellery, money, furniture, and crockery. All they left behind was their dead, who lay lifeless and nameless in the streets.

Many of the farmers were left lamenting the destruction of their entire harvest. Others had lost their houses and all the valuables in them. But it was worst of all for Mushtak. The news that Sarka had disappeared hit him harder than the loss of his possessions. She was not among the dead, nor could she be found anywhere else.

Sofia the midwife helped Sarka's housekeeper to look after the four children. The firstborn, Salman, was just eight, and Elias the youngest was not yet two years old.

All attempts to trace Sarka failed. Two years passed, and Mushtak never had a good night's sleep. When he closed his eyes, he saw her lying naked on a heap of wheat. During the day he longed for her fragrance. Sofia saw him pace up and down her room and heard him crying out in pain. He would take out Sarka's clothes, smell them, tear them up and then gather the pieces together and put them in a big box. When lovesickness began to cut him like a knife, he went to the church of St. Giorgios, where he opened his shirt and showed the Catholic priest, Father Timotheus, a deep cut in the region of his heart.

Timotheus was the son of a rich Damascene family who had fled from the world to find peace in Mala. The villagers regarded the monk as a saint, and it was said that he sometimes levitated, hovering in the air for over an hour while praying. Just before Easter his hands always showed the stigmata of Our Lord, and bled. Timotheus was both modest and stern with himself. That day he laid his hand on the suffering George Mushtak's wound.

"No, not that wound, reverend Father, not that one," said Mushtak.

"Pray for Sarka to come back to me, and I'll give the church my thousand-year-old elm tree." Everyone knew the elm that stood on a distant hill, easily visible from the village square.

"If your prayers help me to warm myself on Sarka again, then the firewood from that ancient tree will keep the church and the presbytery warm for years," Mushtak told the priest as he left.

And Sarka did come back three days later, as if out of a clear blue sky. She was wearing plain but clean peasant clothes, but her mind was hopelessly deranged. Her husband welcomed her with tears of joy.

No one knew where she had been all that time, or how she found her way home. She never spoke another word until the day she died. All she did was wander around the village looking for something. Whenever she heard children's voices she ran towards them, only to collapse in disappointment and shed tears.

Legend upon legend formed around Sarka, but all the tales were just gossip. Some people claimed to have seen her with one of the reapers who had been wounded, going about with him looting and burning. Others were sure she had been abducted out of revenge by the brother of a reaper who had been murdered in the village, and was then driven to madness by poison.

Sarka brought George Mushtak no joy now. He would lie silently in his room, weeping. And so time passed, and the church never got a single branch of that elm tree. When the monk lost patience and reminded the forgetful Mushtak of his promise, Mushtak roared indignantly across the village square, "All that your saints gave me back was a lunatic. She's only half a human being, and for that you'll get only half the tree!"

That very night lightning struck the distant hill. For several long minutes, Mala was as brightly lit as if a thousand suns were shining. The elm tree was struck by the lightning and split in two. In time, one side dried up while the other remained green. Over the years, the two assumed a strange shape. The dead half looked like a waning crescent moon, the green half like a waxing moon. Rain, sun, and human hands carved the split down the middle of the tree into a kind of cave, where lovers and children liked to hide.

Sarka often spent days on end there. Travellers and peasants, passing the elm, had a shock when she suddenly emerged from inside the tree.

Just before her death there were rumours that she had borne a son, but hid the child for fear of her husband, and now she had forgotten where, hence her desperate searching. Children ran after her pulling at her dress and crying, "Here's your son, you blind madwoman!" And they crowed and hit her and threw stones. When she was near the Mushtak property no one dared molest her, but as soon as she was a little way from the walls of the house she became a target for all who really wanted to hurt the founder of the clan, but dared not attack him openly himself. However, when a boy hit the crazed woman with a stone, everyone applauded. Sarka cursed the stone-thrower in her heart, and you could see the hatred in her eyes, but her mouth remained mute.

This time, said Sofia, was the hardest of Mushtak's life. His enemies rejoiced at his suffering, and encouraged everyone to tell more tales of his wife.

Two years after Sarka's return to the village, a peasant woman going to quench her thirst at the little spring near the elm found Mushtak's wife inside the tree. She seemed to be sleeping with a blissful smile on her face. But she never woke again.

BOOK OF THE CLAN I

Arab clans and pyramids ignore the passing of time.

৯৹

DAMASCUS, MALA, BEIRUT 1907–1953

22. The Gulf

The gulf between the Mushtak and Shahin families was deep. Later, no one could say just how their hostility had begun, but even the children of both families were convinced that they would sooner make friends with the devil than one of the enemy clan.

George Mushtak had met Jusuf Shahin on the evening of his arrival in Mala. The two men were almost the same age. They drank together in the house of the village elder Mobate, who had invited all the notables of Mala to meet the stranger seeking shelter there. It was said that George and Jusuf made friends quickly that evening, but came to blows a few days later because Shahin had slighted Mushtak's young wife Sarka and treated her roughly. He didn't like women, in particular blue-eyed women with quick tongues who laughed a lot. Sarka combined all those qualities.

Mobate managed to reconcile the two men, and there was peace for a while. Then came the christening party for the village elder's first-born son. The christening wasn't even over, so the tale went, before trouble flared up between the two rivals. Apparently Jusuf had made a coarse joke at Sarka's expense; because of her blue eyes he was said to have asked whether her mother had conceived her with a Frank, his term for all Europeans. "Oh yes," Sarka was reported as replying, "at the same time as your mother conceived you with a donkey."

"Whore!" he spat at the young woman. Then there was a riot. Jusuf was about to slap Sarka's face, when George Mushtak came between them. Several others tried to part the two men. Jusuf left the house. He had been the only Orthodox Christian at the party anyway.

George Mushtak was deeply offended and swore revenge. Perhaps the origin of all the hostility that followed lay in his disappointment. He had liked Shahin, and had great hopes of their friendship.

When the priest spoke to him, trying to smooth matters over, he merely spat. "If I ever forgive that dog I'll lick my spittle off the ground."

From then on he was always at pains to show who was the most powerful rooster on the Mala dunghill. Many tales were told of his wily tricks in buying everything he could lay hands on, until at last he owned a hectare of land, a house, a horse, a cow, a sheep, and a threshing floor more than his arch-enemy Shahin.

From the very first day Jusuf's wife Samia had seen more in Mushtak than just the threat of a rival for power in the village, which was Jusuf's view of him until that christening party. Then she met the stranger for the first time, and later she told her husband that in his company she felt he was a beast of prey. He had an acquisitive, bloodthirsty look in his eyes, she said. She felt as if her skin were scorching when Mushtak looked at her, and she found his presence uncomfortable.

Shahin's pride was wounded by his initial misjudgement of his opponent. It was only Sarka whom he had despised from the first. So now he used her to strike his next blow at Mushtak. He claimed she was a Muslim woman, the stranger had brought her with him from a brothel, and that was why she never went to church. She didn't even know how to cross herself. That taunt went home.

Mushtak wanted to provide evidence to the contrary next Sunday, but Sarka refused to set foot in the church. They quarrelled bitterly; it was said that he had been very abusive to her during their argument, and that was why she had done all the things she did later, which ultimately led to her early death.

But before that sad event hostility between the two rivals went on steadily growing, and the village split into two clearly divided camps, the supporters of Mushtak and the supporters of Shahin. Attack after attack fuelled rage and hatred on both sides.

For instance, a young man once went to work for Shahin as a groom. After a year he disappeared one night with five of his master's most expensive Arab horses. When it came to Jusuf's ears that George Mushtak had hired the runaway groom, Mushtak's barn burned down two nights later with that year's entire harvest inside it.

In addition, the growing enmity between the two rivals ultimately gave their adherents, Catholic on one side and Orthodox on the other, a clear focus for their mutual dislike, and it took up permanent residence in their minds. Soon the village elder, Mobate, seemed only a pathetic mediator always trying to keep the two real rulers of Mala apart. But there was no chance of that, for the hostility between Catholics and Orthodox Christians is over a thousand years old in the Middle East. Too much blood had flowed in Mala now, and both clans had an excellent memory. Every grief suffered by one side was celebrated as an occasion for joy by the other.

But one of the bitterest defeats ever suffered by George, as founder of the Mushtak clan, was the work not of a Shahin but of his own son Elias, Farid's father. Or perhaps old Mushtak inflicted that defeat on himself, and his son was only the involuntary means to the end.

23. Elias Leaves

The Mushtak clan might be small in numbers, but to the peasants of Mala it seemed infinitely powerful. Its power came not only from its wealth but from its bold determination. Peasants hesitate. The Mushtaks made decisions swiftly and without fear of losses. They always acted with discretion, unlike their arch-enemies the Shahins, who were constantly letting the village know which government minister or high-ranking army officer was now friends with them. It was merely suspected that the Mushtaks had secret links with the men in power in Damascus.

They owned many houses in the capital, but however much those buildings were worth, what mattered to the people of Mala was that they owned the biggest farm in the village and the finest houses on the village square. The most handsome building of all, indisputably, was Elias's summer residence. Farid's father built it in 1950, three years after the death of George Mushtak, founder of the clan, as if to show the village that he had returned victorious. Fifteen years earlier his father had disowned him and disinherited him, for Elias had married not the village elder's daughter Samira Mobate, in line with the patriarch's plans, but Claire Surur from Damascus. However, that was only the official explanation of the war between them, and as in all wars there was another story behind their bitter struggle.

It was long assumed that the striking likeness between them had led to their mutual dislike. Elias was the image of his father, wiry, small, and dashing, like George. But in one thing he was very different.

George, the founder of the clan, had felt sick with envy when he first set eyes on his newborn youngest son. The midwife Sofia said that even at his birth Elias had an erect penis as long as her middle finger. And whenever she told the story, at this point in it she would always spread her large hand and show that impressive finger.

The founder of the clan had slept with half the women in the village, but all his life he fretted because his penis was so small. The women simply called it "Mushtak's olive", which tells us all we need to know about that insatiable skirt-chaser's shame. So on the day of Elias's birth he just looked at the boy with revulsion and left the room, cursing, without a single kind word to his wife.

The boy's prick always horrified his father. At the time, most of the children in Mala used to run about naked or at the most very sparsely clad. Not so Elias. George Mushtak had ordered first Sarka, and after her death the housekeeper, never to let his son go out without trousers and a stout bandage worn under them.

Sarka didn't particularly like Elias either. She felt sorry for him, but quite often she was afraid of him too, because whenever she suckled him that alarmingly erect penis would stick up from his frail little body, to macabre effect. It was hard as a rock and had a strangely penetrating tarry smell, even when she had bathed the baby three times with soap and massaged his penis with pure rosewater.

But obtrusive as Elias's prick appeared, he himself grew to be a handsome, delicately built boy who showed a great gift for languages, even in first grade. Yet he never went to school without feeling apprehensive. In those days, children were beaten daily by their teachers, and indeed parents would encourage the schoolmasters with the proverbial saying: "His flesh and skin are yours, just leave us the bones."

George Mushtak handed Elias over to Father Philippus with those very words. But the boy gave no one much of an opportunity to punish him. He was industrious and obedient, clean and courteous. After less than six months he was teacher's pet, which annoyed his fellow pupils. They took him behind a bush at break and beat him up. The boy trembled at the prospect every morning. He saw the peasants mercilessly beating their little donkeys, and often thought he might be related to those animals. Indeed, the schoolboys who saw his prick shouted, "You're not a boy, you're a donkey!" Elias felt immense love for the donkeys.

In the summer of 1924 Father Julian Baston turned up in Mala, looking for talented boys to join the Jesuit order. Baston was tall and athletically built. A Frenchman by birth, he had thick grey hair and clever little eyes. He was around forty, but looked much older.

Father Julian spotted the ten-year-old on a visit to St. Giorgios elementary school, which all the Catholic village children attended. Elias's bright face in itself was a pleasure to see, among the other scarred and dirty countenances. After talking to the delicate boy, the Jesuit visited Mushtak's house. George received him with great dignity, and was delighted to find that Father Julian spoke perfect Arabic.

Julian Baston was frank. He confided his secret to Elias's father: the country needed more trained priests than the wretched handful left behind by the now defunct Ottoman Empire. "They're not priests, they're Antichrists," said the Jesuit, "they've let our Christian faith degenerate into an Oriental orgy of eating and drinking shrouded by incense fumes. They don't understand a word of the sacred texts they parrot, so anyone who hears the word of Islam won't hold out against it for long."

Father Julian explained his thinking at length. The region was awash with mineral oil, and one day it would be a major centre of the international economy. But Islam was not in any position to manage such wealth. To that end, it was time to begin setting up elite Christian schools. And such schools called for intelligent, well-educated priests.

"We have renovated and reopened several tumbledown monasteries. There's a beautiful Dominican institution that we've refurbished in Damascus. If you agree, that's where Elias would live," the Jesuit went on, in friendly tones.

"But don't the Muslims give you any problems?" asked George Mushtak, sceptically.

"No, we have good relations with several Sunni families who help us get access to the important decision-makers. Our only problems are with the Orthodox Christians, because they realize that Catholicism is gaining ground."

"Ah, they're worse than the Muslims. Here in Mala we have those crafty devils the Shahins to deal with. The man Shahin is a Judas who ruled the whole village before I arrived, and was in league with the local Muslims to enslave good Catholics. Now he can't live with the fact that I, a Catholic, have taken over as leader here. Have you seen our church?"

"Yes, yes, indeed, and I know that your donations and your determination alone made all those repairs possible, all those wonderful frescos. But we in Damascus need your help too, we need your generosity so that our students can get the teaching they need to become good priests. For with all due respect to Islam ..."

George Mushtak hated Islam. He was glad to hear that educated Europeans shared his views. So he interrupted his guest. "I can feel no respect for a gang who murdered my mother and my sister! For cowardly reasons of revenge! Just because a Muslim woman threw in her lot with a Christian man."

"I'm sorry, I don't understand," said the Jesuit quietly.

"No one can understand it," replied Mushtak, and his eyes grew damp.

The visitor, a clever man, sensed that his host was struggling with a bitter memory and trying to keep his composure. All was suddenly still in the large drawing room where cool twilight reigned behind the drawn curtains. George rose to his feet, opened the door, and called to his housekeeper to make some good coffee flavoured with cardamom for his distinguished visitor. Then he closed the door again and returned to the guest, forcing himself to smile.

"Forgive the strength of my reaction, but some memories keep coming up again, like undigested food repeating."

"We must learn to forgive, however," said the priest.

"I can forgive anything but the murder of my mother and my sister."

During his training, the Jesuit had read a great deal about guilt and atonement, revenge and clan feeling among the Arabs, and he knew there were subjects better not discussed with an Arab if you were or wanted to be his friend.

"I understand you," replied the experienced priest. Mushtak felt that he had triumphed. One of the greatest miracles on earth, as he saw it, was to make a European who was also a scholar and a churchman understand well-justified hatred.

Soon after this the fragrant coffee was brought in. The housekeeper had added a plate of butter cookies.

"Elias is a rose who cannot flower among the thistles of Mala," said the priest, returning to his request.

"A rose maybe," replied Mushtak, "but with a huge thorn of a prick. I'll give you the boy and a hundred gold lira."

The priest's wish was like manna from heaven to George. For more than seven years to come he would sleep more easily than ever before, since he wasn't at all interested in what his son did behind the high monastery walls.

Elias didn't mind parting from his family either. He was sorry only for his sister Malake, who shed tears whenever she mentioned his imminent departure. When it was time to say goodbye, his father reluctantly gave the boy his hand. Elias kissed it and pressed it to his forehead, as custom ordained, but George did not return the kiss. The proffered hand was not a bridge, but acted like a barrier keeping his son at a distance. The boy's father went no further than the front gate.

That made Elias feel deeply humiliated. Accompanied by his big brother he reached the bus, gave his case to the conductor, and found a window seat.

"Don't let it bother you. He's not in a good mood today," Salman consoled him. But Elias felt angry with his father, who had given such threadbare reasons to explain why he couldn't take him to the monastery in Damascus himself.

"That's all right," he said, close to tears. He looked over his brother's head, and at that moment he saw his sister, who was four years older than him. She was trying to reach him to say goodbye. But their father slapped her face, pushed her back into the courtyard and quickly closed the door so that she couldn't get out again.

"Look after Malake. Our father will kill her yet," Elias said quietly to his brother. Salman glanced at their father, standing stiffly in front of the gate of his property, and smiled.

"Father wouldn't kill anyone, but Malake is a stubborn goat," he replied.

Their father had never liked Malake either. There had been frequent beatings, but only for the two of them. Just two days ago he had hit Malake during a meal for secretly taking a bite of his own piece of bread. Mushtak had strictly forbidden that kind of thing. Everyone's share of bread was handed out. Not that there was any shortage of food, but Malake's father believed you took years off another person's life if you bit into his bread. Elias thought this superstition was ridiculous, but Malake didn't. "It's not superstition. I'm always eating his bread in secret. Sometimes he catches me at it, that's all."

The bus driver, who had hooted five minutes ago and was now roaring his engine, switched it off and went to have another cup of tea with the barber.

"This could go on for ever," said Salman.

"You don't have to stick around," replied Elias, who was finding his brother's presence more and more of a nuisance, and as if Salman had just been waiting for him to say so he shook hands and hurried back home.

Just then Elias saw his sister running out of a side street. He admired her for her dauntless courage. Malake was beaming all over her face when she came up to him. Old Mushtak, however, gave a start of surprise on seeing her and spoke to Salman, who had just that moment reached him. His eldest son turned briefly, then took his father's arm and led him into the house.

Breathless, Malake flung her arms around Elias's neck and wept. "He didn't want to let me say goodbye properly. But you're my own dear brother." And she sobbed out loud. He began to weep too, not with emotion, not because they were parting, but with the fury of desperation because he couldn't protect his sister. Elias knew that when Malake was home again all hell would be let loose. She had defied her father's orders to stay indoors and climbed over the wall. Several men had certainly seen her do it, and would have laughed at Mushtak. If a girl made her father look ridiculous, that was reason enough to kill her.

Malake seemed to guess what he was thinking. "Oh, my dear brother," she said. "'I don't feel the blows. I pray while he's beating me."

"You pray?" asked Elias, surprised.

"Yes, I pray, I beg the Virgin Mary to make his hand decay and drop off while he's still alive. And then, while he's hitting me, I think how miserable he'll look sitting there and begging me for a sip of water."

The engine of the bus was revving up as she kissed him for the last time. Then she jumped out of it, and for the first time he saw that she was barefoot.

24. A Reception

There was unrest throughout the country, and uncertainty everywhere. The French and the British had taken the Arabs for a ride. In the secret Sykes-Picot agreement of 1916 they had divided up the Middle East between them, even before the Arabs could enjoy the fruits of their revolt against the Ottoman Empire. The countries were recolonized, with Arabia chopped up on the negotiating table in the interests of the two great powers.

One dusty July day in 1920, French troops marched into Damascus, and they stayed until 1946 – a quarter of a century of uprisings, banditry, and fighting between powerful clans.

A week after the French arrived, their High Commissioner, General Gouraud, invited all the important sheikhs and clan chiefs to a reception. And they all came, for it made no difference to them whether the ruler in Damascus spoke Turkish, Arabic, or French. What mattered was that their own clans were not enfeebled and passed over in favour of others. They suspiciously scrutinized the seating order and the presents that the general gave them. They understood not a word of his brief address, and still less could they get their heads around the fact that all the French officers had brought their wives to the reception, as if to give the ladies a look at the defeated natives. Gouraud even had his daughter with him too. The women were pretty and silent, like little Chinese porcelain figures.

The general gave each clan chief a new French sporting gun and a compass, and his guests were as delighted as children with these amazing little clocks that always pointed north. Many of them were playing with their magical devices even during the reception, turning them around and around and roaring with laughter.

It was high summer, and the big table groaned under the weight of the delicacies prepared by Arab cooks. To the horror of the Frenchwomen, the Arabs ate with their bare hands. They slurped and smacked their lips, and soon the tables had grains of rice, pieces of bread and food stains all over them. But none of the Arabs touched the red Bordeaux that was served with the meal.

"Why do you drink only water?" General Gouraud asked the man next to him, Sheikh Yassin Hamdan, head imam of the Ummayad Mosque. He himself raised his glass and drank with relish.

The question surprised Sheikh Yassin. He wondered for a moment if the general could really be as ignorant as he sounded.

"Because the Koran forbids us to drink wine," he replied through his interpreter.

The general grinned, and pointed to the red grapes that the sheikh was eating.

"It is His Excellency's opinion," said the interpreter, "that you eat grapes, yet wine comes from grapes."

The sheikh glanced at the general, who was looking at him blurry-eyed after his eighth glass.

'True, wine comes from grapes. But his daughter comes from his wife. Does he therefore sleep with his daughter?"

This *bon mot* later went the rounds of Damascus as if the sheikh's answer had crushed Gouraud. However, the general remembered nothing of what was said that evening. He was too drunk.

His mission had been to win over the clan chiefs to accept French rule, for if they were well disposed then their subjects would make no more trouble. So he told his adjutant to telegraph Paris, saying: "Mission completed. Clan chiefs well disposed to France. Said not a word about their dead."

25. The Novice

It was late in the evening when Elias finally reached Damascus. The bus had had problems all the way, and its inexperienced driver had been unable to do anything but swear at the engine. About twenty kilometres outside Damascus the bus finally broke down. Beside himself with fury, the driver began throwing stones at his own vehicle and cursing his mother.

Finally, all the passengers had moved to the load area of a truck where twenty sheep had to make room for them. Elias was disgusted because one of the animals had diarrhoea, and the stinking floor of the truck was filthy with it.

The truck driver had to deliver the sheep to various different destinations, disappearing into the house each time for a tea, while his passengers waited in the hot truck.

Elias was drenched with sweat and tired when he finally knocked at the monastery gate. An inscription in Latin letters over the entrance said: *Omnia ad maiorem Dei gloriam*. He didn't understand a word of it. While he waited he thought of his sister Malake and prayed for her.

A monk opened the gate. He smiled at Elias. "We were worrying about you. I hope you didn't have an accident?' he said in a gentle voice, and introduced himself as Brother Andreas.

With those words a time began for the boy that Elias was to describe, later, as "the happiest days of my life." In the monastery all was peace and calm, discipline and cleanliness. No one beat him, no one called him names. Above all, no one told tales of him to the man who had been less of a father to him than prosecutor and prison warder combined. He had enough to eat, and he was taken seriously, although he was still little more than a child. Elias worked hard, and here too he was top of the class in most subjects, but he wasn't teased or beaten up for it. He showed particular talent for maths. After two years Father Samuel Sibate, a mathematical genius himself, let him join his higher mathematics study group. About ten of his students met every Thursday and tried, with Father Samuel himself, to solve those great mathematical problems that still baffled the world. Elias was the only one in the group who was still of school age.

A year after his arrival in Damascus, there was a great uprising against the French occupiers in the south of Syria. The word was that the British would help the rebels against the French. But for a long time all that passed the monastery walls by, and Elias too. Instead, the boy learned to play the piano and speak fluent French with a perfect accent.

He didn't want to spend his vacations with his family, though he could have gone home every other year. To the delight of his teachers, he preferred to go on industriously learning Latin and Spanish, and even the heat of summer in the city couldn't keep him from his books.

Not until seven years after he entered the monastery, in the summer of 1931, did he take two weeks' vacation to go to his brother Salman's wedding back in Mala. His teachers were happy to let the clever, devout novice enjoy this brief period of rest and relaxation.

Elias didn't care about the wedding one way or other, and he probably wouldn't have gone if Malake had not written him a letter in secret, saying she absolutely had to talk to him because a crucial change in her life was imminent.

After three weeks in Mala he came back again, silent and distressed. He was transformed. Suddenly he had lost all interest in the life of the monastery, but no one ever found out why.

In the years before Salman's wedding, however, a great deal had happened in Mala, and that story must now be told.

26. How Mushtak Won Honour

As early as the end of July 1925, soon after the beginning of the rebellion in the south, George Mushtak foresaw that the fighting would spread and affect Mala. Anxious about his second son Hasib, who was clever but not brave, he first sent him to a boarding school run by Jesuits in Beirut. The boy was safe there. Later, when he had taken his high school diploma, the plan was for him to study medicine at the American University of Beirut.

Once all that was fixed, Mushtak felt freer. Elias and Hasib had left. He now had with him only his courageous fifteen-year-old daughter Malake, and his firstborn son Salman, aged seventeen. George loved and admired Salman. Even as a child, the boy had shown an interest in the farm, and by now he was an experienced agriculturalist. He had blue eyes like his mother and her bold heart too. From the other side of his family he inherited his father's taciturn disposition, and he acted even more discreetly. It was on his eldest son that George Mushtak pinned all his hopes of making the clan the most powerful family in Mala in the near future.

But in his heart of hearts he loved Salman most because he was the only child he had given Sarka during their days of stormy passion. All the others bore the mark of the hatred that Sarka had later come to feel for her husband.

Hasib was brilliant, but crazy with jealousy. He saw red if anyone so much as touched his mother, and threw a tantrum if any of the other children were better treated. Malake had inherited her mother's epilepsy and her wild disposition, as if she too were afflicted by the devil who had taken possession of Sarka's soul. She was wilful and stubborn. Later, when a stranger took a fancy to her and was prepared to wait until Salman married, George was pleased with that solution, although he thought the man a fool. As for Elias, he had a prick like a donkey's which turned even George's stomach, and nothing in the world usually daunted him. In addition, the boy was moody, like his mother, and could spoil everything at just the wrong moment.

Only Salman, the son of innocent love, had not only inherited from him, George Mushtak, his strength of character, temperament, and firm disposition, but also had the most beautiful eyes in the world: the eyes of Sarka.

✤

At this time there were rumours going around that bandits were making use of the unrest for their own ends. They avoided big cities so as not to clash with the French. Instead, they attacked rich or Christian villages, killed the men, and raped the women.

Alarmed by these stories, a delegation from Mala set off for Damascus. It consisted of the village elder, the priest, and several other important men, and they were going to ask the French governor to protect the village.

The bus set off at dawn. George Mushtak, accompanying the party, argued on the way with the Catholic priest, who really believed that the French would send a peace-keeping troop as soon as they heard that a Christian village of people who loved France was in danger.

When they arrived at about nine, he paid all their fares. Then he told Mobate that he was going to have a quiet breakfast in the Venecia restaurant while they went to put their case to the governor. They were welcome to join him when the governor had thrown them out, he added.

Around twelve they came in with their tails between their legs. The governor had laughed at them, they said, and recommended them to convert to Islam, saying that he for one couldn't spare any soldiers. The rebels were already threatening the southern suburbs of Damascus.

Mushtak smiled, and invited the delegation to lunch. While they were still eating dessert, a man of perhaps thirty at the most came over to their table. George introduced him as Ahmad Tarabishi. The young man stood there a little stiffly in his European suit and red felt hat as he took George's order for a hundred Mauser rifles. Mushtak put his hand in his pocket, brought out a small velvet bag, and put it on the table. "Here are fifty gold lira; you'll get the other fifty when you deliver them. And if there's anything wrong with a single one of those rifles you'll be sorry, because I will personally knock your skull in."

"You can rely on me, sir, as always," said the dealer quietly. He took the bag, kissed Mushtak's outstretched hand as he took his leave, and hurried away. Speechless, the men of Mala looked at their mysterious companion with admiration.

"You took me in when I was in need, and I promised you then that George Mushtak never forgets anything," he said dryly, almost grimly.

"Are you sure the man won't just abscond with such a large sum of money?" asked Father Johannis.

"Oh, I've done business with his father in the past. Fifty gold lira are small change to the Tarabishis."

"How can I ever repay you?" asked Habib Mobate. But Mushtak did not reply. He never expected gratitude from his subjects.

✺

Friday was market day in Mala. Many farmers from the surrounding villages arrived with their chickens, horses, lambs, and olives. Others came from the distant villages on the plain, where all varieties of melons and mulberries grew and flourished.

One Friday in the late summer of 1925 a farmer stopped there with his horse-drawn cart, which was heavily loaded up with watermelons. The farmer asked for the Mushtak family's residence. He, his cart, and his two horses disappeared through the great gateway, and when he came out again hours later the cart was empty. Soon the village elder learned that the hundred German Mauser rifles had arrived, together with a hundred crates of ammunition.

That winter was bitterly cold. But a volcano was seething in Mushtak's soul. Not until spring 1926 did he finally see his time coming, and that was just when everyone else in the village was sure he had backed the wrong horse. When rumour said that seventy thousand

French soldiers had landed in Syria, armed to the teeth, and law and order would soon prevail again, he disputed it. Now of all times, he told them, when the rebels and bandits would be withdrawing to all four points of the compass, Mala must be on its guard.

But most of the village elder's friends thought as he did: Mushtak just didn't want to admit that his purchase of the weapons had been a mistake. They whispered behind his back that loneliness since his wife's death had embittered him, and his hatred for Muslims had made him blind. Not a few laughed to themselves to think of the high price he had paid for those guns.

Only one man did not laugh: Jusuf Shahin, his arch-enemy. He didn't think that bandits would attack Mala either, but when he heard of the rifles in his adversary's house he had a number of weapons brought over the mountains of Lebanon and, after discussion with the Orthodox convent of St. Thecla, he had them stored in the grotto there.

"May St. Thecla bless the guns," he said to the abbess as he took his leave, placing a friendly hand on her arm, "and guide the bullets on their way to the hearts of Christ's enemies." And then he smiled, because he was sure she thought he meant the Muslims. As he saw it, however, there was no greater enemy of Christ than Mushtak.

Summer passed slowly; the air was hot and dusty. George did not feel inclined to go out in the village square. The other men cast him malicious glances, for it had never been as peaceful in Mala and its surroundings as it was that year. Even in the village itself, people were friendlier to each other than usual these days.

He wondered whether it might not have been wiser to go about the matter as his arch-enemy did. Very few people knew about the large quantity of guns stored in the convent.

At the end of August he woke from a nightmare, bathed in sweat. Day was only just dawning. The children were still asleep. He dressed and left the house with his revolver and his field glasses strapped to his belt. It was still dark when he reached the gate. He looked left, as if he knew that someone over there was watching him. His manservant Basil, relieved, waved from the window of the little hut where he lived in the yard of the property. He kept better watch on the place than the three dogs who roamed free there at night. Mushtak could sleep easily now that he knew nothing escaped Basil's eyes. He had given him a gun and permission to shoot any intruder. His blood feud with the Shahins left no room for any carelessness.

Soon word of this arrangement had gone around the village, and when two young men tried to play a trick on the watchman, apparently for a bet, Basil fired his gun without warning. He hit the pair of them in the buttocks. They had to endure the mockery of the villagers for weeks on end, and from then on no one ventured to set foot in the yard without sending word first. Even when a complaint was laid with the police and they came to search the place, the police chief politely informed Mushtak the day before, telling him that the CID from Damascus was going to search his property for hashish in the morning.

Three jeeps drove down the quiet street to the house at dawn. The ten policemen had brought chisels, a large axe, and saws to dispose of any obstacles they might find in their way. But the gate was open and the dogs in their kennel. Sullenly, the officer went all over the property with his men, but of course they found nothing.

"George Mushtak has dealt in anything that makes money, but never hashish. It is beneath his dignity," George told the police officer, "and so whatever bastard laid that complaint knows." He always spoke of himself in the third person when addressing a social inferior.

The officer, disappointed by his failure, said nothing. He drank the coffee that the housekeeper had given him, and as he left gratefully pocketed the ten lira pressed into his hand by Mushtak, who said almost paternally, "Buy your children some candy." The police officer took the strong hand of the master of the house and whispered, "Jusuf Shahin." George Mushtak merely nodded.

The CID officer knew that by giving away the name he might cause a murder, but he hated peasants and the very smell of them. In the city, he would never have revealed the identity of a man who had laid a complaint, not for all the money in the world.

That incident was now two years in the past. Ever since, Mushtak's men had been doing their utmost to repay Jusuf Shahin in his own coin, but none of what they had suggested so far pleased their master.

He didn't want his enemy's horses or barns, his house or his yard, all he wanted was to strike him to the heart so that the scoundrel would finally keep quiet.

That morning at the end of August 1926, when Mushtak set out at dawn, he closed the gate behind him and walked towards the ravine. It was very quiet, but his mind was seething. He quickened his pace. He was sweating. Soon he was struggling for breath, for the path climbed more steeply all the time.

It was half an hour before he reached the top of the rocky ridge. Mala lay in its shadow, and he had a wide view from here. Still breathing heavily, he raised his field glasses and turned them south. His dry lips moved. Almost inaudibly, he said, "I know you're coming. Here I am, come along. You'll find your grave here. I know you're coming!" There was a pleading note in his voice.

But the distant prospect disappointed him. The rising sun swept the grey from the sky, and a soft blue replaced it. George Mushtak, however felt nothing but an oppressive emptiness. He lowered the hand holding the field glasses, looked around him, and walked slowly home.

Resistance in the south of the country was weakening by the day. The men who had assembled in the village elder's house heard the news on the radio, and breathed a sigh of relief. Two days later, when even Great Britain officially stepped in against the fleeing rebels, ranging itself on the side of France, the entire rising collapsed.

Mushtak withdrew into his property and kept to his darkened bedroom. His son Salman was anxious, but Malake reassured him: the old patriarch was sound as a bell, she said, it was just that his heart was full of longing for something, and none of them, not even she, knew what it was. This time at least it was nothing to do with Shahin. It seemed as if he wanted to answer someone back, settle an old score with him, and he was sick with that longing because he feared he would take it to the grave with him unsatisfied.

One afternoon in September he emerged from his room, sat down on the bench outside the house, took a deep breath and said, "They'll soon be here."

"Who'll soon be here?" asked Salman, who was mending a rent in a saddle on the terrace. He was planning to ride out and pick a basket of ripe grapes. The best grapes in Mala were September grapes, which tasted like drops of honey surrounded by a thin, aromatic skin.

"The bandits. They attacked Daisa today, plundered the village and set fire to the convent of St. Mary. It was on the radio. Those ungodly villains shot fifty men and abducted over twenty women," replied his father almost cheerfully.

"Who was it? And what did the French do?" asked Malake, stirring a spoonful of honey into her peppermint tea.

"It was Hassan Kashat, who else?" replied her father, looking into the distance and shaking his head. "The French, ah, well, the French," he added.

"You know Hassan Kashat, am I right?" asked Salman. He knew that his father hated the man, but not why.

'You're right,' replied Mushtak, and his eyes narrowed. "I know him very well, and I hope he will make the mistake of coming to Mala. But you children wouldn't understand that," he added, dismissing the subject.

Two days later, on the fourteenth of September, the village celebrated the Feast of the Holy Cross. The village elder came to the great bonfire, together with Imam Yunis from the nearby district town of Kulaifa, and Muhammad Abdulkarim, head of the Rifai family, one of the most powerful Muslim clans in the country. Their residence was in the village of Aingose, ten kilometres from Mala. The village elder hoped to show that the religions lived at peace with one another.

Mushtak stayed away from the festivities. Instead, he was oiling the hundred rifles behind closed doors with Salman, Malake, and his faithful manservant Basil. Then he had the guns carefully wrapped in linen cloths and packed in wooden crates, five to a crate. He had given his other ten men twenty piastres and let them have the day off to celebrate as they pleased. He spent all evening cursing the village elder's yielding character, and not until late at night did he let Salman and Malake join the noisy crowd dancing happily in the village square.

Only his servant Basil stayed with him. Even though he had permission to go, he would not leave his master's side. Mushtak was fond of his faithful servant, who was sometimes closer to him and understood him better than his own children. Basil was an orphan. He had grown up with the Mushtak family and venerated the patriarch of the clan.

Salman and Malake were glad to be among the other young people at last. Everyone was gathered around the bonfire in the village square now. The two Muslim dignitaries were joining the celebrations too, and enjoying the presence of the cheerful girls who stayed in the square, mingling with the men, until far into the night. Now and then one of them disappeared into the darkness with a young man, and came back after a while giggling. Even most of the children were still up.

George Mushtak was missed, since he usually donated plenty of wine and three lambs for the spit on this occasion every year. But even when the village elder knocked at his door and invited him to join them in the square, he merely replied dryly that he didn't feel like celebrating anything, and would not open the gate.

Three days later, a Sunday, a cold north wind blew over the village square and the air smelled of snow. Suddenly, during divine service, a shepherd came running down the central aisle of the church of St. Giorgios.

"They're coming, they're coming!" he cried, waving his hands in the air. The priest interrupted his prayers, but not before concluding the last verse of the hymn of praise to the Lord with a *kyrie eleison*.

"Calm yourself, my son. Who are coming?"

"The bandits. The whole plain's black with them. I set off at dawn for the hill beyond the mill with my sheep. When I saw them, I couldn't believe my eyes."

The man was breathing noisily. Apart from that, there was a deathly hush in the crowded church. Someone hushed a crying child. Then nothing could be heard but the congregation whimpering desperately behind their hands.

"How many are there?" asked the village elder.

"Thousands. They're advancing through the whole valley along a wide front," replied the man, tracing a horizontal line in the air with his hand.

Mushtak rose from his seat in the front pew, went up to the altar, crossed himself, and turned around. He looked over the village elder's head.

"I need," he said, in a calm, firm voice, "five brave men on five good horses to hold the bandits back down there while we get our women and children to safety in the caves in the rock."

Twenty men rose briskly to their feet and followed him to his house. The village elder was left behind, ignored, and at that moment, although he was only sixty, he felt older and frailer than the ninety-year-old widow Nasrin in the pew at the back.

Even before Mushtak reached his house, the bells were ringing in all the church towers. It was an ancient signal of danger. People streamed out of their houses into the village square. Many of them were afraid, but there was no sense of panic anywhere.

He stood at his gate deciding which men were to have rifles and which were not. Salman wrote down the names of the men standing ready, rifle in hand. Then the armed men stormed out to the hills that had a good view of the village from the south.

Mala was a rich Christian village. High in the mountains, it had been well protected from most of the adventurers who roamed the country during four hundred years of Ottoman rule, looting and burning. Its inhabitants had also been spared the Bedouin who attacked the villages of the plain in successive waves, trying to escape starvation. Mala had thus become a pearl among villages. Even in the 1920s it had electric light, mains water, and four coffee-houses. Many rich emigrants from Mala had gone to America, Canada, and Australia, and sent money home. The monastery of St. Giorgios and the convent of St. Thecla were famous for their miracles. Prosperous Christians from all over Arabia came to ask the saints for children, a cure, or success, and had given generous donations, transforming those religious houses into rich citadels.

The bandits knew that, and they had descended like the locusts that come out of nowhere and devour everything, before disappearing into nowhere again. It had been like that in 1830, 1848, and 1860. The battle of 1860 was famous all over the country, for not only did the little village hold out for four weeks while it was besieged by over three thousand heavily armed bandits, it then put them to flight. It was such a devastating victory that after it the bandits had avoided Mala for sixty-six years, until now.

Soon the first shots fired at the bandits by the horsemen up in the hills were heard in the village. The line of men at Mushtak's gate was a long one. Even the village elder had to wait his turn. He was given a rifle, not with solemn ceremony, as he had hoped, but not peremptorily either, as he had feared. Mushtak handed him the gun without a word, and was already looking at the next comer.

Mobate envied the man his household servants, who showed him dog-like devotion. Finally, Mushtak himself carefully folded up the list that Salman had handed him, and gave it back to his son. "They are all in your debt. You can always remind them of it later," he said. "Man is a forgetful animal."

Then, accompanied by his son and shouldering a Mauser, he walked out to the village square with his head held high. Many of the men kissed his hand emotionally, as if he were a saint, and thanked him for the rifle, but he just stood there listening to the distant sounds.

Suddenly his glance fell on the line of men forming in the Orthodox quarter. The Shahins were distributing rifles to their own supporters, who were soon perched on the rocks like black ravens, keeping watch on every part of the northern and eastern routes to the village, while the Catholics guarded the roads to the south and west.

Late in the afternoon all the children, old people, and most of the women were safely in the great rocky caves that surrounded the village. Only about fifty women stayed with the men, helping to construct the huge mounds of rubble with which they were trying to block the one weak point in the fortifications, the Damascus road.

Mushtak rode to the hills with a Mauser over his shoulder and his field glasses hanging in front of his chest, giving him the look of a military commander.

It was nearly evening when the men took their first prisoner, a little man with a southern accent who had apparently been scouting around to spy out the village's defences. The furious guards hit and kicked him, and one of them actually wanted to shoot him out of hand.

"Leave the man alone," ordered Mushtak. He turned to the trembling spy, and said, "Have no fear, we'll send you back. Who's your leader?"

"Hassan Kashat, sir," replied the man anxiously.

"Are you sure of that, or do you know it only by hearsay?" Mushtak asked, and before the man had even nodded he was going on, "What mark does Hassan Kashat have on his left hand?"

"Mark?" said the man in surprise. "'He has no mark on his left hand. That hand's crippled. I swear by God I've seen it. He hides it well by resting it on his dagger, but it's crippled."

Mushtak beamed. "You weren't lying. Bring the man a piece of bread and a dish of fresh yoghurt," he told his followers, and then turned back to the prisoner. "Well, my lad, you will eat under my protection now, and after that I'll show you what your friends can expect here. And then you can go back to your leader Hassan Pasha Kashat and tell him: the man who crippled your left hand is waiting for you. Do you understand?"

"The man who crippled your left hand is waiting for you," repeated the man, to show Mushtak that he had learned the message by heart. His voice sounded fearful and uncertain.

While he greedily ate the yoghurt they had brought him, Mushtak hurried away and gave orders for all the men whom the spy was about to pass to keep their faces muffled up, and as soon as he had gone by they were to go and station themselves elsewhere, so that after a while he wouldn't be able to estimate the number of fighting men any more. The spy was released after nightfall, and he hurried away in the darkness down to the plain.

"Will Hassan Kashat withdraw when he learns that you're here?" asked Salman next morning.

"No, he'll stay," replied Mushtak, and he hadn't even finished what he was saying before the besiegers opened fire. The men entrenched in Mala replied, and Hassan Kashat's troops, although they suffered great losses, moved closer and closer. The first villager fell at about ten in the morning. It was Tuma, one of the three village butchers of Mala. A bullet hit him in the forehead just as he was rising to his feet to fetch a crate of ammunition.

Around midday the first cannonball sailed over the men's heads and smashed the window of the church of St. Giorgios. A second cannonball hit the back yard of George Mushtak's house and left a small crater. Two window panes in the grain store were broken. The explosion of the cannonballs and the impact as they struck frightened the beleaguered villagers. Some of the men in the front line began firing at random. Hassan Kashat's troops answered them with more cannon fire, and moved to within five hundred metres of the old mill at the entrance to the village.

Both sides fought fiercely for ten days, but they couldn't get anywhere. The bandits could advance no further towards the village, the defensive ring stood firm as rock. And the climb up from the valley, which wasn't so steep near the village itself, no longer offered the enemy good cover.

But the defenders of Mala could not break through the rampart their enemies had built from rocks and felled trees. The bandit Kashat's troops had entrenched themselves in their positions. Mushtak's face grew darker every day. Finally he told Habib Mobate to summon all the leading men of the village.

"Jusuf Shahin too?" asked the village elder.

"Him too," replied Mushtak dryly. The village elder turned pale.

Mushtak spoke bitterly to the assembled men. He never for a second looked at his rival; it was enough to have had to greet him with a handshake. That was the condition made by the two priests, Catholic and Orthodox. He sensed Shahin's reluctance to be reconciled. The man's hand was cold, as if he had drained the blood out of it.

Mushtak told the assembly that the French were not about to send the village any help, and he expected the besiegers to stay until the people of Mala starved to death.

Shahin waited until everyone else had spoken. Then he said, "No one will starve," and turned his gaze on the priest of his Orthodox community, as if paying attention to no one else. "I've stuffed three of the caves in the rock full of wheat, dried meat, raisins, and nuts from the Lebanon, and two more with maize and lentils, salt and olive oil. That will last us for a while."

Secretly, Mushtak admired his quiet enemy. Shahin had sent all that food to the caves, and not a soul in the village had noticed. Everyone knew, however, that he was an experienced smuggler, and it was said that he had often muffled the hooves of his mules by wrapping them in cloth so that they could pass border guards in silence.

"Tomorrow," Shahin went on, "everyone can take what he needs. The nuns of the convent of St. Thecla will supervise the distribution."

Mushtak quickly pulled himself together again. "And I will make sure this siege doesn't last much longer," he told the assembled men before they dispersed. It sounded more like a loser's defiance.

Jusuf Shahin rose and went away without any leave-taking, but with the dignified bearing of a victor. Followed by his son Salman, who stuck to his side like a shadow throughout the siege, George Mushtak himself set off for home.

Salman kept turning, looking distrustfully to all sides, and surveying the situation. There had been an attack on the sixth day of the siege, allegedly by three men of the enemy troops. The shots had been fired from very close to Mushtak, and though they missed him the men had escaped unrecognized. No one discovered any more about the incident, or knew that their tracks led to the Orthodox quarter. But Salman feared that one of Shahin's killers would take any second opportunity to shoot his father in the general confusion. Salman always carried a loaded revolver under his shirt now, and after that incident he became harder and less approachable. And Mushtak went along with what his stern son wanted.

జ

The cannonballs were falling in the village less frequently now, and had a less devastating effect on the peasants' minds.

Three days after the meeting at the village elder's house, Mushtak and his son rode out to the farthest-flung of the sentry positions at dawn, and observed the enemy camp down in the plain as if waiting for a signal. A tent, a particularly large tent at the far end of the camp near the wild oleander bushes, increasingly attracted his gaze. It was out of reach of the rifle bullets, and very well defended by two trenches, as well as soldiers and a couple of cannon.

On the twenty-third day of the siege, another man fell into the hands of the village guards. They caught him in the olive grove below the mill. He was unarmed and disguised as a peasant from Mala – black trousers, striped shirt, waistcoat, and a black *kuffiyeh* head-cloth. The man claimed to have had a vision a week ago in which he heard the voice of his brother, who had been living in America for the last ten years, and this brother, he said, was calling for him, so he didn't want to fight any more. He had bought the clothes from one of the besiegers, who had taken them from a Mala peasant.

In tears, the man told his captors how Kashat was torturing men who tried to run away. A troop had been stationed to shoot the deserters, or bring them back to camp and torture them to death in front of the others.

"And what about the man whose clothes you're wearing?" one of the villagers asked him.

"He was shot… Kashat takes no prisoners. They cost food and water," the man replied, diffidently.

The men from Mala lost their tempers. One young fellow drew a knife, but Mushtak raised his hand. The prisoner's words dried up in his mouth with fright. He turned pale.

"If you are an honest man," said George, ignoring his followers' indignation, "you'll be taken over the mountains tomorrow, and from there it's two days' journey to Beirut and the sea. But if you are lying you'll wish for death not once but twenty times over." Then he sat down on a stool in the middle of the circle that his men had formed around the prisoner.

"Now, tell me something in confidence. Since you say you hate Kashat, you won't mind what happens to him. So when does Hassan Kashat always leave his tent?"

"Only once. At midnight exactly he inspects the front to make sure his sentries are on watch. He has two adjutants with him, no more."

"What are the adjutants' names?" asked George Mushtak.

"Ahmad Istanbuli and Omar Attar," replied the man.

"What about the Khairi brothers?" asked Mushtak, to the surprise of his men.

"Mustafa fell in the first week, and Yunus a few days ago," replied the prisoner.

That same night, George followed hidden ways winding through the terraced fields of the green valley to the bandits' camp. He knew the narrow paths like the palm of his hand. He often had to go to his fields by night and divert the water of the little river to his land.

Mushtak loved the night hours. By day, he left the irrigation of the crops to his men, but after dark he liked to be in charge of the water himself. He would leap, light-footed, from sluice to sluice, smiling when the water followed him. Sometimes he ran along the dry bed of the channel, anticipating the gush of water that must go the long way around through the sluices before it raced forward like a flock of hungry sheep.

This evening he was accompanied by his son Salman; Nagib, the village elder's bold youngest son; and Tanios, the baker from the Orthodox quarter. Not only was Tanios one of the strongest men in the village, Mushtak also wanted to use him as an eyewitness to report back to his enemy Shahin's supporters on what he, Mushtak, was planning to do in the next few hours.

Even years later, Salman would say how his father suddenly looked young again. On the way to met his deadly enemy Kashat he strode out so fast and vigorously that his son and the other two men had dif-ficulty keeping up with him. Soundless as shadows, they moved past the guards of both front lines that night, and finally they lay in wait for Kashat. He appeared around midnight, a small figure on his way to the furthest outposts of his guards. There were two tall men with him.

When Hassan Kashat reached the ancient walnut tree a moment before his companions, Salman and his father leaped out and flung him to the ground. The other two men from Mala killed the adjutants in silence. Hassan Kashat was frightened to death. He couldn't even call for help, for Mushtak was already stuffing his headcloth into his mouth as a gag.

"You filthy rat, what did I tell you? I'll get you, I said! It's taken me twenty years, but I have you now. All those nights I've been waiting for this moment, and now you're in my hands. You'll die like a dog on a dunghill," he cried, hoarse-voiced, and with Salman's aid he actually did drag the bandit leader, who seemed paralysed, to a heap of dung that he had brought to his field before the siege began. This particular field was just beyond the walnut tree.

It was a clear night, and the full moon shone brightly. The bandit leader looked pitifully pale now. "Do you see this lion my son?" Mushtak continued, clapping Salman's shoulder and kicking his enemy in the kidneys at the same time. "I got him on Laila. I slept with her and she gave me four children. This lion is my firstborn. Look at him! Can you see his eyes? Aren't they the eyes of Laila?" he asked, kicking Kashat again and again.

His captive shook his head, and desperately tried to avoid the kicks as he lay on the ground.

"How could my mother help it if Laila and I were crazy for each other? Why did you kill my mother? And my sister Miriam? Why did you torture her like that? Before my mother's eyes!" cried Mushtak, and then he rammed his knife into his prisoner's belly, pushed him down in the dunghill, and pulled the gag out of his mouth. Kashat widened his eyes, tried to gasp for air and scream, but a fistful of dung was stuffed into his jaws, and Mushtak went on stabbing until his victim's body went limp. At last he stood up, exhausted and weeping.

Only when he felt Salman's hand on his shoulder did he say, quietly, "Let's go." But Nagib the village elder's son had another good idea. After brief discussion, all four of them began shouting in Arabic with a southern accent, "The Christians have attacked us! Our leader Hassan Kashat and his adjutants Ahmad and Omar have been murdered! Listen, everyone! Our leader is dead! Run for your lives!"

Slowly at first, then faster and faster, loud cries from Kashat's own men echoed through the camp. Panic broke out. Mushtak and his three companions made haste to get back to their village. Once there, they quickly summoned all the men, lit torches, and rode down into the valley on their horses and mules, guns in their hands. They drove the fleeing bandits ahead of them, killing many.

When day dawned, the valley was full of corpses down to the Damascus road. All the abandoned horses and weapons were taken to the village square of Mala, but the bodies were put in one of the remote caves. They were walled up inside it, and the entrance was covered with earth. One of the dead was the chief of the Rifai clan, Muhammad Abdulkarim, who had been at the harvest festival.

Kashat had obviously persuaded him that there was good loot to be had in Mala.

People were already coming to the village square at dawn to dance, drink wine, and shout for joy. They had all entirely forgotten the prisoner, but Mushtak finally found the man lying tied up under a fig tree.

He had the prisoner released from his bonds, gave him three gold coins, and called out good wishes for his crossing to America as he left. Then he dropped on the bench outside the door of his house, exhausted and happy, in the firm belief that no less than God had been at work in this victory. And George Mushtak wept for the sublimity of that hour.

27. Weddings

Little by little, Salman had taken over the farming of the land. At first he followed his father's advice and grew all kinds of crops: vines, maize, olives, tobacco, wheat. Like all the farmers, he also raised cattle. But then he went to visit his youngest brother at the monastery and met one of the monks who was an expert on agriculture, and advised Salman to mechanize his farm and switch to products for the export market. Salman made the change at the end of the twenties. Old Mushtak cursed the export market and the French monk's advice, and it took Salman years to convince him of the merits of the new idea. "You're either a big farmer or a big loser these days," he kept explaining.

So he turned the farm into a modern agricultural business, right on the Damascus road, and specialized in roses, almonds, tobacco, and apples. He sold the rosebuds to the perfume industry in France, the almonds went to a marzipan factory in north Germany, and the tobacco to the Netherlands. Day and night, Salman lived for his dream of a thoroughly modern business. He was the first to bring a cross-country vehicle and a tractor to the village. The villagers laughed at Salman, but soon other farmers were wondering whether they too might not be able to take their produce to the capital as fast and get it there as fresh as he did, thereby saving themselves the tedious drive with a donkey and cart.

In time old Mushtak came to trust his son, and enjoyed being driven by that strong, sun-tanned, blue-eyed young man through the village in the open jeep.

Young women liked Salman's blue eyes and dry humour too. When he was twenty, one girl even tried to commit suicide over him. Her life was saved, but her relations spread the story that Salman had made her pregnant. No one ever knew whether that was true. The one certainty was that she came from a penniless family, and that was also the reason for the rumour that old Mushtak had paid her cousin a large sum of money to marry her quickly.

When this tiresome business was dealt with, George called his son to order. "You're marrying Hanan in six months' time," he told him. Salman knew the pale daughter of a rich engineer only distantly, but he knew his father very much better. He agreed. The wedding was to be on the first Sunday of August in 1931.

In addition, their father decreed that six months later Malake was to marry Adel the Lebanese cattle dealer. What he didn't know was that she had been having an affair with that same man for years. Whenever George mentioned him she appeared indifferent, or expressed nothing but contempt for Adel. Malake knew that as soon as she showed her love for him, Salman and her father would find some reason to prevent the marriage. The Mushtaks were nothing out of the ordinary in that respect. Since time immemorial, parents had refused to sanction a marriage if they found out that it would be a love match. A letter was enough, or a poem, for the lovers to be parted for ever. Half of all Arabic lyric poetry tells tales of such tragedies.

Malake was already over twenty, and she had loved Adel since she was fourteen. But the cattle dealer had to wait until Mushtak's first-born son was married. That was what custom demanded in Mala, and Adel waited patiently, because he loved Malake.

They were all to come to Salman's wedding: Hasib, now studying medicine at the American University of Beirut; Elias from Damascus; and Adel from Beirut, who for years had been regarded by everyone as a good friend of the family. The wedding festivities were to last seven days and seven nights. A bishop and six priests were invited from Damascus to celebrate the nuptial Mass. But the biggest surprise was the arrival of the Patriarch of the Catholic Church. George Mushtak kissed his hand, and was moved to tears when the head of the Church embraced him, laughing. "I know you only asked for a bishop, but I would like to bless your son's marriage myself in gratitude for all you have done for the Church."

The villagers couldn't remember ever seeing a Catholic patriarch in Mala before. But since his great victory over the besiegers of the village, old Mushtak was thought capable of anything. And then he had an unpleasant surprise. The day before the wedding, quite by chance, he found his daughter in bed with Adel. He was extremely angry, not because his fiend of a daughter had seduced the simple cattle dealer, but because Malake ignored propriety and his orders, and insisted on having her own way, just like her mother. So after all Malake had been the first to celebrate her marriage in bed, before her brother, which showed that she didn't care in the least for any of her father's decrees or wishes.

Mushtak did not rant and rage, nor did he hit Malake, as he often did when he lost his temper, because this time he feared a scandal. The house was full, the head of the Catholic Church was drinking his coffee in the courtyard under a sun umbrella. Hundreds of people were crowding around him, all wanting to get close to His Excellency, Patriarch of the entire Middle East and the holy city of Jerusalem. He was, after all, the second most powerful man in the Church after Pope Pius XI. They were grateful to the bridegroom's father for giving them this opportunity.

And now his own daughter was sleeping with that simple-minded cattle dealer. Mushtak swore he would hate Malake for it until the day he died. Today, however, he just stood in the doorway. Malake and her lover froze under the bedclothes when they saw him, and Adel regretted his stupidity in leaving his jacket with the revolver in its pocket out of reach. He expected to die, but nothing happened. Leaden minutes crawled by. Mushtak said not a word, just went on staring at the couple.

"We'll celebrate the nuptial Mass tomorrow," he said after an eternity that had, in fact, lasted three minutes. "And after that I never want to see either of you again." His voice cracked. Those were the last words he spoke to Malake and Adel.

But the two of them ran away that night. Malake was afraid that her father's henchmen would abduct her and her husband directly after the ceremony, kill them, and bury them in some distant ravine. She knew her father very well.

When Mushtak's faithful servant Basil whispered the news to him next morning, while everyone was drinking to the wedding, he was surprised by the reaction of his master, who just smiled and nodded. "She's quicksilver, like her mother, she can't be held fast," was all Malake's father said, and then he took the Patriarch's hand and led him to his place at the festive table. He was to sit enthroned there with Salman on his right and Hanan on his left.

The village had never seen a wedding like it before. Over a thousand guests celebrated for seven days on end, local people and strangers from the surrounding villages, from Damascus, Aleppo, Jerusalem, Baghdad, and Beirut.

Not since it was founded had the village seen so much meat and wine, so many pistachios and sweetmeats. It was said that for those seven days you could smell the aroma of roast meat and thyme ten kilometres away. For seven days, people drank themselves into a stupor on huge quantities of wine and arrack. And finally, at the end of the seventh day, when everyone thought the dream was over, George Mushtak announced that a man didn't bring a son like Salman into the world every day, and the party was to go on for another whole week.

28. The Transformation of Elias

As soon as he arrived for the wedding festivities, Elias Mushtak was surrounded by young men teasing him, asking if he'd poked all the cooks and cleaning women in the monastery yet. He didn't answer, but waved the jokes aside. Only once did he lower himself to saying,

"That kind of thing just goes on in your corrupt little minds. The brothers and sisters in the monastery are chaste and devout."

In the village, he heard about his sister's love affair for the first time. Malake herself told him, asking for his blessing. And Elias kissed her and smiled awkwardly. "The way you describe Adel to me, it's a love that deserves the blessing of God himself."

Malake was obviously relieved. She ran off to her lover and told him the good news. She had also taken the opportunity of telling her brother about her plan to escape, and Elias prayed all night that his sister would elude their father's guards.

On the wedding day, when Malake had gone, he was happy at the festivities for his brother's sake, but he wasn't at ease in all the noise made by the drunken guests. He often walked alone along the narrow paths through the terraced fields, and was surprised to find them even more beautiful than he remembered. He spent hours wandering in the hills and valleys, resting under large fig and mulberry trees, and drinking in the view of the landscape.

On the fourth day of the wedding festivities, he was watching a large black donkey in a field repeatedly mounting a pale brown female under an old walnut tree. The donkey was a stray; the remnants of his reins still dangled from his neck. The female donkey couldn't defend herself. She kicked, hitting the male so often that it must hurt him, but he was in a strange state of intoxication, and didn't stop until, after the fifth mating, he collapsed, snorted, and licked white foam from his muzzle. At that moment Elias smelled the sexual arousal of the female, who was probably just beginning to enjoy the love-play.

It was a sweetish smell, like faded roses. He felt a curious arousal in himself, a sensation beyond his control. That moment changed Elias's life for ever. From now on he could scent a woman's arousal from over three metres away, and he was never wrong. Even if at the last moment a woman sometimes took fright and denied feeling desire, he knew better. His nose was a merciless guide, knowing no consideration or morality.

At that extraordinary moment watching the female donkey, however, he felt so beside himself, so aroused, that he rushed at her and penetrated her himself. She brayed under the thrusts of his powerful penis. Elias felt the pulsating muscles inside the creature almost crushing his glans. Suddenly a huge tremor shook his body as if it had been struck by lightning. He cried out so loud that the female donkey froze in alarm, while the male watched with drowsy eyes.

Elias walked slowly home. He knew for certain now that the abstemious Jesuit life was not for him. But he had no idea that two young women had been standing behind a pomegranate bush all the time, watching him. Moist between the legs and giggling, they ran home, promising each other, as they parted, to keep the secret to themselves. In Mala, however, such promises were the surest guarantee that a story would spread like wildfire. It wasn't long before the news of Elias Mushtak's amazing prick was circulating among the village women, and that very night he was seduced by Munira, one of the two girls who had watched him with the donkey.

He spent the days of the wedding feast in a never-ending state of exhilaration. He couldn't get enough of women. So he went around in search of them, and as soon as his nostrils picked up that special aroma he was like a man hypnotized. Elias never found out whether it was their indulgence in meat, nuts, and wine that sent the women wild, or the forbidden thrill of an adventure with a sexually potent novice monk, but it was certain that he caught the sweetish scent more and more often.

The women laughed, pinched him, joked with him. They took him into remote corners and got to work without delay. Samia, the bus driver's wife, worried about his health. She fed him pistachios and the spinal marrow of lambs, foods well known to increase potency. Elias could have done with something to dampen his desires down instead. The women were carried away. When he took them, they often forgot themselves and shouted out loud in their ecstasies. So what was bound to happen finally did.

The whole village was given over to the wedding festivities. So many guests could never have been received and entertained with food and drink in a single house. Every corner of the Mushtaks' entire property was stuffed with provisions. Lambs and calves stood crammed together in their pens, quantities of different beverages were stacked on top of each other. Every day, at six in the morning, carts brought fresh supplies to the churchyard, the village elder's house, and the village square, where bonfires were built ready to be lit. Apart from the Shahins and their allies, all the people of Mala offered guests from outside the village as many beds as their houses could provide. Hundreds still had to sleep out in the open, but the nights were mild, and apart from three or four cases of painful but harmless scorpion stings there was nothing wrong with that. Moreover, the mood remained extremely harmonious in spite of the crowds and the huge quantities of spirits and wine that they imbibed, and if George Mushtak hadn't had his strange accident on the penultimate evening everyone would gone home with the happiest of memories.

That evening he was going back and forth between his own property, the churchyard, the village elder's house, and the village square. He seemed a different man, affable to everyone. He said goodbye almost affectionately to those who were setting off that night. Suddenly he saw that the guests in the churchyard had run short of arrack. He decided to fetch them two canisters each containing five litres of arrack himself. His house wasn't far off, and he also felt strong pressure in his bladder, so he could kill two birds with one stone.

He took two canisters of arrack from the stores, put them down a little way to one side of the courtyard, which was full of guests, and went to the earth closet on the other side of the yard. The long tool shed divided the grounds of the property into two, the front half ornamental, with flowers in containers, fountains, arcades, and benches to sit on, the back half devoted to the farm. There was an earth closet for the farm hands here, a rather better one for the master of the house and his family, a large stable, a sheep pen, a granary, and a kennel for the dogs.

After only a couple of steps he heard the first scream, but he thought he had simply imagined it, or else it came from the guests celebrating in his yard. He went on, lit the oil lamp in the little room with the earth closet, undid his flies and directed his stream of urine into the closet. Suddenly he heard the scream again. Mushtak paused. He listened, and a terrible fear took hold of him. It was a woman's scream, and it came from the nearby granary where wheat and barley were stored in dry lofts. For a moment the old man thought it was his daughter Malake's voice, and his blood boiled with anger. But then he remembered that she wasn't there any more, and smiled. The woman screamed again.

"Let's have no more of this," he growled, hurrying out. Breathlessly, he tried to open the granary door, but it was bolted on the inside. Looking up, he saw that there was a window open on the upper floor: the window of the drying chamber where the clean jute sacks were stored. Now he heard the woman whimpering up there, repeating again and again, gasping for breath, "You'll kill me yet!"

Mushtak looked around and found a ladder. It was one of the heavy kind made of steel tubing. He put it against the wall without a sound and quickly climbed up. His eyes were flashing fire; he was so agitated that he could hardly breathe. When he reached the window four metres up, and was about to haul himself through it, he froze at the sight that met his eyes. The room was dark, but light from the three tall lamps illuminating the inner courtyard came through the open window. In the lamplight he saw someone thrusting into a woman again and again. Although he could see nothing of the man but his back, his bare buttocks, and his mighty member, the sheer extent of the penis told him it was Elias. The woman was laughing and screaming at the same time.

Later, no one could say exactly what happened next, not even Mushtak himself, let alone the terrified couple in the drying chamber.

"You damn son of a whore," he cried, and perhaps he was about to fall on both of them, hit his son, or turn away in disgust to avoid the sight of that terrible prick. He may have tried to do all those things at the same moment, with the result that he suddenly found himself lying in the paved yard below with a broken leg. Elias hurried down, and Nasibe, widow of the butcher Tuma, the first man to die in the siege, ran ahead to the wedding guests, where she cried out the news that quite by chance, she had seen George Mushtak lying on the ground as she was on her way to the earth closet.

The festivities came to an abrupt end. No one felt like singing and dancing any more. A heavy silence fell on the village. Guests took their leave of Salman, who stood at the gate outside the house and wouldn't let anyone but old Dr. Talani disturb his father. The doctor had reassured the family at once, telling them their father was strong enough to be getting around as usual in three months' time. But the festive spirit was gone.

Hanan the bride became nurse at the morose old man's bedside that night, and she remained his nurse until the last day of his life, sixteen years later. For even when his leg was better he took special pleasure in having her care for him. As for Hanan herself, he repelled her, and she nursed him with silent hatred. But old Mushtak never noticed.

On the evening of the accident he absolutely refused to see Elias, and over the next few days he cursed the devil every time his youngest son entered the room. The watchful Salman didn't fail to notice, and asked his father why, but Mushtak gave no answer.

Only when Salman took his brother to the stable on the day before he was due to leave early and whipped him did Elias begin telling the true story. Then Salman stopped beating him and started to laugh.

Mushtak wouldn't bless the novice when he left either. He turned his head away and looked at the wall. Elias's back was burning from the lashes of his brother's whip.

He had never hated his father so much as he did at that moment, when he waited at the window of the old bus until the passengers had hauled aboard all the stuff they were taking to Damascus with them. The village square was full of the travellers' relations, saying goodbye and repeating their last good wishes again.

Some thirty passengers and as many chickens, two large rams, and a young goat filled the bus. Elias sat on his own, feeling chilly. Not a soul came to see him off. His sister Malake had made her escape. Here and there one of the many women whose favours he had enjoyed during the wedding celebrations waved to him surreptitiously or smiled, but none of them dared exchange a word with him.

Then a madman suddenly appeared in the square, pushing his way through the crowd with difficulty. It took Elias some time to realize that the man was making straight for him, and then he turned away.

"Here, it's for you," said the deranged man, smiling and handing him a little bundle. Elias could see fresh grapes and bread. The bundle smelled of pungent sheep's cheese. He was startled, and left at a loss.

"Thank you," he said awkwardly, taking the bundle. The young man's face turned red, and he stayed there under the bus window. At some point in the wedding festivities he had appeared from nowhere. He was dazzlingly beautiful. He spent the night in the village elder's guesthouse, and hadn't attracted any particular attention among hundreds of strangers. But soon people realized that he was crazy. He kept having fits that lasted for about ten minutes, when he fell to the ground and seemed to be possessed by the devil. However, he was gentle and calm when he came to himself again, and in general he was peaceful, although his behaviour was strange. He listened to discussions with such interest that you might have thought him a sensible man, but then he would suddenly begin interrupting the disputants and start to sing, or throw melon peel and dirt picked up in the street. Only when he caught sight of George Mushtak did he instantly become almost rigid with fear. Secrets never lasted long in Mala. Within a short time the whole village knew the identity of the young man who went by the name of Shams. But old Mushtak mustn't know he was here, and so Elias hadn't heard anything about him either.

Yet again he thanked the unknown man, but he stayed there under the window of the bus, and people looked at him and laughed. When the bus finally moved slowly off on its way out of the village, the madman ran after it. Elias was embarrassed. He had a feeling that the bus driver was going extra slowly because he disliked the Mushtaks, and wanted to spin out what Elias felt was his own humiliation. The people in the village square fell about laughing when the madman tried to stop the bus.

"God protect you, brother!" he cried, weeping aloud, and at last he stood still. Only then did the driver step on the gas.

29. Loneliness

Early that evening, Bab Tuma Street, leading to the Jesuit monastery, smelled of jasmine. The bus journey had taken forever; the driver had to stop again and again because the overheated engine was boiling the water in the radiator.

Who, Elias wondered, was the madman? He felt embarrassed that he of all people had called him "brother", while Salman wouldn't give him a brotherly kiss and hadn't even come to see him off. Why was Salman so cold towards him, so harsh?

He knocked at the monastery gate, and was pleased to see Brother Andreas's face. Andreas smiled at him. "You're back early. I thought you were staying two months," he said in surprise. Elias did not reply. He just said good evening to the monk, went to the dormitory, left his case there and then hurried to evening prayers. The bell was just ringing.

As time went on he could find no peace in the monastery. At first he thought it was because he felt guilty about his father. He wrote letter after letter, saying that he prayed daily for his return to health. He was sorry to have caused him such pain, he said. His father did not reply. Two months later a letter came from Salman. It was disappointingly short, cool, and matter-of-fact: *Don't write so many letters, pay attention to your books. Father is well and happy. Your brother, Salman.*

At least this brief missive freed Elias from his fears for his father's condition. Yet still he was not at peace. There was a great deal to do in the monastery, and he flung himself into his work. But he never again felt the old happiness he had known before he went away. He tried not to let anyone see that his thoughts were elsewhere. The women of Mala had taught him another kind of happiness, a wild desire that plagued him, especially at night, when he lay alone in his room. He prayed to withstand the temptation, but as if he had been praying for more temptation instead his longing for women now attacked him by day, as well as following him into his dreams at night.

The monastic life seemed to him more and more like the quiet onset of senility. There were a hundred men there, and not a single woman worth a glance. Three ancient ladies from the neighbourhood came in to clean, cook and wash the dishes, and then went home again. The windows of the building led nowhere; it was as if no female creature lived anywhere near the monastery. He thought of the seething life somewhere beyond its walls. Damascus wasn't a city to him any more but a woman, and the monastery was trying to keep him away from her.

When Elias imagined a woman it was almost always Nasibe, the butcher Tuma's widow, whom he saw in his mind's eye. Merely thinking of her passionate nature aroused him. She wasn't a native of Mala; Tuma had seen her at the cattle markets he visited, and she was twenty years his junior. At the time Tuma had quickly come to an agreement with her father, who was glad to have one of his eleven daughters off his hands. The butcher was rich. He had inherited money and he worked hard. All seemed well, until the day when a bullet struck him in the forehead during the siege of Mala. He was just forty at the time.

After his death Nasibe dressed modestly in black and lived a very quiet life. There had been plenty of would-be suitors for a while, but she didn't want to know about any of them. So after some time the men stayed away, since the grieving widow seemed inconsolable. She was left alone, and women praised her, no longer seeing her as a threat. Nasibe prayed a great deal. She made a living by fattening up kids and lambs which she sold cleverly and at a high price not to the village butchers, but to private customers who had something to celebrate and wanted to serve good meat at a festive meal. She soon had such a high reputation for her wares that she had more than enough work to keep her busy.

Elias had been told to go to the widow Nasibe early in the morning of the eighth day of the wedding feast, to ask if she could let the Mushtaks have another five well fattened lambs and three kids. His father had noticed that the cooks were economizing on meat to make it last through the extended festivities.

So Elias had knocked at the widow's door and delivered his father's request, she quietly asked him in, and when he passed her into her pretty little living room he suddenly smelled her ardent desire. It was only later that she told him how, not long before he arrived, she had overheard two women talking quietly about him under her window, and that had suddenly aroused lust in her again.

Elias sat down on the couch. She knelt on the floor between his feet, caressed him, and looked amorously at him. Slowly, she took off her black dress. It was the greatest surprise of his life. Nasibe seemed to grow out of the fabric. Her body, a moment ago nondescript, stiff and flat, rounded out as she cast off her fetters, liberated into a femininity that Elias had never before seen in such perfection. Nasibe told him that she wore tight clothes to hide her curves from men's eyes. She was almost twenty-five, but her body looked no older than seventeen.

Then she undressed her visitor and led him into the bedroom. A large bed filled the little room. Nasibe quickly pulled the curtains, pushed Elias down on the bed, laughing, and lay on top of him. At that moment he doubted whether she had ever lived without men. She made play with her tongue, and he tasted her saliva, which was sweet as honey. Her lips wandered down his body, tickling him like butterflies. From time to time the tickling became too much to bear, and then he would push her up with both arms and kiss those lips passionately.

Her skin was dark and smooth as a child's. He bent over her; she laughed and yielded to him. He kissed her feet, let his own lips wander over her soft knees and along the insides of her thighs to the source of her perfume. He licked the aroma of her insatiable desire. Nasibe spread her legs and raised them in the air, and then drew Elias to her.

"Slowly," she begged in ecstasy, as if to hold the moment fast. She laughed flirtatiously. He sucked her right breast. Nasibe groaned in a strange way, her voice like the soft whinny of a mare, and he tenderly bit her lip. "More, more," she repeated lustfully. He thrust in, licking her earlobe as he did so. "No, bite me, blow your breath into my ear. Do it, do it, please," she begged.

He lost consciousness, he was flying with her like a feather. She clasped him in her arms to regulate the rhythm of his thrusts, and then they were united, almost bodiless, far from the earth and its force of attraction.

Later he didn't know how often he had made love to her that day, but after that she clung to him. She was eight years his senior, but in her forthright peasant way she had told him he ought to leave the monastery. "I'd suit you better," she had said, laughing. But Elias was aware of the grave intent that showed through her laughter lines.

She kept seeking him out during the wedding festivities and wanting to make love. Sometimes they were very careless about it. Finally he had chosen the safest place he knew, the drying chamber at the back of the yard, for their next rendezvous. And as chance would have it, that was the very place where they were discovered by his father.

When Elias thought of Nasibe now that he was back in the monastery, his loneliness grew high as a mountain, and he wept quietly into his pillows.

30. Arson

One cold February day in 1933, Elias returned to Mala with a suitcase in his hand. No one in the Mushtak household seemed interested in his arrival.

He got out of the bus and walked slowly home. The gate was closed. His sister-in-law Hanan, Salman's wife, opened it and brusquely showed him his room on the first floor near the back entrance. It was the room where his mother had spent her last days, and after that servants had slept there. The room was only sparsely furnished, with a bedstead made of old wooden lathes and a mattress stuffed with dried maize leaves and straw. The mattress stank of urine and sweat, the bedclothes were grey with dirt. Only the pillows and two threadbare towels were at least clean.

"I'll bring you your meal in this room at noon every day. You know the master of the house doesn't want to see you, but you can stay here until you've found somewhere else."

It was Hanan's voice, but the words were his father's, so he couldn't blame her for those two incredible sentences. All the same, he felt humiliated. Here was a stranger showing him where to go in his own father's house, explaining that he must stay in this dismal room and would get only one meal a day. He had to summon up all his strength to keep back the tears.

"What about Salman?" he said, not sure what to ask first: why his brother hadn't come to greet him, or why he was allowing him, Elias, to be treated like a mangy dog.

"Salman's very busy," replied his wife, and left. She fits into the Mushtak household perfectly, he thought, watching Hanan go. She had a strange way of walking, like an old woman. He sat down on the edge of the bed and stared at his brown case.

The burning monastery rose before his mind's eye again. He could clearly hear the screams. Three Jesuits had perished in the flames, the bravest of the Fathers. They had rescued all the students before they burned to death themselves.

The whole dreadful business had begun as early as the summer of 1932. When the unrest started, Elias was on the point of leaving the monastery to find some kind of job working for the French, so that he could live in Damascus and make love to women. There were demonstrations of some kind every day, and they were all against the French in one way or another. Even if they were just demonstrating against the decline of morals, the march ended in anti-French violence every time.

The French governor of the city responded by letting his most brutal forces loose on the demonstrators. The Senegalese were notorious for their ferocity, and struck without mercy. Demonstrators were killed and injured every day.

Brother Andreas was the first to realize that the riots would lead to the closing of the Jesuit mission in Damascus. Everyone laughed at him. As a great power, so Abbot Rafael Herz, an arrogant and greedy man, told him, France was putting all its weight behind them.

"France?" said Brother Andreas in surprise. "France is much too far away, and the rabble are too close." But no one understood what he meant.

On the seventh of October, the Feast of St. Sergius, the first wave of the disaster reached the monastery gates. About a hundred men were shouting as they fled from the cudgels and bayonets of the Senegalese soldiers. "Down with France! Down with the Christians who pray to the cross, down with them, the swine!" They threw stones. One stone hit the cross above the monastery gateway, and it fell to the ground.

There hadn't been a drop of rain throughout the autumn in the south of the country, and when the seed corn dried up in winter thousands of people set off to go north. With images of beautiful green cities before their eyes, they whispered their prayers and hoped to escape starvation.

From then on the rioting was worse and worse. Wherever it raged, it left sheer devastation behind, flattening everything like a desert storm. The French soldiers struck back without mercy. And when the demonstrators retreated, they took their wounded away with them, cursing and swearing revenge.

January was freezing cold, but the sky still grudged the country rain. Soldiers prevented a huge wave of peasants from the south from invading Damascus at the southern city gate of Bab al Sigir. The human torrent stormed on along the city wall, forced its way in through the two gates of Bab Sharki and Bab Tuma, and attacked the Christian quarter. Shops were wrecked, churches and houses set on fire. But only the Jesuit monastery actually went up in flames. Two trucks of soldiers cut off all escape routes and fired into the crowd. Three soldiers and seventy peasants died that day. The Jesuit monastery burned down to its foundations.

As already mentioned, Elias had been feeling for weeks that he must leave the monastery, but he realized that he shrank from explaining his decision to its administration and his father. The monks were too kind to him, regarding him as one of their best novices, while his father, the sphinx of Mala, was already embittered enough. Failure to make it in the monastery would have meant Elias's death sentence.

He was waiting for a good opportunity to get away, and kept only the essentials, next day's clean underclothes, in his small locker. Everything else was in his case under the bed. It was evening when Brother Andreas hurried into the church, crying, "The house is burning!"

Neighbours with buckets of water helped to put out the fire, or at least keep it from spreading to other buildings made of wood and mud. It was a miracle that only the Jesuit monastery went up in flames.

The monastery administration found the students rescued from the fire temporary accommodation in a nearby building belonging to the French Lazarist mission, but a few days later it was decided that the monastery was to be dissolved, the priests and teachers would go to Beirut, and the students must go home. Only Brother Andreas would stay to make the necessary arrangements for selling the site. The ruins could not be restored now.

Andreas waved goodbye with tears in his eyes.

31. Nasibe

Elias was bored in Mala. He had spent nine years studying natural sciences, philosophy, literature, and music, and suddenly he found himself back in a remote mountain village that hadn't moved on at all in those nine years, and knew nothing of the outside world. Mala was intellectually stagnant. Its people seemed to be living on another star, where there were no table manners or mathematics, no civilized social intercourse or Molière. They knew as little of Aristotle as of the exotic plants of South America that Elias had read about in his lessons.

He couldn't find a single book in the village apart from the Bible, which he knew by heart already. The folk music played at weddings and religious festivals could best be described as a shrill kind of snoring. The musicians were unacquainted with notation and the theory of harmony, and scorned purity of tone in playing. Elias couldn't listen without feeling it was driving him crazy, and he thought of his music teacher Brother John, who played the piano and flute so divinely, yet was never satisfied with his performance. He would have had a heart attack if he'd met puffed-up Sarkis who stood with his legs planted wide apart, played out of tune, and was proud of it.

His only comfort at first was Nasibe. But although he could sleep with her – and she was magnificent in that respect – how was he to carry on a conversation about things she didn't understand? She too was only a backwoods peasant woman. At least he could laugh with her, although even that hadn't been so easy recently. For in the middle of their laughter she would suddenly turn serious, and suggest selling everything she had to go to Damascus with him and marry him there.

He didn't say no; he did not want to lose her. Her infatuation with him was all he had to cling to in the village.

But one day he heard of a job with the French administration in Damascus. He asked his brother to get him his father's permission to go back to the capital. He still had to communicate through Salman, for even after six months George Mushtak wouldn't say a word to Elias.

Salman told him curtly, "You can go. Here are five lira for the first few weeks, until you have a salary." And he threw the coins in his lap.

Elias took up his post in Damascus early in July. The work wasn't hard: he was running a provisions store for the French army. In three weeks he learned how to draw up lists and tables of everything that came into the store and went out of it, and a little later, like all his colleagues there, he found out how to earn something on the side as well as his official salary. It was simple: you set aside five kilos of rice and let the grocer have them, then you counted the five kilos in again with supplies for the soldiers' canteen, and you shared the money thus earned fair and square with the cook. Everyone did it. And if an officer came along – an officer with the rank of at least first lieutenant – and said he needed three litres of red wine you didn't stop to argue, you smiled, gave him what he wanted, and added the missing bottles to the accounts for the next party. Who was going to check whether three hundred or three hundred and fifteen bottles of red wine had been drunk at a reception for the French High Commissioner or the governor of Damascus?

"No one," explained his predecessor, giving Elias a list of the maximum quantities to be unofficially allowed to every rank of officer. "There's order even in chaos," the old man went on. "Only generals can have as much as they want."

Elias was living in the Bab Tuma district, lodging with a tight-fisted old widow whom he hated as much as his boss. Neither of them could be described as a genuine human being. If his boss First Lieutenant Mauriac had really been human Elias's life would have taken quite a different turn. But Mauriac was a sadist who enjoyed tormenting his inferiors, a slimy hypocrite who spent all day cleaning his uniform, tidying his desk, or polishing his boots. He had been transferred to administration as a punishment for cowardice on the field of battle, and even that was only because his uncle had been a famous hero in the First World War, or he would have been dishonourably discharged from the army. Every single one of his thirty-five underlings knew it. He was a corrupt, unprincipled man who delighted in humiliating his new employee every morning. "Well, little Syrian?" he would say. "So how are you going to defend France, eh? The rebels will just fart in your face. You'd better be glad we're taking the trouble to put this dunghill of yours in order."

There was nothing to be done about it. Answering back just spurred Mauriac on to think up even worse humiliations. "You have to keep saying, 'Yes, sir, very true, sir,'" Elias's predecessor had told him quietly, "while you secretly wish him an elephant's prick up his arse." Elias laughed, and thought the old administrator had lost his backbone with the advancing years, but he soon found out what happened to those who stood up to Mauriac. The first lieutenant had them beaten and put to cleaning the latrines.

So the former Jesuit student repeated, "Yes, sir, very true, sir," at least three times a day. It was a bitter daily pill that Mauriac made him swallow.

Otherwise, however, there was nothing wrong with the administrative work. Elias and another Syrian called Adnan, under Mauriac's direct supervision, managed a huge store containing not just foodstuffs but luxury goods from all over the world, things that the average Syrian never set eyes on: expensive sweetmeats, textiles, wines, coffee, butter, cognac, champagne, spirits, rock candy, pistachios and peanuts.

Over thirty workmen did what the two managers told them, and before three months were up Elias thought up a good idea for getting around the problem of certain logistical bottlenecks that were delaying the supply of goods. Mauriac was pleased, because the military governor gave him a decoration for it, and "his" procedure was to be adopted in all the other stores too. But Adnan ascribed the fact that the newcomer and not he had won praise, although he had been in the job so much longer, to the general injustice of Christians. He was a Sunni and had never been praised for anything in his ten years working here.

Elias later suspected that Adnan gave him away out of resentment, and took pleasure in his cruel punishment. But something of crucial importance was to happen first.

Nasibe visited him. It was a surprise. He came back from work about five in the afternoon, and there she was standing under the chestnut tree near his lodgings, carrying a small basket. Elias was bewildered. On a short visit to Mala, he had probably told her where he was living in Damascus, but he had never expected her to come and see him.

But now here she was, delighted when he smiled at her and said she was in luck, because that dragon his landlady was away for a week, staying with her daughter in the distant seaport of Latakia. She wouldn't let her lodgers have visitors, either men or women. "Their shoes wear out the stairs," he said, quoting the old lady as he took Nasibe into the house.

However, after a few hours his pleasure in seeing her died down, and on that day he knew he didn't want to live with Nasibe. She, on the other hand, was as happy as ever with his pretended ardour, and took the things she had brought from Mala out of her basket: dried fruits, wheat grits, cheese. He took her hand, led her to the larder and asked her to cook something with these magnificent provisions.

Nasibe sensed no change in Elias, because he still wanted her in bed. Perhaps he didn't make such wild love as before, but he was more affectionate than any other man she knew. Above all, he was very courteous to her, and Nasibe regarded courtesy as one of the cornerstones of love. In the evening he even took her out, and they went walking through the Christian quarter together. He just didn't want her to take his arm.

She stayed with him for five days, cooking, washing, and ironing, and looking forward to his return every evening. Elias was especially courteous to her now, for the very reason that he no longer desired her. He thanked her for every little thing. But she was losing all her power of attraction for him. He tried hard to find her interesting in some kind of way, and drank when he was with her so that he could give his instincts free rein, but even drunk he couldn't make love to her as wildly as he did a few months ago.

She smelled of strong rosewater, sour milk, and rutting billygoats. Even when she put on makeup he thought she looked rustic. She used too much of everything, as if the world were short-sighted and colour-blind. Everything she said and did reminded him more and more of Mala. And Nasibe became more rustic all the time because, out in the street, she noticed that she was inferior to the city women.

He was glad when she left. She had wanted him to take her to the bus, but he pretended he had an urgent inventory of the store to draw up. However, she did not, as he had hoped, sense his coolness. He could feel that when she embraced him in tears behind the door as they said goodbye, and whispered to him almost pleadingly, "Think of me, my little stallion. I'll look forward to your decision. We suit so well together. Did you notice too? Five days, and we haven't spoken a cross word." And her eyes became a gushing fountain of tears.

32. Adnan's Revenge

Mauriac was supposed to be on three days' leave, but suddenly there he was in his uniform. It was after five in the afternoon. He had never before turned up in the store at that time of day, after working hours. Elias had just invited a workman whom he liked to drink a glass of wine with him in a back room. They were sitting among the crates, sipping their wine and eating roasted peanuts from a little dish. The man's name was Burhan, and he was very poor. He worked as a porter, making ends meet as best he could, but he had a quick and clever wit. Elias liked his pointed remarks. A small sack of peanuts had split open that day; he had distributed the contents to the porters, except for this last handful, and then he asked Burhan to stay and chat with him after work. Like Elias himself, Burhan was a bachelor.

Adnan had seen it all from the doorway. But soon after that he left, and Elias hadn't been sorry to see him knock off work early. There wasn't anything more to do. Now, however, Adnan was standing behind the furious Mauriac with a spiteful grin on his face.

"A manager thieving!" shouted Mauriac. "Caught you in the act, you lousy Arab."

He took no notice of the porter at all, and indeed turned his back on him and seized the shocked manager's hand as if he feared Elias might run for it. Burhan quietly made himself scarce, and no one paid him any attention. Elias stood there in front of the open bottle of red wine and the dish of peanuts.

"You thought I wouldn't notice what a thief you are. But you were wrong, and you'll be punished for it."

Then he laughed as if he had exactly the right idea for a punishment in mind. He turned to Adnan. "Tell the commandant of the men on guard that I need two good strong fellows."

Adnan went off and soon came back with two tall guardsmen, both Syrians.

"Hold the thief tight," said Mauriac, and in pleasurable excitement he whispered an order to Adnan, who disappeared into the equipment room and soon came back with a funnel and a small hosepipe.

"And now a bucket of *pour*."

Pour was short for *pour chien*, "for the dog". It was the codeword in the store for a cheap red wine given only to the common soldiers when there was something to celebrate. The two Syrians held Elias's hands, one on each side, and pulled his arms apart so that he slumped between them as if he had been crucified.

Then Adnan roughly forced the hose into his mouth, and Mauriac, laughing, poured the wine into it down the funnel. "Here, drink up," he said, still laughing. Elias thought his end had come. Years later he was still saying that at this, the worst moment of his life, he had understood all the misery of the Arabs. Three Syrians slavishly helping a corrupt, cowardly French officer to torment their fellow countryman.

He swallowed and swallowed, tried to get his breath back and choked, but Mauriac went on pouring. The wine flowed out of the corners of his mouth and down over his throat and chest. Mauriac poured the entire contents of the bucket down through the hose until Elias lost consciousness.

When he came back to his senses, he was lying on a dirty mattress in a dark room. He sat up, his head heavy. His skull was buzzing and there was a bitter taste in his mouth. He didn't know how he came to be in this room or how long he had been lying there.

Slowly, he went out of it. The room was in a poor peasants' house, behind their living room. An old man sat with his wife beside the small hearth, and they were feeding the fire with thin pieces of wood. Elias didn't know either of them. He sat down on the first stool he saw.

"Thank God, you're alive," cried the man. "My wife thought you'd die soon."

"Where did you find me?"

"In the ditch at the roadside, not far from Damascus," said the woman. "We were just coming home from market after selling our walnuts and dried figs," her husband added.

Elias quickly recovered, went back to Damascus, fetched a few possessions from his room, and set out for Mala.

The village knew by now was that he was doing splendidly with the French, and was said to be a store manager. George Mushtak felt a certain pride in that damn son of his who wouldn't let anything get him down, but kept on fighting. He had decided to bury his hatred and forgive the boy next time he came to visit.

Elias came home a broken man, carrying a single case, so he was much moved when Mushtak sent Salman to tell him he could come and receive his father's blessing. He ran upstairs. His father was sitting on the big couch like a king, and Elias's eyes filled with tears when he kissed Mushtak's hand and asked his forgiveness.

"I forgive you everything! You are my son, and you have my blessing," said George Mushtak, equally moved. Salman and his wife were standing in the doorway.

"Why are you standing there like a couple of plaster dummies? Fetch us wine, bread, olives, and cheese, and we'll celebrate!"

The word "wine" was unwelcome to Elias's ears, and indeed he never in his life drank red wine again.

"Water for me, please," he begged.

"Why? You're a man, aren't you?" asked his father, and there was anxiety in his voice.

"Yes, Father, but some red wine gave me bad blood poisoning," Elias replied. He stopped for a moment, and then realized that he was going the wrong way about it. He must be frank. "Father," he said, "I've been tortured. They poured five litres of wine into my belly down a hosepipe." He fell silent as Salman and Hanan carried in two large trays laden with olives, preserved aubergines and sheep's milk cheese. George Mushtak gestured to them to put it all down and keep quiet.

"Who tortured you? And why?" he asked, taking his son by the right shoulder.

Elias told the whole story, laying the blame on Adnan and Mauriac.

"Then now let's celebrate your homecoming, and I swear to you by my mother's soul that neither of them will have the strength to reach their own homes tomorrow," said his father, drinking to his son.

Late that night three men rode towards Damascus behind Elias. They arrived early in the morning. Like his father's three servants, Elias wore peasant clothes, and they lay in wait for Adnan, who always turned up for work at eight. When he appeared, the men looked hard at him and memorized his face and figure. Then Elias pointed out Mauriac, who came to work at nine with all due ceremony, wearing his uniform.

"You can sleep until midday now," he told the men, and they lay down beside a nearby stream. He stayed awake himself. He kept thinking of his father, who had insisted on paying out those who had tormented his son. He woke the men around twelve.

"They'll both come out in half an hour's time," he told them. "God be with you." And he reached for his pistol. They had agreed that he was to stay in the background. The men would attack the two from the store and beat them, and only if they were in danger themselves would Elias give them cover.

Mauriac came marching out of the store first. Adnan, his puny shadow, followed him. Mushtak's men, well muffled up, let them go about a hundred metres to the first bend in the road. Then the peasants from Mala fell on them, threw them to the ground in silence, and beat them about their heads and knees with iron bars. After that they mounted the horses that Elias was holding for them and rode out of town faster than the wind.

His father's welcome, however, was a strange one. George Mushtak stood with his face impassive, listening to his favourite servant Basil's account. When he heard that it had all gone as he wished, he said only, "Good," beckoned to Elias, and took him into his bedroom. He went to the shelf under the picture of St. Giorgios on the wall opposite the big bed. It was a seventeenth-century original that the bishop had given George Mushtak after he made the Church a large donation.

"Put your hand on the Bible," he ordered, "and swear not to fuck a woman again until you marry." Elias was shocked at first. Then he was almost overcome by a fit of laughter. Only his father could utter the words "Bible" and "fuck" in the same sentence. He put his hand on the Bible. He was almost unconscious with weariness after the six hours' ride.

"I swear," he whispered, almost inaudibly.

33. Flight

George Mushtak was less and less intemperate in his dealings with Elias now, but he was truly at ease only with Salman. They were almost like boon companions. George's eyes always flashed with joy and admiration when they rested on his firstborn child. But at least he had made his peace with his youngest son now. Elias had a fine room on the second floor, and was treated with respect by everyone, including his father.

It took Elias some time to recover from his experiences, and then he wondered what to do now. He didn't want to teach at the school in Mala, although the village priest was pressing him to take the job. But the musty damp of the classrooms choked him the moment the priest so much as mentioned the subject, and in any case he never again wanted to work in the service of any authority, even the Catholic Church.

He briefly contemplated starting a small factory to produce natural dried fruits. But one day George Mushtak suggested horse-breeding, a trade at present pursued by only two families in Mala: the hated Shahins and, in a smaller way, the Mobates. And the future of the

Mobate stud farm was uncertain, since the village elder's three sons had shown no interest in the business.

"The beautiful Samira is crazy about horses, the only one among them who is, but she's a woman and needs an intelligent man to guide her," said his father, in an almost conspiratorial tone.

Elias knew Samira only slightly. She wasn't beautiful, but she was large and imposing, which amounted to the same thing for the peasants of Mala. She laughed a lot, very loudly, and she rode like the devil. Everyone knew that Mobate idolized her, and to the great annoyance of her brothers was leaving her a quarter of his large fortune in his will, just as if she were a man.

Elias had no idea that his father and the village elder had already settled everything. He was to marry Samira and start a stud farm of his own with her. Mobate would provide the thoroughbred Arab horses, Mushtak would contribute three hundred gold lira for the stables.

But it was in that summer of 1935 that Elias met Claire and fell in love. Captivated by her as he was, he was impervious to all else. Every hint his father dropped about Samira went unheard. He nodded amiably, but he wasn't listening. And even when he was stopped in the village square at noon one day by the handsome lunatic known to everyone as Shams, the man's strange words did not alarm him at first.

"Brother, don't marry Samira. She loves me, but her father wants to sell her off to you. Look at me, brother, look at me," begged the madman, and his wide eyes showed how deranged he was. "Have I done anything to harm you? Is it too much to ask? You can marry all America, but leave me Samira!"

Elias found this conversation embarrassing. "Hush, there's no need for you to shout. Why would I have anything to do with Samira? I'm happy to leave her to you or anyone else," he replied.

"No, brother, not anyone else, just me, all right? Just me, right?" cried Shams, laughing, and there was a pleading note in his voice. The saliva dribbled uncontrollably from his mouth, yet he was still as handsome as a Greek god, thought Elias.

Only that evening did he learn that the madman had not, like many Arabs, used the word "brother" as a courteous but generalized form of address, but meant it literally.

"He's your half-brother," Salman told him, his tone cold and brittle as usual. "Your mother was unfaithful to my father, and God punished her because he loves George Mushtak. She went crazy, and her son has fits of lunacy."

"Where does he live? What does he do?"

"He's worked as a groom for Mobate ever since he turned up here. They say he's good with horses," replied Salman.

"And what about Samira? Why did he beg me not to marry her? Does Father have plans of some kind?"

"What do you mean, plans? He has no plans at all. You mustn't let any chance-come idiot turn your head," said Salman, lying. He knew very well that Mobate and Mushtak had already fixed the wedding for Christmas. The only snag was that Samira didn't like Elias. She often mocked his slight figure and his liking for books, and she thought his affairs with women ridiculous. She dreamed of an immaculate love as Shams passionately understood it. He described such a love wonderfully.

Elias wasn't interested in Samira either. While the fathers were making their plans he had met, for the first time, a woman who attracted him even though she smelled only of perfume, giving off no aura of desire for him. But her speech was sensuality itself, and when she said "*chéri*" he could have fainted away with happiness.

She spoke fluent French, which sounded to his ears like civilization, liberation from cow dung and the smell of sweat. There was something in her voice that he had never encountered before. It trembled, it sounded almost hoarse, as if Claire had a slight cold. And when she spoke of Molière, Mozart, or Lamartine her vibrant voice gave him a warm feeling and a great sense of longing.

But he often doubted whether Claire loved him back, for she could suddenly be very reserved, keep her distance, sound noncommittal, and then she was only a cold cloud of perfume. So one day he summoned up all his courage and asked her if she loved him.

She gave him a more direct answer than he had ever read in any book about love. Claire spoke softly, but she looked him straight in the eye. She loved him very much, she said, and wanted nothing more fervently than to hold his hand, kiss him, and hold him close. But she didn't know what she was to do without causing a scandal and putting him, Elias, in mortal danger, because she was engaged to a dangerous boxer who worked as a bodyguard.

He wasn't so much alarmed by Claire's frankness as by realizing that he could scent no desire in her. Furthermore, Nasibe warned him against Claire and described her in forthright terms as "that Damascus whore." She was ready to kill the woman, she said, if Claire tried taking Elias away from her.

But when his father had a private conversation with him one morning, saying he would like him to seduce Samira with his charms and make her submissive, because after that she'd be bound to want him, Mala seemed too hot to hold Elias. His father and the powerful Mobate on one hand, Claire's injured fiancé on the other, and then there was the infatuated Nasibe, who was claiming to be pregnant. He knew he mustn't waste another second.

Only flight was left, but to be sure of the girl he wanted to take with him he went to Claire, and made his love and strong feelings for her very clear. He enjoyed the touch of her smooth skin, and although this first sexual experience of hers hurt, she held him close and wouldn't let him go until she had entered Paradise with him several times.

They eloped next morning. Elias never guessed that his flight had saved his life, for Jusuf Shahin had just heard of the plan for him and Samira to set up a stud farm in competition with himself. So old Shahin had sent two men to lie in wait for Elias by night. They were to leave him alive, but mutilate his face. Then the vain Samira wouldn't like the look of him any more, and George Mushtak's son would be nothing but a burden to him.

The two men had waited opposite Tamam's house, where the Surur family was spending the summer. They knew that Elias visited every evening. But they waited there in vain until after midnight. George Mushtak too had been waiting up for his youngest son until dawn. He thought Elias was with Samira, and smiled as he imagined her surprise and pain when that small, slight man thrust into her. He almost felt something like love for his difficult son. He was going to use him to ruin old Shahin.

If he had had the faintest idea of what had already happened by then, he would have wept bitterly at his worst defeat.

34. Defeat of the Master of the House

George Mushtak shut himself up in his bedroom for days on end. He cursed everyone, and he reviled Elias with particular ferocity. Mushtak knew that Shahin would strike now, and he told Salman to tell his men to be very careful and never leave the house unarmed. Many of them smiled at the fears of the master of the house, but soon after that they witnessed an attempted murder, and realized that George Mushtak had not been exaggerating. Shots were fired at Salman.

Mushtak's eldest son was the only one allowed to see his father, and they spent many hours together every day. Salman kept urging his father to show himself to his people, because the wind was turning, blowing against the Mushtaks from a very dangerous quarter.

Shortly after the Feast of the Holy Cross on 14 September, Salman entered his father's room again. That day, he had had a distressing quarrel with three young fellows lounging idly about, who made no move to go back to their work when they saw him coming.

"Father, you must go out to the men," he said. There was sorrow and determination in his voice. "Elias doesn't matter so much. It's a pity that we've lost a supporter now that he's gone, but you have a new son in Basil, which is more than we could have hoped for. The men are waiting for you outside. Of course I've had everything you ordered done, but I can tell that they need your word, your hand."

Salman waited. He did not tell his father that the Shahins had fired on him, or that they were spreading word around the village that Mushtak had suffered a stroke. He passed one hand over the basil plant growing in a pot by the window, and thought how powerful his father was, when his mere absence seduced their enemies into rash confidence. He had recognized the marksman, despite the distance he kept. It was Butros, Jusuf Shahin's eldest son. And Salman thought he would pay him back for that cowardly attack.

"Then let's go out," said George Mushtak, interrupting his son's dark thoughts. He sensed that Salman urgently needed him.

At the end of September he rode out into the mountains, breathing deeply. He stopped on a hill, and let his eyes wander from his property to the Damascus road.

35. Samira and Shams

Mobate was by no means as unhappy as Mushtak when he heard of Elias's flight. He had been very anxious about his daughter, who wouldn't hear of marrying Mushtak's son. She had actually threatened to die rather than become the wife of a dwarf who couldn't even speak the village dialect properly, and instead tried to babble French in a pretentious way, as if his mother came from Paris.

When George left his room again Mobate immediately came to visit, assured him of his friendship, and said that marriage was a matter of fate, not planning. Mushtak did not agree, but he was relieved that the village elder bore him no grudge for his son's flight.

Mobate knew he would have gained power if Samira had become Mushtak's daughter-in-law, but at the same time he would also have lost it through being so clearly related to Mushtak. Clarity in that respect would make him less acceptable in others. The more open to him all houses were, the stronger he was as village elder. And then there was that eternal bloodshed between the Mushtaks and the Shahins. The marriage would have left him constantly involved in it himself.

As for Samira, he wasn't worried about her future. And he was right. After a short, stormy infatuation with the handsome lunatic Shams, she had decided in favour of a marriage that would take her into calmer waters. Shams disappeared from the village and was never seen there again. Some said they had seen him begging in Damascus, others claimed to have come across him preaching in a mosque.

Samira met a man from Damascus who loved horses, and took herself and her fortune off to join him. The couple founded a stud for noble Arab horses that was to become one of the most successful in the country. But that was later, and much was to happen in the village before then.

As already mentioned, two weeks after Elias's flight a marksman shot at Salman for the first time, although he missed. But then, in October and just after the Feast of St. Sergius, the attacker fired another bullet at Salman, and it hit him in the upper arm. It was only a glancing shot, but this time old Mushtak heard about the attack and massively over-retaliated. The Shahins' stable was set on fire. Six horses perished miserably, and the watchman's charred body was found with a hole the width of a finger in his right temple. Everyone knew that the Mushtaks were behind it, but the operation had been so efficiently carried out that no trail led to them. For months Jusuf Shahin mourned his horses, which he loved more than his own children. Old Mushtak knew just where his enemies were most vulnerable.

A counter-attack in the early summer of 1937 failed, thanks to Basil's watchfulness. He set a trap for the three men who climbed into the yard by night after tricking the guard dogs with poisoned meat. The men were caught. After being cruelly tortured at the police station, they finally confessed everything. Jusuf Shahin had to pay a fortune in bribes to avoid going to jail, as the man behind the three of them, and was obliged to sign a humiliating document stating that he would be liable to prosecution for incitement to murder if anything happened to George Mushtak, one of his sons, or even just one of his employees. The verdict would inevitably have been a death sentence.

That evening the Mushtaks celebrated victory with their friends at a meal in the courtyard of the big house, and Mobate, who was sitting beside George, was not exaggerating when, in drinking his health, he said that after this no one, not even Salman or Basil, would take such good care of his safety as his arch-enemy Jusuf Shahin. Everyone laughed.

His old enemy did indeed forbid his sons to make any more attempts on Mushtak's life. And they respected that prohibition until their father's death in the summer of 1938.

BOOK OF THE CLAN II

The clan saved the Arabs from the desert, and at the same time enslaved them.

ॐ

36. Jasmin and Mariam

When Jusuf Shahin died in the summer of 1938, his testicles crushed by an accurately placed kick from his mare Sabah, his arch-enemy George Mushtak told the old village barber who brought him the news that while the snake's tail might be dead, the snake itself was still alive. The barber understood those words as an insult to a dead man. The hostility between the two families didn't even respect the dignity of death. He silently nodded and moved away.

But George Mushtak had told the truth. He feared Samia, the real ruler of the house of Shahin, far more than his old rival Jusuf, who might be unprincipled and malicious but had never been able to see further than the end of his own nose. Samia, on the other hand, was the daughter of a family of considerable importance. She came from Aleppo, and had seen a good deal of the world before finally marrying the rich horse-breeder from Mala who was twenty years her senior.

For decades her father Butros Khuri had been the biggest textiles manufacturer in Aleppo, supplier to the court of the Ottoman Sultan Abdulhamid. He bore the honorary title of Bey, which the Sultan seldom bestowed on Christians. Butros Bey had stipulated that the bridegroom, Jusuf Shahin, must be a strict adherent of the Greek Orthodox Church. He hated Jews, Catholics and the French, and blamed himself all his life for having backed the overthrow of the Sultan, toppled from his throne thirty years before.

Jusuf Shahin was Greek Orthodox but very far from devout, so he was hypocritical in presenting himself to his future father-in-law as a man who would campaign against the Catholics day and night. He got what he wanted: his wife and a great deal of gold in return for his courage.

"The Catholics are even worse than the Muslims. You have to knock their heads in, that's the only language they understand," said Butros.

"And so I will," replied Jusuf unctuously, unaware that in his struggle with his rival Mushtak he was indeed going to become the greatest enemy of the Catholics.

After this conversation with Butros Bey, Jusuf used part of the money to renovate his large property. And he did it exactly as Samia wished, so that she would lack for nothing and could hold her head high in the company of her rich parents and the rest of her family. His was the only house in the village at the time to have a proper bathtub, and coloured marble tiles on the floors of the rooms. A year later Samia moved in.

Loyalty was alien to Jusuf Shahin in both his business dealings and his private life. He was faithful to Samia only because he hated all women. It was said in the village that he allowed her near him only four times in his entire life, on the occasions when he made her pregnant. None the less, she brought eight children into the world. The other four, rumour said, were the result of her love affairs with the young grooms. This, however, was the wildest of gossip. Only her youngest daughter Jasmin was the fruit of a passionate affair, but no one in the village knew anything about that in detail.

Samia went to Aleppo to spend a week with her family and relations there every year. Jusuf never accompanied her, and so she was able to meet the love of her youth secretly in Aleppo. Her cousin Samer was a highly regarded lawyer, although he had made his large fortune by importing exotic woods. Samia and Samer had grown up in the same big house and played together like brother and sister. They had loved each other since childhood, but they couldn't marry because, as a baby, Samer had been breast-fed by Samia's mother for several weeks while his own mother recovered from an inflammation of her nipples. According to the custom of the time, that made Samia and Samer siblings at the breast, and marriage between them would have been incest.

Samer himself was now unhappily married. His father had chosen the daughter of the richest merchant family in Aleppo as his wife.

Samia knew exactly when and where she had conceived Jasmin. In the winter of 1919 Samer was able to welcome her to his own house for the first time. His wife had gone away with their three children, so Samia visited him daily, and they spent a week together in Paradise.

On the first day of their reunion they were hungry for each other, and had already made love in the dining room, on the stairs, in the bathroom, and in the passage under the arcades. When they reached the bedroom on the first floor, they were so exhausted that they fell asleep. Samia woke in alarm two hours later, and had to run back to her parents' house nearby. As a woman, she couldn't on any account spend the night out.

Next morning she went to Samer as early as she could. Her cousin was already waiting for her. He led her to the bedroom, where she stopped in surprise. He had covered the bed with a thick layer of snow-white jasmine flowers, picked early that morning and now filling the room with their intoxicating fragrance. He undressed Samia and carried her carefully to the bed, where he made love to her at length in the sea of jasmine. They perspired freely during their love play, and their bodies were saturated with the scent of the jasmine blossom.

Weeks later, however hard she scrubbed herself in the bath, Samia still smelled of their fragrance. Even her husband, who always stank of his horses and whose nose was anything but sensitive, wondered why she had given off such a flowery scent ever since her return from Aleppo.

So Samia gave the daughter she had conceived that day the name of Jasmin, and she was her favourite child. The girl looked like her mother, but she moved, spoke, and laughed like her real father, although she never met him, for Samia's cousin Samer died in an accident in 1923, when the child was only three years old.

When her other daughter Mariam married Samer's eldest son in the summer of 1938, Samia stayed away from the wedding. She went to bed and claimed to be unwell.

Her husband Jusuf hated wedding festivities, but he was sure that his daughter had won a great prize in Jakub, the son of his father Samer's rich and highly regarded family. However, he was morose and bad-tempered when he went to the wedding with the bride and her older brothers Butros, Bulos, Faris, Basil, and Musa. All his sons were married now, and they brought not only their wives but also their parents-in-law with them. His daughter Amira and her husband Louis came from Damascus. A bus had to be hired just for the family, and another was reserved for Shahin's followers, neighbours, and the leading villagers of Mala.

Jasmin was eighteen at the time. She wanted to go to the wedding too, but she had to stay with her allegedly sick mother and help the housekeeper Salime to look after her. She wept for nights, but it did her no good.

※

Since Jakub's mother was a widow, his grandparents organized the festivities. The powerful textiles manufacturer Khuri gave a wedding party fit for the *Thousand and One Nights*. In between the lavish meals, dancing girls and conjurors entertained the guests for seven days and seven nights. The best Syrian cooks lived not in Damascus but in Aleppo.

Besides the rich gold jewellery that Jusuf gave his daughter, he had thought of a special surprise. He had a noble Arab steed brought to Aleppo, and it was led out by a slim stable lad wearing colourful Arab costume on the wedding day. The stable lad solemnly handed the astonished bridegroom the horse's gold-studded reins. Mariam whispered to him what he must do, and to the surprise of his grandparents and the applause of the guests Jakub, son of that distinguished family, walked the horse around in a circle, with perfect self-assurance, before he gave the reins back to the groom, patted the animal's neck, and returned to sit on the raised seat beside his bride feeling wonderfully happy.

Jusuf looked at the horse with sadness in his eyes. "Go with the grace of God. Sabah will miss you very much," his neighbours heard him whispering. No one guessed that the horse-breeder would pay for parting them with his life. Sabah, his finest mare, loved only this one stallion Shafak, and kicked out at any others.

Shortly after his return Jusuf tried putting a young stallion to his mare. The mare lashed out wildly and would not calm down. After a few days Jusuf lost patience and decided to break her resistance. When he approached her she kicked. Jusuf shot three metres through the air to meet his death.

Jakub was an able man, but he wasn't interested in his father's business dealing in exotic woods. His mind was set on his grandfather's trade, and at the age of twenty-two he opened his own small, modern textiles mill.

Samia was envious. To think that Mariam of all people, the very image of her father, had the luck to live with this wonderful man. All these years she had hoped that Jasmin would make the running, and kept sending her to stay with her grandparents in Aleppo during her vacations. But to Jakub the little girl had been only his pert young cousin, and he was all the more strongly attracted to Mariam, who wasn't particularly beautiful but was mature and energetic. When he was with her he felt a deep need to tell her everything, and he sensed that her readiness to listen in itself lured the words out of his mouth. Only with her would he allow himself to speak of his half-formed ideas, for when she listened they matured into convictions.

And whenever Mariam went home on a visit, Jakub felt a great void in himself. That was love. Not only her own mother but the whole village envied Mariam her happiness. She was also thankful to Jakub for catapulting her out of Mala, eaten up as the place was by quarrels and hostility, and showing her the great world of Aleppo, Venice, and Istanbul. She loved her tall, slim husband, who couldn't look at a woman without ideas of sex in mind, yet remained as faithful to her as a dog. He was a genius, and like most geniuses he was also a grown-up child who needed a firm hand. But happiness is an unreliable companion. Jakub died of a stroke after only a year of marriage. One night he woke and asked for a drink of water. Mariam jumped out of bed. Something alarmed her. And even as she stood in the kitchen she knew that Jakub was dead. She came back with the water, and there was her happiness lying half off the bed with his back bare. He had stretched out his arms as if to save himself from falling. She screamed, the glass flew from her hand and shattered against the wall. Mariam never wanted to go back to Mala. She believed all her life that the jealous villagers had grudged her such happiness and killed her husband with their darts of envy.

She went to Damascus, where she opened a fashion store in the high-class Salihiye quarter with the money she brought with her. From then on she spoke only French, and called herself Marie Shah.

37. Samia

Women meant nothing to Jusuf. He regarded marrying and founding a large family as a duty, important purely in the context of power calculations. On those few nights when he visited his wife, he came to her because she told him it was a good time for her to conceive. After that he left Samia alone in the large, comfortable, cedarwood bed with its soft wool mattresses.

Samia's original infatuation with Jusuf quickly died, and never turned to love. She saw that this man had no place in his life for her. His heart was full of ambitious plans. She was allowed to join him in discussing them, but that was all. It was said in the village – and the Mushtaks encouraged the rumour – that Samia was unable to love because she had a shard of steel where others have a feeling heart, which made her the perfect partner for Jusuf.

George Mushtak hated the woman, sensing that the fortunes of the Shahin family had changed since she came to Mala. The blows Jusuf inflicted on him were suddenly of a different calibre. For instance, it had allegedly been Samia's idea to lay charges of conspiracy against him with the Ottoman governor of Damascus. Mushtak was taken away by night and was already in danger of the gallows when the Catholic Bishop of Damascus intervened.

George was convinced that Shahin's wife was a woman who ruled with a heart of iron. His insinuations about Samia's influence were correct, but the idea that she had an iron heart sprang entirely from his resentment of her clever wits, since her heart was really loving and full of grief.

For she very soon understood that with the marriage ceremony Jusuf had achieved his aims. She had been pregnant with her first child, Butros, a month before the wedding. It was not that Jusuf did not respect her, but he wasn't interested in her as a woman. He never called her Samia again, only "mother of my children".

She lay alone in the great bed every night, wondering what Samer might be doing at this hour. She dared not tell anyone, even Samer himself, for she believed she was in a constant state of sin, she prayed and prayed and suffered from a terribly guilty conscience towards her husband, who never looked at another woman. So she tried to stand by him and lend him moral and practical support. She learned to love horses and hate Mushtaks. It was she who made Jusuf's eyes light up when she told him her plan for giving his despicable adversary trouble. Jusuf looked at her, fascinated, and for a moment she hoped he would take her in his arms and kiss her, but he only smiled and praised her with the saying that he kept repeating for twenty-eight years, until the last day of his life. "The prophet Muhammad himself warned his followers of women's wiles, and *he* knew what he was talking about."

George Mushtak went to excess in everything, eating and drinking, grief and joy, but seldom in his estimation of his enemies.

38. Fifty-One and One

Jusuf Shahin respected his wife deeply, and was thankful for all her advice. He allowed her to choose their children's names herself, which was unusual at that time. As a rich farmer and horse-breeder he had had many affairs before his marriage, but now he seemed to have cut all the threads linking him to his past. Samia's present, on the other hand, appeared to be entangled in threads from the past, a thousand and one of them.

Like a child singing out loud to overcome its fear of the dark, Samia kept telling herself that she could live and laugh even without Samer. She made up her mind never to think of him again, and not to go back to Aleppo until she was firmly in charge in Mala.

She told her heart to stop looking for unhappiness, and held up her life full of family duties for its inspection. But her heart was deaf and wouldn't see reason. When all was silent around her it kept repeating the same question, hour after hour: what is Samer doing now?

The quiet life of the village and the unforthcoming manner of the mountain farmers gave her time and space, and Samer filled them. Sometimes she felt her heart beating fast. Fear and shame filled her when she asked herself: does he think of me too? Such questions were born of her fear of the answer no, and her shame for her selfishness.

She rode through the mountains calling her lover's name out loud to the wind, as if she didn't just want to enjoy its sound in her ears but were telling the wind to carry her cry to him.

She stayed away from Aleppo for three years, but when her father fell sick she took her two children, Butros and Bulos, and went north, full of anxiety. Jusuf didn't want to go with her. When she arrived, her father came to meet her with outstretched arms, smiling mischievously. Not a sign of sickness about him.

"If your husband had come along too, I'd have had to take to my bed," said the old gentleman, confessing that he had longed to see her but didn't like visiting Mala. Her mother had suggested the letter about his poor health. He spoke like a child describing a successful prank, slapping his thigh with delight.

He was a born city dweller. He didn't mind in the least that he couldn't tell the difference between mules proper, a cross born of a male donkey and a mare, and hinnies, the offspring of a stallion and a female donkey or jennet, nor could he distinguish between rye, wheat, spelt, and oats. Even with his eyes blindfolded, however, he could identify any variety of tea from the first sip. And he could also converse with a Turk, an Arab, a Frenchman, and an Italian in their mother tongues.

Being back home with her parents was a strange feeling for Samia in the first few days. She glided around the rooms of the big villa, light as a fairy. Her parents let her have the whole east wing, with its bathroom, bedroom and drawing room, and its own kitchen. She had the services of two women who looked after her sons Butros and Bulos all around the clock. It was only after a while that Samia saw, with alarm, how old her father had grown. He seemed to have shrunk, he was thin, almost frail, his hair was white as snow. Her mother, on the other hand, was the same as ever: reserved, stiff, correct in everything she did.

Suddenly there stood her lover in her drawing room doorway. She was just reading a French magazine. He was tall, slim, and had a breathtakingly beautiful smile on his face. She felt dizzy.

"Holy Mary Mother of God," she whispered.

"No, only Samer Khuri," he replied, laughing. She blushed and could hardly get to her feet. He took her hand and helped her up from the couch. Then Samia's lips touched his mouth with its wonderful fragrance. She breathed in the scent of her beloved, and dissolved in transports of delight. When she came back to her senses they were lying in her bed, drenched in perspiration.

She went back to Mala tormented by her memory of those hours in his arms. She was hungry for him, and at night, when darkness and silence fell over the village, her heart fluttered like a bird trying to escape from its cage.

After that she went to see her parents every year. Soon both she and Jusuf thought of her the visit to Aleppo as normal. Fifty-one weeks of loneliness and one week of ecstasy.

39. The Struggle

For years she felt guilty towards Jusuf. He wasn't jealous, he always showed her respect, and let her visit her parents every time without asking any questions at all. She felt she was behaving badly. Jusuf, on the other hand, seemed to her proud, lofty, and inscrutable, and that made him interesting to her, not that he cared in the least for her interest.

He liked the company of his pure-bred horses better than anything. He was a successful breeder; even the richest Arab and French owners had to go on a waiting list to get a horse from Jusuf Shahin's stables. He had an infallible instinct for the mating that would produce generation after generation of even finer horses.

He seemed to live for his horses alone. His clan respected him and his enemies feared him. And unlike his arch-enemy George Mushtak, whose reputation as a fornicator was known to everyone, who had fathered at least sixty bastard children and even in his latter days was still grabbing at bosoms or behinds in a very undignified way, Jusuf, so the villagers considered, behaved properly around women. There were no whispered rumours about him.

One night Samia woke from a nightmare. The moon was full. She sat up in bed, bathed in sweat. At first she was afraid that something had happened to one of the children. In her dream she had seen the house burning and heard her children's voices behind the impenetrable flames. But when, with her heart beating fast, she went into their room, which was close to hers, her two boys were sleeping as peacefully as little angels. She went back to her room, but a sense of uneasiness came over her again. "The horses!" She leaped up. Without a sound, she went downstairs and crossed the dark yard to the dimly lit stables. There she froze. At first she heard only her husband's whispering and moans, then she saw him.

He was lying over the young stable lad Ahmad's back. Jusuf was thrusting himself into the boy, caressing him all the time, lavishing on him the loving words and kisses that he had never given her. The boy was awkward and sullen, and wouldn't keep still. Her husband, ruler of the large Shahin clan, was begging the stable lad for a little affection like a man deeply in love.

So that's it, she thought on the way back to her room. He likes slender young men.

She never mentioned Jusuf's inclinations to him, but after that night her conscience no longer pricked her, and her relationship with her husband was more serene. Jusuf enjoyed life with Samia at his side. She gave him eight healthy children, and brought them all up to became clever men and women. But now and then it struck him that in any quarrel all his offspring, except for his firstborn son Butros, took their mother's side. He thought it was just the vagaries of fate, and because of it he avoided any argument with his wife in his later years.

The horse-breeder never realized that the children's affection for their mother arose from her care for them in childhood. Samia had the midwife Amine's insight to thank for that. "Only those who have their children's hearts have the future," the woman told her in passing one day. Amine was illiterate, but she had the wisdom of thousands of years behind her.

40. Faris the Patient

Jusuf was the undisputed head of the clan. After him came not his brother Tanius, who had tuberculosis, or his wily youngest brother Suleiman, but his firstborn son Butros, who used bribery and black-mail to unite all their relations behind him. In his lifetime Jusuf invited the most important men of his clan to visit him, and made them put their hands on the Bible and swear that they hoped their arms might wither if they turned against his son Butros after his death.

That was the worst day of Suleiman's life. At the urging of his mother, a severe widow who was under the spell of her eldest son Jusuf, he had to promise his obedience in a loud, clear voice when it came to his turn. Suspicious as Jusuf was, he embraced him and called to those present, "You have been witnesses: my dear brother Suleiman will follow my son, in his own interests and those of us all. And the life of anyone who turns against him is forfeit, and not worth an onion skin to you. Are you of the same opinion?" And they all gave their consent.

Butros was brave and generous as long as you obeyed him. Unlike his father, however, he was pitiless as a scorpion to those who deserted him: silent, cunning, and deadly.

But Faris, Jusuf's third son, considered himself the future head of the clan. He realized that the greatest obstacle in his way was not his father but his eldest brother. The second eldest presented him with no problems. Bulos was simple-minded, and didn't seem to mind whether he held power or the udder of one of his many cows in his hands.

Faris did not think his two younger brothers Basil and Musa were dangerous either. Basil was a boarder at the French school in Damascus, and wanted to go to Paris and continue studying there when he left school. And Musa planned to start a haulage company. His father gave him his first truck when he was nineteen. Jusuf Shahin saw this as a way of bringing the transport routes between Mala and Damascus under his control. However, to the end of his life, which was a short one anyway, Musa thought more about women than his business.

Their father was well aware of his son's love affairs. He gave him a year's leeway and then made him marry Rihane from the seaport of Latakia, a pretty woman who hated life in the village. The wedding was in 1933, and when they were married Rihane kept pestering her husband to move to Latakia. He could build up his haulage business there, she said. To bind Musa to her she bore him two children. The first was a girl called Mona, after the mother of Jusuf, the head of the clan. The second child was a boy. Musa called him Said, "the happy one". But the children made Musa neither domesticated nor faithful. He was said to have a mistress in every village on the Damascus road. And in the end it wasn't his dangerous driving over potholed winding roads, but a pretty blonde American woman who, unintentionally perhaps, summoned the angel of death to Musa. The angel came on 7 April 1941.

Soon after Musa's death his widow received a large sum of money for her husband's share in the family property, and in the village elder's house she signed a document giving up any claim to the inheritance for herself and her children. She moved to Latakia with Mona and Said, before long she married the manager of the arrack distillery there, and from then on she bore his surname, Bustani. She wanted no more to do with the Shahin clan.

Faris's three sisters were no danger to his ambitious plans either. Women had no say in affairs out in the country. For that very reason, Samia had sent all three girls to the boarding school run by the Sisters of the Sacred Heart of Jesus in Damascus: first Amira, then Mariam, and finally her youngest daughter Jasmin. So Faris knew that only Butros need be regarded as a serious rival. But it was also clear to him that if he, Faris, tried to oust him, his brother wouldn't for a moment hesitate to kill him. So he set about it very slowly. Faris first formed his plan in the summer of 1935, when he was only twenty-one years old. He had to wait nearly twenty more years before his chance came. But then he took it without hesitation.

41. Musa and Hasib

Plenty of attempts were made in Mala to reconcile the two clans, but none of them came to anything, and the last, undertaken by two bishops, ended in disaster. Yet it had been hoped that a sign from heaven might perhaps bring the blood feud to a peaceful conclusion.

The bishops of the Catholic and Orthodox Churches of Damascus felt that the enmity between the two families was disgraceful, particularly as the village lay in the middle of a Muslim region. Increasingly dramatic reports of events there greatly distressed the two dignitaries. Visitors from outside were stigmatized as enemies of one of the churches just for donating a piastre to the other. Quite often nuns and abbots refused to let foreign delegations visit their convents and monasteries because the foreigners had been to see their rivals first.

In 1941 there was only a week between the Catholic and Orthodox celebrations of Easter Sunday. The Orthodox Church was celebrating the resurrection of Christ in accordance with the Julian calendar on April 7th, the Catholic Church in accordance with the Gregorian calendar on April 14th. So the two bishops had agreed that festivities to mark the reconciliation should go on all week and thus remain in the peasants' memory for ever. As a sign of fraternization they agreed to celebrate Mass together on Easter Sunday at the beginning of the festivities, close to the Catholic church of St. Giorgios, and later have lunch in the Orthodox convent of St. Thecla. On the following Sunday the village priests would celebrate divine service near the convent of St. Thecla with both clans, and have lunch outside the church of St. Giorgios.

On that Sunday, 7 April 1941, many of the inhabitants of Mala wept tears of emotion, for there had never been such a fine, magnificent church service in the village in their lives. It was held out in the open, in the village square.

All the Mushtaks and Shahins had travelled to Mala, and invited all their friends and allies. There were not two thousand but seven thousand people in the village that day. The sky was blue, the sun shone as if it were summer. After the solemn service, both bishops gave the assembled congregation their blessing and opened the Easter celebrations. Musicians played flutes, lutes and drums to accompany the dancing. Then, at about midday, there was to be a long, solemn procession to the great convent of St. Thecla, where cooks had been preparing for the arrival of the crowds for a week. But it all went wrong.

Around eleven, three shots were heard. The first killed Musa Shahin. His murderer was Hasib Mushtak, George's second son, who had come to Mala from Beirut especially to be with his father on this difficult day.

Hasib had studied medicine at the American University of Beirut. He had been a gifted schoolboy, and Mushtak sent his son to study in Beirut rather than Damascus because in his opinion, "You won't learn to be anything better than a butcher in Damascus." Hasib had completed his studies with the highest distinction in 1937. After that he was going to work at a Beirut hospital for another three years while his American wife Dorothea finished her studies of Arabic. He came home to Mala as often as he could, for he loved the village and his father. And Mushtak was fond of his clever son and his wife, who spoke better Arabic than many an Arab.

Malicious tongues, backed by slanders cleverly spread by the Shahins, claimed that old Mushtak's daughter-in-law didn't take his fumblings seriously, but that Hasib didn't like it. He was extremely touchy if anyone even looked like getting too close to his wife, and he was regarded as very jealous.

After divine service that April day in 1941, there was to be dancing and singing until it was time for the reconciliation banquet. The best place to be was the inner courtyard of the church of St. Giorgios. Soon the two bishops were enthroned on the terrace, watching the dancers near them with benevolent smiles. The spectators stood very close together, arrack was handed around, donated by the two rival clans and symbolically mixed by both bishops in large bottles to make a single beverage. The aniseed spirit, fifty percent proof, soon took effect.

Musa, Jusuf Shahin's third son, although married and the father of two children was, as already mentioned, a skirt-chaser. He had kept touching the tall American woman that day, and was pleased to find her so easy-going.

Musa was a handsome, dashing man. The blonde woman probably liked the awkward charm of his advances. To her, he seemed like a little boy, and she was amused by his attempts to speak English, here at the end of the world. But Musa took her laughter to mean that he was irresistible. He put his hand inside the American woman's blouse. Hardly anyone noticed, but Dorothea suddenly froze rigid with shock.

Hasib, who was slightly tipsy, broke off his conversation and hissed at Musa to leave his wife alone. But Musa, now babbling in his cups, retorted with the humiliating remark that anyone whom old George Mushtak fumbled was fair game for all.

Hasib didn't say a word. He left his wife there and disappeared. The Shahin supporters around Musa laughed in a rather muted way, so that the bishops wouldn't notice. But not for long. Hasib was very soon back again. He aimed at his adversary's forehead, and the last laugh froze on Musa's lips.

The rocks carried the echo of those three shots ringing through the mountain ravines. Panic broke out, and before the crowd could scatter there were over ten members of each clan lying severely injured in the church's inner courtyard.

Musa's body was trampled by the panic-stricken, screaming men and women running for the gate and safety. Later, curiously enough, many of them didn't remember the details of the murder as clearly as the saying of a midwife who had, apparently, told Musa weeks before that she had seen him in a dream being trampled by a herd of cattle.

Hasib calmly took his wife's hand. He walked not to the courtyard gate but through the church. Leaving by its main entrance, he quickly reached his father's courtyard. Hasib kissed the old man's hand and received two fervent kisses on his cheeks.

"You showed the bastard what a Mushtak is," said George, "and by doing so you saved me from hypocrisy. God bless you wherever you go." And he put a bag of gold lira in his son's jacket pocket. "Leave everything here and get away. You can buy what you need in Beirut. Kiss your son for me," he added quietly, and signed to his faithful servant Basil, who led Mushtak's son and his pale wife to the horses standing ready at the back gate of the large property.

In exactly three hours' time the couple were over the Lebanese border.

Hasib reached Beirut next morning. He sold the horses, provided himself, his wife, and his four-year-old son George with the requisite papers, and went to America. His first letter home came three months later. And in the years that followed his father learned, greatly to his satisfaction, that two more sons, Jack and Philip, would carry the name of Mushtak on into the next century. But Hasib's address remained unknown. He knew that Jusuf Shahin had cousins in America.

42. End of a Hope

My God, thought George Mushtak as Hasib disappeared into the western ravine, those two brothers Elias and Hasib are worlds apart. Growing up under the same roof, yet as different as night and day.

Hasib had lived far away in Beirut, yet he had always been close to George's heart. He must have sensed his father's wishes.

For George Mushtak had been in a quandary. He couldn't appear uncooperative in front of the two bishops. But Hasib had come along, heroically helped him out of his fix, and then quietly disappeared again.

Three shots! Musa's blood had flowed like the blood of the dogs that useless good-for-nothing used to run down with his truck.

In his joy Hasib's father forgot everything else, even the pain that he had felt somewhere near his heart for months. That Easter Day at noon he stood on his balcony, watching the turmoil in the village square, and with his son Salman he had laughed till the tears came at the sight of the Catholic Bishop of Damascus, looking lost as he stood among the shouting peasants and desperately searching for his chauffeur. And when he did catch sight of his black limousine, just see how he wielded his mighty crozier to open up a path through the surging crowd of the faithful! He even ignored his Orthodox rival, who was calling after him to wait. He didn't feel safe until he was in the back of his car, cursing the barbarians of this village. When someone knocked on the window and cried, "The Orthodox bishop asks you to stop. Please stop," he didn't even turn around. His car merely raced away.

Elias had come to Mala that Easter, with Claire and the baby Farid, and hired a small apartment, hoping for a reconciliation with his father. The reconciliation planned between those sworn enemies, Mushtak and Shahin, seemed to be just the right opportunity. At a brief meeting with him, Salman had advised Elias to be friendly to the Shahins.

When the shots rang out and the bishops fled in panic, Elias waited for a while. The village square emptied. Claire didn't want him to go to his father. She was afraid that some marksman might shoot him down even before he reached Mushtak's house. But Elias had made up his mind. "It's now or never," he said, and left her behind with little Farid.

Endangering his life, he hurried across the square and, with the last of his courage, knocked at his father's gate. Salman opened it just a crack. Two armed servants stood behind him, and Salman himself had a revolver in his hand.

"What do you want?" he asked curtly, keeping in the shelter of the gateway.

"I want to see my father. I want him to give my son Farid his blessing," replied Elias, close to tears.

"Wait here," ordered Salman, closing the gate. His brother stayed outside. It wasn't long before Salman appeared in that crack in the gateway again.

"He doesn't want to see you." There was triumph in Salman's voice.

43. Butros and Samuel

When Jasmin Shahin's life ended, years later, at the entrance to a Damascus cinema, nine out of ten inhabitants of Mala thought the killer had been a Mushtak again, but they were wrong. The murderer was sixteen-year-old Samuel, one of the Shahin family. Both friends and enemies of the clan recognized that Jasmin's story had not yet been told to its end. For a long time there had been rumours in the village that she had fallen in love with a Muslim, a married man, and had eloped with him. Five years later the couple returned to Damascus.

Jasmin got in touch around now with her niece Rana, who was ten at the time, and her nephew Samuel. She was particularly fond of them both, and hoped that through them she might make her peace with her brother Basil, Rana's father, and her sister Amira, Samuel's mother. They were the two who had moved furthest from the village and its fanaticism. Basil was a successful lawyer. He had studied in Paris and hated antiquated notions. He despised church and mosque alike. His daughter was a sensitive, sharp-eyed, courageous girl who wanted nothing to do with the village.

And Jasmin loved her nephew Samuel as if he were her own son. He was her sister's first child; after him, Amira had brought six girls into the world. She loved parties and dancing. There wasn't a club frequented by the French or by rich Arabs to which she and her husband did not belong, and in spite of her children she still looked as young as on her wedding night in 1934. But she was always short of time, so she had hired two housekeepers who did at least look after the little girls. Samuel hated both the housekeepers, and often spent the night, did his lessons, and ate his meals at his aunt Jasmin's.

Rana didn't like Samuel. As she saw it, he was a show-off and crazy about guns. But he was certainly a good shot, a member of the national team. His parents adorned their drawing room with his photographs and cups, as if the six girls didn't exist at all.

Jasmin nurtured two hopes: she thought that all Samuel needed was loving care to become an affectionate boy himself, and then he might persuade his mother to put in a good word for her, Jasmin, with her mother Samia Shahin who ruled all their lives. After that, she hoped, she might escape the anger of her three brothers Butros, Bulos, and Faris, who still lived in the village. If Samia, Jusuf Shahin's widow, had given her daughter her blessing then no one, not even Butros, would dare to raise his hand against Jasmin. No one would welcome her in, of course, but they wouldn't seek to take her life and her husband's.

Jasmin often went for walks with Rana and told her how much she loved her husband, and how little religion mattered in all decisions of the heart. The best known of all Sufi scholars lies buried in Damascus, Ibn Arabi, who seven hundred years ago cried, "Love is my religion!" The Syrians venerate him so much that they have called the whole quarter of the city around his mosque after him.

But Rana's parents refused to see her aunt. She was a traitor, cried Rana's mother, a woman who had abandoned her religion for a Muslim. Her father said nothing, and acted as if he hadn't even heard his daughter asking him to put in a good word for Aunt Jasmin with Grandmother. Only years later did Rana discover that although Basil had not responded to her at the time out of consideration for his wife, he had gone to Mala in secret and spent a whole night trying to make Samia change her mind.

Samia was obdurate. Her daughter had wounded her personally by keeping the relationship secret from her for years. But she restrained her two hot-tempered sons Butros and Bulos, who had ranted and raged, accusing their brother Basil from Damascus of lacking principles. Butros would actually have thrown Basil out of the house if his mother hadn't stopped him.

"Sit down, boy. As long as I'm alive no one else throws anyone out of this house, certainly not his own brother."

Butros gave way, and Bulos with him. Only Faris kept his temper and took note of everything.

Two weeks later Amira and Mariam arrived with the same request, assuring their mother that no one troubled about a man's religion in Damascus any more, his character was all that mattered, and the Muslims were very accommodating too. A Christian like the legendary Fares al-Khuri could even become prime minister and the parliamentary leader of the Islamic state of Syria.

Their mother didn't react, but nor did she refuse outright this time. Bulos, her second son, talked nonsense, and fell silent only after two reproofs, merely complaining now and then. Without the leadership of Butros he was only a simple cowherd.

Butros sat opposite his mother at the great table, ostentatiously taking his father's place. He was grey-faced and said not a word. At that moment Faris realized that his eldest brother felt their mother was on the point of being reconciled to her favourite daughter.

He knew Butros, and he knew he would do anything to prevent such a reconciliation. From now on he watched his brother's every move and every contact he made. Only in that way did he find out what Butros said to young Samuel when Amira came back to try changing her mother's mind again. This time she brought her husband and their spoilt son, whom Faris did not like. When Butros left the room he followed, silent as his brother's shadow, and overheard his conversation with their nephew.

Faris was hiding behind a haystack when an ingenious plan suddenly formed in his mind. Very close to him, Butros was telling Samuel that the Muslims were to blame for the downfall of Arabia. The boy didn't understand a word of it. Then Butros started talking about heroes who saved the honour and good name of their families and won immortality. After that he held out the prospect of a great reward to the boy: the finest horse in the Shahin stables, and one of the most modern pistols in the world along with a crate of ammunition. Apparently only three men on earth carried such a weapon, and the fourth pistol could be Samuel's. Gradually, the boy fell for the lure, and asked what the penalty would be. Butros told him the prison sentence would be six months at the most, because he was avenging his family's honour, and was still a minor too.

At that moment Faris knew that his sister Jasmin was doomed to die. Finally Butros kissed his nephew and promised to bring the horse to Damascus himself. Samuel cried, "I'll kill her for betraying us."

Faris wondered, but only briefly, if he could save his sister's life. He quickly worked out the answer. No, no one could save her. She had become fair game, she herself had decided to challenge death. If she had fled to America for ever, she could have lived there undisturbed, but she had wanted to flaunt herself. There was something of the daredevil about Jasmin, and she enjoyed the limelight. By standing in it this time, however, she had condemned herself to death.

So Samuel was also releasing Faris from a tiresome duty. If he did give the boy away, this particular attempt on Jasmin's life would probably come to nothing, but then someone else would kill her at Butros's urging. However, if he kept his mouth shut he could at least prove who was behind the much-indulged young murderer. And he knew exactly who would take revenge on the man who had wickedly urged Samuel on: Samia, the mistress of the clan.

He held his peace.

44. A Mother's Lament

Samia wouldn't have her daughter buried in Mala. She decided on Damascus, and chose the church of St. Mary in historic Straight Street. It was the biggest Orthodox church in the country. A bishop and six priests were to conduct her daughter's funeral service.

The church was enormous and the congregation of mourners tiny. Although Samia laid on five buses, less than a hundred people came from Mala and Aleppo. And even those who did, family and friends, attended the funeral only reluctantly, although SamDevia had spread the word that her daughter died as she had lived, in the true Christian faith of the Orthodox Church.

In fact Syrian law does not compel a woman who marries a Muslim to convert to Islam. The children of such a marriage are indeed all Muslims, but Jasmin never had any children.

As far as her immediate family was concerned, Samuel's mother Amira and all Samia's sons and daughters with their own families sat in the front row, or at least they sat there until Samia gave an address for Jasmin which was an impromptu part of the service.

Faris stuck close to his mother that day. He held her arm until proceedings reached the young bishop's luke-warm sermon, which ended up half condemning both the dead woman and her murderer Samuel and half asking forgiveness and mercy for them. At that point old Samia shook her arm free of her son's grasp, went up to the casket at the front of the congregation, and kissed its lid.

"Holy Mary, Mother of God, hear my prayer! I commit into your hands a gentle soul who died innocent. Innocent," said Samia, raising her voice again, "because she followed the dictates of love. Her heart beat for Jesus, who taught us to love our enemies. Then murderers came along and killed her for loving a stranger, and now we're supposed to pray for those who murder a loving woman in the name of honour. What kind of honour is that? What kind of honour?" cried Samia in a voice that broke, looking at the bishop where he stood frozen like a pale statue at the altar. "What kind of honour is it that men seek not on the field of battle, but in a woman whom they utterly despise? What honour do those murderers have who tore my daughter away from me, robbed me of her for ever and ever? Who gave them the right to end a life? Religion? No! A religion that parts God's creatures is the work of the devil."

Samia faltered slightly when two groups of three or four people rose and ostentatiously left the church, making a lot of noise about it. The first to storm out was her son Butros, followed by his wife and his four children. Then Bulos left, with his wife after him.

"Go, daughter," said Samia to Jasmin in her coffin, this time in a sad and loving voice, "go to your Creator in peace, you bear no guilt, go with your pure heart and Paradise will take you in. There's more room for lovers there than on this miserable earth. Go, daughter, go in peace. I will love you always, for as long as my heart beats. Go, my little angel, and God be with you," she concluded her address, in tears, and slowly went back to her seat.

Many wept, Rana among them, although she didn't understand why her grandmother had been talking about murderers in the plural. Later, Rana remembered not so much the words as the reaction of the congregation. They were horrified. Even her father was ashamed that his mother had spoken out so angrily in the house of God.

The bishop bravely went on with his prayers. The funeral procession was a solemn one after all. And when the bishop's old housekeeper indignantly denounced Samia at supper, saying she was a crazy old woman, the bishop surprised her even more than the old widow had done. "Samia Shahin taught me more today with her address," he said, "than I learned in five years studying theology."

45. Amira

It was Amira's thirty-fourth birthday, as she realized only by chance when she cast a glance at her ID before putting it in her handbag. She visited her son Samuel twice a week, and the soldiers on guard and the prison warders always asked to see that document.

She was surprised to think that she was so old already. In fact no one would have taken Amira for more than twenty-five. Her features resembled her mother's. The family looks followed two lines: she, her sister Jasmin, and her brothers Faris and Musa took after their mother; Butros, Bulos, Mariam, and Basil were very like their father.

Amira's large eyes and rounded face emphasized her youthful appearance. She was very feminine, yet she gave the impression of strength.

As she passed a white building in Rauda Street she stopped for a moment at the entrance with its imitation Greek columns. Some kind of restaurant was about to open here. It used to be the Nomade de la Nuit club, and painters were busy obliterating the name, covering it with sky-blue paint. In the 1940s the Nomade de la Nuit had been *the* club for the richest people in Damascus and high-ranking French army officers. When the French left the country and the number of coups scared off the rich Damascenes, the club folded.

She remembered how shy she had been the first time she went there, because her husband had lectured her endlessly on table manners, and the etiquette of dancing, and subjects of conversation to be avoided if you ever wanted to go to the club again. She had been terrified, because it seemed that anything other than breathing quietly could cause a scandal. Louis was a coward. But fear has never been a good teacher to anyone who wanted to find out about the world.

Three or four visits, and Amira had learned the rules of the game and was popular and highly regarded. Her husband, on the other hand, bored everyone by expressing fulsome and diplomatic agreement before his interlocutor had even finished what he was saying. But he was one of the most respected doctors in the city, and a very good match. Sometimes she felt almost grateful to him, for instance when she looked at herself in the big mirror of her bedroom in winter, wearing nothing but Russian mink next to her bare skin, or when she sat beside him in his open Mercedes driving through the streets of Damascus. There were only three Mercedes in the city at the time. Louis Safran was extremely large and stout, but a chance like that came a woman's way only once in her life. She had had to take it at once.

Amira had been happy to go to the boarding school run by the sisters of the Sacred Heart of Jesus in Damascus, where she ultimately met Louis. And she hated her family, who had more time for their blood feud with the Mushtaks than for real life. Her father took no notice of any of his children but Butros, whom he idolized, and if he did happen to recollect that he had other offspring too, Mariam was his favourite among the girls. He treated Bulos like a stranger and a menial, and ignored Amira entirely. As for her mother, she loved only Faris and Jasmin.

When Dr. Louis Safran came to the school to give the girls lessons in hygiene once a week, he took a liking to her. The other girls said he was old and fat, but he was interested in her, and for that alone she was happy to marry him.

She had never for a moment felt any love for him, and love wasn't what Louis Safran needed. He wanted children to show off and a wife at his side. She had to be beautiful. Apart from that, he preferred to occupy himself with his rich patients and his expensive and hard-to-get cars.

Louis never complained. He was always smiling, but he could give neither her nor the children any affection because he had none in him. He had once told her that the Safran family regarded kissing as a sign of a primitive nature.

But he was always pleased when she outdid his expectations, for instance at the club. Soon all the most respected members were asking after his wife, if Amira happened not to have come that day, so he always begged her to accompany him, because the members included the fifty most prominent men in Damascus.

And what a surprise when, one evening in 1943, she was chosen as the club's beauty queen! Over thirty wives had stood for election, four of them Parisiennes. Her husband had been proud as a peacock. That evening she fell in love with Jean-Pierre, a dashing French air force officer, who talked about his adventures until she was lying in his arms in some kind of storeroom. He smelled so virile in his summer uniform. Even as a little girl she had been fascinated by athletic men who wore clean uniforms.

Jean-Pierre was a sportsman, and he captivated her with his ready tongue. French is better for love-making than Arabic, she thought. When her lover said *"chérie"* or *"mon amour"*, she always felt a tingling sensation run from her ears down her legs to the tips of her toes.

He was a passionate lover but also a charming rogue. He had a mistress in every city; oddly enough she had been able to forgive him that. "You can't blame a fox for chasing chickens, *mon amour*," he had told her, laughing like a naughty little boy.

Her husband didn't notice that she was in love with the Frenchman, either that first evening or on any that followed. It was an exciting adventure.

Jean-Pierre was bold. One day he phoned: her children were at school, her husband at his consulting rooms, would she like to go for a flight in an airplane? It was the first time she had known what it was like to see the city and its people from above, and she suddenly had a sensation of lightness in her heart, a kind of sublimity. She felt almost like a goddess.

Her passionate love affair lasted three years. Then her air force officer left the country in 1946 with the French troops, making her no promises.

As she went to the prison that morning, Amira's heart closed itself against grief. She felt her tears evaporating on their way to her eyes. For she felt she had been let down by both her lover and her son. Jean-Pierre had never told her when he was going to leave Damascus, and her son had chosen to take his uncle Butros's advice without a word to her.

She never did learn just what had happened. Her husband was always repeating, like a parrot: that's not women's business. But suddenly Samuel was "her" son. She ought to have brought him up properly, said Louis, instead of entrusting him to that rustic oaf her brother, who had filled the boy's head with nonsense.

He would never visit the prison with her. He hid behind appointments and the bonnets of his motor cars, but Amira knew better: it was his mother, the arrogant widow Safran, who had forbidden him to visit his son.

Amira could see her son twice a week, on Tuesdays and Fridays. She walked from her house in the rich Abu Rummana district to the prison in the old citadel near the Suk al Hamidiye. She needed time to herself. For days, she had felt a strange uneasiness.

What kind of a family was it for whose honour Samuel had sacrificed himself? He was the bravest of all the Shahins. He had done what they all wanted, but no one else dared do it. The others hid behind cowardly excuses. Her eldest brother Butros, who had always despised her way of life, had suddenly turned so friendly to Samuel, and even praised her for raising "such a lion". Only he didn't dare say such a thing publicly. He was afraid of his mother. Was that just? The boy was blamed for everything, while the rest of family quickly went back to their own lives, just as if Samuel had done the deed for himself alone. He had told Amira that he kept seeing Jasmin dancing towards him in his dreams. The surprise in her eyes when the shots rang out tormented him.

Her brother the lawyer, Basil, would have nothing to do with the case. It was a delicate business, he said. His mother was suing her own grandson for premeditated murder and wanted his legal assistance. So did his sister Amira. He asked both parties to understand that there was really nothing he could do.

Butros knew no one in Damascus who could help. Bulos was a simpleton. That fox Faris was on the side of her mother and Mariam. Amira's sister hid behind her cynicism. And as for her mother! She'd been the cause of all this misery, after all, and now she was suddenly making herself out grief-stricken! Jasmin was the only one of Samia's children whom she had loved. She had always been unjust. Whatever Amira or her younger sister Mariam did, she had coldly ignored it and talked only of her wonderful darling.

Jasmin was four years younger than Amira and thought she could trample all over her sister's feelings. She'd always been outrageous. Even at Amira's wedding, she had tried to attract attention to herself; she was only thirteen at the time, but much too mature for her age. She had performed a series of belly dances, and the men of Damascus reached out to touch her, encouraging her to show even more vulgarity. Amira's husband's family, all of them doctors and architects, had been horrified by the girl's conduct. Her father-in-law George Safran was still alive then, he had turned his face away so as not to see Jasmin, and her mother-in-law Victoria was spitting venom.

Amira had to ask her father to control the brat, and when Jusuf Shahin growled something to his wife Jasmin stopped, sulked, and soon left the festivities with her mother. Instead of boxing the girl's ears, her mother even covered up for her, saying that she felt dizzy and they'd both have to go home. Shortly after that, she even said the sight of that poisonous creature Victoria Safran, Amira's mother-in-law, would always give her a headache.

She had tried covering up for Jasmin's treachery and shamelessness yet again, but then Samuel intervened. Her brother Butros told Amira that the boy couldn't be sufficiently honoured for getting in ahead of his grandmother's wicked plan to humiliate the family forever. Samuel, he said, had acted for the honour of the clan, like a razorblade separating a shameful encumbrance from the family name.

Still lost in the labyrinth of her restless thoughts, Amira reached the rusty old gate of the citadel of Damascus, which had seen better days since Saladin's time. It stood on an arm of the river which was now just a stinking sewer. Rats scurried everywhere, disappeared into their holes, came out of other holes and looked suspiciously at human beings. Amira woke from her daydreams in alarm when one of them crossed the street. It had almost passed over her foot. She must have uttered a small scream in her fright.

Then Shukri, that sun-tanned, bright-eyed young officer smiled at her. He was standing in the gateway watching the passers by. Still smiling, he asked in his deep voice what brought such a pretty princess to this grubby area.

"Fate, First Lieutenant," replied Amira, almost bashfully. He shook hands with her. His was a strong hand.

"And what's the name of this fate?" he asked.

"Samuel Safran," she replied.

"Ah, that courageous lad. Well, just come with me," he said, knocking softly at the small spy hole let into the right-hand side of the gate.

A soldier opened the gate, and Amira went down the corridors beside the first lieutenant, whom everyone greeted respectfully. Doors swung open, no one asked to see her ID. The officer led her down a passage to a short staircase, and then entered a large, bright room with flowers in it, a large desk, a new sofa, and two chairs.

"Do sit down until the soldier brings your son," he said politely, picking up the phone and relaying an order. His eyes wandered over her body, and she felt a hot beam of light scorching her skin beneath her dress, not too strongly, but giving her goose bumps. She couldn't help thinking of her old physics teacher. He always tried to tell them that eyes don't emit light. Poor old fool, she thought, moistening her lips to make her lipstick shine, and smiling.

46. The Opportunity

Faris told his mother, only a week after the funeral, that proof existed of the fact that his brother Butros had incited that fool Samuel to attack Jasmin. Samia wouldn't believe it, and still less would she believe the reasons why, as he said, Butros had arranged for his sister's murder in such haste. His main aim, Faris told her, had been to hurt his mother, because if Samia had been reconciled with Jasmin it would have been a bitter pill for Butros to swallow. He wouldn't have been undisputed head of the clan any more, the one who made the life and death decisions. Instead, she would have retained the highest authority. So Butros had passed sentence of death on his sister, and he saw that it was carried out.

Samia listened carefully. She had always feared jealousy among her own sons, so she distrusted any negative remarks made by one of the brothers about another.

"Nonsense, Faris! Butros is a man of high calibre. I never disputed his position as head of the clan, but it wasn't for him or even the President of the state to make decisions about my daughter's life, that was only for Jasmin herself and God. That's why we quarrelled. Anything else is just a wicked insinuation," she reproved him.

Faris kept calm. "He promised him the black stallion," he replied quietly but firmly, "and a very special pistol. He'll take the horse to Damascus himself, Butros said, on the day Samuel comes out of prison. Wait, Mother, and you'll see that your son Faris isn't lying to you."

Faris never returned to the subject. Samia tried to be composed in her treatment of Butros, who was being extremely charming to her. But the doubt that Faris had sown in her mind kept returning. Suppose her son Butros really had ordered her daughter's murder? It was at night most of all that she felt abhorrence for him: a peasant ready to sacrifice a life to win mastery over a dunghill. She discovered that even after decades in Mala she was still a city woman at heart.

One cold day in late February 1951, Amira went to Mala with her husband and young First Lieutenant Shukri, to visit Butros. Faris was able to overhear their conversation from a bedroom above the drawing room of his brother's apartment. He discovered that Samuel was to come out of jail on 10 April, and a party would be held for him. Amira was going to invite her brothers Butros and Bulos. Their mother refused to see Amira and her husband.

Amira praised First Lieutenant Shukri who, she said, had done so much to ease Samuel's time in prison, and Butros gave the man handsome presents of wine, honey, and pistachios. From his hiding place, Faris could also see Amira coming out on the balcony with the officer several times to show him the view of the village, while her husband talked to Butros and his wife.

When the visitors went back to Damascus, Faris hurried off to see his mother. "Butros is going to take his finest horse to Damascus on April the 10th, as a present for Samuel when he comes out of prison," he told her, his voice as quiet as ever.

Samia pretended to take it calmly. "Why, he wouldn't even give his wife that horse!" she said, laughing. But her laughter was full of uncertainty, and matters turned out worse than she had expected. Butros led the horse out to his horse box and drove him to Damascus on 9 April. He planned to be at the prison gates with the horse early next morning. From her window, Samia watched him leave. His wife and two children sat in the Chevrolet, which also belonged to Butros, with Bulos and Bulos's wife.

The brothers hadn't even said goodbye to their mother. They were slipping away like thieves in the night to celebrate a murderer's release, thought Samia, and Faris encouraged her. She considered Bulos far too stupid to take any responsibility for what had happened, and his morale had snapped anyway from the grief of childlessness. At first it had been thought that his wife was infertile, but then the doctors found out that he was the one who couldn't father a child. Since then his wife had humiliated him day and night for the injustice he had done her.

"Butros and no one else is responsible for letting everyone know that Jasmin had gone astray," said Faris after supper. "We ought to have listened to Basil and hushed the scandal up, the way those damn Mushtaks always do."

For the first time Samia felt something akin to hatred for her own son Butros.

"You are right," she agreed. She felt that she herself was partly to blame for her beloved daughter's death, because she had hesitated to forgive her for so long. She hated Butros and Samuel because the murder had humiliated her too, and she lay awake all night, brooding. She imagined the riotous feasting in Damascus. When she fell asleep at last the revellers in her dream were still celebrating, but they were sitting around a large table, cutting up Jasmin and greedily devouring her flesh.

On the third morning she summoned Fahmi, her most faithful manservant. He had been ten when his parents died and he joined the Shahin household. Fahmi had always served Jusuf obediently, but it was Samia whom he idolized. And he was the only one of the servants to have worn black since Jasmin's murder.

"I want you to go straight to that bastard Salman Mushtak and tell him that in four days' time Butros will be getting delivery of a large consignment of guns and over sixty mule-loads of hashish from the Lebanon."

"Oh, madame!" cried the alarmed Fahmi, taking her hand and kissing it with the humility of a slave begging to be released from the performance of an unwelcome task.

"Fahmi, Butros gave the order to have my daughter killed. When he did that, he struck me to the heart. It was attempted murder of me too, and do you know what God says about that?"

Fahmi did not reply, because he too knew that Butros had encouraged young Samuel. But he had hoped and prayed that his mistress wouldn't find out. Now he was horrified to discover that she knew.

"Madame, I can't turn against the hand that feeds me ..."

"Fahmi, you will do as I tell you. And if that son of a whore Salman asks why you come to him of all people, you'll say you want revenge because Butros makes your wife Salma sleep with him once a week, and you found out about it only today."

Fahmi went red with anger and stormed out of his mistress's room. A little later Samia heard the sound of blows and Salma's pleading, and then there was silence. Fahmi rode off on a brown mule, going down to the village square.

Salman disliked double-dealers, but at his faithful servant Basil's urging he listened to Fahmi. He asked him the very question that Samia had predicted. When Fahmi refused the money Mushtak offered him for his information, and said he wanted to avenge his honour, Salman finally believed what he said.

That evening, Butros came back from Damascus. He was going to act the hypocrite and call on his mother. But she cursed him as a Judas and wished death to him and his wife. Butros wasn't about to take this lying down. He replied to her in kind, saying it was his mother's fault that his sister had become a whore, that he was proud of encouraging Samuel to do his heroic deed. She had better retire from public view, he said, and then she could live on his charity, but if she insulted him, the head of the clan, he would throw her out.

His mother did not reply, but went to her room and wept all night. She cursed Jusuf for dying prematurely and leaving her alone.

A week later Salman Mushtak made a phone call to Damascus. That was after his faithful servant Basil had confirmed that columns of mules had been delivering their loads to the Shahins for several nights running, and then went back in the direction of Lebanon as day dawned.

Next morning not only was the whole of his arch-enemies' large property surrounded, the entire village was sealed off by policemen and armoured cars. Evidently armed resistance was expected. There was no way out. Butros was trapped.

Bringing that police force to bear had been worth while. A large store of smuggled goods was found at the Shahins' house. The customs officials couldn't believe their eyes when here, in a small mountain village, they found enough ultra-modern weapons for an army. Several trucks were needed to take away all the machine guns, pistols and hand grenades, not to mention the explosives and ammunition. Another two trucks were loaded up with hashish.

Butros was devastated. He, the leader of his clan, was humiliated in the village square and taken away in handcuffs like a common criminal. His brother Basil, Rana's father, although Butros had had time to alert him, wasn't even allowed into the family home. The lawyer stood on the other side of the police barrier, like everyone else in the village, watching the arrest.

When he saw his brother coming out of the house barefoot, in his pyjamas, and being knocked about by one of the soldiers, he boiled with rage. He turned to the officer commanding the troop. "Captain, is this any way to treat distinguished citizens?" he asked, forcing himself to sound courteous and almost pleading.

The officer looked at him with watery eyes. "No," he said, "but that's no citizen, that's a criminal who was planning to overthrow the government with his weapons."

"I really don't believe it. There must be some mistake. I know the man, and he's a patriot," said Basil, trying to sow doubt in the officer's mind, but the seed fell on stony ground.

"You call that son of a whore a patriot?" replied the captain indignantly. "I wouldn't proclaim your friendship with him so loud if I were you. Those who mingle with pigs will soon smell of the sty." Then he climbed into his jeep and left the dazed Basil standing there, very correct in his collar and tie.

Salman was watching the scene from his balcony, visibly enjoying his view of events in the village square. He drank his tea, slurping out loud, and now and then he whispered, "What a shame you're not here to see this, Father."

That morning he felt he was in the forecourt of Paradise. But he was mistaken in the extent of his rejoicing, for the new head of the house of Shahin was Faris. Equipped with his own high intelligence and his mother's blessing, he intended to make his clan absolute rulers of Mala at long last. Faris abhorred bloodshed, so he had no designs on Salman's life. He wanted to ruin him utterly, and then wish him long life and health.

47. Shaklan's Birthday Party

Torrential rain fell all through December and January. There was no frost that winter, there were no storms. The people thanked God, because rain in this dry country meant rich harvests and green steppes for the flocks of sheep to graze, and this piece of good fortune was ascribed to God's approval of the new Syrian head of state, the devout Colonel Shaklan, who had seized power for the second time at the end of November. This time he didn't intend to go back to his barracks. A year earlier he had led a first successful coup, and then he gave the civilians their chance, but they changed the government five times in eleven months without rescuing the country from chaos.

Shaklan intended to organize Syria with strict military discipline, like a regiment, and make the Syrians observe law and order by handing out generous rewards and merciless punishments. For preference he surrounded himself with young officers. In late December 1951 he told them, in a short speech, that if he were given six years there would be no thieves or smugglers left in Syria, no rebels or injustice. He repeated this promise in his first radio broadcast to the nation in early January 1952, concluding with the words: "I will make you Syrians into Prussians."

Shaklan was fascinated by Prussia, the German army, and above all Hitler. He was impressed by Leni Riefenstahl's movie *Triumph of the Will*, which he watched once a week in the private cinema of the presidential palace. He imitated the Germans even in his uniform and the way he staged his appearances.

Shaklan was at the peak of his power in the spring of 1952. He did not yet guess that only six months later rebellions would be breaking out everywhere. Amira felt there could be no better moment than this to help her disgraced brother Butros. In prison, he had shrunk to a picture of misery.

Amira's lover, First Lieutenant Shukri, advised her to go straight to Colonel Shaklan in this delicate matter. It was beyond his own competence. He had been able to help her with her son's case, but there was nothing he could do here without burning his own fingers.

"You must pluck up courage and go to the very top. Approach Colonel Shaklan through Captain Tallu, his right-hand man, invite the ruler of all Syria to Mala, give him a magnificent banquet, and then send Butros's wife and children in tears to kiss his hand and ask for clemency. They may be able to soften his heart that way, because harsh as he can be, the colonel is very sentimental. Particularly about tearful children," said First Lieutenant Shukri, briefly drawing on his cigarette. "And you can soften up Tallu by giving him a horse. Your brother has plenty of horses," he added, accompanying Amira to the door of his small apartment in the Midan quarter. As they said goodbye he held her close again, kissed her lips, and swung her up in the air in his powerful arms. He was enchanted, as always, by her femininity. Amira felt dizzy with desire, but she had to go. "Don't eat me up with your kisses! I must hurry before Louis gets home. We have the Bishop coming to dinner this evening." She tapped him on the buttocks, and when he looked crestfallen she caressed his face. "Another time, my handsome stallion," she said, laughing, and she left.

Captain Tallu thanked her for the fine horse, and liked the idea of the invitation. He cast a brief glance at the President's engagements diary. "You can give him his birthday party on 12 July. For three hundred people. A hundred to come with him, two hundred from the village. Only Colonel Shaklan himself can pardon Butros, because the penalty for smuggling arms plainly says life imprisonment." Without getting to his feet, he offered her his limp hand. Amira was amazed that such a physically feeble man could be so powerful.

Shukri's advice was pure gold, thought Amira as she left. If she could get her brother out of jail she would be worshipped like a saint in the village. And Butros's wife Susan immediately and enthusiastically went along with her suggestion. So far Susan, from a Damascene family, had lived in her husband's shadow, almost invisible. Now she saw her chance. With this birthday party, she would not only help her husband but defeat her mother-in-law. Everyone would know that her connections reached all the way to the President himself.

12 July 1952 was a hot Saturday. The forecourt of the convent of St. Thecla was sprinkled with water early in the morning and then decorated with loving care. Flowers in pots, rugs, banners and garlands gave it a festive air. Three cooks and countless kitchen maids worked wonders in the great kitchen of the convent, preparing an abundance of everything for the guests. The banquet was to begin at six in the evening, when the temperature had dropped slightly. The President's seat of honour was protected from the heat all day by a sun umbrella. Marksmen were stationed on every rooftop that had a view of the decorated forecourt.

About fifty officials in civilian clothing checked up on the guests with ruthless lack of ceremony, and many of the locals were indignant about such treatment, but Amira mollified them. It was the usual practice, she said, for men to have a hand put between their legs to see if they were concealing a pistol or sharp knife down there. The inspectors also confiscated any other large implements that looked as if they might pose a threat. "You could strike an ox dead with that," one of them roughly told an old man, putting his heavy wooden walking-stick aside for safe keeping. It was fitted with a large, wedge-shaped piece of metal, which did indeed look dangerous, but was really just a harmless key, with wards made to fit exactly into the holes that would unlock his door.

Late that afternoon the first black limousine appeared in the distance. A peasant announced the news, and excitement spread. Then came the second, then a third. In the end there were sixty cars. They wound their way up the last few bends in the road like a black snake.

Teachers and pupils from the school stood at the entrance to the village, waving little flags. It was rather a sparse reception committee, but Mobate the village elder had found it difficult to muster even that number, since none of the Catholics wanted to wave to the head of state. Many of them stayed at home out of loyalty to the Mushtaks.

The column of cars churned up hot dust in the faces of the children and teachers, and went purposefully on across the eerily empty village square and so to the festive forecourt, which could be identified from afar by all the banderols and the colourful flags and banners. Up there all the guests were happy to think that the most powerful man in Syria was going to celebrate his birthday with them. Birthdays were never usually celebrated in Mala.

Mobate stood squarely in fourth place behind the abbess, the Shahin family, and the Orthodox notables of the village.

"Colonel, this is the happiest day of my life. Please consider me your loyal servant," he said, reciting his laboriously learned welcome, and he shook the President's hand vigorously. The President laughed and looked at the next man in line, the stout sheikh of the little village mosque, who was so scared that he mumbled into his beard a quotation from the Koran which even he didn't understand. The President smiled.

Apart from Butros's wife Susan, absent from the reception because she was to make her own entrance, almost all the important men and women of the village were there. Only Samia Shahin was absent, and of course all the adherents of the Mushtaks from the Catholic quarter.

Mariam, Butros's sister, had come on her own, as usual. Bulos, Basil, and Faris, however, had brought their wives with them at their sister Amira's invitation. They all wanted to take their chance of a personal meeting with the most powerful man in the state.

Laying on the charm, Colonel Shaklan cracked jokes with the small group of his hosts, telling them that he had often heard of Mala, but had never had time to visit that beautiful village before. And then, when Captain Tallu whispered something in his ear, he thanked Amira for her kind invitation and warm welcome. She took the hand held out to her, curtsied as she had been taught to do at school, although she had never had any occasion to drop a curtsey before, and said in a faltering voice, "We are all your soldiers, O hero of the Republic."

The seats next to the head of state were carefully allotted. The abbess sat on his right, his friend Captain Tallu on his left. Two bodyguards in black uniforms with their machine guns levelled stood behind his tall chair. No one was to move about behind the President.

The three hundred birthday party guests sat crammed together at the huge circular table that had been set up, but a space about five metres wide was left empty opposite the President so that his view wouldn't be obstructed. There was also a gap in the huge circle opposite the kitchen. Only carefully pre-selected waiters were allowed to approach the President and serve him. Over to one side, but within view of the large table, about fifty soldiers of his special unit were eating without taking their machine guns off their shoulders.

A single person was coordinating the whole occasion: Amira, who had shown amazing talent for making plans and carrying them out in the last few days before the party. By now she knew all the security officers and soldiers who had been checking the region for three days to defuse any bombs that might have been planted. Amira got on well with all of them except a certain Lieutenant Hamad, she didn't know his surname. He was really far too old for his low rank, he wore a baggy uniform, and he had an ugly tattooed nose. Lieutenant Hamad was a Bedouin, and Amira didn't like the Bedouin, whom she considered savages. But he was constantly at her heels, gripping her arm firmly and asking the same stupid questions. He was suspicious and hated Jews, Christians, and women. He was always asking: Where are you going, little lady? Is the cook a Jew? Did he maybe marry a Jewess? You don't look much like a patriot, do you? Is the abbess an Arab? Why does she speak with that accent? And hundreds of other such questions. He kept grabbing her bare upper arms, and his rough fingers bored into her flesh and left red marks behind.

"He's a prodigy of nature," a young officer told her. "He can sniff out truffles and gunpowder three metres away. He used to make his living selling truffles, but then the President discovered him and found out about his wonderful nose." Hamad had already saved the President from three assassination attempts, the officer added, so no one must touch a hair of his head.

The party began. A small group of girls in folk costume did a dance, a singer did his best to perform a hastily written verse celebrating the hero Shaklan's birthday, and Mobate insisted on making a short speech saying nothing at all. Then two of the Shahins' grooms, riding the finest horses, did equestrian tricks in the middle of the large circle surrounded by the tables. Tallu had tears of emotion in his eyes.

Finally the meal was brought in: prettily arranged platters of delicious appetizers, fragrant warm bread, drinks cooled with chunks of ice. A whole truckload of ice had come in from Damascus the day before.

Next the main course was served: lamb stuffed with rice, pistachios and raisins, roasted until it was nicely browned, along with excellent salads, and as if all that wasn't enough it was accompanied by mountains of kibbeh, tabbuleh, and stuffed vine leaves.

By agreement with the security officers, Amira had planned for Susan, Butros's wife, to appear about nine o'clock with her four children Jusuf, Bulos, Taufik and Barbara. Then the abbess would ask His Excellency to give her a hearing, whereupon Susan and the children were to kneel down in front of the table and ask the President to show clemency to Butros, head of their family and the breadwinner. After that they'd see what happened next.

The President's bodyguards and close friends knew that he was a heavy drinker. He might make pious speeches in support of Islam, and he was very good friends with the Saudi royal house, he went on pilgrimage and he prayed in public, but at the same time he loved Irish whiskey. Amira had bought a whole bottle of the best whiskey for him in a Damascus delicatessen.

That evening, however, President Shaklan was trying the sixty-percent strength arrack distilled in Mala, cooled with ice, and he liked it so much that he partook freely. Later he had heavy red wine served, brought at the abbess's request from the convent's own wine cellar. It was a sweet, sticky wine with a seventeen percent alcohol content, and was usually drunk from tiny glasses as an aperitif.

Just before eight Colonel Shaklan cracked a small joke, which Tallu, who knew him well, saw as an indication that in two seconds' time the light in his master's brain would go out. In the darkness now falling over him, the President looked at the abbess and told her, "You're a lovely gazelle. Like Leni Riefenstahl." Then he collapsed face down on the table. Tallu swiftly propped him up again.

The President came back to his senses for a moment or so and was alarmed. "What happened? Don't let anyone leave the room!" he shouted across the square. His words echoed back from the rocks in the silence that had followed the crash as he collapsed. "Don't let anyone leave the room!"

Then the President lapsed back into unconsciousness. He went to sleep lolling sideways in his chair. As if at a word of command, the soldiers of his special unit, who had been laughing and eating just now, took the safety catches off their rifles and moved two or three metres closer to the guests. The abbess sat there white and rigid as an unpainted plaster statue.

It was already getting dark, the last brightness in the sky would disappear any moment now. Large lights came on. The whole table was brightly illuminated, like a film set. But it was a silent film.

Just before nine the unsuspecting Susan came tripping up the steep path from the Shahin property to the square where the festivities were taking place. She reminded her children once again not to forget that the way they behaved now could save their poor father. Jusuf, the eldest, was seventeen, Bulos was fifteen, Taufik fourteen, and Barbara twelve.

But when Susan and the children reached the square, they stopped in alarm at the sight of the soldiers holding at bay the birthday guests around the figure of the President, who was slumped at a strange angle in his chair. For an instant Susan thought he had been shot. The bodyguards in their black uniforms standing stiffly behind the chair reinforced that impression.

"The President's dead," Jusuf whispered into his brother Bulos's ear.

"Keep your mouth shut!" his mother hissed quietly. Barbara giggled with excitement. And Taufik, fascinated, looked at the soldiers in their camouflage gear.

Amira saw her sister-in-law and hurried to meet her. The security officers wouldn't let anyone else move about freely, and she was trying to reassure everyone that the party would soon resume. Mountains of fruit, ices, and nuts were ready in the kitchen. Amira's long black hair lifted behind her in the cool breeze that made it a little easier to sit waiting in suspense.

"Go back with the children," she told Susan breathlessly. "The President's drunk, he's sleeping it off. We'll have to wait. I'll send you word when he wakes up again." There was a note of pleading in her voice, for she could see the bitter disappointment in her sister-in-law's face.

"All right, we'll go back," said Susan, narrow-lipped. "Let's hope this wasn't for nothing. That fine horse, all that money!"

"But I want to wait here," insisted Taufik, who would have liked to stay with the soldiers. Without a word his mother took him by the ear, and he shrieked, although it hadn't hurt him in the least. He was probably toying with the idea that the soldiers might come to his rescue, but no one took any notice of him, and when Jusuf kicked his backside he ran down the steep path, howling.

His grandmother Samia had heard the shouting in her room, and suddenly the rancour vanished from her heart. Smiling broadly, she said with malicious glee, "This is about to go wrong, like everything Amira touches!" And if anything she was understating it.

Out in the square, the President was still asleep. Soon Captain Tallu, who seemed to know just how long his master's slumbers would last, followed his example. But the guests couldn't even talk, and when all the carafes and jugs of water were empty they were offered nothing more to drink. They just sat there in an oppressive silence, staring into space.

A room in the left wing of the convent, with a window looking out on the square, was commandeered as a temporary control centre. The security officers sat feverishly discussing every step to be taken. It was something new, even for them, to see their lord and master suddenly fall asleep in public. But they knew how bad-tempered he was when woken from a nap. Messengers ran down to the officers in the square to whisper instructions, soldiers hurried upstairs with news of the latest developments.

At about one in the morning, when it grew cold, the nuns found lightweight blankets in the convent so that two soldiers could cover the President up carefully, leaving only his head free.

Opposite the control centre, in the right wing of the convent building, the lieutenant with the tattooed nose sat alone in a room that he had requisitioned as his office. From there, he watched the comings and goings in the square. He too had to be asked for permission to bring the blankets, to allay any suspicions he might have.

Amira was running back and forth, and when the nocturnal cold increased she asked the officers whether at least the older guests, still sitting on their uncomfortable chairs, might not be allowed to go home. The officers sent a soldier to ask the control centre. He quickly came back with the answer no. Amira felt contempt in the peasants' weary eyes.

Her husband Louis had already dropped off to sleep. He was never awake after midnight, even at the club. Her brother Faris grinned at her. She went over to him. "What am I to do? Please help me," she pleaded.

"He who leads a donkey to the top of a minaret must lead it down again," he replied. She hated this proverb, much-cited by her mother: quintessential coldness of the heart wrapped up to look like wisdom. Her brothers Basil and Bulos were just sitting there too, but at least they showed some sympathy. The hours dragged slowly by.

Amira was standing in the middle of the circle of tables. Lost in thought, she looked up, and suddenly thought that the abbess had smiled at her and signed to her to come closer. Later she realized that in her weariness she had just imagined it, for even the mistress of the convent had fallen asleep with her eyes half-closed. As Amira took a step towards her she suddenly felt a strong hand pulling her back by her shoulder. A young soldier was smiling awkwardly at her, and showed her where she was to go. Looking up, she saw the lieutenant with the tattooed nose standing at his window. He beckoned her to come up to him.

Ever suspicious as he was, he probably feared she might assassinate the President, she thought, and she laughed on her way up the marble staircase leading to his room. Perhaps she ought to pretend a little, and then ask his advice. Many primitive, small-minded people feel obliged to show magnanimity if you flatter them enough.

She knocked. The door immediately opened, and a rough hand reached for her soft arm. He pulled her into the room so brutally that she lost her balance and stumbled. A blow to her neck sent her flying forward over an empty desk.

"Christian whore! Why are you always stirring up trouble? Why can't you let it alone?"

She didn't understand. She couldn't straighten up either, because he had grabbed her by her long hair, twisting it swiftly into a pony-tail, and was keeping her upper body pushed down on the desk top with his free hand. "Don't move or I'll kill you," he spat. She didn't know what this was all about, but next moment the Bedouin was pulling her panties down and thrusting himself into her. She felt pain. Everything inside her was dry; she couldn't even weep. A slap stifled her scream. "Be glad I'll waste my time on you. I ought really to have you shot. You lured our President into a trap. It'll be the worse for you if his enemies discover that our master drank strong liquor in this Christian dump. I'll slit you open with my own hands," he groaned in a savage voice, hitting her on the back of her head.

She felt terrible fear rising in her. Suddenly she understood why her lover Shukri hadn't wanted to come to the birthday party for the President. He had explained his reasons, but she had reacted indignantly and said he just wanted to let her down. However, Shukri had repeated patiently, "I love you, but I don't like attending such occasions. Rulers are beasts of prey, and when they eat and drink deep, they can strike out blindly and break your neck. I'm not taking part in anything like that until I'm a colonel, and then I'll be a beast of prey myself."

"This is the only kind of language the likes of you understand," said the lieutenant with the tattooed nose, bringing her back from her thoughts into this dark room where she lay on her stomach over the desk, while this monster thrust faster and faster into her from behind. Suddenly he grunted like a boar.

When the man with the tattooed nose let go of her hair and collapsed into an armchair, she pulled up her torn panties and ran out. He didn't try to stop her. She hurried downstairs and along a corridor to the lavatories, where she threw up. Then she spent a long time washing herself, rinsed her mouth with gurgling water, spat it out, and finally ran a broken comb lying beside the mirror through her hair. Finally she left the place.

About four in the morning Colonel Shaklan woke with a start. Amira was sitting hunched on a chair beside her husband. She had stayed awake the whole time, afraid that the lieutenant with the tattooed nose might attack her again. She had chosen a place where the monster couldn't see her from his window.

"Who gave the murderer my address?" shouted the President, his eyes red and confused. He roared it out in such a loud voice that everyone who had nodded off woke up.

Captain Tallu hurried up and immediately took the President to his car. On the way Shaklan told him how he had dreamed, yet again, of a young Druse from the south shooting him at the door of a villa in Brazil. He was still dazed by this recurrent nightmare. So he took no notice of anyone, not even the abbess standing there in the light of dawn offering him her hand. He didn't say goodbye to his hosts, but ignored them all as if they were insects or pebbles.

Captain Tallu, relieved that the party was over, laughed and told Shaklan at length about a book that he had just finished reading. It was called *The Dreams of Rulers*. "Napoleon," said Tallu, "had a recurrent dream of swimming back and forth between Corsica and Sardinia. And Hulagu Khan, who conquered Baghdad in the year 1258 and had the greatest library in the world of his time thrown into the Tigris, was always dreaming that he had turned to stone and was a statue standing at the foot of a mountain, facing the sea. Longing for that unattainable distance stabbed him to the heart, and he was angry with the gulls that kept landing on his head and shitting on him."

They both laughed and got into the armoured car. The other servants of the state and those representatives of its power who had come to Mala with the President followed in the other black limousines. And in the village, two hundred voices cursed both the President and the Shahin clan.

Basil, the Mushtaks' faithful servant, had watched the whole thing from a place where he had been hiding. When the President and his men left, he waited a little longer and then went quietly down the alleys to the village square. Day was only just dawning when he opened the gate of the large Mushtak property. He couldn't wait to tell his news, so he woke his master and told him, with a grin, about the humiliation of the Shahins and their supporters.

The grateful Salman kissed his faithful employee's weary face, and felt stronger than ever before in his life. He decided to donate a large sum to the church of St. Giorgios next Sunday, the thirteenth of July, in thanks for God's grace.

Amira went back to Damascus with her husband without saying goodbye to Susan, who was still waiting. From now on she wore her hair very short, which suited her even better, and she never told her lover Shukri about the man with the tattooed nose.

Shukri, to bring this part of the story quickly to its close, truly loved Amira and remained unmarried for her sake. But Amira didn't want to leave her husband. Shukri made his career in the army, and even rose to the rank of general in 1966. A year later, however, he and a handful of other officers were shot when they tried an amateurish coup, and failed miserably.

At the end of July 1952, two weeks after the disastrous birthday party, Butros Shahin was found stabbed to death in his prison cell. No one ever found out who did it. His widow left Mala for ever, and went to live in Damascus with her three sons and her daughter. She never wanted to see any member of her husband's family again.

In December 1952, when Colonel Shaklan erroneously imagined himself at the height of his power, he arranged for a military parade to show off the latest tanks that he had just bought in France with Saudi money. He returned the salute of the officers driving past him even more punctiliously than usual, and felt proud of their shiny new weapons.

Suddenly one tank driver lost control of his modern vehicle, and the mighty tank went straight into the rows of applauding spectators lining the streets. Heart-rending screams reached the colonel, shaking him badly, and rose to the sky of Damascus. Swallows flew away in fright and didn't come back to the city for days. The tank tracks crushed more than fifty men, women, and children before the fearsome machine crashed into a concrete pillar and finally came to a halt. The tank driver climbed out of his turret, saw the catastrophe, and instantly shot himself.

People said it was a divine portent of imminent downfall. And Colonel Shaklan agreed as he sat alone in the presidential palace that evening, eating his dinner and washing it down with chilled whiskey.

48. Dethroned

Rana never felt at ease in her family. Her father was a lawyer, her mother taught French in an exclusive girls' school. Since they both had careers, they didn't want more than two children.

Rana was pretty, with a delicate look rather like an Indian girl's. She learned fast, and was already quite independent at the age of three.

The first bad experience of her young life was her child-minder, a dissembling woman with hairs on her nose. The girl hated her, and never liked being left with her.

Then her brother Jack was born and laid claim to everything, their mother and father and all the available space. He was fair-skinned, almost blond, rather plump, and he had a powerful pair of lungs. He disliked Rana from the first. She felt the same about him. She pinched him whenever she could, and he yelled blue murder when he so much as set eyes on her. That made their parents take the little boy's side. When Jack came along Rana's mother, who had gone back to teaching six months after her own birth, handing her daughter over to the horrible child-minder, suddenly wanted to give up work and spend all day at home looking after him. But she still sent Rana to the childminder, at least until her daughter rebelled. A year after Jack's birth the delicate little girl developed a strange fever whenever she went to the hairy-nosed woman, but it vanished as soon as she was home again.

Rana had got what she wanted. From then on both children stayed at home. But their mother had time for no one but Jack. Jack did such and such, Jack ate this, Jack said that, it was Jack, Jack, always Jack. Rana had to get by as best she could. As far back as she could remember, her mother had never once asked, "Is there anything you'd like me to explain?" or "Do you need help?" Never.

But when it came to that great hippopotamus Jack, even his first day at school was a major family event. All it lacked was a telegram of congratulations from the President of the state. And from then on Rana's mother spent time with her son every day, following his progress through school. Woe to anyone who trod on the plump little boy's toe; his mother, equipped with every weapon her teacher's training could provide, would sally forth to his school and deal with the teachers there. She was an expert herself.

Jack was not stupid, as his teachers later came to believe. Far from it, he was highly intelligent, but his abilities went the wrong way. At the age of ten he was showing Rana that he had his mother entirely under his thumb. He could succeed in getting his sister slapped when he felt like it, he could have her pocket money docked, make sure she was forbidden to go out or listen to music – all through his mother. He used his mother for his own ends, and she became his slave.

Rana had just begun at high school when she found out for certain that Jack would never be her brother, but always her enemy. She was sitting quietly in her room, playing, when he came in and attacked her for no reason at all. After he had beaten her up brutally, he tore her favourite doll to pieces and ran away. Rana wept, and tried to gather up the rags of her doll. Suddenly her mother appeared and laid into her like a woman deranged. She'd been saying filthy things about the Virgin Mary, said her mother, her brother was sitting in the kitchen crying his eyes out with shame. Rana was baffled. The world was upside down. She had never in her life said a word against the Virgin Mary. Far from it; even as a little girl she had venerated the mother of Jesus.

Her father came home late. He went to see her, sat down on a chair, and looked at her sadly. "Girl, girl, what makes you do these things?" he asked quietly. Rana didn't reply.

That evening she knew that her brother was dead to her, and now living in the family home was easier. Even Jack was nice to her when he sensed her cold indifference, but she didn't care about that.

With much moaning and groaning and the help of three private tutors, he managed to pass the exam for his middle school diploma, and then he left. Rana had taken her high school diploma the same year, with distinction, but her mother didn't even notice. She was busy letting every visitor know how enthusiastically all his teachers spoke of her brilliant son. But she'd decided to take him out of school all the same, she said, because he was such a talented craftsman and his ambition was to be a goldsmith.

He didn't make it, however. He skipped classes for a year and gave up the training course, and after that he became a male nurse. His mother described him as the surgeon's right-hand man. At twenty, to his father's great disappointment, Jack became a professional soldier, and as he had his middle school diploma and was almost two metres tall he became a sergeant in the President's special unit, which was in fact just the thing for him. But that wasn't until much later.

Rana's parents still took no notice of her, but there were advantages to that. It meant that she could make her own decisions, didn't have to ask permission, and wasn't accountable to anyone. She swore to herself that she would take charge of her own life.

When she fell in love with Farid in the spring of 1953, the feud between the Shahins and the Mushtaks was at its height. All the same, Rana ventured to hint to her mother that she had met a nice boy whose surname was Mushtak. Her mother threw a fit. "Mushtaks can't be nice," she shouted, as if Rana were hard of hearing. "They ruined your uncle and cost your father a million lira, and you call one of the Mushtaks *nice?*"

Her mother wouldn't hear another word about the boy. That was sad, but much worse was to come later that afternoon. Jack pushed the door of her room open. "You listen to me, you stupid cow," he shouted, planting himself squarely in front of her. "If I catch you with anyone even distantly related to the Mushtaks, I'll kill you. Do your hear me? I'll kill you! I'm the Samuel in our family, understand?" He shouted so loud that his mother came running and begged him not to over-excite himself.

The word "traitress" escaped from Rana, but no one heard her, because her brother was still ranting in a deafening voice. Later, when she told Farid about it and said she would have to be careful, *he* suddenly threw a fit and began shouting. What kind of life did anyone have in this filthy country, he cried, you'd only just started loving someone and you were threatened with violence and murder! Only later did Rana discover that he had quarrelled with his father that day, and was still upset. He asked her if she had another boyfriend and was just looking for a way to get rid of him, Farid. That was too much. Rana rose to her feet and ran away. It was a week before Easter.

49. Salman

No one knew about his fear. He lay awake for nights on end, staring at the ceiling. His wife Hanan slept peacefully at his side. He went back over his life, searching for something he could hold on to. Since his father's death in 1947 he alone had been at the head of the clan. That was six years ago, but he still hadn't recovered from the loss of the man who was dearer to him than anyone. For thirty-nine years he had been able to shelter in the great Mushtak's shadow from the icy wind blowing their way. Now he had to face it by himself.

Since the spectacular police raid and the arrest of his enemy

Butros, the Shahins had been just waiting for an opportunity to get their revenge. Their new leader Faris was a snake, smooth and dangerous as his mother.

Times were changing. After a series of revenge killings, the government in Damascus had tried to control the situation by passing several death sentences on those who had egged the murderers on. The principle was that of French law, which regards the motive of revenge not as a mitigating circumstance but as incitement to murder, and punishes it with particular severity. These new laws had dealt the moral code of the Arab clans a heavy blow. But their rigour took effect, and feuding families were now trying to hit their adversaries hard some other way.

Salman was sure that the widowed Samia and her son Faris had only one purpose in mind: to ruin him completely.

"A pity you're not here now," he whispered in the darkness, as if his father could hear him. He had learned from George Mushtak that important things should be whispered, not spoken aloud.

For over six years Salman had been trying to prove to the village – friend and foe alike – that he was George Mushtak's true successor, but Mala took no notice. He wasn't even invited to take part in discussions. When his father was still alive, no one would have dared to make a decision without the old man.

Salman believed that several people in the village were hatching a plot. Dogs like that man Ismail would never have dared to ask old Mushtak if he wanted to sell his farm. But now they guessed that in three to five years there would be no stopping him, Salman; he would be the richest farmer in the whole region then. So they were doing all they could to bring him down just before he achieved his ends.

Ismail was only a tool of the widow and her son, that devil Faris. Hadn't he been punished enough by God? Faris's wife, the daughter of a despicable secret service agent, who had married into the Shahin clan just to make her family even more menacing, brought only deformed children into the world. It was said privately in the village that they were the living images of the torture victims in the secret service's cellars. Allegedly Faris and his wife hid their children away in dark rooms and treated them like animals. Two of them hadn't survived their fifth year of life, and the third son, folk said, howled so loud by night that many in the Orthodox quarter woke in alarm. But obviously Faris didn't understand the wrath of God. His heart grew harder and harder.

How lucky, on the other hand, Salman had been with his own sons! He thought of his firstborn, Nassif, who was now working successfully in Damascus as a motor mechanic, along with his three brothers.

Salman's thoughts wandered further back in the depths of time, to the day when George Mushtak had noticed Hanan's belly swelling in her fourth month of pregnancy. He had summoned his son, congratulated him, and then took him walking in the mountains. Out there the sky was wide, the air was pure, and no one would overhear them, his father had said, and then at last he told him the secret of his own life.

His real name was not George Mushtak at all, but Nassif Jasegi. He had called himself George when he reached Mala in flight with his lover Sarka, and discovered that the patron saint of this village was St. Giorgios. And he had thought of Mushtak because at the time he had been obsessed with death, which is the meaning of *mushtak lalmaut*, but he had spared the stupid peasants the mention of death, and just said his name was George Mushtak. Then the name was finally recorded as his during the registration after Syrian independence in 1946.

Here Salman's father had paused for a long time, as if he were suppressing memories. "So I was called Nassif Jasegi," he repeated at last. "My family belonged to the nobility. My father had been a governor in the mountains of Lebanon, and was loyal to the Sultan. His first name was Salman, like yours. After a peasants' uprising against the Sultan he fled and took refuge in Damascus. The peasants' revolt was overthrown with much bloodshed after three years, but my father couldn't go back to the mountains. The Sultan gave him estates south of Damascus, but after being high up in the civil service all his life he knew nothing about farming the land. His tenants and servants soon realized that, of course, and they cheated him wherever they could. He died an embittered man, among other reasons because the Sultan had never given him an office of state again. I learned a lesson for my own life from that: I would never serve anyone. None of my brothers ever wanted to enter the service of the state either. It's an ungrateful master to us Christians."

Once again George Mushtak paused for a long time. Salman kept quiet. "My three brothers, I, and my sister Miriam had to go out early to the fields and the stables, and toil like poor peasants to pay off the debts our father had left on his death. It was my mother who turned the tenants out and took charge of everything herself. She was a lioness who feared nothing, and she passed that attitude on to her sons. Love death, and your enemies will fear you – that was her motto.

We toiled for ten years, and at last the farm was free of debt, and a magnificent sight. We were the main local producers of silk and apricots. The soil was fertile and the irrigation system we had built made us independent of the weather. We grew rich, very rich, and lived well, until that man Kashat ruined everything."

And after that his father told him no more.

⁙

Later, Salman gave his own firstborn son the name of Nassif. The boy took after Hanan in looks and after Salman's father-in-law in character. He had been good with his hands since childhood; he wanted to be a mechanic, and hated farming. Salman smiled when he remembered that at eighteen Nassif had been set on joining the army.

"The army is no place for Christians," Salman had told his son. He had been opposed to the army at the time less from fear than out of distaste for it, a distaste that he had inherited from his own father. "The army is the garbage heap of our country. Only failures join up. Muslims of distinction and their sons strive to get power in the cities, and look for high positions of state. Christians and Jews can live only by trade, by their knowledge and their wits."

Nassif didn't understand him at first, but then he discovered the technical world of motor cars and was absorbed by his new passion. Salman was very glad now that he had followed his father's advice and made the boy change his mind. Since 1949 army officers had been carrying out coups that took them to the summit of state power and back down again into misery.

Who'd have thought that the first to lead a successful coup, Colonel Hablan, would die so miserably after only a hundred and thirty-seven days? Who'd have thought that Colonel Dartan, who overthrew him, would have to run like a rat to Beirut, where he was shot a year later after Colonel Shaklan toppled him in his own turn? And who'd have thought that Shaklan, who still had the people at his feet at the end of 1952, could find himself isolated so quickly and would now, at the end of 1953, be losing more power daily? Salman thought of the birthday party in July given for the colonel by the Shahins, and their humiliation. He smiled in the darkness of his bedroom, grateful for divine providence.

His other sons Latif, Shadi and Fadi were also solely interested in engines. Together with their eldest brother they had made ambitious plans. The future was motorized, they said, and consequently a good garage and workshop in Damascus would be a goldmine, because the Arabs had no car manufacturing plants or factories to make spare parts, so they depended on repairs and ingenious minds to keep the cars they had bought on the road.

Saba and Nasser were still much too young to choose a profession. But Ibtihal, Salman's only daughter, loved agriculture and always wanted to go out to the fields with the men. Funnily enough, she was the only one who looked like a Mushtak. Who knows, thought Salman, his anxieties allayed, perhaps she carries her grandfather's soul in her, and will be the first woman to become a successful farmer some day.

But until they saw whether, in a few years' time, that happened he had to defend the farm alone against his enemies, and most important of all he must get rid of that troublesome Ismail.

What, he asked himself, will Ismail do? Attack the estate? He'd never dare. Side with those damn Shahins against me? A neighbour had told Salman at the barber's that Faris wanted to get a rich man's help to build up a farm twice as large as the Mushtak lands, and growing just the same produce as Salman: apples, almonds, roses, and vegetables.

Salman smiled in the dark. A rich man would be a fool to invest his money in these bleak mountains. Soon he fell asleep. He saw his father smiling at him, and handing him a branch of the pomegranate tree. It was covered with red blossom.

50. Ismail

It was an established fact in Mala: buying land from a Mushtak, even just a handful of earth, was completely impossible. The other farmers were selling off their acres because of the drought and the lure of the oil boom. The preferred to hire themselves out as workers in the Gulf states, where they did in fact earn a great deal of money. Many became millionaires overnight in the Gulf, but most of them lost their money again once they were home. Clever con-men persuaded them to invest in expensive buildings in Damascus and then absconded with the cash. Their victims couldn't return to Mala, because the price of land there had risen steeply in a very short time. Mala had become popular. The village lay high up in the mountains, and its good air and cool summer nights were famous. First the prosperous citizens of Damascus discovered it, then came other Arabs who had plenty of money in their pockets, and soon the price of building plots was as high as in the capital. Farmers who still had their land now grew rich from selling it. And the emigrants who hadn't been conned out of all they had in Damascus, but came back to Mala in time to lay out their money there in the fifties, were the richest of the villagers ten years later.

Old Mushtak had never wanted his children to divide up his property. Division went against the principle of a strong clan, so after his father's death Salman took over the farm uncontested. That was in 1947. Hasib was in America, and received nothing, Elias and Malake had been disinherited. Salman was a good businessman and lavished presents on his siblings, sending sackfuls of rosebuds, apples, raisins, dried figs, and almonds even to the disinherited brother and sister. He was earning extremely well, and even had plans for a perfume factory of his own in Mala. Then disaster suddenly struck.

Ismail Rifai was the son of that Muhammad Abdulkarim who had been at the harvest festival in Mala long ago and then, with his brother-in-law and son-in-law, went over to the side of the attacker Hassan Kashat when he surrounded the village. But after that George Mushtak had killed his arch-enemy Kashat. Muhammad Abdulkarim's brother-in-law and son-in-law managed to escape; he himself had been hit by a ricocheting bullet and died.

Now Ismail, the dead man's son, wanted to buy the Mushtak farm with all its wide lands, and make the place a vacation paradise with the financial support of a French tourist agency. He didn't want just any plot of land, only the Mushtak property, not least because of its incomparable views and good supply of ground water. But there was another reason known to no one but Ismail himself and George Mushtak in his grave. Ismail wanted to settle accounts with the village whose bullets had killed his father.

By now he was a powerful man. Ismail had sold the idea of his father the martyr to the first Syrian government after the country gained independence, and the government, which couldn't legitimately lay claim to any heroic battle for that independence, only to tough fighting for small, indeed tiny concessions, was in bad need of martyrs, as many of them as possible, so as to represent its rise to power as the natural reward for many sacrifices made in the struggle for the Fatherland.

Ismail, son of the alleged great martyr Muhammad Abdulkarim, seized his opportunity and rose to be a state secretary. His father, said the official records and his new tombstone, had fallen fighting French colonialism. In fact, as Ismail knew only too well, his father had been hit in the left temple by that ricochet and fell into a small, muddy pond surrounded by stinging nettles just below the Mala mill, a patch of ground on which no Frenchman had ever set foot.

Ismail's plan to buy the Mushtak farm was like a bombshell dropped on Mala, especially in the Catholic quarter. The land lay on a high plateau reaching from the old elm tree to the mountains of Lebanon. Was it now to go to a stranger rather than someone from the village, to a Muslim whose father was a traitor?

Salman reassured his anxious friends in the barber's shop. "A Mushtak never sells, and will bow to no one," he said in a tone almost of indifference, trying to imitate his father.

"Your father would have cut the messenger's balls off," said a toothless old shepherd, adjusting his headcloth. Salman had always thought this shepherd an unpleasant know-all, and ignored him.

He gave a polite but cold reception to the messenger from the state secretary who wanted to encourage tourism. "Tell your master Ismail Rifai that this is a Christian village, and it's grown neither larger nor smaller over thousands of years. We're not selling. Not at any price. Syria is a large country, and there are plenty of other places for tourism."

Two days later the go-between came back and, with dark hints and threats, offered twice the sum, but this time Salman didn't even look up from the tractor he was repairing. He growled at the envoy, "Didn't I tell you plainly in good Arabic, or is your boss as slow on the uptake as his father? We're not selling." And when the envoy got back into his black car Salman wondered briefly if the shepherd's suggestion hadn't been a good idea after all. The leaves on the trees had already turned brown that October day.

A week before Christmas, persons unknown destroyed all the trees on Mushtak land standing out of sight of the village. No one had heard anything, but later a pigeon-breeder said that his birds had been fluttered around restlessly for three nights on end. However, they calmed down again in the early hours of the morning, which they wouldn't have done before an earthquake, and slept almost all day, only to batter themselves desperately against the walls of their wooden lofts again by night.

The police thought it had all been well organized, and then carried out according to plan during several days of icy December weather. All routes leading to the lands belonging to the Mushtak farm had been blocked by men claiming to be military police. If anyone asked why, they had said there were army manoeuvres on the high plateau.

Not until the third day did Salman and several other farmers in the village who wanted to ride out to their fields become suspicious. They asked at the Mala police station whether there was in fact any manoeuvre going on. The two local policemen, followed by several farmers, drove in Salman's truck to the plantations some three kilometres away, where a terrible sight met their eyes.

The bare, felled trees were covered by hoarfrost. The scene froze Salman's blood in his veins. All his trees and rosebushes lay on the ground as far as the eye could see. Twenty hectares of ravaged orchards, most of the trees grubbed up roots and all, a few old, well-established specimens simply sawn down. The entire irrigation system had been destroyed by bulldozers; pipes and hoses stuck up from the churned soil like skeletons. Several bulldozers, specially equipped trucks, excavators, and tractors must have been used in the operation.

Not a wall, not a water tank had been spared. The watchman's house had collapsed, and they found the poor man under its ruins. His corpse had two large, gaping holes in the chest. His murderers had torn it apart with dumdum bullets.

Salman's face turned grey, and he wept for the first time since his father's death. He just stood there, unable to utter a word. The sympathy of the people around him was no comfort.

In February 1954, two months later, he died of a heart attack, the first villager in Mala ever to suffer one. Heart attacks are almost unknown among the Arabs.

At the time, in the winter of 1953, all the clues pointed to Ismail Rifai, but the case was never cleared up. Ismail was powerful, and Salman's sons were not strong enough to act yet. Their mother Hanan knew that. She wore black for fifteen years, and kept reminding her children of the perpetrator's name. Her sons adopted her own quiet approach, and started planning too.

Hanan, who didn't once smile in all those fifteen years, was a pale woman of iron energy. After the attack she and her children wanted no more to do with farming. She leased the fallow land to several Mala farmers, and divided the rent equally between her husband's siblings. Hasib had disappeared without trace in America, so she donated his share to the religious houses of Mala in his memory. In return, they let her keep old Mushtak's house, which her sons later converted into one of the finest buildings in the village, with an artificial stream that wound its way through the extensive grounds and cascaded from a high rock into a swimming pool. Latif, Nassif, Shadi and Fadi were inseparable. They always liked going out together to Mala, where they partied all night long, and then drove back to Damascus in their big deluxe American limousines.

But to conclude the story of Ismail: in the autumn of 1968, Salman's youngest sons Nasser and Saba, through go-betweens, tricked Ismail Rifai out of his entire fortune. At this time he was also under suspicion of having smuggled weapons and money into the country from Iraq to organize uprisings against the government. Collaboration with neighbouring Iraq was hated in Damascus even more than collaboration with Israel, and always had been.

Ismail denied all accusations, but the evidence was overwhelming. Guns, ammunition, and crates of money were found in his barn. The find had been faultlessly arranged by a secret service man to whom Nassif, Salman's eldest son, gave a 1967 Opel. Ismail was sentenced to life imprisonment.

That day Salman's widow Hanan laughed again for the first time and wore coloured clothing. She hailed her sons as heroes, and gave a lavish party for them in the expensive Ali Baba restaurant that had just been opened in Damascus. Elias and Claire were invited too. Farid wasn't there; he was already in prison at that time.

"It took fifteen years," said Nasser, raising a glass of arrack to his mother, "but we've avenged our father."

"Fifteen years?" asked Elias in surprise. He was sitting between Claire and Ibtihal.

"Yes, uncle," replied Saba, the second youngest son, "it takes a long time to ensnare someone like that. He was a suspicious man."

"A Bedouin," joked Nasser, "would say: well done, lads, but why in such a hurry?"

BOOK OF THE CLAN III

Love is a wildcat with nine lives

ॐ

51. Lucia and Nagib

Claire's memory was not particularly good, but one event in the summer of 1935 was ever-present in her mind. She was seventeen, and had loved Musa Salibi with every fibre of her heart for the last two years. But then she suddenly met a pale young man with the most beautiful hands in the world in the God-forsaken village of Mala, and he spoke to her in French.

She was a city-dweller born and bred, and as a young girl she thought village life boring. She shared her aversion to all things provincial with her father. He made no secret of the fact that he preferred a newspaper and a morning cup of coffee in Damascus to the fresh mountain air. Unlike Claire, however, he could always get out of visiting Mala by claiming that, sad to say, he couldn't take the time off work.

Her mother seemed indifferent to her father's presence or absence. She liked the rugged country life and the primitive villagers who obeyed her slavishly, did everything she asked, and kept calling her "Signora", because she liked to hear the word so much.

Claire's brother Marcel, two years her senior, could imagine no better way of spending the summer than in Mala either. For that very reason Claire took a dislike to the village. But one thing was true: you slept better in the mountains than in the sticky heat of Damascus.

Her mother Lucia was half Venetian. Her father, Antonio Sciamico, had come to Damascus in 1850 with a trade delegation, fell in love with the city, and stayed. He was said to be a nobleman. Large parts of the Italian city of Venice, Lucia liked to say, belonged to his family. However, the only certain fact was that he was a *flâneur* and a playboy.

Antonio Sciamico learned Arabic fast, and renamed himself Anton Shami, which sounded rather like his Italian name, but helped him to blend in more easily. In Arabic, Shami just means *Damascene*, and is a very common surname. Many Jews, Christians, and Muslims bear the name.

After a while he married Josephine, the daughter of Zacharias Asfar, one of the largest silk manufacturers in Syria. Shami himself became a famous trader in the Suk al Buzuriye, the spice market near the Ummayad Mosque. He made a large fortune from spices, silk, and fine woods. But his greatest source of pride was that in 1871 he had eaten supper with his favourite composer Giuseppe Verdi in Cairo, where the Italian genius was giving the première of his opera *Aida* for the opening of the Suez Canal. Anton Shami had the photograph showing him sitting at table with a laughing Verdi greatly enlarged and hung it in the drawing room of his magnificent house, which united Italian and Syrian stylistic features to very beautiful effect. To this day the building bears his name, and is the finest in the whole quarter. When the last German Kaiser, Wilhelm II, visited the East in 1898 he stayed there while he was in Damascus. At the time Lucia was already engaged to Nagib Surur, son of a prosperous family of cloth merchants, but Anton Shami had the betrothal ceremony repeated and photographed in the Kaiser's presence. These pictures hung in Lucia's bedroom, along with those of her Venetian forebears.

She could tell wonderful stories about her grandfather Doge Paolo Sciamico's glass eye and the last German Kaiser's withered hand. And the older she grew the more stories she told. Her fund of stories grew even greater after her husband's death. She began indulging in flights of fancy about a great collection of glass eyes owned by her family in Venice. The glassmakers had had to produce countless eyes, she claimed, until they made one that suited the Doge. She wrote letters to the Italian authorities in Rome and Venice, demanding the return of this valuable collection. But that was not until just before her death in 1959.

In 1900 she married Nagib. Anton Shami liked the elegant, well-connected young man, and hoped that he would help him to expand his business. But Nagib didn't want to work with his father-in-law, or his own father either. First he took a post with a money-changer, and later, after two years of training in Paris, he became technical director of the quality and control department of the Banque de Syrie et du Liban, which as a central bank was allowed to print lira notes. The notes came with an imprint stating that the French government guaranteed the value of the Syrian and Lebanese lira to a maximum of twenty French francs.

In 1910, cholera carried off Anton Shami and his wife. Lucia survived because she and her husband happened to be visiting her family in Venice that summer. She inherited a large fortune which Nagib invested securely with the bank.

His wife was intent on having a large family, and she duly bore ten children, but eight of them died just after their birth. Only Marcel, and two years later Claire, lived.

Until her mid-fifties, Lucia habitually had affairs with young men. Later, her daughter often laughed to think how as a girl she had innocently believed that all her mother's visiting lovers were family members, and called them Uncle, until one day a girlfriend explained it to her. Claire was seventeen by then, and her mother had long since given up the young men.

When her friend enlightened her in the spring of 1935 Claire felt furious, not because of her mother's escapades in themselves but because of the lies and derision to which she had exposed Claire, her own daughter. But she felt truly humiliated and isolated only when she tackled her brother on the subject. He was nineteen, and had been studying law since the beginning of the year. He unfeelingly told her to her face that he had known about it all along, and was glad to see his mother find the love their father couldn't give her.

"But what about me? Why didn't any of you tell me?" asked Claire, close to tears.

"You take after Father, you're as sentimental as he is. You can't accept hard facts," he claimed.

From that moment on her love for her mother and her brother died. She wouldn't give them away, all the same, although when she went into Damascus with her father a week later to eat an ice she broached the subjects of love, faithfulness, and jealousy. She said she'd like to hear his opinion so that she would know more about the way to behave with her fiancé Musa.

Nagib looked askance at his daughter and smiled. "Why does love always have to imply possession?" he asked, shaking his head. Then he fell silent for a while, as if wondering what he should tell her. Claire gave him time. "You should love with composure," he said. "Love should bestow sublimity. It lets you give everything without losing anything. That's its magic. But here people want a contract of marriage concluded in the presence of witnesses. Imagine, witnesses, as if it were some kind of crime," he repeated slowly, allowing her to appreciate the ridiculous aspect. "State and Church supervise the contract. That's not love, it's orders from a higher authority to increase and multiply."

He smiled at his own words. "And any idiot who can't even add up one and one to make two knows, when he loves someone, that he wants to possess that person body as well as soul. He guards his property jealously to ensure that neither heart nor brain, neither liver nor stomach, nor ..." Nagib hesitated for a moment. "Well, you know what I mean," he added, "...will be touched by any other thought, hand or feeling. Jealousy and unhappiness are programmed into the arrangement in advance."

They sat there quietly, and Claire looked at her father as he spooned up his ice, smiling. What a wise man, she thought. He seemed to her like a visitor from a strange world that was now at peace.

She didn't feel like that; it did matter to her when women gazed adoringly at their fiancés or indulged in vulgar behaviour with them.

A week after this conversation in the ice cream parlour, her father was arrested. He was accused of embezzling large sums of money from the bank where he had worked for five years, and he spent three years in prison, until the Catholic Patriarch successfully intervened on his behalf. But he was never exonerated, even by his own wife. However, that was a matter of indifference to Nagib.

52. Tamam and Sarkis

The large house stood on the village square, opposite the gate of St. Giorgios's churchyard. Lucia had the second floor entirely renovated, equipped with the most modern technological devices, and furnished in the latest fashion. The rent was so cheap that she paid it for a whole year in advance, so that she could visit Mala any time she liked.

Tamam, who owned the house, liked her tenants from Damascus because she enjoyed talking to Lucia. She never exchanged a word with the other villagers. She had a large vegetable garden and several vineyards, and bought the rest of her provisions in the neighbouring village of Ainyose, bringing them home on the back of her donkey. So whenever Lucia came to Mala she brought an extra case full of the finest foodstuffs, including chocolate and canned meat. Nothing could have given Tamam greater pleasure.

At the time Claire, like all girls in love, was reading love stories non-stop, especially French novels, but their landlady's own love story cast all those books into the shade.

Tamam was a strange woman. She lived alone with her son Djamil. The villagers thought her eccentric, and people whispered that she was to blame for her husband's early death. She had loved him from her childhood. He and his parents lived in a little house near her family's large property. Her father was a prosperous farmer then. She wasn't beautiful, but several men proposed to her. She turned them down, and her father was glad that she stayed with him when his wife died, and he didn't have to share her with any other man. But when he discovered that she was in love with his neighbours' son, he forbade her to have anything to do with the young man, who barely scraped a living by working in the stone quarry. Tamam loved her father, and was torn between her feelings for him and for her lover. Night after night she wept with longing for Sarkis, who had sworn not to touch any other woman. He suggested elopement, but Tamam didn't want to expose her lonely father to the mockery of the villagers. She hoped that death would bring him release, but death took its time.

The couple waited for twenty years. When Tamam's father did die, Sarkis was forty and she was in her late thirties. They waited another year, until Tamam could put her black mourning clothes aside. Until that day Mala had never known a tale of self-sacrificing lovers with a happy ending. Such stories always ended in tragedy; you couldn't reconcile the harsh peasant life with the tenderness of great love affairs out of fairy tales, set in lush gardens where people wore flowing silken robes, probably because those tales made life in the bleak mountains seem even less bearable.

Tamam was afraid of the wedding night. Her neighbour, an experienced midwife, told her horror stories of the first night when the bride wasn't in her first youth and had a hymen harder than leather. Husbands, she said, quite often needed her, the midwife, to help by sticking her forefinger through it.

Relishing the bride's fears, the woman told her about one man in the village who had fractured his prick when he deflowered his bride. It had a right-angled bend in it ever after. Another husband, she said, thrust in with all his might, but because his bride was thirty-five her maidenhead resisted, bouncing back like a trampoline, and he fell out of bed and hit the back of his head on the floor. The blow left the man's mind confused. He spoke nothing but Spanish thereafter, and he avoided all women.

Tamam felt the iron claws of fear squeezing her heart, and she hoped the midwife was telling lurid tales just to show off. But her own wedding night was worse than all the stories. Sarkis had been drinking to give himself courage. Tamam, who never drank alcohol, was horrified by the stink of her husband, who was sweating heavily, and by his rough hands as he tried to pull her panties off under her dress. She begged him to remember that she wasn't very young now. That infuriated him even more. "I don't need any midwife," he cried, as if he too had heard the neighbour's stories. "I've hardened and sharpened my chisel these thirty years."

Not a word of love, no tender caress. His fingers, although covered in scratches from his work in the quarry, had always been softer than a rose petal when he touched her skin. But now Sarkis's face wasn't fragrant any longer, nor was he her shy lover, but a stranger lying on top of her with all his weight, pressing the air out of her.

He thrust into her dry soul. Tamam screamed so loudly that the musicians, singers, and dancers stopped for a moment, but then they all raised their glasses in rejoicing. Tamam hated them. They were out there eating her bread and applauding her pain.

The night seemed endless. She felt near death, and wept, but that only encouraged Sarkis to push himself into her again and again. Late in the night, his old aunt knocked at the door with the laconic remark, "Proof of honour." Sarkis tore the bloodstained white sheet proving Tamam a virgin from under her and gave it to the old woman. Once again rejoicing broke out among the guests, who went on making merry under the bedroom window until day dawned.

The marriage lasted only two months. Then Tamam summoned up all her strength and threw her husband out. Sarkis did not protest. He went back to his old home, bitterly disappointed in the woman for whom he had waited so long. She had always talked to him of love games with desire in her voice. Now she was acting like a nun, and what a nun! On the wedding night she began screaming the moment he touched her. And then she went to sleep before he had finished doing his conjugal duty.

A week later she had asked him to sleep alone in a small room, saying that when she slept beside him she had nightmares in which he was always raping her. Sleep by himself in a miserable little room? What was the point of getting married, then? Sarkis asked himself that question out loud at the barber's, and the men there nodded with mingled sympathy and derision.

But Sarkis didn't tell the men that he never went back to her because he hated himself. Why had he turned down all those beautiful, willing women? His neighbour's daughter, soft-armed Saide who kept visiting him after his parents' death, had given him a basil plant, saying that a man like him needed a good woman to warm him in bed and bear him fine children. "Look at my breasts, feel my belly," she said. "Aren't they just made for you?" And he had touched her; she had firm, round breasts, and a captivating navel. But in the end he sent her home. How could any man be so idiotic?

Saide had tried for two years, and then she gave up and married the village blacksmith. At the time the blacksmith had been a dirty, intolerably coarse man. But now? Now he looked well groomed, he had three sons, each more handsome than the last, and their mother was bringing up all three as good Christians. The whole village talked about Saide, who had made a miserable dog into the master of a fine household.

And there was the young widow Walide. She had wept for nights at his bedside, begging him to let her get in bed with him, but he was faithful to Tamam and turned down all her advances. "You and I, we're both widowed," said that far-sighted young woman perceptively. "The only difference is that your partner still lies above ground." How right she was, thought Sarkis. Tamam is a living, breathing corpse.

Sarkis disappeared from the village overnight. Four weeks later, children playing found his body in a deep, long-disused pit in the stone quarry.

53. The Rift and the Meeting

The second floor had its own entrance, up a flight of wooden steps behind the house. The Sururs' landlady Tamam lived on the first floor. They always arrived at their summer lodgings two days after the beginning of the long vacation, and usually stayed until the day before school began again in early October. Marcel had found a friend who was glad of his company in Djamil, Tamam's son.

In the summer of 1935 Marcel was nineteen, and had begun studying law. And Nagib Surur had been in prison since May, which meant that Claire would have to go to Mala alone with her mother. So she sought her fiancé's company even more than usual in the last weeks before they left.

But then, just before the last day of school, he shocked her. Just when she most needed him, he seemed to her so strange that she thought she must be losing her mind.

She had met Musa Salibi by chance in 1933, when she was out eating an ice with her father and he came up to their table, a tall, strong, well-dressed figure. He stopped politely and said good day to Nagib. Nagib invited him to join them. Musa looked at Claire, and she felt the ground sway beneath her. He was five years her senior, and looked as elegant as any actor. Her father liked Musa, who was both a good boxer and an excellent shot. With these qualities, he had found a job as bodyguard to the French governor of Damascus.

After that first meeting in the ice cream parlour, he kept visiting the family on one pretext or another. Claire's mother didn't like him. He was only a husk, she said briefly, handsome but empty, and when he called she would leave the drawing room with a theatrical groan. But it was Nagib, not Lucia, who had the last word on Claire's engagement, and he immediately gave his consent when Musa asked to marry his daughter. He took no notice of his wife when she pointed out that Musa had no proper profession; bodyguards were there only to deal with any trouble and die for the governor if necessary.

Claire loved her strong, handsome fiancé, and already saw herself travelling the world under his protection. And once they were officially engaged in the winter of 1934 he was able to drive her around in his car. It was a black Renault, the 1933 model, with leather upholstery, fine wood fittings, and curtains for the back windows.

She felt like a princess, dressed in her best and sinking into the soft back seat, while Musa drove the car through the streets of the New Town.

Claire went to boxing matches with him too. When he was in the ring himself, his athletic torso bared, he looked even more magnificent than he did in a suit. Musa fought elegantly, dancing around his opponent. Women adored him, and he enjoyed the glances they gave him from eyes that were moist with admiration.

Soon after their engagement he was to fight the legendary Syrian champion, Ali Dakko of Aleppo, and the talk at the boxing club was of their good prospects of sending Musa to the French contests in

Paris next year. In her daydreams, Claire already saw herself living in that cosmopolitan capital. Her father, who had been to Paris three times, waxed enthusiastic about the metropolis.

In March it was all settled: Musa would go to Paris if he won a fight against a youthful challenger. This boxer didn't have his opponent's elegance and good footwork, but his fists were like steel. Once, for a bet, he had killed a fully grown bull with a single punch between the ears. The young boxer's name was Rimon Rasmalo, and he was a stonemason by trade.

"It'll just be a little limbering-up exercise for Musa before he goes to Paris," Nagib reassured his daughter. He was standing at the second-floor window, watching his wife prune the roses in the garden on this cold but sunny day. "I've hidden some money in a purse under your mattress. It's for you. Perhaps the two of you will like Paris and want to stay there. Life will be very difficult for us Christians here over the next few years. The Muslims are going to slaughter us." There was grief and despair in his voice. His daughter didn't understand him.

Then on 14 May, a Tuesday and exactly a week after her birthday, he was arrested. Ismail Ballut, a young man in his mid-twenties, had gone to the police station of the Muhayirin quarter just before midnight on Monday 13 May. He was well-dressed and identified himself as an employee of the Banque de Syrie et du Liban in Damascus. He had a large suitcase with him, and said he couldn't sleep at nights. One of the police officers asked why not? Another laughed, and added, "Love or a quarrel with your wife, is it?"

"No, it's the money," he replied, opening the case, which proved to contain fifty-two million Syrian lira. The policemen stared blankly at the money. They were sure the man before them must be a complete idiot. "Nagib Surur is the devil incarnate. He's tricked the machine that stamps old, worn-out, badly damaged banknotes to make them worthless before they're burned in special furnaces. Then the bank produces new notes with the same numbers as the old ones and puts them in circulation," the man painstakingly explained as they took his statement. In answer to a question he further explained that there were now doubles of those notes that Nagib had *not* destroyed, and they weren't forgeries because both series of banknotes were genuine.

They just had the same numbers. The man couldn't say exactly how that devil Nagib had managed to fool the machine. His part in the business, he said, had been only to keep his mouth shut, and sign papers saying that the procedure in the room where the old notes were destroyed had been correct. "The inspector who checks the ashes wasn't allowed into the room, so he never knew anything about it. Nagib gave him newsprint ashes instead, weighed out precisely to the last milligram. How he fixed it all only he knows. He fooled me too."

"Easy enough, with such a simpleton!" whispered a freckled police officer to his colleague as the duty NCO went on interrogating the man, taking down his statement in person. He wrote slowly, and kept asking him to repeat what he had last said.

He, Ismail Ballut, said the man, was supposed to keep the money safe for a few weeks, and then Nagib was going to let him have one-third of it, and use the other two-thirds to bring Syrian boxing up to world-class level. The policemen looked at each other incredulously.

"And as for you, you bastard, I suppose you were just planning to make a bunch of orphaned kids happy with your share of the money!" bellowed the NCO, who had no idea that he was a mind-reader. For Ismail Ballut had indeed wanted to start and run an orphanage. He merely added, quietly, that he had been given a very religious upbringing, for his father was the well-known Sheikh Hassan Ballut. But the devil, disguised in the body of that Christian Nagib, had tempted him, and now he, Ismail, repented of his crime.

The policemen didn't know who Hassan Ballut was, nor did they fully understand the trick allegedly used by the perpetrator to circumvent all the French bank's security systems, so they put the man in the cells, recorded the amount of money in the files, and called their boss Lieutenant Fakhri. For a start Fakhri had the bank clerk tortured, allegedly to find out whether there was more money hidden anywhere else. Torture was a routine police measure at the time.

By the early morning of 14 May, however, it had produced no further information. Three hours later the police arrested Nagib. Unlike the loquacious Ballut, Claire's father was saying nothing, but all Lieutenant Fakhri's incoming phone calls showed that it was incumbent on him to go carefully with the Christian.

Since the entire sum of money was still intact, the verdict of the court, when it came later, was mild. Ballut was given a suspended sentence of six months; Nagib was jailed for five years. He was free again after three of them. Claire welcomed her father as if he had come home from a long journey. But much was to happen before that time.

Just after her father's arrest Claire felt miserable. The others often bullied her at school now, and she had to put up with all kinds of sharp remarks. Sometimes she wept in the washrooms because some of the girls attacked her like a swarm of hysterical wasps. The nuns of the Besançon School acted blind, deaf, and dumb. Only her friend Madeleine stood staunchly by her. Claire never forgot that to her dying day.

She told Madeleine about the bad dreams that tormented her by night. For one thing, she knew that her father had been kept in solitary confinement for months to make him talk. Neither she nor anyone else was allowed to visit him, and one day someone started the rumour that Nagib Surur had died under torture and lay buried in the desert. For another, Musa's fight against Rimon Rasmalo, the man with the steel fists, was to be at the beginning of June.

"It's crazy," said Madeleine one morning, "here are the two of us, best friends, and our menfolk are planning to knock each other's heads in." At first Claire didn't understand. Of course she had told her friend all about Musa, and how they would probably be going to Paris. And of course she knew that Madeleine was also engaged, but her friend didn't talk about her fiancé much, and when she mentioned his job she had just said he was a stonemason. If Nagib or Musa had ever mentioned the name of Musa's opponent to her, reassuring her by saying that he was strong but technically a poor boxer, she had registered it only in passing, and hadn't realized that Musa was to fight her friend Madeleine's fiancé. Only now did the scales fall from her eyes. She was horrified.

Madeleine laughed. "I feel like someone in a trashy novel," she joked. "All it needs is for the two of us to go for each other tooth and nail and climb into the ring ourselves, screeching. But luckily we're not in a novel. I never go to fights. As far as I can see, they're just a silly way to stage a brawl. Why would anyone want to watch that?"

"I wish I were as strong as you," replied Claire. "I always have to go, not because I'm brave but because I'm a coward. I feel as if I might be some help, if the fight's going badly for him, and if he wins he'll be happier because then he can celebrate his victory in front of me."

The fight had been fixed for Sunday 16 June. The boxing club was in the Muslim quarter, but both the defending champion and his challenger were Christians, and they had insisted on Sunday as the day of the match. Claire made up her face and put on her yellow dress, a particular favourite of Musa's. But she didn't feel happy on the way to the club, even when the whole committee welcomed her ceremoniously, expressing their sympathy with her father, an innocent man in jail.

Claire's stomach lurched when her fiancé came into the big hall with the boxing ring in the middle of it. And before he and his large retinue disappeared into the changing rooms, Musa reassured her with his smile. "I'll be a butterfly, you just wait and see," he said. But it didn't turn out that way.

Her fiancé made a majestic entrance by comparison with his opponent's pitiful effort. Musa strode to the ring like a film star, with music and a whole team escorting him. He climbed elegantly up the steps and jumped through the opening in the ropes that his companions had made for him. Up in the ring, he ran a round of honour. The whole hall roared. He blew Claire a kiss and smiled.

When the spectators had calmed down again Rimon Rasmalo appeared. He was short and sturdy. Claire had to stand up to see him. He came in accompanied only by his trainer, who was carrying a worn old bucket. Rimon earned laughter and insulting catcalls. He walked leaning slightly forward, and his arms looked much too long. "Hey, is that ape here just to give Musa a laugh or what?" called a sweating, fat man three seats away for her, and another man replied, "No, he's Musa's hors d'oeuvre, but where's the main dish?"

Rimon climbed into the ring with a grim look, raised his hand reluctantly in a brief salutation, and went to his corner. He seemed to consist entirely of bulges. His neck, his arms, his legs – there were no straight lines about the man. He looked darkly at his opponent as his trainer urgently whispered last-minute advice to him.

None of the speeches, greetings, and expressions of gratitude preceding the fight penetrated Claire's mind. Only the bell aroused her attention again.

From the first, Musa didn't stand a chance.

Rimon made for him like an enraged bumble-bee. The referee kept trying to separate the boxers, but during each clinch Rimon punched Musa mercilessly. Musa did his best to keep his opponent at arm's length, and when he succeeded he too excelled with his elegance and the stylish series of hooks he threw to the other man's head. At those moments the crowd rejoiced in relief. But Rimon took the punishment and then went straight as an arrow past his opponent's fists to get him in a clinch again, neutralizing the advantage of Musa's long arms. When Rimon kept so close to him, Musa was helpless. His adversary's movements had none of that dancing beauty that he himself saw as essential to the sport of boxing. Rimon was rough and square-set, and the ring judge had to warn him three times in the first round for head-butting his opponent.

Musa sat in his corner in the short break between the first two rounds, looking dazed. The trainer was urging him to keep his opponent at a distance, while his second cooled his face with water. But as soon as the bell went Rimon got going like a clockwork tin toy. He shoved, he punched, he pushed and bellowed at his adversary, moving forward like a road roller all the time. Musa stopped dancing. He sought safety in distance, trying to gain a few seconds to pull himself together and remember his technique, but soon a hammer blow from that gorilla Rimon destroyed any kind of technique at all. Rimon battered his head with uppercuts, while digging his elbows into Musa's stomach.

These first rounds lasted forever, and at the end of the third round Rimon landed a punch on Musa Salibi's left temple. It wasn't a hook but a jab, and it was like a chunk of granite flinging Musa away from his challenger. He staggered sideways and fell to the floor. The referee held back Rimon, who in defiance of all the rules was trying to rush his opponent like a beast of prey. Musa struggled up again, and the referee allowed the fight to go on, but the two boxers hadn't had time to make another move before the bell rang.

"You just wait," an elderly gentleman sitting near Claire told his wife, "Musa's worn that appalling amateur out. Now he'll really show what he can do."

Musa dragged himself to his corner, and Claire called out to him to stop fighting. He heard, and looked at her with empty eyes. A man caught her arm roughly. "*Hureime*, little lady, this isn't for women and children. You just sit down or go out in the fresh air." And he pushed her unceremoniously down in her seat. The man hadn't even looked at her. His gaze was fixed on his idol, sitting up there in the right-hand corner of the ring with his eyes swollen.

The fourth round lasted seven seconds. That was the time it took Rimon to get from his corner to the middle of the ring and slip below his adversary's outstretched fists. Then, in the fraction of a second, he planted the full force of his left hook against Musa's chin. A second later his right glove landed a thunderous blow on his tottering opponent's left temple. Musa not only lost his balance but sailed through the air to his right, dropped like a stone, slid half a metre across the ring, unconscious, and came to rest on his back at an awkward angle. Rimon knew there was nothing the handsome man on the floor could do now. Arms outspread, he leaped up in the air, uttering a yell that shattered two light bulbs and did permanent damage to the referee's right eardrum. The audience changed sides, and was now acclaiming Musa's savage conqueror.

Claire didn't know what to do. A number of men jumped up to go and help the ex-champion lying on the floor. She tried climbing into the ring too, to be with Musa, but her uncongenial neighbour held her back. "No women go up there except whores," he said. She could smell his nauseating sweat, and was only just able to keep the contents of her stomach down. Then she shook her arm free. "Don't you touch me," she said, trying to keep calm, "not unless you want trouble." The man showed his bad teeth in a grin, and moved away.

She stood there by herself; no one offered to help her, not even the committee chairman. The men carried Musa past her, one of them calling for a doctor. But when Claire tried following them to the changing rooms, the little caretaker who had always been so deferential to her father planted himself four-square in front of the entrance. "No women in here," he said, staring into the distance. She couldn't take it in; she had always called the man "Uncle", she'd known him since her childhood. How often had he patted her head, how often had her father pressed five lira into his hand, telling him to go and have a good meal out with his wife? At that time a labourer didn't earn as much as five lira for two days' work. And now the caretaker didn't even call her by her name, just spoke of "women".

"But Uncle Sharif, don't you recognise me? I'm Musa's fiancée," she said softly and sadly, for she knew deep down that he had recognized her perfectly well.

"No women allowed in. You'll have to wait here for Musa. We have decent morals here, not like you Christians."

She was confused. Of course she knew the boxing club was in the conservative Muslim quarter, but that was still in the heart of her native Damascus. Where had Musa brought her? Obviously her mother had not been wrong to say, as Claire left, that she didn't like letting her go to that rough part of town, but she supposed her daughter would be under Musa's personal protection the whole time. And now he was lying helpless on the floor himself.

The place emptied, the stream of spectators crowded out through the distant main entrance. Claire found herself at the other side of the hall, near the little back exit next to the changing rooms, showers, and toilets. The hollow silence alarmed her.

The minutes crept by, heavy as lead. She seemed to wait for hours. Even later, she couldn't believe it had really been less than thirty minutes. She heard laughter and other sounds beyond the heavy door. They reached her as if they came from a deep cavern with its entrance blocked.

Two men were coming out of the auditorium, approaching her. A small sturdy man and a tall strong one, with a cigarette in the corner of his mouth.

"Hey, how about us having a nice time together?" asked the tall man, waggling his eyebrows up and down in what he took for a seductive manner.

"Go to hell," said Claire with difficulty. Her voice was failing. Her heart froze to a sharp splinter of ice.

"No need to act like that, we'll pay," replied the small man, thrusting his right forefinger back and fourth through the circle he made with the thumb and forefinger of his left hand.

"Please go away," she begged, but that just encouraged the men. The tall man reached for her breasts. She kicked his shin and swung her bag at the smaller man, who was grasping her buttocks. She screamed, because hitting them wasn't going to get her anywhere. The pair of them quickly seized her arms, one each, and pushed her towards the toilets.

But then something she was never to forget happened, and she often told the story. A man came hurrying out of the door to the changing rooms.

"What the hell do you think you're doing?" he shouted, and without waiting for an answer he picked up a short length of hosepipe lying under the washbasins and began lashing the two men with it.

"Leave the girl alone, you bastards!" The hosepipe whistled through the air and came slapping down on the heads and shoulders of her repulsive assailants. They let Claire go and stumbled away. The smaller man turned just before he reached the exit and shouted back, "Whore!"

Her rescuer stood there looking almost shy, breathing heavily. The man's name was Barkush; he was a police captain and an enthusiastic if unlucky boxer. He kept his distance from her so that she could recover her self-control.

"Thank you," said Claire, and she began to cry.

"What are you doing here?"

"I'm … I'm waiting for my fiancé. He's unconscious."

"Who? Musa? You're Musa's fiancée? He came round some time back, he's drowning his sorrows in chilled arrack with his friends. You can go home, don't worry."

She wanted to ask him to find Musa for her, but suddenly her tongue wouldn't obey her. A rift the size of the rocky ravine in Mala opened up inside her, splitting her heart. She had to make an effort to preserve her composure in front of the man, and dragged herself out.

At the time her mother was living in a villa in Arnus Avenue, an exclusive area. It was about two kilometres away, but she decided to take a cab. Several horse-drawn vehicles were standing ready near the Hidjaz train station. She picked the best and didn't haggle over its price. When the cabby wondered aloud what a woman was doing out and about on her own by night, however, she snapped at him to mind his own business and take her to Arnus Avenue, near the French gendarmerie.

As soon as the old cab driver heard that address he cheered up, for only the rich and powerful lived there. Fares to that quarter always gave generous tips.

"Just as you say, miss, I won't meddle, but I'm a father myself, I'd be worried about such a beautiful young lady. I have three children, you see, my daughter Hayat, she's about your age, and if you'll permit me I'd say she's as pretty as you, not that I mean to give any offence."

Cabbies are always talkative, but this one could compete with my mother's new radio set, thought Claire. His name was Salim, he said, and in the normal way he drove between Beirut and Damascus, but there wasn't much money in it these days, for hardly anyone travelled that road now, so he'd switched to the city, which wasn't so easy, because the regular town cabbies didn't like to see the bread taken out of their mouths. They attacked cabbies from the country and robbed them of their day's takings. But he had no choice, he said, he had those two horses ahead of them to feed, not to mention a wife and three children. That made him braver than a lion, he told her, and the town cabbies sensed it, riffraff that they were, so they left him, Salim, alone if they had any sense.

He talked and talked, and suddenly she didn't mind any more. The cab was driving through the mild summer night. A cool westerly breeze was blowing into the back of the vehicle, and the horses' hooves beat out a soothing rhythm on the cobblestones of the streets.

Claire heaved a sigh of relief when she saw the lighted windows of her home, and paid the cabby generously. Even before she reached the door she could hear the Italian songs that her mother listened to on the radio night after night.

ﻼ

Two weeks later she was sitting beside her mother in the bus to Mala, feeling utterly miserable.

She loved Musa, but something had broken for ever that night at the boxing club. He had come to see her, he'd been very nice to her, and he tried to explain that he'd been ashamed to look her in the face that night. But for the first time she felt a void in her heart not when he left, but while he was sitting there with her.

The village felt bleaker than ever to Claire that summer. Only the French novels and books of poetry that she had brought with her proved to be life-rafts. For days on end she followed Julien Sorel's fate in *Le Rouge et le Noir*, she sought comfort in Verlaine's love poems. She also took refuge in André Gide's *Les Faux Monnayeurs*, George Bernanos's *Sous le Soleil de Satan*, Guy de Maupassant's *Bel Ami*, Colette's *Chéri* and *La Vagabonde*.

Her mother left her alone, was out and about all the time, saw visitors, or stayed close to her radio. For the first time, in her loneliness, Claire felt some kind of kinship with Lucia. And for the first time she briefly sensed a certain closeness when they ate or went for short walks together.

One sunny day in early July, she met Elias. She always laughed about it later, for their meeting place was anything but romantic. It was in the vegetable dealer Tanius's store on the village square. Claire liked Tanius, who was always kindly disposed to her. Whenever she went to the shop he had a joke ready, bringing it out in his broken standard Arabic. As a rule Tanius, like all the villagers, spoke the local dialect.

That day she had just finished reading Stendhal's *Le Rouge et le Noir*, and oddly enough was more moved by Mathilde's fate than by the tragic, dramatic death of her lover Julien Sorel.

In the store, she put a few tiny cucumbers on the scales handed to her over the counter by Tanius. One little cucumber fell to the floor, and suddenly a slender hand was giving it back to her. Claire hadn't noticed the young man before, and now he was looking at her with the eyes of a child who had all the sorrows of the world within him.

"*Merci bien, monsieur.*"

"*Avec plaisir, mademoiselle,*" said the man. He wasn't much taller than Claire herself. He had left the shop again by the time she was through with her mother's order. Tanius smiled when she turned around, expecting to find the stranger still standing behind her. "That's Elias, a fine young man. Amazing that a prickly thistle like George Mushtak could bring such a flower into the world."

When she left the store, with a small errand boy carrying the heavy basket of vegetables for her, she saw Elias walking down the street by himself. He had just reached her house, and she wished he would stop so that she could catch up with him.

And sure enough, he did turn to look at her. Her heart fluttered with joy as if she had just won a prize. Claire was never to forget that moment and the sense of delight that she had never known before. She was rejoicing in a magical power that, at that moment, she had at her command.

"You called to me?" he asked in fluent French. She felt she had to tell him the truth.

"Yes, monsieur, I wanted to ask what an educated man like you is doing in this dusty village?" She sent Butros the errand boy on ahead with the basket of vegetables, telling him to leave it at the door, and gave the boy ten piastres. Butros beamed all over his face, for that was as much as he earned in a week working for the vegetable dealer.

Claire and Elias talked to each other for a long time outside the Sururs' vacation house. Elias knew many of the books she loved, and he could recite Baudelaire's *Les Fleurs du Mal* by heart. When she told him she went to the Besançon school, he smiled. "Besançon is a small town, but it gave mankind a great gift: Victor Hugo."

Claire felt hypnotized. She would have liked to put out her hand and touch Elias, because she could hardly believe all this was real. Here in the middle of a village at the end of the world, a young man had said lovelier things to her in the short time since they met than anyone else in her whole seventeen years of life. She felt a need to sit down and listen to this fascinating man, tell him all the things she kept locked in her heart. She had to make up her mind quickly.

"Will you come in for a coffee in an hour's time?" she asked. And Elias simply said, "*Avec plaisir.*"

In the brief hour before she came back she knew in her heart that she had fallen under this man's spell. She took off her engagement ring and put it away in a little box.

54. Purgatory and Paradise

It was something that Claire had never in her life expected: from visit to visit, she realized that she was counting the hours until Elias came to see her again. Her heart betrayed her, wrecking her intention of waiting for their meetings with calm composure. When he touched her with his gentle hands, she felt violent excitement in every vein. But his mere presence excited her too. He was witty, he could laugh on the slightest provocation, but he could also be very jealous, although that was just an expression of his feelings for her.

They read a great deal together, and talked of love and grief, fulfilment and abstinence, loyalty and longing. Claire felt as if she had only half existed until the day she met Elias, and now had found her missing other half. It did not escape her mother's notice.

"That young man is your own kind – forget about your father's primitive friend and send him back his engagement ring," Lucia advised her at breakfast two weeks later. Claire's jaw dropped with surprise, and her mother remarked dryly, "You'll have to chew, you know, food doesn't go down of its own accord. Elias is from a distinguished family," she continued. "The Mushtaks are real men, rich, generous, made of granite, not like that feeble chauffeur who'll let a dwarf knock him about in the ring." Lucia shook her head. "But Nagib always did keep such dreadful company."

For the first time in years, Claire felt a deep need to hold her mother close. She stood up, hugged her and kissed her. Lucia stroked her head. "You must be very generous in what you offer Elias. The Mushtaks are magnanimous in all they do, and I feel sure this latest sprig of theirs doesn't like people to be faint-hearted either."

She had known and respected George Mushtak for years, and the old man respected the Signora too, although he avoided any close friendship with her. Rumours of her attitude to men kept him away.

She insisted that her lovers must wash thoroughly and shave their pubic hair, and was said to treat them like horses, riding and even whipping them.

Once, when Elias didn't visit for several days, Claire felt quite sick with longing. She summoned Butros the vegetable dealer's errand boy, gave him fifty piastres, and told him to look for Elias and ask him to come and see her at once.

"He goes up to the mountains at dawn and doesn't come back until after dark," the observant boy immediately told her.

"What's he doing in the mountains?"

"I don't know, lady. My master says there was such a quarrel between father and son that everyone in the street could hear them."

"Well, I want you to wait for him first thing tomorrow and ask him to come and see me before sunrise. And don't say a word about it to anyone else. Swear!"

"I swear, lady. I hate tell-tales," said the lad, who wasn't even twelve yet, gratefully pocketing the money.

She couldn't sleep all night, and in those hours of darkness she realized that the purgatory they talked about in church consisted of waiting and longing.

When two roosters crowed by turns in the distance, she got up and went to the window. The night sky was growing pale in the east. Claire looked over at the village square and saw him hurrying along the street, a small and inconspicuous figure.

Her heart beat fast. She groped about for her dress in the dark, couldn't find it, and cursed her own untidiness. Suddenly she felt his hands. She was not alarmed, just surprised by the speed and silence with which he had made his way to her.

"I love you," he said, and he was weeping. He held her close, and she felt his head. It was like the head of a child seeking protection.

"I love you too, dear heart," she whispered, her voice breaking with emotion. Then she kissed his forehead and pressed him to her breast. After a while he calmed down and began telling her his story.

He told her everything, and Claire felt a great need to care for this boy who had stumbled from one misfortune to another. He told her frankly about his desire for women, and his bad luck when his father had caught him with Nasibe. He described his wretched situation when the Muslim peasants, running wild in the hunger riots of 1933, set fire to the Jesuit monastery in Damascus. He had come back to Mala like a whipped dog. But his father wouldn't speak to him, and derided him at every opportunity. As if not the mob but he, Elias, had attacked the Jesuits in Damascus, his father had accused him of failure. And whenever he asked to be sent to study with the Jesuits in Beirut, he had met with a refusal.

He told her about his bad luck working in the French provisions store. Early this summer, however, his father had suddenly turned friendly to him, had even forgiven him for all his faults in front of the assembled family and forbidden his brother Salman to hit him. He wanted him, Elias, to start breeding horses; it was a gold-mine, said old Mushtak. You could get fine Arab horses at a good price from the Bedouin, and then build up a large business.

He had been willing enough, he said, because he loved horses, but now he had found out that his father's sudden change of heart was the result of a secret deal with the village elder Habib Mobate. He, Elias, was to marry Mobate's daughter.

"A miserable bunch of tricksters, that family, but they know how to cheat peasants. And I'm supposed to waste my life among them," groaned Elias, telling her that Habib Mobate had made his money by secretly registering his name with the French as owner of all the land in the neighbourhood that had been common property under the Ottoman Empire. It consisted of fields, mountains, and valleys of incalculable value. The farmers never noticed, for Mobate let them go on using the land for grazing, but when anyone tried cultivating a plot of land, the village elder got the gendarmes to drive him off it, so it was two decades before the village discovered that entire hills and huge expanses of grazing belonged to the Mobate clan.

That morning in July 1935, Elias was badly frightened. He had to make up his mind: if he married Samira, he would be doing his father a great favour, as old Mushtak had told him in friendly tones. He didn't have to love Samira, added Mushtak. He just had to get her pregnant, thus making the Mushtak clan more powerful. With his great virility, he could make love to as many women as his heart desired. Elias knew he would be the richest of George Mushtak's sons, for Samira would inherit as much money as the cash and property of all the Mushtaks put together were worth.

Time was short. Two days ago, the servant Basil had given him away. He had seen him coming out of Claire's house by night, Elias told her. Mushtak had ranted and raged and struck him in the face. He had shouted that city girls were all whores of the French, and he'd have Elias shot if he went to see her again.

"So I've been roaming the mountains for days. I know my father. He might not kill me, but he'll certainly disinherit and disown me if I decide for you and not Samira," he said quietly.

Claire held him close. They were lying naked in her bed now, with Elias's hands moving as light as butterfly wings over the landscape of her body. While he told her the whole story she sensed that he had long ago chosen her, and she felt a wild longing for him.

It was already light in the room, but the curtains dimmed the daylight. He thrust into her, expecting a scream of horror, but she welcomed him, twining her arms and legs around his back.

55. Beirut, or Deliverance

Two days later Claire and Elias fled to Beirut, where they married in a small chapel. Their witnesses were Elias's sister Malake and her husband, who had been living in Beirut since their own elopement in 1931.

At first Elias and Claire hid away in a little hotel by the harbour. They didn't want to stay with Malake, because it was embarrassing to show their love and passionate longing in her house. They made love, wandered along the boulevard by the sea, and ate grilled fish in small restaurants. Then, as if it were a ritual, they lay in the warm sand on the beach and looked up at the sky for a long time.

"What did your fiancé do for a living?" asked Elias.

"He was a bodyguard," said Claire, a little surprised, because she had told him that on the first day they met.

"Thank God he wasn't a good bodyguard, or I wouldn't have had a chance," laughed Elias.

They hid in the harbour city for three years. At the time it sheltered thousands of refugees, soldiers of fortune, and adventurers. For many of them Beirut was the final stage on their journey, the last they would see of Arabia before they left for America.

Elias thanked his sister for all her help, but he was careful not to spend too much time in her house. He was afraid his father would soon get on his trail. Claire had enough money for the first few months. After they had left their first hiding place, the hotel, they lived in two modest rooms in the Daura quarter. And they still lay on the beach every evening and enjoyed the sight of the infinite starlit sky.

Only Lucia had been taken into the secret of their plans for flight, and she fell for none of the charming tricks employed by George Mushtak when, with his injured pride, he tried to find out where the couple were hiding. She put on a convincing performance as an indignant mother, and in private laughed at the old farmer.

 ❧

Claire found work as an interpreter for a shipping company. Elias took a job with a confectioner called Gandur, the father of one of his old school friends in the Jesuit monastery. At first Elias just worked as an assistant, but soon he was enjoying it so much that he learned the trade and its mysteries thoroughly. Before two years were up he was a master of the craft himself.

Gandur the confectioner was a clever businessman. He recognized his young employee's talents, but Elias was far too ambitious to agree to run the branch shop that Gandur was planning. He wanted to go back to Damascus.

When Claire had her first miscarriage, Lucia too urged them to return. After the second miscarriage she came to Beirut herself, and was horrified by her daughter's condition. She wasn't happy with the treatment Claire was getting at the hospital, and talked earnestly to Elias until he gave Lucia his word to return to Damascus as soon as possible, for the sake of his wife's health.

"But what will my father do?" he anxiously asked.

"Oh, we'll bring him around to it. His feelings are a little hurt, that's all," she said. "Apart from that he wouldn't hurt a fly." But there she was wrong.

56. Autumnal Atmosphere

They were lying on the beach surrounded by the warmth of the spring night. It already felt like summer. An easterly breeze carried the fragrance of flowers from the mountains out to sea. Elias held Claire's face in his hands and kissed her eyes. At that moment she felt that a second little heart had begun beating inside her.

"I think I'm pregnant again," she whispered. Elias could have embraced the whole sky. But an invisible hand clutched her heart. She was anxious. Her two miscarriages were still too close: the pain, the fear, and the empty feeling when it was all over. Elias felt for her, and was very affectionate.

Claire remembered the times after her miscarriages. Elias came to the hospital straight from the confectioner's after work every day, exhausted, and sometimes fell asleep on the floor beside her. He felt for her hand again and again in the night, whispering quiet words of love so that the others in the ten-bed ward wouldn't wake up.

Then he slipped out at five in the morning, unwashed and without any breakfast, and went to work. It was touching to watch him leaving the ward with such a youthful spring in his step. Every day Claire fell in love all over again with the small man who could quote any French poet by heart, and now he was working in a confectioner's shop and still kept cheerful.

The other women envied her Elias, who brought them all chocolates every evening. And they loved his wonderful laugh.

Claire's third pregnancy came at a most inconvenient time. They had planned to return to Damascus early in June. Suddenly she was afraid to go back, but Elias's cheerfulness dispelled all dismal thoughts and smoothed out the rugged mountains between Beirut and Damascus into gently rolling hills.

News came from Damascus that her father had been suffering from severe pneumonia since April. She cried a great deal, imagining him sitting in his prison cell and coughing. He had been in jail for three years, and didn't want his wife to visit him. Their only contact was through his cousins, who fetched money and clean clothes from Lucia for him, and told her how he was. He had a sunny cell, they said, and the prison governor played backgammon with him all day. With the money that Lucia sent him Nagib was able to pay an army of servants and bodyguards, who ensured his safety and made life much easier for him. But out of pride he wouldn't let his wife see him behind bars. Lucia was more than happy with that arrangement.

⁂

The move back to Damascus was the beginning of a lucky streak for Elias. He spent three hours explaining his plan to Claire's mother at her kitchen table, showed her his calculations, and asked her for a loan of a hundred thousand Syrian lira. Lucia said she wanted ten percent interest, but after tough negotiations she accepted five. Elias could offer only his handshake as a guarantee.

"But if I give you my hand it's worth more than an agreement with the National Bank of France," he said quietly, and very courteously.

"The Mushtaks keep their word," agreed Lucia, standing up. Ten minutes later she came back with a packet. "You can count them. There's a hundred and ten thousand there. The extra ten thousand are a present; even if you're just renting a place to live you should furnish it in style, because a confectioner lives by his reputation for prosperity. You'll bring me five hundred lira in interest on the first of every month."

Elias was touched, and also full of admiration for his mother-in-law, who was so trusting and generous to him, while at the same time surreptitiously raising the interest by half of one percent. He smiled, and she understood without words that her son-in-law had already worked it all out to the third decimal point. Lucia patted him on the shoulder and said, as he left, "No bank will accept your love for my daughter as surety for a mortgage, you know."

Elias did not reply. Only on their way home did he tell Claire what had been going on in her mother's kitchen while she was reading in the drawing room.

"And she let you have the hundred thousand?"

"A hundred and ten, and now I'm setting to work on my plan," replied Elias.

る

Autumn of the year 1938 was mild and long. Damascus is at its most beautiful in that season. It wasn't so hot now, and the swallows were filling the air with their farewell songs before they left for Africa. Damascus was colourful for the last time, as if the city were showing its full beauty once more before falling into profound, grey hibernation. Claire had known that atmosphere from her childhood. But this autumn, she believed, would remain in her memory as the best of her life. Her father was freed from prison after serving three years.

57. An Unholy Alliance

To his dying day, Musa Salibi didn't believe it had been his fault. And after a long period suffering from Parkinson's disease he died, an embittered old man, in a hostel for indigent Christian senior citizens.

When Rimon Rasmalo defeated him in the ring, he had spent two weeks trying to make his peace with his fiancée, but he thought he could tell that Claire already had someone else.

Then she went off to Mala, and he followed her in the general's car. On the way he went over everything, preparing for a reasonable conversation. But when he reached the village no one would talk to him, and Claire had changed entirely. She turned him away as soon as he arrived. You have to be patient with women, he told himself, and kept calm. Then she threw the little box containing the engagement ring out of the door. He was bewildered. She was acting outrageously, and someone in love never does that. To Musa, it was immediately clear that she was just a whore.

He found her mother as cold as ice too. When he tried getting her to explain herself, she said straight out that she had never liked him. He could always visit his friend in jail and complain to him, she added. Musa took his engagement ring and drove back to Damascus that very evening.

He had been tricked. Mother and daughter, both of them whores! And the malice in that old viper's voice when she told him Claire was in very good hands, so he had better look for a girl of his own class. Just whose hands was Claire in? The woman he had thought of as his future mother-in-law wouldn't say. She simply shut the door in his face.

For a long time he couldn't make out why they had treated him so shabbily, until it came to his ears six months later that Claire had eloped with the son of a rich farmer from Mala. Musa was seething with rage. Eloped – a likely story! The old procuress had fixed it all. He could forget a good deal, but not hypocrisy. Claire always used to say she found the primitive peasants in the village repulsive. Lies, all of it! Camouflage! He had just been used to inflame the desire of other, richer men who took special pleasure in robbing the poor of their women. Musa swore revenge, but until the day when a man came to the boxing club in the summer of 1938 and asked for him he didn't know how to go about it.

Elias had just bought an old olive warehouse in the Christian quarter, in Bab Tuma Street on the corner of Bakri Alley, and in the record time of three weeks he turned it into a modern confectioner's shop with a glass and marble façade. Many rich Christians lived nearby, and the nearest good confectioner's shop belonged to an Armenian, was tiny, and lay in Bab Sharki.

Elias was hoping to be reconciled with his father soon. Claire was in her third pregnancy, and this time he felt sure that, in the safe surroundings of her own city, she would bring a healthy baby into the world. The baby would soften up that old fossil George Mushtak. Nothing in the world touches a man's heart like a grandchild, he told himself.

The opening of his shop at the beginning of September augured well. People crowded in to try the new sweetmeats, and Elias sold his entire stock that day, down to the very last item. Every customer went away with a present: a china plate with a coloured print of the shop on it. This cheap plate, which cost only a couple of piastres, made the new confectioner famous in a day. It was the first advertising campaign in Damascus. Elias had followed the example of his master Gandur, who always brought the latest ideas home from Paris.

Claire's belly was rounding out, and she and Elias were glad that August had passed without any mishap, in spite of the heat. In her first pregnancy she had lost the child after two months, in the second one after three months.

One evening Nuri the flower seller came into the confectioner's shop. He was drunk as usual, but he seemed to have something he was bent on saying. He stood at the counter and waited for the last customers to leave.

"Guess who came asking after you! It's a small world," he said, laughing. "My old school friend Musa," he continued, holding on to the edge of the counter. His gaze strayed around uncertainly for a moment, as if he couldn't make up his mind what he was looking for. Then it fell on Elias, who wasn't really interested in his neighbour's babbling, but like everyone else had to put up with him.

"Musa who?" asked Elias out of politeness.

"Musa who? I know only one Musa – Musa Salibi."

Elias stopped what he was doing. He had been sorting out the day's takings; now his hand froze with the lira notes in it.

Nuri noticed nothing amiss. "I said to him, why are you asking me where he lives? Ask him yourself, I said. He's a nice guy, I'm sure he'll answer your questions. But he didn't want to. Where *do* you live, anyway? I didn't know what to tell him. He wanted to know what time you come here and what time you go home. 'He works from six to six,' I said. That's right, isn't it?"

"Yes, that's right," replied Elias. His throat was dry. He watched Nuri weave his unsteady way back to his flower shop. Almost mechanically, Elias cleared out the till and entered the day's accounts in an exercise book. He listed next day's tasks and orders on a piece of paper, to leave his memory free for more important things. It was a trick he had learned from the Jesuits. He locked the safe and put his keys in his pocket.

Suppose this boxer, whom he had never met but who, according to Claire, was a muscle-man almost two metres tall, humiliated him here in the middle of the Christian quarter? Suppose he came into the shop, picked a quarrel, and demolished the expensive furnishings? The three crystal chandeliers alone had cost a fortune. And his customers? What would his frightened customers think of the new confectioner?

He was still deep in thought when Ali, who ran errands for him, came out of the stock-room and said good night.

"Wait a moment," he cried, for the sight of big, strong Ali had given him an idea.

Ali was a young farmer whose small plot of land stopped producing anything but dust and thistles in the long drought. He had come to Damascus to look for work. Ali was a bachelor, and his arms were incredibly strong. That was why Elias had hired him. He had found him a small, cheap room near the shop, and kept a fatherly eye on the young man.

"I want you to help me," said Elias. "There's a man who bears me a grudge and wants to attack me, I don't know why. But he's two metres tall and a boxer. Could you take him on if the worst comes to the worst?" And he offered the young man a fine Bafra cigarette.

"I don't know how to box, sir, but I was always best in the village at cudgel-fighting. Give me a good stout stick for a cudgel and no one will touch you. A lot of men carry walking sticks these days. A good oak stick would be best," said the young man, his eyes shining.

"But what will we do if he comes into the shop?" asked Elias.

Ali had no answer to that.

"Right," said Elias, "from tomorrow you'll wear a clean white coat and a white cap, and stand out in front at the entrance to help me. You'll welcome the customers in and help the old folk. Then it will look as if you're there as a doorman. And if someone tries making trouble, you take him out quickly and quietly, and once you're well outside you can break all his bones."

"That's fine," said Ali, "but who's going to do my work in the stock-room?"

"Don't worry about that. From now on you're my bodyguard. I can hire someone else for the stock-room work until this cloud has passed over."

"But what after that? Do I get my old job back, or will I have to go home?" asked Ali uncertainly.

"If you do your work well you can stay with me for ever."

"Then I won't let a fly touch you," said Ali.

At six in the morning from then on, Ali was outside the building where Elias and Claire lived. It had a big wooden door and a handsome knocker, a woman's hand made of bronze. For now, Elias had rented three rooms on the second floor. The building was very close to the St. Louis Hospital. Ali accompanied his employer to the confectioner's shop in the morning and saw him safely home again in the evening.

He was reliable and didn't let his master out of his sight. He never grumbled, and he did his job at the shop door with as much charm as if he'd taken at least three courses in etiquette in the finishing school run by the Sisters of the Sacred Heart of Jesus. The customers thanked him for his help and kind attentions, and Elias began seriously wondering whether he might not employ a permanent doorman. Not Ali, but an attractive little boy, dressed like a hotel bellboy, to stand at the door for him. He wouldn't even have to pay a boy wages, for he had noticed the richer customers pressing a couple of piastres into Ali's hand now and then. Usually the tips in his pocket amounted to more than his day's wages by evening.

One evening, on the way home, it occurred to Elias to buy his helpful bodyguard a meal. He could sit with Ali as he ate, read the paper, and drink a coffee in peace before going home himself. The idea came to him suddenly, just as they were passing the entrance of the big Glass Palace restaurant, halfway between the confectioner's shop and his apartment. Elias stopped suddenly and took Ali's arm.

"Come on in here," he said. At that moment a shot rang out. It smashed the glass window and hit a waiter inside the restaurant in the shoulder. Passers by and guests screamed in terror. Elias sprang nimbly through the open doorway into the restaurant and pulled Ali in after him, for the shot had been fired from the building opposite.

A second shot hit a woman walking by in the leg. She collapsed. Chaos ensued. A young police officer raced out of the restaurant with his pistol at the ready. He located the marksman.

"He's in the Hotel Baladi," he called. Three men followed him, while passers by tended the injured woman and the waiter. There was a large police station quite close, so the hotel was quickly surrounded.

The would-be assassin was led out of the building, handcuffed and bleeding from the head. Several people recognized him. Word went from mouth to mouth. "Musa Salibi, that's Musa Salibi."

"You saved my life," Ali told his master.

"The hand of God protected us both. And now let's have something to eat," added Elias, propelling his pale employee into the restaurant. "You can sleep late tomorrow and take the whole day off. I'll give Hassan notice and you can go back to the old job," he told him.

"Why?" asked the naïve Ali.

"Because they've caught the man who was after me," replied Elias.

When Claire heard what had happened she immediately felt a stabbing pain in her belly. Elias made her some herb tea, but the pains became unbearable during the night. Elias ran out in his pyjamas, woke a cab driver and came back with him to the door of the building, where his pregnant wife was standing with a woman neighbour now supporting her. The hospital was only a few doors away, but Elias didn't want Claire to strain herself.

The doctors did their best, but they soon discovered that at best they would save the mother, for the baby was already dead, and they induced a stillbirth.

Elias sat on the steps of the hospital for a long time in his pyjamas, weeping, until the cabby politely asked if he was to wait any longer. Elias sent him away, asking him to come to the confectioner's shop next day, when he would be paid his fare. The cabby knew the confectioner. He pressed his hand. "My wife's lost six children too, only God knows why," he said, much moved, and trotted off to his cab.

Three days later a CID officer came to the confectioner's shop and asked Elias to accompany him to the police station. A young French officer received him there and civilly questioned him. The officer was enchanted by the confectioner's command of his own language, and kept saying that Elias spoke better French than many a Frenchman born.

Asked about the incident, and whether he would give evidence as a witness, Elias told the officer what he had heard from the flower seller, and said that after that he had always gone out with his employee to escort him.

"That bears out exactly what the criminal said," the officer told him. "He was planning to abduct you, monsieur, torture you, and then kill you, but he saw that he wouldn't easily be able to outwit and overcome your companion. So he decided to shoot you, and he wounded two other people instead."

"And he has brought an innocent child to its death," added Elias bitterly.

"Can you tell me why he did it?" asked the officer, who could make nothing of Elias's remark about the dead child.

"I think it was jealousy because his former fiancée left him, good for nothing as he was. She's my wife now," replied Elias, with a certain pride.

"Yes, monsieur, but there's something else too. He said a man with a heavy accent gave him the job to do, provided his German rifle, and paid him five gold lira. He was to have had another twenty gold lira after your murder. Can you think who that man might be? And above all, why anyone would want to murder a decent, able confectioner like yourself? But the assassin may be lying, and there could be something else behind it. We haven't been able to find out by our usual methods of questioning. Would you like to ask him yourself?"

"Yes," said Elias. His throat felt dry.

When the policeman brought in Musa Salibi, Elias was horrified. The "methods" of the French police had made a formerly tall, proud man into a broken, subservient creature. The marks of torture were obvious.

"Sir, I don't know who the man was," stammered the prisoner, "but I've said it a hundred times: I only met him twice, and after that I never saw him again. He was tall and he wore sunglasses. Once they slipped a little, and I saw that he had blue eyes like the French, maybe he was a Frenchman … that's all I know. He, he … but I said it all in my statement. The devil possessed me, and now I'm left paying for it."

"How did the man speak?" asked Elias.

"He spoke … well, it was just the way he spoke, but not like a Damascene. He spoke with an accent like … like the mountain folk. Like the people of Mala."

Musa Salibi fell silent. He was shaking all over.

"Could it be someone from your village?" the officer asked Elias. "Do you know anyone who wanted to kill you for some reason?"

"No," he said, looking at the miserable specimen of humanity before him, a man who had once been such a heart-throb. He rose to his feet. "Do you need me any longer?" he asked the officer.

"No, monsieur, thank you very much," the man replied, and he accompanied Elias to the door while the two police officers took Musa back to his cell.

"The confectioner was lying," said the young Frenchman later to the man who had been taking down the statement. "Did you see him twitch briefly when the gunman said the man who commissioned him to do the job spoke with the accent of his native village?"

The other policeman nodded. "What shall I add?

"Nothing. Sounds like a blood feud, some kind of clan vengeance, and that's none of our business. We have our criminal, and he'll get the maximum sentence."

A week later Elias sent a Jesuit priest who was a friend of his to Mala, entrusting to him the delicate task of finding his father and letting him know, straight out, that Elias had survived the murder attempt, and moreover had proof that his brother Salman had given the criminal Musa Salibi the gun and charged him with his father's mission. He, Elias, wanted an apology and his father's word that he would never plot against his son's life again; otherwise he would go to the CID and give them his evidence against Salman. Under the law of the French occupying forces, the penalty for incitement to murder was death and expropriation of all the guilty man's property. If anything were to happen to Elias, the message said, someone he trusted would take the envelope containing his evidence to the CID.

Father François Saleri was a brave man. He had stayed on in Damascus after the fire in the monastery, and was now teaching mathematics in the schools of the elite Christian classes. He loved Elias like a brother, and was horrified when he heard the story.

He left at once in the luxurious cab provided by his friend, and he did in fact come back to Damascus next day with an apology from Elias's brother and his father's word, sworn with his hand on the Bible.

"I couldn't get any expression of remorse out of old Mushtak, but your brother shed tears. He was ashamed, and that induced your father to give his word. I knew about his fear of God, and I didn't demand a signature, just for him to swear with his hand on the Bible. A powerful man like George Mushtak cares for no signatures, but he does care for the word of God. You can rely on what your friend François says and live in peace," said the priest, taking his leave.

It was midnight when Elias, pale-faced, came back to Claire. She was still in bed. He dropped on the sofa beside her and began to sob pitifully.

"I'll get the better of them all," he said at last. Claire didn't understand, but later she always said that Elias had lost his laughter and all his cheerful bearing that night.

"Why," she wondered aloud, "why do our enemies shape us more than our friends?"

But Elias had fallen asleep, and she couldn't answer her own question.

58. The Lightness of Love

Whenever Claire thought about love she saw in her mind's eye not just that moment in Mala when she first met Elias, but also the radiant face of her former teacher Barbara.

Her love for Elias had been a blazing fire in which her heart flared up, an affection that nothing could hold back. On the night when Elias determined to get the better of his father, all that seemed to be over. But love is a wild cat with nine lives. So that night her desire for

Elias turned to endless concern for his health and constant fear for his life. This new kind of love bound Claire to him more closely than ever. She knew he was his father's victim, but ultimately his battle against his father was a battle for their love.

It was all so different with her teacher Barbara and Fadlo, Barbara's husband. They showed her the essence of a wonderfully light-hearted kind of love, yet one that seemed perfectly natural, a Paradise on earth. Claire had liked her teacher from the day she met her. That was in the eighth grade, when the girls were wondering about the replacement for Sister Helena, who had had an unlucky fall and must now spend months in plaster. No one missed her. Even the headmistress of the Besançon School was secretly grateful to the divine or human hand that had allowed the accident to happen. Although Sister Helena was sixty-eight she wouldn't retire. She was a good mathematician, but unable to communicate what she knew. All the girls she taught had bad marks in her subject. That changed when Barbara came.

Josephine the jeweller's daughter had been joking the day before that she couldn't imagine a maths mistress without a moustache. The others felt sure their new teacher would walk into the classroom in a man's suit, with thick glasses and a book of logarithms in her hand. Madeleine, Claire's best friend, laughed. "And her name is Math al Gebra, and she has three children, Cone, Cube, and Pyramid. Pyramid's the daughter." The girls giggled.

Then she arrived. Barbara was willowy as a schoolgirl herself, but that was just outward show, for she could fight like a lioness for her convictions. She came into the classroom with a spring in her step, and when the girls stood to attention and called out "Good morning" in chorus, the way they used to with Sister Helena, she laughed. "I don't want you standing up when I come into the room. You'll just frighten me," she said, smiling. "It's more important for your brains to wake up, and I don't want you making any statements you can't prove."

After that she told them about herself, and why she loved mathematics, and within half an hour the young woman with short black hair, wearing a pale pullover and a skirt the colour of autumn leaves, had won the girls' hearts. Barbara told them something odd and interesting about the history of mathematics in every lesson: not just what the inconspicuous, apparently worthless zero had brought to it, and what that zero had changed, but also – and this remained imprinted on Claire's mind for ever – stories of how mathematics could put even kings to shame. As in the tale of the inventor of the game of chess, whose king asked what he wanted as a reward, offering the man his own weight in gold. "No, your Majesty," he said. "I will be happy with one grain of wheat in the first square on the chessboard, two on the second, four on the third, sixteen on the fourth square, and so on."

The king and his court laughed at the simple-minded inventor of the game, who asked for nothing but a few grains of wheat. The court mathematician was the first to stop laughing, for after only a few squares the number of grains ran to twenty decimal points, and he knew that the whole kingdom could never provide as much wheat as the inventor had asked.

Barbara mingled the curious and the practical in a magical way that drew the girls into the world of mathematics. The school administration was amazed by their progress after six months with her, and even more by the atmosphere in the class. Barbara was the only teacher who sometimes asked girls home to her house for a cup of tea.

Claire would never forget the first time she went there. Her heart was beating fast as she entered the little house in Bab Tuma, which had a narrow façade, but was on several floors.

On this first visit, Claire was fascinated by Barbara and her husband. They had been married for twenty years, yet they were always kissing as they passed each other in a happy, heartfelt way, as if they had only just fallen in love. She had never before seen such affection between a man and a woman. Lucia and Nagib never kissed, they never held hands, and if for once Nagib caressed his wife Lucia would immediately and suspiciously ask, "I suppose you want me to do something. Why not say it straight out?" Sometimes Claire felt very angry with her mother for her coldness, but Lucia was quite often right, and Nagib came out with the true reason for his show of affection. The tender moments between Barbara and Fadlo, on the other hand, had no ulterior motives.

Claire tried to visit her favourite teacher as often as she could, but Lucia would allow it only once a month. Barbara herself liked to see the attentive, friendly girl. As she and her husband had never had children, she longed for a young creature to whom she could give something special, and she had found just the right girl in her delicately built pupil with the beautiful face. With her, Claire found the warmth she missed at home. Her father Nagib was born to be a bachelor. He did keep trying to be kind and affectionate to her, but most of the time he lived in his own world. Only later, in old age, did he develop a strong and truly loving relationship with his daughter.

Claire's friendship with Barbara had been an ardent one, up to the day before the end of the school year of 1935, the beginning of the vacation when Claire met Elias and fell hopelessly in love with him. After a quarrel between the new headmistress of the school and the maths teacher, Barbara lost her job. She moved north and found another post in an American private school. When she said goodbye to the weeping girls, she told them a great many things that, hearing her through the mists of their grief, they failed to understand and had soon forgotten entirely.

The new headmistress was spiteful, and bent on ensuring that she had no competition in the running of the school. Madeleine pitied Jesus for having to put up with this particular nun in his harem. At the time all nuns wore a plain wedding ring on the ring finger of their right hands, a sign of their virginity and chastity, and the ardour of their relationship with the Son of God, for they were the promised brides of Christ. But in Damascus there was always a touch of the harem about the nuns' rings, making Jesus appear in a rather dubious light.

59. Mirages and Oases

School friendships are usually like mirages and melt away at the end of your schooldays. If they survive the seventh grade, however, they are oases for ever.

Claire was surprised to find how many calls the girls from her old class seemed to have on their time these days, so many that they could hardly stop to be glad of their friend's return from Beirut. Many of them hadn't even realized that she had gone.

In my three years away, Damascus has changed, she thought on her first walk after that last miscarriage. There were guards stationed everywhere these days – tall Africans in French army uniforms much too small for them. And the streets that had seemed so lively and familiar when she was a child were strange now that she had lost touch with the girls who were once at school with her.

But a few days after her return she met Madeleine. While they were in Beirut Claire's mother had told her that her friend was married to the stonemason Rimon Rasmalo now, and they had bought a huge house. "An enormous apartment building with two entrances on different streets," said Lucia. She had gone to congratulate Madeleine on the birth of her first and second children, but stayed away after that. "The place is chaotic, and it stinks," she said with revulsion.

"Is Rimon still boxing?" asked Claire.

Her mother laughed. "No, you know what Madeleine's like. Rimon is a successful building contractor, And the last I heard of it they had another little girl."

The first moments of their reunion were disappointing. Madeleine seemed calm as ever, almost stoical. Her mother, her mother-in-law, and her two older unmarried sisters-in-law looked after her three little girls. She herself wasn't especially interested in what went on in the house, where there were constant comings and goings.

"He wants a son so much, but I only have daughters. I'm pregnant again, and I know it will be another girl," she said, almost with indifference.

Madeleine didn't even absorb the information that Claire had suffered three miscarriages. She was in love with her new radio set, she listened to music all the time, whistled the tunes, chain-smoked, and otherwise hardly seemed to notice anything.

She liked her life with Rimon, but she could just as easily imagine life without him. "What matters is having my music every day," she said, and fell silent as the voice on the radio announced Mozart's

Magic Flute. Claire didn't understand a word of what the announcer was saying, but Madeleine was so captivated by the opera that when the music started it was obvious that her guest was a nuisance and in the way. Claire said goodbye and left.

It was more by accident than on purpose that she and Elias moved into Saitun Alley six months later, early in 1939. You could see into the Rasmalo house from the stairs leading up to the second floor. Only a low building, an aniseed warehouse, separated the two houses.

From then on their old friendship slowly revived – but now it was more mature and easy-going. Madeleine had always been passionately fond of music, and was the only person in Claire's immediate circle of friends to own a modern gramophone. Claire enjoyed visiting her, but she was even happier to invite Madeleine to see her, because the Rasmalo house really was a chaotic place, full of children, grandmothers, and old maids. Her friend lived among them all like their queen. She delegated the jobs to be done early in the morning, and then went shopping. Besides music, shopping was her favourite occupation.

Claire's new home was a jewel. There was plenty of room for a childless young couple, and no one else lived in it, which was unusual for that part of the city, where almost every building accommodated several generations of the same family, or at least a few neighbours. Most people lived crammed together at close quarters. But Elias had managed to buy the whole house at a good price through his connections with diplomatic circles. To do so, he increased his debt to his mother-in-law to two hundred thousand lira in all, staking everything on his success in his business, and indeed it didn't let him down. He supplied sweetmeats to the richest Christians in the city, and soon it was considered good form in the Christian quarter to say that you served your guests cakes, cookies, and other sweetmeats from Elias Mushtak. Elias charged twice as much as other confectioners, but he never stinted on the quantity and quality of his ingredients.

Before three years were up he was even supplying the presidential palace. As ever, he was generous and made the palace staff many small presents. He once told Claire, later, how he had managed to remain confectioner to the palace despite the constant changes of government. They needed a great deal of confectionery there, and his profits were unusually high, because civil servants weren't bothered about the price, and the vain dictators were happy to hear their diplomatic guests enthuse over these Syrian specialities.

"Presidents come and presidents go, but not the head of the palace household, or the head of reception in the palace, or the palace cook either. And I have them all in the hollow of my hand," explained Elias, laughing. Then he added quietly, "But you mustn't tell anyone I said so, even under torture."

Three years after he last asked Lucia for credit, and in the presence of his wife, Elias Mushtak put two hundred thousand lira down on her drawing room table, with a small extra stack of banknotes. "Your money back, with my thanks," he said ceremoniously, "and this is the last of the interest, for the month of May."

"A true Mushtak," said Lucia, feeling sure that her daughter had done well in marrying this capable man. She pressed his hand warmly.

But that wasn't until June 1941, and a few things happened before then, that must be briefly mentioned here.

Claire's miscarriages meant that she had to spend weeks in hospital. It was boring there, so she looked forward to Madeleine's daily visits. Madeleine came laden with magazines and candy, and spent half the day with her. Claire found that she enjoyed her friend's sense of humour just as she used to.

"Rimon weeps every night because he wants a boy. Men are such children, they always want boys because they don't know how to play with girls," Madeleine told her.

"It doesn't matter to my husband which we have, so long as I hang on to the baby for nine months, and I've never yet managed that."

"Oh, it will be all right, and the way I see it you'll have another twelve healthy, beautiful children. I'm afraid all mine take after Rimon. But never mind, I'm sure there are enough short-sighted men around to marry my daughters," said Madeleine, laughing.

Claire was heavily pregnant again, and Elias prayed for her every night. Then, at last, Farid was born. He was healthy, and only a few days after his birth he looked like a little copy of Claire's father, which did not particularly please Elias Mushtak.

And it was Nagib who urged Lucia to sell the expensive villa in Arnus Avenue and move into the old Christian quarter, so that they could live close to their only daughter. Lucia gave way to him, and with Elias's help they found a handsome house in quiet Misq Alley. Nagib was delighted; only a walk of five minutes now separated him from his daughter, or rather from his grandson Farid. But to her dying day Lucia lamented her loss of status in moving to what she thought a far too modest part of town.

60. Water In A Sieve

"Anyone who trusts men," said Madeleine, and a painful tremor crossed her face, "would trust a sieve to hold water." She smiled, but her eyes were bright with the tears she was holding back.

Claire sat quietly on the sofa in Madeleine's sitting room, lost in her own thoughts. It had come so suddenly. She felt paralysed. Hadn't all the pain of her three miscarriages been enough? At last, six months after her baby's birth, she had begun to enjoy some happiness again. She liked being called Um Farid, Farid's mother, as the custom was in Damascus. The personal names of fathers and mothers were lost as soon as they had their first child. They became Abu and Um, Father of or Mother of, with the name of the firstborn child was added. Elias didn't like it. He preferred to be known as Monsieur Elias, as the French called him, but Arabs did not adopt the European style of address. They went on calling him Abu Farid. Elias kept putting them right for a year and then gave up.

Her father's joy made Claire happy too. He visited her daily, and would look after his grandson for as long as she liked. After a while, the old man even learned to change the baby's nappy, feed him and wash him, and then she could get out of the house – often with Madeleine – to enjoy a few hours of the vibrant life of the city. She had thought for a long time, wondering whether she wanted to have more children, and decided that she did. Farid had opened the gate, said Elias, and ten more would follow. And then, suddenly, came the discovery that her husband had been cheating on her, and she was on her own.

"My love," her mother Lucia had said, "men need that to cool their blood, or else their seed rises to the brain and then they fight wars." She lit herself a Hanum, a brand of cigarette popular with women.

For the first time in her life, Claire had shouted at Lucia. She tried to say that life wasn't lived solely between your legs, and love was something to be cherished and cared for. Lucia remained calm. She stroked her daughter's face. "Eternal love, my child," she replied, "is found only in novels and poems, and the more I think about it the more I believe that those who write about such things are the true cheats, not we real men and women with all our weaknesses. That's life, the rest is just paper. Elias is the best man in Damascus, and if you're clever about it you'll get him back. You must open your arms yet wider, make even more of your looks, fix up his home to be even more attractive and inviting, and then he'll come back to you."

For the first time Claire felt curiously ill at ease in her parental home. She could hardly draw breath there, she went out, and only in the street could she breathe deeply again. She didn't reply when her mother called to her. Lucia hadn't understood at all. My mother doesn't even have the courage to look into the depths of my wound, she thought on the way home. She was in despair. Her father, sitting by Farid's cradle in the nursery, looked up and saw her sorrow.

"Can I help you?" he asked quietly.

Claire shook her head. "I have a headache," she lied. Her head had never been so clear or so full of grief.

Nagib went home, and as she prepared the evening meal despair vied with rage in her mind. She wandered around her house. There was no one she could lean on, not her mother, not her father either.

Elias was betraying her with Alexandra, one of the silliest women in the world. She and Claire had been at school together, but in those ten years Claire had spoken to her at the most on three occasions, and even that had been a waste of time. She had heard from Madeleine that the woman was married to a member of parliament twenty-five years her senior. After the wedding Alexandra had insisted on being called Madame Makram Bey, even by her relations and her women friends. Her husband was the latest scion of a rich family of large landowners, and hoped to have a son to carry the name of Makram on into the future. Even if she hadn't been having an affair with Elias, Madeleine couldn't stand the woman.

"Alexandra, of all people!"

She could well imagine how Alexandra had made a conquest of Elias. That woman's backside got her everything she wanted. Even the proud Elias.

Madeleine suggested a trip to the hammam together. Claire hadn't been to a public bathhouse since her wedding. She had her own beautiful bathroom in Damascus, a wonderful bathroom with coloured tiles, showers, and a huge white marble wash-basin. Next Wednesday morning she went along to the hammam with her friend. Silent, lost in thought, she clung to Madeleine's arm.

Her father was happy to look after Farid by himself for a few hours. He didn't even look at her as she left, just turned his transfigured gaze on the sleeping baby.

They were going to the Hammam al Bakri in Bab Tuma, not far from Elias's confectionery shop.

"I once trusted a man myself, but he went away to America, taking my heart and a rich woman with him and leaving me alone with our engagement ring," Madeleine suddenly said quietly, as if to open her own heart just a little.

"You were engaged before Rimon? I never knew," said Claire, amazed.

"I had to keep it secret. I took the engagement ring off every morning and put it on again every evening, because that was when my lover came to see us. My mother liked him. I think she was in love with him herself. He was a charming, witty man," added Madeleine, but then waved the subject away.

"Why did he go off with the other woman?"

"Because she promised him her whole fortune and I had nothing to offer. My father said it was un-Christian to give women a dowry to induce men to come along and marry them. You love either the woman or her money, he thought. But he sometimes went too far. He played a practical joke on Said – that was my fiancé's name – and told him he'd lost everything. I realized that Said wasn't so sure what he wanted then, and asked my father to stop talking such nonsense. After all, he'd made pots of money in the leather trade, but I could see that the love was leaking out of Said's heart now, and however much I filled it up the tank up with more, it was soon empty again.

"Then along came this young widow with all the money she'd inherited, and he went off to America with her, and not a word to me. I lied to everyone, saying it had all been very sudden. But I'd known for months that he was moving away from me. Love is like childhood. When it's gone, it's gone for ever. My father was triumphant, delighted to think he'd seen through the man from the first, he'd known it was money he was after and not love. But I was crushed. Two weeks later I fell sick and I was away from school for six months, do you remember?"

"We thought you had pneumonia, maybe TB as well," Claire recollected.

Madeleine laughed. "That was the official explanation, so that no one in school would know. I tried to take my own life twice, but I was too much of a coward to do it properly. My mother took me to Beirut, and we spent three months with an uncle there. I feel today as if he wasn't an uncle at all, he was a magician who knew all about love and the soul. He spoke to me so understandingly, we talked night after night, and I almost fell in love with *him*, but I stopped myself just in time. He was happily married and much older than me. He wasn't gentle with me, he was honest, he could even be harsh. And a time came when I realized I ought to be glad to be rid of my fiancé at an early stage. He might not have left me until later.

"Since then I've lived sensibly with Rimon, who thinks himself lucky to have married a daughter of the distinguished leather exporter Antoine Ashi. He wants children, I give him children, and the rest of the time he leaves me alone."

At this moment they reached the hammam. Madeleine was a frequent visitor, and knew not only the woman who owned it, the strong masseuse, the old lady who soaped customers and all the assistants, but many of the women who were bathing there too. They came to meet her now with open arms. And Claire was amazed to see how

Madeleine changed as soon as she undressed. She shed her reserve along with her clothes, played around and joked with the women. Her laughter broke out in waves, echoing back from the walls and infecting other women sitting further off.

All of a sudden Claire was among strange women who smiled at her and immediately included her in their conversation, as if she had always been one of them. And soon she too was giving her opinion of some husband or other who was being picked to pieces in his absence. After an hour she was pleasantly tired, and went to sleep on the warm floor. When she woke up she was surprised to find how peaceful she felt. The room was almost empty, the women she had been with had moved on into the next room, where it was warmer. She lay where she was, looking up at the dome with the little stained glass windows that muted the sunlight. She felt safer than she had been for a long time. The world was far away, Elias and Alexandra were far away. Only Farid looked at her with his beautiful eyes that were so strangely like her father's.

If it were possible to feel as secure as she did here, and live with no one but her son, life would be all right, she thought after a while, slowly sitting up. She heard Madeleine laugh again. The assistant – a dark-skinned woman with a friendly face and terribly bad teeth, mere stumps – appeared suddenly, as if she had been waiting for Claire to wake. She handed her dry, snow-white towels, and took away the wet and sweaty ones. Slowly, Claire went into the next room.

She talked for hours with Sarifa and Baraka, two women of wide experience. Sarifa was married for the second time, and very happy with her new husband, the way you can only be in movies. She was the more outspoken of the two, and advised Claire to leave her husband and throw everything into the lap of fate.

Baraka was almost sixty, and was quieter but also more inscrutable. The other women joked about her, calling her Mashnakt Rigal, "a gallows for husbands". Her fourth husband had died a year ago of some strange stomach disease, and his family had accused Baraka of poisoning him. Baraka recommended her to fight back against her rival Alexandra; she mustn't let the other woman off the hook for a moment.

Claire laughed a great deal, and she felt lighter at heart with Madeleine and the other women, as if she had washed off not only her dirt but her grief as well. She liked the company of Sarifa and Baraka, but her love for Elias was something different, so she couldn't take their advice. But she did take something home with her that afternoon: she knew she wasn't alone any more. Both women understood her, and Sarifa made it clear, as they said goodbye, that she would be happy to see Claire in the baths again next Wednesday. And Claire went there with Madeleine not only the following week but almost every Wednesday after that for years.

After the hammam Claire went home feeling relaxed, stepping lightly. But as soon as she was back, and had picked Farid up and said goodbye to her father, her dismal thoughts returned. All the lightness of heart she had felt with the women was gone.

How could Elias do this to her? Why did it have to happen to her? Wasn't what she'd been through with three miscarriages enough? And why did he choose that cackling goose Alexandra who'd already been wiggling her bottom about like a whore at the age of thirteen, and always used to say she knew where a man's brains were: in his balls, semen was his brain-juice and that was why it looked so milky?

How could Elias find happiness between the legs of a stranger, a stupid woman like that? Hadn't she satisfied him? What all his protestations of faithfulness? Perhaps part of the trouble was those long periods of abstinence after her miscarriages. Elias needed sex every day; he had joked about it often enough, hinting at his appetite. She was always tired in the evenings now, after the boy's birth, because she had to get up to feed him three or four times in the night. Elias sat alone, drinking his arrack in silence. Had that driven him into that woman Alexandra's arms? Her head was buzzing with questions all afternoon. She couldn't answer any of them.

She washed and made her face up, but when Elias came home she looked at him with grief in her eyes. He didn't even try to lie to her when she asked, "Is it true about Alexandra?"

"Yes," he said. "I have a relationship with Madame Makram Bey."

In spite of his embarrassment, Elias felt relieved. He had wanted to tell Claire again and again over these last few months. But her silence had left him confused. It was a deep lake threatening to drown him bit by bit. Three times he had brought out Alexandra's name, but Claire had stifled any other words by showing her undisguised contempt for the woman.

His silence had been a lie. How often had he lied? He thought back, remembering how he had sometimes felt he was standing outside himself, as if he were two men. One Elias was talking just to please people, the other Elias said nothing, but registered the lies. Had it happened once or a hundred times? How often had he agreed with Claire that Arab women needed freedom and equal rights? He had noticed that she liked to hear him say so. She had confused love with the attitudes he adopted.

Now he felt relief. "It's not the way you think, though," he said. Claire had promised herself all afternoon to keep calm, but when he said that and put out a hand to placate her she struck it away and wept. "You've deceived me, Elias. I never loved anyone in my life as I've loved you, and now you pay me back by deceiving me. Oh, Elias," she cried, almost inaudibly, as if to say: help me, please, I'm dying. But it was a long time before she could get another word out.

"Elias," she whispered at last, weeping as if for the death of someone she had loved dearly. He sat beside her, lost in thought, and dared not try to touch her again. And for a moment she hoped he would explain that it was all a mistake and put his arm around her shoulders, and then she wouldn't shake it off. She felt he was about to do just that, but then he merely stood up and went to the window, and she knew that he belonged to Alexandra now.

She was intimidated, and said no more. It was more than ten years before she recovered from the shock.

61. Pangs of Conscience

No one was buying the idea that Elias had been very devout since he left the Jesuit school. Many regarded him as a hypocrite. He was on the committees of all the Catholic associations of the city of Damascus and the village of Mala, he dutifully went to church on Sunday, and then he slept around for the rest of the week.

He thought his first affair during his marriage stupid at both the beginning and the end of it, but Alexandra – or Madame Makram Bey, as she liked to be called – was hot as a wasp in full sunlight and smelled of unsatisfied lust for many metres around her. And since he could hardly make love to Claire at all at the time, he fell for the temptation.

It was at a party given by her husband for the deputies who had elected him their parliamentary president. Elias and three of his employees, clad in snow-white coats and caps, were to serve the delicious sweetmeats. Suddenly Alexandra came delicately tripping up to him and said it was she who had persuaded her husband to choose Elias's shop to supply them. And that same evening, as the new parliamentary president was smoking his Cuban cigars, drinking French champagne and talking to the deputies, Alexandra was enjoying her first love-play with Elias in a small bedroom on the third floor of the big house.

Claire refused to believe that he suffered every time he satisfied himself with a woman, but he did. Quite often, when he came away from one of them, he looked for the nearest church, knelt down before Christ, and asked for forgiveness. It was like that with Alexandra. The morning after their night of pleasure he was tormented by pangs of conscience, and begged the supreme judge of all for justice and mercy. For after all he, the creator of all the worlds, had given Elias his prick and his eternal lust for women. So he must surely have a heart open to the sins of his suffering servant.

But with Alexandra, and only with her, Elias felt he was very close to power, and he wanted to prove himself to his father through power and importance. Elias knew that Makram Bey was a slave to his wife and would do anything she wanted, and now Alexandra herself had fallen for Elias in a big way.

By devious means, he let his father know directly after the party that he was friendly with the parliamentary president. Soon after that Salman and his wife had a chance to see the truth of it for themselves when they looked in at the confectioner's shop. Elias had them given a coffee, and while they were drinking it a large limousine drove up, the parliamentary president's wife stepped out, came into the shop, greeted the confectioner himself warmly, and told him her husband would like Elias to visit him that evening for a game of chess. Then she took the elegantly packaged sweetmeats that Elias had prepared for her, and left. The car had been blocking the street outside all this time, but no one waiting behind it dared to hoot or shout angrily, as drivers usually did in Damascus. It had no licence plate, and that was something not many people could afford.

Salman and Hanan were impressed, and when they went back to Mala that evening they told old Mushtak that Salman's little brother did indeed go in and out of Makram Bey's house. After that, George Mushtak was sick with a strange fever for a week. No one knew that Elias had staged the whole scene and asked Alexandra to come to the shop for that very purpose.

His desire for power was one compelling reason why he could tolerate Alexandra at all. Sometimes Elias took his penis in his hand and spoke to it. "My friend, you have more influence than certain powerful farmers."

They parted not, as Alexandra said, because her husband left parliament to devote himself entirely to his large estate and his pure-bred horses, but because she insensitively told Elias what her spouse had said about him.

Makram Bey's private detective always kept him informed about his wife's affairs. He knew all her lovers by name, and even where and how often they met his wife. Why he wanted to know remained his secret. He showed her respect in public, and actually dedicated his reference book on Arab horses to "my loyal wife Alexandra".

It was only in his cups that he called her names. Alexandra had told Elias all about it one day, with a detailed account of how, on this particular occasion, he had sent all the servants home and then laid five pieces of paper out on the drawing room table in front of her. Men's names were written on them. "These are your lovers," her inebriated husband had told her, in a perfectly clear voice. "The photographer's a viper, the hairdresser's an ape, the interior minister is a chameleon and the swimming-pool attendant is a crocodile." Then, she said, he had paused, picked up the piece of paper bearing Elias's name, and fell into a fit of laughter that left her utterly bewildered. "And as for this one," he went on, "he's a donkey from Mala. I ride Arab horses, and a donkey rides my wife." And he had actually whinnied, and then left her standing there while he went to his bedroom. When she followed him he was already snoring. Next morning he was as kind and subservient to her as ever.

Elias was seething with anger, but he kept calm. He didn't understand why such a despicable old man would call him a donkey. But then Alexandra told Elias she'd expect him next Thursday, when her husband would be away spending the night on his estate. "The old fool is so crazy about horses he can't wait for a couple of pedigree mares to foal," she explained, laughing heartily, "and I want to ride my donkey."

Elias felt deeply wounded and humiliated. He told her he didn't want to see her any more, and asked her to leave his shop at once. Alexandra fell silent, and her smile slipped sideways on her face, like a mask. "Lousy peasant," Elias heard her saying angrily as she went out.

After that he never touched another Damascene woman. Instead, he made love to women in Mala, who were grateful for his presents and his money. Not that Elias paid them much, but it was important to him to know that he was buying their love, because he wanted to make the nature of the deal perfectly clear. He was the master, he was helping himself to lonely women whose menfolk had emigrated to the Gulf states in the late forties or early fifties, or were away driving long-distance trucks between Damascus and Kuwait or Riyadh.

He had more than ten mistresses in the village, and went to see them in secret whenever he wanted. And just as he bought olive oil, honey, wine, cracked wheat, raisins, almonds, and sheep's cheese for his household only from Mala, despising all the products on sale in the city, he did the same with women. It was rumoured in the village that many of the emigrants' children were really his sons and daughters, but rumour flourished in the imagination of the villagers.

However, no one in Mala knew that Elias Mushtak hated the women he made love to, because after the act, sober again, he suffered from the pangs of his guilty conscience. He damned the women who had such power over him, and would often say, even before he had done his trousers up again, "You're costing me money now and the torments of Hell later."

62. Practice

Farid was six when he came to Claire's bedside one night. "Mama," he whispered, "Papa's talking to the cupboard." And he pointed to the drawing room. He had woken up because he needed to go to the lavatory, and heard his father's voice.

His mother sat up and stroked her son's head. "Don't worry," she whispered, sitting on the edge of the bed and taking Farid on her lap.

Then she listened, and clearly heard her husband's voice. He was sitting with his face turned to the cupboard. She could see his back from her bed. The cupboard, like the seats in the room and its ceiling, was made of walnut wood elaborately decorated with coloured intarsia work.

Elias was talking to an invisible visitor. He spoke in two voices, one his own, the other and deeper voice obviously his father's.

"So I see you've made your way in life, my dear son," said the deep voice.

"Yes, Father. Thanks to your upbringing and most of all thanks to your blessing. Because I know, even though you threw me out, you loved me in the depths of your heart."

"Congratulations, my son, but haven't you overdone it with this house – didn't I hear that it once belonged to a consul or an ambassador? Have you put any savings aside?"

"Father, I'm cast in the same mould as you. I spend only what I have in abundance. I've saved for everything," said Elias, straightening his back. Then he said softly, "Look in the big drawer beside you." And he sat on the chair where his father was supposed to be sitting.

"Which drawer, my son?"

"The nearest to you," replied Elias.

"Oh, that one," said the deep voice, and Elias pulled the drawer a little way out. It was heavy, for it was filled to the top with gold coins.

"I'm speechless! What an idiot I was!" said the deep voice remorsefully. "I was so wrong."

Elias was weeping with emotion now, probably imagining his father's defeat.

He slowly rose and went back to the sofa, where he sat down and drank his arrack in silence.

"There, it's all right now. You can go to sleep again," Claire whispered to her son, and Farid, barefoot, tiptoed his way back to bed.

But she herself lay awake for a long time.

BOOK OF LOVE IV

At the moment of love there's no place for a strange woman

🕮

DAMASCUS, JULY 1940

63. Disturbances

The copper-coloured turtledoves were beginning to sing their melancholy songs again, and the people of Damascus rose from their siesta. While the heat is unbearable the birds keep silent. Claire sprinkled water on the marble floor of the little inner courtyard, which was burning hot, and opened all the drawing room windows. Heavy heat weighed down on the city.

Farid was sleeping peacefully. His mother drew the curtain that protected his little cot from flies. The baby smiled in his sleep.

The midwife's words and clear laughter were still ringing in her ears. "What a masterpiece! But no wonder, after so much practice. Well, my dear, it was worth it. You wait and see, Nadshla is never wrong. He has the most beautiful eyes I ever saw. He'll soon be winning the hearts of all the ladies." Claire knew that Nadshla was an excellent midwife and also an accomplished liar. Babies change, and Farid was only five weeks old.

She smiled, for she was suddenly wondering why Nadshla would specify the conquest of women's hearts in the child's future. Had it been a reference to her husband's many adventures? Some of the men in the Mushtak clan were obsessed by women: George Mushtak, his son Salman – and indeed, hadn't the rift between her husband and her father-in-law been over a woman too – herself?

Thinking such thoughts, she had come over to the pot of basil in the window. She loved its refreshing fragrance, gently stroked the leaves, and then smelled the palms of her hands. After that she turned, drew the curtain over the baby's cot aside again, and looked at her son. "You will not be a Mushtak, and you'll never conquer anyone. You will be a Surur who loves women." There was bitter determination in her voice.

Her sister-in-law Malake, her cousin, and a few women friends were coming at three. Claire heard shots fired, but far away, possibly in the New Town. The disturbances had been going on for weeks. Famine drove the poor to Damascus, where they looted and held demonstrations. The French soldiers shot at random into the crowd, and over a hundred people had been killed in the streets during the last three weeks. Elias had had iron roller shutters fitted to the confectioner's shop.

Once again several shots rang out in the silence. Claire whispered, "Holy Virgin, I commit Farid to your hands. You know how I've suffered to bring a healthy child into the world. Holy Virgin, hear me. These are difficult times."

The international situation was extremely uncertain. The French were still occupying Syria, but the Germans had invaded France in June. There were rumours that more and more German agents were being infiltrated into Damascus to prepare for the expulsion of the French. "More than a hundred Syrian nationalists, including that bastard Fausi Qawuqji, are already in Berlin with Hitler and will march with him. If he comes," said Elias, "I shall pick up a gun. Better die with honour than live like a dog under Qawuqji."

"Is he so bad?" asked Claire.

"He served here as an officer with both the French and the British. Such unscrupulous lickspittles are the worst. And he attacked Mala."

"Holy Virgin, let's hope the Germans don't come," she whispered.

Her gaze wandered from the drawing room window above the inner courtyard to the rather smaller room opposite. With the big dining room, it formed the north wing of the house. When she looked through the open window, her eye fell on the large brown leather suitcase that had stood there, packed and ready for the last year, in case fighting spread to the whole of Damascus. It contained a few clothes for Elias and her, and a hundred pounds sterling in gold. "The sovereigns would last us a few months," her husband had always said.

"Now we'll need another suitcase for Farid," Claire whispered to herself.

The French occupying power had kept the country more or less peaceful for a long time after the great Syrian uprising of 1925. Elias admired the French high commissioner, whose firm hand had imposed order since the mid-1930s. The smallest misdemeanour was instantly punished with death, and the Arabs knuckled under. Now, however, the cards were being reshuffled.

General Louis Weygand, who had ruled Syria with a rod of iron until May, had been recalled to Paris to lead the French army against Hitler's forces. In Damascus the French had boasted that the Maginot Line was impregnable, and Hitler would perish miserably if he attacked it, but two weeks later the Germans were in the French capital.

The opinion of the colonial troops was split. Many wanted to collaborate with the Germans, and proclaimed their allegiance to Marshal Pétain's government, set up in Vichy by agreement with the Nazis. Others allied themselves with the Free French national committee led from exile in London by a young officer called Charles de Gaulle, to organize resistance to the Germans. There were violent confrontations between the two parties everywhere. The leadership of the French troops in Damascus came down on the side of the Germans, and declared war on Great Britain and the French exiles. There was chaos in the city, and trained German agents contributed to it.

It was said that large British forces were gathering in Palestine, on the southern border of Syria, to occupy the country again and free it of Nazi adherents. The Syrian administration governing under the French occupation didn't last two weeks. It fell, was formed again, fell once more. The chaos of war and the bad harvest brought the first famine since 1918.

The embittered masses carrying their dead to the cemeteries cried out in pain, and saw the French and all other Christians as godless folk whom it was the first duty of Muslims to kill. Many Damascene Christians fortified their houses and kept large supplies of buckets full of water ready, for fire was the rabble's favourite weapon.

64. Sheikh Napoleon

Every time she met her neighbours Claire could feel that they backed Hitler because they hated the French. Madeleine herself thought the French were barbarians, and told horror stories of humiliations inflicted by the soldiers. When Hitler's troops marched into Paris the Syrians hailed it as a victory. They were glad to see the hated French General Weygand, who had shed so much Syrian blood, overthrown by the Germans.

There were two foreign radio stations transmitting Arab news. One was located on Cyprus, and had close links with the British. It reported even the most appalling incidents factually, calmly, and in monotonous Arabic, as if it were reporting the yield of the wheat harvest in Argentina. Elias liked it because it gave detailed information. The other station broadcast from Berlin, and Claire listened to it when Elias wasn't around. The announcer was called Yunus al Bahri. Madeleine had told her about him. People tuned in only in secret in the Christian quarter, for fear of French informers, but in the Muslim quarter Claire saw a large group of men, over forty of them, sitting around a radio set and listening to the tinny voice of Yunus as he breathed out fire and brimstone against the British. The worst he called the French was bastards; the principal targets of his tirades of hatred were always and exclusively the British. They were a race of liars, he cried, hoarse with excitement. He was a master of passionate oratory, he recited poems and suras from the Koran, he reported news and gave vent to insults more freely than Claire ever heard anyone let fly before or indeed later. Yunus did not shrink from crying, after the music of an Austrian march rang out, "You English, here's some good news for you, Hitler's going to fuck your mothers. That's right, fuck your mothers," he repeated, in case any of his hearers thought they couldn't believe their ears.

On another occasion Yunus announced that, in a confidential interview, Hitler had said he was going to convert to Islam after his victory, just as Napoleon, Goethe and all other great men had done before him.

Claire knew that the tale of Goethe's conversion was only a myth, but Napoleon had indeed said he was converting and wore a turban when he was in Egypt, in order to deceive the Egyptians. She was surprised to hear that Hitler was going to become a Muslim, but the news rejoiced the hearts of millions of Arabs.

65. Laila

It was nearly four when the women, talking volubly, arrived at the door. After Claire had taken them into the drawing room and crossed the courtyard to fetch lemonade, she heard a bang in the distance again. She stood still for a moment, then went into the kitchen, took a block of ice out of the big drawer, and used a hammer to strike off a piece of it. Then, wrapping it in a white cloth, she broke the piece of ice into many small splinters.

Once again she heard a bang, followed by hollow thudding sounds. She looked over the courtyard at the drawing room. Her sister-in-law was standing at the window. "They're firing again," called Malake in concern, stepping back into the darkness of the room. Claire picked up the tray of lemonade glasses and went back across the courtyard.

Elias will probably soon be calling the hired cab to take us to Mala, she told herself. "Taking our own car would be suicide," he had said. The road led through Muslim villages. These days only a reliable Muslim cab driver could offer them any security and get them through safely.

"Come here to me," said six-year-old Laila, bending over the baby lying in his small white-curtained cot. Her mother Malake rolled her eyes as her sister-in-law came into the drawing room with the glasses.

The pieces of ice in them made a soft whispering that sounded a little like people chattering in the distance.

"Let her play with him," Claire reassured Malake. "Laila's a sensible girl. She knows how to treat babies." She offered her guests the cool lemonade and some sweetmeats.

Ten women and three children sat down on the heavy, satin-covered sofas in the spacious drawing room. But Malake's little daughter sat on a stool beside the cot, enchanted by the baby. The big chandelier hanging from the intarsia-work ceiling, and the large wooden table with the same inlaid pattern in the middle of the room, gave the place a slightly religious atmosphere, and the women and children sat there stiffly, as if they were in church. Only Laila and the pretty, pale cot seemed out of place in all this weighty solemnity.

Claire had filled her afternoons with the company of women since Farid's birth. She hadn't been prepared for quite so many visitors, and felt both proud and embarrassed. She would never have guessed that she and Elias had so many genuine well-wishers among their friends and relations, or that many of them would face the stress and strain of a long journey from Aleppo or Beirut to come and see her, despite the blazing heat of July and the unrest in the countryside. She was sorry that she had to accommodate those who had come such a long distance in hotels. It had struck her, for the first time, that the house was very splendid but didn't have a single room where a guest could stay. Over the last two months she had been obliged to book twenty-seven hotel rooms. Elias had complained a little of the expense, but he too was happy to have a healthy son after those three miscarriages that had left him not only fearing for his wife's health but anxious in general. He was superstitious, and his father's curse haunted him even in his sleep.

Laila had the baby on her lap now and was gazing at him, her face transfigured. "May Our Lady keep him from envious eyes! He's looking at me as if he understood everything."

"You'll drop the baby. Put him back in his cot like a good girl, and sit down with us and the other children." Her mother was trying to show good manners, but Laila knew her own mind that day.

"Can't I stay the night with Farid? Please, Aunt Claire, let me change his nappy and give him his bath, and then I can sleep the night on the floor beside his cot. It's nicer here than in the hotel."

The women all laughed. "The hotel is fantastic! Claire even thought of flowers for us. And the errand boy says every morning that all her guests are royally treated because she's a queen," said Laila's mother, hastily saving the situation.

Claire smiled, because the errand boys often came three times a day to ask if there was anything else they should do or provide for the hotel guests. Every time they called meant another tip of a few piastres.

However, this was the one house that Elias had wanted to buy, a handsome little palace that was perfect for him. All his life he had aimed to put on a good show, and more than anything he wanted to welcome his father to this house if the bishop's efforts to reconcile them really came to anything. Their reconciliation would take place here, and his father would see that his curse hadn't worked.

Claire was particularly unhappy about the house because of her sister-in-law. The journey from Beirut to Damascus was difficult and sometimes dangerous; bandits and rebels attacked cars and cabs, robbing and murdering their occupants, but all the same, Malake had insisted on coming to congratulate Claire in person.

That afternoon she kept reprimanding her daughter, but Laila took no notice. She was deep in her first conversation with her little boy-friend, and was sure he understood her. The visit lasted two hours, and she was whispering secrets to the baby all the time. Farid looked at her in surprise. Sometimes he laughed, then he frowned again, and his eyes seemed full of grief.

When Claire picked up her son to wish the guests goodbye, he began crying and stretched his little arms out desperately to Laila. She turned back to him once again. "I'll come and see you soon," she whispered softly.

It wasn't until an hour later, when Farid had finally settled down, that Claire was able to collect the glasses, coffee cups, and plates now empty of sweetmeats, and take them to the kitchen. When she looked at the little table that had been standing in front of Laila, she was astonished. The child's lemonade, sugared almonds, and pistachio rolls – Laila's favourite sweetmeats – had not been touched.

૭

Elias was late home from work that evening. He looked tired and desperate. "Shahbandar's been shot," he said quietly, taking a sip of water. It was the first time Claire had heard the name. "One of the leaders of the 1925 uprising. A Syrian agent of the Germans killed him because he wanted to do a deal with the British. They're about to march into Damascus."

"Is that bad news for us?" she asked anxiously.

"The bad part is that people only have to hear a shot fired to start slaughtering each other. After Shahbandar's assassination there'll be gunfire everywhere. A French officer turned his cannon on a village near Damascus and shot the whole place to pieces. It seems that one of his comrades was killed there a year ago. This time there were over twenty dead and a hundred wounded. A whole part of the village lies in ashes," said Elias. His voice was faint, and he ate little that evening.

BOOK OF GROWTH I

Caterpillars dream of flying.

৯৯

DAMASCUS, 1940–1953

66. Childhood

Saitun Alley was short compared to other streets in the Old Town. It was broad and light, and came to an end before it began to get interesting. It lay as open as a weathered seashell, containing no mysteries, only the residence of the Catholic Patriarch of the entire Middle East, the largest Catholic church in Syria, and the Catholic College, one of the three elite schools in Damascus. Beside it, small and unpretentious, stood the elementary school for poor Christian children, which aptly bore the name of St. Nicholas. According to the legend, St. Nicholas saved some children from a wicked man who was going to slaughter and pickle them, and a sculptural group showing him with the three children in the pickling tub stood at the entrance to the school. But unlike the pupils at the elite establishment next door, the children here were taught by an army of sadistic and useless teachers, and often wondered whether they wouldn't rather be pickled than subjected to daily beatings.

The street divided into three narrow blind alleys. One ended at the gate of the big Catholic elite school, the other led to the entrances of private houses. Farid didn't know many people in Saitun Alley. The boys from the neighbouring houses were either much older or much younger than he was. Only Antoinette seemed an oasis in this barren desert for a while, but in the end she turned out to be a mirage, because when she was eleven and he was nine she didn't want to play with him any more. Even years later he remembered the loneliness of the long summer days when he ran up the street to the bus stop and back down to the church over and over again, in what little shade the façades of the buildings offered in the afternoon. All was still, everything seemed to be asleep. Later his cousin Laila told him that far away in Beirut she had heard him calling every day at siesta time.

Farid wasn't allowed out of Saitun Alley. There were a thousand rumours around. It was said that gangs went about kidnapping Christian children and selling them to rich, childless oil sheikhs abroad. So he was a prisoner of the street and his mother's anxiety.

Only one incident from that time stuck in his memory. He was standing in the shade of a building and wanted to play with the dog dozing beside the wall of the house opposite. Suddenly he heard the sensuous sighing of a woman from above. At first he thought that because it was siesta time she was groaning in her sleep, but then he clearly heard a man whispering, and after a little while the woman uttered an alarming cry. It was only much later that Farid realized what had been going on behind the curtains over that window.

Josef, a thin and gloomy boy at his school, fascinated Farid, although many people avoided him because he was so ugly. He talked nineteen to the dozen, but as he had no idea how to defend himself he was always losing fights. One day Farid saw two other boys beating him up. He found a good strong branch and hit out at Josef's two assailants until they ran away, howling. Josef half sat up. "Not bad, confectioner's boy. I thought you were just a little sugar dolly. But why did you have to go barging in? I'd have dealt with those two arseholes on my own."

He certainly talks big! Farid thought. But the boy invited him home that afternoon, which was something special, because Josef didn't trust many people. For the first time in his life Farid saw a house with doors opening on two different streets. It was just right for Josef. "Ideal when you're escaping from secret agents," he whispered. The building was huge; over ten families lived there, sharing the inner courtyard and all the noise.

Josef's room was on the second floor, and smelled pleasantly of aniseed; the window was right above the flat roof of a broad, single-storey aniseed warehouse. Not until he leaned out of the window did Farid realize that this flat roof linked his own house with Josef's, so he had only to climb over the banisters on the second-floor landing at home to go straight across to visit his friend.

Josef didn't even look up from the toy fire engine he was investigating when Farid excitedly told him this news. "I've known that for ages. I've been over to your place twice," he said, as if it were the most natural thing in the world.

"Smells good here," said Farid awkwardly, to hide his surprise.

"Smells horrible. Aniseed all day long, it's like living in a barrel of arrack," grumbled Josef.

"And who lives in the house over there?" Farid pointed to a small building in the middle of a garden that seemed to belong to the aniseed warehouse.

"Two old men, lonely and miserly old men," replied Josef. "They cry every night and call for their wives, who left them. Sometimes I feel sorry for them when it's cold and they stand at the window side by side in their pyjamas." Farid was surprised to find how much he knew about the men.

Josef's room was large and light, and the shelves were laden with foreign toys. He was obviously his father's favourite: the much-wanted son who had finally been born after four daughters. In his first few years of life his mother had been terrified of the neighbours' envy, and she never cut Josef's hair, so that even the devil would take him for a girl and spare him. He filled all her thoughts and feelings so much that when she had yet another baby, another girl this time, she couldn't think of anything to call her but Josephine.

In his youth, Josef's father Rimon had been a famous boxer and a good stonemason. But his wife had faced him with a choice: "It's me or the boxing ring." And while he was still thinking it over she kissed him. That made up his mind.

However, Rimon was allowed to hang a picture in the drawing room, showing him as a boxer with his torso bare, wearing boxing gloves, a proud young man with a strangely gentle, melancholy expression better suited to a poet than a muscle-man with swelling biceps.

One day the bishop, who was enthusiastic about Rimon's skill in carving stone, suggested he might set up as a building contractor. He could get him any number of contracts, said the bishop, for most builders were Muslims. Rimon liked the notion, since he had many ideas for building handsome, solid houses. And the bishop kept his word, so that Josef's father was soon almost overwhelmed with work. By the beginning of the 1940s he was one of the most successful building contractors in the city, and he married Madeleine Ashi, the daughter of a leather exporter.

Claire had no objection to Farid's friendship with Madeleine's son. But after that first visit it was two years before Josef let him come again, and then Farid discovered that he had turned suspicious when his parents congratulated him over-effusively that evening on the new friend he had made.

"I thought," he said apologetically later, "you were one of those creeps – dear little nicely brought up boy and all that – who get to know all about someone and then tell tales of him. They praised you so much I thought you were bound to be an arsehole. But I know now you're okay."

On his first visit Farid had met Josef's entire extended family, who all lived in the house. His two old aunts Afifa and Latifa were dressed like servants, and seemed to be there only to look after Josef's mother and her children.

"They're my father's sisters," he explained. "They once had boy-friends, two brothers. But Afifa and Latifa kept cooking the brothers spaghetti, so they ran away to America."

Josef hated spaghetti. It was only a decade later that he really understood his aunts' tragic story. They had both inherited a great deal of money, but their father's will stipulated that they must live in their elder brother Rimon's care until they married. And he immediately scared off any man who so much as looked at one of the sisters, until they were old and no one wanted them any more. That way he made sure that he kept his sisters' inheritance, and at the same time had two unpaid household helps to toil away for his family for over twelve hours a day.

Two more women also sat in the living room, these two very old indeed, doing crochet work in silence. Not just on this visit but also later, Farid felt as if he had stepped into a convent of nuns.

"Who are those?" he asked.

"My two deaf grandmothers. They hate each other." Josef gave a nasty grin, and then, after greeting both old ladies politely, added, "And *they* cooked spaghetti until their husbands choked on it."

"How come you have two grandmothers?" Farid had asked. Josef laughed at him for years over that question.

67. Grandparents

Later Farid could smile at his own mistake, but when he discovered it at the age of seven he was shocked. Up till then he had firmly believed that he had only one pair of grandparents who once upon a time had somehow produced both his parents, like rabbits and cats who breed together even when they're siblings. It wasn't just childish naivety: the main reason was that he knew only his grandparents Lucia and Nagib. He had neither seen nor heard of any others. Even his mother never mentioned that side of his family. And he talked to his favourite cousin Laila about everything else, but not their relations.

When Laila came from Beirut to visit, their time together was precious. Farid walked through Paradise with her to protect him. They were allowed to go beyond the high garden wall.

Once Josef had explained about grandparents, Claire had to tell her son that his paternal grandmother, a remarkable woman, had died very young. "Your grandfather George Mushtak is a hard-hearted man who hates your father. He hasn't spoken a word to him for ten years, because Elias disobeyed him and married me instead of the daughter of a friend of his. So he cursed your father and disinherited him. But now the Bishop of Damascus himself, who went to school with Elias and is a friend of your grandfather's, is doing all he can to get the old gentleman to bless his own son again. So it could be," Claire concluded, "that you'll soon get to see him." That was in April 1947.

The meeting between father and son was to take place on Sunday 15 June. The bishop had invited the whole Mushtak family to a solemn church service at ten that morning. After it they were all to eat together in Elias's house opposite the church and be reconciled.

George Mushtak died on Friday 13 June, and his son cursed all day long. He kept on shouting, "He bore me malice not only in his lifetime but even in his death." And he went around looking the very image of an embittered man for weeks.

Farid insisted on going to Mala for the funeral with his parents. He wanted to see his other grandfather at least once. But all he saw was the closed casket, and there was such a strong smell of bitter almonds near it that it turned his stomach.

Now he really did have only one grandfather: Nagib Surur.

68. Love

Some children look like their fathers or their mothers, others are a more or less fortunate mixture of both. Farid looked like neither his mother nor his father; he resembled his grandfather. He might have been descended straight from him without any intervention by his parents. From his mop of hair to his little toe, he was such a carbon copy of old Nagib Surur that it quite alarmed many of their relations at first.

Claire had inherited her looks mainly from her mother: her large green eyes, her smooth black hair, her rather broad but beautiful face, her small nose and snow-white skin. Her mother who, as already mentioned, came from a Venetian family, was even said to have aristocratic Austrian blood in her veins.

Nagib, on the other hand, was a Damascene born and bred. His ancestors had been textiles merchants who came from the Yemen in the twelfth century and settled in Damascus. All their descendants had the large dark eyes, finely carved features, and dark skin typical of Yemenis.

Nagib was a slender man, tall and dark-skinned. His general

appearance was extremely virile, although his attractive eyes looked feminine at close quarters because his brows naturally lay like two delicate lines traced above them. Nagib was always being compared to various Egyptian actors, which he didn't particularly like, for he preferred sport to the arts. As a young man he had been an enthusiastic boxer, but he was far too much of a gentleman to survive in the ring. His opponents at the time had been merciless hard-hitters on the fringes of the criminal fraternity; he lost all his fights, and after a while he gave up, but he still had a passion for boxing. Even in great old age he was a member of the boxing club and went to every fight.

His enthusiasm for boxing always led to quarrels with his wife, who was repelled by any kind of sport and much preferred going to large receptions. She and her son-in-law Elias agreed on that, and also on Nagib's involvement in the bank affair of 1935. Farid couldn't make out why it had landed his grandfather in prison for three years. Nagib would never talk about it.

Claire loved her father. She appreciated his gentle nature, his generosity, and in a way even his pliability, which her mother lacked. Lucia was always severe, rigorous with herself as well as others. "It's a wonder she's on speaking terms with herself," her husband often joked.

He came to visit Claire for a coffee every day, since after his dismissal from the bank he had plenty of time on his hands, and his wife didn't want him hanging around the house. After the coffee, Nagib would sit for hours by his grandson's cradle, gazing at him blissfully.

"He's given me the best victory of all," he told Claire, "a victory over death. I shall live on in him, and death itself will feel mortally injured."

As soon as Farid could walk, his grandfather took his hand and showed him the world. He would walk slowly down the streets of Damascus, telling the little boy about the buildings, shops, churches, and mosques of the city. He talked about drinks and spices, sweetmeats and nuts, and let his grandson touch everything and taste much of it.

He kept stopping to call on friends and drink coffee. Then his grandson would sit on his knee, looking at the world around him with wonder. Their friends always smiled at the sight: two versions of the same person, divided only by time.

69. K.O.

For the rest of his life, whenever Farid thought of Damascus he connected the city with his grandfather's warm hand and deep voice. Years later, he could remember the first time they went to a fight together. It was spring, and Farid had already started school. His grandfather dropped in, as he did every afternoon, and Farid ran to meet him.

"Would you like to go into town with me?" asked Nagib. Naturally the boy was delighted.

"But don't be late back. Elias will be home around seven today," Claire called after them.

Grandfather Nagib took Farid's hand and wandered through the suks and past the cafés with him. Then he suddenly asked, "Would you like to see a boxing match?"

Farid was all for that idea. "Oh yes!" he cried enthusiastically.

There were four fights. The first three were amusing, designed to keep the spectators happy and delay the main fight between the Syrian and Egyptian national champions until all the seats were filled. Grandfather Nagib told Farid all about the principles of boxing, right down to the dirtiest tricks. He never again learned so much about any sport in a single day. When the main fight was over it was already dark outside. "We'd better hurry," said Grandfather, and he took a cab. The boxing club was in the New Town. The cab driver was drunk, and kept falling asleep during the journey. His horses stopped as soon as they sensed it, and Nagib had his work cut out for him, shaking the man awake.

At home there was a row between Elias and Nagib, and Farid was sent to bed without any supper. Claire, trying to make the peace, was silenced by her husband's furious outburst. Grandfather kept apologizing, saying it was all his fault and nothing to do with Farid, but Elias was beside himself with rage. He shouted at the old man, forbidding him ever to take his son anywhere again. That silenced Nagib, who was very downcast, and in his bedroom Farid cried because Elias was shouting so dreadfully. Two neighbours came hurrying along and tried to intervene, but in vain.

After that day Grandfather still called, but he avoided going for long walks with his grandson. He took him to the nearby ice cream parlour, but never for more than half an hour, and when they came back they parted company, to be on the safe side. Farid hurried on ahead, and Grandfather strolled slowly in to see his daughter. Elias never suspected anything, and Claire staunchly covered up for both of them, telling lies when it came to protecting her son from his father's wrath.

The night after the fight, Farid dreamed that his father was punching his grandfather, a hook to the chin. Nagib staggered back and lay on the ground unconscious. Grandmother Lucia was the referee; she raised her son-in-law's arm and shouted, "K.O." Farid woke in alarm. It was dark and he felt hungry. When he put the light on, he found a large apple and a glass of water on his bedside table.

70. Temptation

One summer day, when Farid was eight, he went out with his mother. She wanted to do some shopping in the Suk al Hamidiye and then visit a woman friend who lived in Qaimariye, a quarter in the heart of the Old Town near the Ummayad Mosque. Most of the people who lived there were Muslims, but Claire's friend was a Christian. She would rather have lived somewhere else, but her husband had got the apartment cheap through his boss, so she put up with her dislike of the area.

The woman had no children, and Farid felt bored. He asked his mother if he could play in the street until she had finished drinking her coffee. Both women agreed, so Farid went out of doors. The street was almost empty. A pretty little girl was standing in one doorway. When she saw him she asked if he would like to play with her. Farid hesitated for a moment, and then nodded.

From outside, the building looked as unpretentious as all old Arab houses. Built of mud brick, it rose hardly any higher than the other two-storey buildings in the alley, but the inner courtyard was a masterpiece of the Arab art of life. A narrow corridor led to it from the door of the house. With every step the noise of the street died down. Orange and lemon trees protected the courtyard from the blazing sun, and besides the fragrance of their blossoms they cast a magical play of light and shadow on the coloured tiles at every breath of wind. A small marble fountain provided a little moisture and the sound that Arabs most love to hear: the splashing of water. No one window was the same as any of the others; each was a work of art in wood, metal and stained glass.

Farid stood marvelling at the beauty of the courtyard for a long time. Suddenly the little girl turned the tap of the fountain up and laughed out loud as a jet of water shot up to the sky. It drenched her. Her thin dress stuck to her body. He turned the tap down again. Taking his hand, the girl led him past the arcades and into the back part of the courtyard, where a coloured mattress lay on the ground.

"Here!" she said, lying down. Farid didn't know what kind of game this was supposed to be.

"You lie down beside me and we'll play at weddings," she begged him. He was baffled by her boldness. "Aren't your parents here?" he asked, sitting down on the far end of the mattress.

"No," she said, rubbing her leg against his arm. "Don't you want to kiss me?" she added, and she closed her eyes and laughed. There was something crazed in her laughter, and it scared Farid.

"No," he said shyly, and stood up. "Don't you have a ball? Or some marbles or playing cards?"

At that moment two strong boys fell on him, grinning maliciously. The girl cried out in alarm, "Go away, you devils!" But before Farid realized what was going on the stouter boy had grabbed him by the arm.

"Caught you! Let's see your prick! If you're a Muslim you'll have to marry this crazy kid, if you're a Christian we'll circumcize you first."

The girl shouted for help, but the second boy took a large flick-knife out of his pocket and threatened to kill Farid if she didn't shut up. The girl crawled into a corner and looked at him with her mouth open and her eyes wide and crazy.

He hadn't been frightened until the smaller boy took out his knife, but the sight of the sharp blade paralysed him, and he was unable to tear himself away. The smaller boy, who had one eye half stitched up, came towards him. He pressed the point of his knife into Farid's navel and asked, enveloping him with wafts of bad breath, "Are you a Christian?"

"Yes," said Farid, with his throat dry, trembling.

"Trousers down!" cried the stout boy, laughing like someone possessed. He held Farid's head firmly between his legs. A few seconds later his trousers were on the ground.

"Now your underpants!" he shouted. The girl suddenly attacked the smaller boy. He hit back, but she fought grimly to free Farid. Her words still echoed in his ears years later: "Castrate your own friends, not the only friend I have!"

After a while the smaller boy had Farid's underpants down too. This humiliation dispelled the last of Farid's paralysis. He freed his right arm and hit the stout boy in the balls with all his might. The boy bellowed like a steer and writhed in pain. Then Farid ran to the smaller boy, who was slapping the infuriated beauty, grabbed a chair and brought it down on the boy's back until he fell over.

Suddenly a man entered the courtyard and stared wide-eyed at the exhausted combatants. "What the devil's going on here?" he cried in alarm, and fell on the stout boy and the smaller boy. They flew through the air. The lighter boy landed next to the fountain, the larger one head over heels beside the mattress.

"They were going to circumcize me," said Farid, crying and covering his penis with both hands.

"For God's sake! That's the last time I tell you, you dogs!" cried the man. He ran into the kitchen and came back with a long bamboo cane. The stouter boy began whimpering, but the man lashed out at both of them, hardly minding where he hit. "How often do I have to tell you not to touch that knife, how often?" he bellowed.

Farid put his clothes on and was going to slip away. The man stopped for a moment and looked at him with a smile. "You won't tell your parents, will you? They're just a couple of stupid boys and a feeble-minded girl."

The girl laughed and lifted her dress above her head, exposing her buttocks. She was shaking with laughter.

Farid promised not to tell his parents, and at first he didn't want to accept the five-piastre coin held out to him. But the man urged him in friendly tones to take it. So he finally put it in his pocket and ran out. He bought himself a packet of chewing gum and went back to his mother, who was just saying goodbye to her friend.

"Well, did you have a nice time?" she asked.

"You bet!" he muttered. His groin hurt.

On the way home Claire suddenly stopped at a barber's shop where men had gathered around a radio set. The barber had turned the volume right up. "War," Farid heard. He didn't understand.

"Come on, we must get home, quick," said Claire, and her face was clouded.

A few days later he saw the first refugees arriving in Damascus. Someone said they were Palestinians and the Jews had driven them out. People were saying they'd go home again in a few days' time. But Elias shook his head.

71. An Oasis Called Antoinette

Antoinette Farah was dark-skinned and smelled of almonds. Farid had been playing with her as long as he could remember. She lived not far from him, in the blind alley leading to Josef's house.

Antoinette's mother liked Farid very much. She often kissed him, much more often than she kissed her own son. Her husband, on the other hand would rather have seen Farid playing not with his daughter but with his lethargic son Djamil, who was two years older than his sister, but more interested in jam sandwiches than playing games. Farid and Antoinette soon found a way to get rid of Djamil. They told him which of the neighbours was cooking something really delicious that day, and he would be off like a shot to stand at that neighbour's door with a pleading look in his eyes. Everyone liked his generous parents, and accepted greedy Djamil for their sake.

Like Farid, Antoinette thought their own street very boring. She didn't know any other girls of her own age there. It wasn't until later that she made friends with Josef's sister Josephine, who couldn't stand her own brother either.

Farid went to visit her whenever possible. As soon as Djamil had a sandwich in his hands, or was off tracking down a good meal, the two of them disappeared into the children's room. The game that Farid liked best was lying on top of Antoinette, particularly on her back, which made him feel pleasantly hot between the legs. But she didn't like that. It was Djamil who told him one day that Antoinette loved chocolate and would do anything for it. On his next visit Farid brought a chocolate bar with him and showed it to her. Of course she wanted it at once, and he stammered out what Djamil had told him to say. "You can have it if you'll let me do what I want to you."

Antoinette glared furiously at her munching brother, but agreed, and lay on the carpet enjoying the chocolate while Farid rocked back and forth on her back.

Djamil's eyes were glued to the chocolate bar, and he ignored Farid entirely. When Antoinette had finished it and licked her fingers with relish she shook Farid off. "That's enough for today. Bring me another bar and then you can ride on me again," she said calmly, adjusting her clothes.

"That didn't last long," he protested.

"You can ride me for an hour for every chocolate bar," said Djamil. Revolted, Farid turned away from him.

"It may not seem very long to you on top, but it's ages for me underneath. Want to try?" she asked.

He lay on the carpet and Antoinette climbed on top of him. At first he thought it was amusing, but then her rocking weight felt uncomfortable, and the minutes seemed an eternity.

One summer night the Mushtaks visited the Farah family, and after a leisurely meal the grown-ups played cards. Farid had asked to be allowed to sleep over with the Farah children, and the three of them went off to the children's room next to their parents' bedroom on the second floor and played games, looking out of the window now and then at the grown-ups enjoying the cool night air down in the courtyard.

Soon Djamil was asleep, and Antoinette showed Farid her latest discovery. She crawled under her blanket with him and raised her legs to make a tent. Where the wool was thick the roof of the tent was dark, but in some places the blanket let the light of the bright lamp in the room come through.

"Look at the sky, and those are the clouds," she said in the dim light, and then pointed to a tiny hole in the blanket. Light fell through it. "And that's my star. It visits me every day before I go to sleep."

Farid wasn't sure later how long they had played under the blanket. At some point he fell asleep, and his parents had long ago gone home when he suddenly woke up. He heard moans and laughter. When he sat up in the bed he saw that Antoinette was awake too. He could see her face in the light coming into the room from a lamp in the inner courtyard. She put her forefinger to her lips.

"What's going on? Where am I?" he asked softly.

"In our house. Perhaps ..." she said, and hesitated as a loud moan came from the room next door. Her mother was begging for more, and her father was crying breathlessly, "Yes, yes!" again and again.

"They're making love," said Antoinette, smiling. "They do that almost every night."

"Is your Papa hurting your Mama?"

"No, no, he's necking with her. And she wants more."

The sound of the woman's laughter reassured Farid. Antoinette put her head on his chest and stroked his hand. Finally she crawled over to him and kissed him on the lips. Her mouth tasted of peppermint, probably because she had to clean her teeth every evening. It was nice, and Farid kissed her cheek. Her face was hot, and she kissed him on the lips again, holding his hand tight in hers, almost as if she were praying. He pressed it, and felt that she was perspiring. For the first time he smelled her sweat. That night she smelled of almonds and coffee.

She bared her breasts. "You must kiss me here and then they'll grow," she said in the dark, raising herself until her little nipple pushed into his mouth. Farid sucked it, and she laughed because it tickled. "Not so hard, or they'll grow too big," she whispered, giving him her other breast.

72. The Hammam

Later, the word Paradise always made Farid think of the time when he was still a little boy and could go to the hammam with his mother. They went to the Hammam al Bakri, near Bab Tuma. Wednesday was the women's day. Antoinette and her mother were always there.

The hammam was a world of its own. In later years, when Farid saw the paintings of the French Romantics idealizing women in the hammam or the harem, he thought their pictures boring by comparison with what he remembered.

The two most beautiful girls there were Jeannette and Antoinette, although they looked very different. Jeannette had pale skin and green eyes. Antoinette's skin was dark, almost black. Both were maturing rather early, and at the age of ten they already had small breasts and round little backsides.

Jeannette liked playing in the hammam with a blond boy from Ananias Alley. Antoinette, on the other hand, was interested only in Farid. It was she who explained the difference between men and women to him in one of the empty cubicles. Opening her legs, she showed him her vagina. Farid thought it was a wound.

"Have they cut off your little pigeon?" he asked. Children in Damascus called a penis a pigeon in those days, because they thought it looked as if it were sitting on two eggs.

Antoinette giggled. "No, silly. Women keep their little pigeon and its eggs in a nest inside them."

He didn't understand, and she giggled again, but promised to tell him all about it. However, she never did, for directly after this he was torn away from his dream of Paradise. Overnight, he wasn't allowed to go to the hammam with the women any more. Years later Claire told him how the women would hint delicately to a mother that it was time she stopped bringing her son. He laughed, but at the time, aged nine and suddenly banished, he had wept in the courtyard for a whole hour.

"Your son will soon be needing a bride." That was how the coded information went. If a mother didn't catch on, the women put it more clearly. "Next time you'd better bring his father too," they would say.

Claire had taken the hint. "You can go with Papa from now on," she had told Farid next Wednesday, and set off alone with her things.

So Saturday after Saturday he followed his father to the baths. Elias always went on his own, and if he met any acquaintances it was by chance. He didn't mind who was there and who wasn't. The men always conducted boring conversations about business and war, extravagant and unfaithful women, the government and the weather.

And then there was the horrible man who did the soaping and whose eyes followed him every Saturday. He would soap and massage the men for a few piastres. He talked to Elias for a long time until he was persuaded to pay for a massage with his son. You never lay there naked, but always with a towel around you, and the masseur too had a thin apron around his hips. His bare torso was tattooed and not very hairy.

Farid didn't like the heavily built man, so he didn't want to go into a cubicle with him, but said he'd rather stay in the large public room. The masseur muttered, but agreed. He worked away on Farid's back for a while. Then, suddenly, he was lying on top of the boy with his penis erect, massaging him with a sisal glove.

Farid tried to get up, but the man pushed him back on the wet stone floor. Elias was drowsing on a bench above the stove at the far end of the room. Everything went blurred before Farid's eyes and suddenly looked dim and misty. His father appeared to be far away and out of reach. Then he felt the man removing the towel that covered his buttocks. "No!" he cried, rearing his upper body up. Only the man's apron separated his excited penis from the orifice it desired.

Elias briefly opened his eyes. "What?" he muttered, and dozed off again. But another man saw Farid's plight, and emerged from the mists.

"What are you doing with the boy?" he asked quietly. He wasn't sure, because he couldn't see properly in all the steam.

The embarrassed masseur smiled. "He doesn't like being rubbed down with sisal," he claimed. "The boy has skin like a girl's, but he'll soon get used to it."

"No, I won't," protested Farid.

Now the man did see what was going on. "And what's that, then?" he asked, low-voiced, taking hold of the erect penis with the towel. The masseur flinched back, and Farid jumped up.

His father was still asleep.

Farid never let himself be overruled like that again. He didn't want to be either massaged or soaped, and soon he stopped going to the hammam.

But after he had been banished from that female Paradise, Antoinette didn't want to play with him any more. "You're a man now," she said, "and it's not a good idea for a girl to play with men." From then on she spoke sharply to him, just as Josef's sister did. And without Antoinette, Farid's childhood was as boring as white cotton wool, until the day when Josef let him join the gang.

73. The Gang

He was to go to the attic at midnight. It was a warm spring night, and Farid lay awake in his bed. His heart was hopping with excitement like a scared rabbit. When the clock struck twelve he jumped up and slipped out of his room barefoot. He heard a brief cough, and froze beside the fountain. Then he went on to the stairway between the bathroom and the drawing room. At the landing on the second floor, a pleasantly cool breeze blew into his face, smelling of jasmine and aniseed.

Farid stopped by the wooden banisters for a moment, observing the inner courtyards, the gardens, and the roof of the aniseed warehouse below him. When he saw a shadow scurrying up to the attic, he climbed on the low banister rail and jumped.

The attic door was open just a crack. Candlelight flickered. Farid slipped into the large room like a ghost, without opening the door any further. Josef and three other boys were sitting around a large wooden table on which two candles were burning. The only window in the attic was covered with a thick cloth so that the light wouldn't give them away. The room was musty.

Apart from Josef, Farid knew only one boy in the gang: thin Azar from the class above him at school. They were all barefoot and in their pyjamas. He sat down on a chair at the table with his back to the door. That made all of them except Josef laugh. It was only later that he realized why. No one but a beginner, a trusting child, sits with his back to the door.

"This is Farid," said his sponsor Josef in his dry voice. "I've sounded him out. He's okay. I propose him as a candidate." The others nodded agreement.

"So if no one objects, he must take the oath now that he'll never betray anyone from our gang and will keep faith with it for ever," Josef went on. "And if he keeps his word, he'll be a full member in six months' time."

Word for word and parrot-fashion, Farid spoke the pompous sentences that Josef asked him to repeat. Even years later he remembered that meeting. It had impressed him greatly, and gave him experience of a political discussion for the first time in his life. A few days before, at the end of March, Colonel Hablan had led a coup against the civilian government. It was the first coup in Arabia. Rasuk, one of the members of the gang, said that Hablan had gone proudly to Faris Khuri, a famous and brilliant politician. "Well, what do you think of my coup?" Hablan had asked Khuri. "It succeeded without a single shot being fired. Isn't that brilliant?" But the wily politician replied, "I can't be the judge of that. However, you have opened a door that you'll never be able to close again. Someone else will soon come through that door and overthrow you." The colonel had laughed, and left. A few months later, Rasuk told them how another man had carried out a new coup and had Colonel Hablan shot.

The gang met almost daily to discuss their operations, although what effect those operations had was not apparent. Far more important were the nocturnal meetings that strengthened their nerves and made them feel brave. Later, they exchanged banned books and secret plans and ideas. The gang opened the gates of life to Farid, and suddenly he felt as if he had spent his earlier years packed away in cotton wool, like a larva in its cocoon.

74. Boxing

Laila thought boxing the most stupid of all sports. "It's just men making an art out of their wish to beat each other up," she said, when Farid enthusiastically told her how he had been to a fight with his grandfather, sitting in the front row to have a really good view.

Elias had gone to a friend's funeral in Beirut, and Grandfather Nagib just happened to drop in that afternoon, or so he claimed. When Claire told him that her husband had gone away that morning for two days, he simply gave her a mischievous smile.

"Then I can take my young friend for a good long walk in town again, and he can stay the night with us. That way you'll have peace and quiet and you can do as you like for two days."

Claire laughed. "When the cat's away the mice will play."

But she agreed, stipulating only that her boy must come home as early as possible next morning, because his cousin Laila would be passing through Damascus and was going to drop in.

Nagib took Farid to a boxing match in the main hall of the club, where he always had the best, upholstered seats. The first fight was boring. "Beginners," said a spectator to their right.

Grandfather disappeared during the intermission, and didn't come back even when the bell rang for the next fight. Farid, feeling anxious, left his seat and went in search of Nagib. He suddenly felt afraid that his grandfather might have fainted in the men's room, so he ran that way. There were four or five cubicles in a large room. The first two were empty, but as he was about to open the third door he saw his grandfather coming out of a small room a little way off. There was a young man with him. Grandfather adjusted his jacket and checked his flies, then took out his wallet and gave the stranger some money. Obviously overwhelmed by his generosity, the young man kissed

Nagib's hand. Nagib took the man's face in his hands and kissed him on the lips. Farid, who had just been going to hail his grandfather, felt strangely moved, and stood rooted to the spot in the shadow of the door.

When Nagib left, Farid unobtrusively followed him back to their seats. "I was looking for you," he said when they were sitting comfortably next to each other again. Grandfather avoided his inquiring gaze. Some time later, when Farid had almost forgotten this incident, he inadvertently overheard a fierce quarrel between his mother and his grandmother. Claire was defending her father, while Grandmother was talking angrily about Grandfather's liking for young men. It was downright scandalous, she cried. Claire didn't want to tell her son what it was all about. Grandmother was always imagining things, she said briefly, and wouldn't allow her poor father the smallest pleasure.

"She ought to have married my Papa and you ought to have married yours, and then we'd all have been happy," the boy speculated out loud.

Claire looked at him, her eyes wide. "You may well be right, but time decided otherwise. Mama and I have to love our own husbands."

It was Josef who explained to him. "If what your grandmother says is true, it means your grandfather fucks boys."

Farid didn't understand. "How?" he asked, baffled.

"Oh, for goodness' sake, don't you know anything? Or has God sent me an innocent angel? How? How? How many orifices does a man have? Ears and nostrils wouldn't be much use, right? So what's left? Your mouth and your bum, idiot."

75. At the Barber's

The best barber in the Christian quarter was Michel, a distant cousin of Claire's. Like all men of good standing, Farid's and Josef's fathers went to him. His customers even included the Catholic Patriarch and the bishop. Grandfather Nagib went to Michel too, and praised his elegance in the highest terms. He had a very handsome salon, said

Nagib, and was one of the few barbers to wrap warm, moist towels around his customers' faces after shaving them, to give the skin that special smooth, supple look.

Michel's salon had large mirrors and a marble floor. Frescos and Arabic ornamentation adorned the ceiling and walls, and the basins were white marble with brass taps that shone like gold. The barber liked to show people his razors and scissors made in Solingen, which cost a fortune in Damascus. He was also an excellent perfumier, and had a secret book with a thousand and one formulas for fragrances. Men swore by his creations, but Claire laughed at them. "It's all humbug! Michel just adds a few drops of cinnamon, rose, or carnation extract to ordinary distillates of jasmine and lemon blossom, and the men go wild about them."

Farid didn't much like visiting Michel the barber. Twice running he had left the boy to an apprentice, who was a nice lad but inexperienced, and kept pulling his hair. "I'm not letting that stupid little chicken loose on me a third time," muttered Farid on his way home.

Josef too had rebelled against his father and went to a Muslim barber far away near the Ummayad Mosque, where the customers told so many stories that the barber's attention was constantly distracted, and he gave Josef some very odd haircuts. The man also drew teeth. Quite often he would draw a painful tooth for a customer who had arrived in haste, wailing, while he left a man with his face already lathered waiting to be shaved. He also dealt in houses, songbirds and smuggled goods. He was just the barber for Josef.

"It's like being in a movie there," Farid's friend enthused. "You get a really crazy haircut, you hear two or three exciting stories, you see a tooth being drawn or a deal done under the counter, you get to hear canaries singing, then you have a glass of tea, and all that for half a lira." A haircut at Michel's cost at least twice as much.

Farid went looking for a new barber in the Christian quarter, and found a dimly lit salon very close to his own street. He had never noticed it before, although he had passed the dirty wooden door with the smudged little pane of glass in it countless times. This particular day the barber was busy clearing out the salon, so Farid could see into the dark tunnel-shaped room inside. A naked light bulb hung over an ancient mirror. It was left on all day so that the barber could see what he was doing.

"Can I ... can I get my hair cut here?" asked Farid hesitantly.

The old man looked up from his broom. "You of course can. Why not? When I finished." The man spoke broken Arabic like all first-generation Armenians who had escaped the 1915 massacre and found asylum in Syria.

Farid went in. There were a couple of rickety chairs by the wall, and the place looked poor but very clean. Piles of old magazines lay between the chairs. The first page of all of them was missing. Posters of a green landscape with snow-covered hills in the background hung on one wall. There was a picture of the Virgin Mary in the middle of the wall between the posters.

Two large glass jars of water stood close to the barber's chair. The bottoms of the jars seemed to have a black deposit in them. When Farid's eyes had become used to the darkness of the room he saw that they were leeches, which his grandmother thought were very good for treating her inflamed leg. "They suck the blood and take the pressure off places where it hurts," she claimed. Grandfather Nagib spoke of leeches with revulsion, and called anyone he disliked a leech. Here they were, then, swimming about in the two jars, clinging to the inner walls with their front or back suckers. A shudder ran down Farid's spine.

The Armenian was having a long conversation with his neighbour and seemed to be in no hurry. To give himself something else to think about, Farid picked up one of the magazines and leafed through it. It showed pictures of King Farouk of Egypt, looking solemn, fat, and short-sighted, and surrounded by beautiful women. All the pictures were in unnaturally garish colours. Another magazine was devoted to all that was strange and wonderful, and seemed to find nothing but curious facts on this earth. A third was full of jokes and cartoons, a fourth was a fashion magazine.

"Read more or hair cut?" asked the Armenian shyly. Farid looked up and put the magazine back on the pile. Time passed quickly, for the barber was an excellent storyteller who was short on grammar, but not on wit and adventurous experiences.

This first visit was the start of a friendship that lasted three years, until one day Farid found the salon closed, and heard from the cobbler next door that Karabet the barber had been knocked down by a truck in the night after a party, and died in hospital soon after the accident.

Until then, however, Farid had been to him every other week, and the Armenian never charged him more than quarter of a lira. Farid paid him half a lira, and added the other half to his pocket money. Claire laughed at his haircut, but she let him do as he liked, and his father never noticed.

Karabet was often sad or angry when he told his own story. He had lost his mother and father and fled from Armenia on foot, almost starving. Only when he described his childhood did his eyes shine. Then he stopped cutting hair for a moment, and talked about the sunny afternoons when he used to visit his grandmother. She always gave him a roll with a filling of pasturma, that delicate air-dried beef with its piquant crust of sharp spices. He would stand with his back to the mirror, miming the enjoyable consumption of an enormous pasturma roll.

Karabet earned more from his leeches, which he raised in a pond near the city, than from cutting hair. He was very clean and took good care of his "little beasties", as he called them. Doctors, neighbours, even university professors bought them from him in large quantities, paying a lira for ten leeches.

It was in Karabet's salon that Farid learned of the deposition of the king of Egypt, and in the tattered magazines he read about his comfortable life in exile in Rome and St. Moritz. He often went to the salon just to read the magazines. Sometimes Karabet asked him curiously what was in them. He couldn't read them himself, but was given them free by a newsagent once they were several weeks out of date. And when a new supply came he didn't throw the old ones away with the garbage, but passed them on to a neighbouring grocer who carefully folded them to make paper bags.

Farid felt safe in the dark salon, as if he were in a deep cavern. There were seldom any other customers, and those who did come were old Armenians who engaged in heated debate with Karabet. Here, in this secluded shop, the boy learned to know the world through pictures.

Until now life outside his own experience had been only sound and words to him. Elias read nothing but his newspaper, and seldom picked up a book. Claire was a passionate reader of novels. Only years later did she too discover the world of illustrated magazines.

In Karabet's salon Farid saw photographs from distant lands: wonderful beaches, mountains, deserts, lavishly laid tables, exotic fruits, and all in colour. Actors and politicians, scientists and daring adventurers suddenly had faces too, and he looked at them so often that he felt almost familiar with them.

76. Cats and Bandits

The banisters on the staircase were a metre away from the roof of the aniseed warehouse, and the drop between them was four metres. Once Farid had landed safely on the warehouse roof he could make his way to the gang's meeting place unobserved. The other four members walked over the flat rooftops of Damascus too, light of foot and soundless as cats, and met in the attic, which had been disused for years. A large wooden table and a few old chairs had been stored up there for ever. The owners of the building never came up to the attic, and several steps were missing from the stairway leading up from the courtyard of the whole large property.

At Farid's second meeting, Josef brought out a fat book with a black cover. It contained descriptions of all the secret societies in the world. He never said how he came by such books. Some nights he read chapter after chapter aloud, while the others sat on the large chairs with their legs tucked under them, listening. Farid never met anyone who read aloud better than Josef, either before that time or after it. His husky voice increased the sense of mystery and made his hearers shiver. When he stopped for breath, the air was crackling with the boys' desire to hear what came next.

At such moments Farid felt how easily he could take off from the earth and fly, light as a feather, to the times and places that Josef brought to life. He felt a particularly close link with the boy on those nights, one that he never felt later with other friends, even those who shared his hiding places when he went underground.

Their tasks were carefully allotted. Azar was responsible for inventions. Josef called him "Gaber", after the inventor of algebra. Suleiman was to keep on the alert for any rumours. He was nicknamed "Bat", because he listened to everything in silence. Josef himself was responsible for research into conspiracies and secret societies, and Suleiman dubbed him "Massoni", freemason. Farid was given what he himself thought far too grand a title, but Josef, who thought he was very brave, gave him the job of defending the gang and called him "Kamikaze". Rasuk was to report news, and was called just "Journalist". Their names stuck even when the gang broke up.

Meetings always went on until dawn. Then the boys slipped off over the rooftops, like cats returning from their nocturnal rendezvous, and back to their beds.

77. A Series of Coups

When day dawned over Damascus on 31 March 1949, two armoured cars followed by two jeeps and four army trucks coming from the south reached the Old Town, where they divided into two groups. An armoured car, a jeep, and two trucks drove to the Prime Minister's house, the other vehicles went to the radio station.

When the armoured car braked sharply outside the Prime Minister's house, the soldier on sentry duty woke abruptly from an uneasy doze. A sturdily built colonel climbed out of the car. The sentry saluted.

"This is a coup," said the colonel. The soldier didn't know what that meant. It was the first time in Arab history that anyone had mentioned such a thing.

"Shall I wake His Excellency?" asked the soldier uncertainly.

"No need," replied the colonel, turning to his own soldiers, who were now standing to attention. "Fetch him out," he shouted excitedly.

Two men ran past the sentry into the palace and up the stairs. After a short time the Prime Minister could be heard swearing. Accompanied by the two soldiers, he came out of the house and stared at the colonel without a word. He knew the man: Husni Hablan was an unprincipled servant of the French who had also been in touch with the German Nazis in secret. A worthless character.

The Prime Minister was the scion of an ancient and aristocratic Damascene family, and had insisted on getting correctly dressed before going outside with the soldiers.

"You'll go on trial for this insult. And you won't get out of jail again this time," he finally said, in angry tones. Like the sentry on duty, he failed to understand the situation.

Husni Hablan laughed. "You and your trials – you can lick my arse! I'm the law now, and you'll be going to jail yourself because I say so."

The Prime Minister was deeply offended by the colonel's language. "Take him away," ordered the leader of the coup, and the soldiers, though still rather hesitantly, led away the man who had just been their prime minister. As if dazed, he walked to the jeep and sat down in his black suit between two unwashed soldiers.

"And now for that other idiot," cried the officer, telling his column to drive to the hospital where the seriously ill President was waiting for a stomach operation.

Soon the ten men who until now had been the most important people in the state found themselves in prison. That same morning the radio station broadcast some Austrian marching music and then the first communiqué from Husni Hablan, leader of the coup. The Damascenes, who had always hated their governments, rejoiced and danced for days.

Colonel Hablan moved into the palace with his wife and promoted himself to Field Marshal two weeks later. When he discovered from an illustrated magazine that field marshals always carried a baton, he ordered one made of pure gold from a jeweller. The baton, Hablan decreed, was to be large and its shape unique. But the jeweller, though he was pleased to have the order, had never seen a field marshal's baton in his life, so he modelled it on a rolling pin that he happened to have bought the previous day because he liked its shape.

The Syrians, with their talent for ridiculing all their rulers, said the dictator was under his wife's thumb. She was always waiting for him with a rolling pin when he came home drunk after visiting whores, and now he'd show her a thing or two!

Husni Hablan acclaimed his own rise to power enthusiastically and often, especially at the American and French embassies. But he soon sensed that the French and Americans wanted to keep him down. He turned away from these allies, feeling suspicious of them. Then he met Anton Saade, an ambitious young adventurer who admired and tried to emulate Hitler. His supporters called themselves Syrian Nationalists, wore black shirts, and copied the swastika as their symbol, but giving it rounded corners that made it look like a toy windmill. The ambitious Saade wanted to unite Lebanon, Syria, parts of Palestine, Iraq, and Jordan under Syria's leadership. As dictator of Damascus, Hablan applauded the young nationalist's brilliant idea, and hoped for more respectful treatment from the French and Americans once it was a *fait accompli.*

Saade was a fanatic, capable of anything, an intellectual with ambitious political plans but no experience of armed conflict. His first attempt to occupy a police station in the mountains of Lebanon failed miserably. His men were shot down, he himself escaped to Damascus, and fled to the protection of his patron Hablan.

Soon after that, however, the American ambassador called on Hablan and told him brusquely that, as the new ruler of Syria, he had embarked upon an extremely dangerous venture. Lebanon was part of the French protectorate, and if he did not hand the terrorist Saade over to the Lebanese at once the United States couldn't protect him any longer.

Hablan was frightened, and he did indeed deliver his ally up to the Lebanese, who executed Saade within twenty-four hours, even before the man who was such a threat to them could give away his contacts, naming any persons and governments behind his movement. Anton Saade's death for his ideal made him a martyr to his followers. The Syrian Nationalists, who were politically insignificant but well organized and shrank from nothing, now had a new enemy: the cowardly Husni Hablan.

On 14 August 1949, a hundred and thirty-seven days after his coup, the dictator was overthrown. It was just like a movie. A troop of soldiers marched into the capital. To avoid bloodshed the head of the secret service, one of those involved in the new coup, got in touch with the lieutenant commanding the guard of the presidential palace. The lieutenant received a large sum of money for unobtrusively disappearing that morning and telling his men to keep the peace until he was back.

The Field Marshal was still asleep when the troop arrived at the palace. Colonel Dartan, leader of the coup, sent a young first lieutenant to Hablan. The name of this athletic officer was Mansur, he was a loyal supporter of the executed Anton Saade, and he thirsted for revenge. Mansur drew his pistol and stormed up the broad marble stairway. Colonel Hablan was just coming out of his bedroom in a rage when the young, powerful officer in his camouflage gear reached the landing. Before the colonel found out what all this noise meant, the lieutenant's large hand, the hand of a farmer's son, landed on his cheek. The small, stocky dictator lost his balance and fell to the floor. "That's what you get for betraying the martyred Anton, you son of a whore!"

The dictator shouted for help, imbuing his words with all the weighty importance of the state, only to discover that the state wasn't at all important now. Only his wife went to stand by him, but she was sent back. Pale as death, she obeyed.

First Lieutenant Mansur kicked Hablan to start him going down the stairs. The dictator, stumbling, cursed, and begged, and when he reached the bottom his face was bleeding.

"Filthy dog," snarled Mansur. Colonel Dartan was standing some way off, disguised by a pair of sunglasses, unmoved as he watched the man who until just now had been his supreme commander. Two soldiers tied the dictator up with an old rope stinking of dung. "Put him up on the bonnet of the car," called First Lieutenant Mansur, while Dartan got into his own vehicle and went to the radio station to deliver his first communiqué personally.

Mansur drove his armoured car with the screaming dictator on the bonnet through the streets of Damascus, and then out towards Mazze. Once on the narrow country road he stopped at an agreed place, and waited for a second car to arrive with the overthrown Prime Minister Barasi. The scene had been well rehearsed and went exactly as planned. Four soldiers used their rifle butts to drive the dictator and his loyal prime minister, both in their pyjamas, out into the fields barefoot and with their hands tied. Mansur went up to them and shouted that they were going to be executed as CIA agents and traitors to the Syrian nation. Then he shot them both. Barasi said not a word. He had appeared dazed all the time. The first bullet hit and killed him. But Hablan, who was only wounded, screamed and cursed the cowards who were deserting him now. Mansur levelled his pistol at the dictator's forehead one last time as Hablan lay on his back and called out, loud enough for all the soldiers to hear him, "Anton Saade sends you this bullet, my dear leader." Then one final shot rang out in the silence.

Colonel Dartan, who had led the new coup, preferred to pull the strings backstage, and installed a civilian government loyal to him. But it didn't last long. On 19 December 1949 Colonel Shaklan, another early supporter of the nationalist Anton Saade, carried out a coup of his own. Shaklan, a wary and hardboiled character, was an enemy of the British and a friend of the Germans and the French. He ruled Syria with an iron hand until the end of February 1954, when Colonel Batlan carried out his own coup and put him to flight.

78. The Alley

Abbara Alley became Farid's province. In the afternoon he could hardly wait to be through with his homework and allowed to go out with Josef. He met more children and young people now. There was no other street where so many girls met every day to play games and whisper secrets. Word of that got around, of course, and the reputation of Abbara Alley attracted other boys.

And some strange people lived there, the kind you didn't find anywhere else in Damascus. The cab driver Salim was the best liar of all time; Riyad could talk to birds; and Basil, a lonely widower, had a dog who drank strong liquor with his master every day. Crazy Sa'dia wore seven dresses one on top of the other, and whenever she set eyes on a man she called out, "Don't you want to marry me? See how many dresses I have." Then she would begin lifting her skirts one by one. Bassam could shed tears to order, and Jusuf could walk upstairs and downstairs on his hands.

The inhabitants of Farid's own street exchanged polite salutations but otherwise kept themselves to themselves. At most, they knew their neighbours in the two or three nearest houses, whereas here in Abbara Alley people lived at such close quarters that they were like brothers and sisters, and everyone called old people Auntie and Uncle. The front doors of the buildings were never locked, and you could get into the inner courtyards any time you liked.

The alley divided at the end. To the right, it led to Jews' Alley, and to the left to the small but famous Bulos Chapel by the wall of the Old Town. Crowds of tourists passed by every day, and the children shouted, "Mister, mister, this boy is the son of holy Paulus," pointing to the only fair-haired boy among them, Toni the perfumier Dimitri's son. Toni just stood there, munching a flatbread filled with Dutch cheese, and as usual understood none of what was going on.

Farid had been spellbound the moment he stepped into Abbara Alley. It was the place of his dreams, just as he had imagined it during his solitary wanderings. It pulsated with life. The boys would often spend a couple of hours playing football, marbles, or cops and robbers in the street or its many back yards, and then four or five of them went along to see Uncle Salim and listen to his stories and tales of adventure.

But if they wanted to be private they went to Rasuk's place. With his father's help, Rasuk had converted an old tool shed in the garden into a room where he and his friends could be undisturbed, coming and going as they liked at any time.

Rasuk's elder brother Elias was a tiler. He was a cheerful character, and very nice so long as you didn't lend him any money. He danced beautifully, sang, and always looked slightly raffish with his oiled hair and open shirt. It wasn't long before Farid fell for his tricks. A little cat had broken its leg, Elias told him, but the vet wanted five lira and he had only four. Could Farid help out with the other lira? It was touching: the poor tiler, who earned two lira day at most, seemed very surprised to find that Farid loved cats more than any other animal. "I can see you're a noble, brave boy. Only the brave and noble like cats," he praised him.

Farid ran home as if those words had lent him wings, raided his piggybank, returned to Elias breathless and handed him the lira. When he told Josef about the cat's operation later, with much emotion, Josef laughed pityingly. "That trickster!" he said "He can't stand cats. He scores at least one hit with a stone on any stray cat around here. And now he's cheated you of the lira you carefully saved up." But on seeing his friend's horrified face, he consoled him. "We all get cheated by Elias some time or other. He wangled a lira out of me too," he added, shaking his head gloomily. After the cat story, Farid avoided Rasuk's brother.

Toni always had the best cigarettes, but he also brought chocolate and Dutch cheese to Rasuk's little hideout. They all liked the cigarettes except Farid, who didn't smoke. He preferred chocolate. The ever-hungry Azar used to fall on the cheese. He was very poor but highly intelligent. His father was a street trader who sold vegetables, fruits, or sometimes household implements from his wooden handcart, depending on the season, pushing the cart through the streets from sunrise to sunset, crying his wares. He had to feed nine children from the proceeds.

Azar's mother did what she could to help out by earning a little money. She embroidered Arab robes and dresses for a textiles dealer, she knitted pullovers, woollen caps and scarves. Her children always wore the most colourful pullovers in the whole alley because they were made with odds and ends of leftover wool. Her most tedious job, however, was wrapping caramels and other sweets in coloured paper for a large confectionery factory. The work itself was easy, but Azar's mother had a hard time protecting the delicious sweets from her hungry children. They were all carefully weighed and counted, and she had to pay out of her own pocket for every one that went missing. Once, when the children were left unsupervised and ate about forty, the poor woman had to wrap four hundred extra sweets to pay for those she had lost. She gave up that job in the end and wrapped socks instead.

Azar, who loved and honoured his parents, was able to go to the elite school in spite of the family's poverty, because he was extremely gifted and the Catholic Church paid his fees.

The Jewish boy Saki was different. Farid had never known anyone who made fun of his own parents before. Saki called his father "Old Skinflint" and his mother "Liverish" because of her liver disorder.

It was a year before Farid visited Saki's home for the first time. The family lived in nearby Jews' Alley, in a fine house with wood and marble panelling on its interior walls. Saki was doing an injustice to his father, a calm and courteous man with a melancholy face. His mother, however, was much worse than Saki described her. She was always suffering from some ailment or other, and expected everyone to feel sorry for her. Her husband did the housework for her, and suffered in silence from the diabetes that finally killed him at the age of sixty.

But to Farid, the greatest surprise was Saki's sister Sarah. Sarah was a beauty. She had her mother's blue eyes and her father's gentle, melancholy face. She was two or three years older than Saki and had matured early. At the age of twelve she went about looking very raffish, dolled up like a diva. One day, when Farid's gaze lingered on her backside, she turned and grinned at him. "Don't even think about it! I'm not marrying you. You're only a little boy."

He felt caught in the act, for at that very moment he had in fact been thinking that Sarah's behind was even prettier than Antoinette's, and he would like to marry her and lie on top of her back. Saki, who knew his sister, laughed. "He can't marry you anyway. He's a Jew gone wrong. He seriously believes the Messiah already came to earth to let a few useless characters crucify him."

Farid understood none of this. When he told Josef about it, his friend said the only difference between Jews and Christians was that one bunch thought Jesus had already come into the world and the other didn't. Only now did Farid understand Rasuk and Saki's game when they grabbed each other by the collar for a joke and kept shouting the same things.

"The Messiah came to earth – go on, say it!" Rasuk would bellow.

"No he didn't come to earth – go on, say it!" Saki would reply, even louder, until finally both boys punched each other in the ribs, grinning.

"What about Sarah?" asked Farid.

"Oh, never mind her," replied Josef. "She's a silly cow, mad keen to get married, that's all she has in her head. She wants to be married before her bloom wears off, because then there'll be nothing left but her stupidity."

Her brother Saki couldn't stand Sarah either. "She's thirteen, and she already knows what kind of meals she'll be cooking when she's fifty," he said with derision.

But Sarah was nice to Toni, and only to him, and closed both eyes to any faults. Perhaps because he looked like a blonde girl, perhaps because he was always giving her perfume. It was only when his father beat him one day for giving Sarah two wickedly expensive bottles of scent, and Toni had to go to see her empty-handed, that she gave him too the cold shoulder. Saki laughed at him. "You're nothing to Sarah without perfume," he told him in Rasuk's shed. As usual, Toni didn't understand.

79. An Angel's Weak Point

Aznar was really far too pale and thin for the part, so everyone was surprised when he was picked for the role of the angel that year.

Father Michael, who taught religious instruction, read out the names of all the pupils who were be in the end of year celebrations. This time Molière's *The Miser* was one of the items on the programme. The twelfth grade had been rehearsing twice a week since January. Farid, who had recited a long poem last year, was to do the same again too. He was known for his good memory and ability to get through a piece without getting stage fright. A gigantic tombola with many prizes donated by rich Christians was to boost the school funds. The Minister of Culture, the Patriarch of all the churches in Damascus, and the Vatican ambassador were invited to the festivities, which acted annually as an advertisement for the elite school. Forty or fifty rich families also had invitations.

Everything was going smoothly. The pupils taking part were let off homework on rehearsal days. Farid was very pleased. He had only to read his poem through twice before he knew it off by heart, but he didn't mention the fact, thus ensuring that he still had time off.

Azar rehearsed endlessly, practising how to move elegantly in his long white robe and manage his large, snow-white wings. The wings got in the way, and he kept falling over sideways. He looked pathetically clumsy. In the end the priest realized that he'd have to find him smaller wings, and after that Azar played his part brilliantly.

The great day came. Over five hundred seats in the school yard were all occupied, and over three hundred pupils and the school servants had to make do with standing room.

Opening the show, Mr Mansur the Arabic teacher read out a long, patriotic poem about Palestine and love of the homeland. Apparently his grief for Palestine made him weak and sick. Farid thought red-faced Mr Mansur, who was bursting with rude health, was rather too stout to be convincing. The pupils didn't understand the poem, but they had to clap at a signal from their teacher in order to impress the minister of culture.

Then came the play. It was a huge success, for nothing makes Arabs laugh as heartily as a miser. Finally Farid recited his poem with so much feeling than many women in the audience wept. But something went wrong with Azar's part in the proceedings. He was supposed to hover past the distinguished guests in the front row during the brief intermissions, offering them chocolates from a tray held in front of him and disguised as a cloud. But temptation was too strong.

When Farid joined the others he saw Mr Mansur who was so upset about Palestine, and the art teacher Madame Marierose, both laying into Azar, who was weeping with his mouth full. There was a pile of chocolate wrappings.

"What a thing to do!" cried the indignant Madame Marierose. "He ate all the chocolates! Every last one!" Azar shed more tears. One of his wings was hanging hopelessly askew.

80. A Message

Farid was fascinated by Sarah, but she simply ignored him. She walked past him and the other boys who visited her brother without a word of greeting, as if they weren't there at all.

You might have thought she was blind, for even when Farid put on his best clothes and asked for Saki at the door she merely said her brother wasn't in. Farid was well aware of that, having just seen his friend with her father in the family textiles store. Then she would turn and go away. Yet about every tenth time she said something that had him thinking for nights on end.

"Grey doesn't suit you. If I were you I'd try black and white and make the most of the contrast," she once advised him. So she *was* noticing him after all.

Next day, when Saki was working with his father in the store, Farid turned up not in contrasting colours but in white trousers and a white shirt. However, Sarah simply looked through him and said, "Saki's out." She didn't notice that he hadn't taken her advice, nor did she ask how he was. Nothing, no sign of interest, and that was worse than if she had called him and all his ancestors bad names. But just before turning she examined him scornfully once more, and said, barely audibly, "Black suits you better." Then the door closed.

"There's a secret message to you somewhere in all those remarks," said Josef, when Farid told him about it. Farid felt the same, but he didn't understand the message.

One night he dreamed of Sarah. She was lying on the marble floor of the hammam beside him. Steam hovered above them, and they were both perspiring. Sarah smelled of jasmine, her favourite perfume. She looked intently at him with her blue eyes, and he could have died of love.

"Now you must be brave or I can't marry you," she said, coming closer and kissing him on the lips, and then she lay down on her back beside him again and held his right hand. Suddenly he heard the voice of Claire's cousin Michel the barber.

"What's he doing here?" he asked.

"He has the best knives. Made in Solingen," she replied. And suddenly he felt a heavy weight on his outstretched thighs. Michel in his barber's coat was sitting on his thighs, holding his penis firmly between the thumb and forefinger of his left hand, and a razor blade flashed in his right hand. Farid wanted to jump up, but his body was heavy as lead. He heard the barber laugh. "You'll be a Jew in a minute," he cried, and Farid felt a sharp pain on his glans.

Breathing heavily and sweating, he sat up. His room was dark. Two cats were fighting on a rooftop somewhere. They hissed loudly, and then all was still. His prick hurt. He got up and put on a light. His foreskin was intact, but the glans was slightly inflamed.

81. Going to the Movies

"We just have to see that movie," said Josef up in the attic. It was Charlie Chaplin's *The Kid*. Josef loved films. But as all the cinemas were in the new part of town, and his parents worried about him; he always had to keep his cinema-going secret.

Although he was only nine, Josef had seen all the films about Flash Gordon the space traveller, and he knew the names of all the American film actors. He didn't like Arab film stars. "They just aim to make women cry. That's not what boys want to watch," was his crushing verdict.

"You have to see Chaplin before you die," he announced portentously, as if hatching a conspiracy. Rasuk was keen to go off to the cinema at once. He thought Chaplin was a genius. Saki and two other boys joined them, and at the last moment Toni said he'd come, but Josef didn't want him tagging along. "He'll only attract sex maniacs in those shorts of his."

So Toni went off to change and arrived at the bus stop, gasping for breath, just in time. His long trousers weren't properly buttoned up yet, and he was still fumbling with his flies.

"There are two people with congenital defects in this street," said Josef. "Aida ought to have been born a boy and Toni a girl." Suleiman's sturdy little sister could compete with any boy. Her stone-throwing was feared, for she always hit her mark.

It was Farid's first visit ever to the cinema. The man on the door took their tickets and laughed. "Here come Ali Baba and his thieves." He seemed to know Josef well.

When the lights went out Farid's heart raced with excitement. However many movies he saw later, *The Kid* was always his favourite, because of the magic of that first film show. He soon forgot everything around him and plunged into the world of the little orphan boy to whom the large-eyed tramp took such a fancy. Unfortunately the film kept tearing, and the light coming on in the auditorium was like a cold shower.

The show wasn't over until half an hour later than scheduled, and they ran for the bus. The driver took his time, stopping at every other store on his way through the bazaar to pick up people who had booked seats. This seemed to be his last trip of the day, and he was in no hurry.

It was after seven when Farid walked through the front door at home. He could hear his father's angry voice in the drawing room.

"Hello," he said, but he got no further. Before Claire could say a word, Elias had jumped up and hit him in the face. Farid fell backward and crashed into the door of the room. His nose was bleeding.

Claire begged her husband to stop, but he was like an angry bull. He grabbed the boy by the collar, kicked his backside and hit him on the head. Then he pushed him out into the courtyard and over to the storeroom near the kitchen. He thrust him inside and locked the door. Farid lay there for a while, but finally sat up. There was a light switch, but nothing to sit on, only shelves of foodstuffs, cans, rice, flour, salt, sugar. He crouched on the floor and tried to stop his nosebleed by raising his right arm and putting his head back. It did begin to dry up, but the pain in the back of his head, his ears, and his back was still there. He heard Claire crying and Elias shouting, telling her she'd be responsible if anything happened to her son on the street in the evening.

The memory of Chaplin's slapstick routines made Farid smile. All was quiet outside now, and it was late when he heard soft footsteps.

"How are you doing?" whispered Claire.

"I'm okay, don't worry," said Farid.

"I can't let you out. Elias has the key. But I can slip something under the door. I can ..."

"Oh yes, please, some bread and my geography exercise book. And a pencil. I have to draw the solar system. And I need an eraser too."

"I'll be right back," said Claire.

Soon after that she pushed his exercise book, ruler, compasses, a pencil, and an eraser under the door, as well as two flatbreads and a slab of chocolate in a flat paper bag.

Only later did he find a note between the flatbreads. "I love you!" it said, and, "I want to hear all about the movie tomorrow."

His solar system was not a huge success, but better than nothing. The geography teacher was strict, and seemed to have his hand welded to his cane. He rapped the pupils' knuckles for the least little thing. The children were afraid of him, and learned the lengths of rivers and the heights of mountains by heart, parrot-fashion.

Next morning a number of them were punished, including Josef and Suleiman. Farid escaped because of his drawing, and he thought gratefully of Claire. For the first time he understood what mother-love really means.

"How did you manage to get your drawing done?" asked Josef curiously at break, not without envy.

"The nights are long in my father's prison," he replied, aiming for a tone of histrionic pathos.

82. The Short Memory of Chickens

Aunt Salime wasn't really any relation; Claire and Elias just bought their eggs and chickens from her when they were in Mala, and called her Aunt out of civility and respect.

She had been a brave woman all her life. Wonderful tales were told of incidents in which she had played a prominent part, usually showing more courage than all the men in the village put together. Perhaps that was why she had never married.

If anyone asked why men avoided her, she said, "It's because they eat too much meat steeped in fear. Meat is digested in the body and everything that was in it goes its own way, the nutrients into the blood, the waste matter out again, and the fear into the heart."

She herself knew no fear and ate no meat, whether beef, mutton, or goat, because in her view not all the seasonings in the world could do away with the fear felt in its last moments by an animal going to slaughter.

Aunt Salime raised chickens and lived from selling their eggs, which were in great demand, because she fed them only the best grain. And when she had nothing else to do she sat with them and sang them nursery rhymes in a quiet voice. The chickens seemed to like her singing. They clucked quietly and melodiously, as if echoing Aunt Salime's voice.

She told her fowls tales of love, loyalty, and treachery. Claire was amused by them, and said Aunt Salime had a brain no bigger than her chickens did, that was why she understood them so well. But Farid thought her stories were exciting.

One day she told him about a hen who put up with all kinds of dangers and humiliations for love. She refused the advances of the magnificent rooster who ruled Aunt Salime's poultry yard, and instead went through a hole in the fence to the yard next door, where a gaunt white rooster lived. She made love with him until he fell over, exhausted, and only then did the hen go home. Aunt Salime's jealous rooster pecked her and flapped his wings, but the hen took her punishment, and went back day after day on her amorous outings. When Farid saw Aunt Salime's magnificent rooster, he doubted her story. The bird was a fine specimen, with all the colours of the rainbow in his tail.

"There, look at that! What did I tell you?" she suddenly said. The hen was on her way through the fence. Farid stood up and saw the two lovers dancing around each other. Then the white rooster mounted Aunt Salime's hen, who willingly squatted down and raised her rear end for him. Meanwhile Aunt Salime's rooster was throwing a fit of rage and jealousy, crowing himself hoarse. But the lovers took no notice. He couldn't get through the small hole in the fence; Aunt Salime had made sure of that. Whenever the white rooster finished the hen wooed him again with her dance, until he mounted her once more. And just as Aunt Salime had said, she didn't come home until the white rooster was lying in the sun half dead, and didn't even have the strength to keep his eyes open.

Farid shooed the jealous rooster away, and wouldn't let him get near the love-sick hen.

When a chicken was too old to lay, Aunt Salime killed it and sold it to one of her family or the neighbours. The way she killed the chickens so as to keep their meat free of fear was an impressive sight. When she had chosen an old hen, she took a long, very sharp knife and went out. She fed the chickens. She lured the bird whose life was about to end to a wooden platform set up in the middle of her meadow, drove all the others away from this raised dais, and finally made a great fuss of the hen, feeding her a few nuts and grains. The hen pecked, felt happy, and suspected nothing. Aunt Salime sang songs to her.

Then, quick as lightning, she drew the knife from its sheath, which she wore on her back, and stabbed, but not like a butcher, more like a dancer. Seconds later the knife had disappeared again. Her hand, now free, moved gracefully back to the bowl of corn. The other chickens were alarmed for a split second or so, but next moment they were greedily pecking at the grain that Aunt Salime scattered around the platform, while the star of the day performed a headless flight. It looked as if she were going to loop the loop in the air by way of farewell, but before she had finished she fell to the ground a few metres away, and Aunt Salime quickly vanished into the kitchen with the dead fowl.

"Okay, so that one left this life without fear, but what about the others?" asked Farid. "They've seen their companion die. How will they ever get up on that platform without feeling afraid?"

"Yes, the chickens do see it," replied Aunt Salime, "but they have very short memories – if they didn't, they'd have stopped laying eggs long ago."

83. The Devil's Daughters

His family's summer residence was not in a pleasant location. In the hot season, when Damascus was unbearable, his parents fled to Mala in the mountains, and Farid was woken every morning by a terrible sound: the bleating of sheep on their last journey through the village.

Nothing ever changed in Mala. Grapes, figs, sweet corn and tomatoes certainly tasted better there than anywhere else, but the butchers still slaughtered animals right outside their doors. There were three butchers in all, and one of them had his shop opposite Farid's house. The butcher was one-eyed but witty, and his fine voice was popular with the women.

Every morning he led one of the sheep from his distant sheds to his butcher's shop. He did it with the composure of a conqueror. He walked patiently behind the sheep, and kept stopping when it stopped and bleated pitifully, obviously with some presentiment of misfortune ahead. It was a short-winded, bloodcurdling bleat. The sheep looked around with its eyes wide. The butcher sang soft folk songs about longing and loneliness, and pushed the animal almost considerately forward. The sheep seemed to rouse itself from its sense of loss. It walked on as if automatically for a while, only to stop again. Interestingly, it was more hesitant and bleated louder the closer it came to the shop. It wouldn't walk the last few metres at all. All its legs seemed to go rigid, but with the ease of long practice the butcher pushed the poor animal to the door, tied it up to a metal ring there and opened the shop. At this time of morning Farid was already sitting out on the balcony.

The butcher soon came back from the shop with a knife and a tin bowl to catch the blood. He skilfully caught the sheep by both front and back hooves, threw it over like a judo fighter, and pressed his knee against the animal's head. It was taken by surprise and made no more noise. The knife flashed quickly and the sheep began bleeding to death. Its last twitchings pursued Farid into his dreams.

Once a week there was goat meat at the butcher's. Usually it came from young animals, but now and then an old billygoat had his throat cut. On goat days Claire stayed well away from the shop. She was fond of the little kids, and didn't want to see them slaughtered. The elderly billygoats smelled too strong for her, even if they had been washed before slaughter and the flavour of their meat was disguised by large quantities of choice spices.

The goats never took a step towards the shop of their own accord. The butcher hauled them there on a rope, and they resisted with all their might, bleating not pathetically but indignantly. In the end he had to carry them. He never sang to the goats at all.

"It's worth resisting even in the slaughterhouse," said Claire, who sometimes consoled Farid in this early and sorrowful hour on the balcony by bringing him a coffee.

In the afternoon – by which time all the meat was sold – the butcher rose from a brief siesta and strolled through the village and past his shop with his goats, about ten of them, and his sheep, taking them to the nearby fields to graze on thyme, thistles, basil, parsley, grapes, roses and anything else they found. That was what made the meat he sold so popular. The surprising thing, however, was that as they passed his shop the goats looked at it, stopped, bleated in agitation for a moment, and only then did they obey the butcher's imperious call.

"The nanny-goats know all about it. They don't just wail like the sheep, they're telling their friends exactly where they're going," said Claire, who affectionately called the animals "the Devil's daughters".

84. Secrets

The school vacation hadn't even begun when Farid realized, in horror, that his father had planned the summer ahead for him in every detail. If Elias didn't want to go to Mala he thought up some reason to keep his family in Damascus too. This time it was repairs to the house that Claire must supervise, since he had more than enough to do at the confectioner's shop. There were ten weddings imminent in the Christian quarter alone, and he had to provide mountains of sweetmeats for each of them.

"And I've found you two jobs," he casually told Farid, as if the matter had only just crossed his mind. "You'll spend the mornings with Abdullah the calligrapher, and the afternoons with the perfumier Sheikh Attar. He's the best creator of fragrances in town. You'll like working with both of them."

"Why two?" asked Claire. "Wouldn't one job be enough?"

Elias ignored her. "You start with Abdullah at nine on Monday." Farid knew the calligrapher's workshop; Abdullah was a friend of his father's. Whenever he went there with Farid they spent some time together, and Elias sometimes felt embarrassed about it and bought some examples of fine calligraphy, usually quotations from the Koran. Later, at some suitable opportunity, he would give them to his own Muslim customers, since he wasn't about to hang up passages from the Koran at home.

"So where's the perfumier's shop?" asked Farid, knowing that his father wouldn't put up with any protests.

"Ten minutes' walk from here, on the way to the Buzuriye. You'll learn a lot from old Sheikh Attar, he's a real magician."

The calligrapher was a shy, stiff, elderly gentleman. Farid had to start by polishing the workshop until it shone, and then he spent several days learning how to clean, sharpen, and trim pencils, pens, quills, and reeds and set them out for his master. Weeks passed before Abdullah finally said anything about calligraphic script itself. "It is the shadow of the voice," he said quietly, and handwritten script must be as clearly formed as shadows under the Arabian sun.

Farid learned what the calligrapher told him, made tea for him and his customers, fetched water and ran errands for his master. It was very hard work. All the same, he was happier there than at the perfumier's shop, where he went after the siesta. At first he liked Sheikh Attar's smile, but then he found out that it was only a mask. The man was cold as ice. He just wanted to use Farid as cheap labour. He put a seat outside the shop for him, and the boy was supposed to encourage passers by to go in and visit the master perfumier. But Farid himself was never to enter the place.

When he told Claire about it in the evening she didn't believe him, but next day she checked for herself, watching from a distance and seeing her son sitting on a stool outside the shop, looking forlorn. The sight did away with any scruples she might have had.

"This is not what we sent him here for. He isn't learning anything at all," she informed the perfumier in civil but determined tones.

"I don't have any other job for him," replied the master, with his mask-like smile. "I can't let anyone into the secret of my perfumes."

"Then we'll part company, with thanks for your hospitality," said Claire, patting Farid on the shoulder. "Come along, let's go."

They went to eat an ice at the Bakdash ice cream parlour in the Suk el Hamidiye, and then set cheerfully off for home. Claire said she would tell Elias about the end of this particular job that evening.

But Farid enjoyed going to the calligrapher, and Abdullah himself liked his young employee and his interested questions. He even began to smile a little. And when the summer was over, he had at least told the boy about the mistakes that a calligrapher must not make, and had agreed that the boy could go on coming to help him out any time.

So during the following school year Farid continued his training with the calligrapher. Whenever he felt like it he took the bus to go and see Abdullah, who always gave him some work to do. Usually it was filling in the characters on large advertising posters. The master painted the outlines of the characters with a thin brush, and the rest of it was tedious, time-consuming work, but it taught Farid patience.

He spent six weeks with Abdullah next summer too, before going to Mala with Claire and Elias for their vacation. From then on Abdullah even gave him exercises to take home. Usually he had to write out certain sayings in one of the seven different kinds of script that he now knew.

Later his master taught him the technique of calligraphic reflection. This was pure pleasure to Farid, and quite often it made him forget the time entirely. Playing with reflections fascinated him so much that even at home he could sit up until late at night over a picture in which a triangular calligraphic figure was reflected six times around the centre of a circle, producing a geometrical game and a maze for the eye to follow.

His father was deeply moved when, at Christmas, Farid gave him a calligraphic version of the name "Elias Mushtak" in the form of a circular ornament. The script was in gold on an olive green background;

both were his father's favourite colours. Elias couldn't take his eyes off the picture.

"Did you do that all by yourself? Did Master Abdullah help you?"

"No, no, I did it by myself here at home. I'm sure Master Abdullah would find all sorts of mistakes in it. I'd rather you didn't let him see it," said Farid, smiling awkwardly.

Elias gave his son ten lira that day. He had never given him so much money all at once before. "Go and buy yourself the best paints, brushes and pens. And if the money isn't enough, come back to me," he said. Two days later his name in Farid's fine calligraphy was hanging in a frame on the wall over the cash desk at the confectioner's shop.

Farid scribbled and practised on every piece of paper that he found. Before two years were up he was known as "the boy with the beautiful handwriting". He was only eleven.

He didn't guess what his reputation might do for him. Girls weren't very interested in the pieces of paper on which he wrote their names in curving script, but their mothers suddenly discovered his talents. They asked him in, turned on the charm for him, and after a while they came to the point. Would he write a letter for them, please? Those were strange sessions, in rooms where the daylight was dimmed because the women drew their curtains to guard against the neighbours' prying eyes, and sent their children out to play in the street when they were going to tell Farid what was on their minds. They had loving letters to send their absent husbands, sons, siblings, and friends.

At first he just wrote down everything the women poured out to him, but as time went on he reworked the texts himself so that they really did sound like love letters. Later came a third phase in which he listened only to the main points and then used his own intuition to write the love letter. Once he had found the right way to say something he repeated it word for word to all the husbands. Their wives rewarded Farid with chocolate, delicious rolls, and candies, and if they were really delighted with their letters they even gave him a hug.

His best letter of all was written for young Shafika. She lived at the cobbler Abdo's house in Abbara Alley, two buildings away from Josef.

One day she beckoned to him and asked, in the abrupt manner of all northern Syrians, how much a letter like that to her husband would cost. He told her it was all right, he didn't charge, and when she asked him in he followed her.

Farid knew Shafika only from hearsay; Josef had once said what a beautiful body she had. After she had offered him a seat she sat down too and asked him to write. He wrote in a kind of daze, for the young woman spoke sadly, in very brief and concentrated language, without any of the usual hackneyed phrases and without repeating herself. She dictated him a wonderful love letter, and he had only to put her words down on paper. The letter was about her loneliness and her longing for her husband, who was working on a building site in Saudi Arabia to pay off the debts he had incurred in Damascus when his little bus company failed.

After an hour the woman fell silent. Her letter covered six pages. Farid stood up when he had addressed the envelope.

"Would you like something to eat?" she asked, without looking at him.

"No, thank you," he replied. "I'm not hungry. I'll be happy to write letters for you any time you like." And with these words he quickly left. He was sorry he hadn't had a chance to discover whether what Josef said was true and she really did have an enchanting body, and whether, as many said, she smelled of thyme.

When he told his friends later about this commission they laughed at him. "No wonder women invite him in to write letters for them. Our Farid is just a big, innocent baby," said Josef.

Suleiman looked thoughtfully at Farid. "I think that's the trick of it," he murmured.

The beautiful Shafika never asked him to write another letter. Her husband had been angry, she told Farid. He said he was dying a hundred deaths daily there in the hot sand with the Saudis, while she sat in lush, shady Damascus, filling her head with all that nonsense about love as if life were some trashy Egyptian movie.

85. Death

The building next door to Farid's house had once been very beautiful. You couldn't tell from outside, for the façade was unpretentious, made of mud brick and wood, like most of the houses in the Old Town. People preferred to keep their riches away from envious eyes. The religious minorities were twice as cautious as the Muslims, for they always had to remember that any display of wealth might injure the vanity of the city governor. Then he would exercise his powers and confiscate a house for the flimsiest of reasons. That had happened to the Jew Josef Anbar, a rich merchant who had a wonderful house built in Damascus. He guilelessly showed his neighbours what he was creating within his four walls. Envious souls among them went straight to the governor claiming that the Jew had said his house would be finer than the governor's when it was finished. Next day Josef Anbar was arrested and the house confiscated.

So a wise man let only friends and family see his domain. The handsome architecture of the house next to Farid's was a wonderful interplay of form and colour. The arches around the inner courtyard on the first floor and the mingled pink and white stones of the columns and walls made it look larger, while their recurring patterns and lines delighted the eye. An octagonal fountain of coloured marble stood in the centre of the courtyard.

The man who built this house, Djamil Khuri, had inherited a large fortune. His father, a ship-owner, came from Egypt, and when riots broke out there in the nineteenth century and Christians were at risk he sold his shipping company and went to Damascus, where he grew even richer as a money changer. He married the daughter of an old but poverty-stricken Damascene family. His wife gave him a son, this Djamil Khuri, but before the baby was a month old his mother took her own life. No one could explain why, since she had always seemed happy. Only after her death was it discovered that she had been forced to marry the rich Egyptian. Her family owed him a lot of money.

The suicide and the rumours about it hurt her husband, who had thought he was giving his wife a Paradise on earth. Soon after her death he began drinking, and he was dead within a year.

His son Djamil was brought up by his grandmother. He was cared for well enough, but no one could take his burden from him. As a young man he swore that he would never marry, for he never wanted to do to any child of his own what his parents had done to him. He left the house and all his money to the Catholic Church on condition that the rooms would be let only to poor, needy Christians.

More than ten families had lived there since Djamil's death, and the building was now in very poor repair. Firewood and drums of heating oil were stored where the fountain once used to play. The walls were filthy, and many window panes had been replaced by cardboard or plywood.

"They're not poor, they're just mean," said Josef, when Farid said he supposed the state of the house was due to its tenants' poverty. "They won't pay a piastre for repairs. Those are cunning folk – they live there for almost nothing, pretending to the Church to be poor."

But Josef was being spiteful. The young widow Salma, who lived on the first floor near the way into the building, really was as poor as a church mouse. Claire and Antoinette's mother Hanan used to give her clothes and sometimes food or money. Even when Salma's husband was alive they had been so poor that they could hardly feed their six children.

And then her husband died one day without any warning. Salma's mother and sister happened to be visiting at the time, and when news of the death reached one of her husband's brothers he and his wife arrived in haste. After the scanty supper she gave them they stayed, even though there was so little space. Salma put her guests to sleep with the children in the main room, and she herself slept with her sister in the next room, where her dead husband was lying. It was a hot summer, and in the night the corpse began to smell of decomposition. Only slightly, but Salma picked it up. If you live in cramped conditions you're quick to notice any unpleasant smell. She cursed death, who had robbed her of her husband and left her alone with the children. Towards morning her eyes closed with exhaustion.

86. On the Rooftops

From Josef's room, you could reach the flat roof down a stairway, and from there you had a clear view of the big building next door and into most of its rooms.

"All the doors and windows are left open, and the walls are so thin that neighbours hear you coughing, farting, and snoring. They know what you eat, what you say, and what you want to keep secret," said Josef, laughing. His rooftop had a balustrade around it, so he was allowed to sleep up there on hot nights. "You never saw such things. A movie without a screen. A new story in every window," he assured his friend.

Farid's father despised the Damascene habit of sleeping out of doors in summer. Those who did, he said, were all uncivilized Bedouin who wanted to feel they were still in the desert, as if no one had ever invented houses. Claire didn't share his views, but she dared not contradict her husband. However, she told Farid that, to her mother's annoyance, she had sometimes spent summer nights with her father on their own roof as a girl. She thought it delightful, and had felt very close to the moon up there.

Elias Mushtak greatly respected the Rasmalo family, so he had no objection to his son's spending the night with Josef now and then. Unlike Claire, however, he never discovered that the two boys slept out on the roof together.

Farid felt as if he were in a theatre with several different stages when he first spent a night in the open air with Josef. Somewhere in the building opposite a play would begin, build to its climax, break off abruptly or continue after a short interval, while a second and then a third drama began in parallel on one of the stages above or below the first. Farid's marvelling gaze wandered back and forth. The characters in the dramas were quarrelling, playing, weeping, loving, laughing. Josef knew the programme by heart; he could say when and where men and women made love, how they did it, and how long for. To Farid it was all entirely new.

"He screws her seven times a week," commented Josef as they saw the traffic cop Maaruf through one of the semi-circular windows above the doors. He was thrusting vigorously into his wife as she knelt in front of him. She was pleading, her face twisted in pain, begging him to stop, but the man pushed himself in harder than ever, slapping her buttocks with the flat of his hand. The woman began to weep.

"Same thing every night. Her screams make him even randier. She doesn't fancy him at all, she loves Said who lives on the second floor next to Fahime," said Josef, pointing to the big corner room, whose tenant was walking up and down in it, wearing a pair of shorts. "She'll be there with him in exactly half an hour," he prophesied.

The attractive man in shorts was a bachelor from the north. He was blessed with an athletic body, almost blond hair, and sky-blue eyes, but he was not particularly bright, and he was also regarded as rather suspect. It was thought that he worked for the secret service on its lowest level, so people avoided him. All the same, women cast him amorous glances.

"You're joking!" Farid protested. "She must be half dead of pain down there, she won't want to do anything but rest."

Josef looked at him with a supercilious expression. "You don't know anything about women. They have eight souls and the Devil has only seven, so he can never get hold of a woman. She takes refuge in her eighth soul where the Devil can't reach her any more," he said, just as Fahime put on the light and began watering her flowers. "Look, she always waits until it's cool. It's better for the plants then," whispered Josef.

Fahime lived in a two-roomed apartment with her husband and three children. Like many Damascenes, she had the art of making ordinary cans, drums, tin containers, and old buckets into the most fascinating colourful pots for flowers, and she had adorned her windows, the stairs and the little terrace with them. Cacti, oleander, small-leaved basil, avocados, jasmine, hibiscus and carnations grew and flourished in these containers.

Even as Farid's eyes were wandering over all the plants, a fight broke out between two girls in a bedroom to the left of the stairs up to the second floor. Miserly Masud lived there with his wife, who was twenty years his junior, and their two girls, who took after their mother and squinted just like her too. They were having a pillow fight and were in the middle of it when Masud ran into the room, slapped their faces hard and switched off the light. The girls whimpered at first, but then Farid saw them lying side by side in the faint light of a small electric bulb, laughing quietly but heartily at their father's fury.

At the same time, on their left, the male nurse Butros was quarrelling with his wife over a broken vase. He was trying desperately to stick it together again. Josef giggled. "Maybe he put his prick in that vase." It was said that the male nurse would stick his penis into any orifice he chanced to find. But his wife was a particularly devout woman, who dressed their three daughters in such old-fashioned clothes that the girls looked like old women before their time. The neighbours often told tales of fights raging in the marital bedroom. Butros wanted to sleep with his wife every night, but she wouldn't let him.

A narrow corridor led past the male nurse's apartment to the old sailor Gibran's room. It was dark in there.

"What did I tell you?" whispered Josef, when something suddenly flitted past on the dark first floor of the house next door.

"What? I can't see anything," said Farid.

"She's waiting down there for Fahime to draw her curtains and go to bed," said Josef.

Fahime was the only tenant in the building who had thick curtains. The others had either none at all or very threadbare curtains that showed more than they concealed.

Ten minutes later Fahime put out her light, and next minute Samira the traffic cop's wife, barefoot, was on her way upstairs to the second floor. Silent as a shadow, she floated into Said's room.

"You've never in your life seen a dance of love like this," whispered the excited Josef. His voice held a promise of much to come. The electric light in Said's room went out, then there was the brief flicker of a match, and a candle was lit. Its light was so faint that Farid could only guess at the lovers' bodies. They both kept completely quiet, for the window was open and the curtain thin.

At last the game of love began. The man carried his lover around the room, and she twined her arms and legs around him. He danced with her, pressed her against the wall, laid her tenderly on the bed, lay down on her only to pick her up again as if she weighed no more than a feather. He whirled around in a circle with her, and then sat down on a chair while the woman rode him, perched on his lap. Her upper body moved rhythmically up and down, as if she were sitting on a trotting horse. After a while the man carried her around the room and slowly let her down to stand on her feet again, then embracing her like a dancer from behind. Farid was sure that Samira was smiling; he knew her face. She was pale, with white skin and blue-black hair.

How long they danced and made love in their dancing he didn't know later, for suddenly old Gibran's window caught his eye. It was said that the old man had seen both sides of the world. He was wrecked and all adrift, but the Catholic Church had caught him and found him a room in the big building. He had certainly declined to spend a single night in the St. Anastasius Old Folks' Home. Gibran had once been a sea captain, so the story went, and had made a great deal of money, especially by arms smuggling, but then he lost it all by night in the taverns and brothels of harbour towns and went back empty-handed to Damascus, no better off than when he left the city forty-five years ago as a young seaman.

Gibran told a great many stories, but most of them were lies and often macabre too. However, the young people of the Christian quarter loved him. He was ready to tell a story in return for a cigarette, and if there were women in the story he would want an extra five piastres to buy a shot of arrack. If he was drunk he would tell stories for free, but he needed half a litre of high-proof arrack to get drunk in the first place.

That August night Gibran was walking around in circles, looking at a picture on the wall, weeping, laughing, talking to the invisible hearers who seemed to populate his room.

"What do you bet he's talking about the crusades again, or his love affairs in Hawaii or Honolulu?" said Josef, who knew the picture on the wall. "All it shows is an ugly old freighter with a tiny little captain waving from somewhere on top of it. Gibran always says that's him."

Farid had never visited the old sailor, even though he lived so close. Claire wouldn't let him. She didn't like the grubby old man, she didn't even believe he had ever been to sea. And she said Gibran put too much nonsense about the seafaring life into young people's heads, more than was good for them.

87. Forbidden Reading

"It's not suitable for you," said Elias, when Farid saw him sitting over a fat book one day and asked what he was reading. His father's repressive reply intrigued him, and he went looking for the book with the brown cover next day. It wasn't in the modest library in the living room, or lying on any of the tables. Even days later it didn't reappear. Josef said that when fathers hid books they must be about sex. He'd just have to go on looking for that book, Josef added, and bring it to the attic.

Farid kept wriggling out of the proposition, but Josef didn't forget it. When he reminded his friend for the third time, Farid decided to search the wardrobe in his parents' bedroom, although he had never done such a thing before. Somehow that bedroom was taboo. Elias didn't like to see him there, and Claire herself always contrived to visit Farid in his own room before he thought of entering his parents'.

Heart thudding, he pulled the heavy door of the wooden wardrobe open. Farid suspected that he might find a secret compartment for forbidden books behind it. But the book lay in full view inside the wardrobe, wrapped in a red cloth. It was a book not about sex but about famous murders in history, and it said expressly, under the long title, that it was unsuitable for women and young people.

"That's because authors usually don't know the first thing about women," said Josef. "They ought to live here with a house full of females, like me, then they'd find out what strong nerves women have. We men are weaklings by comparison."

Then he read aloud. The book contained accounts of over fifty murders and the punishments, some of them very cruel, inflicted on the murderers. One such execution imprinted itself on Farid's mind for ever. It was for the murder of General Kléber, Napoleon's representative in Egypt. The murderer was a destitute student aged twenty-three called Suleiman al Halabi, a Syrian fanatic from Aleppo, who had come to Cairo on purpose to kill the victorious unbeliever. He made his way into the well-guarded French headquarters and stabbed him.

The French staged his execution as a grisly theatrical show. Suleiman al Halabi stepped up on the huge stage, watched by thousands of spectators. After nights of torture, he was a pitiful sight. But appearances were deceptive.

French music played, and a cannon shot announced the opening of the show. The verdict was read aloud. Four sheikhs accused of being in the plot were beheaded. That was just the prelude. An officer stepped up and explained that the hand raised against France was to be burned, and the man's screams were not to arouse any pity among the spectators, for the condemned man deserved none.

Two soldiers placed the man's right hand in a brazier where a fierce fire was burning and kept it in place until it was charred and dropped off. But Suleiman al Halabi neither screamed nor wept. He stood there as if he were in another world, looking absently at his torturers.

The little man never uttered another sound until the moment of his death, even under further cruel tortures.

The French occupying power took a final revenge on the city that had sheltered a man like Suleiman al Halabi by bombarding the Old Quarter of Cairo with cannon fire. More than eight hundred dead were found among the ruins.

"Compared to the stories in this book," said Josef as he reached the last page four nights later, "what our teachers call history lessons are pure distilled shit."

88. The Photograph

If he tried to remember the first time in his life when he seriously rebelled against anyone, he always thought of a little photograph of himself that he had had taken when he was a boy. He had been twelve at the time. The photo looked harmless enough. Farid was gazing into the distance, seen at a slight angle in the manner then usual for photographic portraits. There was a touch of melancholy in his eyes, although his gaze was determined, almost defiant. His mouth had made only a faint attempt to sketch the friendly smile requested by the photographer.

That day Farid was wearing a dark brown shirt with a broad collar showing above a fawn jacket. In the photo his shirt looked black and his jacket grey. His wavy hair was combed back.

A week earlier Sarah, Saki's sister, had told him he had beautiful hair, but it would look even better if he rubbed hair oil in and then combed it. That way it would look more elegant, and its black would be more brilliant than his natural muted near-black.

He couldn't find any hair oil at home. He fished a lira out of his piggy bank and went to the Armenian barber. Claire beamed at him when he came home, and went straight to find her in the kitchen to see if she'd notice.

"What a handsome boy," she said, hugging him. Then she looked at him again and kissed him on the forehead. "If I were a young girl I'd fall in love with you on the spot. But alas, I must make way for others now."

He was rather surprised to see so many baking sheets in the kitchen, full of meat pasties and stuffed flatbreads, and the mountains of vegetables waiting to be cooked. The table was also laden with generously filled dishes of salad, rice, and pine kernels. But Farid had no time to linger and ask questions. He went straight over to see Josef, and was surprised to find that his friend didn't notice any change in him. Then he met Rasuk, Suleiman, Aida, and Antoinette in Abbara Alley, and they didn't marvel at the new glory of his hair either. He couldn't go around to Sarah's place because her brother was in the street with the others at this moment, explaining why he couldn't invite anyone home. "We can go there again tomorrow, but today they're all cleaning like crazy because of this big Jewish festival coming up, and the moment they see someone just sitting they find him work to do."

Disappointed, and cursing his bad luck, Farid mooched off home again, unaware that his father had invited twenty other confectioners to supper. It was only in the front hall of the house that he heard the cheerful noise from the drawing room. He stood still for a moment, glancing at the inner courtyard. There was no one there. He hurried to the right, past the store-room, and into the kitchen. Claire was there, eating by herself at a small table.

"What's going on?" he asked breathlessly.

"Your father has invited his colleagues to supper to thank them for electing him."

"Electing him to what?" asked Farid, looking through the kitchen window and into the drawing room, where the tipsy men had just burst into a roar of laughter.

"Your Papa is the top confectioner in Damascus now. It's a great honour. No Christian has ever held the post before."

Farid nodded his head in acknowledgement, and hungry as he was quickly put a flatbread stuffed with meat into his mouth. Then he took a second stuffed with sheep's milk cheese.

"You should sit down to eat," said Claire. "Or better still, go and say hello to your Papa and his guests first, and then come back here to have a proper meal."

"Must I?" asked Farid unwillingly. "Why aren't you with them?"

"It wouldn't do. They're Muslims, and it's not the Muslim custom to eat with strange women. Off you go, now. You only have to say hello and then come back."

To please her, he went, although he didn't want to. When he entered the drawing room, a cloud of smoke and the aroma of aniseed met him. The men were laughing.

"Ah, here comes the crown prince," cried a fat confectioner with bushy eyebrows. Silence followed his words.

"Good evening," Farid greeted them, almost inaudibly.

"What on earth do you think you look like?" bellowed his father, who was enthroned at one end of the table, and he pointed to Farid's oiled hair. "Say hello nicely to the gentlemen and then come here to me."

Elias was drunk. Farid felt miserable with rage and shame. He shook hands with all the guests one by one and tried to ignore their mocking remarks about his hair, although he also heard some of them speaking up for him. He went on to where his father was sitting, walked past him to go down past the other half of the confectioners' association, saying good evening to all the men there as well. He began to feel less flustered, for by now the men had stopped taking any notice of him. They were talking to each other again, and merely gave him limp handshakes. But the last man, who was sitting by the door, held Farid's hand tightly in one of his own and stroked his cheek with the other.

"Won't you give me a little kiss? Uncle Hamid likes good boys," he said, his wet lips smiling to show yellow teeth.

"No," muttered Farid, pulling his hand away with a jerk. Then he went back to his father.

"Good evening, Papa," he said. Elias turned his vacant gaze on him, took a fabric napkin in his left hand, grabbed his son's collar with his right hand and pulled him close.

"My son is no American sissy." His aniseed-laden breath was horrible. It made Farid retch. But his father pulled him even closer and began rubbing his head with the large napkin as if towelling it dry. The men laughed.

"Young people have to be brought up properly," announced one of them.

"Yes, the saying goes: God's blessing be on the man who beat me, not the man who indulged me."

There followed a babbling of confused voices, and Elias's grip tightened. Farid's scalp was burning. His father's hand was holding the collar of his shirt so tightly that he could hardly breathe. He felt he was choking. With a violent movement he freed himself, and fell over backward. Elias was alarmed when he heard his son hit the floor.

"You fool!" he stammered in alarm. "You could have broken something!"

Farid got to his feet and rushed out of the dining room to the sound of laughter from the men. He saw Claire coming out of the kitchen, ran past her to his room and locked himself in.

She followed and knocked softly on the door, but he didn't want to see her. In this humiliating defeat, he would feel ashamed to meet her sympathetic eyes. And he was angry with her for sending him in to his father. Farid felt lonely and desperate. The world had turned its back on him.

After a while, however, he straightened up again and saw his hair in the mirror, looking as windblown as a wheatfield after a stormy night. Suddenly he couldn't help laughing. That one crucial second stayed in his memory for ever. He decided to get the better of his father. "I'll keep my hair like this even if you die of rage," he whispered.

Claire was surprised to see him storm out of his room, and when she heard the door of the house bang a little later she knew that her husband had handled the situation badly yet again.

Farid didn't have to look far. The photographic "Studio of the Stars" was just before the Kishle road junction. Basil the photographer was not a little surprised when the boy paid him the price he asked in advance, and without haggling either, bringing out a heap of piastres which, as the photographer rightly suspected, was all his savings. The boy carefully counted the money, put the remaining piastres back in his pocket, looked proudly at the photographer, and said, "And for that, I want the best photo you ever took. I'm going to keep it all my life."

The photographer had no idea what the boy wanted the picture for, but somehow he felt tremendously keen to take a good photograph, so much so that it made him slightly dizzy. He suggested that the boy might like to comb his hair, because the camera would record everything. He himself took a sip of water and then watched closely, rather taken aback to see Farid carefully arranged his oiled hair in front of the mirror, putting every lock in order.

"You look like that famous young actor; his name escapes me for the moment," he flattered the boy.

Three days later the photo was ready. Farid was more than satisfied, and from then on he took it with him wherever he went.

89. The Inventor

As they were sitting on the ground outside Josef's house, listening with bated breath to the story Suleiman was telling, a woman neighbour called out to Azar: would he come and mend her broken iron? Azar wasn't thirteen yet, but he was as efficient as if he were a mechanic, an electrician and a joiner all in one.

Suleiman had just seen the latest Errol Flynn movie, and was telling his friends about *The Adventures of Don Juan*. Since children weren't allowed in to see the film, Suleiman had bribed the doorman with Spanish cigarettes.

Farid was sure that the movie was only half as exciting as his friend's account of it, for once Suleiman got into his stride he used only the basic outline of any film and made up his own story on that foundation. The story changed track even more when his audience interrupted him.

Azar, who never tired of Suleiman's stories, called back to the neighbour, "It'll cost you twenty piastres."

"My God, you're getting pricier all the time. Look, come around here, I'm sure we can reach some agreement," the woman said.

"No, twenty piastres or I'm not doing it," replied Azar. "Last time," he muttered quietly, "she fobbed me off with an orange and a slobbery kiss on my cheek. Talk about a nightmare! I can't stand the way she stinks of fish and oranges."

"All right," called the woman, "but I'm only paying fifteen piastres, that's all I have."

Azar got to his feet and turned to Suleiman. "Don't go on with the story until I'm back." Don Juan was just holding his beloved in his arms.

"Tell her to pay you the twenty and I'll screw her," smirked Josef.

"Heavens above, she'd suck you in and spit out your bones, and then what do I tell your Mama?" sniped Azar.

Quarter of an hour later he was back, cursing the woman, who had paid him with just ten piastres and two oranges.

90. Laila's New House

Farid had really met his Uncle Adel properly only on two or three visits to Beirut, and when he and his parents went to stay with Aunt

Malake he had eyes and ears only for Laila. He knew he had once seen Uncle Adel sitting at the end of the table at lunch, but even then Laila's father had failed to make any great impression. It was Elias and Malake who dominated the table. Back in Damascus, Farid could hardly even remember the man's face.

Laila always looked after her little cousin so lovingly that Claire could have those days in Beirut to herself, left at leisure to go on long shopping expeditions with her sister-in-law. In the 1940s Beirut was a window on the west, a city of exotic goods and customs from all over the world. By way of contrast, Damascus was still something of a sleepy provincial town in the middle of farming country.

One day in the winter of 1951 a telephone call brought the bad news that Uncle Adel had unexpectedly died of a heart attack. He had woken in the night and felt thirsty, but he obviously never made it to the refrigerator. He fell down dead in the corridor.

Elias sent telex messages to his brothers Salman in Mala and Hasib in America. Salman still bore his sister a grudge, and refused to come to his brother-in-law's funeral. Hasib wrote a few civil platitudes, and didn't come either. Elias himself, however, set off that evening with Claire and Farid, and reached Beirut late at night. Malake was grateful to them, for her husband's family was also hostile to her, so she and her daughters had no one else to stand by them.

Her daughter Barbara was nineteen. In temperament and strength of character, as Elias realized with amazement, she was the image of old George Mushtak. Laila was seventeen at the time, and Farid was surprised by the pallor of her face. He felt alarmed at the sight of her, and later, when she was resting on a sofa with her eyes closed, he actually thought she had died. Isabelle, the youngest girl, was just nine, and to Farid she was a silly little thing whom he ignored. He spent most of the time sitting with Laila and comforting her by stroking her hand.

Malake was lamenting the fact that next spring Adel had been going to give her the promised honeymoon they'd never had. He was planning to take her to Rome, Venice, Paris, Vienna, and London. Barbara had encouraged them to go, saying she and Laila could easily look after little Isabelle.

A year later Elias was helping his sister to find a house in the exclusive Salihiye quarter of Damascus. Malake had sold the factory and their villa in Beirut for a good price, and in the summer of 1953 she and her daughters returned to the Syrian capital. But she refused ever to set foot in Mala again.

They lived in style in a large, handsome house built in the eighteenth century by a relation of the Ottoman Sultan, and Farid, who knew the mysteries of calligraphy, was able to decipher all the sayings on the ceilings and walls for his aunt and her daughters. Poetic and religious Sufi quotations adorned the walls, columns, and ceilings of rooms in line with their functions. Barbara carefully wrote everything down, and Laila, her gaze transfigured, watched the boy. Everything he did touched her heart. He looked handsome and noble as a prince's son, she thought, as he stood there deciphering the Arabic texts word by word, and once he had disentangled the calligraphic labyrinth of a saying it was clear to her for ever. The bathroom alone had thirty of them, all to do with water and Paradise.

Malake was a capable woman. With her brother's help, she bought some large and dusty fields lying fallow to the north-east of the Old Town at a very reasonable price. Later on, this area became a large, elegant middle-class housing estate. After ten years plots of land here cost almost a hundred times what she had paid.

Normally Farid would have been glad of his favourite cousin's return to Damascus, but instead he bewailed his bad luck, for he had to leave the city himself.

"When the angels visit a house," joked Laila, "the devils run for it." She looked at him and laughed to hide her own regret, but she couldn't deceive Farid.

91. Grandfather's Death

It was a sunny February day, and as Grandmother Lucia told the story, Nagib had found one of his rabbits sick that morning. Grandfather loved rabbits, and had built his pets a beautiful hutch. He never had many of them, at most six or seven. Farid didn't like the rabbits, so he never went to the east-facing terrace of his grandparents' house where the hutch stood, although hutch was hardly the word for it. Grandfather had lovingly built a natural enclosure with a stream of water, caves, and sunny terraces, all surrounded by wire netting. There was a bench opposite the hutch where he often sat for hours on end, happy as a child as he watched his rabbits running about. Grandmother Lucia hated them.

So that morning Grandfather had been sitting on his bench, as he so often did. There was a big black rabbit on the old man's lap. He was worried; it wasn't well. Grandmother had looked out of the kitchen and saw Nagib sitting there without a scarf. She opened the kitchen window and called to him to put something warmer on, but he told her he'd come in soon. Lucia made coffee. When she turned to look again, he was sitting there all hunched up while the black rabbit hopped merrily about the terrace.

"Nagib," cried Grandmother, full of foreboding. But Grandfather couldn't hear her any more.

❧

Farid had just come home from school when the phone rang. "Oh, no, for God's sake! I'll come at once!" Claire called down the receiver, and she rushed out of the room.

"What's happened?" he asked.

"My father's dead."

Grandfather was lying on the bed. Neighbours and relations were there already, and Claire was crying like a little girl. Farid had never seen her shed tears before. She reacted to neither friends nor family members, and he had a feeling that she didn't even recognise him. She just wept and kept kissing her father's hands and forehead, and she was talking to him. "Why did you leave me so quickly, why didn't you say goodbye?" Nothing could comfort her.

Claire heard nothing and no one. Even when Elias arrived and embraced her lovingly she didn't notice him, but sat lost in her thoughts beside Grandfather's body.

"I'll have to go now, there's a lot to organize," Elias whispered to his son. "You stay with Mama and help her."

Even when Lucia went to bed, Claire and Farid stayed with the dead man. Farid didn't feel at all tired. "Do you see his smile?" Claire asked in a low voice at about midnight. And indeed Grandfather was smiling with as much amusement as if his death were a joke. Farid noticed Grandfather's new shoes, and he remembered other corpses who had worn brand-new shoes in their coffins. Presumably God set great store by cleanliness.

"Do you know why he's smiling?" asked Claire, with the ghost of a grin around her mouth. "He's laughing at Grandmother's superstitions and our own horror."

"What superstitions?" asked Farid.

"She believes the rabbit was mortally sick, it palmed its own death off on Grandfather, and that cured it. She told everyone so, and late this afternoon she gave the butcher all the rabbits for free."

"But that's stupid," he said. "The poor creatures can't help it."

"Come out with me a minute, but put something warm on," Claire said suddenly.

Farid put on his jacket and followed her. She left the second-floor drawing room, went along the arcades around the inner courtyard to the terrace on the east of the house, wrapped herself in a rug, and sat on the bench. Shivering, Farid sat down beside her. It was full moon.

"This is where he was sitting with the rabbit on his lap, and then his head tipped a little way forward as if he'd gone to sleep. Grandmother knew at once that he was dead, because he never fell asleep when he was with his rabbits. He was always far too curious and interested in everything for that."

The enclosure was empty. Even the little stream of water had stopped flowing. Farid felt a strange loneliness. He pressed close to his mother, and Claire wrapped her rug around him.

92. Going to Church

Farid's had strange feelings when he went to church. He took little notice of the Mass itself; in spite of the incense and gorgeously coloured vestments, it left him cold. But his gaze strayed, and when it fixed on one of the pictures on the walls, he wandered back in time to the dramatic events recorded there in oils.

It was obligatory for the pupils at the elite Catholic school to show up in the school yard washed and neatly dressed on Sundays, and then proceed two abreast to the church. He was happy enough to go, but he didn't like having his presence checked on the way into church every Sunday. Anyone who didn't come was punished first thing in the morning on Monday in front of the whole school. Only Muslims and Jews were excused attendance at Mass.

For years he made the church service into a memory game. He divided the Mass up to fit the fifty kilometres of road between Damascus and Mala. Both Mass and the journey to Mala lasted about an hour. The idea of the game was to suit every sentence spoken or act performed in the service to one of the various places that the bus passed on the way to Mala. Farid assigned a village, a factory, a ruin, or a tree to every *kyrie eleison* and every hymn.

He also liked to imagine the bus constantly losing parts of itself along the way, cutting curves so that women and children screamed and the chickens who always travelled under the seats with their feet tied flapped their wings. And when his bus finally reached Mala, clattering, hooting its horn and raising dust, he was glad because the church service was over.

But after a while his imaginary bus ride bored him, and he found wandering among the pictures and statues in the church more exciting. For almost three years he always sat in the same place, a pew with a good view of almost all the paintings hanging near the altar.

He liked the angels best. They were not gentle but often looked positively violent, armed with swords, spears, and fire. They were strange beings, their faces radiating feminine charm, while their bodies and posture were warlike and virile. For Farid, however, their greatest fascination lay not in this contradiction but in imagining how it would feel to be such a creature himself, both airy and of the earth, able to walk on foot or rise in the air with powerful wings, free of all earthly bonds.

He had favourite pictures, but the light decided which painting or which figure attracted his attention on any given Sunday. However, the great cross behind the altar where Jesus had died with an infinitely sorrowful expression on his face was always at the centre. The letters I.N.R.I. stood above the Saviour's head, and Farid always tried to understand this word INRI as a secret message.

Every time he saw the crucified Jesus he couldn't help thinking of his friend Kamal Sabuni, who like a few other sons of prosperous Muslim families went to the elite Christian school. Kamal thought Christianity interesting, but he could make nothing of the crucifixion of a God who could have turned the entire Roman Empire into a swamp and the Caesars and their soldiers into ants, just by lifting his little finger. And the young Muslim thought the Trinity of Father, Son, and Holy Ghost a very strange idea.

"Muslims are too primitive to understand it," said Farid's father, but even he couldn't explain the Holy Ghost, although he knew a lot about religion.

INRI. What message lay behind it? The religious instruction teacher at school explained the meaning of the letters in Arabic: Jesus of Nazareth, King of the Jews. But that wasn't mysterious enough for Farid. Why did INRI have such an effect on him?

"It was all part of the big theatrical show," said Josef portentously. "He had to be killed in the Roman way. They were the rulers, so the notice had to be written in their language."

In his mind's eye, as Josef talked, Farid saw Pilate the Roman governor standing pale, slender-boned, and full of revulsion before the rabble of what, to him, was a strange and dusty province.

"Pilate found himself on a kind of stage," Josef went on, "facing a trembling young man, and he, the Roman, quite liked him: a young Easterner condemned to death and abandoned by his whole clan. So there stood sensitive Pilate, a man who didn't like the death penalty, and opposite him was a young revolutionary who simply wanted to get dying over and done with and didn't even notice when he was offered a way out. Anyway, but for the Romans his death wouldn't have had any INRI or the huge symbolical weight of the cross. Jesus would have died a miserable death by stoning, that was the usual kind of execution in the Middle East at the time. A heap of stones as a symbol wouldn't have lasted for even a century. But," said Josef, lowering his voice as he always did when he was about to broach the subject of conspiracies, "I.N.R.I. didn't just mean Iesus Nazarenus Rex Iudaeorum, it was a coded message to the Romans saying: Iustum necare reges Italiae: It is just to kill the kings of Italy. That's what it says in this book," concluded Josef, showing Farid a work about Italian secret societies.

93. Saying Goodbye

"Parents are weird," said Josef. "They never ask if you want to be born, they just go ahead and produce you. And they don't often ask any children they already have if they want a new baby in the family. They have it off with each other and expect the rest of the family to be glad. But in terms of the actual results, the cost of those five minutes of pleasure would give even a math teacher goose bumps.

I mean, what harm did I ever do Rimon and Madeleine for them to dump me in this house full of females? Did I ask them to do it? I'd have liked to be an only child with two ordinary parents, mother and father, and then I'd have some peace now. 'Mind what you're doing, Josef! That's not a thing to say to a girl! Josef, dear, we don't say that kind of thing when there are women in the room! Josef, that's no way to speak to your sister! Josef! Josef! Josef! The hell with their Josef! He's not me. I'm not him. I've been secretly calling myself Jacob for some time, so when they call for Josef I don't feel as if it's me they want.

And what about your own respected father? Did he ask the rest of us if he could put you in a monastery? He'd have had a shock if he did. Elias Mushtak, sir, we'd have said, we don't give a damn for your monks. Leave Farid here with us. He hates the monastery idea. We don't mind praying for the elm tree that burned down, but leave your son here. I'm just beginning to like him. But what does your good father go and do?

I overheard Madeleine and Claire talking yesterday, and they're dead against it too, but they don't get a chance to open their mouths."

Josef looked up, and for the first time ever Farid saw tears in his tough friend's eyes. This was at the beginning of June 1953, a week before he left for the monastery.

BOOK OF LAUGHTER I

*The world of the imagination welcomes children
more kindly than their parental home.*

৯৹

DAMASCUS, 1940–1953

94. Damascus

Damascus isn't so much a city, a place marked in an atlas, as a fairy
tale clothed in houses and streets, stories, scents and rumours.

The Old Town has fallen victim to epidemics, wars and fire countless times in its eight thousand years of history, and for want of anywhere better was always rebuilt on the same site. The hand that has
moulded Damascus to this day was that of a Greek town planner,
Hippodamos of Miletus. He divided the city into strictly geometrical
quarters with fine streets, all laid out at right angles. The Greeks loved
straight lines, whereas the Arabs preferred curves and bends. Some
say it has something to do with their exhausting journeys straight
across the desert. A bend shortens the distance, at least for the eye.
Others claim that life is expressed in curves: the olive tree bows
under the weight of its fruits, a pregnant woman's belly is curved, the
branches of a palm tree form a rounded shape. The old Damascenes
had a more prosaic explanation: the more bends in your streets, the
easier they are to defend.

Once you start talking about Damascus you must be careful not
to founder, for Damascus is a sea of stories. The city knows that, so

for all the Arab love of winding streets and alleys it retains a single Straight Street, which is called just that. It is the guideline and point of reference for every walk and every story. If the countless bends in the winding alleys confuse you, then you can always turn back to Straight Street. It's an outsize compass that for over three thousand years has shown people the way from east to west.

Once upon a time, they say, it was over twenty metres wide, a magnificent avenue with columns and arcades. But the traders moved their stalls further and further out into the street from both sides, and today parts of it are not even ten metres wide. The traders of Damascus are masters of the technique of land-grabbing. They unobtrusively extend the area occupied by their stalls with a crate of vegetables, a little pyramid of inlaid boxes, or a tray of pistachios put out on the sidewalk for a few hours to dry in the sun. Then they put up a light-weight wooden stand and cover it with an even lighter cloth, to protect their wares when the sun is too hot. Once passers by and the police are used to the look of it, the wooden stand sometimes falls over, and the trader finds himself obliged to replace the wobbly structure with something more solid. Then the whole thing gets a door, so that he can enjoy his siesta without fearing thieves, and soon there's a small window with a curtain over it. A week later the thin wood of the construction has been reinforced as if magically with mud brick, and after a covert nocturnal operation the little building is suddenly bright with whitewash, and its doors and window frames are freshly painted blue. Soon there's yet another vegetable crate standing outside it, just to attract the customers' attention. The police officer on duty grumbles, but he is placated with much volubility and a cup of coffee – until the time comes when he is transferred somewhere else. And the new policeman could swear that there'd always been a bend in the road here.

Damascus has seen and endured Arabs, Romans, Greeks, Aramaics, and another thirty-six peoples of different cultures. They ruled the city in succession, or sometimes at the same time, and no race has ever moved on without leaving its own mark on Damascus, so it has become a historical patchwork, a lost luggage office of cultures. Many compare it to a mosaic with pieces that have been fitted together by travellers over a period of eight thousand years.

Its builders have given the Damascenes all kinds of presents. Here you see a Greek column; a Roman bridge; a modest wall built with stones from the palaces of past millennia. There you find plants brought from Africa by slaves. To this day you seem to hear words in the street that were spoken by foreigners hundreds of years ago. And you meet people, whether vegetable sellers or doctors, whose forebears came from Spain, the Yemen, or Italy, but who still think of themselves as genuine Damascenes. The odd thing is that they're right.

Damascus has been a fruitful oasis in the desert of Arabia. At the end of the 1940s several large textiles companies were founded near the city, many schools were opened, the university was enlarged, and newspapers and magazines filled the kiosks, bearing witness to the cultural wealth of Damascus. Cinemas became fashionable. They all had special days when women could go, and sometimes a man in love would wait in the street for three hours just to set eyes on his beloved when she came out. He would have to take the greatest care that no one noticed him smiling at her, but if she returned his smile it was like a foretaste of Paradise.

95. The Cat-Lover

Grandfather held his grandson's hand tight, for he was afraid of losing little Farid in the crowded souks. He stopped at the entrance to a caravanserai and spoke to a spice merchant. Meanwhile Farid stared curiously at the interior of the great building. Horses and mules were tied up in the yard, and he saw many porters hurrying into large storerooms full of sacks. They carried the sacks out on their shoulders as if they hardly weighed anything, and loaded them up on the carts waiting in the yard. A pale man in a dark suit wrote down what the porters had stacked on the carts. A driver cracked his whip and the horses, who had been dozing with their heads bent, woke up and trotted out. The driver shouted to people to clear the road, so that they wouldn't get their clothes dirty. It worked: a passage was opened up for his vehicle, and then the crowd closed up again to continue their conversations.

Suddenly Farid saw a camel butcher in a distant corner of the caravanserai. Camel meat is not eaten in the Christian quarter, so Farid had never before seen anything like this, and he was never to forget the horror of the scene.

The tall, distinguished-looking animal stood at the door of the butcher shop. It was looking at Farid, its eyes wide with fear. A dwarfish butcher was whetting his big knife while he talked to another man stitching jute sacks nearby.

With difficulty, two men finally got the camel to kneel down. The animal was still looking at Farid as if pleading for his help. Then the butcher passed his big knife over the camel's throat, as if he were drawing a bow over violin strings. Blood spurted, and fell into a huge bowl. The camel's empty eyes now gazed into eternity. The man stitching the sacks didn't even give the scene a glance. He turned the jute sack he had just finished inside out again, and then added it to a large pile of other sacks.

Farid and his grandfather strolled on from the caravanserai through the Qaimariye quarter that had once been the commercial centre of Damascus, and was now a residential area with a few workshops. On the way he saw a strange sight. A man was sitting on the floor in the middle of his store, reading aloud from the Koran. About thirty cats surrounded him. They were sitting on his lap, on the shelves, on the floor, and in the display window of the otherwise empty room.

"Does he sell cats?" asked Farid.

"No, no," said Grandfather. "He's a holy man who looks after all the local cats."

The cats clambered over the man as he sat there, jumped from his shoulder to the shelves and then back again, but he went on reading undisturbed. Grandfather took a lira bill from his wallet and put it in a copper dish near the entrance.

"My thanks for your kind heart," said the man, and turned back to his Koran. Three cats crossed the street. Making purposefully for the store, they put their catch of three mice down outside the door and went in. The man looked up.

"Ah, those are their love letters," he said, and smiled when the mouse in the middle suddenly jumped up and disappeared, quick as a flash, through the window of a cellar on the other side of the road.

"A good actor, that mouse," said Grandfather, turning home with Farid.

96. The Scooter

Farid was about ten when scooters became the latest craze. Toni, the perfumier Dimitri's son, was the first to take his out on the street the day after Easter. It was a top-of-the-range model in red-painted metal tubing, and the children stared as if Toni were an astronaut.

Toni often got presents of foreign toys from his father, who travelled the world tracking down new fragrance ingredients, but the scooter was the best yet. The girls, particularly Jeannette and Antoinette, were fascinated. They all wanted a ride with him, and he raced past the envious boys with his girl passengers.

Before the week was up, Azar appeared with a clunking, clattering wooden scooter. Its footboard was joined to the vertical steering handle by simple angle irons, but all the same Azar's scooter was a successful imitation. The wheels consisted of large, indestructible ball bearings. They made a racket calculated to bring tears of delight to the boys' eyes. Like Azar himself, the scooter was robust, straightforward, and practical.

"My scooter's not for girls," he said, when his sister asked for a ride on it. And it was indeed much harder to steer and keep balanced than Toni's scooter with its rubber tyres. But it was all his own work.

Farid could hardly sleep for the next few nights. In his dreams he saw himself racing around on a scooter. Once he even had the parrot Coco on his shoulder. Perhaps the parrot featured in his dream because it had stopped talking since the day when Azar went down the road on his scooter, and just made loud squawking sounds in imitation of the noisy ball bearings. A week later the bird's owner stopped hanging its cage on the window looking out on the street and gave it a view of the interior courtyard as seen from her kitchen window instead.

The local car repair workshops were suddenly swamped with requests for ball bearings. It was only after a long search that Farid found a pair. They were larger than Azar's, but the larger your wheels the faster you could go.

"You can have them for three afternoons clearing out the workshop, making the men's tea, and fetching their bread and falafel from the restaurant," said the owner of the place. "Is it a deal?"

It was definitely a deal. Farid spent three afternoons sweeping, scouring, and polishing the workshop until it was clean and neat, and serving tea, sweetmeats, and fresh water. He made good tea for a ten-year-old. The men and their master were very happy, because Farid never gave them tea in dirty glasses, which was what they were used to. He washed the glasses well, and after the men had drunk their tea he rinsed them out again quickly with hot water, so that they steamed and then shone. He had learned that from his father.

In the end Farid got not just the ball bearings but the fixings he would need for them, as well as hinged steering joints with their pins and screws. But the useful tips the men gave him were better than all these presents. Finally, the workshop owner even handed him a simple prop stand, made out of a small metal rod bent into a U shape.

"Fit that on, and your scooter can stand upright anywhere, proud as a Vespa, and it won't have to lean against the wall like a tired old bike," he said. The workshop owner looked like a baddie in an American B-movie Western, but he was kindness itself.

His most junior employee, a young man of equally sinister appearance with tousled hair, surprisingly gave Farid the most valuable item of all: a brake. Neither Toni nor Azar had brakes on their scooters. It was a piece of rubber tyre, and Farid fixed it to the back wheel like a mudguard.

Finally Farid went off with his bag full of metal parts to his cousin George, who was apprenticed to a joiner, a tight-fisted man. Farid waited until the joiner had gone home at midday, and then slipped into the workshop. He didn't mention the scooter at first, just stood around asking after George's health and how his family was. As he talked he kept putting the bag down in different places, until his cousin asked what was jingling about inside it. Farid told him it was parts for a scooter, and all he needed now was the wood.

"Why didn't you say so at once, you idiot?" laughed George, and asked Farid to tell him what the scooter was supposed to look like. That didn't take long. George abandoned the jobs he had been doing, and within half an hour he had prepared all the wooden parts, tied them up in a bundle, and put them over Farid's shoulder.

"Now get out before that old skinflint shows up. I guess you can screw it all together yourself, but you'll have to glue the parts first," he said, and he gave the boy some adhesive too. Farid ran home. Ran? No, he was so happy that he positively flew. He worked for two hours, and then, feeling pleased with himself, stood back to look at the wonderful scooter he had made.

Finally he helped himself to a small rear mirror from his father's worn-out old bicycle and fixed it to the left of the steering handle. And his grandfather gave him several small stars and moons made of coloured tin for decoration.

Last of all Farid found a piece of card and wrote out a charm against envious eyes that he had seen on a mirror in his mother's cousin Michel's salon, showing the palm of a hand with a blue eye in the middle of it, and an arrow piercing the eye. Under it, in beautiful Arabic script, were the words: May the eye of the envious be blinded. As a barber, Michel had a great fondness for handsome polished glass mirrors. A particularly fine example had once broken soon after a customer said, with envy in his voice and salivating greedily, "What a lovely mirror!" The man was famous for casting envious looks, and people said that if he envied a pigeon he could kill it in flight with his glance.

Farid used shiny brass tacks to fix the oval piece of card with the lucky charm on it to the front of his rather broad handlebars. He painted a sunflower and a canary on the scooter too, and next Sunday, his hair combed and perfumed, in white shirt, blue trousers, and tennis shoes, he took his scooter out into Abbara Alley.

"Terrific!" called Azar, and after taking Farid's scooter for a ride himself he braked it, balanced on the spot for a minute, and folded the stand down. The pedal scooter stood upright in the street in all its glory. If Azar described something as "terrific", the other boys all took notice, for it wasn't easy to satisfy such a gifted handyman.

Less than three weeks later, ten wooden pedal scooters with ball bearing wheels were racing down the street, and the boys' mothers were cursing the car repair workshops which were to blame for all this racket. And each new scooter was better than the last, so that Farid's "terrific" construction was soon quite ordinary and occupied only a modest place among them. Now there were scooters with ostrich feathers, with bells and horns, and several with padded seats for little brothers and sisters, or the neighbourhood girls. Farid made a basket for Tutu, a spaniel who enjoyed a ride too.

Khalil was the first to master the art of drinking lemonade while riding a scooter. The bottle was securely fixed in a holder in the middle of the handlebars, and a straw enabled the clever inventor to drink without taking his hands off the steering handle or his eyes off the road.

Soon Abbara Alley wasn't large enough for so many scooters, so all the boys adopted Josef's suggestion of moving to parallel Saitun Alley, where Farid lived. The women of Abbara Alley blessed St. Joseph that day.

From then on a wonderful spectacle was to be seen in Farid's street every Sunday afternoon. Ten boys, all spruced up, rode their scooters in a line two abreast to the forecourt of the Catholic church, and slowly paraded there before the eyes of the girls who, equally smartly dressed, were waiting for the scooters to arrive. The riders dismounted with solemn, almost majestic mien, folded down their prop stands in slow motion, and sat on the stone benches opposite. They crossed their legs and began talking about their scooters.

"Can I have a go on yours? Just to the tobacconist's and back," Toni begged humbly one day. He had never let Farid touch a single one of his many toys.

"Yes, okay, but be careful," said Farid.

"That's right, you watch out," called Khalil. "His scooter bites children ..."

"... who eat Dutch cheese," Azar added, laughing. Josef grinned too, and his laughter infected the others too. For the first time Toni's scooter was left lying on the ground, and no one condescended even to look at it.

97. Hashish

Arabs have all kinds of celebrations, but they never celebrate birthdays. They believe that just makes you grow old faster.

But early in the fifties, upper-class Christians began to adopt the European custom of marking birthdays. Elias, Farid's father, who was on all the committees of the Catholic Church, had a good business idea: why not encourage rich Christians to make larger donations by celebrating their birthdays publicly? So he found out the dates of birth of the richest Catholics, and took the bishop and six priests into his confidence. The millionaire Bardoni's secretary, wife and housekeeper knew that he was to be woken early in the morning by the Catholic Pathfinders' brass band, and the day-long festivities would open with a folk dance performed outside his house. Two newspapers and Radio Damascus had also been told about the forthcoming event.

Then the plan was for the birthday boy to be led in solemn procession, amidst singing and dancing, to the church forecourt, where a festive table would be waiting for him and the guests.

After the meal, a singer was to keep the celebrations going from afternoon until well into the evening, his performance interspersed by occasional songs from the orphanage choir, while the St. Nicholas School for poor Christian children put on an amusing little play, and a sturdy pensioner delivered a rhymed greeting from the Old Folks' Home.

What with all the organization, Elias was in a state of agitation for days before the birthday. He complained to Claire of the difficulty of teaching Arabs good manners. "They can't even sing a little song in an orderly way," he groaned on the Tuesday. "Everyone's singing by himself, bawling out the tune regardless, no idea of harmony, just as if they were on their own in the desert and had never realized that we live in cities now."

On Wednesday he was complaining of Bardoni's powerful house-keeper. "His wife has no objection, oh no, but that old crone doesn't want him woken by the sound of drums, cymbals, and trombones. Just try telling the bandleader that he must do without one-third of his musicians! But there's nothing we can do against that woman's will. Monsieur Antoine Bardoni is her slave. He may shout at his wife, he never shouts at his housekeeper."

On Friday Elias couldn't sleep. "There's an insoluble problem," he told Claire. "We managed to hire Monsieur Antoine's favourite singer. His secretary told us that in private the eminent Monsieur Bardoni listens to records by the Egyptian singer Abdulmuttaleb. Amazing! The son of one of our richest Christian families, a fan of this hashish-smoker from Egypt! Well, we were in luck: the singer happens to be in Damascus, appearing in the evenings at the Scheherazade nightclub, where they don't pay much. So he was glad of the idea of earning something extra, and he agreed. Then comes disaster: he can't sing, he tells us this afternoon, because he's clean out of hashish. His head's empty, would you believe it? He can't find the melodies, they've gone into hiding, or so he claimed – what a childish excuse! – he needs hashish to entice them out of the closets and drawers of his memory. I thought I must be going crazy. A singer who can't remember his tunes! Would you believe it, he wants to go back to Egypt because he doesn't know his way around Damascus, and the nightclub owner won't get him any hashish? Which is understandable, because they come down on you hard for possession: as little as five grams will get you a life sentence. But if he flies back to Egypt tomorrow the heart goes out of our birthday surprise."

"Why don't you just lay in a day's supply for him?" replied Claire equably. "He can fly anywhere he likes after the event. The main thing for you and your friends is to have him there performing."

"Where would we get the hashish? Here I am trying to organize a birthday party, that's all! Do you see me landing in jail for the rest of my life?" Elias laughed bitterly.

"You could always ask my cousin," said Claire after a moment. "Butros is legal adviser to the CID. He told me they have tons of con-fiscated hashish there waiting to be destroyed. Why don't we simply abstract a little of it from the CID offices and give it to the singer? Butros is friendly with the head of the anti-drugs department. He's won a case for him twice already."

Bewildered, Elias looked into his wife's unfathomable eyes. "Then … then call him and ask if he'll help us out," he stammered.

Next day Claire came back from the CID headquarters with a lump of best Lebanese hashish the size of a tennis ball. She gave Elias the handkerchief containing her valuable loot. "That would make even an elephant sing," she said.

Elias turned pale. In Damascus, you could get three life sentences for possession of such a large quantity of hashish. But that evening, when the singer said he'd never smoked such fine hash before, he was happy.

Sunday came at long last, and the party began. Later Elias said the unfortunate outcome was because the first person he met that day happened to be the hunchbacked, one-eyed widow Mathilde, and she had grinned at him and shouted, "It'll all go wrong!" Elias hated the widow.

"So then the band didn't play cheerful tunes, it churned out Austrian marching music instead, the stuff they usually broadcast over the radio when there's a coup. The millionaire was frightened to death and ran down to the cellar in his pyjamas. It was difficult to convince him that it had all been arranged specially for his birthday," said Elias, taking a sip of water to moisten his dry throat. "Well, so he reluctantly followed the procession to the Catholic church, and he didn't cheer up until the Patriarch of the Middle East and the Bishop of Damascus welcomed him at the church door. He was pleased as punch then, and the lavish meal was the very best quality. I supplied the cakes and cookies myself, made with the finest butter as usual. But it all still went wrong. The Egyptian singer made for the wide blue yonder before he was due to perform."

"Why on earth did he do that?" asked the incredulous Claire.

"Because when he'd just smoked his third hashish cigarette, some joker backstage asked if he knew where the stuff came from. When the singer shook his head – he had no idea – that son of a whore whispered, 'It's from the CID.' Then the singer cracked up. Maybe he'd smoked too much hash, or maybe fright turned his brain. Anyway, he started screaming that he'd been lured into a trap and they'd put him in prison. And then he was gone, said he wouldn't stay in Damascus a moment longer."

98. The Photographer

Few things fascinated Farid as a child more than photographs. In the first few years after his birth they were rarer than pictures of saints. Seven pictures of the Virgin Mary hung on the walls at home, along with two crosses made from the wood of the olive tree in Jerusalem, which was in great demand. A small statue of St. Anthony of Padua with the child Jesus stood in a niche in the dining room. It was a copy of the famous work by Juan de Juni, and such things were distributed by the Franciscans all over the world. The abbot of the Franciscan monastery had given it to Elias shortly before Farid's birth, not only in thanks for his generous donation, but because St. Anthony was the patron saint of bakers, and also stood by women in childbirth and helped people to find things they had lost. The abbot enumerated over ten instances in which the saint's protection had apparently been beneficial, and Elias fervently hoped that Anthony of Padua would both find his keys for him and help Claire in childbirth after all her miscarriages.

However, only three photographs hung in the drawing room: one of Farid's mother when she was sixteen, another of both his parents, his father in a dark suit and his mother in a white wedding dress. The suit and the wedding dress had been borrowed. The third photo was of Farid himself aged two, in a sailor suit. He was asleep on his mother's lap, and she was smiling at the photographer. His father stood stiffly beside her, looking gravely past the camera. Behind Farid's parents stood Grandfather Nagib and Grandmother Lucia. Lucia posed looking as stiff as her son-in-law, but Grandfather was laughing and glancing up with his head on one side.

At the end of the forties, Basil opened the first modern photographic studio in the Old Town. He called it the Studio of Stars, and tried to give his customers a touch of Hollywood gloss when they posed for his camera.

Farid felt there was something mysterious about a photo. The people in it were alive, yet frozen on a piece of paper. But he understood the deep dimension of the magic only when he saw a photographer at work in the street. Farid was just seven that summer, and for some reason his grandfather urgently needed a picture of himself.

"Come on, we're going to the photographer's," he told Farid.

Close to Bab Tuma, three photographers stood in front of their remarkable apparatus, large wooden boxes on adjustable tripods also made of wood. Their customers sat on folding stools in the open air, in front of a wall with a black cloth over it.

Farid and his grandfather had to wait. There were two farmers and a young man in line ahead of them. One of the farmers was cross because he didn't want to puff out his cheeks as the photographer asked. The photographer snapped at the farmer to do as he was told or his face would look like a crumpled pair of underpants in the photo. The other farmer was afraid that the photograph might steal his soul.

"Don't worry, it's like painting," the photographer assured him.

"But the Prophet forbade it," explained the man.

The photographer was losing his temper. "The Prophet didn't need ID to claim a legacy. You do. Take a deep breath and hold it," he ordered. The man fell silent and blew out his cheeks until they were smooth and round.

"But who's doing the painting there inside your box?" he asked, when the photographer had finished with him.

"The light," replied the photographer.

"Ah," said the farmer, mulling it over. He stepped back, looking baffled and muttering to himself, "The light, the light."

Next was a young man who wanted a photograph of his wife taken, so that she could get a passport for the pilgrimage to Mecca. But a furious quarrel broke out when the man refused to let her lift her veil in front of so many men. Farid's grandfather tried to make the peace, but it was no good.

"I can't take her picture with that black veil on, you might as well have a photo of an aubergine," said the photographer venomously.

The man took his wife's hand and marched angrily away. She could be heard abusing him, complaining that he and his mother were making trouble because they didn't want her to go on the pilgrimage.

Farid was surprised when the photographer disappeared under a black cloth fixed behind his camera. It was some time before he came out again, and then he opened a drawer filled with some kind of liquid at the side of the apparatus and took out a small, dark picture with a few lighter patches on it, which Grandfather called a negative. Finally the man fastened the little picture to a board and briefly held it in front of the lens, only for his head to disappear inside his cloth tunnel again. After quite a while he emerged, sweating and looking as if he'd been fighting a demon. Once again he opened the curious little drawer at the side and took out the second photograph. It was a perfect likeness of the man who hadn't wanted to puff out his cheeks at first, and sure enough he looked much healthier in the picture than in real life.

As for Grandfather, he went home that day with four photographs, none of them any good, because he kept on smiling at the last minute. The photographer was cross with him, although Grandfather paid for all the pictures. They were amusing. Farid got them as a present and kept them in a box like a valuable treasure.

"I'll go back again tomorrow," said Grandfather.

"But why are the pictures no good?" asked Farid. "They're lovely."

"Officials don't like photographs where you're smiling. It makes them think you don't take them and their check-ups seriously."

99. Suleiman and the Chickens

Suleiman's father Abdallah was chauffeur to the Spanish consul. He was a man of elegant appearance and limited intellect, but because he never said much he gave an impression of wisdom. He was happy in his job, and did his work conscientiously.

His wife Salma came from a peasant family in the south. She was wily and distrustful by nature. Salma always looked just a little too elegant for Abbara Alley, because she wore the consul's wife's cast-off clothes. The Spanish lady was sturdily built, like Salma herself, so the clothes fitted perfectly.

Abdallah and Salma had two children, Suleiman and Aida, who both took after their mother. They were short, sturdy, and born tricksters. One day the chauffeur was planning a visit to his parents-in-law. He was allowed to use the consul's limousine, because the consul himself was in Spain. Suleiman's mother was in the seventh heaven. She put on her best dress, and after an hour's drive climbed out into the dusty village square as majestically as a queen. The peasants marvelled at the transformation, sang Salma's praises, and suddenly remembered that they'd always known this enterprising woman would make something of herself.

But not all her relations admired and flattered her. Salma's cousin, the biggest building contractor in the village, had never got over the fact that she had chosen to marry not him but a useless townsman, and always tried to present Abdallah as a weakling. He was married himself now and had three children, but his heart still belonged to Salma. So almost every visit ended in a quarrel between him and Abdallah. The quarrel broke out this time when he boasted that his own children were braver and healthier than Salma's, and to prove it he wanted the children to behead the five chickens destined for the midday meal.

His three boys seized a chicken each, wrung their heads off their bodies with their bare hands, and dropped the fluttering fowls carelessly on the ground. At this point Aida rose to her feet, unasked, and went over to the two remaining chickens, which were lying beside a tree stump with their legs tied. She picked up the hatchet ready beside them with her right hand, grabbed a russet-coloured chicken with her left hand, and quickly struck off its head. Then, her expression untroubled, she returned to her place at the big table laid in the shade of the walnut tree for the occasion.

"Aida takes after her mother," said the spiteful cousin, "and that townie there has nothing to do with it. Now let's see what his son is like."

Suleiman was a crafty boy, and brave when it came to defending a friend from his own street against a stranger, but he couldn't stand the sight of blood.

"Show this boastful fellow what you're like," called his father. But Suleiman couldn't do that without letting his father down.

All eyes were now on him. He stood up with his heart racing, took the hatchet, seized the chicken by one wing and put it on the tree stump. The bird looked at him in alarm and cackled.

"Holy Virgin, help me," whispered Suleiman, bringing the hatchet down where he thought the chicken's neck would be. For the fraction of a second he closed his eyes. When he opened them again, the chicken's head was rising in the air, its reproachful eyes bent on him, and then it fell lifeless to the ground.

"A master stroke," said Suleiman's father triumphantly. Late that night, just before they went to sleep, Aida assured her brother that no one had noticed how scared he was.

100. Sugar Dollies

It was usual in the Christian quarter for children to find jobs in the long vacation, which lasted three months, something to earn them some pocket money, give them a taste of working life, and let their parents have a little peace. Many families had up to ten children.

The children worked as general dogsbodies for the barber, the vegetable seller, the ice seller or the tailor. The joiner Michel was popular, and no one wanted to work for Mahmud the butcher, although Michel was bad-tempered and grasping while Mahmud was a generous soul. But the children would rather work with wood than with blood, fat, and meat.

Anyone with a little money set up in trade on his own account, bought sugar dollies, cheap cookies, chewing gum, and lollies in the Suk al Buzuriye, and went around the streets selling them for twice the price he had paid. You might make a profit of a lira by the end of the week, which was good going. With that capital, you could buy even more wares and offer a larger selection on your sales tray.

Those who thought it beneath their dignity to walk through the streets just sat at the doors of their own houses, offering their wares to children and passers by. But you might have bad luck and find ten children sitting outside their doors at the same time, trying to entice everyone who went down the street with the same offers. Strange children stood no chance in these streets. The brothers and sisters of the local sweetmeat sellers called them names until they ran away.

Farid begged and begged until Claire finally let him fill a tray of his own with sugar dollies, chewing gum and lollipops. With great patience, he made a fly-whisk out of strips of paper and a small wooden stick, to keep insects and the hands of greedy children off his tray.

Elias didn't like to see Farid sitting in the alley, selling cheap sweetmeats. That was more to do with his pride as a confectioner than with educational ideas, as Farid later discovered.

The night before he went out in the streets with his tray for the first time, he was so excited that he could hardly sleep. He saw himself in his waking dreams as a successful trader with children thronging to his round sales tray.

Next morning he hurried to the Suk al Buzuriye with Josef, bought stuff there cheaply, and as Josef kept squinting at the chewing gum on their way back Farid gave his friend a little packet. An hour later they were home, and Farid sat in the shade of his house with a magnificent tray full of brightly coloured, delicious sweetmeats. Josef, with his grumpy expression, proved an excellent deterrent to competitors.

Farid felt proud, and was glad to see no rivals in the form of neighbouring children from his alley. His first customer was Claire. She bought three sugar dollies and a lollipop, and hardly haggled at all. For a moment Farid felt ashamed to take money from her, when she had provided his starting capital, but that was how she wanted it.

Then Antoinette came along. She just stood there at first, admiring him, and admiring the chewing gum even more. After a while she asked how much a packet cost, giggled coyly and licked her lips, making her mouth shine. In her red dress she looked even sweeter than Farid's sugar dollies.

He gave her a present of two packets of chewing gum, and she patted his face. "You're so cute," she said, running away. Not five minutes later her fat brother Djamil rolled up, as usual puffing and panting unattractively. "Either I get a sugar dolly or I'll tell on you and Antoinette and what you do together," he demanded, salivating. Farid looked around him. Then, feeling very anxious, he looked back at the plump boy, who was waving his arms about excitedly and almost lost his balance. He saw the moment coming when Djamil would fall over and land with his fat behind on the sugar dollies. So he took one that had turned out a rather ugly shape, handed it to Djamil, and snapped, "You get out of here, tell-tale, or I'll get Josef to give you a thrashing, understand?"

Djamil looked at Josef, who was standing nearby making a stout twig whistle as he lashed it through the air. The fat boy took his sugar dolly and disappeared.

No child came to buy anything that first morning. Saitun Alley might have been swept clean. At midday, Farid hid his tray in the pantry, where his father never went, and hoped for better business next day, for the heat was unbearable in the afternoon.

"You must think up rhyming slogans to attract children. Advertising works wonders," Claire advised him.

Farid remembered the cries of the Damascene street traders. They always made him feel cheerful. So he thought up three street cries, one for sugar dollies, one for chewing gum, one for lollipops, and set to work with new courage next day. Josef kept watch on the entrance of the alley. He was dressed like a cowboy today, with the hat and pistols that his father had given him for Christmas, and looked as if he were expecting a hold-up any moment.

Farid was very surprised to find a number of children already waiting for him. They all came from the big building next door where the tenants were poor Christians. Soon he couldn't help realizing that though they were licking their lips as they looked at his wares, they didn't have a piastre in their pockets.

A little later Antoinette turned up with Josephine, Josef's youngest sister. Antoinette forced a path for herself through the assembled children, dragging Josephine after her, and if anyone barred her way she said indignantly, "He's my friend, so you just let me by." When she reached the tray, which was now under siege, Farid was knocked backward yet again by her pretty looks. She was wearing a blue summer dress, a necklace of coloured beads, and two amusing hairgrips.

"Josephine won't believe that you gave me some chewing gum yesterday. So did you or didn't you?" she asked in challenging tones.

"Yes, yes, I did," said Farid.

"But he's not going to give you any today," said Josephine in an equally challenging manner. Antoinette, who hadn't expected this, looked at Farid for help, and he didn't know what to do. Djamil was leaning against the wall listening hard.

"There, see, he isn't giving you anything!" Josephine repeated in a loud voice. Antoinette's eyes suddenly filled with tears.

"Yes, I am," Farid stammered softly, "I am so giving her something today!" And he handed Antoinette another packet of chewing gum.

"How about me? I mean, you're *my* brother's friend," said the indignant Josephine. "Do you want me telling him you give things to everyone except me?" And she angrily stamped her foot until Josef noticed and came over. Meanwhile, Antoinette was chewing her gum with relish. Her tears had dried up as suddenly as if she had swallowed them.

"All right, you'll get something," sighed Farid, and he reluctantly gave Josephine too a packet of gum. She took it, laughed, and pushed out through the crowd of children again. He heard her calling, "He's giving away sugar dollies and chewing gum, he's giving them away." As for what happened next, he would never forget it. As if some invisible conductor had brought the children together into a harmonious choir, they all chattered and wept together.

"Why doesn't anyone give us sugar dollies? *Why not?*" And that last "Why not?" was a long-drawn-out cry of exaggerated pain. The children's song was more persuasive than the Catholic church choir on Good Friday. It wasn't long before Claire appeared at the door.

"Just a moment, children," she called. "Just a moment!" She stretched her arms out to pacify them. The children suddenly fell silent.

"Everyone gets a sugar dolly, and I'm paying."

"But I don't want a dolly. I want chewing gum!" cried a little girl with a snotty nose. Farid had tears in his eyes. He felt like throwing his tray at the children. Josef shook his head sympathetically and went home.

Claire distributed her son's sweetmeats among the children, and didn't say a word when Djamil came back three times for another sugar dolly.

"You're no Mushtak, you're a Surur," she told Farid later, giving him two lira, more than all the dollies, lollipops and chewing gum could have earned him. "We've never been any good at haggling in my family," she added, laughing.

101. Quo Vadis?

A hundred and thirty-two schoolchildren occupied several rows of seats in the biggest cinema in Damascus. They were seeing the movie at a reduced price, so it wasn't surprising that even Rasuk's father, who had scorned the art of film all his life and never entered a cinema, gave permission. And the teacher had assured everyone that the movie reinforced the Christian faith.

Rasuk's father made the sole condition that he must tell his father about the film that evening, for hearing stories while he was drinking tea seemed to him like a foretaste of Paradise.

"But I had to lie to him," Rasuk told his friends that night in the attic, "not because I was afraid but to spare his nerves. So I censored everything, the way grown-ups do when a child suddenly comes into the room. 'Tell it from A to Z,' my father told me, which is what he says when he wants to hear all about something from beginning to end, but I just couldn't possibly tell him about the trailer. It was for a Western where the Indians were the baddies, and my father would have thrown a fit. He thinks native American culture was wonderful, and when anyone mentions the name of Columbus he crosses himself and spits three times. And how could I have told him about the second trailer, with Humphrey Bogart in one of his darkest roles?

So I told him how the first Christians had to go underground in 'Quo Vadis?'. I told him about the catacombs, and Peter Ustinov playing Nero so brilliantly, and the Eternal City of Rome burning, and then more about the persecution of the Christians. My father was so moved he even forgot to drink his tea. Tears came to his eyes. But I didn't say that after the movie we were in a big punch-up with some Muslim kids. It's a pity you guys weren't there.

The Muslim kids were in the two rows in front of us, and they'd come with their teacher to get to know about Christianity. But when the lights went up again one of the Muslim boys had to go and tell his mates, 'Come on, let's see if that bunch are good Christians.' And he pointed at us, hit my friend Gabriel in the face, and shouted, acting all naïve and innocent, 'Okay, so now you turn the other cheek, right?'

Gabriel was startled for a moment, but then he grabbed the boy, who wasn't very big, lifted him in the air and threw him over the heads of the audience to land three rows forward. Then all hell was let loose. The teachers didn't know what to do. They said they were ashamed of their pupils. Of course I didn't tell my father a word about that.

So on Saturday I had to go to confession. 'I told lies,' I admitted, kneeling.

'Why did you do that, my son? Was it out of greed, or fear of punishment, or to get some advantage for yourself?'

'No, it was for humanitarian reasons,' I said. There was total silence in my confessional. Finally Father Athanasias told me to say a prayer of repentance and three Our Fathers, to cleanse my soul of the sin of lying. He didn't understand at all, so I didn't say any of the prayers."

102. Jokers

Each season had its own game. Who decided when one period of games began and when it ended remained a mystery of childhood. Only marbles could be played at any time of the year.

In winter the children played with nuts and olive and date stones.

The winners ate the nuts and took the olive and date stones to the bri-
quette factory. They burned well, and the children earned a few piastres that way. And they played cards more in winter than in spring.

Just before Easter they played with hardboiled eggs. Farid was never
allowed to join in, because Elias and Claire thought egg-cracking was
a primitive game of chance played only by the lower classes. They
didn't mean harmless egg-cracking at home, something all Christians
did as an Easter custom, but cracking eggs in competition, when you
won or lost the eggs you had staked. All the same, Farid slunk off to
the road junction with Jews' Alley, so that at least he could watch.

The game involved all kinds of cheating and fixing, and no day ever
ended peacefully. Someone was always caught cheating, and then
there was shouting and sometimes fighting. Suleiman was an artful
devil. He purposely went looking for innocent children who had
brought one or two hardboiled eggs from home to try their luck, and
challenged them. Azar had once given him an Easter egg that couldn't
be cracked because of the clever way its young inventor had prepared
it. Only he could have thought of such a thing. First he bored a tiny
hole in the shell of the raw egg and sucked out the contents, then he
filled it with liquid plaster and waited for the plaster to dry hard as
stone inside the shell. But Azar himself didn't have the nerve to cheat,
so he gave Suleiman the prepared egg, and Suleiman won at least fifty
eggs with it every Easter. If a grown-up got suspicious and asked to
look at the egg he quickly disappeared into the crowd.

Just after Easter they began playing with apricot kernels, which
were in great demand because they brought in a lot of money. There
were the expensive sweet kernels, which were ground to a kind of
marzipan, and almond oil was pressed from the rather smaller, bitter
kernels.

Then the season came for balls to come flying out of the houses,
while the children ran after them to work off all the pent-up energy
of the winter months. Football and basketball were the two favourite
games. There were always jokers playing in the ball games. Jokers –
called after the joker in a pack of cards and known in some streets as
"migrant birds" – were children who were too small and too young
for the game, but wanted to play all the same. They could go out on

the pitch with the others, run around with them, and fling themselves into playing for one team or the other. They kicked the balls all
over the place, threw themselves into the spirit of the thing and were
accepted and always treated kindly, as they didn't belong to either
team. Their goals didn't count, but they played, changed sides, and
were happy in the belief that they were really part of the game.

When school closed at the end of June, and the streets were hard as
stone in the drought, the children played with pebbles. There were all
kinds of different games with both pebbles and marbles, all of them
calling for stamina, a sure aim, and a good sense of height and speed.

There was constant cheating and trickery. A joke even claimed that
Jesus, who wouldn't work miracles to save himself even on the cross,
fell for the temptation when he was playing a game. One day, so the
children in Farid's street said, Jesus and Muhammad were playing
backgammon in heaven. When Jesus was losing and had reached the
point where his last throw couldn't win the game even if was two
sixes, Muhammad scoffed at him. "Give up, lad!" he said. "Nothing
can help you out of this fix!" But his broad grin froze when Jesus,
smiling, threw the dice and they landed on the board – two sevens!
Muhammad was furious. "You just listen to me," he spat. "That's no
miracle, that's cheating!"

103. Superstition

Josef's neighbour Halime had finally borne a healthy baby after three
miscarriages. She was just twenty-two, and Josef said she was very
superstitious. During her pregnancy she had done everything the
midwife advised, and although she was a Christian she even went
with her mother to a sheikh who lived nearby to get talismans from
him.

Her mother-in-law had driven her nearly crazy, for she had been
against the marriage all along, and was always trying to turn her son
against his wife. Whenever he visited his mother he came home in a
bad temper, and would shout at Halime for the least little thing.

Her own mother was an attractive woman of forty who looked younger and more feminine than her only daughter. She worried about Halime terribly, and was ready to do anything for her. She gave the Virgin Mary candles, she gave St. Anthony incense, she gave St. Barbara a silver heart. And she donated to charity three times running, because the sheikh said it was possible that the soul of some female ancestor of hers was in need of grace. In such cases the people of Damascus donated food or drink to passers by in the street. The charity offered in summer was usually *sus*, a black, bitter-sweet brew that tasted of liquorice. The passers by refreshed themselves with it, and wished for God to have mercy on the dead.

When Halime was in her sixth month of pregnancy she donated a huge vat of *sus* every week. The drinks sellers stood in Abbara Alley and generously handed it out to passers by, until one day a neighbour went to see the expectant mother and told her he kept dreaming of his dead father, who had seen Halime's ancestors, and they were in Paradise too. But they were calling for help, because great waves of *sus* were flooding the place. Many of the saints were already up in the treetops, begging for the charitable donations to stop. Halime listened to this request, and in the end she had a pretty and most important of all a healthy baby.

But her mother wanted to take precautions, and hurried off to visit the sheikh again. In the meantime, however, he had died, and his son was running the business now. He told her to be very careful to protect her grandchild from attack by the envious, and sold her large quantities of talismans to hang around the little baby. When the attractive woman left he held her hand for a long time and looked deep into her eyes. "We ought to get to know one another better in the baby's interests," he said in conspiratorial tones. She felt her heart racing, but she suppressed her excitement and hurried back to her daughter. By night, however, as she lay beside her husband, she thought of the young sheikh.

Halime hung the talismans all around the baby. The attack would come from a blue-eyed woman, so the stars had told the sheikh. Her mother carefully kept watch on every woman who came to call, and if someone looked at the baby too long, or was too fulsome in her praise of his good health, she would nudge Halime and prompt her to say, "God protect the boy and blind the envious." And as soon as the visitor was gone Halime's mother softly recited two sayings from the Koran for protection against envy.

The baby stayed healthy. His mother fed him from full breasts. But then the inevitable happened. Halime's mother-in-law took her chance while the baby's other grandmother was in the kitchen making coffee. She glanced at the child, who had milk trickling from one corner of his mouth, and hissed like a snake. That was when it happened. Halime felt a stabbing pain in her nipple.

Next day her breasts were hanging as flat and limp as two empty bags, and she couldn't squeeze a drop of milk out of them. Her mother raised the alarm, the sheikh came at once, and listened to the story with a gloomy expression. It was clear to him at once who had hissed the spell specially designed to draw the milk out of a mother's breast. He asked for one of the mother-in-law's dresses with her smell still on it, or even better, three items of her clothing. He would see to the rest, he said.

Once Halime's mother had found a neighbour who was a nursing mother and could suckle her daughter's child too for a while, she hurried off to call on the mother-in-law and made up an excuse to go into the bathroom. There she abstracted two pairs of panties and a dress from the laundry basket. The sheikh burned the clothes in a copper cauldron, muttering something incomprehensible, while Halime's mother recited the suras from the Koran that were supposed to fend off the envious woman's ill will.

Finally the young sheikh sat down on the sofa with Halime's mother, murmured a mysterious spell, and looked at her with his large dark eyes in a way that made her feel weak at the knees. Taking her hand, he laid it on his heart. His ardent gaze rested on her nipples, and she felt like tearing off her clothes. The young sheikh spoke softly and urgently to her, while the room gradually filled with dense incense smoke.

"Now you must be very strong. Only you and your loving heart can help me to reach your daughter. You must pass through the spiral, and I will pass into it through you, and together we will free your daughter." So saying, he moved the woman's hand down from his heart to his lap. She didn't know what spiral he meant, but she felt his penis and found herself gasping for air.

"For heaven's sake, God protect it from envious eyes, but it will tear me apart," she said, stroking his prick without looking down. It was huge, and hard as a stone. The woman could tell that the sheikh wasn't wearing any underpants.

"Then let's hang a couple of sesame rings between us," said the sheikh, rising to his feet. His prick made his robe stick out like an Arab tent. He fetched five of the hand-sized sesame rings that are eaten in the morning and with tea in the afternoon in Damascus. Each ring was almost three centimetres thick. The woman glanced at the rings, and she thought she could just about manage the length that would be left.

"Good," she said, relieved. "What must I do?"

The sheikh brought a large sheet of paper, the size of an unfolded newspaper, and the woman saw a saying in black ink written on it in the form of a spiral. The sheikh spread the paper out on the rug and asked the baby's grandmother to lie down on her belly so that her mouth was exactly over the word at the centre of the spiral. Then she was to begin slowly reading without moving the paper. This was the crucial part, he said, and she must concentrate on the words. He himself would have to work through her to reach her daughter, and she mustn't stop reading the saying aloud whatever happened.

"But put the sesame rings on," she begged him.

The words of the spiral were written in Arabic characters, but apart from her daughter's name at the centre she couldn't understand a word of it. However, she tried hard to decipher the chain of written words, for she fervently desired to help Halime. Suddenly she felt him. A cry escaped her, but she read on. Soon she felt the fire inside her, and began thrusting in response. A little later she got up on her knees, propping her hands on the large sheet of paper.

"Break off one of the sesame rings," she begged, for the fire was blazing higher and higher. Her longing grew ever greater, and the sheikh broke off ring after ring. Halime's mother came to the end of the spiral and entered a heaven she had never known before. Suddenly she felt light as a feather. She was airborne, dazed half by pleasure and half by the incense.

Three days later the milk came back into Halime's breasts. After that her mother visited the young sheikh every week, and she never forgot to take five sesame rings with her.

104. Grandfather's Glasses

Suleiman's grandfather read a single book over and over again all through his life: the Bible. He read slowly, very slowly. His image was indelibly imprinted on the memory of all who saw him: bending over the big book, stealing a little more light to read by from the last rays of the setting sun. He would never read by artificial light.

And when he was asked what he wanted most he would reply, "A good copy of the Bible in heaven." He would sit under a tree there, he said, and read day and night, for in heaven the sun never sets.

As the years passed his eyes grew weak, and he bought a pair of glasses. There were no opticians or eye specialists around at the time, you just went to the general stores where all kinds of glasses were hanging, and tried them on until you found one that was right for you.

The glasses changed Grandfather's face. He didn't look kindly and wise any more, but tense, fearful, and constantly surprised. When Suleiman said so to his grandmother, she laughed. "Yes, he's some-times tense with fear, and he's been surprised ever since he was born."

One day Grandfather died. Suleiman had been away for three days with his mother. When they came back he was lying in the living room, already stiff in death. The boy grieved for a long time. The old man had been the best grandfather in the world, an excellent and patient craftsman, and a good friend to his grandson.

Two weeks later Suleiman found Grandfather's glasses. They were lying on the shelf behind the Bible. He hurried to his grandmother with them. "Grandma," he cried breathlessly, "Grandfather won't be able to read in heaven."

His grandmother looked at him for a moment, rather confused, and then she smiled. "He'll be finding his way around heaven for now, and when I join him I'll take him his glasses."

Six months later Grandmother fell very ill, and when Suleiman heard his mother tell his uncle at lunch that she was afraid Grandma would soon follow Grandpa, the boy heaved a sigh of relief. He ran to his room, fetched the glasses, and put them down on his grandmother's bed.

"Don't forget the glasses," he whispered, and she laughed so much that she had a coughing fit. Then she stroked his head and picked the glasses up.

Three days later she was dead. The neighbours were not a little surprised when they saw what was in the coffin with her. Usually people put a rosary in a dead woman's hands. But Grandmother's hands were holding Grandfather's glasses.

"It was her express wish," Suleiman's mother told the disapproving priest, and now the boy knew for sure that his grandfather would be able to start reading again that day.

105. Gibran

The man whose name was Gibran sat on the steps leading up to a small house, drunk, with over ten children crowding around him and wanting to hear his stories. By day he wandered the streets of Damascus looking for people who would give him food, cigarettes, and arrack. In return he told stories.

"Another one," Suleiman was demanding as Farid and Josef came down the street. They saw their friend giving the man a Spanish cigarette that he had certainly stolen from his father.

"It's not cut with anything, is it?" he asked suspiciously. "Hashish doesn't agree with me." He was drunk but not incoherent, although his eyes seemed unable to rest on anything, and roamed unsteadily through space and time.

"No, no, just perfumed, for the high-up diplomats. Now tell us the one about the Frank and his wife again. That's the kind of story Josef likes."

"Ah, that's an old tale, one I read on board ship in the Caribbean. We had to wait for a repair to be done, and we killed rats and time by turn with anything that came to hand. I found a shabby old book without a cover in the hold. It was full of stories. One of them mentioned our quarter here in Damascus and the Hammam Bakri near Bab Tuma. True as I'm sitting here," he assured them, drawing on his cigarette.

"Well, once upon a time there must have been a Frank around here. The Franks were brave warriors. They marched from their homeland three thousand kilometres away to save Christians, but when they arrived they couldn't tell Christians, Jews, and Muslims apart, so they killed anyone who got in their way just to be on the safe side. Then they conquered several cities, among them Jerusalem, but they never took Damascus.

"In a long war like that, lasting over two hundred years, there were many breaks, and at those times the Arabs could go into the crusader castles, and the Franks could wander around the towns they hadn't conquered and buy things. So one day this Frank came to Damascus. He had only just arrived in the Middle East as a crusader, he didn't know anything about the people here. And he'd ended up in a castle further down south, where he was a guard and his wife was cook to the lord of the castle.

"The city gates were open. The Frank wandered about. In those days Damascus was a jewel among cities; the Mongols hadn't arrived yet. The crusader couldn't get over his amazement. He started at the southern gate, the Bab al Sigir, he passed through the spice market, and then went on to our quarter. And suddenly he saw the entrance to a hammam, and couldn't make out why there were so many men going in and out of the place. He looked cautiously behind the curtain, and the hammam attendant, who knew the Frankish language, invited him in with flowery words and friendly gestures. But the crusader was scared, because he didn't know the custom. He was a bold, fierce warrior, but bathing naked with other men seemed to him like the devil's work. However, the attendant stayed close to him, persuading him, until the Frank paid and agreed to try the hammam. The attendant sent a lad to undress the man, scared as he was, until he stood there with nothing on, white as snow and stinking like a pig.

"'Look at this,' the attendant called to his Arab guests, who were resting in the hall and drinking peppermint tea. 'They're as wild and fierce as lions in the field, but a little soap scares them.' The men laughed, and looked at the Frank as he hesitantly followed the lad into the dark interior of the baths. There he was soaped, massaged, shaved and washed. A young fellow carefully removed his pubic hair. The Frank rested, and fell asleep now and then. When he woke up and saw handsome youths wandering around in the twilight, he thought he had died and gone to heaven. Only when the man who did the soaping came up and indicated by gestures that he was going to wash him for the last time did he realize that he was still on earth. He happily drank his hot peppermint tea and listened to the water playing in the fountain. When his visit to the baths was over, he dressed, thanked the hammam attendant, and went cheerfully away.

"Two days later he came back hand in hand with his wife. The hammam attendant was just about frightened to death. He tried to explain to the Frank that women weren't allowed to bathe with men, but the Frank insisted on enjoying the same pleasure as before, only with his wife this time. A great tumult broke out in the doorway. The men who had finished bathing and were resting in the hall near the entrance fled in fear from the lady, whose blue eyes scrutinized them with interest, and escaped back into the baths.

"Women from the neighbourhood came hurrying along, some of them calling the shameless Frankish woman bad names, while others wanted to bathe too. The hammam attendant begged the Frank to take his wife away quickly, before there was a massacre. Surprised and rather disappointed, the couple left. Later the hammam attendant said he had heard the crusader telling his wife, 'It's a strange thing, they're supposed to be fierce warriors who don't fear death, and they run scared at the sight of a woman!'"

106. Salma and St. John

Suleiman's mother Salma loved John the Baptist with all her heart. She wasn't alone in this: the Damascenes are devoted to the beheaded saint. After Salome's notorious dance, the legend goes, his head was brought from Palestine to Damascus, and his shrine lies in the middle of the prayer hall of the Ummayad Mosque, where the Muslims venerate it.

Salma often went to look at the oil painting of the saint in the Catholic church, lit a candle, prayed devoutly and told him all her troubles. And she swore to Josef's mother that everything she asked John the Baptist for was granted.

But one wish of hers remained unfulfilled. Salma kept repeating her request, but in vain. She gave even more candles, but nothing happened. Salma reminded the saint first gently, then more and more forcefully, that she had already given nearly seventy candles for this one request and he hadn't heard her. The priest of the church sometimes had to wait a long time for her to finish her conversations with St. John. It was a nuisance, because if he was tired, hungry, or in a hurry he couldn't just lock the church door and leave.

One day he had an idea. The large painting stood on a marble table with plenty of room behind it. When all the congregation who had come to Mass had left, and Salma was exchanging a few words with a woman neighbour, the young priest saw his chance. He quickly got behind the picture and waited, standing perfectly still. Soon Salma came along and began explaining volubly that she was disappointed, because St. John had failed her even though she'd already given him seventy-eight candles.

"This is my last," she said.

"Why so sad, my daughter? Your requests have not yet reached me. What exactly do you want?"

Salma was alarmed, but she pulled herself together, explained her wish at length, and promised that if St. John granted it she would give the church a hundred lira.

"Why the church? There are a thousand and one saints here, and they'll all want something too."

"Very well," said Salma, "then the hundred lira will be just for you."

"But I don't want money," replied the priest behind the painting of St. John. "What else can you offer?" It was hard work to keep himself from laughing out loud, for he could guess how baffled the woman was looking at this moment.

"What do you want? Candles? I could light you a hundred," offered Salma.

"Oh, how I hate candles," groaned the priest.

"Would you like me to slaughter a sheep and distribute it to the poor?"

"Those poor sheep, I can't stand the sight of blood. Don't you know I was a vegetarian?"

"A silver cross?"

"You're mixing me up with Jesus."

"A, a ..." But Salma couldn't think of anything else. "An outing for all the children in the Catholic orphanage, or ..."

"You could never pay for that," the priest interrupted her, speaking for the saint.

"Just you leave that to me. I'll bargain for a good price, the manager of the bus company is my husband's distant cousin, and there are plenty of cheap restaurants where the poor little souls can eat their fill."

"And what do I get out of that?"

"Well, what do you want, then?" asked Salma, her nerves all on edge. "Tell me what I'm to do for you to grant my wish."

"I want you to scrub the church three times a week for three months."

"Oh yes? Scrub the church!" Salma snapped angrily. "I can do without that, thank you very much, but I'll tell you one thing: I'm not a bit surprised they chopped your head off, you old misery-guts!" she cried, and she hurried out of the church. From that day on she avoided the picture of John the Baptist.

107. When the Tram Stopped

Farid liked riding on the trams. Unlike a bus, a tram was never too crowded and was always pleasantly airy. In summer it drove slowly along with the windows open. He was fascinated by the elegant uniforms: the tram driver in grey, with a handsome cap, the conductor with his box of tickets and the ticket inspector both in sombre blue. The ticket inspector's uniform was the finest. Apart from looking at tickets the man really had nothing to do, for it was the conductor who never took his eyes off the passengers. The tram went from Bab Tuma to the terminus in the New Town and back again. Suleiman could get a free ride in return for lending the conductor a hand, and Farid sometimes went with him. While the conductor and driver drank tea together at the terminus, Suleiman would clean the tramcar and then switch the trolley arm around. The latter was a delicate job that the conductor wouldn't entrust to many people. The trolley arm – a metal rod three metres long – had a copper wheel at the far end with a groove for the cable. A large steel spring on the roof of the tram pressed the rod and wheel against the electric cable. A cord was fitted below the wheel, and when the tram had reached the terminus the cord was used to turn the trolley arm. Suleiman had to brace his whole weight against the strong spring, and then walk around the tramcar and fit the wheel correctly back on the electric cable so that the trolley arm was pointing the way the tram would be going. Finally, while the driver and conductor were still sipping their tea, he took out the steering handle and went to the other end of the platform to fit it into the engine block there. He did all this as naturally as if he had worked on the trams all his life. The conductor and driver admired the little fellow who had the strength of an adult. Suleiman was the only boy who got to shake hands with all the conductors and didn't need to buy a ticket wherever he boarded the tram. He often brought the men things from his home: sandwiches, apples, sometimes Spanish cigarettes. His father brought large quantities of these cigarettes back from the embassy.

Of course Farid paid when he rode on the tram. Claire had made sure of that. "You mustn't cost other people money."

One day he wanted to ride the tram nowhere in particular, just looking at people. He sat down by the window with a big bag of peanuts and watched the passers by in the streets. The great advantage of the tram was that it went along at a very gentle pace, and unlike bus drivers the men who drove the tramcars never stopped on some whim of their own to talk to friends. Somehow tram drivers didn't just wear uniforms but seemed more serious in every way than bus drivers.

On the outward journey Farid could pick jasmine and oleander flowers through the open window, from bushes growing wild very close to the rails. At one point he suddenly spotted the lunatic who had been looking for his horse for years. Apparently the man, a Bedouin, had once owned the finest horse in the world. One day President Shaklan saw it and wanted to buy it no matter what it cost, but the proud Bedouin despised money and threats left him cold. However, the secret service had the Bedouin arrested and took his horse. The man went crazy with grief in prison. After a while he was released, and he had been roaming the streets ever since, knocking gates and calling out, "Here I am, Sabah." Then he listened for an answering whinny from a horse. Sometimes he would begin to weep pitifully. People felt sorry for him, and gave him food, old clothes, water, even money. He went barefoot in summer and winter alike.

On the way back Farid couldn't help laughing. A crook who had already tricked several women in Farid's quarter was standing at a stop where a crowd of people were waiting for the tram. He sold sweetened, coloured water as a miracle cure for worms. And almost the entire population of the city had worms.

"Look at this, look at this, will you?" he cried, showing a jar containing small snakes and an assortment of worms pickled in alcohol. "Only the other day these worms were living it up in the belly of one of my customers, oh yes, they were holding wedding parties, until he took three of my miracle drops on an empty stomach, and out they rushed like kids going down a slide."

The people looked anxiously at the big jar. Its contents could have filled the stomach of a cow. The tram driver himself was so impressed that he rose to his feet and followed the words of the alleged miracle-worker from the door with his mouth open.

"So how do we know if we have worms?" called one of the passers by.

"Does your breath smell? That's the worms farting. And if you want to be quite sure, run your fingernail or a smooth piece of wood over your teeth first thing in the morning when you get up. If you find a yellowish, smelly smear on the wood, you have worms. It's their shit," replied the fraudster.

The tram driver scratched something off his teeth with one fingernail, smelled it, shook his head in horror, and hurried back to his seat in alarm as the next tram approached, ringing its bell loudly.

108. Children's Games

Azar soon thought up a good way for Suleiman to get his own back on the policeman who had called him names and slapped his face. Suleiman had won ten packets of chewing gum from the policeman's son during a game. The game was a very simple one: everyone threw his little packet of gum towards a wall, and the one that landed closest had won. There were no tricks involved; only practice counted. But Suleiman had been a little unfair because he was a world class chewing-gum thrower, and had persuaded the unsuspecting boy that with a little luck he too could win. The policeman's son had spent all his money on ten packets of gum, and every one of them ended up in Suleiman's pocket. Then the boy began crying inconsolably. Before long his father, a large and portly police officer, came hurrying down the street, seized Suleiman by the collar, shook him, slapped his face hard and took away all his packets of gum, including those that other players had lost to him that day. Josef always said that Lady Luck herself avoided playing games with Suleiman because she knew she didn't stand a chance.

"He's taken away all my chewing gum! That's worse than him hitting me, because now I don't have any capital left. How am I going to carry on playing?" wailed Suleiman. His face was red and swollen where the policeman had hit him, but he could take a punch. All the same, he was furious with the policeman's children, who were all standing at the window up on the second floor, chewing gum and laughing. And their father, with his hairy chest bared, looked triumphantly down over the children's heads at Suleiman and the other boys.

That night the gang met in the attic and decided to get their own back on the policeman. But it was a week before Azar could put his wily plan into practice. It was a mild summer night. The policeman was sleeping next to an open window with his pillow almost on the sill when something suddenly exploded right beside him. When he sat up with a roaring in his ears, there was a second explosion. This time he saw a bluish globe of fire floating towards him out of nowhere.

"War, it's war," he cried. He pushed his wife from the bed to the floor and flung himself on top of her. The woman, frightened to death, cried angrily that he had crushed her ribs; he'd better get off her at once, she said, and go and see to the children. However, they were sleeping peacefully in the back room, which looked out on the inner courtyard, and like all the neighbours had heard nothing.

Azar's idea had been to put zinc and hydrochloric acid in a bottle to make hydrogen. He blew two balloons up with the hydrogen, fitting them over the neck of the bottle. The balloons rose into the night air without a sound, while Azar and Suleiman, down in the street, held their long, thin strings and manipulated them. Large firecrackers hung just under the balloons. When the right moment came Azar put a match to one of the strings, which had been soaked in kerosene. The flame shot up it and ignited the firecracker. The force freed the balloon, and it rose towards the sky. The second firecracker was just a little too close to its hydrogen balloon, which went off with a huge bang immediately after the firecracker had ignited. But by that time Azar and Suleiman were well away.

109. Festival of Sacrifice

Farid was just twelve when he ventured into the Muslim quarter on his own for the fist time. He knew from school that this was the day when the Muslims held their great festival of sacrifice. Josef didn't want to go with him; he thought it would be too noisy and dirty for him there.

Although they lived so close to each other, the Muslim way of life and celebrations were very different from Christian customs. To Farid, Muslims seemed like an exotic race of people who were somehow more physical, colourful, noisier, more forthright than Christians. Later he found another way of putting it: they were more natural.

The cries of the street sellers at their fairground stalls sounded more cheerful than usual. All the houses were decorated, with coloured cloths and rugs hanging from their balconies like banners. Groups of people kept gathering around two or more men performing mock fights. Farid saw a couple of young men in traditional robes, carrying curved swords and small, round, steel shields. They hopped and danced and struck the paving stones with their swords, making sparks fly. Then they attacked one another. It was all well rehearsed, and blows fell only on their swords and shields in a prearranged rhythm.

A few metres away a man was making his horse dance. The horse was decorated too. The man assured onlookers that it was an Arab, although many of them volubly expressed their doubts of his claim, for Arabs are proud horses and run like the wind, but would never dance. Anyway, the animal had much too plump a body for an *assil*, a genuine Arab horse.

Elsewhere, a fight with bamboo canes looked much more dangerous than the swordfight. The two combatants carried long, thin canes and hard, round leather shields padded with cotton. They met in the middle of a circle formed by the spectators, kissed one another's fingertips, and took three steps back to show that they were cautious and respected their opponents. Finally they began, each dancing around on his own and striking his shield or the ground with his cane. The canes whirled through the air with a whistling sound that gave you goose bumps. Finally the men went for each other, and the blows they gave were real and not just for show like those in the swordfight. A referee was in charge of the fight and gave the sign when it came to an end.

When the two men acknowledged the applause, gasping for breath, Farid saw the red weals left by the canes coming down on their arms, necks, and faces.

Farid moved on, and for the first time he saw a shadow theatre. Damascus was famous for them at the time. There were none in the Christian quarter, but the Muslim boys at school were always going into raptures about the shadow theatre. A small stage with a screen behind it had been set up in a café, and the place was full. Adults and children alike sat there, enjoying a play about the shadow figure Karagös, a character who was always playing tricks but lost out every time. Farid was surprised to find that the narrator behind the screen on which the shadows moved didn't care about his language or the sensitivities of the audience. His story was full of terms like "son of a whore", and "pimp". The main characters in the story had arses rather than backsides or buttocks, and they didn't break wind but farted, very loudly. One of them could even work a mill with his farting and keep his whole family on the proceeds. The spectators laughed and slapped their thighs. Suddenly they were all like children. Farid didn't quite understand what the play was about, but he couldn't help chuckling too, because Karagös kept doing everything wrong and coming off worst.

The whole quarter was out in the streets celebrating. The houses seemed empty. Christian festivals were the other way round: the streets were empty then, and the houses full of visitors who moved at least once from one building to another, to go on celebrating somewhere new.

Farid happily roamed the streets, eating something now and then, drinking juice and *airan*, a chilled yoghurt drink, buying himself bags of pumpkin seeds, and several sweetmeats dripping with fat and syrup. He didn't realize that he was slowly but surely giving himself indigestion. However, although he had terrible diarrhoea that evening he thought he'd never had a better time than at the Muslim festival of sacrifice.

110. Riding a Bicycle

Bicycles were expensive in Damascus at the beginning of the fifties. They were imported, usually from England or the Netherlands, and they cost a fortune. Two or three men at the most in any street owned such a luxurious means of transport. However, there was a bicycle hire place in every quarter. The man who hired out bikes in the Bab Sharki district had his shop on Straight Street, right between Saitun Alley and Abbara Alley. He was a Muslim, and bad-tempered, he looked a mess, and he was always working away on his bicycles. Farid couldn't remember ever seeing the man drinking tea, smoking cigarettes, or simply sitting about. He was always bent over one of his bikes, or pumping up one of countless tyres. He wasn't uncivil, but he was taciturn, and in Damascus that was regarded as unfriendly. However, people bought and hired bicycles from him because he asked less than his rival in Bab Tuma. And his bikes were sturdy.

Farid was fascinated by bicycles, but he couldn't ride one, and didn't feel brave enough to hire a bike and learn. Azar and Suleiman had learned very quickly. How they did it no one knew, but it was as if they had been riding bikes all their lives. Suleiman could even ride with his hands free, or stand on the saddle and spread his arms. Azar could fling the front wheel up in the air and ride on the back wheel alone. It all looked so easy, but the moment Farid so much as touched the handlebars of a bike it seemed to want to fall over, or at least go in a different direction. It wouldn't even let him push it.

Josef was no better, but that very fact was a challenge to him. He paid a lira to hire a bike for two hours.

"And if I can't ride the wretched thing after that, you can throw me into the sewers," he growled with determination.

Farid laughed. "Or call an ambulance."

"No way! You wait and see, I'll come riding it back shouting, 'Look, no hands!'"

But their plans fell through. The man at the hire shop took the lira and didn't ask if Josef could ride a bicycle, just pointed to a red one and mumbled morosely, "You better be back by five, or I'll charge for another hour." And he added, as he did with all children, "I know your father."

It was quarter to three now, so he'd given them an extra fifteen minutes. Josef beamed and pushed the bicycle towards Saitun Alley, rigid with excitement.

"It'll be easier in your street, it's better paved," he claimed. He wanted to avoid the mockery of the boys and girls in Abbara Alley.

Saitun Alley was quieter than a graveyard at this time of day. There wasn't a human soul in sight as Josef and Farid turned into it. But suddenly a man appeared.

"Hello," he said, "what a nice bike! You two look like beginners – has anyone tested the brakes for you? I have a friend who put his brakes on too hard. He flew over the handlebars and landed on his head. He's spoken nothing but English since. A medical phenomenon. Let's see how those brakes are working." And before Josef had fully grasped the situation, the man had gently removed his hands from the handlebars, jumped on the saddle, and rode off towards the Catholic church. There he turned and raced back towards them. Josef stood in the middle of the street waving to the man to stop, but the man called, "The brakes don't work!" shot past him like an arrow and turned right into Straight Street. Josef and Farid ran after him, but the man had almost reached the eastern gate already. And then he was out of sight.

"I'm an idiot. I ought to have kicked him in the balls. He was a thief, and now the bike's gone," said Josef gloomily.

They stood there, silent and lost in thought, watching the street sweepers who sprinkled the road surface with water in the afternoons in summer, and swept up the worst of the refuse.

"Come on, let's go to my place," said Farid at last, but Josef just stood there. He was wondering how to break the news of the loss gently to the man in the hire shop without having him seize him by the throat or demand large sums of money from his mother.

"I'll help you," Farid went on. "I've saved over fifteen lira, and I bet Grandfather Nagib will come up with fifty. I'm sure I can get another ten out of Claire, so that comes to seventy-five. That's almost the price of a bicycle."

Josef's face brightened, and a smile showed, although a smile clad in grief and gratitude. He put a hand on Farid's shoulder, saying in a shaky voice, "Thanks. You really are my friend."

"Of course I'm your friend. And when we've paid for the bicycle we'll go and find that bastard and smash his balls to scrambled egg," proclaimed Farid grandly, to make it even more impressive.

They couldn't say later how long they had been standing there like that, but suddenly Josef froze with surprise, for the man appeared again. Shouting cheerfully, he rode past them to the Catholic church.

"He's not getting away from me this time. I'm going after him," growled Josef. Farid planned to grab the bicycle from behind as soon as the man rode past him. But it never came to that. The man rode around in an elegant curve in front of the church porch, dismounted, leaned the bike against the wall, and adjusted his shirt and trousers. Then he went into the church. For some reason its doors were standing wide open.

"What's he planning to do?" asked Farid.

"He's trying to lure us in."

"You run and fetch the bike and I'll wait here. If he gets in your way, shout for help," said Josef, picking up a large stone lying by the wall.

Farid's heart was thudding, but he ran. The sun, suddenly hotter than ever, was blazing down on his head. He was sweating, and so scared that the air flickered before his eyes, but he could feel Josef's eyes on his back, so there was no way he could change his mind now. When he reached the bike he swiftly seized the handlebars, started pushing it, and for once, oddly enough, it obeyed him and went along beside him like a faithful dog. Josef put the stone down and came over to his friend. Relieved, he took the bike.

"It's five," he said.

The man in the hire shop just looked up briefly from his work, pointed to the wall where he wanted Josef to lean the bike, and took no more notice of the boys.

Josef and Farid quickly went back to the church to find the man, but the church was empty, and the old sexton Abdullah hadn't seen anyone come in or go out.

On the way home, Josef swore that he would never touch a bicycle again in his life. And sure enough, he never did.

111. Maaruf Directing Traffic

Maaruf lived with his wife Samira and their four children in two rooms of the big apartment building next to Farid's house. Samira was a tall woman with white skin and black hair. She wasn't beautiful, but her white skin had men turning to look at her.

Her husband was tall and massive. Farid had never seen him looking as if he had just washed; he was sweaty even early in the morning. Most traffic cops in Damascus were extremely elegant in appearance, but not Maaruf. He looked like a jailbird on the run who had just stolen a traffic cop's uniform.

He earned very little. It might have been enough for him on his own, but with a wife who in his opinion couldn't keep house, and four children whose appetites were never satisfied, even two salaries wouldn't have been enough. And he had his old parents to support as well.

Claire had never liked Samira and Maaruf, and since the incident with her brother Marcel she wouldn't even pass the time of day with them. Maaruf had stopped Marcel close to Bab Tuma. Marcel gave the policeman a friendly greeting and said, casually, that he knew him and his delightful wife, since Maaruf was his sister Claire's neighbour in Saitun Alley.

"I don't know any Claire," claimed Maaruf, and he also denied living in Saitun Alley. "You hooted, that costs ten lira, you have vapour coming out of your exhaust, that costs twenty lira, and you're driving without lights, that costs thirty lira. Pick your fine. I don't want to be unjust."

Marcel was trapped. He decided for the cheapest fine on offer, but he could find only a twenty-lira note in his wallet. He gave that to the policeman, saying, "I'll have the hooting."

The policeman grinned and said, "Very sensible of you." And turned away.

"But I want my ten lira change," protested Marcel.

Maaruf put the twenty lira in his shirt pocket and said generously, "For the second ten lira, you can hoot your horn again."

112. Raining Sugar-Coated Fennel Seeds

One summer morning in the year 1952 the inhabitants of the Christian quarter found that a miracle had happened. By now coups and miracles were everyday occurrences for the Damascenes, although so far miracles had befallen only individuals, not whole parts of the city.

Almost all the inner courtyards, balconies and rooftops were sprinkled with little coloured things that looked like grain. People cautiously tasted them, and were delighted to find that it had been raining fennel seeds. In Damascus, fennel seeds are coated in coloured sugar and used to decorate sweet dishes, or simply put in the mouth to be chewed after a spicy dish. Fennel is good for the digestion and perfumes your breath.

The neighbours picked up the delicious seeds and ate them thoughtfully. Many decided that they had never tasted so good before, others claimed to have been cured of chronic stomach ailments the day after eating them.

So this was a time of blessings. Now that Colonel Shaklan had risen to power in Damascus, heaven appeared to be content. There had been plenty of rain last winter, which augured well for a record harvest in summer. And now sugar-coated fennel seeds had fallen from heaven. Some of the neighbours were reminded of the manna that God had fed to the children of Israel on their flight through the desert. Was this a sign from heaven that the lord of the universe was pleased with President Shaklan? The ever-suspicious Josef suspected that government airplanes had dropped the sugar-coated seeds, but no one had seen or heard any planes.

The gang sat in the attic above the aniseed storehouse, thinking about it. Azar joined them late that evening, and brought the answer to the riddle with him.

"It was Burhan and me," he said. "A thank-you to the neighbours."

Burhan was not a man of many words, and found talking hard work, but when he did come out with complete sentences he sounded surprisingly clever. Normally he was regarded as simple-minded for the time it took him to put two words together – hours, days, even weeks.

Burhan was small and strong and had a job that suited him perfectly: he was a stonemason. Stonemasons are silent folk, and he liked to keep quiet.

He worked as a labourer for Josef's father, he was a bachelor, and he lived only a couple of houses away. He and his sister had inherited their house. He lived on the second floor, she lived on the first floor with her husband and four children. Burhan didn't want to get married. Marriage would have meant talking a lot, which would be too much of a strain on him. He liked best spending time with his pigeons. He had over a hundred, and knew every single one of them better than he knew some of his neighbours.

He paid his sister a third of his wages, and for that he shared her family's meals. He spent another third on his pigeons, and with what was left he allowed himself a small pleasure here and there. Burhan was at ease with himself and the world. He ate what was put in front of him, he found fault with nothing, but he never praised anything either.

Josef's father liked Burhan but not his love for his pigeons, because it meant that the man always put his hammer down on the dot of four in the afternoon to go and see to his birds.

Pigeon breeders had a bad reputation in the city. They were considered obsessive and lazy, and their witness statements were worth nothing in a court of law because they were regarded as notorious liars. Furthermore, they were always up on their rooftops, where they could spy on other people's houses. And their neighbours were bothered by the pigeon breeders' calls and whistles, and all the garbage that they threw at hawks, cats, or even their own birds if they turned awkward. The garbage often landed in inner courtyards, even on tables where people were eating, and the pigeons themselves were lavish with their droppings.

All that was true of pigeon breeders in general, but Burhan was different. He loved his pigeons, and never threw anything at them. He conducted them the way a musician conducts an orchestra, and he always tried not to bother anyone. Curiosity was far too strenuous for him.

Josef, Farid, and the other boys in the gang had no great opinion of pigeons. Azar was the only one who liked them, and as he couldn't afford any of his own he went to see Burhan almost every day and admired his birds, which had a very high reputation in the pigeon fancy. Over the years, Azar became almost like Burhan's assistant. On Sundays he was even allowed to go to the Pigeon Café in the Suk el Sinaniye with him, where breeders met and offered their birds for sale.

Like Burhan, Azar was silent and given to brooding, so the two of them got on well. One day Burhan asked Azar how he could thank the neighbours for their patience with him and his pigeons. Azar immediately had an idea. He made little boxes of lightweight card, and fastened them to the pigeons with short rubber bands cut from the inner tube of an old bicycle tyre. The boxes had little holes in their bases, and just before the pigeons took off the boxes were filled with the sugar-coated fennel seeds.

Then, early that summer morning at the first light of dawn, Burhan sent fifty pigeons up into the air. He guided them soundlessly on their round trip, and before anyone had begun getting up in the morning, the pigeons were back from their flight over the Christian quarter of the city.

113. Grandfather's Salt

Farid hated the idea of leaving Damascus for the monastery, but he sometimes consoled himself with the thought of being closer to the Mediterranean. Josef, Suleiman, and Azar had never been away from the city for long. Of the friends, only Rasuk had once spent two years outside the country, in the Lebanese monastery of Christ the Redeemer.

One night, two weeks before Farid's departure, Rasuk came up to the attic where they were all sitting gloomily. No one was saying a word about the Flash Gordon movie they'd all seen together that afternoon.

"You'll like the sea, Farid, I'm sure you will," he began. "I was eight when I saw it for the first time. I spent hours, fascinated, sitting on a rock outside the monastery the day after I arrived. I could look down on the waves from up there, and a week later I found a huge book all about the Mediterranean in the monastery library, with illustrations. The underwater sights, the sea creatures, the amphorae, the shipwrecks – they were all there in large, hand-coloured photographs. It was the mysterious blue of the sea that I liked. I played by the water whenever I could. Later I learned to swim, and the salty taste of seawater surprised me.

"Then I came back here to Damascus in the summer vacation, and my parents took us away from the heat, the way they do every year, to our home village of Sabadani, fifteen hundred metres above sea level up in the mountains, where we always stayed with my grandparents.

"One afternoon I was sitting on the terrace with my grandfather. He used to drink coffee there just before sunset. The coffee was spiced with cardamom and smelled delicious. I loved my grandfather, because he told good stories.

'Tell me about the sea, Grandfather,' I asked him.

"He smiled slightly. 'I can't tell you much about the sea. Ask your grandmother. She comes from Latakia, the northern harbour town.' But Grandmother was away with her family for three weeks just then, and when she came back my vacation would be over and I'd have to be back at the monastery. So I said what bad luck that was, and the old man nodded and took a big gulp of coffee. 'The sea,' he whispered, and then he fell silent. 'The sea is – well, the sea's quite something,' he added, finishing his thought out loud at last. He stood up. 'The Mediterranean lies over in the west, beyond the mountains, and I can tell you a little story about that. Thirty years ago I was planning to escape the First World War and emigrate to America, but when I saw the sea, and I found out that an even mightier ocean lay beyond that great stretch of water, and I'd have to cross it, I decided to stay in port for the time being. So I leased a tavern. Evening after evening I listened to the bragging tales of sailors, smugglers, adventurers. One day an Englishman gave me a lot of money to go to Cyprus with him and smuggle gold and weapons to Beirut for Lawrence of Arabia. So I stepped into his rotten boat. But I couldn't swim, and the sea was rough ...'

"And Grandfather told me such a long tale of weapons, gold, and smugglers that I can't repeat it all to you now, but he was so excited that every now and then his voice sounded hoarse, as if he were reliving the moment when he was near drowning, but a dolphin rescued him and brought him safe ashore.

'And ever since then,' he concluded, 'salt oozes from my skin when I tell stories of the sea.' And he reached his wrinkled brown hand out to me. 'Taste it,' he said, smiling. I licked it carefully, and sure enough, his hand was as salty as the sea at the foot of the monastery of Christ the Redeemer."

BOOK OF LONELINESS I

Loneliness is death's twin brother.

જી

114. The Journey

Arriving as suddenly as a summer storm, a small truck with no licence plate appeared on the winding road, overtook the bus, and came to a halt right across the carriageway. The words "secret service" went back and forth among the passengers. The bus driver braked sharply and cursed under his breath. A bearded traveller and a stout woman, sitting on the front seats near the door, trod on invisible pedals in parallel with him and noisily sucked air in through their teeth. The vehicle lurched to one side, and didn't come to rest until it reached the soft verge of the road. Gravel fell to the abyss below.

Seconds later the bus was surrounded by four armed men in civilian clothes, while two more searched the passengers. A large, handsomely ornamented dagger earned its owner a slap in the face. After taking his punishment the peasant, a figure of impressive masculinity, stared dejectedly out of the side window. The consolations offered by his neighbours didn't get through to him; the dagger was all he had inherited from his late father.

Cameras were also frowned upon in the mountains where rebels held sway. An Egyptian tourist had to hand over his, with all the films. Smuggled goods, however, didn't interest the inspectors. They were looking for books, newspapers and weapons.

Colonel Shaklan had hardly any allies left in Damascus in this, the fourth year of his dictatorship. The army was muttering more and more audibly. Riots and mutinies were breaking out everywhere. The secret service was the one weapon he had left. When he sent it in, death would not be far behind.

A young teacher was hauled out of the bus for hiding a French newspaper. From the angry abuse hurled at him, the other passengers gathered that the newspaper carried an article about a Syrian government in exile in Baghdad. The young man was kicked and pushed into the truck. Everyone could clearly hear his pleas.

Only after this prelude did the first lieutenant in charge of the party get into the bus himself. It was baking hot by now in the July sun. Almost politely, he demanded to see the passengers' papers. He was charming to the children. His gaze moved back and forth between the passengers' ID and his lists.

On coming to a bearded doctor he asked, in passing, what would cure his migraine. The doctor hesitated, fearing that the question was a trap. Everyone waited with bated breath for his answer.

"Aspirin," he said at last, hoarsely, swallowing hard. "Don't smoke too much, no alcohol, and get plenty of sleep."

The officer laughed and shook his head. His laughter gave all the passengers a moment's respite. Some heaved a sigh of relief, others cast a quick glance at the photos in their ID cards, as if they feared they might find forged papers there.

Farid felt no fear, and even enjoyed the sight of his father's pallor. Elias kept muttering to himself, "We ought to have taken the coastal road, it's safer." When things went wrong he liked to use the first person plural, as if to avoid taking the blame himself. Claire had recommended the coastal road, but it meant a longer journey, and as usual his father was in a hurry. Farid had to get up at four in the morning, so that his father could be back in Damascus at eight that evening for a meeting of the confectioners' association.

⚓

Encouraged by his undaunted passengers, the bus driver had over-taken trucks and other buses on the good blacktop road going north from Damascus. After four hours, he had turned off and taken the protesting vehicle up the endlessly winding country road, which was more detritus and potholes than asphalt.

Worse than the potholes, however, were the many checkpoints. Farid had counted four barriers guarded by soldiers along a twenty-kilometre stretch.

An elderly smith sitting on the other side of the aisle had told Farid's father that the region was under the control of a rebel called Tanios. Whole villages and forests had once belonged to a single clan. The peasants had attacked it again and again, but they had all been butchered until this man Tanios came along. He was a Christian, although hostile tongues said he was in league with the devil. Under his influence, the young peasants suddenly became brave as lions. Even Muslims flocked to join him, crazy men who now bore arms too. What poor soldier was going to hold out against the rebels here for the ridiculous wage of fourteen lira a month?

115. Tanios and Asma

Only later did Farid learn that until Tanios's uprising, the peasants of this mountain region had not been allowed to have lights in their houses. And every virgin had to spend her wedding night with the landowner – she couldn't be taken home by her bridegroom until next morning. It was the custom of the *droit de seigneur,* entitling the master to the first night.

Tanios was a proud man, and he loved Asma. At their betrothal, he swore to her before friends that Sheikh Mustafa, the mighty owner of the whole area, would never touch her. They were to marry at Easter. Tanios bought black patent leather shoes in the nearby harbour town of Latakia, and at Asma's wish he was going to wear them at the wedding. He spent his entire savings, for he liked nothing in the world better than seeing tears of joy in his bride's eyes.

On the wedding day Asma stared spellbound at his patent leather shoes the whole time. What her bridegroom promised, he performed. Suddenly, in the middle of the *Kyrie eleison*, she longed for the touch of his hands on her naked skin.

But two birds of ill omen were waiting outside the church, Sheikh Mustafa's black-clad guards, saying that they had come to fetch the bride and the patent leather shoes, for only great men might wear shoes like that.

Tanios roared, "Now death will taste sweet as honey!", and that roar echoed through the mountains for weeks to come. He fell on the two messengers like a lion and killed them. Thereupon hundreds of angry peasants and serfs stormed Mustafa's magnificent estate as if they were drunk on blood, killing him and his three sons. They drove his three wives and ten daughters away. When the peasants saw how easy it was to murder a lord, they conquered two more mountainous valleys.

Only in the valley of the Three Rivers was the onward march of the rebel peasants halted, for here they met with the troops of another rebel called Salman Sufi, who ruled the mountain chain down to the Mediterranean. The government was still partly in control of the road leading through the mountains to the sea, but no more.

The peasants who followed Tanios divided the land and money they had taken between them, and they all bought patent leather shoes to wear every Sunday. And now they also lit lamps in their houses. Asma was the first poor peasant's wife to lose her virginity in a night of love.

When Colonel Shaklan, the son of a small farmer himself, carried out his coup and made himself president, he felt sympathy for Tanios, whose heroic story had spread like wildfire. He wrote him a letter saying that the feudal period was over, the peasants could safely place their cause in the hands of the father of their country and lay down their arms. He, President of the Republic and father of the great Syrian family, gave Tanios his word that the government wished for peace with him. All he, Shaklan, wanted was Salman Sufi's head.

In return the colonel received a barely legible letter written in pencil, which ran:

From Tanios, the slave of God, to Colonel
Shaklan, who calls himself lord of Damascus.
God alone is lord of all cities and all creatures. We
do not trust city folk. First agree to our demands, and
have them read out in all churches and mosques,
and put in all the newspapers.

The earth, like the sun, belongs to all men.
Every farmer may plant and eat as much as he needs.
Every man may light a lamp whenever he wishes.
The right to the first night is repealed.
All peasants may wear patent leather shoes.

Colonel Shaklan smiled at the peasant's naivety, but his advisers warned him that what Tanios was asking was the first step towards communism. Shaklan had better send his troops to kill the peasant leader, they said.

Three thousand infantry set out into the mountains in February 1953. Exactly a week later, Damascus had lost all contact with the expedition. Together with their cannon, military transports, and fifteen trucks carrying ammunition, they had disappeared into the impenetrable green vegetation of the mountains. Two weeks later, a truck reached the capital with the bodies of twenty-three officers. Rumour said that Tanios had cast a spell over the common soldiers, who had shot all the officers and gone over to the rebel side.

It was a devastating defeat. Colonel Shaklan swore revenge, but then, in May 1953, a great rebellion broke out among the Druses in the south of the country. So the colonel had to send his troops there, but he reinforced supervision of the roads in the north with checkpoints and mobile units of men.

⁂

The bus driver seemed to be experienced. At every barrier he had replied to the questions put by the NCOs, which were always the same, in a casual and almost bored tone. He seemed to have all the time in the world, and on their way had kept stopping at some shabby kiosk where only soldiers sat around on old wooden crates drinking tea. They all seemed to know him well.

But now that these armed civilians had stopped him he suddenly fell silent and huddled further and further back in his seat. The officer didn't seem to trust him. He waved the driver's ID in front of his face. "In my opinion," he said, "a man who drives more than three times through the region of these godless folk and hasn't been shot yet is one of them himself. But unfortunately the government in Damascus won't listen to me, so you can enjoy your life for a little while longer," he added with an unpleasant grin, and handed the bus driver his ID back. He did not speak angrily or in loud and threatening tones, but with quiet emphasis, and for that very reason his words had the ring of death in them.

When the officer asked Farid's father his name, he replied in a hesitant, indistinct voice, "Elias ... Elias Mushtak, sir."

"Are you related to Mustafa Mushtak?" asked the officer.

"No, sir, certainly not," replied Elias, and he felt a stabbing pain in his larynx.

"What makes you so sure?"

"We're Christians, and Mustafa is a Muslim name," said Elias, and he knew the officer was acting dumb on purpose to lure him into a trap.

"Your profession?" he heard the officer ask.

"Confectioner," replied Elias quietly.

"And what's a confectioner from Damascus doing here?"

"I'm taking my son to the monastery of St. Sebastian. He wants to be a priest."

"A priest?" repeated the officer incredulously, scrutinizing Farid. "The boy doesn't look to me as if he'll be a priest." He fell silent. Then he asked, casually, "The monastery is in the area controlled by the godless Salman Sufi, am I right?"

"We didn't know that in Damascus. The news didn't mention any unrest. I first heard that name in the bus this morning."

Elias's voice was gradually growing stronger again in his indignation, as he realized that the authorities were suppressing all news of anything like epidemics and rebels.

"Do you expect the government to put out propaganda for the criminals? We shall soon crush them, but by the Prophet Muhammad, your son's never going to be a priest. Why would he want to? What's your name, my boy?"

Elias Mushtak felt the derision in the man's words like a knife stabbing him. Who gave this lousy Muslim the right to say whether or not Farid had a vocation for the priesthood?

"Farid Mushtak," he heard his son answer fearlessly. The officer entered the name in his list, as he had with the other passengers. Farid thought it was all for show. Why bother to write down the names of hundreds of people who happened to be driving through rebel territory?

The officer turned to the next passengers. Now Elias took out his handkerchief with a steady hand and mopped his face dry. Soon the officer got out, and the armed men disappeared as quickly as they had come. The column of cars, carts, and trucks that had been waiting behind the bus in silence all this time gradually moved on up the narrow mountain track.

When the bus driver reached the next stop, he parked in the shade of an ancient elm tree and joined the customers in the kiosk. "Fifteen minutes' rest for everyone!" he called to his passengers. His voice sounded friendly but exhausted. The passengers were grateful to him.

Farid tried not to look at the elm tree. He didn't want to get out. His father, however, joined the men in the kiosk. Farid closed his eyes, and suddenly he saw the elm surrounded by tall flames.

Back in the Easter vacation in Mala, the flames had blazed through the night. The fire hadn't gone out until nearly four in the morning, when only the green, right-hand half of the tree was left. No one except his father thought Farid had set fire to it. At the time, however, in the village elder's house, Elias Mushtak had decided with all the severity of a judge that his son would atone by entering the monastery of St. Sebastian.

Farid was alone in the bus now, except for three chickens cackling faintly and wearily under one of the front seats. They sounded like a distant radio station transmitting in a foreign language.

After a while the engine roared again, and the travellers were quick to get back into the bus. The driver looked in the rear-view mirror and saw that one seat was still empty. He hooted three times, and a pretty young peasant girl climbed in. Farid thought she had the most beautiful ears, eyes, and lips he had ever seen.

Later he kept thinking of what lay ahead of him. He had been told just before they left that the former Jesuit monastery was notorious for its strict discipline, but the most important bishops of Syria and Lebanon had studied there.

Elias Mushtak considered it important that the monastery of St. Sebastian, although officially in Arab hands, still trained its students in the modern but strict Jesuit manner. Strict discipline was exactly what his son needed, everything came too easily to him, Elias had said in defending his decision to Claire. Farid was wasting his clever mind. And he didn't want him ending up as priest in some lousy little village, he had the makings of a great theologian.

None of these ideas cut any ice with Farid. As he saw it, entering a monastery was a punishment. And what for? The rotten half of a miserable elm tree at the back of beyond.

A bitter taste, acrid as smoke, rose in his throat and tears came to his eyes. His father had fallen asleep. For a second Farid toyed with the idea of getting quietly to his feet, jumping out of the large, open window and disappearing into the undergrowth. Any chance-met robber would understand him better than the man beside him. The bus was going very slowly, because there were small rocks and large branches all over the road. The driver had to steer past these obstacles at snail's pace.

Most of the passengers were sleeping, exhausted, in the pleasant cool breeze with its fragrance of resin, thyme, and damp soil. Farid peered into the impenetrable green. He couldn't see the faintest trace of any human figure, yet he was sure that sharp eyes were keeping a close watch on the bus. Soon the forest became so dense that Farid could actually touch the leaves and branches of the trees if he put his hand out of the window.

The driver stopped and climbed out. Farid saw him take a jute sack from a hiding place under the bonnet and put it under a tree by the roadside. After that he got back in and drove on. Farid was just in time to see two men slipping out of the bushes and disappearing again with the sack, quick as a flash of lightning.

116. Elopement

Rana was sitting on a park bench with Farid, staring into space. She had just heard that he was to go into the monastery, and tears were running down her cheeks. "Why are they taking you away from me? What will I do without you?" she asked.

Rana never talked much, but her words were always harbingers of her deeds. Nor did she say much at this meeting, as usual, but she told Farid she had decided to run away with him. Only now did he see her little case beside the bench.

Her words touched Farid, and the sight of that case made him feel both deeply uneasy and furiously angry with his father. When those two emotions clashed, there was only one thing he could do: he agreed to the elopement.

If this delicate girl was brave enough, why must he always be a coward and do as he was told? He hurried home, packed his pyjamas, two pairs of trousers, two shirts, a large quantity of underwear, all Rana's love letters and his entire savings: 100 Syrian lira. Finally he wrote a single sentence on a piece of paper and put it in his mother's cosmetics bag: *Mama, I love you.*

Farid and Rana quickly agreed on their destination: Beirut, the Lebanese capital. Once there, they planned to earn money and travel to America with forged passports.

They found a taxi. The driver, a young man with a practised eye, knew after they had gone ten kilometres that they were eloping. He had to smile, because he himself had once done something similar. In his case, he told them, the love story had ended with a reconciliation and not a hole in the head. He too had hidden in Beirut with his wife for five years, until the storm at home died down with the birth of his first child. Today his father-in-law, who had once sent a killer to track him down, positively idolized him, he said.

Farid and Rana felt more hopeful. The taxi driver was willing to help them. He knew an old woman in Beirut, he told them, very discreet, he was sure she would rent them a room.

Twenty kilometres before the border, however, his smile froze as he sat behind the steering wheel, when he found out that naïve as they were, Farid and Rana expected to get into Lebanon without any papers. But in spite of his initial horror, he went on being helpful. He drove a long way around through several villages, dropped them off at an abandoned mill, showed them an old, ruinous railroad embankment, and told them how to find a secret path into Lebanon. He promised to wait for them on the Lebanese side of the border.

They both ducked into the tall grass, waited until the border guards had finished their hourly patrol, and then ran across the embankment and easily climbed over the rusty barbed wire fence, which was falling down anyway. After that they had to cross an open field. They ran for their lives. Twice Farid imagined that he heard someone calling, "Stop, this is the police!" but nothing was going to stop him now.

At last they reached a road leading to a village. It ran through orchards, and the taxi was parked in the shade of a house. Their guardian angel was sitting in it.

"Welcome to Lebanon!" he said, beaming, and he got out of the car to greet them. "You made it. No one will bother you any more here," he said as he raced away with them. Only now did Farid realize that his case had been in the back of the car the whole time. All his money was in it.

"Where's yours?" he asked Rana quietly. She smiled at him, and patted her stomach. "Here, in a thin leather bag."

ॐ

They were brother and sister, said the taxi driver, and they had to live in hiding for a few months because of a blood feud. This story was necessary, for otherwise no one would have taken in such young lovers. The old widow looked at them with narrowed eyes.

"A blood feud," she repeated, and nodded.

That first night with Rana was so exciting that Farid couldn't sleep at all. They kissed, feeling very nervous. He had never seen Rana naked before. He knelt down by the bed and adored her body, which was shivering with excitement and got goosebumps whenever he touched her. Farid had found her most sensitive spot, her nipples, and when he tenderly sucked them the demons of inhibition slunk out of the room. The two of them licked and kissed each other, curious and hungry for more. Suddenly Rana's body was like a wave of the sea. She swayed up and down and let out a soft cry. It sounded like the cry of a gull, and satisfied Farid to the depths of his heart. Only at dawn did they fall asleep.

They did not guess that their landlady, who had been shut out of this Paradise ever since her husband's early death fifty years before, was listening to it all outside the door. An inexorable knocking woke Farid abruptly. For a moment he didn't know where he was and why Rana was lying naked beside him.

He asked the widow to wait a moment and dressed. The woman nagged about immorality and her conscience. For twice the rent of the room, however, she said she was prepared to let the two of them go on staying there.

When they had negotiated this deal, their days in Beirut were wonderfully peaceful. Rana and Farid felt that they belonged together. Every conversation, every plan, every touch brought them closer. Soon they found out that travelling to America on expertly forged passports was by no means impossible.

At the time the city of Beirut was a handsome seaport. Rana and Farid walked by the sea as often as they could. That spring was particularly cold, and the beaches were empty. They sang together in competition with the breaking waves, and talked about their future life in America. They ate very little, but Farid never again enjoyed eating as much as he did in those days, sitting on a park bench beside Rana and sharing a falafel with her.

As soon as they had closed the door of their room behind them, they fell into one another's arms. At first Rana pecked at his tenderness like a pampered bird, and Farid swallowed hers like a hungry wolf, but as the days went by his greed was less demanding, while Rana became increasingly insatiable.

After a week Farid found work selling newspapers, and he bought Rana a wristwatch with his first wages. That same day the old woman turned up again, talking about the loss she was suffering with the rent they had been paying so far. She wanted to double what was already a high price for the room. Farid, alarmed to see how their reserves were dwindling, refused, and decided that they would move, but that point never came.

Just after midnight they were at the police station. It was a cold night. The officers soothed Rana and gave her tea to drink, but she kept on crying.

"Please let us go!" she begged the police officers. "We want to go to America."

"I'm afraid you can't, little one, you're still a minor," said the officer, a stout Lebanese with huge bags under his eyes. He hit Farid and accused him of seducing little girls. A woman took Rana into the next room with her, wrapped her in a blanket and held her close like an anxious mother. "You must say it was all his fault, and then they'll let you go," she said. Rana indignantly freed herself from the woman's embrace. "He didn't do anything. I was the one who abducted him," she cried angrily.

Three hours later they were driven to the border and handed over to the Syrian police. "I'll wait for you until eternity," said Rana.

The two Lebanese officers were much amused. "Is someone shooting a movie around here?" one of them asked.

"No, the child's seen too many Egyptian tearjerkers," replied the other.

The Syrians police spoke angrily to the two young people at the border. A stout woman took Rana into a cell and once again tried to persuade her to say that Farid had abducted her. Rana screamed as loudly as she could, because she heard the blows raining down on Farid in the next room, where two police officers kept shouting, "Pimp!"

After half an hour, all was quiet at last.

When Farid came back to his senses, it was early in the afternoon. A middle-aged police officer led him out of the cell. "Your fiancée's father isn't going to bring charges, to avoid any scandal. My word, kid, you're lucky! If it had been my daughter I'd have shot you."

Elias Mushtak, his face dark, was waiting in the office of the police station to collect Farid. In the dusty car park, blind with rage, he hit out at his son. Farid staggered and could hardly breathe. He dimly saw the concerned faces of the passengers in the buses waiting at the border to have their papers checked. A child cried and pointed out of the window at Farid. In spite of all his pain, he felt ashamed.

One of the bus drivers went up to Elias and tried to calm him. That made him even angrier. "It's a disgrace. First a fire-raiser, now he abducts a minor."

And so saying he hit Farid full in the ribs. Farid lost consciousness and fell to the ground.

At that moment Rana came out of the building. She saw Farid lying there and wanted to go to him at once, but her father – in his light summer suit, and carrying her case – pushed her courteously but firmly into his parked black Citroën.

Elias Mushtak watched the car drive away, then looked back at Farid, and went to his Fiat, bent with exhaustion. He dropped the small case on the back seat, got into the car, and started the engine. With difficulty, Farid hauled himself into the passenger seat.

They were home in an hour's time. Farid was in so much pain that he could hardly get out of the car. His knees were grazed, his face was swollen, but his ribs hurt worst. He still found breathing difficult. Helplessly, he began to cry.

The Mushtaks, Claire often used to say in jest (but accurately hitting the bull's-eye) have their moments of insanity. When Elias lost his temper he ranted like a madman, but never for more than five minutes. After that he was ashamed of failing to control himself better. Farid's grandfather had been just the same.

Claire came out of the door. At the sight of her son she was rooted to the spot with shock, but only when they were all inside the house, and she had carefully closed the door, did she explode. "What have you been doing to my son? My only son!" she shouted at Elias. For the first time in her life she felt she actually hated this narrow-minded, deranged confectioner who was now sitting there in silence, staring at the fountain in the inner courtyard.

"It's a disgrace. First he sets the tree on fire, then he runs away with our arch-enemies' daughter. Now we're at their mercy. They have the police records in their hands, they can put your son in jail any time," he replied. His voice sounded sad and weary. But Claire was not pacified.

"I'm asking you again," she shouted, "are you a father? Welcoming your prodigal son with violence – what kind of father is that? You're a violent lunatic, you belong behind bars. Your arch-enemies the Shahins are decent people. They haven't even raised their hand against our son, and you have to beat him like that? Farid is a child, a child, and you all mistreat him!"

Claire didn't say another word to Elias that evening, but gave all her attention to Farid, and slept on a couch at his bedside. What her husband did was a matter of indifference to her. Later, the doctor diagnosed the boy with two broken ribs and severe contusions.

Only on the third day did Claire find out about the violence of the Syrian border guards. She telephoned around until she learned the name of the officer responsible, and then threatened to charge him with child abuse.

The officer at the other end of the line laughed. "You do that, madame. Then I'll get promotion," he said, claiming to have been defending Arab morality. Then he hung up.

But Claire was as good as her word. Through a distant cousin who was highly placed in the Interior Ministry, she did have the officer charged, and he was transferred to the Euphrates region for disciplinary reasons. There he complained bitterly until the day of his retirement that there was no saving Syria now, when a whore could have a first lieutenant transferred to the wilderness just for doing his duty and slapping a badly behaved boy about a bit.

117. The Gate

The bus driver was making for the summit of the last mountain before the coast. In the distance, the mighty monastery perching on top of it like an eagle's eyrie was already visible. Its white walls shone in the afternoon sun.

As if liberated, the driver stepped on the gas again, raced the last few metres to the monastery wall, and finally braked so forcefully that two of his passengers, who could hardly wait for the end of the long drive and were already standing in the aisle, tumbled forward. That didn't bother the bus driver. When he had switched the engine off he took his comb out of his shirt pocket and parted his oiled hair neatly, looking in the rear view mirror. For a moment he examined his well-tended, thin moustache, then smiled at himself with satisfaction and got out of the bus, whistling.

He looked at the clock on the church tower, compared the time with his watch, and adjusted the watch.

"More than twelve hours of driving," said Elias Mushtak in surprise, as he climbed out of the door at the back and glanced at his own watch. He realized that he wouldn't be able to go back until next morning.

Elias looked at the bus driver. Men with oiled hair revolted him. Depending on their age, they looked like either rent boys or pimps. The driver threw a few foreign cigarettes to the farm hands and impoverished-looking workers standing around, and they thanked him. A stray dog scented something for his hungry belly, and cautiously approached, wagging his tail. But the bus driver kicked him hard in the side, sending the animal scampering away and yowling with pain.

"That's not normal, is it?" said Elias indignantly. "A dog is one of God's creatures too – did you see that, a poor hungry dog, and what does that pimp do? Kicks it in the ribs," he said angrily but quietly to one of the peasants who had been on the bus.

"All townies are bastards," the man replied, sending a waft of bad breath Elias's way. Farid's father felt like kicking *him* in the ribs.

The bus driver strutted around his vehicle, put a ladder up and climbed to the roof, which was loaded with cases, crates, and bags. He picked up one piece of baggage after another, called out, "Whose is this, then?" and before any owner could speak up it was flying down to the waiting crowd. Elias Mushtak shook his head in annoyance when his own case landed roughly on the ground. "Bloody bastard," he muttered. It was followed by a smaller case in which Claire had packed underwear, socks and towels. Everything, as required by the monastery, bore the initials FM and his date of birth: 230640. The large case contained coats, pullovers, and other winter clothes. Trousers and shirts were not needed, because everyone wore the same black monastic habit.

Farid moved away from the noisy crowd outside the bus and went up to the great gate by himself. It seemed to him more impenetrable than the high stone wall that made the monastery look like a castle. "Mother," he heard himself whisper. "Mother, where are you? Mother!" He felt abandoned as never before, and knew that tears were running down his face.

"What's the matter with you?" His father's voice brought him back to reality.

"I want to go home," he said, and looked at his father through a mist of tears.

"Pull yourself together. You're not a baby now," his father replied quietly.

Farid picked up the smaller case and followed him.

Although it was high summer, musty, cold air met them when a tall man opened the gate. He was smiling like a lunatic. His large, shaven skull was covered with scars. The man had hands like shovels sticking out of his habit, which was much too small for him. The black of its fabric was worn grey on the shoulders and elbows.

"We're to see Abbot Maximus Haddad. The bus was ..."

"He's expecting you," the man interrupted Elias brusquely, and went ahead. Elias Mushtak made his way after him with the heavy case, panting. They went along endless corridors, until the man stopped outside a door on the second floor. When Farid had caught up, the monk knocked and pushed down the door handle without waiting for a reply. Then he stepped aside to let the two new arrivals in.

"Put the cases down and come in. Brother John will see to them," said the abbot, coming out from behind his large desk. "Monsieur Elias, what a pleasure for me to greet the son of that great hero George Mushtak."

That took Elias's breath away. He had expected anything, but not to find that his father's reputation had come all the way to this monastery. Farid was surprised that the abbot was so young, forty at the most. He imagined abbots as old men with snow-white beards and bent backs. This man was athletic, bursting with health, and had a thick, black beard. His face was friendly, his voice melodious. He spoke classic Arabic, but Farid detected a slight Lebanese accent.

"Forgive us for arriving late, the bus …" began Elias, trying to apologize.

"Oh, dear me, yes," the abbot interrupted, "we know about the dangerous roads, we're glad you managed to get here at all today. The parents of seven other new pupils have put off their journey for the time being, in view of the situation. Today is Thursday. Your son can rest until Sunday evening. The intensive French language course begins on Monday. He can attend that from the start. Regular school lessons don't begin until October, and they will be given in French."

"We're happy that you have accepted Farid. My wife and I appreciate it. I studied in a monastery in Damascus myself as a boy, and those were the best days of my life, although cut sadly short. I'm sure you remember the tragic end of the Jesuit monastery," Elias added quietly.

"How could I forget? A black day for Christianity and the whole of civilization. My uncle died in the fire. He was the librarian there."

"What? Father Antonios Haddad … your uncle?" said Elias in amazement.

The abbot nodded. "What a small world it is! You knew my uncle, while as a student in the monastery here I prayed for a hero called George Mushtak who saved a Christian village. And that man was your father. May God bless his soul."

"Thank you," whispered Elias in subdued tones. Farid noticed the mask of humility that his father always assumed when he was speaking to churchmen.

Only now did the abbot turn to Farid. "Welcome, my son," he said, shaking his hand with a powerful grip. Then he asked them both to sit down, and seated himself with his back to the big windows. Through the window on the left, Farid could see the grounds and the mighty trees with their branches rising to the monastery walls. The sun was still shining brightly, but was visibly sinking towards the distant line of the horizon.

Abbot Maximus addressed Elias again. "We try to educate our pupils and novices well. They can continue their studies later in Rome and Paris, and do good service to Mother Church. As you know, we have excellent connections with the Jesuits in both those cities, and we thank God's grace that to date we may count twelve bishops, two patriarchs, three cardinals, fourteen theologians, and a world-famous doctor of medicine among former students at this monastery. Those with talent have a duty. With the help of God and by his grace, your son Farid will put his talent to the service of Christianity, just as his grandfather did."

The door opened quietly, but the abbot merely looked up briefly and went on with his remarks about talent and duty. A thin man brought in a tray with two glasses of water. Elias was so spellbound by what the abbot was saying that he jumped when the man, who was insubstantial as a ghost, politely handed him the water.

Farid smiled at the skinny monk. He was about forty, and the abbot called him Brother Gabriel. Farid took his glass and put it down on the little table between the two armchairs where he and his father were sitting.

The monk remained by the door, attracting no attention. Farid thought that the man had an aura of kindness and calm about him. Suddenly he heard Maximus Haddad's voice rising a little. "Your son Farid," he said solemnly, and from his tone it was clear that the interview was coming to an end, "will now be our son and brother, and will be known as Barnaba."

The abbot stopped for a moment, as if guessing at the surprise that both Elias and his son felt at this moment. He smiled, and cast a glance at the page of a fat book lying open in front of him. "In the monastery," he went on, in a slightly lower voice, "all the pupils bear saints' names. Farid is a good Arabic name, but unfortunately no saint ever bore it." He glanced quickly at Farid. "Not yet, anyway," he added, smiling, pleased with this idea. "And a new name is the symbol of a new life. Farid will remain as a memory in his parental home, and Barnaba comes into the world here. Barnaba because today is June the 11th. And that, as we know from this book of saints, is the day of Barnaba. He was one of the first Christian martyrs, a friend and companion of Bulos, founder of the Church. His name in Aramaic means *Son of Comfort*. How lucky you are, my dear Barnaba," he concluded, smiling at his new pupil. Farid felt neither lucky nor comforted. What a weird name, he thought.

Only weeks later did he discover that Barnaba was one of the early Christians, and had spoken up to the disciples of Jesus on behalf of Bulos, known as Saul to the other Christians. They distrusted Bulos. Later Barnaba and Bulos did missionary work together for a while, but finally they fell out with one another and went their separate ways.

"And now," he heard the abbot proclaim solemnly, "your son Farid will leave you, and as Barnaba, a pupil in this monastery, he will enter the fields of Jesus Christ, whose devoted servant he is to be."

Farid felt paralysed by fear. He hadn't expected the parting with his father to come so soon.

"A room in the guesthouse has been reserved for you," the abbot told Elias, offering his right hand in farewell. "You are welcome here for tonight. Tomorrow a bus leaves very early for Damascus."

The abbot came out from behind his table, and now placed his hand on Farid's head. Farid stood perfectly still, but his heart was thudding. Elias Mushtak wiped away his tears with his handkerchief, which was already drenched in sweat after the journey.

"God bless you on your way," said the abbot, "God make you brave, unselfish, obedient, and ready to do everything to spread the teaching of Christ. May God protect you in all you do."

118. The Tonsure

"Right, little Barnaba, let's go," said emaciated Brother Gabriel. His deep voice surprised Farid. When they left the office the cases had disappeared. Gabriel noticed the boy's questioning glance, and smiled.

"Brother John has taken them to your place in the dormitory. You have a little locker for your things there. But come with me now – he's waiting to give you your tonsure."

"What's a tonsure?" asked Farid, bewildered.

Gabriel smiled. "A shaven head. After that you get the habit, and then you're really one of us."

Farid entered the room known as Brother John's workshop. John was the general factotum: plumber, postman, porter, barber, but he also inflicted physical punishment when the monastery authorities thought it necessary. The workshop consisted of two rooms, one in front of the other, with a connecting door between them. The front room contained bicycles, metal trestles, chests of drawers and a workbench. It smelled strongly of engine oil, but was meticulously tidy. John was sitting in the back room on a mattress, trying to repair the broken handle of a wicker basket with his calloused hands.

When Farid came in with Gabriel, John looked up and grinned. He stank of sweat and old socks. Nothing in the place was even remotely reminiscent of a barber's salon. The one cheerful touch was a sunbeam falling in through a round window on the west wall of the room.

John put the basket down and stood up. He pulled a small stool to the middle of the room and gestured to Farid to sit down on it. As soon as Farid was seated, he pushed his head down and began shaving it with an old pair of clippers. The clippers pulled out whole tufts at a time. It was a painful business.

"What's our new boy called?" Farid heard John ask.

"Barnaba," said Gabriel.

John repeated the name in a childish singsong, gradually turning it into its Greek version of Barnabas, then into Barabbas, the name of the robber whom the Jews chose to free instead of Jesus on the feast of Passover. John kept chanting this new name with enthusiasm. "Barabbas! Barabbas!" Although it wasn't the robber's fault, the early Christians hated that name as the symbol of a life saved at the cost of the Lord's own. It seemed that Barabbas couldn't live with that thought, and had hanged himself soon after he was set free.

"So now you're one of us," cried John in his singsong voice. Then, suddenly, his rough hand hit Farid right in the face. He had really meant to give the newcomer a pat on the back of his shaven head, but Farid had turned at just that moment.

The blow struck him full on. Farid lost his balance and fell off the stool. He was trying to stand up when he suddenly felt a thin hand on his shoulder, turned around, and looked straight into Gabriel's face.

"Let's go, Barnaba. John's a lout," said the monk. He helped Farid up and led him out of the workshop.

"Hey, I didn't mean to do it," cried John, putting out his hand to the boy, but Farid had already reached the door and slammed it behind him. John was left behind with his jaw dropping.

119. The First Night

The habit felt strange. It billowed between Farid's bare legs, and made him walk unsteadily. When he passed one of the mirrors that were fitted at every landing on the stairs, he was startled. A bald-headed stranger in a black sack stared back at him from the mirror, eyes wide with shock. Josef would have a heart attack if he could see his friend in this outfit.

Evening dusk was already falling over the quiet inner courtyard. Farid stopped for a moment, and then followed Gabriel down to the cellars, where he heard a babble of voices. The cellar area had a high, vaulted roof of polished white stone. The doors to the refectory were open, and as Farid stood on the stairs leading down he could already see hundreds of monastery pupils, all with shaven heads and in black habits, sitting at three long rows of tables. At right angles to them, and slightly raised, stood a large table for the Fathers, and roughly in the middle of the room there was a kind of pulpit beside the wall. One of the older pupils stood at it, leafing through a thick book. His narrow leather belt told Farid that he was a novice. The Brothers and the Fathers wore broader belts.

Farid waited awkwardly near the door while Gabriel hurried up to the table where the Fathers sat, and whispered something to a rather stout priest. The priest looked at Farid and then stood up. There was silence at once, and Farid felt the eyes of the pupils and novices burning on his scalp. He looked down.

"In the name of the Father, the Son and the Holy Spirit," said the priest, crossing himself. All the pupils did the same, repeating the words after him. Farid hastily made the sign of the cross too. "In the name of Abbot Maximus, who can't be with us this evening," said the priest, "I am happy to welcome our new pupil Barnaba. He is in the seventh grade, one of ten new students in all who have come to swell our ranks. Welcome, my son. Now sit down, and we can begin the reading."

Gabriel moved his head in response to Farid's glance at him asking for help. Then he saw the empty place. A napkin and cutlery were already laid.

The pupils started talking again, and his twenty companions at the table showered him with questions. They were all speaking French. Farid understood a good deal of what they said, but he confined himself to simple answers to avoid making mistakes. The pupils seemed eager to hear about the outside world. Only later did he discover that neither they, nor the novices and monks, were allowed to leave the monastery walls. Unlike ordinary boarding schools and many liberal monasteries, the order of St. Sebastian wouldn't even let its pupils go home for the vacation.

The reading was in French too. All Farid understood was that it was the story of St. Barnaba. His companions told him that they had the story of a saint read to them every day before supper.

"Some of them are as exciting as thrillers, some are as colourful as movies, but some are just plain boring," said a boy whom the others called Marcel. He sat opposite Farid and was beaming at him. As far as Farid could make out Marcel, who was rather stout, came from Alexandria in Egypt.

It was also Marcel who told him, briefly and graphically, about the hierarchy of the monastery that first evening. "The monastery pupils are squires, the novices are knights, the monks are princes, the Fathers are kings, and the Abbot – well, he's God in person."

"Why are some of them still just Brothers although they look old enough to be ordained priests by now?"

"Only God knows. They probably have a screw loose somewhere," said Marcel.

"What about Brother Gabriel?" asked Farid.

"Gabriel's the only ordinary monk allowed to sit at the top table with the Fathers and the Abbot," Marcel told him. "He's cleverer than all the rest put together. But he can't be a priest, all the same."

"Why not?" whispered Farid, leaning over the table.

"He's sick in the head," replied a small pupil next to Marcel. The others called him Timotheus. Marcel dug him in the ribs with his elbow. Obviously he didn't approve of this explanation.

"Doolally," said another.

"Oh, shut up," snapped Marcel. "The Pope himself is afraid of Gabriel because he knows so many secrets," he whispered in conspiratorial tones. The others fell silent, exchanged meaning glances, and looked surreptitiously at Gabriel.

"All those secrets probably sent him crazy," said Timotheus.

A bell rang, and the pupils began folding up their napkins, putting them into small drawers under the table top.

"What happens now?" Farid asked in Arabic.

Marcel smiled slightly. "Well, in the summer vacation we have free time. We play cards or chess, or we go for walks in the yard and talk about people behind their backs. It's prayers at ten, and then we go to bed."

When the bell rang for the second time they stood up. A short prayer followed. Farid kept his mouth shut and looked helplessly at Gabriel, but he was one of the few who were entirely absorbed in praying. When they all crossed themselves at the end of the prayer, Gabriel became aware of his surroundings again, including Farid, and signed to him to stay in the room.

"Let's start here," said Gabriel, when all the others had gone. "You know the refectory now. We all eat the same food that you get, even Abbot Maximus. No one has any privileges in our order. The food is prepared here in the kitchen." As they approached it, two elderly women in white overalls were pushing a trolley through the kitchen door and began to clear the dirty plates off the tables.

The kitchen was enormous. Several men and women were cleaning and scrubbing in it, some of them polishing up the stoves and the big white marble work surface. The floor of the kitchen, like the refectory floor, was made of polished slabs of red-tinged stone. About twenty people worked here. Farid noticed one of the cooks in particular. Her name was Josephine, and she looked out of place among the others. It didn't seem right for her to be wearing an overall and working in the kitchen. She had blue-green eyes and fair hair, and she looked like a marble goddess. She smiled at Farid, but he soon discovered that she spoke an unattractive dialect, coughing words out with no melody to them, as if she were having a fit,.

"So this is our new boy – handsome, isn't he?" she smiled, putting her hands on her hips.

"Good evening," said Gabriel.

"And good evening to you too, Brother Gabriel. Are we getting this handsome lad to help out here?"

Gabriel dismissed the idea with a smile. "Well, so how is Joan of Arc getting along?"

"Oh, my word, if I'd known how much work there was in it I'd have said no. Working away all day here and then rehearsing in the evening!"

"I'm sure you're right. It's too much even for a bundle of energy like you," agreed Brother Gabriel sympathetically, and he went on his way with Farid. When they reached the corridor he whispered, "A very gifted woman. She was once one of the star pupils in St. Mary's Convent, she knows French and Latin perfectly. But the porter there seduced her, and she was pregnant at the age of sixteen. So they had to get married in haste, and of course he was fired from the convent. He found another job only with difficulty, thanks to the kindness of Abbot Maximus, who got him work in a horse-breeder's stables. But the man was useless and lazy, and a week later he was out on his ear."

Farid was surprised not just by the frank way Gabriel spoke, but by the decided tone of his judgement.

"And this is our treasure, the library," Gabriel interrupted his thoughts. "One of the best in the Middle East." He pushed the heavy wooden door open. Farid's eyes were bright with amazement. He had never seen such a library before. It was at least as large as the refectory, with endlessly long, tall shelves on which all the books were neatly arranged. Most of them had leather bindings.

Between the shelves and the tall stone columns there were little tables, each with a chair and a reading lamp. A large table with over twenty seats stood in the middle of the room. Several monastery pupils and Fathers sat there, immersed in reading.

On the wall opposite the door stood glass-fronted cupboards where scrolls and old manuscripts were kept.

"Those are the words of St. John of Damascus, or St. John of the Golden Mouth," said Gabriel. Farid knew a lot about St. John, the writer and orator who was the pride of all the Damascene Christians.

He would have liked to spend longer in the library, but Gabriel gently impelled him out again. There was still a lot to see, and Gabriel needed to go to the lavatory.

Farid waited for him in the corridor. The cellar was enormous, apparently extending under the entire monastery building and the inner courtyard. Two thirds of it were occupied by the refectory and the library, which lay side by side, and that area was surrounded by storerooms as well as the lavatories and the little printing press and book-binding shop. All the rooms had thick, heavy doors.

A fresh breeze swept briefly over the inner courtyard, which was lit only faintly by a lantern at the entrance gate, but light fell from the rooms on to the arcades surrounding the courtyard on the west and the south.

The north side was occupied by the great church, the entrance gate, Brother John's workshop and the visitors' room. Brother Gabriel explained that the monastery pupils and novices could be visited, under supervision, by close family members. The visitors' room had a narrow door of its own opening on to the car park.

"Over there," Gabriel said, pointing north, "is the church of St. Sebastian, our patron saint. I'm sure you've read his story and the history of the monastery in the little book given to every future pupil here."

Farid nodded, hoping that the monk wouldn't ask him for details, for all that stuck in his memory was the image of Sebastian with a transfigured expression on his face, tied to a tree trunk and pierced by three arrows. As he read, Farid had imagined Sebastian dying among native American Indians, and that idea had taken firmer root in his mind that the legend of the martyr.

Luckily one of the monastery pupils was coming their way, and called out to Gabriel, in French, 'Good! At last! I can pass the signal on to you!"

"Not now," protested Gabriel, laughing. "I'm busy showing Barnaba the ropes as quickly as possible, so that he'll know his way around."

"Excuses, excuses!" replied the boy, laughing too.

"Speaking Arabic is forbidden," explained Gabriel, as he turned back to Farid, "and that applies to everyone. Anyone caught at it is given a round, thin, wooden disk with the letter S for 'Signal' on it. He has to carry the signal about with him until he finds someone else speaking Arabic, and then he gets rid of the little disk by passing it on to him."

"But suppose whoever it is denies speaking Arabic? Or suppose he's older and stronger than the person carrying the signal?"

"Large or small, old or young, it makes no difference. The carrier of the signal will have witnesses, because no one talks out loud to himself alone. And it's best for the guilty party to take the disk, or everyone will know he's looking out for someone speaking Arabic, and they'll avoid him like the plague."

"But suppose he doesn't catch anyone else?"

"Then he eats his dinner kneeling, and the signal is taken away from him and given secretly to a scout known as the Starter, who goes around listening for Arabic."

"But that's espionage. Do you approve?"

Gabriel froze. The question seemed to have gone home. "Personally, no, but the monastery administration uses the system to make sure pupils are well disciplined and learn to speak French quickly. Oh, look, it's time for night prayers! We must hurry," he added, glancing at his watch.

The church of St. Sebastian had been built in the seventeenth century to plans designed in Rome. It wasn't large, but it was magnificently furnished. The nave had no columns, so there was a clear view of the high altar wherever you were. Stylistically, the interior was a mixture of the Baroque, Jesuit magnificence, and Oriental opulence. Large paintings hung on the walls, showing Biblical texts, angels, and Jesus and Mary in royal splendour. Farid thought the church was cluttered by comparison with the Catholic church in his street at home.

To the right of the altar hung a large painting of St. Sebastian, a copy of the original Italian work of Guido Reni, as Farid later discovered. The altar itself was dominated by a magnificent statue of Jesus Christ. Tall arched windows surrounded the nave of the church.

Gabriel motioned to his charge to go further forward, while he himself found a place with the other monks near the door. Farid looked desperately around the sea of shaven heads and black habits for someone he knew. A slight nod of the head and a shy smile came to his rescue: Marcel. Farid made his way along the long pew, knelt down beside Marcel, and whispered, "Thanks!"

Night prayers didn't last long. Then, silently and well disciplined, the monastery pupils, monks, and Fathers moved out in an orderly line. Farid followed Marcel. Out in the dark courtyard, the pupils dispersed into smaller groups and went on climbing the stairs to the dormitories in silence. Farid was strangely restless. His heart seemed painfully constricted, and he felt estranged from himself and abandoned.

There was absolute silence in the dormitory too. Farid unpacked his underwear and put it away in his small locker, washed, and got into bed.

Almost a hundred and twenty of the younger monastery pupils slept in the west wing. About a hundred older pupils and the novices slept in the east wing. The rooms for the monks and the Fathers lay in between.

It was a mild night, and the sea sounded closer in the silence and darkness. Farid couldn't get to sleep for a long time. The dormitory was not entirely dark; several little lamps fastened to the wall gave a muted light.

Near the entrance of every dormitory a monk slept in a small room, furnished in extremely Spartan style with a bed, desk, and medicine cabinet. The only ornament was a picture of the Virgin Mary illuminated by flickering light. A different monk was on duty supervising the pupils every week; only Brother John was excused that duty.

The monk on duty on Farid's first night stood at the big window in the dark for a long time, keeping an eye on the dormitory. Then he did his rounds, stopping briefly by every bed. Farid closed his eyes and did his best to breathe regularly.

"Try to sleep," whispered the monk, and went on. He said something quietly to a boy at the end of the aisle near the washroom too. When Farid slowly opened his eyes again a little while later, he had disappeared.

How beautiful his time with Rana had been, thought Farid. "Love tastes and smells so wonderful," she had said one night. He had laughed then. Was she thinking of him now? She had promised not to let a single hour of her life pass without thinking of him. And what Rana promised she always performed. He was ashamed to realize that he sometimes forgot her for hours at a time.

Now he was thinking of her breasts. He had never seen anything so lovely before. They didn't look like the apples or pomegranates so often mentioned in Arabic poetry, no, Rana had breasts with nipples like the tips of a lemon, pointing slightly upward and outward. The mere sight of them aroused him.

He turned on his side and pressed the light blanket between his legs.

The sea slipped away on velvet soles.

120. Summer Days

Next morning Marcel showed Farid a piece of paper on the door, setting out the timetable for the day during the vacation:

"6.30, get up. Wash. Make beds. Leave lockers open. Brother to close them after checking. Short morning prayers. Breakfast. Work. Lunch eaten at work place. End of work 15.00 hours. Wash. Summer academy from 15.30 hours. Evening prayers. Supper. Games. Night prayers. Bedtime. Sunday is free."

The days followed this pattern, and after a time they all merged into each other. If it hadn't been for Sundays, Farid would soon have lost all sense of time.

During the first week he was sent to work with the builders who repaired any damage to the monastery walls during the summer months. He and two other school students took them the construction materials. It was hard work climbing ladders in a habit, carrying stones and mortar, and the builders laughed at the boys' clumsiness.

A week later Farid changed to the metalworking shop. The master in charge here was an unassuming, silent man. This work was hard too, but interesting. Master Rimon liked the boy at first sight. He told him that he had once been a priest himself, but then he fell in love with a young widow. He had confessed it at once to the abbot of the time, so he was allowed to go on earning a living in the monastery metalworking shop. Two years after the wedding, his wife died when their son was born, and he had brought up the boy on his own. But at the age of twenty his son had emigrated to America, and Rimon now lived by himself down in the village at the foot of the mountain where the monastery stood.

Farid could happily have spent the whole summer with Rimon, but that wasn't permitted. Every pupil at the monastery had to take his turn with all the different jobs. Next was farming. Working with the reapers was hell; following them through the fields day after day in the blazing sun drained all his strength. He had hallucinations. The reapers were usually strong, experienced older pupils and monks who cut the blades of wheat with sickles. A troop of younger pupils went behind them, fanning out over a broad front, gathering the blades into sheaves and piling them up on carts to be taken to the threshing floors, where hot dust filled your mouth and nose, and husks and chopped straw stuck in your collar, rubbing your skin sore. Those days seemed endless.

Again and again, Farid's loneliness overwhelmed him. The older monastery pupils took no notice of him, the childishness of the younger boys bored him. He saw Marcel and a few other familiar faces only at supper, and was never in the same working group with any of them. That was intentional, so that everyone would get to know everyone else, according to the monastery administration. "So that we don't gang up together and refuse to work," was how Marcel put it.

Sometimes Farid thought he was going crazy. Not only did most of the monks remain strangers to him, he felt that this Barnaba going around in a habit, staring back at him from the mirror with his sunburned face and the ugly, peeling skin on his scalp, was a stranger too. His hands were covered with painful weals and blisters.

When Farid was moved from reaping to the joiner's workshop he felt as if he had won a prize, for he loved working with wood. The master joiner was a gloomy man who said not a word all day, but his journeyman understood all his gestures, and passed the gist of them on to the newcomer.

Every evening Farid was jolted by the sight of monastery pupils who had been lumbered with the signal kneeling in the centre aisle of the refectory. Apparently there were three of the little disks in circulation, although no one was quite sure of that.

"What, even in the vacation?" cried Farid indignantly at the sight of one pupil who was almost falling asleep with weariness and couldn't even eat. His sore, limp hands were dangling.

"The signal takes no vacations and never sleeps," said Marcel, who was often handed it himself, but was clever enough to pass the little wooden disk on again in good time. Only once did Marcel fail, and then he had to eat his supper kneeling. Farid was horrified to find his neighbours at table suddenly turning spiteful. He snapped at them to shut up, but they went on taunting Marcel.

As a newcomer, Farid couldn't yet be given the signal himself, so he didn't have to kneel if he spoke Arabic, but whenever he did the others looked at him in alarm, as if he came from another star. So he said as little as possible, and was soon regarded as a silent boy. That showed him even more clearly what a stranger this shy boy Barnaba was, for Farid's effervescent loquacity had been famous in Damascus.

Father Basilius was a good language teacher who made French lessons lively and amusing. The fact that he also looked like a vulture lent a touch of comedy to everything he told them. The language came easily to Farid, and when he began dreaming in French he realized that he was making good progress. Music was different. He didn't care in the least for highly-strung Father Constantine, who had an aura of great unrest about him, and he couldn't get on with the musical instruments. There was no doubt that the Father was a musical genius, said to have composed several hymns, as well as the music for all the plays performed annually on the feast day of St. Ignatius. But like many another genius he was incapable of explaining anything to other people. Marcel told Farid that the musician, who was still a young man, was in love with the cook Josephine, and had suggested her for the part of Joan of Arc.

One day Brother Gabriel, who was still keeping an eye on Farid, came up with a wonderful idea. In his despair at getting nowhere with music lessons, Farid had told him about the pleasures of learning calligraphy in Damascus, and Gabriel persuaded the monastery administration to let him give up music in the afternoons and instead take the advanced calligraphy course, since he had already mastered the basic rules. The art of calligraphy was very highly regarded in the monastery, for although French was spoken as the everyday language and in lessons, the liturgy and the Bible were in Arabic. The monks were anxious to use perfect script for the products of their own printing press, and were always looking for new young talent. The monastery press had received major commissions from outside because of its high reputation.

Gabriel's idea was Farid's salvation. After the end of August, he found life in the monastery rather more tolerable. Father Makarios the calligrapher, who also ran the printing shop, was both as down to earth as the printing presses and as fanciful as Arabic script. He had such a sure hand that he never hesitated for the fraction of a second in his calligraphy, as if he already saw the words he was going to write on the blank sheet of paper before him. Farid soon became his star pupil.

The mists of disappointment and opposition dispersed, and he began to pay more attention to his surroundings. To his own surprise, it was only now that he got to know Butros, who sat opposite him in the refectory, always ate in silence, and hardly ever laughed. He was shy and suspicious. But at the beginning of September he began telling Farid about himself.

The brothers Markus and Luka sat one on each side of Farid. They were twins, a boring couple who had been in the monastery for three years, always accepting everything and approving of it like good boys.

Marcel knew why. "They have to be ultra-obedient, they're here only through the bishop's good graces. Their father ran off to America and their mother can't feed them. It's because she's the bishop's distant cousin that those two are here at all. Outside, all they can expect is work in the fish factory and beatings from their mother's lovers, and they know it."

In spite of their sad story, Farid thought they were a dismal pair, and once it occurred to him that if Jesus had been obliged to sit between those two in the refectory, he'd have died not on the cross but of boredom.

121. Joan of Arc

Everything was to be bright and shining on the feast day of St. Ignatius. The floor, the columns, the walls of the inner courtyard were scrubbed, the car park outside the monastery was whitewashed, and all the windows were cleaned.

Then the big stage was erected. A play was traditionally performed on 31 July in honour of the order's founder, and here in this desolate part of the country it was a great event. Over five hundred chairs already filled the inner courtyard, although only the seats in the front row were upholstered.

In the afternoon all the employees, peasants, and labourers who worked for the monastery came streaming in. Everyone was still talking about last year's play, *Pietas victrix*. The translated title hung above the stage in Arabic had proclaimed, "The Victory of Piety".

Father Samuel the language teacher had written the play, and Father Constantine had composed the music, but the best part came from the workshop of ingenious Father Antonios. He taught physics, and his brilliant ideas had made the play into a positive firework display to delight the senses. He used steel wires, lights and stage effects to bring thunder and lightning down from the sky to the stage. Swords, angels, and spectres hovered weightlessly in the air and took the audience's breath away. He had also stationed two monastery pupils behind the stage to howl like wolves or hoot like owls. It was truly gruesome, and gave even the most sceptical of the audience goosebumps.

This year the play was to be *Joan of Arc*. A magnificent show was anticipated, but it all went wrong. Marcel had already whispered to Farid at midday, "Theodore wants his revenge on his teacher – he hates Samuel." At the end of July it was still vacation, so Farid knew neither the teacher nor his pupil.

"Why?" he asked.

"Why? Because Samuel's horrible. But Theodore is wily. He'll play his trick so cleverly that he won't get punished."

"How?"

"I don't know exactly, I just know Father Samuel has been torment-ing poor Theodore for four years. He made him repeat a school year twice, in grades nine and ten. You don't get far here without good marks for language, and Samuel is in charge of teaching both French and Arabic. Theodore is twenty and still only in grade eleven."

That evening St. Ignatius himself seemed to want to celebrate, and tempered the fierce July heat with a pleasantly cool temperature. Soon medieval torches were flickering on stage. Two violins played a soft melody, and then the play began.

The audience fell silent. The curtain went up. Soldiers and peas-ants stormed forward, crying, "Long live the good Catholic country of France!" But then English soldiers entered left and attacked them, and there was a battle scene involving over forty pupils and monks.

The English won. The French troops took their dead and wounded into a corner. Now the music was slow and heavy, and a guitar imi-tated bells tolling for a funeral. Wounded men said their last prayers. A priest, played by a twelfth-grade student, gave them absolution and his blessing.

Then Joan of Arc came on stage, and the audience loved every-thing she did and said. Josephine was acting very well. When she said that she must die a martyr's death for Christ, the Virgin Mary and France, many a tough Father wiped a tear from his eye and blew his nose loudly, while women in the audience wept with emotion.

Farid admired the cook, who spoke her complicated part in French so well that he could understand everything. He felt attracted by her.

And when, at the coronation of Charles VII in Reims Cathedral, she knelt before the King with the banner of victory in her hand, and cried, "Noble lord, now is God's will fulfilled!" the audience clapped so loud and so long that no one could hear what the King said in reply.

Farid was beginning to doubt what Marcel had said, for the play was three-quarters over, and nothing untoward had happened. He glanced at his friend, sitting a few chairs away from him. Marcel caught his eye, and made a gesture which said: just wait, any minute now.

Soon after that Joan of Arc was taken prisoner, and the judge ordered her to be tortured until she confessed to being a witch. She was to tell her followers to surrender to the English, he said. Joan of Arc bravely refused.

The torturer came on stage, and Farid knew who was under the mask he wore. Theodore seized the cook by her long blonde hair and laid her down on a table that was doing duty for a rack. Then he tied Josephine's hands to a large metal ring.

The lighting effects made a fire seem to blaze up in one corner of the stage. A pupil was working a pair of bellows to fan the flames higher. The torturer picked a black triangular item out of this mock fire: a piece of wood the size of Josephine's upper body. There were curious red protuberances at its three angles. The torturer took the triangle to the front of the stage and told the audience, "These red-hot metal balls will burn their way so deep into the witch's body that she'll wish she had never been born."

Then he went back to the cook, stood between her legs, and placed the triangular wooden board on her body. The corners of the triangle were now lying on her breasts and her mount of Venus, and he began rocking it back and forth.

All was so quiet in the auditorium that you could almost hear the spectators' hearts beating. The torturer rocked the wooden triangle again, pressing it firmly down on Josephine's body, and cried, "Confess that you're in league with the Devil, witch! Confess it!" The cook began to moan. It was only because Farid was in the know, and watching closely, that he saw Theodore not just pressing the board down over her genital area but vibrating it slightly every time.

Josephine tried to struggle, which made the scene even more credible. She opened her eyes and whispered a plea. "No, please don't!"

But that just spurred Theodore on.

"Confess, you witch!"

The cook responded with moans that grew ever louder and wilder. She twisted and turned to escape the hand making the triangle vibrate, but Theodore just stepped up the pace. Now her cries were ardent. They echoed around the courtyard, they made their way right into the bodies of the audience. The Fathers in the two front rows looked around in embarrassment.

Apparently on the point of orgasm, the cook was no longer calling for help but just moaning, "Yes, yes, yes!" Her voice made the stones of the building tremble. Some of the Fathers and monks rose in anger and left the courtyard.

Suddenly everyone heard a loud cry, this time not from the stage but from an attic window. The spellbound audience looked up. There stood a thin figure clad in white, illuminated by demonic radiance. For a split second Farid thought that it was part of the show.

"Get all that damned fornication off the stage! It's the Devil's work!" cried the elderly protester.

Abbot Maximus rose abruptly from his seat and shouted in the direction of the platform, "Bring the curtain down! The play's over!"

The curtain fell, and Father Samuel, the principal loser in the whole affair, sat hunched on his own in the front row, while the audience left the inner courtyard. He never wrote another play again. Abbot Maximus decided to end the tradition of a dramatic performance on St. Ignatius's Day. There was in fact another attempt to produce one two years later, by popular request, but when that too was a failure, plays performed in honour of the founder of the order on his saint's day were finally over.

On 1 August 1953, a day after the performance of *Joan of Arc*, the monastery pupils took the stage down again. Farid and Marcel lent the electrician a hand.

"You knew more than you were letting on," said Farid quietly, but with a reproachful note in his voice.

"Yes," said Marcel, "I knew Theodore had found out how quickly

Josephine comes if you just put a bit of pressure on her mount of Venus."

"Mount of what?" asked Farid. It was the first time he had heard the term.

"Mount of Venus," explained Marcel, showing off. "That hairy triangle above a woman's cunt, get it?" Farid nodded. "If you just rub that place a bit, and touch her breasts, she goes right out of her mind in no time at all," Marcel added.

"And who was that weird old man shouting from the attic window?" asked Farid.

"I'll tell you later," Marcel murmured.

122. Nights in Autumn

September was the harvest month. The great heat of summer was over, but there was even more work. Not only were the grapes ripe, but figs and other fruit were ready to be dried too. Farid felt increasingly that he wanted to be out in the open air and hated staying indoors in a workshop.

Early in September he was given the job of drying figs. He worked for a week on a gigantic threshing floor paved with white stone. The figs were laid out side by side and close together in rectangles, with narrow paths left between them, so that the fruits could be turned once a day without any danger of being trodden on.

The grapes ripened at the same time and attracted more insects, although butterflies liked the figs. Farid, who did not find the work here hard, followed the course of their flight with interest. He felt something like happiness, watching the butterflies in flight as he sat in the shade of a simple shelter made of poplar branches.

But then something happened that was to haunt him in his dreams for years. It was a Tuesday afternoon. Farid was sitting in the shade of his shelter, looking down into the valley. There was much coming and going in the fields and on the threshing floors. A column of three mules had been going between the threshing floors and barns for days, bringing in huge sacks of hay. On the outward journey an experienced monk went on foot, leading the mules downhill, on the way back he always rode one of the animals and led the others after him on a rope.

But now the mules were suddenly racing round the bend in the path of their own accord, and at great speed. The hay on their backs had caught fire.

Terrible screams filled the air. The mules disappeared into the valley leading to the sea, apparently in search of water to save themselves, and so they did not turn to the monastery but galloped through the village. Two peasants' huts caught fire, and an old woman trying to halt the animals was trampled to death. The mules never stopped until they reached the sea below. One of the animals escaped with a singed mane because it had thrown off its blazing load in time, the other two died horribly of their burns. Rumour in the monastery that evening said it was arson, and the hay had been soaked with petrol. Farid slept badly that night, and was distressed for several days. No one ever found out who was behind the incident.

❧

"You want to know how I am?" Farid whispered one September night, full of longing for Rana. "Not too bad. I have three props to support me here. What? Yes, to support me, like legs. Gabriel, Marcel, and Butros. And if I get a fourth leg then I'll be a donkey. No, not a table, a donkey, I like donkeys," he whispered into his imaginary telephone. Then he smiled at his idea, never guessing that he had just made a prophesy.

The fourth leg was Bulos.

123. The Inquisitor

The vacation lasted until early October. A week after the Feast of the Holy Cross on September the 14th, Farid was back working with the builders, who were now repairing a large crack in the monastery wall. He hated the master builder so much that he could already feel cramps in his stomach on the way to join the site. Four pupils from grades eight and nine were in the same working party, but before an hour was up the four had ganged up with the builder and his men against Farid. Soon they were all leaning against the scaffolding, laughing at him.

Farid knew that refusing to work would bring a harsh punishment, and an entry in his monastery records that would never be deleted. Was it worth it, just for that lousy, ugly man on the scaffolding? He gritted his teeth and said to his fellow pupils, low-voiced, "You cowardly traitors!" They just laughed even louder. When the master builder heard what Farid had said he knocked the basket of stones off his shoulder and shouted at him. "I don't like cheek from my boys. Fetch larger stones!"

As Farid hauled the empty basket after him he began shedding tears. Suddenly he saw a pupil four or five years older than him, standing behind a pomegranate tree.

"Come here!" he called.

"Do you mean me?" asked Farid uncertainly.

"Of course," replied the pupil, grinning. "Give me that basket and watch me."

For a moment Farid thought that the older boy who had so unexpectedly come to his aid was a guardian angel in a habit.

"My name's Bulos," said the pupil, taking the basket from him. He filled it with dusty soil and shouldered it so that the basket hid his face. The monastery pupils leaning against the scaffolding were still laughing and didn't notice him. Bulos walked rapidly towards them and emptied the basket over their heads. Taken completely by surprise, the boys coughed and spat as they tried to knock the dirt out of their habits. One began shouting that he would complain of Bulos. That seemed to be just what Bulos had been waiting for; he jumped at the boy and twisted his arm behind his back.

"Come on then, let's go straight to Abbot Maximus, and you can tell him how you were ganging up on your comrade Barnaba with those lousy builders, and you watched and laughed when they tormented him. What do you think Abbot Maximus will say about that?" he inquired, hitting the boy on the neck. By now the pupil was begging not to be taken to the Abbot.

"Then you and the other idiots here can apologize to Barnaba," ordered Bulos, letting him go. "And all I have to tell you," he added, turning to the master builder, "is that if you treat one of the boys so badly ever again I'll make very sure the Abbot fires you. I promise you I will."

The man went pale, as grey in the face as his own cement, and just nodded.

"Right, you can have a few peaceful days with these rats now," Bulos whispered to Farid, and he went away.

That evening Farid looked for his guardian angel in the refectory, and saw him sitting at the eleventh grade table, deep in a discussion with one of his companions. Farid went up to him, tapped his shoulder from behind and said, "Thank you very much." Bulos turned and beamed at him.

"Oh, it's you! Everything okay?"

"Yes, thanks to your help," replied Farid.

"It was nothing. I just couldn't stand by and watch the way they were treating you."

The bell rang, and Farid hurried back to his own place. Then the bell rang a second time, and all the pupils rose to say grace.

From that day on he met his rescuer daily in every free moment he had. Bulos was intelligent and wily, but extremely distrustful. He was proud of his Syrian origins, and despised the Arabs. They were just Bedouin, he said, who had destroyed the great civilization of his forebears the Assyrians with their swords. Farid didn't understand any of this.

Bulos didn't talk much, and you never knew exactly what he was getting at, but he always seemed to know what other people were thinking. And when you saw his blazing eyes you guessed that he would shrink from nothing.

"So why are *you* here?" he asked Farid on one of their first walks together in the monastery gardens.

Farid didn't want to talk about the burning of the elm tree in Mala.

"My father wanted me to come," he said. "He never got to be a theologian himself, so I was supposed to make his dreams come true for him. I'm afraid he'll be disappointed. I'm not cut out for the life here." He shrugged, and shook his head.

"Nor am I," said Bulos, "but I'll have to put up with it. My stepfather won't let me back in his house. He made me go into this monastery so that he could be alone with my mother. I was in the way. Now I'll have to stay here until I take my high school diploma, but after that I'm going to study law."

"Why law?"

"With a law degree you can get to be a high-ranking police officer or a judge. I'd be happy with either," he replied, narrow-lipped, and looked into the distance. Farid could well imagine that at this moment, in his mind, Bulos was torturing his stepfather.

☙

At the end of September Farid wrote his mother his first letter home of any length. So far his letters to his parents had consisted only of five lines of polite clichés and an assurance that he was all right. Now he wanted to give a fuller account.

Dear Claire, dearest Mother,

I'm all right. There's a lot to learn here, particularly French, but I've already made friends. One is called Marcel, he's a born joker, another is Butros, a good friend. The third is called Gabriel and is a clever man. And the fourth is my guardian angel Bulos. I'm sorry, I can't tell you their surnames; surnames aren't used here in the monastery. It seems they're secular, so to everyone except myself I'm Barnaba. The monastery never gives the same name twice, which means there's no danger of any mix-ups.

Marcel is the funniest of my friends, and Bulos is the most interesting of them all. Bulos gets on well with his mother, but very badly with his stepfather. His own father was killed when he was little. Isn't that dreadful?

His stepfather doesn't let Bulos's mother visit her son very often. He misses her, but he's a guardian angel to me.

I wanted to write so that you'd know I'm not choking to death in this dreary monastery, and I love you and miss you very much. I miss your cooking too, what with the inedible food they give us here. Apparently enjoying good food is a sin. I pray for you every day, Mama, asking God to forgive you for enjoying the pleasures of life. Greetings to Papa.

Your son in exile.

Farid

Next day he was summoned to one of the Fathers whom he didn't know, Father Istfan. When he told Bulos this, Bulos frowned. "Did you write anyone a letter?" he asked. Farid was alarmed.

"They call Istfan 'the Inquisitor,'" Bulos explained. "He censors all letters. There's nothing for you to worry about, but your letter will be handed back to you. Every pupil goes through this – it's a baptism of fire. But only idiots fall into the Inquisitor's hands a second time. His halitosis is enough to cure idiocy on its own."

Father Istfan more than lived up to his reputation. His expression was alarmingly gloomy, and he had very bad breath which made Farid think of something decomposing.

"Your letters," he began, taking the folded sheet out of an envelope that had been slit open, and on which Farid recognized his own handwriting, "will be handed in to us in unsealed envelopes in future. We will be happy to advise you how to write them, so as to make sure there's nothing in them to give your parents cause for concern, and we can point out any spelling mistakes. There are a number of untruths here," he said slowly, breathing out air from the graveyard inside him. "First: Gabriel is a Brother, not some playmate of yours. Second: your name is Barnaba and not Farid. Third: exaggerations will only confuse your parents. Bulos is a pupil here, not anyone's guardian angel. Fourth: you write that life here is dreary. That is not true. If you are bored, there are plenty of things you can do for the common good. My son, I wouldn't like you to make your parents anxious with such exaggerations. And fifth, I see that you are in the best of health, so what you say about the food is clearly nonsense. You should describe life here honestly and in positive terms."

Farid's fury stifled the words in his throat. He took his letter from the Inquisitor's hand and stormed out, with tears in his eyes.

"They check up on everything, but you have to write home at least six times a year," said Bulos, who was waiting outside for him. "It's compulsory. Anyone who doesn't write attracts their attention, and they suspect him of smuggling letters."

"Well, I'm not going to write if that ghoul is going to read what I say privately to my mother. That's not ...'"

"You *have* to write," replied Bulos. "Beat them with their own weapons: write letters that don't say anything much, and if you want a real letter taken out in secret then give it to me, and it will be in Damascus next day." Bulos smiled.

"Really?" asked Farid incredulously.

His guardian angel nodded.

Two days later Father Istfan summoned him again. Once again, his room stank of decay. "My son, a letter for you from a person by the name of Rana Shahin arrived today," he informed Farid. "In your own interests and hers we have destroyed that letter. You are allowed to receive letters only from close family members."

Farid could have hit Father Istfan, but he swallowed and said nothing. Bulos's support was a help to him. He wrote Rana a passionate letter, telling her that he loved her and thought of her every second of the day, adding that her letter sent to the monastery had been intercepted, so it would be better if she didn't write until he had found a way to get around that problem. But she was to talk to him at night, and despite the distance between them he would hear her voice.

Then he folded the letter, put it in an envelope, and wrote on it the one word "Rana". He put this letter inside a second addressed to Laila, in which he vented his anger at the censorship in the monastery. He asked her to pass his letter on to Rana and confirm, in an answer apparently coming from his Aunt Malake, that his girlfriend had really received it. She was to write the following sentence: "The Virgin Mary was gracious to me, and my operation went well." He gave this letter to Bulos, promising him to pay back the lira that the bus driver asked as soon as possible.

He was able to do so when his mother visited him two weeks later. He whispered to her that although it was forbidden in the monastery, he needed money. The monk who had to supervise visits was an amiable man who stood at the far end of the room with his back to them the whole time, looking out of the window.

Quick as lightning, Claire handed him a hundred lira.

"All that?" Farid marvelled.

"Nothing's too much if it helps you. Be generous, that will open doors to you."

He also learned from Claire on this visit that his cousin Laila had married a violinist, but to her family's chagrin insisted that she didn't want a wedding party.

"What's her husband like?" asked Farid.

"Well, it's a strange world. A hundred men would have given anything to marry Laila, but she takes no notice of any of them and sets her heart on this fiddler."

"Yes, but what's he like?"

"I don't care for him. He has a shifty look, and he flatters people too much. And he's idle, but Laila has come into a good inheritance."

Farid felt curiously disappointed. Why had Laila never said a word to him about any of this?

Claire smiled bravely when she said goodbye, although according to the monastery regulations it would be a year before she was allowed to see him again. Farid felt miserable for days after her visit.

124. A Shipwrecked Sailor

Life in the monastery seemed harder and more dangerous the better he came to understand it. He was increasingly surprised that he had noticed so little of the churning emotions around him during his first few months. Farid himself felt like a shipwrecked sailor adrift on a stormy sea.

Once he had thought that a monastery would be a place of silence and tranquillity. None of that was true of the monastery of St. Sebastian. It was as if, by withdrawing from the world, the Fathers and their pupils had opened the door to those very passions against which they meant to protect themselves within the monastery walls. The more closely he looked at it, the more blurred seemed the boundary between love and hate.

For himself, he was surprised to find how quickly and warmly he had taken Gabriel, Marcel, Butros and Bulos to his heart. He knew that his soul could rest on those four foundations. By way of contrast, the signs of affection that Markus, one of the twins, kept lavishing on him were alarming. The boy had spoken of his own loneliness with fiery, feverish eyes. Marcel told him that evening that Markus would rather have been born a girl.

But the extremes of hatred to be found in the monastery alarmed Farid even more than this excessive affection. He kept finding pupils in the lavatories who had been brutally beaten up. Only gradually, and with the help of Marcel and Bulos, did he discover that the lavatories were obviously regarded as the best place to settle old scores. Not all of them were equally suitable, although they were all unsupervised, but the more remote they were the greater the danger. Among the most dangerous were those on the third floor, and by night those in the cellars, where really harsh punishment was inflicted. The first floor lavatories were the place to settle minor quarrels. The safest lavatories of all were on the second floor near the administration offices and the Abbot's rooms, but people who only ever went to these lavatories were teased by the others as scaredy-cats. The scaredy-cats included Marcel, although he didn't seem to mind.

"I like to shit in peace," he said, laughing at himself.

It was a long time before Farid realized that he too was regarded as a coward. First Bulos told him not to be so anxious all the time; that would encourage even the most faint-hearted to attack him. He could perfectly well go to the first-floor lavatories, he assured Farid. But his heart thudded every time he saw three or four youths hitting another pupil. Bulos had warned him never to get involved himself, and above all never to tell on anyone to the supervisors.

Only once did Farid get involved, one Saturday when three ninth-grade pupils dragged Marcel into the lavatories in the cellars and laid into him there. Farid had been reading until late in the library, which was permitted only on Saturdays. A moment came when he needed to go to the lavatory himself, and heard what was happening to Marcel. He immediately flung himself on the three boys and hit out at them, shouting. At first they tried to attack him too, but when he shouted even louder they ran off, just before several monks and pupils in the library noticed.

"Why were they beating you up?" asked Farid later, when he was alone with Marcel.

"I hit the little one, he's a terrible tell-tale," replied Marcel. "First I lay in wait until he was finally sitting on one of the first-floor lavatories. Then I tipped a whole can of piss over his head from above. And then he fetched his cousin and a friend to get his revenge," said Marcel cheerfully.

Farid could make nothing of this. Suddenly Marcel seemed like a stranger. Marcel, who had been surrounded by servants at home in his parents' house, had never needed to fight anyone, yet he had a particularly sharp tongue. He provoked others and then couldn't defend himself. At mealtimes other boys, often listening fascinated to his stories, would steal the best bits of meat off his plate. Or they would smuggle the fat they had left on theirs into his helping, and he would absent-mindedly eat it. Farid watched this disgusting game for a few weeks before his patience snapped. He knocked the fork out of the hand of a pupil who was just spearing a good piece of meat on Marcel's plate.

"What's going on there?" It was the voice of Father Basilius, who was on supervision duty on the podium that day.

No one replied.

❧

Farid had to accept that Gabriel had less and less time for him now. Not only was he busy teaching, every Saturday afternoon he also ran a study group in the great hall on the subject of early Christianity, in which only a select few could take part. Marcel and Bulos laughed at the participants, who apparently danced with each other and held hands, ate large quantities of bread, and drank wine. Bulos didn't like Gabriel. "He's a snake in the grass. Smooth outside, venomous inside," he said. He suspected that Gabriel was the head of a secret society and, under cover of being a simple monk, controlled the entire monastery.

"I'll wake you up and show you something tonight," said Marcel quietly, when they were leaving the refectory three days after the scuffle in the lavatories.

"Why at night?" asked Farid.

Marcel looked cautiously around, to make sure no tale-bearers were lurking. "It wouldn't be any good in the day. They'd catch us at it."

"Do I keep my habit on?"

"No, you can wear your pyjamas, and I'll fetch you as soon as the duty monk's asleep."

It was after midnight when Marcel soundlessly nudged him. Farid jumped up and quietly followed his friend. They crossed the wash-room and then went through a door that Farid had never noticed before. It led to a stairway. Farid could smell damp air. His heart was hammering.

"We're going up to the attics," whispered Marcel, and before Farid could ask any more Marcel was hurrying up the small, steep staircase. It creaked beneath his feet. Beyond the door at the top was a heavy curtain insulating the attic yet further from the stairwell. When Marcel pushed it aside, Farid saw that the room on the other side was not entirely dark. Candlelight flickered in four small cells. Farid froze, for there were people behind the gratings over the cell doors: ancient, desiccated monks who could have climbed straight out of a medieval painting. One was kneeling in front of a picture. Farid recognized him as the figure who had hurled denunciations from the attic window during the performance of *Joan of Arc*. All that Farid could make out in the picture was Jesus on the cross. In the second cell a slightly younger monk lay stretched out, face down, with his arms and legs in a cross shape. An old man with hair down to his shoulders crouched in the third cell. He was chained to a pillar. And the fourth cell held a monk immersed in a book lying open on a stool in front of him. Two more cells were dark and empty. Their doors were open. The doors of the other cells were only closed, not padlocked.

"Who are they?"

"Nutcases. Let's go, the others are waiting," said Marcel. He led Farid on along a narrow corridor, past discarded furniture, implements, and large pots and pans.

"Harmless nutcases born a few centuries too late. The one stretching all his limbs out was a famous theologian once, until he started having conversations with God. He and the others are stashed away here like these pieces of furniture," said Marcel, pointing to an old cupboard.

When they left the west wing and went down the central corridor, Marcel mentioned that they were right above the bedrooms where the monks and the Fathers slept.

"But don't worry, they wouldn't hear a herd of elephants down there. This ceiling is very well insulated, and when they couldn't get the third-floor bedrooms warm enough in winter they thought it was because of the height of the rooms. They built in false ceilings lower down, and those are well insulated too," he assured his friend. "All you ever hear is the mice and rats who fall through cracks in the attic floor, and scurry about on top of the false ceilings until they die. There's no way for them to get out of the trap. It can be horrible."

Now Farid heard soft whispering behind a mountain of old furniture. He stopped, rooted to the spot, but Marcel tugged his sleeve. "Come on, those are my friends," he said.

Five of the older boys were sitting in a niche behind the cupboards on old couches and armchairs. They were smoking and drinking wine from a large beaker that was passed around in a circle. A candle on a large tin plate burned on the table in the middle of the party. Beside it lay photos of naked women dating from the 1920s. Farid saw another shabby piece of card bearing the inscription "The Nightclub".

"This is my friend Barnaba, he's another lunatic, he ought to be a member of our nightclub," said Marcel. Farid had to smile.

"Can he be trusted?" asked a thin boy, scrutinizing Farid suspiciously.

"He's okay," replied Marcel, sitting down on a large couch. He signed to Farid to join him there.

Marcel was appreciated in this circle; no one teased him or made snide remarks. Farid took a couple of puffs at the cigarette that was being handed around, but had to cough, for it was curiously sharp in flavour. The wine, on the other hand, was sweet and sticky.

They spent about an hour up there, cracking jokes about the Fathers and nuns. It was cold in the attic, but the boys didn't seem to notice. Farid didn't feel at ease. This was not the kind of company he liked, and he was glad when the meeting ended.

Next time Marcel invited him to join them at the Nightclub, he thanked him but said no, he'd rather sleep. After that night, however, he often lay awake for a long time, staring into the darkness and thinking of the gang at home in Damascus, of Josef, and the attic above the aniseed warehouse. What were his friends doing now?

125. Silence

On Ash Wednesday, 3 March 1954, the world of the monastery fell silent. The idea was that you spent seven days cleansing your soul. To Farid, it was a misfortune. He loved the sound of words, the music of language, and regarded silence as the province of death, not life.

But Abbot Maximus thought otherwise. His remarks announcing the advent of a period of silence sanctified it. "Only when your lips are closed do you hear the voice of the heart," he said, smiling kindly and looking around. "We learn thoughtfulness and patience best in silence. And only in stillness, dear brothers in Christ, do we find our way to the light."

Observance of the commandment of silence was strictly supervised. "One word and you're made to kneel down on the spot," said Marcel, "and you have to stay there until the bell goes for the next meal." He himself had once had to kneel on the ice-cold stone floor for three hours.

Everything fell silent. Even the chattering sparrows avoided the inner courtyard, for the heavy silence scared them away. The monastery became a house of deaf mutes. School and work were in abeyance. It was a week of meditation for all right-thinking people. The church and the library were open to everyone.

Farid almost lost his mind in this silence, but the sight of someone kneeling cured him of any wish to speak. The outward calm left his mind in turmoil. He didn't want to be a priest. Why was he here at all? He dreamed of exploring the world and its secrets, he could be a pilot or a sea captain. So what was he doing behind these dank walls?

The inner courtyard, where the monastery pupils and the Fathers walked without making a sound, seemed positively ghostly in the evening twilight. Farid sat on a bench for a long time watching their silent perambulations, with a yawning void inside his head. He went into the church and immersed himself in the details of the large paintings. Just as he reached St. Giorgios the bell rang for supper, bringing release. Farid cast a last glance at the dragon. The creature looked pitiful, and he felt sorry for it. The horse was muscular, yet wrongly proportioned in some way. Its hindquarters occupied almost a quarter of the picture, and St. Giorgios seemed to be driving his spear into the dragon rather lethargically.

After supper Farid fled to the library, where he found Bulos, who seemed to be buried in a book. Bulos looked up, a smile tried to form on his lips, but he suppressed it and went on reading. *The Rise of Nations*, said the title on the cover of his book.

That evening Farid discovered Jules Verne's first novel, *Five Weeks In A Balloon*. And suddenly a week's silence was no longer a threat. He spent twelve hours a day reading now. Sometimes he even missed a meal to follow an exciting incident to its conclusion. During that week, he realized that books could be a life-raft in an ocean of silence and grief. And when he lay in bed at night with his back aching from sitting and reading so long, he felt Rana's hand in the darkness and travelled with her through the world of the stories he had read.

Jules Verne had been merely the one who opened the door, the magician who revealed the world of books to him. Soon after that, Farid was wandering through nineteenth-century France with Balzac, India with Kipling, Russia with Tolstoy, America with Jack London.

But in the middle of that week of silence, Laila's letter arrived. Brother John handed out the mail without a word. Farid was startled when the monk – in his usual rough style – just threw the letter down on his book and went on.

Rana understood him and would love him for ever. Clever Laila had skilfully smuggled him the message that he longed to hear between the lines of her letter. The camouflage was brilliant. Her seven-year old daughter Rana, wrote Laila, idolized him and spoke of nothing but her dear Uncle Farid who was in a monastery. She wanted to join a convent herself later, and be a nun in Africa. Farid grinned when he imagined the satisfaction on the censor's face.

He had been writing Rana a letter every month since September, and sending it via Bulos under cover of another letter to Laila. The bus driver was extremely happy to have the lira that Farid paid him for every delivery.

And Laila answered once a month. So as not to attract attention, she sometimes signed her letters with the name of her mother Malake.

A great peal of bells announced the end of the week of silence. Farid took more pleasure in regaining the use of language than in the festive meal served that day.

The day was set aside for recreation. All the gates were open, the inmates could go out and take walks around the monastery. For a moment, the world was a whole dimension larger.

126. Rebels

Farid spent a long time standing in front of the glass cases in the library where the valuable scrolls with the poems of seventh-century St. John Damascene were kept.

The saint was also known as St. John of the Golden Mouth for his lyrical style. A short account of his life lay beside one of the scrolls. His right hand had been severed by a blow from a sword during a pogrom, but the story went that he picked it up, put it back on his arm, and finished writing his poem.

Brother Gabriel made fun of this heroic legend. However, when Farid asked about the large greasy marks on the scrolls, his face darkened. They had been left by the sardine cans of the peasant rebels who captured the monastery in the 1930s, drove the monks out, and misused the building as their barracks.

"They couldn't make anything of the scrolls, so they used them as tablecloths," said Gabriel. "They wreaked havoc here in the monastery for two years, until the French army of occupation drove them out. When the monks returned they found a sad scene of destruction. It took three million dollars and four years of work to restore the monastery. That's why our Abbot pays protection money rather than face such devastation again."

"What kind of protection money?"

"We're in the region dominated by the rebel Salman. He's fought off all attacks by the government to date. His headquarters in the Eagle Mountains is impregnable, and he's absolute ruler here. He demands fifty thousand lira every year, and we pay up. In return, his bandits can't so much as pick a blade of wheat from our fields."

"Fifty thousand – why, that's a vast sum!" said Farid in amazement.

"Yes, indeed, but every painting in the church, the marble altar, the library, they're all priceless treasures. And what does the money matter? We can live in safety," replied Gabriel.

"Do the bandits stick to your agreement?"

"Salman's a decent man at heart. A pity he's a Muslim. He is a great Sufi and admires Christ more than many a Christian." Gabriel hesitated, as if he felt awkward about going on. "But unfortunately he admires him with a weapon in his hand."

"And how does he get the money? Do his robbers come to the monastery?" asked Farid curiously. That interested him more than the elevated ideas of the rebel Sufi.

"No, no," said Gabriel. "I take it to him in his citadel. He insists on that, to show that he and not the monastery is the ruler here."

"What? *You* mix with the robbers?"

"It's not as exciting as you may think. The monastery sends word that I'll be coming, then I go, I hand over the money, I get a sealed receipt and come back."

Farid felt very restless. That night he waited until the monk on supervision duty was asleep, and then got up and sat on the broad window sill. It was a warm April night, and the windows were open. The full moon turned the sea into a silver platter with a fishing boat slowly gliding over it. The sea was as still as if the moon had calmed the soul of the waves.

Out there, somewhere in the Eagle Mountains, was an invincible rebel who was popular with the poor, and was said to be so small of stature that if an egg fell out of his trouser pocket it wouldn't break when it hit the ground.

How can such a small man lead robbers, Farid wondered? Perhaps he enchants them with the power of his tongue and they never notice his size.

Farid had clearly sensed that Gabriel secretly liked Salman, even if the rebel did blackmail the monastery for large sums.

The sea was glittering strangely, as if stars had fallen into it. Suddenly Rana was there. "Can you hear me?" he whispered drowsily.

꙳

Very little news made its way to the monastery in the summer of 1954. They heard that Shaklan had been toppled, but it was another year before the monastery felt the first results of his fall. The rebel Tanios, he of the patent leather shoes, was happy with General Batlan's new government, for the President had appointed one of his sons as agriculture minister. Tanios laid down his arms and allowed governmental troops to pass through his own region and surround the second and far more dangerous rebel, Salman. The fighting went on for weeks, and it was said that the rebels fought fiercely, but when their leader Salman was captured and shot in an olive grove, they surrendered. Only the women would not capitulate, and defended their last bastion, a small and ruinous fortress. For a long time the soldiers dared not attack; horror stories were told about the rebels' women. But when they stormed the fortress, greatly outnumbering its defenders, they found out that all the women had committed suicide.

The defeat of the rebels was a relief to the monastery. No more protection money had to be paid from now on.

127. An Excursion

October was almost as hot as August that year. For once, the pupils in the monastery were allowed to go on an excursion to the sea, escorted by Father Constantine the music teacher. They had to walk in line, two by two, but they could choose who to walk with. Farid joined Bulos, who had just received a letter from his mother by courtesy of the bus driver. All the way down he was swearing at the stepfather who beat her.

"I could murder him. A fragile woman like that, he sits on her chest and breaks three ribs. And what does she do? She tells the doctor she fell off a ladder while she was doing housework."

Bulos was trembling all over, and went on to describe, at length, an occasion when his stepfather had tied his mother to a chair and then tortured him, Bulos, before her eyes. He told this tale with as much detachment as if he had merely seen it all in a movie. Farid could hardly believe the story, but Bulos was straightforward in everything he did. Farid shuddered to think of the terrible revenge that Bulos would take on his stepfather some day.

It was a relief when they arrived down on the beach and the line could break up and scatter. There wasn't another soul in the little bay. The pupils undressed. They had no bathing trunks; they were to bathe in their shorts and keep a second, dry pair to change into later.

Marcel was the first to run into the waves, but at that moment Father Constantine ordered them, in tones of alarm, to leave again. Just as the boys were laughing at Marcel's leap into the water, a pair of lovers had come on the scene. A muscular man and a blonde woman tourist had chosen the bay below the monastery for their own outing. They ignored Father Constantine's request to them to find another bay, and undressed. Reluctantly, the monastery pupils left, feeling furious, and all of them without exception thought nothing could be more ridiculous than Father Constantine's suggestion that on the way back they should all pray for the lovers' souls, and hope they would remain chaste.

"How such an idiot can make such brilliant music is a mystery to me," whispered Bulos.

128. The Syrian Brothers

More and more often, Farid longed to hear the sound of Arabic. Sometimes he went off on his own to taste a few Arabic words, letting them melt one by one on his tongue. Twice he got so high on them that he forgot himself and recited some Arabic verses out loud. He was startled to feel someone slipping the little disk with the letter S into his pocket. As he refused to pass the disk on to anyone else, he had to eat his supper kneeling.

"I admire your noble attitude. I'll be thinking of you," whispered Bulos in passing, squeezing his shoulder. Marcel and Butros gave him an affectionate wave too, while the twins Luka and Markus acted as if they didn't know him. Farid also refused to eat, but the monk on supervision duty took this gesture to be mortification of the flesh and not a protest.

A little later, as they were walking in the monastery grounds, Bulos told him about a secret society whose members were interesting boys, and would like to get to know him, Farid.

He was first admitted to a meeting of this secret society chaired by Bulos, the Syrian Brothers, in mid-November. The members were ten pupils from different grades. To Farid's great surprise they included Marcel, who had had to leave the Nightclub in order to join. Bulos had insisted on it.

Farid didn't understand what the aims of the society were, but it was an exciting change from routine, and when they swore loyalty in the twilight of the attic where they met, and Bulos spoke of the power of their association, Farid remembered that other attic back in Damascus and his friend Josef. Bulos appeared to be convinced that the Syrian Brothers would take over power in the monastery one day.

At first Farid thought Bulos was only joking, but when he insisted on the swearing of an oath against treachery and tale-bearing, he realized that his friend meant it seriously. Enemies of the Syrian Brothers were attacked in the lavatories after dark and beaten up without much discussion. The punishment squad consisted of Bulos and three strong tenth-grade boys. The victims could not identify their tormentors, who were well disguised, but afterwards they knew who they had to keep quiet about. And the threat of the signal was instantly reduced for the Syrian Brothers. If a member of the secret society was handed the hated wooden disk, all the others would go hunting until they caught someone else speaking Arabic.

One day Bulos explained that it was important for them to have a secret language that no one else would understand. Every week from then on, he taught his friends ten to twenty new words and phrases invented by himself. He hoped that within a year they would be able to talk to each other in this secret language. Farid was surprised to find how eagerly everyone set about learning it. And sure enough, they were very soon able to greet each other in it at their meetings or in the school yard, exchanging brief secret messages that no outsider could understand.

129. Discord

The January of 1955 was particularly cold. It snowed overnight, and the world seemed to be frozen under a sugar coating. Now the monastery building showed its structural faults. None of the big windows fitted properly; the wood of the frames had warped in the heat and drought of the long summer months. Farid froze in bed at night, even though the nearest window had been draught-proofed with old rags.

Outside, the ground was slippery as glass. No motor vehicle could venture up the narrow dirt road to the monastery. The inner courtyard had become an ice rink. The pupils, the cooks, and the Fathers slid about on it, and someone was always falling down.

Farid was standing near the stairway under the arcades, watching his breath emerging as vapour from his mouth, like cigarette smoke, when Marcel waved to him. "Bulos is looking for you." And he added, in their secret language, "There's a meeting this evening."

Bulos was angry. Markos, a ninth-grade pupil and a member of the Syrian Brothers, had been turned, he said. The boy wouldn't give the society away, but he wasn't coming to any more meetings because he felt more comfortable with Gabriel's Early Christians group.

These remarks reminded Farid how Butros had often warned him to avoid Bulos and attend the Saturday group instead. Bulos was waxing indignant about Gabriel, calling him a Jewish communist, and Farid was startled by the mounting hatred of his tone. The others just nodded. But when Bulos began contemplating a punitive operation against Gabriel out loud, Farid's alarm changed to cold anger. The others were also paying more attention now, and didn't go along with Bulos's idea. Gabriel was frail and sick, said Marcel.

Farid felt something break inside him. "I won't join in. I think we should leave Gabriel alone," he said hoarsely, looking Bulos in the eye. Disappointed, Bulos shrugged.

"I tell you, he's a snake in the grass, but if you don't want to do anything about it, we'll leave him alone for now."

130. Epilepsy

He couldn't wake up, although he heard the bell. Only when Marcel shook him did Farid slowly come to his senses and sit up in bed. He felt a painful throbbing in his right temple. He'd rather have stayed in bed, but he was afraid of his fellow pupils' scorn, for laziness was regarded as disloyalty: the others would have to do his work as well as their own. It was a fiendish system, and meant that even the Fathers and the monks must turn up for work looking keen so as not to lose face. Farid was due to work in the orange grove with five other pupils after lessons.

So he tried to get up, and almost fainted. He clung to the bedstead until he felt a little better. Finally he staggered into the washroom and put his head under a jet of cold water.

He felt a little fresher in lessons. But then, soon after prayers for Nones at three in the afternoon, it happened. He was just marking out a circle around a young orange tree with a spade, as instructed by Brother Jakob, who himself worked hard enough for three, and then he was going to weed the earth inside it. Suddenly everything went black in front of his eyes, he lost consciousness, and collapsed. When he came to his senses the first thing he heard was Gabriel's voice. He opened his eyes and saw Brother Jakob's concerned face. At that moment Bulos walked past a little way off, taking no notice of him. "Where's Claire?" asked Farid softly, but then he realized he had seen her only in a dream. The back of his head hurt where it had hit the ground. Brother Jakob told him he had fallen backward as stiff as a post. Farid wiped the saliva from the corners of his mouth. It's the falling sickness, he thought, frightened, and remembered the street seller Hassan who sold ice in Saitun Alley in summer and sweetmeats in winter. Hassan fell down in a faint at least once a year, and people said that because the djinn loved him they sometimes stole him away to sing to them.

Gabriel accompanied the sick boy to the dormitory, and stayed for a while when Farid sat down on his bed, exhausted. "I see you're my brother in misfortune," he said, stroking Farid's forehead, and then he left.

131. Spiritual Welfare

Anyone with problems was supposed to turn to his grade teacher, although if they were serious or of an intimate nature, every grade also had another experienced monk available. Then there was the confessional for downright sins.

However, Farid never made use of any of these opportunities. At the end of March, just after the week of silence, a monk called

Christian told him he had to confess before he partook of the body of Christ. When Farid replied that he wasn't committing any sins in the monastery, the bearded monk laughed. "And there's your first sin: pride. Seek and ye shall find, oh yes," he added, and went away. Next day Farid set about looking for some small sin that wouldn't mean too many prayers to be said in penance. Marcel warned him, "Thinking of Josephine's legs will cost you a prayer of repentance, two Our Fathers and three Hail Marys. Farting in divine service costs a prayer of repentance and one Our Father. The cheapest sins are small wishes and wanting better food."

So Farid cobbled together his first lie for confession. It turned out exactly as Marcel had predicted. Farid was satisfied with the results. Once, however, sheer curiosity made him want to find out how the Fathers would react to the sin of sexual desire, and he confessed to the priest that whenever he saw Josephine he wanted to put his arms around her and kiss her lips. At that the priest lumbered him with a whole litany of prayers. Farid never said a single one of them. He didn't feel sinful, for he had never wanted to kiss Josephine's lips, and his confessor knew nothing at all about Rana and hers.

Farid solved his everyday problems with the help of Gabriel, Marcel, or Bulos, but the monastery administration didn't approve of that kind of thing. In May the monk responsible for his grade sent for him, and Bulos advised him to act naïve and come up with small problems of some kind. "Then the Brother will be pleased to have helped someone," he said, "and next time you can tell him it worked a treat and then dish up some even sillier story. After about the fifth time he won't want to see you any more."

"Suppose I don't tell him anything?" asked Farid.

"Then he'll keep asking questions and get people to spy on you. That man works hand in hand with the monastery administration, and they're keen to pick out potential troublemakers."

So Farid went for a session of spiritual welfare, presenting himself as a boy plagued by minor anxieties. And yet again it worked exactly as Bulos had said it would.

At the beginning of 1955 the Syrian Brothers had fifteen members. Bulos felt like a little ruler. He had come up with the idea that if an informer was caught at it twice, next time he would be beaten up and then the punishment squad would pee all over him. A week after the first such punishment was carried out the news spread like wildfire, and the authorities lost most of their informers. The monks were going around in circles. They knew nothing about the Syrian Brothers, and that gave the group the power of which Bulos always dreamed. He was a genius when it came to choosing his supporters. The group grew slowly, but it stuck together like a block of marble.

Over the next few weeks and months Bulos didn't say much about Gabriel. Farid thought his friend had finally realized that he was wrong about the monk. It was a long time before he found out that he himself had been mistaken.

132. Fire and Water

A playwriting competition for the eleventh and twelfth grades was held in January, and Bulos won it with a work entitled *The Sufferings of the Christians in China*. Apparently Brother Gabriel was the only member of the jury to have voted against his victory.

Rehearsals began in early March. Farid and Marcel joined in out of friendship for Bulos. The other members of the Syrian Brothers declined to take part; they weren't interested in the theatre. Bulos swallowed this rebuff, but he was obviously disappointed, although there were more people in the monastery who wanted to be in the play than he needed.

Farid was to act the part of a devout Catholic who was imprisoned at the end of the play. The communists were ruling the country, all of them small of stature and wearing uniform, with conspicuous red stars on their caps. They drank rice wine and mistreated the mission-aries and their pupils. Bulos picked tall boys from the upper school to play the missionaries, while the youngest of the monastery pupils acted the parts of small Chinese.

Producing his play was a considerable strain on Bulos, particularly as the secret society was involved in its first serious crisis just then. In May, Farid and the other members found out that Bulos had secretly formed a second group to operate in the monastery without the knowledge of the first. Bulos explained that his secrecy was intended to protect all concerned. But this time the crack that Farid heard inside himself was ear-splitting. His faith in Bulos was badly shaken. However, he kept quiet, and only Andreas, an eleventh-grade student, left the society of his own accord. He said he didn't want any more to do with the group, but they could count on him not to give anyone away. Andreas had been one of the bravest of the members.

Bulos controlled his fury with difficulty, and repaid the defection with contempt. He felt sure that only the threat of harsh punishment could prevent betrayal, not the integrity of someone like Andreas.

Unlike Gabriel, who quietly followed his own route like water, taking the long way around where necessary, Bulos was blazing fire, instantly burning all doubts and obstacles in his path. He and Gabriel, each in his own way, were recruiting supporters. Farid gradually realized that their ideals were irreconcilable, and thought how agonized and hypocritical his friendship for two people at such odds with one another made him personally feel.

But a letter from his father at the end of May took his mind right off these matters. Claire had been in hospital in March, said the letter, for an operation. Farid felt dazed, and breathed a sigh of relief only when he read that she was now in very good health again, and was coming to see him at the end of July.

The letter ended with the news that Matta Blota, the strong boy from Mala who had been one of the party when the elm tree burned, and who ran away over two years ago, had now been caught and had seen sense. He would soon be entering the monastery of St. Sebastian.

Farid smiled at his memories of the boy who had been supposed to join the monastery as a pupil in the summer of 1953, and he remembered Matta's ability to swing like a monkey from branch to branch in the trees, as if he were Tarzan. Two days later, Gabriel confirmed the news that Farid had heard from Damascus.

During June and the last phase of rehearsals, Bulos had been very irritable. He doubted everything and was satisfied with nothing. His anger was more and more clearly aimed at Gabriel, whom he suspected of being behind everything that went wrong. In mid-June came the first major dispute, when Gabriel criticized him in public during a rehearsal. Bulos rejected the criticism brusquely, and in the attic that night he raged against the monk. The Syrian Brothers said nothing. Bulos was beside himself. Gabriel was a communist, he said, and the only reason why he didn't like the play was that it called the communists to account. He was gay as well, said Bulos, he needed two boys from the top grade to satisfy him every night.

Farid exploded. His voice breaking, he shouted at Bulos, "So why would we be interested in Gabriel's arse? Tell me that, will you? What business of ours is it who screws or who gets screwed? Gabriel, Gabriel, Gabriel. Can't you think of anything but how much you hate him?"

Bulos froze. His face was pale and his lips quivered. He had never before looked so ugly. He held his breath and stared back at Farid. There was a deathly hush.

"You're right," he said quietly, his voice icy cold. "I must control myself. We ought to occupy our minds with something more worthwhile than Gabriel."

After that calm returned to the group for some days, and the name of Gabriel wasn't mentioned again.

Matta did not arrive until the end of June. On those hot June nights, Farid thought of his own arrival two years ago. That first year had seemed to him endlessly long, the second was fainter in his memory and was going fast. Time appeared to him to pass not as a linear series of hours and days, but like the squeezing of an accordion.

133. Claire's Second Visit

About ten days before the Feast of St. Ignatius, Brother John told Farid, in his usual uncouth way, that his mother had arrived. Farid was startled. He was in the middle of a game of chess against the invincible Bulos, who laughed. "Mothers are reliable guardian angels. Yours has turned up just two moves before you were bound to be checkmated! Oh well, off you go. Give her my regards," he added.

Farid ran out of the games room feeling that he wanted to do three things at once: wash his face, pick some flowers from the garden, and shout for joy. In the inner courtyard he hesitated for a moment and then, walking slowly, made for the visitors' room near the front entrance.

When Farid opened the door, Claire smiled radiantly at him and spread her arms wide. There was a large box of sweetmeats on the table in front of her.

"My little priest!" she cried.

"Mama," said Farid, but his voice failed him. "Mama," he whispered again, hugging her. When she lovingly ran her hand over his shorn hair, he began crying.

Claire turned to the monk sitting silently on a stool in the corner. "Could you ask in the Abbot's office if I may go for a walk with my son? The weather is much too fine for us to sit indoors," she said in perfect French.

"That is not permitted, madame," said the monk curtly.

"I was asking Abbot Maximus's permission, not yours. So would you be kind enough to bring me his answer, or shall I go and look for him myself?" replied Claire firmly.

The monk stood up and slowly went to the door.

"As always, you're wonderful." Farid hugged his mother again.

"Your father has given me five thousand lira as a donation for the monastery. If they won't let us go for a walk, well, too bad, they won't see a single lira of it."

The monk returned to the visitors' room with his head bent. "You may walk as long as you like with Brother Barnaba. But Abbot Maximus would be glad if you would visit him for a little while when you come back. He has a letter he'd like to give you for your husband," he said, and went away again.

"A letter?" asked Farid.

Claire laughed. "I believe I've already brought the answer."

They left the monastery hand in hand, and walked down the path to the sea in silence. When they came out on the beach, Claire took her shoes off and ran along the water's edge, dancing about happily. Farid took off his own sandals and ran after her.

"And how are you, dear heart?" asked Claire, sitting down on a weather-beaten bench.

"Not too good. Life in a monastery isn't right for me," said Farid.

"What is it you don't like here?"

"Everything. They're dreadfully strict, and …" Farid hesitated only for a moment, and then took his mother's face in his hands and kissed her ardently. "And there are no kisses like that here."

"I miss you badly," she said, "and I'm not supposed to say so, because good mothers don't do such things to their children in a monastery, but there you are, I never was a good mother." She smiled, but her eyes were gleaming with unshed tears.

They went back two hours later. Claire had quietly handed Farid a thousand lira for any necessary expenses, and decided not to give the Abbot anything but the sweetmeats from her husband's shop.

Next day she started her journey home with the abbot's begging letter to Elias Mushtak, and the first time the bus stopped for a break she tore it up and threw it in a rubbish bin.

But she gave the fat envelope with the letter for Rana, as Farid asked, to his cousin Laila.

134. The Sufferings of the Christians

Brother Gabriel didn't attend the performance of the play in July. He thought it was stupid, but he had only one vote on the committee, and the other members had been enthusiastic. It was meant to show people living in freedom what sacrifices their brothers and sisters had to make to defend Christianity in a dictatorship.

But it was a disaster. Bulos hated the communists so much that his play veered towards the ridiculous, arousing laughter in the hall instead of pity and terror. The mirth proved infectious, and by the end of the play even the actors on stage were laughing.

Abbot Maximus had no option but to stop the show. Not only that, he immediately declared an end to all theatrical performances in the monastery for ever. In future, he said, the Feast of St. Ignatius would be celebrated with a magnificent church service and a long reading from Ignatius's famous book *Exercitia spiritualia*.

Bulos said nothing at all for several days. The first words he spoke, at a meeting of the Syrian Brothers, were a furious denunciation of Gabriel.

135. Matta

Matta arrived a week later. "They beat me as hard as if I were a mangy dog," he told Farid.

Matta hadn't wanted to go into the monastery, but the bishop had been worried for years about the falling number of pupils. Almost no novices from the cities joined any more, so he had sent a circular letter to all priests asking them to search every Christian village for boys to be trained as priests at various monasteries. They would be fast-tracked in a course lasting only three years. Matta's father had seized this chance to get rid of his son, but Matta refused to go. At that his father had beaten him so hard that he saw no alternative but to run away.

He hid with a shepherd in the mountains. One day, however, a farmer recognized him and told his parents. His father kept him tied up in the stables until the papers for his admission to the monastery were ready.

"Why would I want to be a priest?" asked Matta. "Spending my whole life in a monk's habit and the confessional! I want to be free, I want to breathe fresh air and follow the sheep and goats with Aida, I want to run around and laugh with them." He stopped, sighed, and glanced down at his habit. "I mean, just look at me," he said, pulling up its skirts to show his big feet and bow legs. "I ask you, do I look like a priest?"

Farid couldn't help laughing. Matta did in fact look strange, and the scars on his head that Farid had never noticed before were unattractively conspicuous now that he had the tonsure. His face appeared even more simple-minded without any whiskers. Matta's hands were as big and horny as any farmer's.

Farid knew about the passionate love between Matta and his cousin Aida. But it was a forbidden love, for Aida, who was exactly Matta's own age, had had to be breast-fed by his mother. That made her and Matta siblings at the breast, and they were not allowed to marry.

A vigorous peasant girl who matured early, Aida had been turning the heads of bachelors in Mala since her thirteenth birthday, but she didn't want any of the men who proposed to her. She loved only this boy who looked like a gorilla, and had only just managed to make it into the fourth grade at school when he was fourteen.

Farid was sorry for Matta, who looked like a lost child. He helped the newcomer through his first few days in the monastery. At least he had been allowed to keep his own name, since none of the other pupils was called Matta, after the Evangelist.

"You're my one piece of good luck," Matta kept saying. He had difficulty with French, and indeed with books in general.

When Bulos first met Matta, he liked the boy at once. He seemed like a force of nature, wild, strong, and lovable. Bulos thought of him as a brother, and soon after his arrival he was admitted to the secret society of Syrian Brothers.

Summer and outdoor agricultural work helped Matta to settle in. Out of doors, he was better than anyone else at harvesting crops and milking livestock. Once Matta had fresh air in his nostrils he was in his element. Bulos admired his strength as he worked, climbed trees as nimbly as a monkey, and then fooled around like a circus artiste up in the branches.

A jute sack full of wheat weighed over sixty kilos. That was no problem to Matta. He did a dance with the sack on his back, making even Brother Jakob applaud and laugh until the tears came to his eyes.

But the moment Matta was back in the monastery he was useless.

He couldn't even write a short essay about the day he had just spent out of doors. Farid gave him coaching daily, with increasing desperation as the beginning of the school term approached.

Matta's mind was somewhere else entirely, not only in lessons but during Farid's coaching. He couldn't get the simplest calculations into his head. Instead, he told Farid at every opportunity that, without fail, he was going to run away. "The time will come," he said mysteriously.

Only in the secret society of the Syrian Brothers was he wide awake and full of energy. And he did everything that Bulos asked him to do.

136. Brother Nicholas

Rana was dancing naked. Her body glowed pink in the firelight from the elm. Farid, also naked, was sitting in the damp grass. Everything was dark except for Rana. But his back was warm from the heat of the burning tree. Suddenly Rana sat astride his lap with her legs spread. Her face was burning. Someone sprayed cold water on Farid's thighs, and a shudder ran through all his limbs.

He woke up. It was still dark. Farid felt that everything under him was wet. He quickly took off his underpants, wiped his wet balls with them, put a clean pair on, and then put his pyjama trousers over it. He placed the wet underpants between his mattress and the iron bedstead. There was no way he could hand them in to the laundry.

❧

Brother Nicholas was a small, dark-skinned man. It was said that as a pupil he had been outstanding with his bold essays on difficult theological questions. But shortly before he was to be ordained priest, he fell out of a tree at harvest time. He lay in a coma for a long time after that, and when he came out of it he was simple-minded and, although he wanted to go on serving the monastery, was capable only of basic tasks. So now he worked in the laundry.

Every week, the pupils had to hand in their dirty washing in a laundry bag. To avoid getting clothes mixed up, every item was marked with its owner's date of birth and initials. Marcel said that Nicholas sniffed all the garments in turn, and as soon as he detected the smell of semen on anything he handed it over to Father Istfan. And Father Istfan gave the pupil concerned a lesson "liable to keep his prick down and out for good, believe you me," concluded Marcel. Farid thought he was joking.

But one day he actually saw Brother Nicholas sniffing pair after pair of underpants with his eyes closed, and then throwing them into a big laundry cart with the vests. He came to one, and suddenly stopped, sniffed it again, and then let out a yelp. It sounded like a whinny of "Yes!" Then he looked for the owner's initials and date of birth, and noted them down.

≫●

Farid's erotic dreams came more and more often these days. He felt Rana closer to him than ever before, and when it was over he stuffed his sticky underpants beneath the mattress.

Some people washed theirs in secret after a wet dream and hung them in the attic to dry. Farid was revolted by the sight of the dried garments hanging there rigid as boards. And he knew from Marcel that it didn't help. "Brother Nicholas gets them anyway," he said. He himself got an uncle to keep bringing him new underpants, and he threw the soiled ones, well wrapped up, into the big rubbish bin, cutting out his initials to be on the safe side.

When Farid had buried fourteen pairs of underpants under his mattress, he wrote his mother a letter and sent it by the secret route via the bus driver. In it he asked her for a dozen pairs of underpants with the usual mark FM230640.

Three weeks later Bulos brought him the package.

Dear heart,
Here are the underpants. That's a funny sort of monastery. What on earth do you do with so many pairs? Laila was here

and helped me sew the initials in. We laughed a lot, and she said that if your father heard you were getting through more pairs of underpants than rosaries he'd probably convert to Islam.

Laila suspects you must all be so hungry there, you have to nibble your underpants.

With love, your devoted provider of underwear,

Claire

Farid happily put the new undergarments away in his locker and then ran out into the courtyard, where the other monastery pupils were spending the short time before the bell went for supper.

"You can visit me more often now," he whispered softly in his mind to Rana as he went downstairs, and he took the last four steps in one great leap.

137. Spectres by Night

Matta and Bulos were different in every way, but complemented one another perfectly. Each admired the other's abilities. Matta was brave and had enormously powerful hands. He was trusting, straightforward, and believed everything he was told.

And it seemed miraculous that Matta, who tied himself in knots trying to finish a single sentence in French, turned out better than anyone at learning Bulos's secret language. That was another reason why Bulos liked him. As soon as Matta heard a new word in the secret language it was imprinted on his memory, and he spoke it without any accent. Soon he could converse easily in it with Bulos.

At the end of August, Bulos had a violent argument with Father Athanasius, an unpleasant and short-tempered theologian whom most of the monastery pupils avoided. After their quarrel, Athanasius went to the Abbot and accused Bulos of calling Jesus a bandit leader.

That wasn't true. Bulos thought Jesus the greatest revolutionary of all time, but the dull-minded theologian thought revolutionaries were exactly the same as bandits.

Maximus showed no mercy. He didn't let Bulos finish his explanation, but pronounced sentence at once: either he left the monastery or he did penance. Bulos accepted penance. It was extremely humiliating. He had to kneel in the inner courtyard and ask pardon of the tale-teller Athanasius in front of all the pupils and all the Fathers.

Bulos repeated his request for forgiveness twice, parrot-fashion and with an unmoved expression, because Athanasius claimed not to have heard the words properly. Tears came to Matta's eyes at the sight of his friend, and Farid cursed the priest from the bottom of his heart.

৯০

On 14 September the monastery celebrated the annual Feast of the Holy Cross. It began in the afternoon, with a huge bonfire out in the car park. According to legend the Empress Helena, mother of the first Christian Emperor of Rome, Constantine, found the True Cross on which Jesus died in Jerusalem on 14 September 326. At the time, said the story, she had found three crosses. To discover which was Our Lord's she placed the three crosses on a man who was very sick. Two struck a musical note, and then she was sure that the third was the cross of the bad thief who was crucified on the left hand of the Lord, and who mocked him to the last.

Now she had to find out which of the other two crosses belonged to the Lord and which to the good thief crucified on his right hand. St. Helena, the clever daughter of an innkeeper whose beauty and brains had helped her rise to become empress, and whose influence on her son Constantine changed the course of world history, knew what to do. She placed the crosses on two dead bodies. One of them came back to life as if waking from a deep sleep, so the cross laid on that body had been the Lord's. Helena had fiery beacons lit to carry the message of the finding of the cross from Palestine by way of Lebanon and Syria and so to Constantinople. To this day, many Christian mountain villages celebrate the bringing of that news by lighting large bonfires on 14 September, just as the monastery of St. Sebastian did.

The pupils, novices, monks, and Fathers all celebrated together until nearly midnight.

That night, however, Father Athanasius obviously went out of his mind. Just before dawn he was suddenly heard shouting for help. Some of the Fathers woke and ran to him. But his room was locked. When they finally opened the door with a duplicate key, there was a strong smell of arrack, and the Father was sitting on his bed in a daze, dead drunk and, so it was said later, soaked with piss.

Black spectres had come in through his window, babbled the theologian, overpowered him in his sleep, tipped half a bottle of spirits down his throat, and finally peed on him.

His story was rather incoherent. Grey-faced, Maximus said nothing. And when the entire event was repeated a week later, he gave orders for the priest to be moved to a nearby hospital, which sent him back to the monastery three weeks later.

Athanasius was still in a highly nervous state, so Maximus gave him a bedroom shared with a deaf old priest, and Father Istfan took over religious instruction.

From then on Athanasius was considered crazy, and was the butt of all the monastery pupils. Only one of them, quietly triumphant, refrained from mocking him, and that was Bulos.

Later, Farid learned from Matta that it was he and Bulos who had haunted Athanasius. The idea originated with Bulos, but he hadn't lifted a finger to put it into practice; Matta did the dangerous part. Farid felt not so much admiration as a sense of distance and isolation, but also some envy, because Matta and Bulos seemed to trust each other so unconditionally.

138. Drifting Apart

Father Daniel, the monastery's mathematician, was a tall, thin man. The pupils called him "Monsieur Integral", which made him laugh heartily. He was a man with a good sense of humour. He liked Bulos, too, and often expressed his indignation at the penance he had been forced to do, which Father Daniel had been alone in opposing. But the disciplinary committee had been intent on making an example of someone.

One day in September Bulos asked Farid to go and visit Father Daniel with him. They drank tea and ate particularly savoury rolls. Bulos argued with the priest as openly as if they were brothers. Later they played chess. Daniel was better at the game than Bulos, but wasn't at all arrogant about it. "I don't let you win so that you'll be encouraged to play even better next time," he consoled him.

Finally the conversation came around to Gabriel. Farid was surprised to hear Father Daniel speak so frankly of the monk's weaknesses.

"Gabriel won't rise any higher," he said. "He criticizes the Catholic Church too much. He's cleverer than Loyola and Luther, but without the heroic courage of either." For once Bulos was diplomatic, and said nothing malicious about his enemy.

In early October, after years of patient work, Gabriel managed to get the custom of passing the signal around abolished, and the unattractive sight of a kneeling sinner was no longer seen in the refectory.

Only Bulos appeared upset. Once there was no signal any more, several of the pupils saw no more need for a secret society, and distanced themselves from the group.

139. Encounters

It was a fine, warm Sunday when Brother Gabriel asked Farid to have another talk with him. As Farid was about to sit down, Gabriel looked out of the window and said, "No, let's go out and enjoy this December sun."

The monastery administration was concerned about the many cases of flu and persistent colds that had been plaguing the pupils, so they were letting everyone go out. The gate was wide open, and after their midday meal a number of the pupils went for a walk or sat on benches in the grounds, basking in the sun. Farid followed Gabriel along the path past the orange groves and down to the sea.

The waves were rough, and roared as they broke on the beach. Spray rose from the breakers. Farid took a deep breath, then removed his sandals and went barefoot.

"When I was small," Gabriel told him, "I lived with my grandmother. My mother died in the sardine canning factory where she worked. It was a tragic accident; a reversing truck ran over her as she was sweeping the yard. My father blamed the truck driver and said he had killed her on purpose because she had turned him down."

"Do you believe that?" asked Farid.

"No, but my mother's death drove my father out of his mind. When nothing could calm him, he was fired from the factory. He went back to sea-fishing. He had been a fisherman before he married. My father loved the sea and the loneliness of it. He didn't know how to deal with children, so he handed us – my sister, my younger brother, and me – over to his parents. They were peasants. My grandfather was a strong, simple-minded man, but my grandmother was crazy and had the second sight. We didn't understand much about it. One Sunday I was going to Mass with her. Grandfather never went to church. Just outside the church she suddenly stopped. 'Do you hear the rafters creaking and groaning?' she asked. I listened, but I couldn't hear anything.

'We won't go into the church,' she said firmly. 'It's about to fall down.' And then she took my hand and walked home with a firm step. Grandfather laughed at her crazy ideas.

"As we sat on the terrace, we could see the village square and the church from up on the hill. Bells were ringing for the beginning of Mass. Grandmother closed her eyes and kept still. Suddenly, without any warning, the whole church collapsed. The bell in the tower rang just once more, and then it fell silent as dust rose. First the roof and then the walls fell in, burying seventy people under their stones. Only five adults and three children survived the disaster, badly injured. To this day I don't know why my grandmother didn't warn the congregation."

Gabriel fell silent, pressing his feet more firmly into the sand. Then, without looking at Farid, he said, "Keep away from Bulos. His heart is full of hatred. That's not Christian." He looked into the distance. Farid walked along beside him in silence, expecting Gabriel to invite him to join the Saturday meetings of the Early Christians group at this point, but the monk said no more, only smiled with relief as if he had been suffering from bearing the weight of his warning.

They were about to turn back when Bulos appeared with a few other pupils, all on their way back to the monastery. Bulos greeted Gabriel, gazing hard at him as if intent on ignoring Farid.

That evening Matta said Bulos had had a letter from his mother, who wanted to come and visit him soon. Then Matta changed the subject; it seemed as if he had something he wanted to get off his chest. He'd been surprised, he said, by Bulos's startled look when he, Matta, happened to mention the name of Farid Mushtak. Bulos had asked twice if he was quite sure that Farid's surname was Mushtak and he came from Mala. He didn't say why he was so surprised, said Matta.

When Farid met Bulos himself next day, his manner was strangely cool.

"How's your mother?" asked Farid. Bulos didn't reply at once, but gave him a dark look.

"What's that to you?" he snapped. "*You* don't tell *me* why you're so thick with Gabriel these days, do you?"

Farid was baffled for a moment. He hadn't expected this coldness.

"You have it all wrong. Brother Gabriel was only being friendly, as usual."

But it was like talking to a brick wall.

140. Matta Runs Away

The teachers were very indulgent to the pupils taking the fast-track course to become village priests, but no leniency and patience could do anything for Matta. It was Brother Gabriel's view that the boy should be sent home as soon as possible. But the monastery administration took no notice, regarding it as a challenge to discipline him instead.

The teachers obeyed, and so Matta's ordeal began that December. Whenever he made a mistake, however small, he had to kneel down, and if that didn't work he was made to stand facing the wall for the entire lesson. Matta bore it all with the patience of a camel. The next punishment was more painful: he wasn't allowed out into the yard for a breath of fresh air during the break between lessons, but had to stay in the classroom writing out meaningless lines. Farid and Bulos forgot the coolness between them for a while as they tried to help Matta. They offered to give him extra coaching, but Abbot Maximus turned the idea down. The trouble with Matta, he said, wasn't ignorance but a lack of self-discipline.

Farid could see how much his friend was suffering. His laughter had gone, and although he tried hard with his work he just fell further and further behind.

During that icy January Bulos's mother came to visit him. Wishing to please him and be back on good terms, Farid said he hoped he'd enjoy the visit, and offered him some money so that he could give his mother a present. Bulos just looked straight through him. Farid was worried. He tried to find out from Matta what had made Bulos so hostile, but Matta didn't know either.

Not until fourteen years later, in a place very far from the monastery, was Farid to discover the answer from Bulos himself.

꒰ꘒ꒱

The next night Matta jumped out of the washroom window into a tree, and then fled into the darkness. When the monk on duty raised the alarm next morning, Abbot Maximus sent for Marcel, Bulos, and Barnaba.

Bulos was pale with rage, and scented treachery. But he couldn't say much, for Maximus was cool to Farid as well, and was acting the part of detective.

"I know you're all in league together," said Maximus sharply. He looked straight at Bulos. "And as for you, you should have told us that our son Matta needed help."

Bulos lowered his eyes.

"Barnaba, did you know that Matta was planning to run away?" asked the Abbot.

Farid took fright. "No," he lied.

Marcel was the only member of the trio who had really had no idea, but it was a fact that Matta, in desperation, had asked Bulos and Farid for help. He had to run away or he would choke here, he said. After their offer to the Abbot to give him extra coaching failed, Farid gave Matta a hundred lira, and Bulos told him two addresses in the port of Latakia where he could hide.

When Marcel too denied having known anything about Matta's flight, the Abbot was beside himself, and said that all three must eat every meal on their knees for a week. It was one of the most humiliating punishments that could be given.

From now on Bulos would speak to neither Farid nor Marcel. He exchanged his place in class with another pupil, and avoided all eye contact with the other two as they knelt. Farid was less bothered by that than by his guilty conscience over Marcel, who had been dragged into this even though he was an innocent party. Kneeling on the icy cold floor didn't hurt nearly as much as knowing that he and Bulos had obviously planned Matta's escape so clumsily that Maximus was able to track them down at once as his helpers. Since none of the other monastery pupils showed any sympathy, Farid began to feel that the Syrian Brothers had been infiltrated.

But Bulos wouldn't hear of any such idea. Gabriel had been spying on them, he said, and told tales to Maximus. Farid couldn't help thinking that when Bulos said "Gabriel" he was also accusing him.

It was true that the monk was suddenly keeping his distance, and just shook his head whenever Farid's eyes met his. There was little regret in his glance. He ate and spoke as if he didn't see three of the monastery students being tormented before his eyes at that very moment. He, the sensitive soul who never punished a pupil, suddenly seemed unmoved. That hurt Farid, and he couldn't help thinking of Matta's last words to him. "I'll miss you so much. That's the only bad part of running away."

Farid would have liked to run away too.

On the twenty-first day after his escape, Matta was found in a village not far from the monastery and brought back. Next time he celebrated Mass, Abbot Maximus thanked God for what he called

Matta's return of his own free will. He told the pupils that the prodigal son needed a period of rest and reflection to become his normal self again.

Farid would never have believed the upright Maximus could tell such outrageous lies. Matta was consigned to the House of Job, an out-of-the-way building behind the stables. "It's a prison for students who sin really badly. It's hell," said Bulos. "They'll send him crazy there. We have to tell him we'll soon get him out, and then he must go straight to Damascus and hide there." And Bulos had the perfect plan.

Two days later, when lessons stopped for the midday break, Farid stole into the visitors' room, which had a door to the car park. He walked through it and with a firm tread went on to the stables, as Bulos had told him to do, as if he had been sent to look at the animals.

Wet snow was drizzling down. There wasn't a soul in sight. When he reached the stables he quickly went around the corner, and then he was in front of the small door. The key fitted. He slipped into the dark hut and quickly closed the door behind him.

He was in complete darkness. He listened for a while until he heard whimpering from the floor above. Cautiously, he groped his way up the stairs.

Two tiny windows covered with moss and slushy snow gave a faint light that showed the single room on this second floor. Matta was crouching in a corner, chained to the wall.

"Matta," whispered Farid.

The boy wept when Farid hugged him and kissed his forehead. "They beat me almost to death," he said.

"But they won't get you down. You're from Mala. Who beat you? Who did it?" Farid asked, suddenly furious when he saw his friend's swollen face. His head was encrusted with dried blood in several places, and his hands and feet were red.

"Brother John," murmured Matta. Suddenly he looked at Farid, and asked, "You have come to let me out of here, haven't you?"

"Yes, but you must hang on for a few more days, until we've been in touch with the bus driver. He'll take you with him, and once you're in Damascus no one can bring you back."

"A few more days?" asked Matta. His mouth was dry. "Get these chains off me, and I'll make my own way to Damascus. A few more days?" he repeated, almost giving way. "Look at me, see what they've done to me, look at me!"

Farid felt wretched. "You must be patient. I'll get you out of here. Trust me. You're still too weak. They'd catch up with you and bring you back before you'd gone far. Trust me."

"I do, I trust you more than anyone else in the world, but John beats me every day, and he kicks me in the head with his boots. He wants me to go crazy, and now you tell me I must stay here?", he sobbed.

The keys to unlock the chains were hanging on the wall, but Farid knew that Matta would never survive another escape attempt. He rose. "I'll be back just as soon as I can. Don't worry. We'll see to John," said Farid, tearing himself away. He felt as if he were chained up there too.

"Oh, Mother, help me," he heard Matta say before he closed the door of the little building behind him.

Large snowflakes were falling outside now. Fortunately the door of the visitors' room wasn't locked, and the cleaners were busy sweeping it out. Farid waved to them and strode past at a steady pace. Only in the inner courtyard did he begin to run. He went straight to Bulos.

"I'm going to Gabriel right away. He must tell John to stop it," Farid finished his account.

Bulos looked at him, horrified. "Are you out of your mind? Gabriel? Gabriel! He'll know at once that you've seen Matta, which means you'll be giving us away. And what for? To persuade that miserable wretch to show mercy? Don't you remember we've been kneeling on the icy floor for a whole week now, right in front of his nose? No, we'll deal with John ourselves."

"How do you mean, deal with him?" asked Farid, but just then the bell rang for afternoon lessons.

141. Punishment

A thick blanket of snow lay over the landscape, softening all its out-lines. Because it was so cold, the snow turned to a dry powder that blew through every crack. The students muffled themselves up in scarves and caps to walk the short distance to lessons.

The monastery administration extended the midday break from two hours to three, and let the students play in the snow outside the walls. The inner courtyard was left almost empty.

Bulos briefly observed the busy scene, and then beckoned to Farid, who pushed his warm cap further down over his face, and followed. Bulos was making for John's workshop, and quickly slipped in with Farid after him.

John was lying on his plank bed in the back room, arms and legs outstretched, snoring loudly. Bulos picked up a piece of metal pipe, taking care to make no sound. Next moment he was standing over the colossus, pressing the end of the pipe to his throat. John woke with a start. He sat up, making a loud gurgling noise which sounded like, "What's going on?"

Staring at Farid with red, bewildered eyes, he tried to stand up, but a blow crashed down on his forehead. Farid jumped, and briefly closed his eyes. He heard John's body fall back on the bed. When he opened his eyes again he saw the man's bleeding forehead. Bulos was standing in front of John impassively, leaning on the piece of pipe like a fencer on his foil.

Suddenly he swung it back.

"What are you doing?" whispered Farid in alarm.

"Breaking the hand that tortured Matta," replied Bulos, and before Farid had taken in what he was saying, Brother John's right hand shattered under the blow. It sounded like wood splitting.

"Come on, quick, let's get out of here," gasped Bulos, throwing the piece of pipe aside and slipping out of the door again.

When Farid himself came out, Bulos had already disappeared. Farid felt his throat tighten with fear. He couldn't go and join the others romping around in the snow. He had to be alone. Just before he reached the gateway he turned, and trudged through the snow to the flight of steps beside the church. His stomach hurt, and there was a throbbing in his temples.

He sat down in the library under the small, semi-circular window, took Kipling's *Jungle Book* off a shelf, and began to read. But he couldn't take anything in. The sentences meant nothing. He kept hearing a voice inside him repeating: John is dying.

His relief was great when he suddenly heard John's voice echoing across the courtyard. The monastery pupils stopped playing and stood still. The monk was calling for help. Farid let out a deep breath, and was trying to read again when he felt a hand on his shoulder.

"What's that you're reading?" asked Gabriel, smiling.

"Oh, Kipling, just to pass the time," replied Farid, and he looked at the table in front of him. When he raised his eyes again, he saw Bulos's head looking in at the library door, just for a moment. Then it disappeared again.

"Brother Gabriel," another pupil called from the door next minute. His face was pale. Gabriel turned in annoyance, and was about to put his forefinger to his lips. "Brother John's been attacked. Abbot Maximus wants you to come quickly," the boy went on excitedly.

Gabriel's hand stopped half-way to his mouth. "For God's sake!" he cried, and he hurried off at once. Bulos came in, as if he had been waiting outside the door all the time.

"What did that Judas want with you?" he asked, clearly distrustful.

"Nothing," said Farid.

"Sure?"

"Sure," Farid replied.

Bulos turned to leave, but his look of scorn burned Farid's skin.

When Bulos was questioned a week later, Farid was at a loss to know why. Marcel claimed that one of the Fathers, looking out of his window, had seen Bulos leave the workshop.

"Oh, but that can't be right," Farid spontaneously replied. For if so, then the alleged eye-witness must have seen him too, he thought.

"What makes you so sure?" asked Marcel suspiciously. Farid bit his lip and said nothing.

"I just don't think Bulos would do a thing like that," he replied at last, trying hard to sound naïve.

"You've no idea what things he'd do," said Marcel scornfully, turning away.

142. Marcel

It was two weeks before the bus driver brought warm clothes and boots for Matta. As Brother Tuma, standing in for John, was gentle by nature, the boy had a chance to recover a little. Farid and Bulos smuggled him some food in his prison every day, and Brother Tuma turned a blind eye.

Brother John came back early in February. His head was still bandaged, and his right arm was in plaster up to the shoulder. He said little, and walked up and down in the courtyard all day.

Matta ran away again in mid-February. But for some reason or other his flight was quickly discovered this time, and the police, who had been alerted, stopped the bus just before it reached the main road. Maximus didn't want Matta back in the monastery. He asked the police to inform the boy's parents.

The next rumour was that his father had gone to the police station and beat his son so badly that the boy lost consciousness and fell on his head. When he came to his senses, he was different, and spoke in a strange, confused way. The police recommended his father to take him to the al-Asfuriye mental hospital.

Bulos was interrogated again and again, from the end of February to the middle of March, but to no avail. The worst questions came from Gabriel, who seemed to know a great deal about the Syrian Brothers. Bulos now doubted the loyalty of every member of the society, Farid in particular. He might not say so explicitly, but Farid sensed his suspicion behind every remark he made. Finally the group broke up. Bulos was about to take the exams for his high school diploma, and had other aims in mind now.

"He's acting all pious because he wants to get a stipend after the exams," claimed Marcel. "Then he can go and study in Rome or Paris."

The weather was extremely changeable in early April. Farid felt miserable, and so weak that he fainted several times and had to stay in bed. All his friends visited him, and Gabriel kept looking in as well. Only Bulos never showed up.

Marcel came several times a day, told jokes and passed on gossip, and always brought Farid something special to eat. One day he confided to Farid that he was going to leave the monastery at the end of the school year, and none of the Fathers were allowed to touch him or punish him any more.

"How on earth did you manage that?" asked Farid in amazement.

"Simple. I found out that no one works in the secretarial office at siesta time, and the phone isn't watched. The only problem was Abbot Maximus, because he spends that time of day in his own office. So I waited until he was away, and then I opened the door of the secretarial office with a piece of wire. I called home and told my father he had to get me out of here or I'd kill myself, and when he asked where I was calling from I told him about the wire and the empty office. My father shouted like a madman. He was scared out of his wits that I was learning to be a criminal in the monastery. That settled it. He blamed Abbot Maximus for letting me go to the bad, and he warned him to leave me alone for the rest of the school year."

"I don't want to stay either," said Farid. "Could you call my mother and tell her to come at once? If my father answers the phone hang up again at once. It's useless trying to talk to him."

Two days later Marcel brought news that Claire would come as soon as she possibly could. But he also told Farid that Bulos had been questioned yet again, by a CID man, no less. Marcel reported that Bulos had said very some angry things about Brother Gabriel and Farid.

The scene in the library went through Farid's mind, the time when Bulos had seen him with Gabriel on the day they did the deed. And at that moment he knew that Bulos was accusing him of treachery.

143. Farewell

Gabriel came to see him once more. He had his gentle smile on his face, and he explained at length that Bulos had been difficult recently, and it had been suggested that he should leave the monastery of his own accord or he might be thrown out. Bulos had gone to pieces, asking to be allowed to take his exams, but the monastery administration refused. The CID was as good as certain that he had taken part in the attack on Brother John, although in the monastery's interests they were willing to drop the case to avoid a scandal in the press.

However, he added, he had now managed to get Bulos a reprieve. He would have to leave the monastery, but he could spend the last months until the examinations in early June at a nearby boarding school. He didn't want to see Bulos ruined and sent home without any diploma at all, said Gabriel.

Farid heard the malice in his voice, and hated him for it. He was overcome by a strange fear that Bulos might hear of Gabriel's visit to him, and then his friend would feel that his darkest suspicions were confirmed. So Farid told Gabriel apologetically that he was very tired, and he lay down. Realizing that his presence was no longer wanted, Gabriel broke off in the middle of his explanations, and left the room.

That night Farid ran a temperature, and when he wanted to go to the lavatory he fell and hit his head. He lost consciousness. When he came back to his senses he felt wretched. Over ten anxious faces were looking down on him. His head was bandaged, his temple hurt. Marcel was smiling at him and kept patting his hand.

Next day Father Simeon, the monastery doctor, visited him. He entered without a word of greeting and began taking his things out of an old leather bag. "Come on, do you need a written invitation to show me your chest?" he growled.

He ran an ice-cold stethoscope over Farid's back and chest. Then he put his things away again. Just then Father Istfan, the Inquisitor, came through the doorway. He spoke quietly to the doctor, and for the first time in his life Farid heard the word "malingerer".

The Inquisitor nodded, and glanced at Farid, who was putting his pyjama jacket on again.

"My son," said the Inquisitor, enveloping him in a dense cloud of bad breath, "you must trust me. I only want to help you. What is troubling you, what makes you withdraw from the school and your comrades? What makes you injure your head like that? Is it perhaps connected with what your friend Bulos did? You can tell me everything."

Farid hated the weakness that kept him confined to the bed. He felt driven into a corner. Why couldn't he just fly out of the window like a bird?

"Take care, my son, for if you won't let us help you, Father Simeon will tell the Abbot that you're only pretending to be sick, and that will be punished as deception."

So that's it, thought Farid, this lousy Inquisitor wants to worm it all out of me because they're not quite sure about Bulos yet. They don't know anything about him. It's Gabriel's cheap revenge. That snake! They're not sorry for Bulos at all, they're tormenting him.

"Mama!" cried Farid, in as loud and shrill a voice as he could. Father Istfan was scared out of his wits. He flung himself on the boy, but Farid slipped out of the other side of the bed and ran to the open window, still shouting "Mama!" again and again. Istfan stumbled after him, but suddenly hesitated, stopped, and put out his hands almost imploringly. Then, however, he hurried out of the dormitory.

Outside, spring was bright with fresh colours. But it was still cold as ice in the dormitory. More and more people were gathering in the car park outside. Farid recognized the bus driver, the mechanic, Brother Nicholas from the laundry, and others. He was shouting for all he was worth, and didn't stop even when powerful hands took him by the shoulder. Turning, he saw Brother John looking at him pityingly. Other monks stood behind John. Among them was Gabriel, pale-faced. Farid tore himself away from John. "Let me go, you criminal!" he shouted, moving away until there were two beds between him and John, who wasn't in fact trying to catch hold of Farid, but was just looking at him with his mouth open.

"Calm down, Barnaba," begged Gabriel softly, going towards him. Farid backed away. "Mama!" he shouted again, as if out of his mind.

At that moment, far away in Damascus, Claire heard someone

calling her. She looked out of her kitchen window, and then went back to the sink.

"Holy Mary Mother of God, I hope nothing's happened to Farid," she whispered.

144. A Lioness

When Farid regained consciousness his mouth was parched with thirst, and there was a grey veil over his vision. The dormitory where he was lying was empty. His head felt leaden. He tried to sit up, but found that he couldn't move his arms and legs. It took him some time to realize that he was strapped down to the bed. Gradually, he remembered someone seizing him from behind while he was speaking to Gabriel. Then he had been thrown on a bed, and they had given him an injection in his upper arm. He had no idea how many hours or days he had been asleep.

Marcel looked in about midday. "Your mother's here. She's raising hell," he whispered, and then he turned and hurried out again.

Soon after that Gabriel turned up, with a rather more powerful monk whom Farid had never seen before. Gabriel was visibly nervous.

'Your mother has arrived. Did you write her a letter or anything?"

"No," said Farid, as Gabriel's stronger companion loosened the buckles of the straps.

"She's worried, but we don't want her to see you sick in bed. Can you stand up?" asked Gabriel, as if he were genuinely concerned for Farid's mother. Farid straightened up. He still felt dazed, but he had to get to Claire. The monk helped him into his habit and did up the buckles of his sandals. Farid wouldn't let him remove the bandage from his head.

"She's in the visitors' room," said Gabriel, standing at the window and gazing out at the sea, as if to avoid looking at Farid. Then he tried to offer his support, but Farid declined it. He was walking unsteadily, but he wanted to be alone on the way to his mother.

When he opened the door of the visitors' room his heart was

thudding wildly. There was Claire, in a yellow summer dress. "Holy Virgin !" she cried, putting both hands to her mouth as if ashamed of her own horror. Only a glance in the large mirror opposite the door showed Farid what had alarmed his mother so much. With his bandaged head, and his pale, gaunt face, he looked as if he had just come out of an operating theatre.

"Dear heart, what have they done to you?" she cried, embracing Farid. She kissed his eyes, forehead, and cheeks. "Farid, my Farid!" she kept saying as her tears flowed.

"Oh, Mama, it's hell here. I'm not staying a second longer. They ill-treat us. I've been very sick, but the doctor says I'm only pretending, and when I fainted and hurt my head they didn't believe me and didn't take me to a doctor, they strapped me down to the bed," he said, all in a rush, as if afraid someone would come and forbid him to tell his mother the truth. "And they gave me an injection to anesthetize me, Mama."

"My God, what criminals! What vipers!"

"Calm down, madame," interrupted the monk supervising them anxiously. This was the first time Farid had noticed him sitting in the shadows at the far end of the room.

"Calm down?" Claire snapped. "Be quiet and take me to the Abbot this minute. Or shall I go straight to him myself?"

The monk froze, but then moved slowly out of the room. Supporting Farid, Claire went carefully to the stairs with him.

It seemed that the Abbot had just gone out. Several Fathers and Brothers hurried to find other members of the monastery administration. When Claire and Farid arrived in the office they found themselves facing a solid wall of seven or eight men in black habits.

"What have you done to my son? Is this the Farid who came to you?"

"Madame, do please calm down," said Father Istfan. "It was an accident. He hurt his head slightly."

"Accident? You miserable hypocrite! I've been told three different versions within an hour. What do you do to these poor boys? They're children, and you turn them into careworn old men. So you strapped my son to his bed instead of sending him straight to hospital? I'll take you to court for this."

There was an awkward silence. Gabriel's face was grey.

"My son is coming with me, right away. He has to go to hospital, and you'll give him a good report for this year's work."

"But madame, we can't do that. The school year isn't over yet," Gabriel pointed out.

"In that case I'm getting in touch with my cousin in the police to lay charges of child abuse against you. And then you might as well close this monastery down. I have no more time to spare, I'm going to pack my son's case now, and if you haven't brought me that report by the time we leave you must hold yourselves responsible for the consequences. Don't say I didn't warn you," she snapped, and she left the office with Farid, holding him close to her side.

The case was quickly packed. With relief, Farid threw the habit on his bed. He was back in his own clothes again, but he still looked terrible. His sickness had left him thin, so he could still fit into his old trousers, shirt and jacket, but they were all too short in the arms and legs, and made him look like a scarecrow.

Gabriel was standing at the monastery gates with an envelope in his hand. "I hope you'll reconsider this. Barnaba has been an excellent student. Some of the other pupils have been a bad influence on him, but from now on I am sure he'd enjoy life here."

Claire said not a word. She quickly tore the envelope open and read the report. It satisfied her. "Right, there we are," she said, turning to Farid and ignoring Gabriel.

"Goodbye, Barnaba," said the monk quietly, and he turned and walked away.

There was a taxi waiting at the monastery entrance.

145. Going Back

The tiny town of Manara was a fishing port with a few houses, a high street, a school, and a police station. The only hotel, a yellow, single-storey building with small balconies, looked out on the beach. A sign hanging crooked bore the inscription: Hotel Panorama.

"On a clear day you can see Cyprus from here," the hotelier said.

The double room had a balcony, and was plainly furnished but clean, the price so low that you suspected no tourists ever came this way. The little town was not attractive. Everything seemed to be rusting away. The small harbour, built by the Greeks two thousand years ago, was no longer of any importance in modern times, and was gradually falling into ruin. The bay was stony and the coast a steep, dark grey, bleak and rocky landscape. A tiny beach had been laid out in the twenties, but otherwise Manara consisted only of a row of houses along the main street. The inhabitants lived more from passing trade than on what little fish they caught.

There was a story that five hundred years ago a shipwrecked sailor, cast up on this inhospitable coast, had built the lighthouse, *manara* in Arabic, and lived in it, keeping the lamp burning night after night and making sure that it sent enough light out to sea. He was said to have saved many lives. One day he rescued a woman who had jumped overboard from a ship to escape her husband. The woman took a liking to the lighthouse keeper, and the two of them lived happily together until, one stormy night, they rescued another shipwrecked sailor, a sea captain whose ship had broken up in the high seas off the coast. It was the woman's former husband. He had changed a great deal in the meantime, and the woman liked him again. But she didn't want to leave the lighthouse keeper.

So the sea captain opened a restaurant in the bay, close to the harbour, and the woman lived in the lighthouse for three days and at the restaurant for three days. She liked to spend the seventh day by herself.

The present owner of the hotel was a descendant of the captain. In the evening he cooked Claire and Farid a wonderful fish dish, perch with black olives, garlic, white wine, herbs, and olive oil, and he entertained his guests for a long time with his stories.

But something seemed to be weighing on Claire's mind, and kept her from going straight back to Damascus. On the third day, feeling restless, Farid asked her what the matter was.

She looked at him for some time. "I wanted a little peace and calm to prepare you for seeing your father again. I'm extremely glad you're out of that prison, but Elias thinks differently, so he's disappointed. He'd have liked to see you end up a bishop," she explained, a smile hovering around her lips.

"I can set your mind at rest there," said Farid, "I couldn't care less if he's disappointed. He almost ruined my life with his crazy ideas and that monastery. Why doesn't he go and join it himself?" And he laughed at the thought of his father in a black habit, with his head shaved.

"Oh no, he's not as bad as all that. That's what makes it difficult for me. I'm right on your side, but I love him, and I know he's a good man. However, he was very deeply wounded by his own father, and I don't want you to inherit those wounds. Try to understand me. I'd like to keep you from inheriting that Mushtak temper of his and wasting your own precious life fighting him, the way he lost his own happiness and humour and lightness of heart in fighting his father."

Farid did understand Claire, but he was not to be so quickly mollified. He thought his father a coward, pretending to be disappointed instead of admitting his mistake. The hell with him, he thought.

"He may be a good husband to you, Mama, but if men had to pass a test to see if they were suitable to be fathers Elias Mushtak would have failed it." He grinned at his own idea. Claire smiled too, but she shook her head.

"No, no," she said, "I won't have that. You mustn't bear a grudge even if he does make mistakes. He's your father, and he's anxious about you. Disappointed, yes, but when I left he told me to indulge you a little on the way home. Your father can be different from the way you know him."

This conversation was leading nowhere, and to escape such a blind alley Farid asked his mother about Matta.

"Oh, the poor boy," Claire replied, "they left him in a very bad state. He had a terrible time in a mental hospital, where they treated him with electric shocks, and then two months ago he came to Damascus. But crazy as he may be, he knows one thing for certain: he never wants to go back to Mala. He's living with his aunt in Masbak Alley, quite close to us. He's broken psychologically, but physically active. He works running errands for several souvenir shops and a few families," she added.

"What's his aunt like?" asked Farid.

"Nice, very nice. She has no children, and she's glad to have a quiet young man about the house. Who knows, perhaps going crazy saved him. She treats him as lovingly as if he were her own son. In Mala he'd have been living in stables and caves and infested with lice. But now he's indispensable to a number of people, because when Matta does something he does it thoroughly. He's at the door on the dot every morning, asking for his errands, and he carries them out conscientiously."

"What kind of errands?"

"Oh, getting in everything a household needs when the woman of the house doesn't have time for it."

"Are you generous when Matta does something for you?"

"That's another story; he won't take money from me. He says he owes you his life, he'll never forget all your goodness to him, you're his only brother on earth. So I go to see his aunt on the quiet and give her double what he asks from other people, which heaven knows is little enough. What *did* you do for him that was so good?"

"Nothing," he said. "I was nice to him, that's all."

❧

It was late when Claire and Farid returned to the hotel on their fourth evening, feeling exhausted. Claire was looking forward to that evening's fish dinner. Promising aromas were wafting out of the kitchen.

Farid stood on the balcony for a while, looking out at the sea over which so many conquerors had come. The wind had died down. Fishing boats and sailing ships seemed to be glued to the shining surface of the water.

That night's fish dish was a sight to gladden the eyes, it was music to the palate, in short, it was a work of art on which Italians, Greeks, Turks, and Arabs had worked for several centuries.

"Do you begin to feel like going home?" Claire asked later, in the dark. The balcony door was open, and the surging breakers of the sea sent a cool breeze into the room.

"Yes," said Farid. "I'm better. Now I want to see Rana as soon as I can."

"Ah, yes," smiled Claire. "We haven't talked about Rana much, have we? Are you still fond of her?"

"Oh yes. I love her," he replied.

"She loves you too. Your cousin met her at an ice-cream parlour in the Suk al Hamidiye. She flung her arms around Laila and kissed her passionately. Laila felt quite uncomfortable. It was for you, Rana said, and Laila was to pass it all on."

Farid smiled. "It's crazy," he said. "Crazy to be in love with someone and not even able to show it. I feel like a dog who wants to wag his tail and doesn't have one."

"If I know you, you'll be barking out your love for all to hear, so go to sleep now, my handsome little dog."

He turned over, and soon he heard Claire's regular breathing.

BOOK OF GROWTH II

He who reads books in spite of school will become a master.

જી

DAMASCUS, 1956–1960

146. Coming Home

When Farid got out of the taxi with Claire that afternoon he took a deep breath, savouring all the aromas of his street. Bitter orange and lemon trees grew in the interior courtyards of the houses, roses, oleander, and jasmine. He knew he wouldn't be able to see Rana at once, but he decided to get up as early as possible next morning and wait for her on her way to school.

He wanted to call in on his friend Josef, but Claire insisted on him going to see his father at the confectioner's shop first. Farid was afraid of that encounter, but not visiting him would have meant more trouble.

"You wait, he'll be pleased," she said as Farid turned back once more at the door of the house. He strolled slowly off to Bab Tuma. Nothing here had changed. Posters for the candidates in past elections were still stuck to the walls, showing a set of men with artificial smiles on smooth faces that gave nothing away.

The confectioner's shop looked to Farid majestic, but he thought his father seemed smaller than he remembered him. Elias was busy putting the finishing touches to a large order, packing sweetmeats into boxes with the firm's elegant logo.

"Hello, Papa," called Farid, trying hard to seem cheerful. Elias Mushtak looked up, murmured a greeting, and devoted himself to packing up his pastries again. Farid stood waiting, but his father, who was talking to everyone else, didn't deign to look at him a second time.

"Can I help, Papa?" Farid asked at last, helplessly.

"Go over to Salman and fold sheets of card with him," replied Elias, without looking up from the scales on which he had just put a number of filled puff pastries.

Disappointed, Farid joined the young employee in the stockroom and helped to fold twenty more boxes bearing the shop's logo. When they were ready he went back to the shop itself, where Elias was still at work behind the scales. Farid waited at the counter for his father to say something, but he seemed to have been struck mute.

"Tell your mother I won't be home until nine today," he growled at last. "I have to go to a meeting of the confectioners' guild. You needn't wait supper for me."

Farid went home feeling angry. When he told Claire about it tears rose to his eyes, and he hated himself for it. He quickly washed and went to see Josef.

When he knocked, he found that a clever construction now opened the door automatically. Josef could pull a cord up on the second floor that undid the lock of the front entrance. Farid came in and stopped at the foot of the steep staircase. Josef appeared at the top of the stairs and he let out a yell of delight. "Farid's back! Farid's back!" And he ran down the stairs taking three steps at a time.

"You're still alive! Oh, that's marvellous!" he cried, embracing his friend, patting his head, and making incoherent noises like a lunatic. The entire family now appeared in the stairwell. Farid was touched. His own father was cold to him, but the family next door rejoiced at his return as if he were their own son. All of them, Josef's father, mother, aunts, grandmother, and those of his siblings who were still living at home welcomed him heartily. Even Josephine the rebel, who didn't like either Josef or his friends, came and gave him a kiss on the cheek. "Well done," she said. "I was afraid you'd be idiot enough to come back in a black habit and with a long beard." She grinned.

"I have to admit, a few of my brother's friends do have something like intelligence." Then she quickly stepped aside, avoiding a playful punch from her brother.

Josef liberated his friend from the family's clutches and took him to his room, where Farid marvelled at the new shelves, stuffed to the ceiling with books.

"What are the others doing these days?"

"Oh, a lot's changed. Our gang doesn't meet any more. We've grown bigger and older. Hey, I'm really glad you're back. There was hardly anyone left to discuss interesting subjects with me. But now, tell me what you've been up to in the monastery."

※

When Farid went home after a long conversation with his friend, he was surprised by his mother's raised voice, which he could hear even before he went indoors. He had never heard Claire so angry before. "You'll have to decide. It's either me or the whores," she finally shouted. Then all was still.

Elias was extremely nice to Claire at supper, although he still took no notice of Farid. When Farid said goodnight and rose to go to bed, Claire followed him to the bathroom.

"What's going on?" he asked anxiously.

"Don't ask. I'll tell you the whole story some day. But don't worry, I have everything under control. All right?" She put her hand out to him.

Farid kissed his mother's cheek, pressed her hand, and whispered in conspiratorial tones, "Well, watch out for yourself, Princess, and if the dragon roars too angrily, wake me up so that I can face him instead of you."

Only thirteen years later did Claire tell him that his return from the monastery had brought about a great change in her. At the time, Elias was having countless affairs with other women, and she was constantly afraid of losing him. But then he made two bad mistakes in quick succession. He had endangered Farid's life for the sake of a vain whim. And because he was disappointed that his son wasn't

BOOK OF GROWTH II

going to be a theologian after all, he went to a brothel on the evening when his wife and son came home. That had horrified and humiliated Claire so much that suddenly she wasn't afraid any more. While Farid was out visiting Josef, she had changed her clothes and marched off to confront the businesslike widow who welcomed rich men to her apartment and provided them with young prostitutes. Claire knew that Elias had been spending every other evening there for quite some time. The lady, a plump and bloated figure, had been arrogant and vulgar and tried to turn her away, but after two sharp slaps in the face she began wailing and begging Claire to understand her, she had four children to feed. Claire stayed where she was in the doorway, shouting, "Fetch my husband, or I'll make such a scene that none of your customers will ever set foot in this house again." There was nothing the widow could do but go and find the sheepish Elias.

So that had been his meeting of the confectioners' guild. Claire wasn't going to keep quiet a moment longer, and she issued Elias with an ultimatum. If he ever touched another woman again, she said, she would go away overnight with Farid without any further warning. Elias gave in. The shock had frightened him badly, and from that day on he was as faithful as a dog.

147. Josephine

"We thought you were in Paradise. We expected you back here any day to bless us, a young bishop and so on," said Josef a few days later. "That's what my old man heard from your father at a meeting of the Catholic Men's League. You'd love it in the monastery and get to be incredibly clever, your father said, you were bound to be a cardinal within fifteen years. Suddenly my old man felt all envious and looked around, and who should his eye fall on but Josephine? Well, he thought, better a nun or an abbess than an extra woman about the house."

"So what did she say?"

"When my father said a career as a nun would be just the thing for her, and he'd already made some inquiries at the Carmelite convent, maybe she could try it for a couple of years, nuns lived like princesses, and so on and so forth. Josephine just stared at him in silence. Next day he repeated his wish, politely, which isn't usual with my father. You know him, he's gruff and harsh with everyone except my mother. Josephine just stared at him again and calmly ate her salad. And when she'd finished, she said in a very soft voice, 'Papa, if you start on about that again I'm converting to Islam. I've made my own inquiries about that, and it's dead easy.' Wham! Crash! K.O. in the second round! That went home. Josephine went on spooning up her rice and beans. My powerful father the ex-boxer was left totally bewildered. My mother fitted his lower jaw back in place to keep the flies from shitting in his mouth."

Josef was still laughing when the doorbell rang. "Oh, there you are, Matta!" cried his aunt Afifa. Farid had already tried to visit Matta, but he'd been out of luck.

"I was beginning to think you wouldn't be coming today. Did you get everything?" the boys heard Aunt Afifa call out in the corridor.

"All here," replied Matta. Farid ran straight out of the room, and saw his friend coming upstairs heavily laden with cartons and bags. He carefully put the things down on the floor.

"Mary Mother of God protect you," cried Afifa, who admired Matta's strength. As she tried to pick up the big sack of rice herself, Matta took it from her hand. "I'll do that," he said, carrying the large, full sack into the kitchen after Josef's aunt. Farid saw that his head was covered with stubble and scars, and there were two shiny burn marks on his temples.

When Matta came out of the kitchen, Farid went up to him, and Matta's mouth opened in a grin of surprise.

"Brother," he whispered, pointing to Farid. He said no more, although he was visibly moved. Afifa anxiously accompanied him downstairs.

"Why does that crazy boy call you brother?" asked Josef when they were alone again.

"Why? Well, everyone gets called brother," replied Farid with some annoyance, because Arabs use the word *achi*, meaning "my brother", all the time instead of just saying "you" or "my dear fellow".

"He gave it a special sort of emphasis, though," said Josef, shrugging.

148. Matta's Ordeal

Matta remembered hardly anything, except that Farid had given him warm clothes, stout boots, money, and provisions. His flight from the monastery had ended suddenly and in great confusion. The police were already waiting at the checkpoint on the main road. When he saw them he jumped out of the bus window, stumbled, and fell. His father, seething with fury, was waiting for him at the police station. After that it was all a blank.

He woke up in a shabby bed. His head hurt, but he could sit up. The walls of the room were smeared with graffiti and dirt. There was a white door and a narrow, barred window. Everything here was strange, so obviously he wasn't in the monastery's detention cell. He cautiously stood on the only chair, and found himself looking down at a park where men were walking around, laughing or talking to themselves. One of them kept banging his head against the trunk of a birch tree.

What is this place? he wondered. There was a knock at the door, and a young male nurse in a grubby white coat came in to put a bowl of vegetable soup and a piece of bread on the small table. The man's right eye was fixed and motionless, like the eye of a slaughtered sheep. "Feeling better now?" he asked, and then he was gone again.

Matta felt extraordinarily weary. He saw himself in the middle of a flock of snow-white sheep and lambs, playing a flute. The lambs looked up inquisitively, while the sheep kept their heads bent and went on grazing. Aida appeared in the distance, with a blue bundle full of provisions. As she came closer she stopped, and her expression became thoughtful, almost sad. "Why are you herding pigs? Surely you always wanted to be a shepherd, keeping sheep and lambs?"

"What pigs?" asked Matta, and then he looked and saw, to his horror, that his flock really had turned into a herd of pigs, all grinning at him. He woke up with a bad taste in his mouth. He couldn't swallow, his throat was too dry.

A red-haired young nurse came into the room. Without a word, she gave him two tablets and a sip of water. The medicine tasted bitter. When the nurse went out again she was marching like a soldier.

No one spoke to him. Where was Aida? He shouted for her, but it was the male nurse with the fixed eye who came in. At least he was kind and didn't beat him, like Brother John, but smiled. He held Matta firmly, saying that Aida was far away and couldn't hear him. Matta wouldn't eat any more. He was convinced that Aida had been killed. The male nurse tried to calm him, without success. "Bring her here, then, if she's alive," Matta shouted at him. The male nurse did not reply, but looked fixedly at him again. Only later did Matta realize that the man had a glass eye.

Matta asked the red-haired nurse why he had been brought here, but she didn't answer, just turned and marched away. Perhaps she's a mute, thought Matta.

He was allowed to spend an hour in the gardens to get some fresh air, and met some odd people there. A wild-eyed young man in pyjamas approached him. "I wrote the Bible. I did, I was the one who wrote it!" he claimed. Another man took Matta's sleeve and drew him behind an old birch tree. "Listen carefully. I know the secret of the factory," he whispered. His teeth were just black stumps.

"What factory?" asked Matta.

"The underground factory where they make human beings. Oh yes, I know about it, and if the United Nations find out the whole world will explode. Crash! Bang! But don't tell anyone." As he spoke, he kept looking anxiously around. Saliva dribbled from his mouth. Then he stood to attention and saluted. "Step forward!" he called. A man in military uniform with a twig tucked under his arm was coming towards them. "How's it going at the Front?" asked the uniformed man, making the V for victory sign.

"Good morning, Sir Churchill," said the man who knew the great secret of the factory.

Later, Matta learned that the man addressed as "Churchill" had once been an army officer, but an explosion had blown his wits away.

ॐ

Two days later, the male nurse came to take him to a large room containing a huge, dark desk. The notice on the door said "Dr Salam".

A dwarf with a bald patch and a red tie was sitting at the table. When Matta saw him he thought the man looked funny, and chuckled. Then he laughed louder and louder, wagging his forefinger at the male nurse to show that he'd better watch the dwarf, because he was about to do a handstand on the desk. However, the man with the glass eye was not impressed. The mute red-haired nurse was there too, standing motionless by the door.

Matta felt a painful pressure in his bladder. It wasn't his fault; they had forgotten to let him go to the bathroom that day. He saw a potted palm in a corner of the room, and went over to pee in the container, but he hadn't finished when a slap in the face knocked him down. Lying on the floor, he saw the male nurse standing over him, shouting something. Matta went on peeing. The jet of urine rose in a small curve and rained down on his trouser leg. The male nurse lifted him, stood him up, and tucked his penis back inside his flies.

The dwarf didn't do a handstand, but went red in the face and shouted something incomprehensible. The mute red-haired nurse was already bringing a bucket and a cloth. They all calmed down again. Then they laid Matta on a bed at the other end of the room. He was terrified. The male nurse put broad leather straps over his shoulders, stomach, legs, and ankles, and tightened them. Matta felt even more frightened. He could hardly breathe, and thought they had wound a cocoon around him. As a child, he had watched spiders anesthetizing the flies they caught by stinging them, and then wrapping them in silken threads.

"I'm not a fly," he told the male nurse gravely.

The man smiled. "Nor am I." Somehow that was reassuring.

"I want to go home," said Matta, thinking of an extraordinary moment one day at dawn, when he had been alone with his uncle's sheep. The sun was just rising above the mountains to bathe the hilly landscape in light. The sheep were grazing, and he sat down under an old tree. At that moment, a butterfly tried to emerge from its cocoon which was wet with dew. The butterfly slowly worked its way out. It was a very large insect, hanging upside down. After a while it spread its brightly coloured wings and went on hanging there, swaying in the morning breeze, as if to let its wings dry, and then it glided weightlessly into the air.

The dwarf was standing close to Matta's head. The mute nurse put a pair of forceps to his temples. The silence in the room laid a cold hand on his heart. Lightning flashed through his brain, he felt his head hitting hard rocks, stars sparkled before his eyes. It was like the time when he had slipped while climbing and a small rock fall came down on him. He clung to the bed and screamed.

When the nurse took the forceps away, his temples were burning, and he felt thick, warm liquid flowing over his mouth.

"He's bleeding," said the woman. Those were the first words she had spoken.

"Tell me your name," said the man with the glass eye in a friendly tone. "Mine is Adnan. What are you called?"

He wanted to reply, "Matta", but his tongue would not obey him.

The dwarf spoke to the woman, whom he addressed as Kadira, and she put the forceps to his temples again.

There was another flash of lightning. This time it felt like the sting of the scorpion that had once bitten his forefinger when he incautiously turned over a large rock. Fiery fluid chased through his veins, like lava looking for a way out. He flapped about like a slaughtered chicken and screamed, but soundlessly. The man with the glass eye put a piece of rubber between his teeth. Matta was falling apart, and felt nothing more.

He woke up in his little room, with his throat and his temples burning. The friendly man with the glass eye had left him a jug of water on the bedside table.

Two hours later, Adnan came back, helped him to get dressed, and led him to the hospital gates, where he gave him an envelope, explaining that it contained his papers. Then he pressed Matta's hand. "You can go home now, your voice will soon recover," he said, at the same time starting off after a patient trying to get out into the street in his pyjamas.

Matta ran and ran until, hours later, he reached his aunt's house in Ananias Alley. The sight of him horrified her. She wept and hugged him. "It's all right, nothing can hurt you here, dear boy," she said. Although Matta was enormously relieved, he was still mute. His tongue wouldn't obey him, and the sounds that came from his throat were like the hissing of a snake.

When his parents arrived two days later, he ran away. He roamed the rooftops of the Old Town, eating whatever he could find, sleeping in abandoned sheds, and didn't come back for three days, an hour after his parents had left. His aunt flung her arms around him and told him she'd been afraid he might have fallen, or someone might have caught him on the rooftops and told the police. She said she'd asked her sister Nasibe and her brother-in-law not to come back for a while.

For the first time in his life, Matta realized that there was someone else in the world, besides Farid and Aida, who cared for him.

149. Rana

The muezzins' chorus woke him. Farid was no longer used to the chanting of over two hundred sheikhs at once, calling the faithful to prayer from their minarets early in the morning, each of them trying to extend the range of his own *Allahu Akbar* as far as possible.

He knew that his father woke at this hour, spent half an hour reading the Bible that always lay open on his bedside table, and then got up and went into the bathroom. Quarter of an hour later he was in the drawing room drinking black tea with milk but no sugar, and talking to Claire for a little while. Only then did he leave the house, singing quietly.

That was always at six-thirty. Elias walked fast; he was freshly shaved, perfumed, and wore a clean white shirt and dark blue trousers. He had large stocks of both.

For some time now, all he had done at the shop was to weigh out the precise quantities of ingredients, leaving everything else to his employees, who thought very highly of him. He was popular with them for his cheerfulness. Claire often said that life with her husband would be like Paradise if only he were as cheerful at home as in his business.

In all those years Elias never once managed to go from Saitun Alley to his confectioner's shop, just outside Bab Tuma, without stopping to crack a joke, exchange the latest gossip, or drink the coffee that one of the tradesmen along the way just happened to have ordered for him. But at seven on the dot he was always raising the iron grille over the shop front as he counted the chimes ringing out from the church of St Anthony of Padua, which rose above all the surrounding buildings.

At seven on the dot today, however, Farid was also out and about, dressed in summery white and boarding the Number 5 bus to the Salihiye quarter, where he planned to wait for Rana outside her school.

He had never seen so many of the military in the city before. There were armed soldiers everywhere, outside the banks, the post office, the radio station, at all the major intersections.

And suddenly here was Rana. She came running around the corner and collided with him. When she had recovered from the shock of it, she stammered, her eyes shining, "You? What are you doing here?"

"Looking for you," he said, holding her hand tight.

"I don't have my watch on today. I thought I was going to be late," replied Rana, almost breathlessly. Farid seemed to have grown taller and more masculine.

"When can we see each other?" he asked, quickly kissing her cheek.

"Here in half an hour's time," she replied, looking around shyly. "I'm going to feel unwell the moment I get to school and ask permission to go home." She pressed his hand, and he stroked her cheek.

"See you soon," she called, and walked on slowly, turning back again and again.

It was over an hour before Rana came back. "It took longer than I expected, because the maths teacher we have for the first two lessons was away. So everything was chaotic, but now the time's all ours," she said triumphantly.

Rana was as tall as he was now, and wore her hair tied back in a ponytail. Her eyes seemed to him larger; her curves were not those of a girl any more, but the figure of a slender woman.

"Where are we going?" asked Farid.

"To Aunt Mariam's apartment. My parents are in Beirut with her and Aunt Amira's whole family. They're going to celebrate the engagement of Aunt Amira's son Samuel."

"Your parents are away too?"

"Yes, and thank God they've even taken Jack with them, because he and Samuel are friends. Monsters always like getting together, so Mama took Jack out of school for a week."

"Samuel? What Samuel? The one who murdered your aunt?" Farid inquired.

"Yes, that's him." Rana hesitated for a moment. "What kind of family is happy to have that spoiled murderer for a son-in-law I can't imagine. He's been thrown out of all the schools he ever went to, but his father's connections got him a job as a sales rep with some kind of pharmaceuticals company."

Rana took him home with her, and while he sat in her parents' drawing room drinking cold lemonade she went to change her clothes. When she came back she looked completely different. She was wearing a summer dress instead of the ugly school uniform, and now her hair lay loose on her shoulders, thick and blue-black. Rana perched her sunglasses flirtatiously on her nose.

He gave a wolf-whistle, laughing. "You could be straight out of a movie."

She sat down on his lap and flung her arms around him. "Well, now I want to kiss you and go back into the movie. It's called *A Thousand and One Nights of Dreams Come True*. Or were you away longer than that?"

"Yes, longer," he said, kissing her nose and then her lips. He took her sunglasses off again. She kept perfectly still. Her cheeks flushed pink.

The colour of love, he thought, and kissed her mouth.

"Let's go to Aunt Mariam's. I have to water her flowers every day, I can even stay there overnight if I want. I don't feel comfortable here. It all smells of my family, it's not good enough for you. I feel as if the furniture, the radio, the bookshelves and the books were all watching us. Come on," she said, kissing him on the forehead and jumping up.

150. Three Days of Dreams Come True

When Rana's parents came back they were surprised to find their daughter so happy, but they were still too elated after the big engagement party to entertain any real suspicions. Only Jack, out of sheer spite, came dangerously close to the truth with his dig at her. "She always gets pink cheeks when she's been meeting that rat of a Mushtak," he said.

"Oh, come on, the old goat's son is a novice at a monastery in the north now," his mother pointed out.

Rana didn't have to strain her ears to overhear their conversation in the kitchen. Jack was bellowing, and her mother too was shouting to make herself heard, because the kerosene stoves used for cooking in Damascus made a terrible noise. Rana went into the bathroom. Her cheeks were red.

Three days with her beloved Farid. She had felt his breath on her skin from morning to night. His voice had found its way deep into her heart. His hands on her body were so gentle.

He had gone through so much, and his love was so great, making him cry out for her so often! She had told him about her own nights, when she couldn't sleep and there was no one she could talk to about her feelings.

They spent all day in her aunt's apartment, cooking and eating properly with knives and forks, but sitting at the big table naked. They kept going back to lie down on the bed, playing under the covers like two small children. When Farid embraced Rana she lost herself in him.

"For a girl who's off school sick," said Farid, gasping for air, "you're remarkably fit and well!" And they went on tussling with each other.

"I've had plenty of time to think about our love," said Rana, lying across the bed with her head on Farid's stomach. "I'm myself only when I'm either with you or completely alone. Others complain of loneliness if they're on their own for five minutes together. I like being alone, and I long for you and your love, I'm addicted to it." Rana paused for a moment, turned over on her front, worked her way up to Farid's face and kissed him until she felt dizzy.

"I thought of you every day," Farid told her. "I was desperate, because I didn't think I'd ever get out of there again. But now I'd do anything to stay close to you." He paused briefly. "And I never want to set foot in that horrible village Mala again."

"Let me hold your hand," said Rana, because a memory had come into her mind, and it frightened her. About a year ago the elder brother of a friend of Jack's began calling to see them rather often, always making out it was just coincidence. Her mother pretended to be dim, and often left Rana alone with this man. He was courteous, so she was all the more shocked when he told her one day that he'd like to sleep with her. She replied that she was only just fifteen and she wanted to study. "Studying just makes women ugly," he said. "It would be a pity to lose your femininity."

Rana left him sitting there and went straight to the kitchen to find her mother and Jack.

"That man's randy. I can't stand him. How can you let him tell me what I ought to do and what not? I don't want to meet a man looking out for a wife, and I'll tell Papa so this evening."

"Silly cow! How about being civil to a guest?" said her brother angrily, making haste to take his acquaintance a coffee by way of mollifying him.

There was a scene that evening, but this time her father was clearly on her side. If Jack ever got to be half as good at school as Rana, he said, then he would allow him to be the judge of whether or not girls should study. The fact was, he added, that he had to pay good money for special coaching for her brother, and he still wasn't getting anywhere at school.

When Rana remembered all this she felt afraid. Suppose her father weakened when the next man came along? And what would Farid do if he was urged to marry another woman?

"Let me hold your hand," she said again, in a voice that shook, "and promise me never, whatever happens, to doubt my love for a single second."

"I promise," replied Farid, with no idea why Rana's voice was suddenly faltering. He was sure that no power on earth could part them, and held her hand tightly as if to crush her fears. Then he kissed Rana, and only now did he taste her tears.

"Crying?"

"Whenever I want our love to give you the strength for something, you give me back more than I could ever have dreamed of. I'm crying for happiness, that's all."

151. Laila

It was unbearably hot. Farid had slept badly that night and didn't want anything to eat at lunch-time. Claire went back to the bedroom for her siesta. He lay down too, but he couldn't sleep.

He picked up the weekly magazine that his parents always read: revelations of Stalin's crimes in Russia ... Archbishop Makarios, leader of the independence movement in Cyprus, arrested for arms smuggling and deported to the Seychelles ... world heavyweight champion Rocky Marciano retires unbeaten ... American actress Grace Kelly marries Prince Rainier of Monaco ... Italian actress Sophia Loren praised for her role in the film *Woman of the River*. Farid was startled by the Italian star's resemblance to Laila.

"Laila," he whispered. He badly wanted to see her, but he had to wait for Claire to wake up before he could find out his cousin's new address. The siesta hour had never seemed as long as it did today. When the turtledoves began cooing again, he breathed a sigh of relief and looked at the time. It was just after three.

Two hours later he was in the bus. Just before the eastern gate, he suddenly saw Matta pulling his heavily laden handcart along. It was a large one with two heavy wheels, and a leather strap at the front that Matta had put over his shoulder. Packages, sacks, canisters and several pots and pans were fastened to its large load area with cords.

The bus driver was thoughtful enough to slow down until the street widened and there was room for Matta to let the bus go by. He waved cheerfully to the driver and stopped for a moment's rest.

When Farid knocked on Laila's door, she opened it and froze in amazement. "Farid," she whispered. "Wherever have you come from?" She was wearing a sleeveless beige house-dress, and a red dress on

BOOK OF GROWTH II

which she was probably working at the moment was flung over her arm. Her face was prettier than Sophia Loren's, and her slender figure surprised Farid. He remembered her as larger.

"Come in," said Laila, hugging him. "My God, how you've grown! I'll soon need a ladder to kiss you." She closed the door and stood still for a moment in the shady entrance, watching Farid, who had gone ahead and was now waiting for her in the inner courtyard of the little house.

The house was in a side street behind the Al-Amir cinema. The dressmaker's workshop was on the first floor, and two other women were at work there, one making a long dress, the other ironing a white blouse.

"I have just too many orders at the moment," groaned Laila, taking Farid into a small reception area and from there into the tiny dining room cum kitchen.

Her husband's spacious, well-lit music room was on the second floor. Several violins stood in a glass-fronted cupboard, and old stringed instruments from every continent in the world hung on the walls, making the place look like a museum. Otherwise the room was empty.

From the music room you could see across the courtyard and into the bedroom, which was in total chaos. The large room, with a window looking out on the main road, contained a broad bed, a couch, and a massive wardrobe. The bed was unmade, and dirty laundry lay about everywhere. No one had cleaned the big bathroom for ages. On the third floor there was a guest room with a bathroom, a lumber room, and a picturesque terrace with a table and chairs and a jasmine trained to grow over it.

Farid was surprised to find that the question of why Laila had never told him about her wedding suddenly seemed entirely unimportant. He felt oddly happy just to be near her, and that happiness had wiped all the resentment away from his heart, like a sponge.

"Tell me about those birds of ill omen at the monastery. You can say anything here without being censored!" she said.

He described his life in the monastery at length, she kept asking for details, and he never even noticed her employees leaving, or dusk falling outside. Laila filled his world with curiosity and laughter.

"Ah, so who do we have here? Let me guess. You must be my wife's beloved Farid." It was Simon, Laila's husband. Farid hadn't heard anyone coming.

"Goodness, how did you get in?" asked Laila, herself surprised.

"Like most people," said Simon, smiling. He put his violin down on a corner table and went towards Farid. "Through the front door." He offered his hand.

"I imagined you much more handsome, from your cousin's paeans of praise," he said, looking Farid up and down critically. "The nose could be a little smaller, the mouth and eyes a little larger. And more flesh on your bones wouldn't be a bad idea," he added.

"My husband," Laila interrupted, turning to Farid to console him, "ought to have been a butcher. He likes fat meat, but don't let him bother you, you're the most handsome man in all Damascus."

"So what do you know about handsome men?" asked Simon. Farid felt that the man had something cold about him, and shook the proffered hand rather more heartily than he really wished to.

"And for you Laila drops everything, even her work and my supper, am I right?"

"I'd do anything for Farid, but there's plenty of food in the fridge."

Soon the three of them were eating and talking together. Simon didn't like monasteries or the Church. He had spent three years in a boarding school as a child, and called it a madhouse.

After supper he changed, took his violin, and left the house to play in a concert.

"What's he like to you?" asked Farid.

"Delightful," said Laila. "Once you're used to his sarcasm he's wonderful."

Farid felt distrustful of Simon, although he didn't know why. When he left, Laila barred his way. "Well? Are you going without a hug? Without a goodbye kiss, my lord Cardinal?"

"By no means, my lady Abbess," he replied, grinning. "If my father heard us, he'd disinherit me." And he kissed Laila on the cheek.

Laila took his face in her hands, closed her eyes, and gave him a long kiss on the lips. "That's what I call kissing, my lord Cardinal."

152. Women Visiting

Those were happy months for Farid just after his return. He didn't have to go to school again until autumn, after the three-month summer vacation, and then he could go straight into the ninth grade. His reports were excellent, and the elite school in Saitun Alley attended by all his friends was happy to take its former student back. His father was on the finance committee of the Catholic Church, which made decisions on the fate of the school.

Oddly enough, Farid didn't find it difficult to get used to his father's indifference to him. Elias never asked about him or his plans. There was nothing between them any more apart from civil greetings. Claire was upset, but Farid pacified her. "There are advantages, because now he's leaving me alone I do feel something like respect for him and his achievements. He's useless as a father, but a fine man in many other ways."

Claire laughed with relief. "I've known that for a long time. That's why I love him."

⁂

One day, Farid was lying on a shabby old couch in what he called the loft, reading old French magazines that his mother had kept. The loft had been his favourite room for as long as he could remember. It was light and airy, with large glazed windows, and occupied the whole east side of the house. The kitchen and pantry were directly below it.

Everything his parents had ever decided to put away was stored there, and he could sit for hours on end reading, rummaging about, rediscovering old metal and wooden toys, putting them together again. There was always a piece missing, but it all had a charm that appealed to him.

So he was lying on the couch with its worn cover, reading an account of the wedding of Princess Elizabeth of Great Britain in a French magazine from the forties. He felt tired. Josef had been telling him about his plans last night, and they sat up until two in the morning.

Farid fell asleep. The last thing he heard was his mother at work in the kitchen below him. She was making a large tabbouleh salad, because she expected her women friends to come visiting that afternoon. Farid intended to go to the cinema while they were there. The performance began at three.

When he woke up the heat had died down, but he still didn't feel like getting up, and he couldn't go to the cinema now anyway, since it was already quarter past three. He lay there and thought of those three days with Rana. Suddenly he heard Madeleine greeting his mother as she sat down on one of the chairs arranged around the fountain. The courtyard was shady now, and Claire had sprayed all the flowers and the ground with water.

Farid stayed where he was, and smiled when he heard her telling Madeleine that she had prepared everything and then even had an hour's siesta. Farid had gone to the cinema, she added, without saying goodbye. He probably hadn't wanted to disturb her.

Next to arrive was the midwife Nadime, whom his mother welcomed particularly warmly, followed by several other women. Farid couldn't identify them by their voices, but he was sure that Suleiman's mother, Salma, was among them, and Antoinette's mother, Hanan, too.

Claire offered lemonade chilled with ice, and after a while Madeleine said, "Let's hear what those fine fingers of yours can do with the strings." The others backed her up.

"Very well, I'll play, but you must all sing," replied the woman addressed, and there was silence. The music she conjured from her lute delighted Farid. She sang an old love song, and the other women softly joined in the refrain. It was a conversation between a man and his lover, who bravely seeks him out at night because she longs for him. Unusual poem, thought Farid, who was more familiar with the reverse situation, when men hung around outside their lovers' houses by night.

The women went on singing for a while, then the tabbouleh was brought in, and Claire served diluted, ice-cold arrack with it. "But don't drink too much, or your husbands will blame me," she said.

"That's not my problem," said the midwife Nadime, who was a widow.

"None for me, thank you," cried another woman. "This is Wednesday, and if my dear husband wants to suck my breasts he'll get tipsy."

The women ate tabbouleh, drank arrack, and laughed more and more often. Farid couldn't follow the thread of the conversation any more. It was all just laughter and confused scraps of sentences.

How long it went on he couldn't say, but at last he heard his mother clear away the tabbouleh dish, stack the empty plates, and carry them into the kitchen. She was gone for only a short time, for she had prepared large bowls of roasted, salted pistachios, peanuts, melon and pumpkin seeds well in advance. There was silence again. All Farid heard was the faint cracking of nuts.

"My turn now," Farid heard one of the women say, and the others agreed. For a brief moment he thought a man had joined the party, but then he realized that the woman was imitating her husband's voice. The others applauded, and then Madeleine took her turn, and so did the others, all of them mocking their husbands' comical behaviour. His own mother wasn't at all bad at imitating one of Elias's furious outbursts.

After this role-play, Claire brought in coffee with cardamom. The fragrance rose to the sky. Her guests sipped with relish, and whispered together. For a while they were all talking at once. Suddenly Farid heard Madeleine's voice. "Yes, I do love hands. Rimon's hands were once so soft. His fingers were as long as a pianist's and smooth as marble. They had strength and elegance in them, tenderness and power. Now they've suffered from working with stone all these years. They're so callused that I hate to look at them, let alone feel them on my skin. No heartfelt feeling comes through those horny hands, no warmth, nothing. And oddly enough the only person I think of when I feel his hands is my father, which takes all my desire away. So I ask him not to touch me during our love play. He's good and sticks to that rule, and if he forgets, well, he gets nothing from me for two weeks."

"And he puts up with it?" asked Claire. Madeleine's answer was lost in the general laughter. Confused voices followed. They were talking about cunning tricks, but Farid couldn't make much of the fragmentary conversation he heard. He went on reading his magazine, and the women seemed far away. At last he heard the midwife Nadime exclaim, in mock horror, that it was nearly six already, and the party broke up.

"Come with me," Madeleine asked his mother. "There's something I want to show you."

Soon after that the women left the house. Claire went with her friend, and of course she didn't come home at once, since she had to have a coffee first.

When she did return it was just after six-thirty. Farid was sitting by the fountain, cracking a few leftover pistachios.

"Oh, you're back," said Claire, beaming. He nodded. "How was the movie?"

"Oh, well ... too much talk, not enough action," he replied, feeling that that was a fair summary.

153. Saki's Flight

Damascus was full of life again. There was a new democracy in power, governing with an elected parliament, and the newspapers were making full use of the freedom they had regained. But at the same time, the Syrians noticed the radical changes being made by the now very popular President Satlan of Egypt. His speeches were followed with mingled enthusiasm and dislike in Damascus, Baghdad, Algiers and Mecca. He had a wonderful voice. People heard it on the radio and said it was as captivating as the voice of the famous Egyptian singer Um Kulthum. Satlan had wit and charisma.

No Syrian politician could compete with him. Even those who never discussed politics suddenly began abusing the British, just because Satlan condemned them.

At home, Farid couldn't even mention Satlan's fine voice, for to Elias and Claire the Egyptian was a dangerous demagogue who took money from Arabs and stirred up mob feeling against Christians. Elias even claimed that Satlan had once been a member of the Muslim Brotherhood, and attacked the British and the French only because they were Christians.

Farid woke up every morning feeling curious about life these days. Those three years in the monastery seemed to him like a long, deep sleep.

Matta seemed to be getting better all the time, returning to life. He came to find out what errands Claire wanted him to do, stood in the courtyard awkwardly when he came back, and usually wouldn't eat or drink anything. But sometimes Claire persuaded him to take some refreshment. Then he would sit by the fountain as he drank, and he always said, "Thank you, brother," when he saw Farid. After a while he would rise with a smile and leave.

Matta was very much on Farid's mind, but he was saddened by what he heard from Josef about his Jewish friend Saki. Saki had turned quieter and quieter over the last year, said hardly a word, and when he did speak he gave nothing away. His words were just covering up for his silence. Then he suddenly disappeared. He was less that fifteen at the time. He planned to go south to Israel, and had hung around the Golan Heights hoping to get out of the country with the smugglers who knew all the paths there, but someone gave him away, and he was arrested.

After that Saki, once a lively boy, went through hell. He had been accused of espionage, he was tortured and interrogated, and he wasn't set free until a year later. Now he was distrustful; he never came out into Abbara Alley any more, and he mixed only with other Jews. He prayed a great deal and worked for his father, whose anxiety about his son had made him sick. Josef said that over a thousand Jews out of what was only a tiny Jewish community anyway had already fled to Israel by way of Cyprus or Istanbul.

"The funny thing is," he said thoughtfully, "the government says the Jews are well off in Syria, and life in Israel is miserable, but then why do so many Jews leave all their worldly goods behind and flee to Israel? Either they're total idiots or our government is lying."

Saki had fled for the second time just before Farid's return in the spring of 1956, this time with his sister Sarah and forged papers, making for Tel Aviv by way of Beirut and Paris. His parents had been questioned and humiliated, but they hadn't known anything about his plans.

154. Turmoil

"Suleiman and I are going to the New Town," Josef told Farid one day. "Students demonstrate in the streets every day there."

"What's it like, demonstrating?"

"Oh, people shout slogans and carry banners saying what they want, and pretty soon it's reported all over the world."

"And," added Suleiman, his eyes gleaming, "some time or other there's bound to be a clash, scuffles break out between opposing sides, and it turns into a street battle. Sometimes it spreads all over the New Town. I've been there three times and joined in." He rubbed his hands with glee.

"How do you mean, joined in? On whose side?" asked Farid

"Suleiman doesn't mind," said Josef, with a dig at his friend, "just so long as he can hand out punishment."

The demonstration was impressive. Farid followed the procession, Josef and Suleiman were right in the middle of it. Josef was shouting slogans along with everyone else. Farid couldn't help laughing at his friend. He'd hardly have known him. Josef of all people, that thin, much-indulged boy, leaping in the air, clapping and yelling as he demanded instant union with Egypt. Good heavens, thought Farid in surprise. Suleiman didn't shout at all. He ran around more like an American Indian in a Western, expecting trouble and always looking out for any kind of threat. But there was no counter-demonstration, and the police provided an escort for the demonstrators and were extremely friendly.

Two men, much struck by Josef's show of spirit, raised the thin boy on their shoulders so that he could be heard better. Josef's voice cracked, sounding as hoarse as a young rooster's. Farid applauded, the men chanted Josef's slogan.

A week later Satlan made a passionate speech denouncing the British and the French who, he said, were trying to blackmail him, and suddenly, to the surprise of millions of listeners, he addressed the demonstrators in Damascus directly. "My brothers in Damascus," he said, proudly repeating their slogans, which he claimed encouraged him in Cairo to promote union between Egypt and Syria.

Josef couldn't sleep that night. He regarded Satlan as a new Saladin who would unite the Arabs into a rich and powerful nation.

That day in the summer of 1956 people streamed out of all the surrounding streets, houses, schools, and shops. Motor traffic came to a standstill until the procession of demonstrators reached the Square of Seven Fountains.

Farid was amazed by the atmosphere. He had never known anything like it: thousands of people all shouting the name of Satlan, praising him to the skies. When the procession passed Rana's house, he felt his heart beat faster. What would she say if she saw him? He didn't know.

None of her family appeared at the windows.

৯

Later, when Josef, Suleiman and Farid were on the bus going home, Josef was hoarse and exhausted. Suleiman was disappointed because it had all passed off so peacefully.

Wanting to cheer him up, Farid asked how Lamia was. He knew the two of them had been in love since they were seven, but he wasn't aware that he was probing a deep wound. Only two weeks earlier Lamia had been married against her will, and had moved to the north with her husband.

155. Suleiman and Lamia

Lamia had lived in the house next door, separated just by a wall from Suleiman's family. His sister Aida always mocked the couple. "My brother is a chocolate addict," she once said. "If Jesus Christ asked him for a piece, he'd convert to Islam straight away. But he'll give Lamia a whole chocolate bar and watch lovingly as she lets piece after piece melt in her mouth."

When they were small, of course, Suleiman and Lamia had played together, but all that changed when she was twelve. Suddenly she wasn't allowed to visit him, and he couldn't touch her or give her presents any more.

He was in despair, but Azar had a bright idea: they could bore a hole in the wall between the two buildings, and then talk to each other or exchange letters through the small opening. The mud-brick wall was thin, so it wasn't difficult to bore the hole. A trickier business was finding a place on both sides of it where they wouldn't be disturbed. In the end they decided on the lavatory on Lamia's side, while Suleiman had to disappear into a small broom cupboard under the stairs. He let his sister into the secret so that she could cover up for him if necessary. In spite of her sharp tongue, Aida could always be relied on.

All went well for months. But one day Lamia's elder brother Ihsan discovered the hole, waited until his sister went to the lavatory, stood outside the door and eavesdropped on her love-talk. She was given a beating, and the hole was bricked up.

For a while Lamia's best friend Nadia carried messages between the lovers when they arranged secret meetings in the New Town. But Nadia's father saw his daughter three times speaking privately to Suleiman, and suspected that she herself had a relationship with the son of the consul's chauffeur, now that Lamia's parents had ended his affair with their own daughter.

Nadia was brave and didn't give the lovers away, even when she was beaten. In his room, Suleiman could hear her screams after every blow, and wept with rage.

In her desperation, Lamia now turned to her favourite brother Usama as a messenger. He was only five, and she gave him a piece of chocolate for every letter he delivered. She thought he was a guileless child, but he began blackmailing his sister and had soon drained her of all her pocket money. When she couldn't pay any more he gave her away. This time her parents didn't beat her or lock her up, but in secret they frantically looked around for a man who would marry her even though she was so young. Soon they succeeded, and found a teacher urgently searching for a wife. He was twenty years older than Lamia, and came from the north.

At the sight of the young girl he felt suspicious. But when a woman doctor confirmed that Lamia really was still a virgin he married her.

156. Indian Movies

Claire's mother had just celebrated her eightieth birthday when she had a fever that left her mentally confused. She needed care all around the clock now, and even though Claire didn't do it herself she had to be constantly within reach of the nuns who were looking after Lucia. There was no way she could go to Mala for the summer vacation as usual.

Farid consoled his mother, saying he'd rather stay in Damascus anyway, he never wanted to set foot in Mala again. She raised her eyebrows. "Your father won't like that," she said.

"He ignores me anyway, so it can't make any difference to him where I am. I hate Mala." Claire stroked his head.

Elias didn't know how to behave with his sick mother-in-law, and visited her once a month just out of politeness. He complained daily of the heat in Damascus, bewailing the fact that their lovely cool house in Mala was standing empty. However, Claire was not to be moved.

So Farid spent that summer in the city. Josef, Suleiman, and the other boys stayed in Damascus as well, but Rana had to go to Greece for two months with her parents. She phoned Farid a week before they left.

"Why Greece?" he asked on the telephone.

"A friend of my father's has a house there."

"Can we see each other before you go?"

"Tomorrow, if you like. We could go to the cinema. Dunia and I have tickets. I could persuade her to let you have hers, and my parents wouldn't know."

"Wonderful," cried Farid. "When does the film begin?"

"At three in the afternoon . I'll wait for you outside the entrance."

"Aren't you afraid of Jack? Suppose he ..."

"Never mind Jack," she interrupted. "We'll meet outside the cinema."

He was there half an hour early, and Rana herself turned up quarter of an hour before the appointed time. "My mother's such a viper!" she said angrily as they sat down in a small café in the cinema building. "Ten minutes before I was about to leave, she said Jack had better go along to look after me and my girlfriend. Think of that! What was I to do? I told myself to keep calm, and I told him, 'All right, come with us, then. We're going to this marvellous Indian movie.' Because I know Jack hates Indian movies. He thinks they're badly made, the actors are too fat, the stories are too thin, and the songs are dead boring. But I still held another trump card."

Farid looked at her inquiringly.

"It's a love story. Jack hates love stories worse even than maths," she explained. "So my mother was still trying to lumber me with Jack, and tempted him with a lot of money, saying he could take me and Dunia out for an ice after the film. Then I played my trump card and told him it was a particularly good love story. That did the trick!"

Rana and Farid sat side by side in the dark cinema, holding hands. It was one of those mammoth Indian films that spend three hours telling a story in which the lovers do their utmost to be unhappy and keep singing at each other without warning. One-third of it was singing that no one could understand.

Farid managed to kiss Rana surreptitiously twice, and was surprised by the tears that ran down her cheeks when she looked at him.

When the film was over she handed him a letter, dropped a quick goodbye kiss on his cheek and whispered, "Think of me." Then she pushed her way through the audience to the main exit. Farid left more slowly, choosing the side exit.

He read Rana's letter in the bus, and had difficulty in keeping back his own tears.

157. Gibran the Sailor

He sat on the edge of his old camp bed with a bottle of arrack in one hand and a cigarette in the other. About ten young men sat on the floor of his poorly furnished room, all of them smoking. A dense cloud of smoke floated out of the open window, as if Gibran's room were a kebab restaurant.

It was the first time Farid had joined them. Josef had been pressing him to go almost every day since his return from the monastery. He was really missing something, Josef said, for when Gibran was drunk he could tell a story better than the best of the *hakawati* storytellers in the city. And today Gibran was so drunk that he never even noticed when they came in. Farid found a place near the window where he could get some fresh air.

"My story today is about a tragic love affair. The tale of Laila and Madjnun is sweet lemonade by comparison. The heroine and hero are Juliana and Arnus, and you must remember those names."

"Why?" some of the young men asked.

Gibran took a large gulp from his bottle and drew on his cigarette. "Arnus. Arnus and Juliana," he repeated.

"Isn't that the name of an avenue in Damascus?" asked Toni. Gibran took another large gulp and grunted.

"And wasn't Arnus the son who went to war against his father?"

"What war?" asked Suleiman. "I thought Arnus meant a corn cob."

"No, my boy. Arnus may sound like the Arabic for a corn cob, but it's a Roman name. Sultan Aziz of Damascus was a young and very clever ruler in the days when the crusaders had occupied the entire coastline."

That was the beginning of the long love story that Gibran told. He talked and talked, and never stopped drinking all the time, holding the normally restless young men so spellbound that they all listened in silence. One of them even shed tears when the Sultan's son Arnus was put in prison, and Sultan Aziz saw around his neck the medallion that he had given his beloved wife Juliana many years ago.

Gibran ended his story, put the empty liquor bottle down on a crate where a full ashtray and several crumpled books already lay, and fell backward on the bed. He began snoring at once, and the young men stole out of his room.

158. The Club

The new club in Abbara Alley, founded during Farid's absence in the monastery, had been there for some time now. It had its premises in a large backyard belonging to the Catholic Church.

Its founders, a handful of young men, were proud of having made a pleasant place out of a dilapidated yard full of mountains of rubbish and old junk. Determined to make their idea succeed, the members had collected donations from the Christian community, reminding the rich that it was time to do something for the young if they were to hold their own with the Muslim majority in Damascus. When they approached atheists, nationalists, and communists, on the other hand, they pointed out the advantages of having healthy young people around, brought in from the street by the club to keep them from drugs, gambling games, and knife fights. Instead they could play basketball and volleyball, table tennis and chess on the club's new premises.

Such lavish donations had come in that, besides a well-equipped playing field, the club also had an office, a large table tennis room, and ten modern showering and changing cubicles in the single-storey building next to the yard. There was even a café.

From the first everything had been open to boys and girls alike, and as prices in the café were affordable it became a favourite meeting place for young people. In less than three years the club had acquired two hundred active members and a hundred honorary members, including the minister of culture, who was a Christian and could always call on the club members as voluntary assistants in election campaigns.

All Farid's friends were already in the club, and his father was an honorary member and generous with his donations. Two weeks after he came home from the monastery, Farid joined. He played chess well, he was reasonably good at basketball, and very good at table tennis.

All the inhabitants of the buildings around the square took down the boards that had been nailed over their windows. Vermin, the penetrating stink, and the unappetizing garbage lying around the yard had made it impossible for them to have them open before. Now they sat at their windows, cracking roasted nuts and drinking tea, while they watched a strange, foreign game in which young men struggled for possession of a large red ball, aiming to throw it up and through a dangling, basket-like construction. Before two years were up, all the neighbours knew so much about the game that they sometimes even whistled derisively at the referee.

Now that this new meeting place was available Farid's friends seldom met in the attic or at Rasuk's place. They preferred going to the club. And someone else started coming to it every day: the old seaman Gibran. He became best friends with Taufik, who leased the café. It turned out that they had known each other in their youth, but then lost track of one another for decades.

Gibran helped Taufik to clean the café, water the flowers, and buy supplies. In return he could eat and drink as much as he wanted there. He stopped wandering around town and cast anchor at the club. There was only one thing he couldn't do there, and that was to drink alcohol. Taufik was inflexible on that point. He himself never drank, and one day when Gibran turned up tipsy Taufik wouldn't let him in, hard as the young people begged him. They had hoped to hear one of the old seaman's spicy stories.

159. Amin

Farid met Amin in September over a game of chess. He said of him later that no one else apart from Claire and Rana had such an enduring influence on his life as the small tiler. Even years later, Farid remembered their first meeting. He had of course seen Amin at the club before, but only that day, during their game of chess, did he first talk to him. At the time there were no very good chess players in the club, so Farid, with the sketchy knowledge of the game that he had picked up in the monastery, was like a one-eyed man in the kingdom of the blind and beat everyone. One September afternoon, Amin came over and asked him to teach him how to play chess.

Amin was five years older than Farid, he worked laying tiles, and he laughed a great deal at the evening meetings. You could tell from his sharp comments that he knew a lot about politics. Josef had always kept a respectful distance from him. Now and then they did argue, but they always stayed friendly.

Amin got Farid to tell him all about chess, and learned with an eagerness and gratitude that were all his own, marvelling at the thought processes behind the moves. He was an emotional player who swore volubly when he lost.

On that first day the game lasted only ten minutes. Amin invited Farid to have a tea, and when Taufik served the slender glasses, the tiler sipped his and then asked, with interest, "I hear you were in the monastery, is that so?"

"Yes, but it doesn't mean anything to me. I had a horrible time there, and the place was anti-Christian anyway."

"How do you mean, anti-Christian?" asked Amin in some surprise.

"Because Christ preached love but they practise hate, pure hate. Jesus never tortured anyone, and shared his bread with all comers. But the monks torture people until they collapse or get to be as heartless as they are."

Amin lit a cigarette. "It's odd what the Church has made of Jesus, don't you think?" he said. "He sided with the poor of this world, but the Church is always on the side of the rich and powerful."

"You're right. A friend of mine in the monastery said the Church makes the way to God not shorter but longer."

"Building in curves, barriers, and detours along the route," added Amin grimly. "And charging tolls and admission tickets whenever it likes."

Josef came in and went up to them. "Hello, Amin, trying to palm a Stalin icon off on him?" he joked.

Amin shook his head, grinning. "No, they're all sold out, and I'm not selling any of Satlan."

Josef forced a smile, but there was discord in the air. Soon Rasuk, Toni, Suleiman and a number of others joined the two opponents. Farid had no idea what it was all about, but he sensed that each was trying to hold the other's ideas and convictions up to ridicule.

Suddenly they were all talking at once, and Farid couldn't keep up. He felt like a small child, inferior to the rest of them as they pronounced instant judgement, juggled names and events, and defended their claims with fanatical zeal. He could think of nothing and no one, apart from Rana and Claire, whom he could defend knowing so certainly that he was in the right.

Unobtrusively, he withdrew from their circle and sat down in the café.

"It's all just froth," said Gibran, who was sitting there too, nodding in the direction of the fighting-cocks out on the terrace. "All just froth," he repeated after a while. His voice faltered, and sounded as lonely as Farid's soul.

Farid read a magazine lying on the counter. Taufik kept carrying tea and coffee out to his customers on the terrace, where over thirty men and women were now involved in a debate that was getting nowhere, but was frequently interrupted by roars of laughter.

"Do you feel like a walk?" he suddenly heard Amin say. "We can't hear ourselves speak any more here."

"Good idea," said Farid. He paid, and waited for Amin, who had to go to the men's room first.

"Off already?" asked Josef, suddenly materializing behind him.

"Yes," replied Farid.

"Will you drop in at my place later?"

"What if it's late?"

"Doesn't matter. I'll wait for you upstairs." Farid realized that he meant in the attic.

Amin seemed to know Farid's family. He lived close to Grandmother Lucia, near the Ananias Church. When Farid went home three hours later, he was feeling remarkably cheerful. He knew that he had made a friend who talked to him like a big brother that evening. Amin was knowledgeable and very witty, yet he could well have complained day and night of the hard times his family had suffered. They had been resettled time and time again over the generations, and every time they lost all they had. His father, descended from a highly regarded Christian nobleman, worked as a doorman in Damascus, and his wages only just paid for his cigarettes and arrack. Amin had had to leave school early and start work to feed the family, including three younger sisters who were still at school. But none of that could quench his love of life. He saw his poverty not as a private misfortune, but as part of even greater wretchedness all over the world that left millions of people starving and suffering. He said he would lend Farid books about world poverty, and they agreed to meet again.

Farid's parents were already asleep when he came home. He went quietly up to the second floor and from there to the attic above the aniseed warehouse. Josef was sitting at the table, reading.

"There you are at last," he said.

"Have you been waiting long?"

"No," said Josef, and then there was a long silence that troubled Farid. "Amin's a nice guy," said Josef at last, without looking at his friend, "but he's a dangerous communist. You want to go carefully with him."

"Why?" asked Farid, who hadn't thought the tiler seemed at all threatening, but was very sensitive and straightforward.

"Because communists never love their country. They get their orders from Moscow and carry them out, and if the comrades there tell them, 'Kill your sister,' they do just that."

"Thank God I don't have a sister, but I do have you. And comrade or no comrade, if the Pope himself tells me, 'Kill Josef,' I'll convert to Islam right away. Satisfied?"

"Don't act so stupid. First they train you, then they inject a love of Moscow into you, and after that you have no will of your own. They're not naïve enough to order you to do something that repels you, they do it much more subtly, telling you to do things you don't think bad at all. And suddenly you may be a decent, honest human being, but you're a murderer and a traitor all the same."

"But I'd never do anything to harm my country, my family, or my religion."

"My God, how simple-minded can you get? The communists don't even recognise God, religion, and the family. They'd sleep with their own sisters."

"Nonsense," growled Farid angrily, remembering that Amin was sacrificing his life for his parents and siblings, while the pampered Josef couldn't stand any of his sisters.

"I only wanted to warn you because I'm your friend and I'm fond of you," said Josef. He sounded sad and resigned.

"Then calm down, Papa, going for a single walk with Amin doesn't make me a communist," replied Farid cheerfully.

"Not yet, not yet," whispered Josef despairingly. For he was firmly convinced that Farid had taken a fatal step.

And he was not mistaken.

160. Hakawati of the Night

One night just before school began again in early October, Gibran played the part of *hakawati*, the traditional Syrian storyteller.

Members were still at the club after midnight, but only sitting in the café and in the table tennis room. Out on the terrace, the noise they made would have disturbed the quiet of the night. However, they could stay in both rooms as long as Taufik let them, and he kept late hours himself. He was always glad to have company, for he felt lonely all by himself in his tiny room in the tenement block at the end of the street.

There was room for ten people in the café, but the big table tennis room would take a hundred chairs. Michel the joiner's clever design for the large green table meant that it could be folded up in a couple of moves and wheeled away to be stored in a cupboard, leaving a spacious lecture hall. Chairs and benches were stacked in a nearby room.

One evening Farid came to the club and found a number of young people sitting around Rasuk in the table tennis room, drinking tea and laughing. Farid entered quietly, found a chair and joined them. Rasuk was in the middle of a story, but Farid soon realized who it was about: their neighbour Saide, who else? Most of those present knew Saide; in the alley they used to say she had a body like marble and a mouth like a radio station. Men spoke of her as a daring woman married to a simple-minded skinflint. Her husband Sadik was a vegetable dealer. His large store was near the mouth of Abbara Alley, and he was a man of few intellectual gifts, but great malice. His best trick was his well-feigned innocence; his baby face would deceive any customer. Claire couldn't stand him, and very seldom bought from him. If she did, once she was home she found vegetables in her bag that weren't as good as those she had chosen and often had even placed on the scales herself. Elias didn't like Sadik either, and would never shake hands with him, saying he was afraid that if he did he'd lose at least one finger to that rogue. "Even his name, Sadik, *the honourable man*, is a disguise," Elias had said.

Saide joked with men and liked it when they gave her presents. In return, she made anyone who gave her something feel that he had conquered her heart.

"She goes to hang out washing on her large rooftop terrace every Tuesday and Thursday afternoon," Rasuk went on, and Farid noticed a fiendish smile on that sophisticated storyteller's face, for he knew very well that his male hearers were thirsting for every sentence, so he slowed down. "Want me to go on?" he asked, looking around as he took a long drink from his glass of tea. Of course he knew what the answer would be.

"Right, so she's stretched her washing line where she can be seen by people in the surrounding buildings, just as if she were presented to them on a platter. Then she begins to sing, and young men in all four buildings run for the lavatories with doors or windows looking out on Saide's rooftop.

Soon she acts as if her skirt is getting in her way as she moves around, so she tucks the hem up into her belt, showing her bare legs, walks around the outside of the terrace, and she knows that behind those doors the young men's eyes are popping out of their heads, practically lodging their pupils in the cracks in the walls. When she's in the mood, she does a little dance in front of every door until she thinks she can feel the hot breath of the boy behind it, and then she goes on to the next, and while the first young man, quietly and hunched with exhaustion and shame, creeps out of the lavatory, she turns her charm on the second and then goes on to the third."

"And are you in the audience yourself?" asked Suleiman boldly, but Rasuk wasn't to be shaken.

"Of course. Who told you I was made of stone?" he replied, to the sound of murmured agreement. "But sometimes she's in a bad temper, or she doesn't feel like playing tricks on the boys. Then she lures them into the lavatories but she does her round very quickly, without stopping anywhere, and then ..." Rasuk broke off his story and drank some more tea. The air was crackling.

"Yes, what then?" asked Toni the perfumier's son impatiently. The others laughed.

"Then she leaves the poor milkmen in the lurch," said Rasuk.

"What milkmen? What are they milking?" asked the naïve Toni. The company roared with laughter. "They're milking their billygoats," cried Suleiman.

"How do you mean? What billygoats?"

"Someone had better tell Toni the facts of life some time," cried Masu'd, a strong builder's assistant with unruly hair.

"Then what happens?" asked Samir, the mechanic's son.

"Then she goes away leaving the laundry basket there," replied Rasuk. "She stays in her apartment for hours, clearing up, cooking, or drinking coffee with a woman neighbour. She takes wicked pleasure in thinking of all those young men gradually emerging from the lavatories again."

As if Rasuk's story had been the newsreel before the main film show, Gibran now rose and came forward. He asked Rasuk for his place, and Rasuk moved to sit next to Farid in the back row. Meanwhile, Taufik came in with twenty glasses of tea on a large tray and offered them to the audience. Everyone who took a glass put ten piastres on the tray, leaned back, and enjoyed the fragrant aroma.

Gibran sat down, put his glass to one side, and for a while he just looked gravely at the men in the audience. "Rasuk's story," he began slowly, "reminds me of another clever woman."

"Even the Prophet Muhammad feared women's wiles," agreed Taufik, taking a glass of tea himself, and sitting where he had a view through the window of the table tennis room and could see if anyone came into the café.

"However that may be, we were living in the outskirts of Damascus at the time, near the south gate of the city, Bab al Sigir. My parents were poor peasants. A woman whose name was Balkis lived near us. Her husband was big and strong as a camel, but he was almost blind. He owned a flour mill behind their house, and vegetable gardens and vineyards, which ensured him a certain amount of prosperity. Balkis was very beautiful. Indeed, to be honest I've seen many women on my travels, but only one more beautiful than Balkis, and she was a Berber from the Atlas Mountains whom I met in a nightclub in Marseille harbour, but that's another story, and I'll tell it another time.

Balkis lived a happy life except that she had a neighbour who pestered her, and that neighbour was my father. He thought himself irresistible, and kept pressing his attentions on Balkis.

It annoyed her, so one day she had a word with my mother, and the two of them thought up a fiendish plan. Do you want me to go on with the story?"

"Yes, yes, go on!" cried the massed ranks of his audience.

"I need a good cigarette if I'm not to forget any of it," said Gibran craftily. Old Taufik laughed and shook his head. Five or six cigarettes were handed to Gibran. He collected them all, lit one, and put the others in his baggy shirt pocket.

"Early one evening, then, Balkis told my father that her husband had work to do in the fields, and she asked if he'd like to come and see her. What a question! The old goat was there within minutes. She told him to undress and get into bed, she was just going to freshen herself up a little and then she'd join him.

My father, who was usually slower than a lame turtle, was stark naked in seconds.

But instead of preparing for love-play, Balkis came running into the bedroom, still fully dressed, and said in a voice made almost inaudible by terror that her husband had come home and was at the yard gate. And if she knew him, he'd lock the gate before he came indoors.

'I'm lost!' wailed my father. He was sure that if her husband caught him he'd pound him to mush in his rage.

'There's only one way,' whispered Balkis. 'A door leads from the bedroom to the terrace, and you can get into the mill from there. Once you're inside, you must turn the millstone as if you were our donkey, and the moment my husband is asleep I'll get the key from his trouser pocket and open the gate for you."

'Oh, thank you, you've saved my life,' whispered my father, and he ran through the back door to the terrace and on into the mill. Then he began going around in a circle, pushing the beam that turned the heavy millstone ahead of him. Every time the beam had gone right around once, a little bell rang. That told the farmer out in the yard when the donkey had stopped.

There was a hole up in the roof, and wheat was poured down into the mill through it. My father heard the man coming home and asking his wife what she'd been doing all day.

'Grinding wheat,' she replied. The farmer pricked up his ears and heard the bell.

'You're a good hard-working woman. But at this late hour?' he asked in some concern.

'Ah, well, the donkey slept half the day. It was dreadfully hot. It's cooler now, and he woke up, so I thought he might as well grind a few more sacks of grain,' replied his wife.

'You must hit him a couple of times. He's been too well fed recently and very contrary,' said her husband.

'No, no, he works for me like a lamb,' replied Balkis. My father made haste to turn and turn the millstone until he felt quite queasy. The farmer tipped another sack of wheat through the hopper that carried the grain down to the millstone.

Balkis and her husband sat out on the terrace for a good deal longer. It was a night of full moon, and they were talking contentedly. And whenever my father wanted to stop and get his breath back, the husband said crossly, 'There goes that donkey, stopping again. I ought to give him a taste of my whip.' But Balkis begged him to stay with her, and my father scurried around in circles as if he had a bumble bee on his tail.

When Balkis finally brought him his clothes, long after midnight, and opened the gate, my father couldn't even walk straight any more.

A week later Balkis asked if he fancied visiting her again. And she gave a very sly smile as she spoke.

'Why?' my father spat at her. 'Do you and your husband need more flour ground?'"

ა

When they were all on their way out, Farid saw that Matta was there too, sitting at the back of the room. "Brother," he cried, and came up to Farid. Farid took Matta's outstretched right hand in both his. He felt a strange warmth.

161. Wars Large and Small

There are certain turns of phrase slipped unobtrusively into conversation in Damascus to find out if someone you don't know well is of your own religion. If a Muslim suddenly cries, "God bless the Prophet Muhammad, on whom be peace!" then another Muslim will reply in the same words. "God bless the Prophet Muhammad, on whom be peace!" But a Jew or a Christian will say, "God bless all the prophets."

Farid had to master countless such secret messages and rituals.

Claire had warned him from his childhood to remember those who fasted during Ramadan, and never eat or drink in a Muslim quarter at that time. The Muslims reckon time by the short lunar months, and so Ramadan wanders through all seasons of the year. Going without a drop of water from sunrise to sunset in the hellish temperatures of summer was bad enough; provocation from those of other faiths would not be tolerated.

Until now almost all Farid's friends had been Christians, and at school his few Muslim fellow pupils like Kamal Sabuni came from rich families and understood Christian customs. So the attitude of the butcher Mahmud's errand boy horrified him. It was the summer of 1956, and the radio was constantly broadcasting reports of imminent war between the British and French on one side, and Egypt on the other. Farid had heard from his father that the bone of contention was the Suez Canal, but that was all he knew. Suddenly an ugly boy who always stank of mutton fat stood squarely in his way.

"If the Christians and Jews attack Egypt we'll burn your quarter down," he threatened, and to emphasize his words he lit a match and threw it at Farid. Farid didn't even know the boy, only that he had recently been working as assistant to the butcher Mahmud. All the butchers in the Christian quarter were Muslims, but he had never thought anything of it before. Even as a child he used to go to see Mahmud. Claire and Elias trusted the man, and Farid thought him witty. His shop in Straight Street had verses pinned up all over it praising patience or condemning envy. The best maxim, which Farid knew by heart, hung right above the chopping block: *As a poet I begged from dogs, today dogs beg from me.*

"He must be crazy," said Claire. "Reciting poems while he chops meat and cracks bones! Did you ever hear of anything like it?"

Early in October, Britain, France, and Israel attacked Egypt. Farid had nightmares. There was a Muslim butcher in every street, and if what the butcher's boy had told him was true, the entire Christian quarter might go up in flames at any moment. He confided his fears to Josef, who didn't laugh, as Farid had feared, but just said, "A stupid boy, and a dangerous idea too. The buildings are wood and mudbrick. They'd burn like a torch."

One night Farid dreamed that he was leading the Christians of the burning quarter across a river into a safe, green countryside. Josef grinned. "Rehearsing for the part of Moses?" He clapped Farid on the shoulder. "Come on, I know a secret tunnel used by Christians centuries ago to escape. You get into it below the underground chapel of Ananias."

They went to the chapel, and as it was empty they went straight to the side door, which led into a dark passage. Farid shuddered. It smelled of mould and moisture. But Josef went ahead undeterred, carrying a flashlight. The corridor came to an abrupt end, and the foundation walls of new buildings and sewerage shafts blocked the tunnel. "No way of escape any more," whispered Josef gloomily as they retraced their steps.

Two days later the whole quarter was rejoicing. The Syrian Jules Gammal, a young Christian officer stationed in Egypt for training, had rammed the French naval destroyer *Jean-Bart* off Port Said with his torpedo boat, dying a martyr's death. His portrait, swiftly painted in oils on canvas, was hung up everywhere. All of a sudden the entire quarter felt joyful release. The young officer's death had resolved the guilt feelings of the Christians. "Our own Jules Gammal has liberated Egypt," they told each other. It was not in fact true, but to them he was a hero who had stopped all the Europeans in their tracks. Later on streets, squares, and schools all over the country were named after him.

The facts were that the young officer died in a desperate action against the superior forces of the French and British, who had landed in the harbour city of Port Said at the northern end of the Suez Canal. He set out at random with his torpedo boat. The fires of hell were spewing out from the horizon at the city, whose inhabitants would not surrender.

Finally he rammed the French destroyer *Jean-Bart* with his explosive vessel. The destroyer was not sunk, but the impact rendered it unable to manoeuvre. It was not until three hours later that a second fast torpedo boat blew it up.

Neither Jules Gammal nor anyone else, apart from a single British Navy man, knew that he very nearly took all the war strategists to their deaths with him. His torpedo boat raced past the British warship H.M.S. *Tyne* with only three metres between them. All the British and French war chiefs were assembled on board, only one sailor was standing in the bows. He saw the boat and shouted, but his voice was drowned in the noise of the engines and explosions ringing out in the Suez Canal. He watched the boat race on until it rammed the French warship and went up in flames.

"What about that, then, Stinker?" cried Josef three days later, looking in at the butcher's shop. Mahmud had no customers at that moment, and was reading a book about pre-Islamic poetry. He looked up in surprise. After all, he knew Josef and Farid. His assistant was standing there with his head bent, looking like a beaten dog.

"Now, now, Josef! Who do you mean by Stinker?" asked the butcher, displeased.

"Your butcher's boy was going to set our quarter on fire. He thinks we Christians are traitors."

"Who? The fool said that?" Mahmud put the poetry book down on the chopping block and turned to his apprentice. "This lad can't even

tell fillet steak from ground beef – so now he's meddling in politics?"
A ringing slap landed on the boy's face. "You bastard, insult my customers, would you?" And a second slap landed on his other cheek.

"I'm sorry, master. I'll never talk politics again. I kiss your hand,
spare me your blows," the boy begged, submissively reaching for his
master's arm. The butcher shook him off like a fly, and turned to Josef
and Farid. "It must have been a mistake, but if he does it again just let
me know, and I'll cut off his balls and throw them to the dogs."

162. Backgammon

Chess ranked highest among the games played at the club. Drafts and
dominoes were played by the very old and very young members, but
card games were forbidden. They were regarded as primitive games
of chance that merely caused quarrels and enmity. No one would
commit himself about backgammon. It wasn't forbidden, but it wasn't
encouraged. Taufik who ran the café was not pleased about that.

"It's only because the committee members don't play it well," he said
scornfully. Farid could play a great many games – chess, draughts,
dominoes – but no one in his family used to play backgammon. It had
been forbidden in the monastery. Josef knew how to play, but it was
forbidden in his home too. A game for the lazy, said his father crossly.

One day Farid came into the club and saw Josef and Taufik sitting
at the backgammon board. He watched the two of them, fascinated.
Josef was cursing quietly because he was losing game after game. The
variant they were playing was called *Frandjiye,* the Frankish game.
When it ended with a score of 5–0, Taufik suggested other variants,
and Josef decided on *Maghrebiye,* the Morocco game. But after half an
hour Taufik was victorious again, although only just.

"Perhaps we ought to try *Mahbusse,* the prisoners' game. You beat
me twice running at that one recently."

Josef waved the idea away. "The dice aren't falling well for me
today."

"What kind of a game is it?" asked Farid.

"An annoying one," said Josef, "but it gets you addicted." He stretched.

"It's a complete philosophy," said Taufik. "Take a look. Chess is iron logic and strategy. A game that leaves no room in it for life, luck, or chance. The whole world praises it because it is indeed a game for clever people. I don't play chess. It's too cold and calculating for me. If you play against a pro you don't have the slightest chance, he'll destroy your army in meticulously planned moves. But with backgammon, as in life, everything is still possible. And there's something else about it too – look, this is what Gibran showed me.

"Two players represent two lives, two dice are two ways to go. Each dice has six numbers on it.

One is God.
Two is heaven and hell, good and evil, man and woman.
Three is father, mother, and son.
Four is the seasons of the year and the points of the compass.
Five is the number of fingers and senses.
Six is the number of harmony, the number of colours in the
    rainbow.

Each set of two numbers opposite each other on the dice add up to seven. Seven is a holy number.

"Each side on the backgammon board has twelve triangles, known as points, twelve spaces for the twelve months of the year. Between them the players have twenty-four points, as many as the day has hours. They play with thirty pieces, which are the days of the month, half of them black for night and the other half white for day. Or you could say for grief and joy, for happiness and sorrow.

"The player tries to use skill, and in contrast to the game of chess he must consult his luck, his oracle, before every move: he must throw the dice, and the victor can quickly become the loser and vice versa, sometimes not until the last minute. The greatest luck in throwing the dice doesn't help you if you play without skill. And that," he concluded his description, "that's life."

That evening Farid asked Taufik to teach him the rules of all the variants of backgammon. And for the first time he had a glimpse of what lay behind the mask of the apparently unassuming licensee of the café.

163. Nourishment

Entirely unexpectedly, Rana phoned. The Greek vacation was over. She wanted to see him, she said, and she had good news too: her Aunt Mariam was flying to Milan for a week to buy the latest fashions for her shop. Rana was to water the flowers and keep an eye on the apartment. In return her aunt would bring her a leather bag from Italy.

"I'd have done it for free, anyway," cried Rana excitedly. He could enjoy Rana's company seven times, thought Farid that first evening, when he had done his school homework and was on the bus. He could hardly believe his luck. They could be together and undisturbed for three or four hours every day. Jack suspected nothing. Rana was right: those hours were stolen from Paradise, and beyond the grave would surely be docked from their time there.

Later, at the worst moments of his life, Farid was to think of those days again and again, and the extraordinary peace that he knew only near Rana. He felt both safe and light as air, so that at some moments he almost thought he could fly. Rana was only a few months older than he was, but she was always a little way ahead of him. He loved talking to her, and was never for a moment bored. And then there was her hair, and her eyes! He loved to kiss her on the lips. They were always sweet, and had her own special fragrance.

He liked it when she read aloud to him. He himself loved to tell stories, but she preferred reading. During those seven days they read *L'Étranger* and *La Peste* together. Even years later, he always thought of Rana's voice in connection with the works of Camus. And in those days Rana told him for the first time how, whenever she had been with him, she waited as long as she could before showering, so that she could take the smell of him to bed with her.

She also confessed that it was he who had taught her the joys of kissing. No one in her family ever kissed.

"What, never?" exclaimed the surprised Farid, who couldn't go a day without kissing his mother.

"No, as I said. My mother doesn't kiss anyone, not even Jack, and he's her favourite. She certainly doesn't kiss me."

"What about your father?"

"He once patted my head when I wasn't well, but he's incapable of hugging anyone. And if you hug *him* he doesn't know what to make of it. It was you who taught me that kissing is nourishment just like bread, water, and olives," she said.

When Farid took her in his arms and kissed her for a long time, she laughed. "Kind sir, you'll eat me up!" And then she tickled him. "I said kissing was nourishment, understand? Not Rana Shahin."

"Very well, madame, very well, but somehow your kiss is a strange kind of nourishment, because the more I have of it the hungrier I am."

164. The End of a Dream

During that week Farid came to know the thousand reasons why he loved Rana. Her way of laughing at anything fascinated him. On their last afternoon in Aunt Mariam's apartment, she told him how badly disappointed her father had been by the Greeks, and she couldn't stop chuckling. "He expected every taverna proprietor to be a grandson of Socrates, every bureaucrat a descendant of Plato, every poor baggage carrier to be Diogenes in person." And she described the way her brother had given himself alcohol poisoning with the sweet wine of Samos. He had to stay in bed for three days, and his Mama had stayed in bed too, to be on the safe side. Her father never wanted to hear the word retsina again.

⁂

Then they sat in the kitchen drinking tea, while Rana read aloud the last few pages of Camus's *La Peste*. Suddenly Farid gave a start. He felt icy cold.

"What's the matter?" she asked.

"How late is it?" he asked in return, because he had left his watch at home. He was white as a sheet.

"Just after six. Aunt Mariam won't be back until tomorrow," she reassured him.

"All the same, we ought to go."

But Rana wanted to finish the book. She felt very peaceful; she had already cleaned the apartment and removed all traces of their presence.

Next moment, however, they both started in surprise. Through the open kitchen doorway, they saw Aunt Mariam carefully pushing her large suitcase into the apartment. Mariam froze when she saw Rana with a boy. Then she recognized Farid, and forgot all about her case.

"I don't believe it," she said, slowly coming towards them. She left the front door of the apartment open. "How dare you meet a Mushtak in my apartment?" she cried, hoarse with anger.

Question after question whirled around Farid's mind. Had someone given Rana away? Was that why her aunt had come home early? What was he to do? He couldn't leave Rana alone now. How could they calm this Fury down?

The two young people stood there as if turned to stone.

"But Aunt Mariam," said Rana, to break the silence, "we were only drinking tea and reading a book."

"You have brought a Mushtak into my most private place! Is he brave enough to take me into his parents' bedroom? Well, is he? I trusted you, I asked you to do me this small service, and you bring a Mushtak into my apartment!"

"But Aunt, I thought you'd understand us. We're young, we were born here in Damascus, what can we do about the feud between our parents and grandparents? Farid and I have both sworn never to go to Mala again," she went on, almost pleadingly.

"Tell him to get out of my apartment. I will never in my life exchange words with a Mushtak."

Farid left the kitchen, walking past Rana's heavily perfumed aunt.

"And now for you, madame!" screeched Aunt Mariam. "Isn't it enough that Jasmin had to die? Isn't that enough for you? Do you want another murder in the family? Don't interrupt me," she snapped when Rana merely raised a hand. "Your brother Jack was right. You're playing with fire. He told me someone had told him you were friendly with one of those Mushtaks. He's going to keep a close watch on you. And if he catches you with that Mushtak, it's him and not you that he'll shoot. Is that what you want? If you're after another bloodbath, then go on meeting this boy, but never come into my apartment again."

Farid waited in the stairwell outside the open front door. It was already dark.

"Aunt Mariam," cried Rana in one last attempt, stretching out her arms as if to embrace her aunt.

"Go away, go away!" the woman shouted, retreating from her. When Rana left the apartment, her infuriated aunt slammed the door behind her.

Farid didn't want to put the light on. They slowly went downstairs.

On the last landing, Rana placed herself in front of him and flung her arms around him. He kissed her lips. They tasted salty.

165. Training

Farid was proud to be a part of the secret life that pulsated beneath the calm surface of the city. Since the autumn of 1956 he had been in the Communist Party youth organization. Meetings of the Young Communists were held at different places every time, and members went separately so as not to arouse suspicion. He liked that in itself. He felt like a secret agent, although owing no allegiance either to Moscow or its Communist Party, only to a future society in which he could live freely with Rana, their heads held high.

The whole idea had the magnetic attraction of forbidden fruit. Like the others, he had a cover name for security reasons, and he regularly attended training courses. The young people he met there came, like himself, from rich families. Communist writings spoke of the workers and proletarians, but he never met one of them in all those years, and he didn't much like that. How could the workers in Russia,

England, and Germany come out on the streets with such militant
self-confidence, going on strike, even forming something called the
Labour Movement, while here they trudged submissively from home
to work and back again, in fear?

When, at a meeting of his own Party cell, he suggested explaining communism to the workers, he was warned not even to try it. It
would just scare people. He discussed the matter with the members
of his old gang, Rasuk, Azar, Suleiman, and Josef, and encountered
outright opposition. Josef was the only one who bought the illegal
Communist Party journal *Youth* from him. The others wouldn't touch
it. But in his own mind, Farid felt this was the right way. He was full
of impatience in his early years in the Party, and genuinely believed
that the revolution was imminent. In his daydreams, he imagined
himself at Rana's side, storming palaces of some kind in which dictators, feudal lords, and also (rather comically) Catholic priests who
had been overthrown begged for mercy. Tears came to his eyes at
the idea of himself standing before these defeated enemies, showing
magnanimity and sending them all off to an agricultural commune
to live by the labour of their own hands at last. But if he so much as
hinted anything of the kind to Josef, his friend laughed at him. "A bad
Russian movie," was Josef's succinct comment.

Farid read a great deal, and since his French was perfect he was
able to translate short texts for his comrades. Before a year was up he
was voted onto the editorial committee of the youth magazine. His
job was to write about literature and culture; other members wrote on
economics and history, and others again on contemporary politics.

Working on *Youth* was a great responsibility, and one that spurred
him on to try gathering together the best, most audacious, and most
revolutionary short stories and poems of world literature, and offering them to the journal's young readers. A few months later he was
praised by the Central Committee, which reported that many readers
turned to the literary page first.

In those weeks he lay awake at night, wondering why people didn't
fight for their freedom. The basic principles of socialism, as he gleaned
them from his reading, were so illuminating, and not at all far from
Christ's own ideas, yet when he tried to talk about them, people acted

as if he were offering them drugs or pornographic pictures. Some were polite, others snapped angrily and asked him to spare them such dangerous naivety.

Farid liked working on the journal, but after a year he still couldn't describe anyone on the editorial team as a friend. He felt a strange chill, a wall dividing him from them. Quite unlike the infuriating Josef, who worshipped Satlan, hated communists, and yet was still close to Farid.

166. The President's Jacket

The communists were convinced that the union of Syria and Egypt, which was rushed through in 1958, had been a bad and over-hasty idea. Satlan, they pointed out, was a confirmed anti-communist, and the government had brought him to Damascus in such haste only to crush communism. Sure enough, persecution of the Party soon began, and the majority of its Syrian leadership went into exile in Moscow.

When Satlan came to Damascus, Josef was keen to seize his chance and approach that charismatic figure. He begged Farid to go with him, because he was afraid to be on his own. However, the Communist Party had strictly forbidden any of its members to attend occasions held in honour of Satlan. All the same, Farid went to the ceremony with Josef, and when one of his Party comrades claimed later to have seen him from his balcony among the jubilant crowd, Farid denied it and mollified the suspicious underground fighters by pointing out, "Every other Damascene looks like me."

It was a beautiful spring day when Satlan was to drive through the city streets in an open car. Schools took the day off, packed their pupils into buses, and went to join the happy throng. Factories and offices were closed. The Christian elite schools were not enthusiastic about union with Egypt, but as everyone knew that the leadership was firmly in pro-Egyptian hands, and the majority of the government were close to the Muslim Brotherhood, they too gave their students and teachers the day off, leaving it to them to decide whether they took part in the rejoicings or stayed at home.

The streets of the New Town were lined with crowds even at nine in the morning. Soldiers stood along the carriageway, making sure that no one left the sidewalk. Josef and Farid managed to push and shove their way through to the front row. Finally they were standing in a good spot, and agreed that as soon as the President's big limousine showed up they would rush forward to greet him. Recently the newsreels had repeatedly shown pictures of a smiling Satlan shaking hands with his admirers. To shake hands with the President himself was Josef's dream.

Along came the black Cadillac. Josef ran that way, with Farid after him. The car was surrounded by rejoicing, dancing men, all shaking the President's hand. Farid pushed Josef closer to the car, which was moving forward at the pace of a tortoise. They avoided the soldiers who were now busy trying to keep the rest of the happy crowd away from the road. "Let us through," cried Josef, reaching out his arms to Satlan. Farid saw the President close up. He was much taller, and his skin much darker than they had expected. And he was talking to his two vice-presidents, while he shook the hands held out to him.

Suddenly one of the joyful crowd turned and struck out ferociously at Josef and Farid. It was confusing. Josef called him angry names, thinking he was just selfish and wouldn't let anyone else near the President, but that was a mistake. Speaking an Egyptian dialect, the man summoned another in a white shirt and told him to "deal with" these two troublemakers. Only now did Josef realized that all the dancing, happy figures were really secret service men. This realization came too late. Blows went on raining down on them both until the car had moved away. Then the men left them and ran after it.

Josef and Farid went home with headaches and a rushing in their ears. Just before they parted, and Josef turned into Abbara Abbey, he mumbled, through swollen lips, "But I did get to touch his jacket."

167. Gibran's Love

The rain was pouring down outside, but it was warm in the table tennis room, for Taufik had kept the oil stove turned right up since that afternoon. Damp, chilly weather was very bad for his friend Gibran, who had a cold.

When he went to see if the stove was still on around seven o'clock, the hall was already full to the last row. There was only one person missing: Gibran. His chair on the knee-high platform that the joiner Michel had made for the club was empty.

Taufik went out once more to look up the street. A few dim street lights did little to illuminate the darkness, and there was no sign of Gibran. Taufik cursed him and went back into the hall, drenched. He was sure the seaman was getting drunk somewhere again.

However, he was wrong. Gibran turned up punctually at eight, with Karime. Many of the company knew her. Her late husband had been one of the richest jewellers in the city, and had left her a large fortune. She was now in her late fifties, but with the help of thick make-up, modern jewellery and clothes in bright colours tried to look at least two decades younger. Unfortunately she didn't succeed. The youthful beauty with which, as a penniless singer, she had turned the jeweller's head so that he cast his family's disapproval to the winds, had faded forever.

Gibran was a new man. He looked frailer and more elegant. This evening he was wearing a blue suit over a wine-red roll neck pullover of fine wool, with new shoes and a beret that suited him very well. He was even freshly shaved and perfumed.

"Gibran's been plundering the jeweller's safe," Taufik whispered to Josef and Farid with a touch of envy.

The old sailor escorted Karime solicitously to the front row, and asked a boy there to give her his seat. Then, standing in front of the platform, he told a love story from the time of the Crusades. It was the first time anyone had heard Gibran tell a story standing up.

The story itself was not particularly exciting, but the staging of it by the two lovers was impressive. Gibran seemed to dwell in particular on all the scenes in which the hero held his beloved in his arms, or caressed her, and enjoyed acting it out with Karime in front of the audience. It was touching and comical to see the old sailor come to life, so anxious to tell an impressive story that he exaggerated his postures, gestures and mimicry like an actor in a silent movie. He pressed both hands to his heart, and kissed Karime's hand so ardently that there was perfect silence rather than merriment in the hall. Karime played along, and the game really did rejuvenate her. You couldn't have wished for a better actress to play the Frankish girl who fell in love with an Arab prisoner in the crusaders' camp.

There was one particularly dramatic scene in the story. The girl fell sick, but the Arab prisoner who loved her was a doctor. He was horrified by the barbaric Frankish treatment of their sick with the axe and fire. In Damascus, which at the time had the biggest and most modern hospital in the world, patients were treated with medicaments and by the arts of language and music. So he offered to try to cure the girl, although he knew that if he failed he would die, and then she would have her head split with an axe to drive the devil out of it.

She was cured, and they both disappeared into the night before anyone who envied them could harm them and their love.

ᴣᴏ

It had stopped raining outside, and as soon as he had finished his story Gibran left the club with Karime. Taufik was waiting with fifty steaming glasses of tea. Each member of the grateful audience put ten piastres on the tray and took a glass. Matta hesitated, but Taufik handed him one. "You're Farid's guest," he explained. He had already made a mark on his list; after ten such marks, Farid paid him a lira. "Thank you, brother," said Matta shyly, and he drank his tea and then left. Farid and Josef stayed behind, talking about the performance. "Gibran wasn't at his best today. He was thinking about his lady love more than the lovers in the story, but it went down well anyway, the audience liked his theatrically amorous show, and that's what counts," was Josef's conciliatory verdict.

A little later, however, he started an argument in which Michel the joiner and Amin immediately joined. "We mustn't forget that before the crusaders attacked the east, the Arabs were divided into a thousand sects and clans, all at war with each other. Almost like today. And whenever the Arabs were at odds, they offered their countries to foreigners for free," he claimed. Then he sat down and waited. The fire had been laid.

Michel spoke up for the crusaders. "But we mustn't forget how the Christians and Jews had suffered for centuries before," he said heatedly. "Caliph after caliph humiliated them. Caliph al Hakim the Deranged alone destroyed three thousand churches and chapels just before the crusades, forced all Jews to wear a large bell around their necks and all Christians a heavy cross. That needs to be said loud and clear," he added.

Amin objected that both the Franks and the Arabs had been stupid, and they had both lost. Only the Vatican had profited. The Crusades had not just been wars against Islam, he said, but battles to set the seal on the power of Rome. "It was all about the destruction of power in Constantinople, Alexandria, Antioch, and Jerusalem. None of those centres meant anything after the Crusades, and Rome ruled the world."

"That's Russian propaganda," said Michel angrily.

"Those two never could stand each other," said Josef to Farid, who had kept well out of the argument. Josef rubbed his hands.

"We'll have to ask Gibran to tell different kinds of stories, not that Crusader stuff," said Taufik, regretfully shaking his head.

168. Alone

It rained for three weeks, and the mud roofs softened. Water dripped into all the buildings. As usual, the city's drainage system was overtaxed, and water filled the streets and turned them into large ponds. A few children hopped about in the water, but it was icy cold. When the sun found its way through the clouds at last, Damascus was steaming like a freshly baked flatbread.

The change in the weather had given Farid repeated migraine

attacks, but he was out and about all the time. Ever since the union of Syria and Egypt, the communists had been feverishly trying to organize an opposition, but they were completely isolated. The secret service dealt them some severe blows. Their printing press blew up, many Party members and sympathizers were arrested, and the population at large had not a spark of sympathy for the communists. Farid had to take care, for there were secret service informers everywhere.

Josef regretted the persecution of communists, but blamed the Russians for stirring up feeling against Satlan. Otherwise, he just urged Farid to leave the Communist Party as soon as possible.

And now, of all times, Farid had another violent quarrel with his father. Elias Mushtak hated communists. By pure chance, he discovered a large stack of copies of *Youth* magazine in the cellar of his house. His son had carefully hidden them there, never suspecting that a burst water pipe would bring them to light.

"Here am I, working like a dog," ranted Elias, "sending him to the elite school, and what does he do? He turns communist! My son," he bellowed, "turns into a godless slave of Stalin. And why?"

"To fight for justice and freedom for mankind," replied Farid defiantly.

Elias uttered a bitter laugh. "I could weep for fools like you! So my son wants to save the world? Who do you think you are, boy? Jesus? They crucified him. And who do you want to save? A mob of folk who can't even flush the lavatory when they've filled it with shit? Who look you in the face and rob you at the same moment? You want to save them? Our country needs morality and education, not communism, understand?" His voice was getting hoarse. He ranted for an hour, never letting Farid get a word in. Then he took a sip of water and gave his son an ultimatum. He must leave either the Party or this house within twenty-four hours. But Claire, although she shared her husband's dislike of communism, intervened.

"Whatever else he is, he'll always be my son," she said. "Give him time, and he'll part with those stupid communists." Elias controlled his anger, and did not reply.

169. Women Helping Out

Claire was expecting eight women that afternoon. A huge quantity of mini-aubergines grown in the gardens of Damascus had to be cooked, slit open, stuffed with garlic, walnuts, peppers, and salt, and then preserved in olive oil.

The women told stories as they worked, so the time passed quickly, and they met again next day at the next neighbour's house. Home was no place for their menfolk during these hours, so Claire suggested to both Elias and Farid that they needn't be back too early.

This banishment didn't suit Farid at all. He had been glued to the radio for days. There had been a revolution in Baghdad. Colonel Damian, a communist sympathizer, had overthrown King Feisal and proclaimed a republic. Over six thousand US marines had landed in Beirut, and the British had sent a brigade of paratroopers to Jordan to protect its king.

The air crackled with tension. But there was no placating Claire; she didn't want Farid in the house. The women didn't feel comfortable with men eavesdropping on their conversations, she explained.

"But I'll be listening to the radio, and I'd close the door," he pleaded.

Claire shook her head, gave him five lira, and said, "Go and amuse yourself with Josef." However, Farid had been at odds with Josef for days because of the Iraqi revolution. Josef claimed that the new regime in Baghdad had been infiltrated by Russian agents.

Farid phoned Laila. She was glad to hear from him, and invited him round at once, since she was going away with her husband on a two-week concert tour in a few days' time.

His cousin made no effort to hide her dislike of the communists either. She abused Damian of Iraq, describing him as an ass whom the Russians took for an eagle. When Farid frankly told her that he was in the Party, she laughed bitterly and said that just made her hate the communists all the more for exploiting clever, sensitive young people and putting them in danger. In fact, she said, they were even worse than the stupid Oriental dictators. "You don't fight cholera with the plague."

Farid was surprised not by the frankness of Laila's opposition to communism but by her harsh and uncompromising condemnation of it. "I've no quarrel with justice," she said, "but all these ideas – whether it's communism, national socialism, or socialism – bring some allegedly infallible, inspired dictator to power, and we can have shady characters of our own for free. At least they speak Arabic and not Russian."

Farid was angry, but Laila soon changed the subject. "Would you like to go to the cinema?" She was very keen to see *The Bridge on the River Kwai* with Alec Guinness, which had been showing to packed houses in Damascus for months. The music from the soundtrack was whistled everywhere in the streets.

They appreciated the air conditioning in the cinema. Out of doors, the July heat had been stifling for days. Both cousins enjoyed the film, and sat together eating ices after it.

"Would you like the key to my apartment?" Laila surprisingly asked as he walked home with her. "You can see Rana there any time, and the two of you can do as you like except one thing; you must keep out of my husband's music room, understand?"

"Really? You'd let me have a key?" asked Farid incredulously.

"Of course, but only for you and Rana. Your Communist Party stays outside," she said, pinching his earlobe.

"By all means, my lady Abbess," he promised.

When he got home the women had left, and four large glass jars of stuffed aubergines, enough to last a year, were standing ready on the kitchen table.

"Rana called," said Claire. "She sounded sad. She says she'd try again tomorrow, about three in the afternoon."

Farid wished he could wind time forward. Next morning he visited his school friend Kamal Sabuni, at whose house he had first met Rana, hoping Kamal's sister Dunia might be able to tell him what the matter was.

But she wasn't in, and Kamal, who was in deep gloom that day, didn't know anything about Rana. His family had lost everything in the nationalization of their textiles factory only just after they'd paid a fortune to modernize the looms. His mother spent all night in tears, he said.

Farid soon left and took the bus home. But a broken-down truck was blocking the road at the spice market, and the bus driver simply switched off his engine and went to drink a glass of tea somewhere.

Farid kept looking nervously at the time. It was two already. In the end he got out of the bus and ran home down Straight Street. He was out of breath when he arrived. Claire had just finished her siesta and was making herself a mocha in the kitchen. She called out cheerfully, "Rana hasn't phoned yet." Secretly she was glad that her son was in love with this girl. She knew that God loves lovers, yet a cold hand reached out for her heart when she thought of what the two clans had already done to each other.

Rana called at three exactly. At first she just stammered a little and asked how he was. Farid knew at once that she had bad news for him. All of a sudden she stopped. His heart was racing.

"Are you still there?" he asked, thinking at the same time what a silly and superfluous question that was. "I love you," he quickly added.

"I love you too," said Rana, and she began to cry. Aunt Mariam had given her away. Now she wasn't allowed out of the house on her own. She was with a girlfriend at the moment, she said, calling from the friend's place, and her brother Jack was sitting in a café down below, waiting for her. He was like a menacing shadow, she added, and he kept reminding her of her Aunt Jasmin's fate. He frightened her.

170. Rasuk and Elizabeth

For the first time since Farid had known him, Josef's father was despondent. "I keep losing my most capable workers and best stone-masons. They go to Kuwait or Saudi Arabia where they can earn ten times what they get here, and I'm left with idiots who can't even hold a chisel."

"Poultry cages" was his term for the modern concrete buildings that began to disfigure the face of the city at the end of the fifties. "I hate those grey boxes. They're falling into ruin even before the scaffolding's taken down," he said, shaking his head.

"You have to move with the times. People think that style of building is very chic now, and it's cheaper," said Madeleine. Her husband just waved the idea away, looking gloomy.

Josef and Farid thought they would go to the club that afternoon. When they were far enough from home, Josef told his friend that his father was getting hardly any construction contracts now, and was thinking of going to Saudi Arabia himself. "The rich men there have their palaces built of the very best stone. But Madeleine's against it. We have enough in reserve, she said, she doesn't want to lose my father to the desert."

"What did he say?"

"He may be able to stand up to an army but he can't stand up to his wife. So he's staying here," said Josef, regretfully.

When they reached the club they found a surprise waiting for them. Rasuk was sitting in the café with a young woman. They both looked happy. The woman had red hair and a pretty, fair-complexioned face, freckled all over.

"This is Elizabeth. She comes from England. My name is Rasuk. I come from Damascus," said Rasuk in English, imitating the manner of someone just beginning to learn the language. He turned back to the red-haired woman and went on, still in English. "And these are my friends Farid and Josef. They speak very well English and very bad Arabic."

"Hi," said the woman. That was all. Her eyes were fixed on Rasuk like suckers. She took hardly any notice of Farid and Josef. Disappointed, the two of them sat down at the bar and left the couple alone.

"Isn't Gibran here?" Josef asked the licensee of the café. Taufik, who usually knew as much about his protégé as any sporting manager, had no idea whether he was coming or not.

"We ought to hang up a calendar in the club and mark Gibran's appearances on it," suggested Josef.

"Not a bad idea," agreed Taufik, looking at the Englishwoman, who had risen to her feet. She was wearing a brightly coloured summer dress, and walked gracefully. When she disappeared through the door leading to the ladies' room, Josef and Farid turned to look at Rasuk. He was beaming with delight.

"Where did you dredge her up from, then?" asked Josef.

"She asked me where the Bulos Chapel was, though she was stand-ing right outside it. That made us both laugh, and then I showed her the Old Town. Elizabeth is very amusing," replied Rasuk proudly.

"Is she a tourist?" asked Taufik.

"No, a student. She's planning to study Arabic here for a year and then go back to Cambridge."

"Aha," said Josef, "then I don't suppose we'll be seeing much of you for the next twelve months." There was a touch of envy in his voice.

"Oh no, I'll be coming here often," Rasuk assured them. But when Elizabeth came back he paid at once and left the café with her. As they reached the door she stopped, turned to the men, and called, "*Salam aleikhum.*"

"Goodbye, Miss Elizabeth, hope to see you again," replied old Taufik in perfect English without any trace of accent. Josef and Farid stared at him, taken aback. "Thirteen years in the British army," Taufik explained. "That's when I met Gibran."

"Don't you mean you were in the navy?" asked Farid.

"No, no, the army. I was stationed in Aqaba on the Red Sea. I was guarding the commissariat."

"What about Gibran?"

"Gibran was a mechanic on a destroyer, but he spent more time in the cells than on board. He was a brilliant mechanic, but he just didn't get on with the others, and when he lost his temper he used to throw anything he happened to be holding at them. He kept breaking out of jail, and he was always picked up again, until he disappeared once and for all in 1940. People said he'd drowned. It wasn't until I leased the café here that I saw him again for the first time in sixteen years. He hadn't drowned at all, unless it was in drink."

171. The Debts of Venice

The year 1959 began badly. A wave of arrests rolled over the country. Farid's Party training was interrupted because the man who ran the courses was in prison. He called himself Comrade Bassam, but his real name was Josef Kassis, and he was the son of one of the richest importers in Damascus. Comrade Bassam was a tall, smooth-skinned man with a droning, monotonous voice. He talked nineteen to the dozen, as if he had diarrhoea of the mouth. When he started on about some Marxist concept, Farid always felt an enormous urge to drop off to sleep, and sometimes, with unfortunate consequences, he couldn't resist it.

"Comrade," Bassam the Marxist expert had reproved him, "a fighter with no knowledge of economics is just a romantic adventurer. He will betray the working class the moment he gets a chance."

Farid had no intention of doing that, but all the same he was obliged to agree that Bassam who ran the training courses was right, for if you contradicted him his sermon was immediately dragged out to three times its original length, and the other comrades would hold a grudge against you. So Farid merely complained to Amin privately about the boring Bassam. Amin couldn't stand him, and called him a rich upstart. "His father imports washing machines, and son Bassam has one in his head, with a drum going around all the time," he said, grinning.

Under pressure from the government of President Satlan, the Party feverishly extended its activities. Farid had to risk his life distributing pamphlets inveighing against the oppression of communists, and finally even found himself leading the youth organization.

❧

At the end of March, Grandmother Lucia's health deteriorated. She lived in her own deranged world, as if in a constant fever. The situation upset Claire. One day when she entered the house the whole place smelled of incense, jasmine blossom, and thyme. Claire called for the nursing nun and her mother, but there was no reply. When she finally found her, Lucia was dancing naked around a small fire that she had lit in the middle of the room. She was throwing spices on it and uttering cries of glee. The nun was nowhere to be seen.

After that Lucia slept for three days, and when she woke up she summoned Claire, who was now caring for her round the clock, and asked for notepaper and envelopes. From now until her death she wrote letters, asking the Venetian authorities to return her grandfather's collection of glass eyes. When that nobleman lost his right eye, he had apparently had three thousand glass eyes made by a famous glassmaker on Murano until he found one that fitted him perfectly.

Farid was afraid of his grandmother's delusions, and would visit her only in Claire's company. Whenever he saw Lucia she was surrounded by ancient journals and papers. She wrote the mayor of Venice letter after letter, and to everyone's surprise received interested replies. In fact they were written by Claire. As Lucia lay in a fever shortly before her death, the postman brought her a letter with the sender's name given as "Mayor of Venice". Claire read it aloud. It was written in French, and the mayor was inviting Lucia to spend a week in the city. She would stay in the finest house there as a guest of honour, and could visit the Murano Museum and see the magnificent collection of glass eyes that her grandfather had left to Venice in his will.

Lucia was very weak, but all the same she slowly raised her head and propped herself up on her elbows. "So there are still some decent people left in the world," she said triumphantly, and her eyes shone with fevered delusion and endless longing for Venice. "But what glass eyes does he mean?" she asked, suddenly at a loss. Then a mischievous smile flitted over her face.

Claire said nothing, and helped her mother to lie down again. That night Lucia slept peacefully, embracing her pillow as if it were a lover, and never woke up again.

172. Paths Crossing

Farid passed the exam for his high school diploma at the end of June 1959, achieving good marks that allowed him to register at the university. He wanted to study mathematics, physics and chemistry, and be a teacher. Josef, whose average marks were not so good, registered to study geography and history. He wanted to go into politics, and was perfectly happy with those subjects. "A politician who doesn't know anything about history and geography is no use, and will lead his country to ruin," he said succinctly. He and Farid were the only members of their set with marks good enough for them to study at university.

It had been late summer when the new candidates for further education streamed towards the university. The authorities had put up a low-roofed building outside the entrance to help them deal with the crush. It had over ten windows side by side, like the ticket office at a rail station. The officials received application forms through a slit in the window, and seemed to have the calm of Buddha and the time of all eternity at their disposal, while the young candidates for university places roasted in the full sun outside.

Farid and Josef talked to the other applicants. Many of them came from the country and had never been in Damascus before. They had to go back to their distant villages that evening or spend the night on a park bench, since none of them had the money for a hotel. Some had even brought bread, olives, sheep's milk cheese, and hardboiled eggs from home so that they wouldn't have to spend anything on food. All the dialects of the country could be heard. There were two separate windows to one side for women candidates, and all was calm and orderly there. Few women managed to take their high school diploma and then go on to further studies.

A young man called Amran with an expressionless face was just ahead of Josef and Farid in line. He was almost sure, he said, that he wouldn't be accepted by the university, he thought his marks weren't good enough. But no one knew if such pessimism was well-founded. The man with him complained of the lazy officials, and enumerated the buses that had already left for his village in the north and those that would still be running from now until evening.

When Amran's turn came to go up to the window, everyone around heard the humiliating remarks made by a fat Damascene clerk to the peasant's son, after the poor man had been waiting for four hours.

"What do you expect to do with these results?" asked the sweating colossus behind the glass pane scornfully.

"Study something, anything," replied Amran, not exactly quietly but in a tone that all could hear. He would be happy with any subject, he continued; the main thing was that a university degree would open gates for him.

"You wouldn't even get a job as a porter with marks like these," scoffed the clerk.

"Why not? I've passed my high school diploma, and there's no law saying you have to have certain marks before you can study," said Amran, in as level a tone as if the point at issue were not his place at university but something of no importance at all.

"Hmm. No, there is not in fact any such law. The university itself decides on its new students, depending on their numbers and average marks. But if we're talking about laws," said the clerk in a loud voice, grinning, "you can't quote me one obliging me to accept you either."

"What am I going to do now?" asked Amran, rather more quietly.

"Oh, join the army. They'll take anyone," replied the clerk. His derision was palpable, pouring out of the window. Some of the bystanders laughed. Farid was seething with fury, but he was afraid to say anything.

"I don't like armies," said Amran. His voice suddenly faltered.

"Nor do I, but someone has to defend the Fatherland," barked the clerk, pushing the thin folder with Amran's application form back through the window. "Next," he said, without any emotion. But the next was Amran's companion. He went up to the window. "My marks are even worse than my friend's, so I guess I'll go straight off to join the army, and do you know why?" he asked with assumed civility.

The clerk, for his own part, pretended to be curious. "No, why?"

"Not to defend this filthy Fatherland but so I can fuck your mother without being prosecuted for it. You wait and see, you bastard of a Timur-Leng," he said. He turned, and walked away at a deliberately slow pace.

The clerk froze. Leaving his window to punish the boy who had insulted him would have been too risky. The other angry peasants' sons who weren't admitted would have lynched him.

That was the first time Farid heard the term of abuse frequently used by peasants from the country to insult the Damascenes.

Timur-Leng came from Mongolia and had captured the city with his wild horde in 1400, after a long siege. His revenge for the resistance that he encountered was terrible. He had a third of the population driven into the great Ummayad Mosque and set the place on fire. None of the thirty thousand people inside survived. He allowed his soldiers a week in which to rape the women who had not been driven into the mosque, and from those who had survived his revenge he sent scholars, craftsmen, and artists to his capital of Samarkand, leaving only a handful of wretches behind on a smoking pile of rubble. It was said that the Damascenes were so crafty because they were Timur-Leng's bastards.

Eight years after the incident outside the university, in the autumn of 1967, a young army captain by the name of Amran led a coup. Two days later he appointed himself general, and soon after that President of Syria. He issued a decree giving peasants' sons bonus points for university entrance. Two years later, President Amran received five honorary doctorates at the University of Damascus, in the faculties of philosophy, literature, mathematics, political science, and medicine. Moscow followed suit. In recognition of a large order from Amran to the Soviet arms industry, it appointed him Honorary Doctor of Philosophy of Moscow University.

173. The State of God

Madeleine opened the door to Farid. "Thank goodness you're here. He's beside himself," she said, concerned, and took him to Josef. Josef was a changed man. He looked at Farid red-eyed.

"Those bastards, they've made a second attempt on President Satlan's life, would you believe it? Suppose the hand grenade had gone off? The criminals, I could murder them all!" Farid didn't know what to say. Josef sounded as if he were under the influence of drugs. He was snorting rather than breathing, his words came out as if he were retching instead of speaking. It took Farid some time to grasp the fact that one of the Muslim Brotherhood had thrown a hand grenade at the President. Satlan had escaped unscathed while the young fanatic fell, riddled by bullets from the President's bodyguard.

Farid kept quiet and let Josef rant on. He could understand his friend's grief and rage, but the assassination attempt meant nothing to him personally. He had been rejoicing all day over news from Rana. She would be alone for an hour in a small church next Sunday, she said, when her brother Jack had to go to the tennis club with his father. Farid was to wait for her under the picture of St. Barbara.

If he had opened his mouth, the only word to emerge would have been "Rana". So he kept quiet and listened to Josef. Later, Rasuk joined them. He had heard about the attempt on the President's life on the BBC World Service. The Arab radio stations were saying nothing about it.

"Elizabeth asked me if these were the new Assassins," he said. "I don't know much about them – they sound odd. I thought I'd ask you," he added, turning to Josef.

"Myths and legends proliferate around the Assassins. They are described as murderers, religious fanatics, paid killers, and most often of all as 'hashish eaters'. At the time no one knew about smoking hashish, people chewed it," explained Josef, sounding like a walking encyclopaedia. Then he went on. "Well, yes, the Muslim Brotherhood are just like the Assassins of the old days. They murder when the leader of their sect tells them to, they don't fear death because they already have one foot in Paradise. So you can't even frighten them."

"And do they pump themselves full of hashish first?" asked Rasuk.

"No, that bit's nonsense," said Josef. "Hashish just makes it easier to get through to other realities. It makes meditation deeper, guides the eye to the essentials, and it's a help in attaining wisdom."

This was the first time Farid had ever heard anyone speak in favour of hashish; his parents and his school, his Church and the Party all condemned drugs as harmful.

"But," objected Rasuk, "Marco Polo said the leaders pumped all new members full of hashish and opium until they were out of their minds. Then servants took the new warrior into a beautiful garden full of naked youths and women dancing about and satisfying all his desires, and he thought he was in Paradise. Later, he was taken back to his lodgings in a dazed state. When he returned to his senses, he was told he would go straight back to that Paradise once he'd carried out the leader's orders and died a martyr's death. Don't laugh," Rasuk told Farid. "It says so in a book about the Assassins."

"Yes, you can find an amazing amount of nonsense in books, said Josef dismissively. "Hashish is soothing, it makes you drowsy and sexy. Not exactly the qualities of a fanatical killer who carries out his mission without any thought of loss. A man like the legendary Hassan Sabah, the leader of the sect known as the Assassins, was an ascetic, philosopher, and mathematician and could never have inspired fear if his army was high on drugs. His men wouldn't have occupied a single village. But they say that Sabah had fifty-three citadels between northern Persia and Damascus in his power by 1092. Marco Polo was certainly an honest man, but how could a traveller with hardly a word of Arabic grasp the principles of such a secretive organization?"

"Why did Marco Polo put all this nonsense together, then?" asked Farid.

"Well, if he'd written honestly after such a long journey that he still didn't understand many cultures and their customs, people would have taken no notice of him. But if you don't tell the truth, if you put your audience's imagination into words instead, they believe you and you're popular. Those orgies in the Assassins' citadels really did take place in Marco Polo's fantasies about the East."

"What drove them to do it, though, if it wasn't expecting to have all their desires satisfied in Paradise?" asked Rasuk, interested.

"Exactly what drives today's fanatics: a sense of divine mission that makes them the elect. It's the only drug that can enable young men who enjoy life to overcome the fear of death and despise life itself. The idea of going to Paradise is the most dangerous of all civilized inventions. That's where communism and religion meet, and the only difference is in defining its location. In this world, say the communists. No, in the next world, says religion. The Muslim Brotherhood tried to synthesize the two. They want to set up the state of God here on earth, because they think that would solve all problems. Although it's the biggest problem of all in itself."

"Do they really want that, or are you just making fun of them?" asked Rasuk.

"It's all in the stuff they write. You two ought to do a bit more reading," Josef said, so worked up now that his voice was hoarse.

"And what does the Muslim Brotherhood plan to do about us Christians?"

"Oh, they're clear about that too – either you emigrate or you become second-class citizens," said Josef.

"I'd rather emigrate," Rasuk decided.

174. The Trap

"I don't know what I'd do without Matta," said Claire, the day before her mother's funeral. Farid could see for himself how hard his friend was working, collecting flowers and wreaths for the coffin, getting food and drink in for the wake after the funeral, and candles for the church. No errand was too far for him to go. He was also willing to be one of the six men carrying the coffin from the dead woman's house to the Catholic cemetery outside the city walls.

Elias surreptitiously slipped a hundred lira into Matta's aunt's bag as she sat with the other mourners. The old lady wept with gratitude and embarrassed Elias by trying to kiss his hand. He dropped a kiss on her forehead. "We're all fond of Matta," he whispered, and patted her on the shoulder.

"God bless you and your Claire, and may the Merciful One protect Farid," replied Matta's aunt, much moved, and she slowly made her way home. The size of the funeral procession surprised Farid. He had no idea that his family had so many well-wishers in Damascus. Josef and Azar walked beside him, just behind his parents and Claire's brother.

This was the first time Farid had seen his Uncle Marcel, his mother's only brother, at close quarters. He was tall and massive, and when he stood next to Claire you sensed that they had nothing in common. There was something shapeless about Marcel, whose face was scarred and pitted by chronic acne. When Farid expressed his condolences, the ugly colossus failed to recognise his nephew, and absently offered his limp, sweating hand.

Later, at the wake, Farid also saw his mother's cousin Sana, whom he had met quite often at his grandmother's house during the last two years. She was almost thirty and already had four or five children, but she looked like a girl of twenty. Her husband Habib worked for the tram company as an electrician. Sana laughed a lot. There was something wild about her that fascinated Farid.

Not long before Grandmother's death she had invited Farid to visit her, but at the time Claire had asked him not to go. "She's a slut," she briefly explained.

But Farid had never noticed any sign of that about her. Sana was always elegantly dressed and smelled of expensive perfume. Of course she was very feminine, and her clothes emphasized her curves, but blaming her for that seemed to him excessively Catholic. So he decided to visit Sana a little while after the funeral. She lived quite close, in Kassabah Alley.

When Farid entered the inner courtyard of the two-storey house, she saw him from the kitchen window. "Oh, how nice! My cousin has come to visit," she cried out loud, as if she wanted to let the whole street know. The stairs were crammed with toys, shoes, and cartons.

She hurried to meet him, trying to button up her open house-dress. But the buttonholes were too big, and she couldn't manage it.

"One of my fine relations comes visiting at last," she said, kissing Farid. She smelled of cigarettes and cooking fat.

The apartment was a dump. An old woman sat in a faded green armchair in the sitting room to which Sana steered him. She looked as stiff and desiccated as a cast-off straw doll.

Children were crawling about, screaming, or running back and forth in the chaos. Sana ignored them. She made a way for Farid through the dirt to some seats in a corner around a low table. There was a smell of stagnant water. Farid soon discovered the source of it: a huge plant pot containing a dead papyrus, with black water in the saucer under it.

Sana disappeared to make coffee, and was gone for a long time.

"He comes every day," said the desiccated figure suddenly, "he beats my son in front of the children every day, he takes his wife away from him." Farid started with shock, and wished he could get out of there. The old woman went on sadly, and when he looked at her, he saw that hers was really a beautiful face, but marred by sickness, dirt and grief.

"He comes home tired from work," she went on, "and he has to feed me, and wash his children, and then the joiner comes and she tells him how many times he's to hit her husband, right there in front of the children, and the joiner knocks him about. My son weeps, and I can't do anything to help him. Habib was a pretty boy like you, but after he married that whore he became a hunchback. My poor son! Can you get me a pistol?" Farid didn't reply. "No? No, I suppose not," she muttered despairingly, and relapsed into her silent grief. She did not say another word.

"I heard from Michel," Sana began, putting the tray of coffee cups down on the table, "that you're very popular with women." She gave him a broad grin. "Just like your father. And that you often go to the club," she added, pushing the scratched tray over to him. Two coffee cups of different patterns stood on saucers that didn't match either of them.

"What Michel?" asked Farid, taking a sip.

"What Michel do you suppose? *The* Michel. He's done a lot of your carpentry at the club," she said indignantly, sitting down and spreading her legs so wide that he could see her red panties.

Farid guessed that Michel was her lover.

"I don't know him," he said obstinately, by way of taking sides with the old woman, who must be Sana's mother-in-law.

Sana was speechless. She looked sideways at him. "You don't?" she said incredulously.

Farid drank his coffee in silence. To his surprise, it tasted even better than Claire's. He kept glancing at the old lady in the dilapidated chair. She was looking at him with eyes wide open, but didn't move a muscle.

"Old viper," whispered Sana, seeing the direction of Farid's gaze. "She'll live to be two hundred. She shits all the time, but I'm not cleaning her up. Her son can do that." There was cold contempt in her voice.

Farid drank the last of his coffee, stood up and walked firmly out. He felt that if he stayed there a moment longer he'd throw up.

"Where are you going in such a hurry?" Sana called after him. The air was fresher out in the corridor. He stopped, leaning against the window sill, and feeling ashamed of his flight.

"I have to go home. There's a meeting at the club this evening, and I must look in at home first," he lied, looking down into the yard. A young father was playing with his son, a boy of about five, laughing and tickling him, and then suddenly he shouted, "Hold still there!" It sounded as if he were training a dog. The child couldn't manage to keep still just like that. He fidgeted and went on laughing, at the same time looking at his father's right hand in alarm. It landed right in the boy's face, knocking him down. He screamed with pain, his father picked him up, carried him about, soothed him, gave him five piastres and began tickling him again. The boy, totally confused, began laughing once more, then his father put him down, laughed with him, gave him a candy, tickled him, and cried, "Hold still there!" And once again the hand came down on the boy's face.

Farid was about to shout at the man when he felt Sana's hand on his back. "Why in such a hurry, cousin?" She was gently flattering him. For a brief moment he forgot Rana, his mother, the old woman in the chair, the noisy children, the garbage and the sadist in the courtyard, and wanted to kiss her lips. She smiled as if she knew what he was after.

Farid ran to the stairs. Sana did not reply to his hastily murmured, "Goodbye." She knew as well as he did that this was his first and last visit to her.

ज०

Farid was drinking tea on the terrace of the club late that evening when Michel the joiner came in. He seemed to be looking for someone among those present, and finally came over to their table.

"The bet's on," whispered Josef, who thought Farid's entire story about his cousin and her lover was the old lady's fantasy.

"A friend of mine," began the joiner, "tells me you said today you didn't know me, although we've known each other for years." As he finished this remark he wondered why the two of them were suddenly roaring and choking with laughter. "Pay up!" Farid told Josef.

"And you're a fool," Josef said to the joiner accusingly. "My clever friend here set a trap and you fell right into it. So it's true. You're screwing his cousin Sana and now I'm paying for his tea." Josef and Farid left Michel standing there and set off for home.

⁊𐎂

It was just before midnight. Two men were running down the street. They stopped for a moment, looking up at the rooftops. The smaller of the two was holding a pistol.

"He went over the roofs and escaped down Jews' Alley," said the smaller man breathlessly. He put the pistol back in his jacket pocket.

175. The Prayer

He had already been waiting quarter of an hour for the bus in vain when a taxi drove up. The driver got out, saying, "The bus driver's had a heart attack. At this moment they're treating him, he can't drive any more today. The next bus will be along in an hour."

Farid didn't think about it for long, but got into the shared taxi. The driver seemed to be trying to pick up everyone he saw at the roadside today, and even stopped when a man who only wanted a match to light his cigarette waved to him. At his leisure, he gave the man his booklet of matches and asked at least ten times if he was sure he didn't want to go anywhere. "Times are bad," he said apologetically to the passengers he already had. "You have to be patient." At the next bus stop he told a different story about the bus driver, who this time had allegedly murdered his conductor, so that was why he couldn't drive any more that day. There was still plenty of room in the taxi. But no one got in, and the taxi driver made for the next bus stop. It didn't bother him at all when, at the fifth or sixth stop, the bus came up right behind him and its driver hooted the horn.

Farid was slightly late at the church. Rana was standing deep in thought under the picture of St. Barbara. He went quietly up to her, and looked around before he touched her, dropping a quick kiss on her neck. Rana started, and then smiled.

They sat in a corner near the confessionals right at the back of the church and held hands. The service was just beginning, and there were only a few worshippers, sitting in the three front rows.

"For once my father was wonderful. My mother's been wanting me to marry my cousin Rami, her brother's son, as soon as I'd taken my high school diploma and left school. He's a first lieutenant in the army. But Papa said I was to study at the university first and then we'd see."

"Well, that's good news. If you're studying we'll have four years' respite, and we're sure to have thought of something by then."

"Yes, but my mother isn't letting it go at that. She keeps looking out for any opportunity to say bad things about me to my father. And you know how hopeless Jack is at school. Even with private tutors he only just got his middle school diploma. Now he's sick of studying and wants to work and earn money. It's a bitter defeat for my mother, and she can't come to terms with the idea that I might succeed at university too. Yesterday she and my brother were saying it would only make me more rebellious, and guess what, they simply decided to marry me off to Rami in a hurry."

Farid shook his head. "Can't you tell your father?"

"I did. He thinks I'm imagining things."

"Listen, if it gets to be a real threat we'll run away again. Don't worry, I'm always there for you, and Claire will back us up too. After all, I'm the result of an elopement myself."

"Believe it or not, when I heard what the two of them were saying I packed my bag at once. You'll remember it: the one I had in Beirut. But then I unpacked it again, because I didn't want to show that I know their plans. If the worst comes to the worst, I can run away without a bag," she said.

Farid kissed her ear. "And I'll love you even without clothes and a toothbrush," he whispered. His breath tickled Rana. She laughed nervously, and moved a little way off.

"I have more than enough money hidden away," she said firmly.

The service ended too quickly for Farid. Rana left the church on her own. At first he just sat there, looking at the pictures. When he was alone he went up to a statue of Christ and began talking to Jesus. "Can you hear me?" he whispered. "This is your friend Farid. I know I haven't spoken to you for years, the monastery spoiled all that for me. And yes, I'm a communist now, but I still believe in you, it's just the Church I don't believe in. Please help Rana and protect her. She's so brave in a cowardly world, and her mother is a viper. Can you hear me? Help her. You don't have to help me too. I can manage on my own."

Farid spoke to the statue for a long time. Finally, when he noticed a young priest standing behind him, keeping at a courteous distance and waiting, he smiled awkwardly, crossed himself, and left the church, walking fast.

176. Hunter and Hunted

"You'd better watch out for Suleiman," said Josef, looking concerned. "I discovered yesterday that he's an informer. Since when I don't know, but he certainly is one." He was speaking very fast, as if anxious to get the words off his chest.

Farid looked at him and said nothing.

"Yes, of course he's working for the state, and yes, I think our President is the saviour of the Arabs, but I despise informers. And you may be idiot enough to go running around with communists, but you're still my best friend. Yesterday he was making up to you just too obviously in the club. What did he want?"

"He was inviting me out hunting," said Farid. "His father's given him a gun that the Spanish consul got from France, but he didn't want it, so he gave it to his chauffeur. Do you think I should go?"

"Yes, of course, and either act as if you didn't know anything or tell him what you suspect straight out. Only you mustn't show any fear, or he'll finish you off."

"Me, afraid of him? Are you joking?"

"No, you stupid Kamikaze. Informers are cowards, but once they taste blood they get amazingly greedy."

"I can't get my head around this. Why would he try it with me?"

"How do I know what you get up to at night? I suppose his bunch just want to know more about you."

Farid sat perfectly still. Grief overcame him. He had liked the lively and mischievous Suleiman. After getting his middle school diploma Suleiman had left school, worked for a while as a taxi driver, and now, at nineteen, he already owned half a taxi. That seemed to Farid too soon for someone earning an honest living. Some said that Suleiman had been involved in smuggling for a while, and invested the money cleverly. Others spread the rumour that the clever young man had, appropriately enough, taken all the taxi owners who employed him for a ride.

But why would he be an informer? Why would he give away people who had never done him any harm? Could he be behind the arrest of Marwan, the new maths teacher, who had suddenly disappeared? No one knew if he was still alive. And who had reported Nadim the barber to the police?

"Informers are monsters," said Farid. "I just can't get it into my head that our friend Suleiman is that kind of a creep."

"There's a hell of a lot you can't get into your head. But our childhood's over now. And a great many people go through the gate to adulthood as perfectly harmless men and women, while others turn out to be monsters. Want me to begin with my family or yours?" asked Josef in friendly tones.

જ

Farid was to be waiting at the door at three next morning, with provisions and a canteen for the expedition. Suleiman was picking him up. They had to be in the game reserve at four, before sunrise.

All night he tossed and turned in bed. He had already warned Amin, but even Amin couldn't tell him how to deal with Suleiman.

What could he do? Wild answers shot through Farid's head. Clichés out of movies and novels: grab Suleiman's gun, point it at his head, heart, or balls, and make him talk that way? And suppose he refused to talk? Could he bring himself to pull the trigger, he sheepishly wondered? The answer was no. He cursed his cowardice.

What would Suleiman say if Farid reminded him of their hours together in the attic with the gang? Too sentimental. He was a trained informer, and their childhood was definitely over.

He slept for only three hours and then sat up in bed with a start. In his dreams, Suleiman had been shot and stowed under Farid's own bed. Not until he put the light on and looked at his room did he calm down again.

It was just after two-thirty already. He dressed and went to the front door, where he met Claire in her dressing gown. She gave him a kiss and a picnic bag.

Suleiman arrived punctually, looking as if he had had a good night's sleep. His hunting rifle was on the back seat. Farid threw his picnic bag in beside it and got into the car. They drove about forty kilometres through the dark to an oasis visited by birds, hares and gazelles. Date palms, pomegranates, figs, wild grapevines, cacti and walnut trees grew there. Only the spring of water was disappointingly tiny. But there were plenty of birds, and when the first rays of the sun came through, and the dawn chorus began, Suleiman fired. He missed, but the shot had made a lot of noise. Farid was surprised by the gun's strong recoil. Suleiman cursed the birds, the wind, the trees, and his own bad luck, and kept firing into the air.

He hit only once, but the injured bird could still fly. Farid ran after it while Suleiman waited. Finally Farid found the bird, which was only slightly wounded in the wing, under a wild pomegranate bush. He didn't know what kind of bird it was – rather like a turtle dove in size, but brightly coloured and with a straight, strong beak. That evening Amin told him it had been a warwar, a bee-eater from Africa.

The bird looked at Farid, its eyes frightened, its beak wide open, and uttered a hiss that sounded more like a snake. Farid stopped. "Found it?" he heard Suleiman call.

"No," said Farid, and he let the branches of the pomegranate spring back into place.

When Suleiman had fired three-quarters of his cartridges, they stopped for breakfast.

"This oasis stinks of gunpowder so much, no bird will be able to survive without a gas mask," said Suleiman, laughing. They sat down beside the water hole and began eating their sandwiches.

"Did you hear about Simon being arrested?" Suleiman suddenly asked.

Even when he was telling Josef about it that evening, Farid couldn't say how the words to save him had risen to his lips. "What Simon? My cousin Laila's husband? What has he done?"

Suleiman faltered. "Is Laila's husband the violinist called Simon too?" he asked in surprise, but he couldn't hide his disappointment.

"Of course. You saw him at that benefit performance for the Catholic Church last Christmas. What about him?" Farid was acting stupid. Of course he knew perfectly well what Simon the informer meant. He was one of the soldiers who belonged to a communist cell, a brave, hot-tempered man.

"No, I didn't mean your cousin's husband. I mean the one who lived near Bab Tuma. A poor soldier suspected of plotting a revolt. Don't you know him? He sometimes used to go to the club and drink tea with your friend Amin," said Suleiman.

"No, I don't know him, I'm afraid. Amin has a lot of friends, and I've never seen this one, but if he comes to the club again you can point him out to me," replied Farid naïvely.

"He won't be back. My aunt's been weeping her eyes out. He was her daughter's fiancé, such a brave young man," said the hypocritical Suleiman. Farid didn't know if Suleiman had an aunt with daughters at all, but at that moment all his feelings for his former friend died, and he was surprised to find how unattractive Suleiman suddenly looked to him.

Three months later Farid and all other members of the Communist Party received orders from the leadership to break off all contact with soldiers. Only years later did he discover that work inside the army had been halted on instructions from Moscow.

177. The Wine Cellar

Josef's family were celebrating the engagement of his sisters Balkis and Jasmin to Samir and Amir, the old pharmacist's sons. Between them, they owned a large pharmacy near the Italian hospital. Everyone in the neighbouring streets knew about the party. The sight of Matta racing around for a week in advance, getting in all kinds of supplies for Josef's family, was a better advertisement than a hundred posters.

On the day of the party itself Matta was among the guests, spruced up in well ironed clothes and along with his aunt, also in her best. It was Madeleine's express wish that Matta wasn't to do any more work at the party.

Farid himself had little chance to enjoy it. He, Azar, Rasuk, and Toni were helping their friend Josef to make sure all the three hundred guests had somewhere to sit, were served drinks, knew their way to the lavatories, and above all could find their old places when they came back again. All this had to be done without a sharp word. They were constantly having to mollify the guests, find more chairs, and wipe dirt off the floor and bad-tempered expressions off faces.

But the master of the house was in charge of the wine and arrack. He himself brought bottles up from the cellar and poured drinks for his guests. Josef said his father had enough wine and arrack in the cellar to get the entire Republic drunk – all excellent vintages that he had ordered when he was still earning well.

Josef's cousin Nawal kept touching Farid when he went into the kitchen. She wore a comical pair of nickel-framed glasses with round lenses, and squinted slightly.

"You be careful, that girl's a loose cannon and fires powerful shots," commented Josef. Nothing escaped him. "She's been having affairs with one or other of her teachers ever since she was eight."

Nawal heard him speaking ill of her, and threw a radish at him. He swore, and called out to his mother that now she knew why he'd rather keep out of the kitchen. The girls fell about laughing.

"You're cute," Nawal whispered to Farid from behind him. "Give me a call some time," she added quietly, as he put down a tray of empty coffee cups. And when he turned to look at her, she quickly slipped a note into his trouser pocket. This rather embarrassed Farid, who didn't think much of her.

What he did appreciate, however, was the fact that the food at the engagement party tasted as fantastic as it looked. Over twenty cold starters and five hot dishes were enough to make anyone's mouth water. In addition, there were three pyramids of fresh fruit standing around the fountain. Madeleine and Rimon had always been generous hosts.

Josef whispered to Farid that the guests were eating the apartment that his father had sold especially for this stupid party, room by room. "Can't wait to see when they'll get to the WC," he added. Farid didn't entirely understand what he was talking about, but joined in Josef's laughter. It went on like that: most scraps of conversation were drowned out by the noise of the party, and there was no time for explanations.

The skills of the singer who had been booked for the party left something to be desired, but she was pretty as a picture, and the men liked that. The more they drank the better they liked her voice, and they even began comparing her with Feiruz, the best woman singer in Arabia. Many of their wives, on the other hand, said sharply that the singer would get no further than the nearest bed.

Around midnight two large groups of guests were still lingering at the party. Farid and his parents had already left. Then something happened to cheer Josef as much as if he'd won a game of chess against the world champion Mikhail Botvinnik.

One group, consisting of about twenty of his father's friends and relations, was sitting under the old vine on the south-facing terrace. The members of the other group, his mother's relations and the pharmacist's family, were sitting around the large fountain in the inner courtyard.

The wine was running out. Madeleine signalled to her husband, and he set straight off to fetch more. The cellar vault, made of white stone, was kept at the right temperature by a clever system of small windows let into it at ground level. Bronze lamps on the walls, handsome shelves, and oak tables, chairs, and cupboards gave it almost the look of a sacred building.

Josef's father had been keeping his best vintages for this late hour. The storeroom under the south terrace was well stocked with wines from Lebanon, every bottle worth a fortune. He hesitated briefly in front of the shelves, and finally chose ten bottles of red wine. As he was standing under the three little windows, he suddenly heard his brother Farhan's voice. "Rimon always liked to show off. Even as a child he just had to be the strongest all the time. Well, as you all know, he was only a third-rate boxer."

Rimon froze. His failure of a brother, whom he had helped out financially several times, was laughing at him at his own daughters' engagement party! Rimon was furious; the blood went to his head. He felt like shouting, "You envious, ungrateful sod!" when he heard his favourite cousin Maria's voice.

"And his wife, too! She's ruined the idiot entirely, and now she's riding high on his back. My cousin was always a donkey. The idea of marrying her daughters to those two feeble-minded pharmacists was hers, and Rimon goes along with anything she says. And Madeleine isn't beautiful or a good mother either, let alone a good housewife. My God, did you notice? Most of those dishes came from a restaurant so that our fine lady wouldn't ruin her fingernails," she said venomously.

Maria! Soft-spoken Maria, who was always telling Rimon, when they were on their own, what luck he had with Madeleine, quite unlike his brother Farhan, whose wife was a silly goose.

"Not only is it expensive," Rimon heard his old aunt adding her contribution, "it tastes horrible too. I hardly touched a bite." She was lying. He hadn't counted, but every time he topped up her glass of arrack she had a new plate heaped high with delicacies in front of her.

"Nor did I," said one after another of the company.

"No wonder, with such nasty stuff, and I'll tell him so to his face," announced his brother, stepping up his indignation a notch.

"Oh, don't do that, you're always sacrificing yourself, and then his wife just says you're envious. Let him alone. What is it they say? If your enemy is suffering then wish him long life."

They all roared approval, instead of slapping the speaker's face – that slut who cuckolded his brother!

"And now, now," cried Rimon's cousin Girgi, a lawyer, "here we've been sitting for ages in the dry. I told Madeleine her guests needed something to drink, but she just gave me a silly smile."

"You know something?" Rimon heard his brother reply in a low voice. "I hear he's ruined. I wouldn't be surprised if he declared himself bankrupt soon."

That's it, thought Rimon. Leaving the wine where it was, he stormed up the steps and made for the south terrace. But at the sight of all those people suddenly beaming at him in the friendliest fashion, he could only laugh. He laughed and laughed, until his relations thought he was out of his mind. Rimon had to sit down, laughing harder than ever at the stupidity of all these people who had no idea that he had overheard their slanders.

When his brother Farhan leaned over him and asked, with pretended concern, if he was drunk, Rimon, still laughing, gave him his famous upward hook. Farhan flew backward, landed on his aunt's lap, and fell to the ground with her.

He stood up indignantly, collected his wife, and left. "And you can take our dear auntie home too," called Rimon, spluttering with laughter. He turned his back on the sour, stony faces of his family, and without another word went to join his wife and the guests by the fountain.

178. Masculine Honour

By the autumn, Rasuk's English girlfriend Elizabeth spoke Arabic remarkably well. She had an English accent, but it sounded amusing, and she could swear like a street urchin.

Rasuk loved Elizabeth more than ever. Proudly, he told his friends about all the men who had made eyes at her, only to be turned down flat. She loved no one but him, and they suited each other perfectly.

He wanted to get his military service done as quickly as possible, because then he could apply for a passport to travel. "No passport without military service first, and I don't want to travel illegally. If only because Elizabeth loves Damascus so much, I want to be able to come back any time," he said. With her help, he was planning to open an Oriental bazaar in England, and he already had ten Damascus suppliers lined up who would be glad to sell their craft products abroad: items made of wood, brass, steel and textiles.

When Rasuk talked about Elizabeth he praised her frankness, courage, and above all her respect for his freedom. "We don't have that kind of thing in Syria. If people here love you, they cling. Your personal freedom is a disruptive factor, it endangers love. That's why we try to give our partners as little freedom as possible. Elizabeth is just the opposite. She sees my freedom as sacrosanct," he told Amin and the others one afternoon at the club.

"But somehow Europeans don't really fit in with us," said Amin. It surprised Farid that he of all people said so. He had always believed that Amin thought nothing of ideas like nationalism and the Fatherland. However, he didn't comment.

"Yes, perhaps they love freedom more, but they don't understand the concept of honour," claimed Badi, an elementary school teacher from the south.

"Every human being has honour. It's stupid to think we have a monopoly on it," replied Rasuk brusquely.

"That's not what I meant," responded the teacher. "Every nation lives with its own scale of values. To some, conquering new territory for the Fatherland comes first, to others it's the happiness of the family, to others again it's the honour of their women, don't you understand?"

"And here we come to the heart of the matter," said Taufik. "Would anyone like more tea before the debate begins? I don't want to miss something later."

Four wanted tea, the rest ordered water or coffee.

"Then keep quiet and wait for me. I'll be back in a moment."

When Taufik had brought the drinks and been paid, he sat down in the back row, where he could keep an eye on the café, and said, "Fire away."

"What Badi was saying is exactly the kind of honour I can live without," said Rasuk, taking up the thread of the argument again. "We've been beaten, humiliated, and robbed for five hundred years, and we confine our idea of honour entirely to a scrap of skin in a woman's most private place. That's not normal, is it?"

Protests broke out.

"He's been going out for a few months with an Englishwoman," cried Michel the joiner, "and now he won't hear of masculine honour any more."

"You listen to me, young man," added Sadik the vegetable dealer, "you can take everything from an Arab except his honour. Europeans may be in advance of us in many ways, but not on that point. Where honour is concerned we're way ahead of them."

Rasuk cast Farid a glance that spoke volumes. Sadik, of all people, who was always cheating his customers! And that skinflint spoke of Arab honour!

"In your place," Farid told him sharply, "I wouldn't talk about Arab values so much. Do you know what quality our ancestors most abhorred?"

"Well, what was it?" asked Sadik with his naïve expression.

"Avarice," replied Farid, and a chorus of laughter and chuckling, catcalls and whistles broke out against the vegetable dealer.

"But Sadik is right all the same," cried Badi the teacher and Basil the construction worker above the din. "We've had everything taken from us, but our honour remains. I'd rather die than marry a woman if other men had slept with her first," added Basil. Several of the company nodded. They included Amin, who was friendly with Basil and Badi.

"And you don't think that's odd?" asked Azar quietly.

"Louder," Taufik demanded. "I can't hear a word."

"Don't you think it's odd for virginity to be so sacred to us?"

"What's odd about it?" growled a small man whom Farid didn't know, but whose name was Edward.

"The odd thing is for men, who pay hardly any attention to women in the usual way, to situate all their honour in the place where they pee! What miserable, dishonoured men those Europeans are, conquering the air and the seas, venturing into the world of atoms, while our proud men twirl their moustaches and live with antiquated ideas – but they can feel superior because they've married women who were still virgins."

Angry murmurs of protest against Azar were heard from several quarters.

"And I'm sure you all know," said Rasuk, coming to his aid, "that a few gynaecologists here do nothing but sew up the hymen again. They study in America, they sacrifice years of their lives, just to come home and spend all their time cobbling up the damage for the sake of masculine honour."

⁂

At the end of October Rasuk was drafted into the army, expecting to have finished his military service in January 1961. Then he would marry Elizabeth a month later, and they would move to England. She would have finished her studies in Damascus by then.

But it all turned out quite differently.

179. Listening to Films

Claire loved films. She could never have enough of them.

"Films are magic," she said. "There was a man sitting beside me in the cinema, weeping buckets of tears over the sad story of a woman prevented by her parents from marrying the man she loved. He went on crying until the end, when she was on her deathbed, and her last words were for her lover who was far away. But at home this man who wept floods of tears in the cinema would forbid his daughter to meet *her* lover. He'd even assure her that he knows who the right man for her is better than she does. I bet you anything he would."

When Claire hadn't been to the cinema for some time she would get Farid to tell her the plots of movies he had seen with the other young men. Claire called this "listening to films". The only ones she didn't want to hear about were Westerns, science fiction, and movies about the days of chivalry.

Once there had been some very good movies on for three weeks, but nothing suitable for Claire, although she was desperate to listen to another film. When Farid woke up from his siesta one hot after-noon, he found her in the inner courtyard. She had freshened it up by spraying water around, and in the shade there was a place to sit with a table, two comfortable bamboo chairs, and a large plate of pistachio nuts. Now he knew why his mother had asked three times at lunch whether he was doing anything that afternoon. She couldn't go on any longer without listening to the story of a film.

For want of a suitable film, he told her the tale of a tragic murder case that he had just heard from Josef. It was the story of a woman who – like Josef's own aunts – was prevented from loving because she had inherited a fortune, but lived under her brother's thumb. He chased away any men who came too close to his sister. Cheated as she had been, the woman kept quiet for a long time, until she fell in love with a spice merchant and begged her brother to agree to the mar-riage. She was already thirty, but as usual her brother found about three hundred things wrong with the man, insulted him, and sent him packing. The woman took her revenge: she poisoned her brother and his family, and then hanged herself. It took the CID a long time to fit all the pieces of the puzzle together and solve the case.

Some time later, when Farid had left the courtyard and Claire was still wondering which of her own women friends might be capable of such an act of murder and suicide, the doorbell rang. Matta was standing outside the front door, with a woman who smiled at Claire.

"This … is Faride … my fiancée," said Matta quietly. "Is my brother … Farid … at home?"

180. Fatima and Josef

Josef was in love too. Fatima had fascinated him from the moment when he first saw her. They had met at the big demonstration in October, when half a million people gathered in the streets to show their support for President Satlan.

As time went on, Josef came to love Fatima as he had never loved anyone before. She had what he lacked: courage, cheerfulness, and spontaneity, and she showed him what she was thinking and feeling. Fatima also read countless books, and Josef had to work hard to keep up with her. When women fall in love with an idea, he sometimes thought, they can be more fanatical than any man.

He met her some ten times in the six months after that first meeting, in the Café Vienna. They always sat at the same table, talked, dreamed of a strong, united Arabia led by Satlan, drank coffee, and kissed.

Fatima loved voices. She didn't mind what people looked like at all, so long as they had good voices. She told Josef that even in her mother's womb she had graded her relations by the sound of their voices, and she hadn't changed her mind to this day. She couldn't resist Satlan's voice, or Josef's either.

From a distance, Josef looked spectrally thin and ugly, but when he spoke Fatima felt elated, light at heart. And there was another reason for her to like Josef's company: his clever mind left no room for boredom. He was amusing and laughed at himself. "The fire in his heart," Fatima told Farid once, "has melted any fat he ever had on him."

Fatima was passionately pro-Satlan. He promised the rise of a great nation moving on to pastures new, and to her he was not so much a politician as a saint. He spoke directly to her and millions of other women in every speech he made, urging them to rise and fight. That was why she had been one of the first Syrian women to stand side by side with men, united in a sea of sympathy for Satlan. And suddenly some men at that October demonstration in 1959 had placed the thin boy whose voice made her go weak at the knees on their shoulders and carried him with them. She had loved him ever since.

⋙

One day her mother took her aside, and told her it had come to the ears of her brothers Isam and Ahmad that she was keeping company with one of those godless Christians. Fatima reassured her mother, saying those tale-bearers were just blinded by hatred. The man with whom she'd exchanged a word or so at the bus stop outside her school was her girlfriend Rashide's brother. "Those two fools are so stupid they don't even know that Rashide is a Muslim," said Fatima scornfully.

Her mother, a kindly and devout woman, patted her head. "I told your brothers, Fatima is a good girl and a true believer! You just keep your mind on school and not on men."

Fatima was sure that her brothers couldn't have found out about Josef, and were just full of spite because their sister venerated Satlan, while they both belonged to the Muslim Brotherhood, which was equipped by the Saudis with money and arms to be used against him.

That stupid bearded couple of brothers would never get on her trail, she thought on the way to the Café Vienna.

It was a sunny but very cold March day, and she was looking forward to seeing Josef. She changed from one bus to another three times, always checking carefully in case anyone was following her. She felt that she was not observed. But appearances were deceptive.

"It's crazy," she told Josef later in the café, still thinking of her mother. "Muslims and Christians can fight each other, trade, mourn, celebrate, live and die with each other, they're just not allowed to love each other. And if a couple do dare to love all the same, the answer is death. Arabs are more consistent on that point than in anything else." And she squeezed Josef's hand so hard that his fingers hurt.

"I hate the idea of delivering anyone up to death because I love them," said Josef. "I'd feel like someone inviting an innocent person to come for a drive in a car, even though he knows its brakes aren't working. The whole idea sends me crazy. A Christian does a Muslim woman no good by loving her. Sometimes I hate myself for it."

"And what about your own life? It's not you luring me into danger, it's love, but I wouldn't want it any other way."

"Aren't you afraid?" asked Josef.

"No," said Fatima, and she thought of her Aunt Sharife, who had fallen in love with a Damascene Jew and now lived happily with him in New York. In fact she was happier than anyone Fatima knew. She laughed.

"What's the joke?" asked Josef.

"It's said that your enemies' curse is a blessing for forbidden love," replied Fatima. "And there isn't another woman in my entire large family who's as happy as Aunt Sharife."

"Do you really think our love has any chance of surviving that pack of fanatics?" asked Josef. He had no idea that Farid would be asking Rana the same question a couple of hours later in the Sufaniye Park.

"Of course," said Fatima. "We just have to want it enough, as the great Satlan says. Without a strong will, love is just a longing felt by the weak."

Fatima's answer sounded to Josef like a quotation from all the slushy love films that his mother saw week after week in the cinema. She always enthusiastically told him the plot later. As a rule, it was the man who said such things in the films. Josef grinned at the idea of finding himself in the wrong kind of movie.

He paid, and was first to leave the café. Fatima wasn't going to go out into the street and take the bus home until ten minutes later.

Whistling, Josef strolled along the street to the stop for the Number 5 bus home, never guessing that he had just seen Fatima for the last time. Two bearded figures, silent as shadows, were following him.

Near the Fardus bus stop, Josef passed the time by reading the headlines of the newspapers displayed at a kiosk. Suddenly a smell of decay met his nostrils. It came from a bearded man roughly pushing in between him and the newspaper stand. Nauseated, Josef took a quick step to one side.

Years later, he was still blessing his sensitive nose for saving his life, for just as he flinched away from the stench, the bearded man turned around and stabbed him. The knife went into Josef's right shoulder instead of his heart. Josef kicked his attacker in the balls and shouted, "Help, one of the Muslim Brotherhood is trying to murder me!" Three men standing near the kiosk rushed the bearded attacker, but his accomplice, lurking nearby, struck out at them with a chain, enabling himself and the would-be murderer to escape. They both got away unrecognized.

Josef's wound was worse than the doctors had thought at first. He was in hospital for weeks, and there was a danger that his right arm would be paralysed, but he was lucky, and it healed up, although the scar always throbbed badly in winter.

When Josef first left home again without his arm in a sling, he tried to get in touch with Fatima, but it was as if the earth had opened and swallowed her up.

Only much later did he discover that her brothers had kept her imprisoned in a dark cellar in their parents' house for months, until she agreed to marry a rich relation in Kuwait. She went to live there with the man's other three wives, and never saw her own city of Damascus again.

BOOK OF LAUGHTER II

Faith seldom moves mountains, but superstition moves whole nations.

やみ

181. Nerves

Rana phoned and said she had to see him. Farid was to keep the Sunday after next free, because Kamal Sabuni would be inviting him to a small party. "And Dunia has promised me to do all she can to make sure her brother doesn't forget about you."

Two days later, sure enough, Kamal invited him. Dunia arranged for Rana and Farid to be able to get away from the party for an hour on their own.

Rana was very cheerful that afternoon. She laughed exuberantly at her brother, and just as much at a neighbour who, she said, was chasing all the married women of the neighbourhood, making very offensive remarks, even to her own mother. "And then he turns out to be jealous," she went on. "Woe to any man who smiles at *his* wife. Most women don't like these importunate advances of his at all, including Warde. But she's a clever woman, with a tongue like pepperoni. First she tried politely turning him down, but that just made him keener than ever. One day he seized her by the arms and said he was going to have a nibble of her some time, just to compare her with his wife and see which of them tasted better. Warde smiled, freed herself from his embrace, and said, in as loud a voice as she could manage, 'Not a bad

idea, but you can always ask my husband's opinion. He's tried us both.'
After that he let her alone."

When Rana told a story Farid was always captivated. Her voice was
soft but a little husky, as if she had a slight cold.

They had settled comfortably on the couch in Dunia's room. Farid,
who was lying on top of Rana, tried to bite her lower lip, but she
wouldn't let him. "I have to tell you about something I did in the last
two weeks." She kissed him.

"Later," he said, kissing her back.

"No, not later. I can't tell you about it outside this room, or on the
phone." Rana tickled him to make him stop.

Reluctantly, he let her go, sat on the edge of the couch and pulled
her dress back down over her knees. Rana smiled, clasped her hands
behind her head, stretched luxuriously, and then lay there, totally
relaxed.

"My mother's been sleeping very badly these last few months," she
began.

"My heart bleeds for her," said Farid sarcastically.

"Oh, do be quiet! Her mind was absolutely set on marrying me
off, and finally she won my father over too, just as I'd feared. But who
do you think they picked for me? Even in my worst nightmares I'd
never have expected it to be my cousin Kafi. He's my Uncle Sami's son.
Do you remember Sami Kudsi who was always doing shady business
deals? That's his father."

Farid shook his head at the mere idea.

"Anyway, he has five sons and they're all in the army. The youngest, Kafi, is my own age. A religious fanatic, quite dreadful. I always
thought he was certain to found a sect of his own some day. As he sees
it, the Catholic Church is a hotbed of atheists and you Catholics are
well on the way to damnation. Once, much to my mother's delight,
he said that Catholics and Protestants are all devil-worshippers. He's
always trying to convert people. Very embarrassing – and to think
someone like that is my cousin!

"So my mother didn't just want to be rid of me, she wanted to
punish me by inflicting this fanatic on me. I knew making a fuss
wouldn't help. I had to keep calm about it.

"On his first visit I made myself up like a tart. As for him, he came in uniform, looking incredibly old and stiff-necked. Of course my mother noticed my trick, and said thank goodness Kafi would cure me of all that vain frippery. And he smiled, very sure of himself, and launched straight into a sermon on the decline of morality.

"Suddenly my mother went away, and Jack, who never usually takes his eyes off me, disappeared too. There I was, left alone in the drawing room with this bore. I was full of plans for making him dislike me. So I told him I didn't really believe in anything, but I was thinking of converting to Islam just for fun, because I thought Christianity preached too much suffering and abstinence for this life, short as it is anyway.

"Instead of being shocked, my cousin Kafi, who could send anyone to sleep, suddenly turned really enthusiastic. He was dead set on preserving me from such a mistake. He didn't come just once a week any more, he came every day, hanging around with a stack of religious tracts to convince me that Orthodox Christianity was the right way. And my mother beamed at me because her nephew praised my frankness and my clever mind.

"When I was alone with Kafi again, I told him coldly that I couldn't stand him, and any marriage between us would bring him only grief. But that made him even keener, and he said oh, that was as nothing by comparison with Our Lord's suffering on the cross, and for love of the Lord he would bear the cross of my dislike.

"I was beginning to panic now. For days I couldn't think about anything but ways to shake off this leech. He brought me huge quantities of Arabic editions of *Reader's Digest,* all going on about the miracle of love and marriage. The *Reader's Digest* was where he got every miserable thing he knew. I was in a trap.

"Then I found a chink in his armour after all. There's nothing he fears more than strong-minded women. The kind of women he likes are poor weak souls who need him to save them, but he'd see a woman who has power, or would like power, as a major disaster. I'd listened to him long enough to find that out.

"So next time he visited I told him that I really trusted him now, and I was going to tell him a secret. He pricked up his ears. I went on to say that for a year I'd been a member of a religious group which firmly believes Jesus was really a woman in disguise, and the Gospels were forged later, by men. 'We're fighting for there to be priestesses in the Orthodox Church, and we won't just have female bishops and matriarchs, we're aiming for a female Pope to head the Church some day, and she will terrify the Catholic Pope.' He might like to join us, I suggested. Several carefully selected men had been accepted into the group already.

"Kafi backed out of the drawing room without even saying goodbye, and he never came to visit again. He hasn't said a word to my mother since that day either," Rana finished her story, and she embraced Farid, gurgling with laughter.

182. Azar's Machines

How Azar came by all his ideas was a mystery. There wasn't a single book on technology in his home. While Farid was in the monastery, all the same, he had built a water clock that kept perfect time. Similarly, he had already found out how the gang could tell the time at their nocturnal meetings in the attic, even without a watch. He used to bring a candle with small pins stuck into it all the way up, at a distance of about two centimetres from each other.

"When a pin falls out, an hour has passed," he had explained, and indeed his method worked. The principle was simple, but the brilliance of Azar's inventions lay in their very simplicity.

The big water clock stood in the inner courtyard of the Catholic bishop's palace until it was stolen in 1965. You could tell the time by it almost to the minute. A valve with a float ensured that the water pressure in the upper compartment was constant.

"And what did the Patriarch give him for it?" asked Farid.

"His blessing," replied Josef, with a wry smile.

Later, Azar built solar collectors out of old barrels which he painted black. He put them on the roof, and they provided his family with hot water for the kitchen and bathroom. At the age of seventeen he invented a small vacuum pump in physics at school, thereby astonishing his teacher.

At the same time he developed another brilliant idea for his family's use. They were living in a large tenement block with ten neighbours, and had two rooms on the second floor. Every time someone knocked at the front door of the building, all the neighbours emerged from their apartments to see who it was.

But there was no need for Azar's family to do that any more. They went downstairs only if the visitor really was for them. Just how they knew was a mystery to the other families for months, but it was all done with a length of pipe and two mirrors that Azar connected up so that you could stand in the kitchen and see who was downstairs.

"That'll protect you from annoying strangers," said Azar.

"And annoying relations too," agreed his mother.

જ

Next he made an automatic flatbread press out of the old roller from the drum of a washing machine, adding a tiny engine. It saved his mother a lot of hard work.

A neighbour saw this device and bought it from her for the fabulous sum of a hundred lira. Azar's father didn't earn that in a whole month, and Azar could easily build another machine from materials costing ten lira.

But he hadn't reckoned with one thing: soon after buying it, the neighbour put the dough roller on the market as a mass-produced item. It cost a lot of money, and all the bakeries bought one to help with making flatbread. The man made a fortune, and moved into a villa in the new quarter north of the Old Town. There was nothing Azar could do about it. He ended up as a poor vegetable dealer.

183. A Women's Meeting

"I was just drinking my coffee this morning when I saw all the women of the quarter streaming into Samira's inner courtyard to see her." Gibran sipped his tea. "You all know Samira, the traffic cop Maaruf's wife. At first I was afraid Maaruf might have died. I expect you heard he's been in hospital for a week after stopping a driver who went over the pavement, the flower beds, and a traffic island. Maaruf asked for the man's papers, but he was hopelessly drunk, he didn't have either his driving licence or his vehicle registration document with him, and he swore at Maaruf and told him to clear off. Maaruf looked at this young man in his sharp suit, thinking there might be money in this – well, you all know Maaruf, he'll turn a blind eye any time if the colour of your money is right. And the blue of the hundred-lira banknote is his favourite colour." Gibran grinned. "But the man shouted that he wasn't going to pay anyway, he called Maaruf a bastard and told him just to write out a parking ticket. Then, at the very latest, Maaruf ought to have woken up to the facts. I mean, who calls a cop a bastard? But Maaruf was slow on the uptake that morning. Samira said later he'd been absent-minded for days, she thought he had a relationship with some woman.

"Whether he did or not, Maaruf checked the front of the car and there was no number-plate, he went around behind the car and there was no number-plate there either. He really ought to have given up then. Well, who drives over pavements and traffic islands in a car without plates? But no, friend Maaruf was dead set on that blue hundred-lira note. Very well, he thought, if this driver keeps on being so obstinate he'll get to know Maaruf better. 'Drunk at the wheel, no driving licence, no papers for the car, no plates! That'll add up to more than I guess you have on you, kid,' he said, leaning over to the man at the wheel. He was going to haul him out of the car and take him to the nearest police station, but the driver hit him full in the face. He was lashing out like crazy. It was none other than Colonel Adnan, one of the worst of that secret service bunch.

"I visited Maaruf three days ago. He's slowly recovering, and he's grateful not to have been thrown out of the police.

"Well, like I said, I thought he'd died, but I was wrong. His wife Samira just wanted to celebrate with her women friends. They made tabbouleh, they drank arrack, they sang and danced and played games like little girls. They didn't notice me at all. I might have been air.

"Finally Samira began to sing. She sang the song that's a single question repeated over and over, with witty replies from the chorus. I'm sure you know it. Samira has a wonderful voice, so she sang the questions.

'Who, oh who's that handsome man?" she cried. "The lover who visits every night,' replied the women.

'Who, oh who's that handsome man?' she repeated. The women laughed and replied, 'Only your tired old husband, alas.'

"So the song went on for a while. When she was just repeating the question about the handsome man for the tenth or maybe the twentieth time – how would I know? – the postman came into the courtyard. You know him, vain as a peacock, knows more about winking at women than delivering mail. He heard the question and immediately thought they meant him. 'Muhammad Ali, madam, at your service!' he replied, working his eyebrows up and down.

'Then give him his due, girls! Fart for the gentleman!' sang their hostess in the same delightful voice.

"And the women, who had been sitting around and relaxing, stood up, turned their backs to the postman, and farted in a number of different registers.

"Startled to death, he took to his heels, with letters sailing out of the full bag he carried slung around him. And I laughed so much that I spilled coffee on my trousers."

184. A Little Worm

"My Uncle Salam was twenty when he decided to marry, but he didn't trust women," Kamal Sabuni began his story, sipping tea from a slender glass. Farid had invited several of his old school friends to be his guests that day, as an advertisement for the club. But the young men just wanted to talk about sex.

"My uncle was very conservative," Kamal went on, "and he thought it was a sin for a woman to go out in the street without wearing seven veils. But he was rich, so a good many girls dreamed of marrying him. However, that didn't make him happy, only more suspicious. In the end he told his mother that if she found him a suitable wife, he'd want to spend five minutes alone with her, talking to her, and after that he would decide if she was the one for him.

"Well, his mother found him a pretty girl, a virgin who was a teacher's daughter. Her parents thought the condition a strange one, but the man was a good match, and they went along with it.

"So there was my uncle sitting with the veiled woman, and he opened his flies, took out his prick, and asked her, 'What's that?'

"The young woman was horrified, but she plucked up all her courage and said, with her throat dry, 'It's a penis.'

'Case closed,' he said, putting his prick back inside his trousers, and he went out.

'She's not the wife for me,' he told his mother. 'She's been with men.'

"The girl, who really was a virgin, assured her parents that she had not for a single moment raised her veil. But she dared not tell them any more except that the man had asked questions, and no, he hadn't touched her.

"The second candidate chose a synonym for the penis that we use widely in Damascus. She said it was a pigeon.

'Case closed,' said my uncle, and he repeated this rejection with thirteen more women, all of whom offered one of the thirty-seven well-known synonyms for the word 'penis'.

"Then came the fifteenth. 'What's that?' asked my uncle.

'A little worm, a little worm! Oh, how cute!' she said happily. He was delighted by her simple naivety, and he married her. On the wedding night he was rather surprised by the enthusiasm with which she entered into the game of love, but he thought she must have a natural talent for it.

"When he finally stopped for a rest, he took an apple from the fruit bowl and gave it to his bride. He felt like Adam about give his very own Eve the fruit of knowledge.

'My dear, I must enlighten you. You are not a girl any more now, but a mature woman. And this,' said my uncle kindly, sounding like a thoughtful teacher as he pointed to his limp member, 'this is not a little worm, but a penis.'

"His bride laughed until she almost choked on the apple. 'Call that a penis? Oh, my dear, you've no idea! Compared to the great big things I've known, yours really is a little worm.'"

185. Crazy Hours

He was to call Rana back at four when she would be alone. Phoning her at home was a strange idea. He saw her before him, throwing back her long, straight hair as she spoke over the phone, examining the ends to see if they were split.

He waited impatiently, and called at five to four. Rana disguised her voice. "Hello, this is Widad Kudsi speaking, Dr. Basil Shahin's wife. Whom have I the honour of addressing?"

Farid tried to keep a straight face. "George Mushtak in person, the avenger of lost honour. Will you marry me, madame?"

"Yes, of course, right away, monsieur. Pack your pyjamas and we'll meet at the taxi rank. Let's go to Venice or Honolulu this time," said Rana happily. Her laughter tickled his ear. "My parents have gone to a wedding and Jack's away. I thought this kind of opportunity won't come again in a hurry. Will you come and see me?"

"Right away," he replied.

"It's very romantic down in the cellar where my father stores olive oil and red wine, and no one can take us by surprise there. In an emergency the cellar even has its own way out of the house, but I don't think they'll be back before midnight."

Farid hung up and went straight to the bus stop. His heart was in his mouth as he entered the house. Rana closed the door behind him and flung her arms around his neck. "You didn't expect a chance like this, admit it!" she said, kissing him on the lips and thus stifling his answer.

They went down the stairs. It wasn't the usual kind of cellar;

because the house was built on a slope, a door led straight from it into the garden, and beyond the garden lay a street. Rana had provided for all eventualities; the door was not locked.

"Doesn't your father ever come in through the garden?" asked Farid.

"No, he parks the car at the front of the house. Anyway, using a back entrance is beneath Dr. Shahin's dignity."

The cellar contained a workshop, a storeroom for wine, another for olive oil and other provisions, two guest rooms, a large bathroom, and Rana's father's study.

The study was the best room. It had a large couch completely filling one wall, a small table in front of it, and the room was surrounded by bookshelves of walnut wood. A large picture by Miró hung on the wall behind the desk. A ventilator hummed in the ceiling.

"Is that an original?" asked Farid, pointing to the Spanish painter's blue picture.

"Oh no, a fake, like everything else in this house," said Rana, and put one hand quickly in front of her mouth as if the remark had slipped out by mistake, but she was laughing through her delicate fingers. Farid loved the sound of her laughter, which reminded him of distant bells. He put both arms out to her.

It was Rana's idea to open a bottle of the best Lebanese red wine. As they drank it, they pictured the life they would lead together some day. Rana kept breaking into her clear laughter, and Farid heard in that recurrent note the twittering of cheerful sparrows, which amused him. After about an hour, however, he noticed that she was tipsy. A little later she could hardly speak, and after another glass of wine she fell asleep, smiling blissfully. Alarm abruptly drove the alcohol out of Farid's own veins. Rana was lying on the couch like a corpse. When he touched her she uttered a whistling sound, like a rubber duck.

What was he to do? It was already after ten in the evening. He sat her up, but she kept falling back again. Finally he bent down and put her over his shoulder. Her weight was no problem, but the alcohol suddenly rose to his head again, making him sway. His view of the stairs was blurred. None the less, he made it up to the first floor and then the second floor. Once there, he found her room and laid her carefully on the bed.

He began laughing himself, and fell on his knees beside the bed, with his upper body over Rana's stomach.

A little later a sound roused him from his drowsy state. He felt as if he had just heard someone closing the front door of the house. For a second he thought of hiding in the wardrobe, but then he realized that no one had come in after all. It was probably the wind blowing the cellar door shut. He undressed Rana, got her into her nightdress, laid her in her bed again and kissed her forehead. In her dreams she moaned.

The bottle, he suddenly thought, and he ran down to the cellar, picked the wine bottle up, cast a glance around the room to check for any other traces, switched off all the lights, and left the house.

He kept his head bent until he reached the next side street. Finally he stopped, disposed of the bottle under the dense branches of a bush, and went to the bus stop. On the way back he imagined the expression on Rana's mother's face if she had entered the house just as he was coming up from the cellar with her daughter over his shoulder. He couldn't stop chuckling, until two women sitting in front of him moved to sit elsewhere.

"Not quite right in the head, if you ask me," said one of them.

186. The Oath

They were sitting in an apartment on the outskirts of the city. Judging by the stuffy atmosphere and the overflowing ashtrays, it must be a bachelor pad. This was Farid's first meeting as a full Communist Party member.

The comrade who led this cell of the Party, which had four members, called himself Said. Apparently he was a bank clerk. Apart from him, only Farid had an important function in the youth organization; the others were ordinary members. Comrade Kamil, a Kurd, had abandoned his studies and now worked as an olive oil salesman. He had a slightly rancid smell about him. The Shi'ite Comrade Samad, on the other hand, always turned up freshly shaven. He was a ladies' hairdresser, and there was something slightly feminine in the way he himself spoke. Comrade Edward, an Assyrian from the Euphrates region, was a maths teacher and an eternal sceptic who doubted everything, especially himself.

"I am happy to open the first meeting of our Party cell. Between you, you represent the living image of our country," said Comrade Said happily, overlooking the fact that the majority of the country's population, Sunni Arabs, was not represented among them at all. "Before we begin our meeting we will swear to be loyal, to die for one another, and to live for the working class. We despise anyone who betrays us. Your word will be enough for this oath now. When I was still young, members of the Muslim Brotherhood placed their hands on the Koran and a pistol. We communists had the hammer and sickle lying beside Marx's *Das Kapital* and a picture of Lenin. But those days are gone now. We had neither cars nor telephones, but we were clever and had nerves made of steel. I still remember a raid on my apartment. I don't mean to boast, but I was famous for my strong nerves and my quick repartee. When the police stormed my place, they saw the big picture of Marx, Lenin, and Stalin, and one of the policemen asked me who the three men were. I told him in friendly tones, 'The man with the beard is St. Anthony, the man with the bald patch next to him is the Apostle Butros, and the man with the big moustache is the Apostle Bulos. The policeman nodded and told his colleagues that I couldn't be a communist. It was a fact, he said, that Christians prayed to pictures of their saints. But time changes everything, even us. So your word alone will do for me. Who's volunteering to go first?" he asked.

Of course no one wanted to be first. The four of them all looked around.

"The youngest of us should have the courage to be first," said Kamil.

"No," replied Farid. "I'll let you go first out of respect for your age."

"Oh, very well, very well, I'll start," said Edward. "I swear by Lenin and my eyesight that I will always be true to communism, and even under torture I will not betray my Party."

"I swear by ..." Samad said next, in his soft voice, "I swear by ..." he repeated, not quite sure who or what to cite, "I swear by my love for the Party that I will never betray my comrades, whether male or female," was the solution he finally hit upon.

Samad was the only one to mention female comrades at all. Farid saw, from Said's slight smile, that this had not escaped the notice of the old Party fox.

"And I swear by my mother and my eyesight that I will never betray the Party or give a comrade away," said Farid hastily, and felt relieved.

"I swear by my people," said the Kurd, and was going to go on to protest his loyalty, but Comrade Said, leader of the cell, raised one hand.

"Wait a moment, what do you mean, your people? Are you going to claim that all Kurdish pimps, speculators, Ba'athists and nationalists are saints?"

"Oh, for goodness' sake! I swear by our General Secretary Comrade Khalid Malis, a Kurd like myself, that I will keep faith in life and in death," Kamil proudly concluded.

187. Of Cats and Clever Women

Azar's neighbour Zachariah was a cook at a pumping station in the desert that sent oil from Iraq on through a pipeline to the Mediterranean. His wife Bahia, at home in Bab Tuma, suffered less from her husband's absence than from his stingy ways. He earned well, but gave her and the children nothing. All four of them were pale, undernourished, and dressed like beggars.

Bahia swore to her neighbours that if her husband died she was going to give a big party, and just to make him turn in his grave she would say out loud that it had been his express wish for her to spend a lot of money on her guests. The neighbours laughed with her, though out of pity rather than anything else.

When Zachariah came home for two days once a month he insisted on eating fish, because they never had fish at the pumping station. It was like a ritual. After the long drive through the desert, the bus arrived punctually in Bab Tuma at nine in the morning. The bus stop was only ten metres from the fish stall. He went to it before going on home and bought a kilo of whatever was the cheapest on offer, paying in advance for another kilo that the owner of the stall was to store overnight in his refrigerator for him.

At home, Zacharia ate the two kilos of fish on the terrace by himself, and when he had eaten enough, his wife and the children might be allowed to scrape what was left off the bones.

His children hated this large, ugly man with the scarred face and huge nose who turned up once a month, put everyone in a bad mood for two days, and at twelve noon precisely on both those days sat on a stool, looking as round as a barrel, and ate all that fish, smacking his lips.

One day when their father came home again the three brothers Sami, Hani, and Kamil, with several other children from their street, searched the whole quarter for cats and caught over twenty. When Zachariah finally sat down on the terrace, waiting for his fish, the boys stole close to the steps up to the terrace with the cats. The animals could smell the delicious fish dinner and were restless, but the children petted them and calmed them down.

Then Bahia came out with the steaming, fragrant platter, and Zachariah hadn't swallowed his first mouthful before twenty hungry cats suddenly chased up. He was sitting with his back to the steps, and for a moment didn't know where all the mewing came from. When he turned around, he froze with his mouth full and wide open. The cats looked at the white flesh of the fish hanging out of this large creature's mouth, and mewed their hungry hearts out.

Zachariah's eyes were wide with anger, and he yelled so loud that even three buildings away the neighbours stopped whatever they were doing in alarm. The poor cats had never heard such roaring before either, and froze in mid-leap.

Then Zachariah ceremoniously reached for his slipper, which was too small for him and just hung from his toes for the look of the thing. His reaching for a shoe, a threatening gesture familiar to all the cats of Damascus, released them from their paralysis and sent them racing away again in all directions, like lightning. Only one scarred, black tom who had lost his tail jumped up on the table with a death-defying leap, snatched a fish from the platter, and ran away. Zachariah went back to his fish dinner.

A year later he fell severely sick with fish poisoning. There was much whispering in the street. Some said Bahia had poisoned him, others spoke of "that disease", without saying what it was, for they believed that if you said the word "cancer" out loud you would get it yourself.

When Zachariah recovered, the skinflint made bad worse by turning fanatically religious. He had given up his job as a cook, and now he went to Mass every day. One day he told his wife that he was going to leave half of all he had to the Catholic Church. As he couldn't read or write himself, he said he had already asked the priest to draw up a will.

Bahia consulted with her women neighbours for a long time, and in the end she made an ingenious plan. Josef's mother Madeleine, in her neat handwriting, drew up another document in which Zachariah revoked all previous wills. It was witnessed by three women: Madeleine, Azar's mother Aziza, and Suleiman's mother Salma.

Zachariah died early one morning in the summer of 1958. His widow Bahia sent the children to school, took her husband's right hand, which was still warm, and pressed his thumb down firmly on an ink pad and then on the will. That was the legally recognized signature of all illiterates at the time.

A week later Father Basilius politely asked the widow if she would like to discuss her husband's will with him. He had a copy of it himself, he said. "Many children in Africa and Asia are waiting hopefully for your late husband's generous donation," he added unctuously.

"Oh, your reverence," smiled Bahia, "you didn't know my husband and his moods. He drew up a new will and left his property to his three children, leaving me and the Catholic Church right out of it." And she made a great business of looking for the document and showing it to the priest, who had turned pale. After that he had some difficulty in finding his way back to the Catholic presbytery in Saitun Alley.

188. Matta's Fiancée

Kamal and Josef had been playing backgammon with Farid, who lost. They had gone home and he had put the game away. He was just going to lie down for half an hour when the bell rang. Matta and his fiancée were standing at the door.

"Brother," began Matta happily, and then stopped. The woman beside him greeted Farid with a hearty handshake and stepped into the house, almost dancing for joy.

"So you're Farid. Matta reveres you like a saint," she said. Faride was much more feminine than her handshake and his mother's description had led him to expect. She was lively and bright, and had all the qualities that Matta lacked.

"Brother," said Matta after a while, and his fiancée Faride stopped talking in mid-sentence to attend to him. "We're getting … married at Christ … Christmas. We're …" Farid sensed what a strain his friend found it to get the words out. "At … Christmas," Matta repeated. "Brother, we'd like you to be … to be our witness."

"There, what did I tell you? It's only with you that he speaks more than three words together. How happy I am!" rejoiced Faride, standing up to kiss Matta on the forehead and both eyes.

189. The Night of Jokes

The atmosphere in the club was gloomy. Amin had been arrested as he left home. Rasuk was being interrogated because of Elizabeth, and two other neighbours from their street had been tortured for a week, apparently because they had been confused with a couple of dangerous criminals. But word was going around that there were arbitrary arrests in almost every street, to intimidate the population.

Spring had been very late in 1960, but now it was suddenly like summer. The nights were warm. At the club, they decided they could sit outside again.

It was after eight o'clock when Gibran came to the club that evening on his own. "Karime is visiting her ancient old aunt," he said briefly, when Taufik asked him. Josef was glad. He didn't like Karime, and thought she was eating Gibran alive. It was a fact that since the old seaman fell in love with her, he hardly came to the club any more.

But when Gibran said she was visiting her old aunt a number of the members laughed, for in the spring of 1960 to say, "So-and-so is visiting his aunt," was code for, "So-and-so is in jail for political reasons."

"Karime and politics?" he replied, shaking his head. "That's like fire and water. She can't even bear to hear the news. I have to come to the café to find out what's going on in the world."

That day it was Butros the tiler who opened the door to the jokes told in Damascus on such mild evenings, and it wouldn't be closed until dawn. "An American, a Frenchman, and a Damascene went to hell," said Butros. "After a year they asked the Devil if they could phone home and tell their families they had ended up there, so it wasn't worth the trouble of lighting candles or giving charity to the poor on their behalf any more. The Devil agreed. The American talked on the phone for five minutes, and when he came back the Devil said that would cost him a thousand dollars. When the Frenchman too came back after five minutes, the Devil asked him for the same sum of money. As for the man from Damascus, he spent two hours on the phone, because his entire family wanted to talk to him, and they were all keen to know if you had to pay rent in hell, and what kind of fuel kept the eternal fires burning. When he came back, the Devil said, 'That'll be twenty cents.'

'Why does he have to pay so little?' asked the American and the Frenchman indignantly.

'It was a local call,' explained the Devil."

"I know a better one," said Gibran. "One morning the Interior Minister, who is brother-in-law to the President, was passing the monument to a national hero when he heard the bronze statue complaining, 'What an ungrateful government we have! I lost my young life fighting the colonialists, and now I've been standing here for fifty years. My legs ache. I have varicose veins. And that general over there gets to sit on a horse!' And the monument pointed to the statue of the last President, who had died in a car crash soon after his successful coup. 'What did he ever do for the Fatherland?' the national hero went on. 'He led some stupid coup, and he couldn't drive a car properly. And now he has a noble Arab steed. I want a horse too.'

The Interior Minister went off to the Palace of the Republic, where he told the President's assembled cousins, sons-in-law, and brothers-in-law, 'Our national hero Ismail wants a horse!'

'What? Our hero who? Ismail who died fifty years ago?" cried the company, and they fell about laughing, because they knew how fond the Interior Minister was of arrack. The President jumped up. 'It'll be the worse for you if you're lying,' he said. 'I want to hear this for myself.'

So they both strode out of the Palace, and as they approached the monument they heard the bronze man complaining at the top of his voice, 'A horse, I said! Don't you idiots understand plain language? It's a noble horse I want, not a donkey!'

Everyone spluttered with laughter except Josef.

"Not bad, but mine is even better," claimed Michel the joiner. "One day Satlan sends his favourite ministers out hunting. He is very fond of monkeys, and he says whoever brings him a monkey will get to be Vice-President.

"After a few days, the Foreign Minister and the Finance Minister come back empty-handed. 'There *are* no monkeys in Syria,' they explain.

"Then along comes the Interior Minister, proudly leading a donkey. 'But that's not a monkey,' protests the President. "It's a donkey."

'You just wait until my men have questioned it, and you'll see how quickly it confesses to being a monkey,' replies the Interior Minister. So he's the one who gets to be Vice-President."

Gibran wasn't owning himself beaten. 'You won't improve on my next joke. I had it from a beggar for the price of a cigarette. There's this supporter of the President who goes for a walk with his wife. He sees a street seller on the avenue sidewalk, with all kinds of pictures of singers, saints, and politicians for sale.

'How much is the big picture of Jesus?' he asks.

'Ten lira.'

'What about the picture of President Satlan?'

'One lira.'

'One lira? Don't you think it's outrageous to charge ten lira for Jesus and only one lira for the picture of our beloved President?'

'Crucify him and I'll sell his picture for fifty,' says the street seller."

Josef thought this was a tasteless joke, but all the others except Suleiman were on Gibran's side, and they accused Josef of having no sense of humour. Josef was out on a limb, for the mood in Damascus had changed since the wave of arrests began. More and more dislike of Satlan and the Egyptians was being expressed these days.

When they parted, Taufik embraced old Gibran and whispered to him and the others, "God preserve us from the consequences of our laughter."

Neither Gibran nor the others knew how prophetically Taufik had spoken.

BOOK OF LOVE V

Happiness often lies in delaying misfortune.

సౌ

DAMASCUS, SPRING 1960

190. The Man Who Saw With His Ears

"I should have known I couldn't steal so many happy moments and get away with it," said Rana to her friend Dunia, "but I was intoxicated by love and thought no further than the end of my own nose. I didn't want to see the black clouds of misfortune looming. I just enjoyed what time I could spend with Farid as if it would last for ever."

Back then in the spring of 1960, when she was studying and could meet Farid often, she had discovered how little a human being needs to be happy. Farid was easily pleased. When he made tea she felt he was in an invisible Paradise because he smiled at her so cheerfully, rubbing his hands and dancing around the little teapot. And when he poured the tea into warmed glasses, he beamed all over his face. He was always thinking of ways to entice laughter out of her. He was addicted to her laughter, the way other men are addicted to hashish or alcohol. He knew no other sound in the world that fell so refreshingly on his heart, like a waterfall.

Then there was the incident with Uncle Mahmud the blind beggar. He was a small man with a friendly face, not yet fifty but prematurely grey, and was known as "Uncle" out of affection and respect. Rumour said he was a Sufi scholar. Rana didn't know if that was true, but she was sure he had the keenest ears in the world. He could recognise all who spoke to him by their voices, even if he was standing in one of the busiest streets in the city.

One evening she was just coming out of the cinema with Farid, and as they passed Uncle Mahmud she said hello and put twenty piastres into the blind man's hand. "Rana," he cried, "what a coincidence! Your Papa was here just two minutes ago." Rana looked up, and saw her father a few metres away, looking into a shop window. She turned swiftly and went away in the other direction with Farid. Her heart was thudding, her temples throbbed. Finally they found a safe corner, and watched her father until he got into his car and drove away.

"Thank you for saving us," whispered Farid in relief, giving the beggar fifty piastres.

"Saving you? What do you mean? And who are you?" asked the beggar, putting the coin in his pocket. "I don't know your voice."

"This is my friend Farid," Rana explained.

"Ah, I understand," said the beggar, laughing. "Well, no harm can come to you as long as blind guardian angels watch where you go."

From then on he always greeted Farid by his name. One Sunday afternoon, Farid and Rana were just coming out of their favourite café when they saw Uncle Mahmud slumped outside the entrance to a building.

"Are you all right?" asked Farid, concerned.

"I've been mugged, but I'll be better soon. Can you two help me home?"

Uncle Mahmud could hardly walk, and Farid kept asking him if he didn't want to go to a doctor or to hospital. The blind beggar said no.

"There were these three men. They said they were police, and I tried to sound harmless, cracking a small joke and laughing a little. I'm a fool, I ought to have noticed that there were three of them. The city police patrol these parts, but they always come one at a time, and they'll usually look the other way, or just say you'd better clear off for a while because of a minister or a state guest driving by. But several policemen all at once? I ought to have shouted for help in that busy street, but they overpowered me and dragged me into a small van. They wanted money. Some idiot had told them I was rolling in it.

They hit me and threatened to strangle me, but since I didn't have anything there was nothing I could give them. They took what money I had from my pocket, threw me out of the van and raced away."

Uncle Mahmud lived in a room at the top of an old house. It was extremely clean and tidy. Rana was surprised. She nudged Farid, and without a word indicated what she was thinking. Farid nodded.

"My neighbour Salime helps me out," said the beggar, as if he had seen Rana and Farid discussing his room in sign language.

"Mahmud, Mahmud!" they heard a woman's voice suddenly calling from the inner courtyard. The blind beggar went to the window and called back, "Hello."

"Where have you been all this time?"

"Don't worry, a couple of friends brought me home. You're welcome to come up and meet them. Then you can tell me later what they look like."

He left the window and sat down on the edge of the bed, pushed the toe of his right shoe against his left shoe until it came off, and then reached into it with a mischievous smile. He straightened up with three lira notes clutched in his fist.

"My safe. The fools never thought of that."

Next moment Salime, the wife of the owner of the building, came in. On hearing that Mahmud had been attacked she embraced him, kissing his forehead, cheeks, and then his lips for a long time. "What trouble you do get yourself into!" she kept saying.

Mahmud's hands sank into the woman's soft arms and equally soft buttocks. To Rana, their lack of inhibition seemed odd and embarrassing. She looked at Farid. He pressed her hand.

"Oh, they were just small-time idiots, my little pigeon," the blind man reassured Salime, burying his head in her ample bosom." I learned a lesson today – never go with anyone unless someone I know is with me." He gave Salime a long kiss. She tenderly slapped his hand as it tried slyly to slip between her legs.

"Now that's enough," she whispered affectionately. "What will these young people think of us?"

Salime loved Mahmud. He lived in her house for free, and she looked after him as well as her husband and her two boys.

"Has he ever played you his flute?" she asked Rana and Farid. "I'm sure you'd enjoy it."

"Oh, Salime, it's not something they'd like ..."

But when Rana and Farid asked him, he did play for them, and it was the kind of music that makes you think of the great expanses of the desert and its silence. Mahmud didn't so much play his flute as caress it, he spoke to it, he put all of himself into it, and the mute wood came alive, unfolding its melodies and giving them back to him.

Salime was greatly moved, and looked ecstatic, but then her husband called and she had to leave them.

"God took my eyes from me, but he gave me better ears and an internal clock instead. He is merciful. He doesn't let something disappear for no reason. I see with my ears and I can feel the time in my heart," Mahmud explained to them later as they sat together for a little longer.

At last Rana and Farid left the house hand in hand. Rana was going to walk the last part of the way back to the street on her own, and then take a taxi home. Farid was to go in the opposite direction, and find another street where he could catch his bus.

Outside the building it was pitch dark. Farid drew Rana close once more, and kissed her mouth for a long while. "You are my time to me," he whispered, and kissed her yet again.

191. Karime

"Karime leaves Gibran sated and lethargic, and she's eating his brain," claimed Josef. "Since he fell in love with her he tells such stupid stories."

Other members of the club spoke ill of Karime too. She had only been satisfying her hunger for love with the old seaman, they said, she had bought him to warm her cold bed. However, Karime's love wasn't a single thread of emotion, but an entire skein of very different yearnings.

With her, Gibran led a life free of care. In return, he banished boredom from the widow's handsome house, opened the mouldering windows in her heart, and blew fresh air in. And she yearned for all the stories he told, she enticed the words out of him, and saw new landscapes rise before her where the two of them went walking. He loved the care with which she went about everything. No one had ever shown such consideration for him before. She, for her part, liked his sometimes painful honesty, which was refreshing after years of lies from her husband. And she liked Gibran's courage in taking a positive view of young people. He showed her that old age is more easily kept at bay by an ever-inquiring mind than by any creams and lotions.

That first evening with him at the club was something she would never forget. Gibran had insisted on taking her. She felt it was an impossible idea. What would she do in such company, at the age of sixty? "Laugh," he said. She was sure she would disappoint him, and felt nervous.

Gibran was a huge, gnarled oak tree. He might let her get him into a good suit, a new shirt, and new shoes, he might let her persuade him to shave his stubbly chin, but inside he was still the same wild, undomesticated tree. But now he was asking her to leave the protection of her familiar snail shell. She felt weak at the knees. Suppose the young people laughed at her and cat-called? It wasn't considered normal for old people to fall in love. Her neighbour Alime, whose venom made a cobra's appear like mild and milky coffee, had seen Gibran in a pair of silk pyjamas on her balcony, and next thing she was shouting abuse of the enamoured widow to another woman three buildings away. Her voice was loud enough for not only Karime and Gibran to hear her but even the President of the country away on his state visit to Moscow. Gibran took it calmly. "We'll be famous. The names of Karime and Gibran will go together like Madjnun and Leila or Romeo and Juliet," he said encouragingly.

In the end she went with him, trembling, and suddenly it had all seemed quite simple. After five minutes she felt the warmth among the young people. And when they were home again she made love with Gibran for many hours, until the dawn of day. At last she fell asleep in his arms, and felt as if she were in a sailing boat.

Karime also loved Gibran because she liked to care for him. She thought it a shame for such a fine man to live in poverty. When she first visited him she had wept. A room, bare apart from a shelf with a few books that were falling apart, an iron bedstead with a stinking mattress and pillows stiff with dirt, a bedside table and two or three raffia stools, and that was all. He didn't even have a wardrobe; his few worn-out shirts and trousers hung from nails. A man who had seen the world as Gibran had couldn't possibly stay in this dump.

And in addition she liked him because he wasn't bitter. He loved humanity. "In spite of everything?" she asked. "Because of everything," he replied.

Most of all, however, she appreciated Gibran because he knew how to treat women. He could caress Karime with his eyes so that she burned beneath her skin with longing for the touch of his hands. And he could always make her laugh. She loved him because he spoiled her as her husband never had; he had slept with her merely to satisfy himself. Loveplay with Gibran had been a bridge for Karime, a way to forget how much had separated her from her husband. She had been young when they met, and he had lavished gifts on her that made her soft and willing, but he could never work on her senses to make music as Gibran did.

And unlike her late husband, Gibran liked listening to her. She had told him more in a single year than she ever told her husband in twenty. With her husband, she had never been able to speak of her past. Her adventurous youth was interred on the altar of marriage. From then on, she had been obliged to play the part of happy wife to a rich, respected man.

Gibran, on the other hand, always encouraged her to tell him about her experiences as a young singer. At that time she had called herself Bint el Sahra, "daughter of the desert", not just to arouse the curiosity of the public but also to spare her family shame, for women singers were then regarded as whores. Karime told Gibran how she had sometimes started brawls when she appeared in cafés and nightclubs, when one of the men drank a glass too many and climbed up on stage to kiss her, thus making the others envious or even jealous, and chairs would go flying through the air. Karime and her accompanists

joined in with a will until the place was wrecked. Gibran never tired
of hearing such stories.

Their happiness, however, lasted only two years, and during those
years Gibran and Karime seemed to be growing younger and closer
together all the time. The two of them would even sing duets for a
whole evening, and you could hear that Karime still had a wonderful
voice. But early in the summer of 1960, a terrible thing happened and
ruined everything.

192. Breathless

Rana had expected anything but the stalker that late afternoon. She
had been to the cinema with Farid. The chance came out of a clear
sky, and Farid had responded at once. Half an hour after her phone
call, he was holding her hand in the dark auditorium of the cinema.
Friends had recommended Kazan's film *East of Eden*, with James
Dean in the lead. Rana thought the story harsh, and unlike her
school friends she didn't find James Dean virile, but rather effemi-
nate. But she was deeply moved by the character of the rebel Cal
whom he played, a man who both respected and fought his father,
as Farid did.

Later, when they left separately, Rana watched as her lover was
making his way to the bus stop. It was at that moment that she saw
the man. He was the same age as Farid and herself, he was leaning
against a lamp post, and he wolf-whistled at her. He wore expensive
American clothes and had combed his oiled hair into an Elvis Presley
style. Rana didn't like either Elvis or Bill Haley, with their ridiculous
greasy locks. Her favourite male singer was the Egyptian Abdulhalim,
and most of the other girls in Damascus were his fans too. He had a
warm, melancholy voice, and looked like any poor Arab boy in love,
not like the smooth and slippery Elvis.

She had first seen the stalker at the beginning of the school year
outside the parliament building, where she met her friend Silvia
every morning. He had followed them, and Silvia made the mistake

of turning around. She had even smiled at him, and then he was glued to them until they reached the school gates.

He was still there at midday. Silvia said boys were like hunters and beggars. "Each of them has his own preserves. This one's obviously set his sights on us."

When the friends separated again at the parliament building, he decided to follow Silvia, and the relieved Rana was able to continue on her way home. But that afternoon Silvia told her that when he began pestering her she had stopped and slapped his face. From then on he stalked Rana like a troublesome shadow. Early in the morning, at twelve noon, after the midday break at two o'clock, and when school closed at five. He was always waiting by the same street lamp, and the girls at school soon thought he was Rana's boyfriend. He seemed to have an endless supply of chewing gum. However, he kept in the background, merely getting a friend of his to call out his name from the other side of the street, as boys often did, to make sure that she knew it: Dured, an unusual name, made famous only years later by a popular comedian.

She began to hate him. Rana liked school, and felt liberated from her family as soon as she stepped outside their front door. Going out, to her, meant plunging into the stream of passers by who populated the streets. She was surrounded by cheerful, attractive faces, school students, office workers, army officers. Best of all she liked the look of the old people who seemed to have all the time in the world.

Fashion boutiques, flower shops, cafés, and cinemas lined her way to school, along with well-tended trees and pretty street lamps. She took her time, was never in a hurry, met up with girlfriends who lived nearby, first Salma, then Silvia, then Fatima, Mona, and the others. Sometimes there were ten of them in the party by the time they reached the school gates.

Now all that was over. She felt hunted, and hurried to school and back every day looking cautiously around her. After Silvia had slapped the stalker's face he stuck to Rana, probably guessing that she would never strike a man.

"Just don't let him know where you live, or he'll be standing beside your bed, and your parents will think you're in a relationship with him," Silvia warned her. A nightmare! Rana was rescued by chance. One day, not far from the street where she lived, she saw him coming closer and closer. Desperately, she fled into a large building with its front door open. He had never come so close and been such a nuisance before. She stood in the stairwell, breathless, and watched him through a dusty window pane. He took up his position right opposite the front door.

"What's the matter, my dear?" she heard a kindly voice behind her, and jumped. A middle-aged woman was looking down at her from the door of her second-floor apartment.

"There's a man who pesters me following me around," explained Rana.

"That's no problem," the woman reassured her. "You're in the right building. If you open that door," and she pointed to her left, "you can go down another staircase and get out into the alley behind this house, and it will take you to the tram depot. Do you live a long way off?"

"Not far from the depot," Rana replied, thanked the woman, ran upstairs, opened the door to the other, providential staircase, and breathed a sigh of relief when she was back home and in her room.

That had been six months ago. Since then he had believed that she really lived in the big building, and she disappeared into it every day to escape him. She meant to do the same when she came out of the cinema that afternoon, but Dured the stalker caught up with her just outside the building. "Don't make a scene. You don't live here. I found that out yesterday," he said.

She felt a strange fear that she was never able to explain to anyone later, not even Farid. As if Damascus were suddenly empty of people. As if this character was the most powerful man on earth, and she was only a little beetle to be trodden underfoot any time he liked. She stopped, feeling as if she no longer had feet, just two lumps of lead in her shoes. Rana wanted to scream, but she couldn't utter a sound.

"I won't hurt you. I just want you to have a coffee with me and be friendly. Is that too much to ask?" he said, standing squarely opposite her, immovable as a mountain.

"Let me by, please," she begged, trying to keep calm.

"I'm not going to touch you, but if you won't have a coffee with me I'll follow you to your front door and tell your parents you go out every morning with a whore who's the daughter of a well-known belly dancer, and you were at the cinema with a man today, and I won't be lying. I can describe him in detail."

"Silvia isn't a whore." Those were the only words that Rana could utter in her indignation.

"Oh yes, she is. Who else would hit a man in the face? Only women of that kind, and she's learned it from her mother," he said in a quiet but venomous voice. Enormous anger suddenly freed Rana from the clutches of her fear. "And you carry tales," she cried, striking him in the face so hard that he almost fell over, but regained his balance at the last moment. Before he knew what she was about, however, Rana kicked him in the balls. Silvia had shown her how to do it.

"Well done!" said an old man who happened to be passing. "That's the only kind of language such pests understand."

Dured limped away, groaning. Deep in her dreams, she could still hear him shouting, "Christian whore!"

193. Moon Woman

Something had happened. He sensed it very clearly.

Farid was just eating lunch when the bell rang. He was alone in the house. Their neighbour Gurios was standing at the door, out of breath.

"What's going on in the city?" he asked without preamble. "My daughter's just come home terrified. The police stopped her bus, all the passengers had to get out, and they were searched for weapons. People are saying there's been an attempted coup. Is that possible?"

"Attempted coup?" repeated Farid incredulously. Damascus had been on constant alert since January. It was said that Damian the Iraqi dictator was likely to attack the country, and there was increasing hostility between him and President Satlan. Not a day went by without bitter accusations. President Satlan, obviously with his reputation in mind, had spent a month travelling around the cities of Syria, making fiery speeches against Iraq and the Syrian communists who were flirting with Baghdad. Rumours were rife, and said that Damian was preparing to fight for Damascus with the aid of communist guerrilla troops.

Gurios wouldn't come in for a coffee, so Farid went back to his lunch, but he had no appetite now. Something made him feel infinitely sad. He phoned Rana. "I'm sorry, you have a wrong number," she said calmly, so he knew that she wasn't alone.

The sense of happiness that just hearing her voice gave him was soon gone. A coffee later, he called his cousin Laila. She was taciturn. When he asked what was going on she burst into tears and could say no more. Farid dropped everything and went to see her.

There was no one at the bus stop just outside her street. The bus itself hadn't been as crowded as usual, and the driver had turned up the volume on his radio. It was broadcasting a report on the catastrophe in Morocco, where an earthquake and an extraordinary spring tide had destroyed the harbour town of Agadir at the beginning of March, and ten thousand lives had been lost.

Farid saw several army trucks in Abbasid Square. Armed paratroopers in camouflage uniform were standing around everywhere. Even in the New Town, soldiers were posted at every street intersection.

Laila wasn't well. She had given her employees the day off so that she could rest; she was running a temperature and looked very pale. Her husband was on tour in the north with the Radio Orchestra. The apartment looked like a dump. Farid kissed Laila and made her get back into bed. Then he spent two hours busily tidying and cleaning the place, opening all the windows and letting in fresh air.

"My goodness, if Claire could see this!" said Laila faintly when she went to the lavatory, and saw the results of Farid's labours. She was smiling.

"She mustn't hear a word about it. I wouldn't do it for anyone but you. Usually I act like a pasha," called Farid from the kitchen, where he was making tea after all those chores.

Funny, he thought, how love alters people. After taking her high school diploma Laila had begun to study history, and wanted to write about the historical development of Arabia from the women's viewpoint. Although she was a Christian, she knew a great deal about the Sufi philosophy, and men had swarmed around her at the university, not least because of her erotic aura. However, she turned down both Djamil the professor of philosophy and Samuel the architect.

The Mushtak clan derided her for failing to take her university finals because she had fallen in love with her musician, and for thinking that she was a good dressmaker after only a short training course. Laila was trying to make a name for herself, and she did indeed have many customers, but unfortunately her abilities were limited. Farid was convinced that his mother ordered a dress from her every year only to bolster her morale, for Claire never wore the dresses. Elias laughed at Laila too.

Aunt Malake had thought long and hard in wondering whether to agree to her daughter's marriage. Musicians, apart from a few celebrities, were not highly regarded in Damascus. Many Christians were pioneers of the theater, film, and music. Famous women singers like Marie Gibran, Karawan, and Nadira Shami, the first Syrian woman to act in a film, were Christians too. They were all regarded as immoral. All the same, Malake had finally said she was happy for the marriage to take place, for she felt how much Laila loved Simon.

Simon made Farid nervous, he didn't know why. Sometimes he thought perhaps it was to do with his own guilty conscience, because his body was always forgetting that he must love Laila only platonically. Yet ever since he could remember, he had felt an enormous physical attraction to her.

He was just bringing the tea from the kitchen when he saw Laila sitting up in bed, rolling herself a cigarette and crumbling hashish over the tobacco. He was shocked, but quickly regained his composure. "Smoking in bed?" he laughingly reproved her.

"I smoke everywhere," she said, without looking at him.

"And what are you smoking now?" he asked, uncertainly.

"Hash, Lebanese quality, the best from Baalbek. It's food for my soul, and I won't hide that from you anymore. I don't let my husband know, or my family, or the rest of the world, but after all you're the other half of my soul."

"But hashish is a dangerous drug," he said in concern, handing her the tea.

"Nonsense. The Arabs, Persians, and Indians have used it for thousands of years, and at the same time they philosophized, invented mathematics, observed the stars, and wrote the most beautiful poetry." She licked the edge of her cigarette paper.

"How long have you been taking it?" Farid asked hesitantly. He had never been able to pretend in front of Laila.

'Calm down, Comrade," she replied, "you're starting to interrogate me. Commissar, I started at nineteen, I'm twenty-six now, that makes seven years. A lucky number, don't you think? Yes, I know it carries a life sentence in the Syrian civil code, so you don't have to preach morality to me." She lit the cigarette.

"Very funny," snapped Farid. "But why do you want to dull your mind?"

"Dull my mind?" she repeated defiantly. "My head is clear as glass when I've been smoking a joint. Only communists get befuddled, by order of the Central Committee. All mystics have eaten or smoked hashish, and do you know why? Because you can never get into other people's souls if you don't leave your own cocoon. Hashish makes a hole in the wall, opens up a way for you. It's just your bad luck that Lenin didn't smoke it."

"Leave Lenin out of this. Seriously, do you think it's a good idea?"

"Yes, a very good idea," she insisted, her voice soft but firm. She drew on the cigarette. "Whenever I feel that sadness is stifling me, but I have some important problem to solve, I smoke a joint, and suddenly I find new hope and sometimes even a solution. Try it, go on," she said, offering the cigarette in her hand. Farid waved it away.

"No, never," he said curtly. He drank his tea in silence. "Anyway, what problem did you have to solve today?"

"A very important one, it's been on my mind for days, and I think that's why I'm feverish. Ever since I was a child I've always run a temperature in such situations."

She said nothing for a while, and Farid poured her more tea. The room smelled of hashish, and for the first time it struck him that the drug smelled rather like incense. He realized that his cousin was serious, and he let her take her time.

"I wasn't eight yet," said Laila, "and as you know we were living in Beirut at the time. One day my mother took me by the hand and whispered, 'Today is a great day for you.'

We crossed several streets and soon reached the old quarter of the city of Beirut, where she went to the hammam. It was the first time in my life I'd been in a hammam – after all, we had two European bathrooms in my parents' villa. But here was another world – and funnily enough I felt at ease in it from the first moment. Just before we went into the baths my mother had bought a great many salted pumpkin seeds, pistachios, and baklava and other sweetmeats.

The bathhouse looked like a mosque from the outside, with a beautiful marble façade. When we were inside, the noise died away and we were surrounded by a silence that made my heart beat faster. We went in under the great dome, and I saw women bathing, soaping each other and themselves, laughing, pouring water over one another or drinking tea. Somewhere even further in about twenty women, young and old, were sitting in a circle, smiling at us in a friendly way as we joined them, wrapped in our white towels. That was when I met the Moon Women."

Laila sipped her freshly poured tea, drew on her cigarette one last time, and stubbed it out in the ashtray.

"They were celebrating my acceptance as one of them. I was the youngest member of their secret society. An older woman told me at length, and very emotionally, that from now on I was a special girl, and the sign I would carry on me from that day on represented not a privilege but a duty to commit my whole life to women and to love. I was so excited that I didn't understand very much of it, but I was impressed to feel her warm, damp arm and see the circle of Moon Women sitting around me. In the distance a bluish glass window gleamed in the light of the sun falling on it. I held my breath, really thinking that the moon would come in.

"And I felt very proud that of her three daughters, I was the one my mother had chosen. In the end they all kissed me. My mother was weeping for joy. Finally one of the women tattooed the sign of the secret society just above my heart. Then we all celebrated in the baths.

"On the way back I felt that now my mother had become a wise woman and my comrade. We sang together so cheerfully that passers by turned to look at us, but that just encouraged us to sing louder. From then on I went with my mother to the hammam where the Moon Women met every Wednesday. There weren't very many of them at the time, but they kept in close touch and helped each other out with advice and money."

Laila paused for some time, and Farid felt that she was struggling with herself. He kept quiet.

"I was fourteen, and by now there were over three hundred of us Moon Sisters, when some of the members chose to go the wrong way. Out of sheer impatience, and driven by the hatred of thousands of years, they wanted to put things right all at once. The leaders of that group began carrying out punitive action against obvious misogynists. Their weapon was poison. They didn't want to wait for the state to see justice done, they made their own justice, and it was deadly. More than ten men died of poisoning in Beirut – judges, a couple of pimps, the chief of police, and two rapists who had been given lenient sentences in the courts. They all died of a dose of the arsenic that women used as a depilatory on their legs in the public baths at the time.

"Finding those responsible was child's play for the CID after the diagnosis of arsenic poisoning. Several women were given life sentences, the others, including my mother, were shadowed. The whole Moon Women group was broken up."

"Sounds exciting," commented Farid, still unsure just what to think of this story. Laila was looking at him with gentleness in her eyes, sensing his uncertainty. Finally she rolled herself a second cigarette.

"We don't want to make that mistake again," she continued her story, as if she hadn't noticed Farid's remark. "By now I've found out one reason why we failed to achieve our freedom as women back then. We know nothing about ourselves, our souls, and our history, or at least not enough. Men have described everything from their own point of view, and when they enslaved us a thousand and one years ago they said we ought to be glad, thankful that they would keep us and feed us.

"Look at Damascus University. Any woman who wants to get a degree mustn't break taboos or ask any awkward questions. We have to accept that as women we get knowledge as men have mastered it poured into our heads, and it stinks.

"When I realized that, I left the university. It wasn't because of Simon, as our family always claims, it was because the university wasn't getting me anywhere in my quest. I wanted to be with other women, looking for our souls and our history, which means ourselves. And how do you get to meet a great many women in this country? As either a hairdresser or a dressmaker. I opted for dressmaking. Now you know." Laila sighed with relief, sensing that Farid understood her.

"So I'm a Moon Woman, and Moon Women choose their husbands not by the criteria of society, which approves of a man more if he keeps a woman under strict control, we choose by how far he'll let a woman live at liberty. That's what matters to me, not the university, not money. Simon knows all about me and accepts me without any ifs and buts, so that's why he is my husband."

"And does he know everything about me too?" asked Farid.

"Yes, he knows I love you. He didn't care for that at first, but when he met you he liked you very much. He understood me, and didn't feel jealous any more. He turned against you only when he learned that you're a fanatical communist – he hates communists."

"Have you found many other women to support you yet?" asked Farid quickly, trying to avoid this tricky subject.

"There are over a hundred of us in Damascus, meeting in small groups, determined to go all the way to the very end. There's no alternative if we want to preserve our dignity."

"And why were you crying on the phone?" he finally asked.

Laila sat still. She put her hands around her knees and stared at a point on the floor. He went to her, sat down on the bed, and took her head in his hands. She smelled as wonderful as ever.

Laila looked at him, and sobbed. "They've taken Nada away. They beat her half to death in front of all the neighbours, and no one went to help her."

"Nada? What Nada?"

"Nada Faris who works in the textiles factory. The secret service picked her up yesterday because they don't yet know who organized the first big strike in the factory after it was nationalized. It employs only women and pays starvation wages. They're raped and beaten, and there's always an army of other poor women standing outside begging for work, which makes the state management even more pitiless."

"Was the strike successful?" asked Farid, rather confused, since he had heard nothing of it either in the press or at his Party meetings.

"There's been no work done for a week, but none of the political parties will support the women. The secret service was furious. A strike organized by women, without any political backing? They needed someone as a scapegoat, and poor Nada was ideal for them. She had as much to do with the strike as any other woman worker, no more and no less, but she was popular, and she's a poverty-stricken unemployed academic keeping herself by working in the factory."

Laila calmed down a little, took Farid's handkerchief from his hand and blew her nose loudly.

"Three jeeps surrounded the little house where she lives in the village of Kabun. The soldiers set up their big machine guns. A helicopter was circling above the place. You might have thought they were about to attack Israel. Nada didn't stand a chance. To spare her family, she went out with her hands up. They beat her until she was unconscious, and then the soldiers dragged her over the ground and threw her into one of the jeeps like a bloodstained rag. Nothing's been heard of her since."

Laila was still sobbing. Farid pressed her head to his chest, and she clung to him.

"Stay with me. I'm frightened," she said.

Just before midnight the leaden silence in the street made its way into the apartment. Laila was the first to notice it. She stood behind the curtains at the window and looked down. "There's something wrong. The street looks as if it had been swept empty," she whispered in alarm. "Switch the radio on."

The radio brought certainty: there was a curfew because of a revolt allegedly planned somewhere abroad. The population were to keep calm, and not go out of doors from ten in the evening until six in the morning without police permission.

A cool breeze heavily laden with the scent of lemon blossom blew over Damascus from Mount Qassiun. Farid picked up the telephone and called home. His mother answered at once.

"Have you heard? There's a curfew," he said.

"Where are you?" asked Claire, relieved to hear his voice.

"At Laila's. I won't be able to get home now. I just wanted to tell you."

"Yes, stay the night with her. And give her my love, and tell her not to let you come home in the morning until you've had breakfast." Claire laughed.

"Yes, Mama, anything else?"

"I want a kiss or I'll come over to you and Laila, curfew or no curfew."

Farid blew her a kiss down the telephone. "Good night, Mama, and tell your husband good night from me too."

"He's been snoring for ages. He has to go out early. His special permission is under his pillow," she said, and hung up.

ᴖ

He slept on the couch opposite his cousin's big bed. When he woke up, Laila had already made tea and prepared a modest breakfast.

"Good morning, dear fugitive," she said, and kissed him on the forehead. He was still drowsy. She dragged him after her to the bathroom like a stubborn donkey.

When Farid left the house he felt lighter than a feather. He thought this was the way you would feel in Paradise, if it existed.

"And now back to real life," he told himself as he saw a military jeep racing past. He did not guess that hell was about to open its gates to him.

BOOK OF HELL I

If we are to respect the freedom of others
we must first respect ourselves.

১১

194. Lilo

The bus made its way along Straight Street, which was crowded with carts, men carrying loads, pedestrians, and street sellers. People deep in conversation in the middle of the road refused to take any notice of it, and had to be alerted by loud hooting before they would step back at least far enough for it to squeeze past, but involuntarily brushing their clothes against it. The driver cursed and kept stepping hard on the brakes, because foolhardy pedestrians would insist on filling the gap that the bus had just left, and then crossed the street right in front of its hood.

Amidst this dangerous chaos, the bus driver still found time to satisfy his vanity by looking in the rear-view mirror and smiling at a woman who preened under his glance. He was a rather portly man in his mid-forties, with a safari shirt and a haircut that emphasized a certain similarity to Robert Mitchum, whose film *The Night of the Hunter* had just been showing for three months in Damascus. In the same way as James Dean had been the idol of young people and adolescents since *Rebel Without A Cause*, Robert Mitchum was the model for all bachelors who weren't as young as they used to be. But however much oil they put on their hair, and even with their shirts unbuttoned to reveal their chest hair, they still oozed loneliness from every pore.

The driver leaned out of his small side window several times, cursing the crowd or hailing someone in a loud voice. It was obvious that he had been driving the Number 5 route through the Old Town for a long time.

Farid left the bus at the stop nearest to his street. As he got out he passed the time of day with Lilo, a rather mediocre barber with an astonishingly ready tongue. Even in the Middle East, that tongue was in a class of its own.

Lilo smiled at him and asked, with a wave of his hand, if he had time for a little tea. A samovar with its fragrant contents stood ready in his shop day in, day out, and when he had no customers Lilo would stand at the door inviting his friends and neighbours in for a cup. His motto was: a barber's shop should always be full, that brings the curious in, and before they know it they're leaving their hair behind, or at least a story.

Farid thanked him but declined, and was about to turn into his own street when he noticed two figures who looked like extra-terrestrials: a colossus two metres tall, and a man shaped like a cube with sides measuring one metre fifty. They were both standing four-square a few metres in front of him. The colossus swiftly stepped up to Farid and took him by the collar. "Era uoy diraf kathsum?" he asked. Farid didn't understand a word of it. This evidently displeased the colossus, and he hit him full in the face with his left hand. The features of the attacker's face suggested Egyptian nationality. "Nos fo a erohw! Uoy tnaw ot worhtrevo eht tnemnrevog? Nos fo a erohw!" Farid heard him roar, as the force of the blow sent him flying backward.

Leaden fear came over him, pressing down on his lungs. When he hit the ground he could scarcely breathe. Now the second, cubic figure came up to him. He approached as slowly as if he had to struggle against the earth's force of attraction. Then he picked Farid up as if he weighed nothing at all, or had turned into a grasshopper, and dealt him another blow in the face. This one sent its victim flying right against the other nightmare figure. At this moment Farid saw the old tailor Marwan looking out of his shop, white with fear.

Finally Farid heard the sturdy man say to the colossus, "That'll do for a start. Let's go."

They were speaking Arabic now, but with an Egyptian accent. Egyptians had made their way into the state everywhere since union with Egypt. Nothing humiliated a Syrian more than to be arrested by Egyptian secret service men in his own country.

The colossus took his victim by the collar for the second time and dragged him to a jeep parked nearby. Farid tried to get away, and half-way to the vehicle kicked the colossus in the balls. The kick struck home, and the man let go of him. But the second Egyptian reacted like lightning, slamming his fist into Farid's stomach. As he fell, Farid saw Lilo standing there frozen with horror, his mouth open and his hands raised.

In his fury the colossus hit Farid in the kidneys, grabbed his prisoner's right hand and swiftly twisted it behind his back, then did the same with his left hand. Farid felt handcuffs digging into his flesh. Now both men picked him up and went on dragging him towards the jeep. The neighbours were standing at many doors and windows, pale-faced, staring at the scene.

The vehicle raced through the eastern gate and turned left. Only now did screams emerge from the neighbours' open mouths.

195. Interrogation

From outside, the building to which they drove in the middle of the modern part of Damascus looked like any ordinary office block. The only unusual thing was the strict guard kept on the entrance. The small plate at the entrance bore the words: Interior Ministry.

The jeep drove into an underground garage. The men took Farid one floor down, through a stairwell with neon lighting, and handed him over to two jailers, who opened a large iron door and pushed him through it.

Farid was in darkness, and an acrid stink rose to his nostrils. It reminded him of a hyena that a farmer had once put on show at the fair in a tiny cage, tormenting the animal with a sharp stick until it howled. The cage had been smeared with its excrement.

Very slowly, his eyes adjusted to the lighting conditions. A tiny crack between the door and the wall let a little light from the corridor into this room. Gradually Farid made out faces; there were over twenty children, adults, and old people shut up in here. They lay on the bare concrete floor, which was covered with faeces and urine.

One of the children crawled over to him on all fours and begged for a cigarette. But Farid had none. The stink filled his lungs, and he could hardly breathe. When would Rana hear about his arrest? He thought of Josef and his mother, and was sure they were thinking of him at this moment. Suddenly he felt warmth protecting him.

Someone shouted his name. He woke up. The jailers were standing in the doorway with flashlights, sweeping their beams around in circles. Two men in civilian clothes were already waiting in the brightly lit corridor. They led him through the stairwell again, up to the first floor this time, and then down a long corridor past waiting men and into an office without any windows. At the door they handed him over to a dark-skinned man with an ugly, tattooed face.

In the office itself a young, clean-shaven first lieutenant was sitting behind a desk. The man with the tattooed face led Farid to a chair and pushed him down in it without a word. Then he took the handcuffs off.

"Try anything stupid and you're dead," he said with an Egyptian accent before he left the room.

The officer spoke the Damascus dialect, and was courteous but pedantic as he took down personal details. A soldier came in and told Farid to place any valuables as well as his belt and shoelaces in the carton he was holding out to him. The officer watched with indifference.

Farid was in the grip of a strange fear. The officer reached for the telephone and dialled a single digit. "I'm ready. You can collect him now," he said, unmoved.

Soon two tall soldiers came in, and having handcuffed Farid again they led him back to the cellars below. This time he counted four floors before the soldiers opened a metal door and pushed him into a corridor.

It was dark, and again it stank of urine. Naked light bulbs, spaced far apart, hung from the concrete ceiling on rigid cables. They passed iron cell doors through which Farid heard the sound of blows, and men and women screaming. His heart was racing and his knees felt weak, but the soldiers drove him on. There was no window anywhere. Corridor followed corridor in a labyrinthine system. He felt dizzy. At last the doorway to the staircase reappeared, and the soldiers drove him into the corridor yet again. Then they stopped, as if at an order.

Farid tried to steady his breathing, and listened. He hear raucous laughter and a stifled scream nearby. One of the soldiers took a step back, stopped at the door, pushed a metal flap aside and looked through the peephole. His face was briefly lit. He beckoned to the other soldier, who led Farid over to the peephole.

The room was almost empty, lit by three large neon lights that made the white walls look like ice. A naked man lay on his back on a table in the middle of the room. His feet were tied to ropes descending from the ceiling. In front of the table stood a soldier with his trousers down, forcing his mighty penis into the man. The man was bleeding. He screamed, his eyes wide with pain and horror. But only a whimper could get past the gag in his mouth. A second soldier stood there, smoking, and laughed at every scream.

Farid turned his eyes away. A blow immediately struck him in the face.

"Take a good look, you bastard," said his guard. Farid felt no pain, he just thought he was going to throw up. After a while the soldiers led him on again and opened another door. The room behind it was almost empty, except for a rusty metal chair and a dirty old table with an ashtray full of cigarette ends on it. Farid had to stand in front of the table. One of the soldiers disappeared, the other stayed with him.

A little later the first soldier came back and stood to attention as he held the door open. A rather stout officer entered the room, with a thick folder under his arm. He was dark-skinned, and wore a sweaty uniform and strong glasses that made his eyes shrink to the size of small marbles.

"So whom have we here?" he asked in an accent that Farid knew from Egyptian films.

"Farid Mushtak, a communist. Head of their youth organization," replied the soldier.

"Let's keep this short and sweet," said the officer in almost paternal tones, while he looked Farid up and down. "You're a good lad from a distinguished family. You've been led astray, lured into this imported foreign communism." He sat down on the chair, opened the folder, and took a sheet of paper out of it. "Here, sign this and then clear out. Your mother will be worrying about you."

The officer pushed the sheet of paper over to him. Farid knew what it was from many Party reports: a standard declaration in which you expressed remorse and total submission to the President of the state. By signing it you were saying you condemned the communists and would do anything to serve the Fatherland. The Party's orders were for no communist to sign in any circumstances. Anyone who did would be expelled from the party and publicly branded a traitor. Neither sickness nor weakness was any excuse. So Communist Party members were in a dilemma: either you died or you were a traitor. Farid decided to die. He shook his head.

"Did you two ever see anything like this?" the officer asked the soldiers. "I speak to him as a friend, and he shakes his head, stubborn as a donkey. What do you think of that?" He didn't wait for an answer, but turned back to Farid and pointed to the sheet of paper.

"Sign it and you're out of here. You can go to the cinema, kiss your girlfriend, sleep soundly at home. The alternative is to die, and no one will trouble about your fate. Think about it. One of these days you'll tell yourself: oh, if only I'd listened to Captain Muhsin, what a fool I was. Because once you get into here you'll never get out again. Well, do we want to reconsider?"

"I'm not signing anything," said Farid firmly. A blow struck the back of his head, knocking him to the ground.

"You son of a dog, you have to begin and end everything you say with 'sir,'" he heard the soldier standing over him say.

"No, no, Ismail. You mean well, but he's not one of those primitive fellows. He's a leading light of the movement and a student. So restrain yourself a little and help him get up, please," said the officer mildly. He turned back to his victim, speaking in a gentle, explanatory tone. "Why do you hate our dear Fatherland so much? Surely there can be no reason." For the first time bitter rage rose in Farid. Here, of all places, in this torture chamber, the lying serpent before him spoke of the dear Fatherland.

Farid would have liked to reply, "You know something, sir? You're the biggest asshole on this earth." But he was badly scared, so he just shook his head.

Then the soldiers waded in. Farid fell to the floor. One of them drew his leg back and kicked him in the kidneys. The last thing he felt was a stabbing pain.

196. The Forecourt of Hell

Loud noise roused him from his uneasy sleep. "Get up! Get up!" shouted a warder, and he was already unlocking the next cell with the same amount of racket. Farid didn't know what the time was. He had forgotten how many days had passed since his interrogation too. His internal clock had stopped working, and there was nothing to help him measure the rhythm of time. Sometimes the warders left him without any food for ages, then they would bring some horrible soup and a piece of bread in quick succession.

The prisoners had to stand by their cell doors. In the end about fifty men were standing in the corridors. Soon after that they were taken to the level of the garage where a truck with a box-like super-structure was waiting to take them to a camp. All the prisoners were chained together for the journey.

Outside it was light. Some whispered that they were going to the camp at Gahan in the steppes north of Damascus, others that they were to be taken to Tad, the worst camp of all, far away in the desert to the north-east of the capital. The driver steered the truck through the New Town. The prisoners peered through the slits between the boards of the superstructure. Some recognized the streets where they lived, and started crying. When the truck was stuck in a traffic jam a few hundred metres further on, Farid saw a boy of about six sitting in a garden under a maple tree, eating an ice cream. His mother was sitting beside him doing crochet work. Farid thought of Claire, and convulsively bit his lip.

A few metres away a man was standing outside his door, drying his hands on a towel. When he saw the truck he called to someone in the house. A woman joined him, barefoot, and they both looked at the truck. Farid would have liked to call out to them, but he knew it was useless.

After a while they went on. The truck drove out of the city and set off north. Farid knew this road; it was the way to Mala. Soon, however, the driver turned right. One man knew this route. "It's the way to Gahan," he whispered, "Gahan." Most of the prisoners were relieved that they were not bound for Tad, but their relief was of short duration.

About an hour later the truck stopped. An NCO opened the tail-gate and told the prisoners to get out and squat on the ground.

They were in the middle of the steppes. The sight of the guards made Farid feel sick. They stood in two rows, forming a corridor to the camp gate, and they did not carry weapons, but were armed with heavy branches and stout twigs.

The guards laughed. Farid desperately looked for a face containing at least some spark of humanity, but they all wore the same sadistic grin. The prisoners were told to go down the corridor two by two to the gate, where a high-ranking officer, flanked by two others, sat at a large table. The first two prisoners started walking past the rows of soldiers, and the branches and twigs whipped down on them. Anyone who fell was beaten even harder. One of the NCOs kept calling out, "Next two!"

Many of the prisoners collapsed, blocking the way for the men coming after them. The guards rained blows down more and more harshly.

Farid's first blow hit him when he had gone one-third of the way. He stumbled over another prisoner, but quickly got up and ran on towards the table. More blows kept striking him, and at last he fell to the ground. The prisoners were leaping back and forth as if in a wild dance, coming together and scattering again. Farid's back was burning from the blows. His hands, arms, and knees were grazed by the gravel.

When they had all reached the gate they had to undress. Many of the guards laughed, grabbed their own balls, and pointed at the prisoners' backsides.

Human beings are repulsive, thought Farid at the sight of them. Dirty as the guards themselves were, stained and scarred, they were laughing at the prisoners. One of the officers at the table grinned cynically and said, "Those aren't noble Syrians, they're American Indians." And he pointed to the coloured stains on them.

Two of the camp staff shaved the newcomers' heads in turn, doing it so brutally that many of them bled. One prisoner cried like a child, calling out, "Mama, Mama, I need you, Mama!"

It was heart-rending. Even the soldiers stared in bewilderment at the man, who must have been sixty. Other prisoners suddenly began weeping too. The officers laughed at the crazy old man, and the guards obediently joined in their derision.

A pharmacist who was a cultural functionary of the Muslim Brotherhood whispered incredulously, "This can't be true. We're not in Syria, we've been abducted and taken to Israel. It's not possible for us to be treated like this in our own country. I swear by Allah, these are unbelievers! How could Muslims torment their brothers in the faith like this?"

A blow struck him in the face, and he fell silent. Yet again, the officers asked each prisoner whether he was ready to repent and sign the statement. Three men agreed to sign. One called out aloud, "Forgive me, comrades, I can't take any more of this." The other prisoners stood there in silence with their heads bent. They were driven through the gate into the camp, naked and with their heads shaved.

Suddenly they heard the old man who had been crying and calling out for his mother laugh. "Is the party still going on?" he kept calling. Soon after that he and the three repentant sinners were sent back to Damascus in a minibus. A rumour spread among the prisoners that they were taking him to the al-Asfuriye mental hospital.

Farid and the other newcomers were alone in the yard now. A prisoner who seemed to have been here for some time pushed around a large handcart piled with items of grey camp clothing. When he reached the middle of the yard he tipped his cargo out on the ground and went slowly to a long building behind the huts. Farid suspected that it was the kitchen and clothing depot, since he saw smoke rising from the building. The man came back several times with his handcart and added more clothes to the heap.

That night, unable to sleep, Farid tried to think of Rana, but she appeared only briefly before his mind's eye and then sank back into deep darkness. Laila escaped him too.

Then he saw his mother wiping away a tear, smiling awkwardly, and finally running away. He ran after her, she went faster and faster, at last he caught up and took her by the shoulders. She turned, and he was shocked to see a strange woman. He woke up, and all was quiet except for a barking dog.

Days in the camp, like the prisoners themselves, lost their names. By chance he heard one of the guards saying he was looking forward to tomorrow because he liked Thursdays best.

In another, distant life he used to study physical chemistry on a Thursday, then mechanics, then two hours of algebra with long, long equations, the calculation of differentials, and logarithm tables. They were difficult subjects. Farid loved organic chemistry, and given a choice would have spent all his time in the laboratory where, synthesizing new compounds, he felt like a real chemist.

They'll be doing their finals around now. His friends wouldn't be thinking of him but of the questions they'd be asked. It was strange; he himself had never wondered about the students who suddenly stopped coming to lectures.

He turned over and fell asleep.

197. Said

Next day he was taken to the camp commandant. Captain Hamdi was over fifty, and seemed too old for his low rank. He put the usual questions again. Farid despised them, and did not reply. But when the officer called him a son of a whore he lost the last vestiges of his fear.

"I am not the son of a whore. I suppose even your own mother isn't a whore either."

This answer paralysed the officer for a moment, but then something seemed to snap in him. He leaped for Farid, hitting out and kicking him. As if thousands of years of civilization had been extinguished, he was suddenly an ape crouching on the bound prisoner's chest, letting out yelps.

When Farid came back to his senses he was in the hut, surrounded by prisoners who were all looking at him with concern. He could hardly move.

"What did they do to you, my boy?" asked an old man. His name was Said, and he had been arrested as a hostage in his son's place, to induce the son, a Muslim Brother, to turn himself in. Said was over seventy and, surprisingly, a complete unbeliever, but now he was imprisoned for his son's erroneous and extremist beliefs.

Farid couldn't move his mouth, and his jaw hurt.

"Sometimes," said Said, shaking his head, "there's a blasphemous voice that speaks up inside me, addressing God. If you exist, God, it says, then turn the camp commandant into a rat in front of everyone. But it won't happen."

"You're right, it *is* blasphemy," a bearded young man shouted at him.

"To be honest, I don't think much of any Almighty God who leaves his worshippers in the lurch to face such a miserable enemy," replied Said, with a bitter laugh. He stroked Farid's forehead.

"He called," Farid managed to say with great difficulty, "he called my mother a whore. I contradicted him. That's all."

The old man nodded.

198. The Chinese

Not a day passed without someone being taken out of his hut and brought back hours later, an almost lifeless bundle. There was no need for any particular reason. The camp guards had a free hand to torture prisoners as and when they liked.

One of the prisoners in Farid's hut was a well-known composer who was always beating out rhythms with a spoon or a stick. One day he played an exacting composition on the bars with two spoons. The guard Abu Satur came along and asked, "Who's that telegraph message for?"

"My mother," replied the prisoner, startled. Everyone laughed, and the crestfallen Abu Satur walked a couple of steps further, but then stopped, came back, hauled the musician into the yard and whipped him. The whip cut his skin like a razorblade.

"That damned Chinese," swore another prisoner, who was standing beside Farid at the fence near the way into camp. Farid had heard a few days earlier that two or three of the guards liked to lick fresh blood from their whips. Abu Satur, nicknamed "the Chinese", was the worst of them. He was a tall, sturdy man with Asiatic features, and enormously strong. The sight of blood when he was whipping a man intoxicated him, and then his anger gave way to a smile that smoothed his face into a Chinese mask. Abu Satur felt exhilarated when he could torment prisoners until the blood flowed. He knew he was one of the lowest on the social scale; like a pimp or executioner, he could never mention his job out loud. Yet he didn't want to be anything but what he was, for here in the camp others feared him. Here he could be revenged on all the distinguished men who were now just miserable, stinking wrecks. Abu Satur felt boundless satisfaction when he, formerly a starving boy who spent every other year in jail, heard them begging him for mercy. How often had he himself been whipped in the past? Now he relished his revenge, particularly when his victims were the educated men who had once been so infinitely far above him: professors, journalists, doctors, ministers, parliamentary deputies, even police chiefs. Now he whipped them.

Abu Satur was happy in this camp. He saved all his wages and gave his wife more presents every other week than she had ever seen before. The prisoners would give anything for a little hashish, a bottle of arrack, or some bread. Captain Hamdi was an experienced man, and let the guards do these little deals so as to keep them sweet in their bleak surroundings.

On the afternoon when Abu Satur whipped the composer in the yard, his victim lost consciousness. The Chinese left him lying there in the blazing sun and went away. Later, two soldiers picked the man up, dragged him to the hut, and asked, "What did the poor devil do?"

"He was composing a love song," said old Said.

"I can't make these people out," said the smaller of the two soldiers. "Here they are in the middle of hell, and they still have just that one thing on their minds."

199. The Children of Job

Five hundred prisoners were terrorized night and day by over a hundred armed soldiers and guards. Farid realized that the aim of the camp administration was to make intelligent men into animals by beating, starving, and above all deliberately humiliating them. The prisoners might be forced to imitate a donkey, a dog, or a sheep. Farid was bewildered by the sight of a professor of mathematics being made to follow Abu Satur about the yard on all fours, barking like a dog.

Apparently the imitation of animals was an established part of camp discipline, for he noticed that the guards were always demanding this exercise. They would sit under a sun umbrella humiliating their prisoners, and woe to anyone who refused to do as he was told, or stopped before the guards said he could. These were deeply degrading scenes.

When Said was the chosen victim, Farid wept at the sight of the old man, who couldn't follow a guard fast enough on all fours, being dragged across the entire yard by a leather collar around his neck. Said slid over the ground on his stomach, gasping for breath. The guard kept kicking him in the side and mocking him.

That evening all the prisoners from Farid's hut gathered around the old man to discuss their situation. A man called Farhan said, "They don't mean to kill us, or they'd have shot us by now. They want to turn us into animals, make us forget that we are fine, valuable human beings with eight thousand years of culture behind us."

The humiliation of old Said suddenly put an end to all hostility between the Muslim Brothers, the communists, and other groups. Everyone was now determined to resist the plans of the camp authorities. Word was passed on to all the other huts. It was on 15 August that the "Humanity" programme of what, at Said's suggestion, they called the University of Job was set up, under the secret leadership of some ten prisoners. It was all done by word of mouth, for there were no pencils or paper in the camp.

Anyone who knew a subject gave lectures on it, and the others, whatever their own education, were the students and could learn anything. In Farid's hut, they had lectures on history, religion, chemistry, car repairs, nutrition, first aid, philosophy, chess, backgammon, card games, and geography. In another hut a famous expert lectured on pre-Islamic Arabic poetry, in yet another there was an authority on Persian miniatures. Professors and men of letters in the hut next to the kitchen taught the works of Shakespeare, Lord Byron, T.S. Eliot, William Faulkner, and Pablo Neruda. The prisoners were moved to tears by Gorki's *Mother*, and laughed heartily at the books of the Anglo-Irish satirist Jonathan Swift.

Some of the men told the stories of Tolstoy's novels, and recited Nazim Hikmet's poems on freedom. A young student from Hut 4 knew the plots of several novels by Balzac. An older man presented Scheherazade's tales from the *Thousand and One Nights* in a lively, graphic style that captivated his audience.

One of the most brilliant storytellers among them was a criminal, a former pimp and multiple murderer. He had landed in this camp because one of his victims was a high-ranking secret service officer who was his competitor in Damascus.

Farid was astonished by this man, whose behaviour to the other inmates of the camp was always charming. He was a fanatical film buff who had spent most of his time in the cinema in his days as a pimp; he used to go from cinema to cinema in Damascus, from morning to early evening, and then he took his stable of three whores out to eat and then cashed up his accounts that night. Sometimes he had paid a cinema proprietor for all the seats in the place, asking the owner to show *Casablanca* or *Gone With the Wind* just for him, when he sat in the exact middle of the auditorium and sobbed like a desolate child at the dramatic scenes.

Because he had seen all the films so often he was able to perform them in the camp, complete with dialogue, mimicry, gestures, and sound effects. He had a divine voice, and used it to imitate up to ten characters and an endless variety of natural noises. His audience could feel the heat and dust of Westerns, or dance and sing with Charlie Chaplin in *The Gold Rush*.

There were evenings of satire, song, and recitations, but serial stories were the most popular of all. Many prisoners could spin out a single story for twenty evenings, some even for fifty, without ever losing the thread.

The random transfer of prisoners from hut to hut, a systematic method of punishment in the camp to prevent them from forming friendship, was all to the good for the University of Job, because it brought variety into the cultural programme.

200. The Power of Words

Two journalists started the first and probably the only paperless magazine in the world. They called it *The Rose of Jericho*, because that desert plant curls its dry stems into a ball and rolls back and forth over the steppes, dry and lifeless, until the rains come, when it revives and turns green again.

There were leading articles, interviews, news stories, readers' letters and editorial answers, satire, caricatures, poetry, but all orally transmitted. And the prisoners in Hut 9, where *The Rose* was published, enjoyed it page by page.

Some men with particularly good memories had the job of learning the newspaper by heart. Then they could quote from the latest edition to prisoners from other huts, who in turn passed sections of it on. Not a week went by without more than ten different copies of the same edition being in circulation.

Two former radio presenters put on a satirical radio programme, calling their station "Radio Earth Closet". The programme went out at night, and contained news, advice, quizzes, and songs.

One of the presenters was a Palestinian, the other a communist from Damascus, with whom Farid quickly made friends. Torture had left this man blind in his right eye. The two presenters collected news all day. Some of the soldiers would tell them what they had read in the daily papers. Then, in the silence of the night, the two men broadcast the news to the sky. It was in this way that Farid learned about the civil war in the Congo, the suicide of the American writer Ernest Hemingway, and the bombing attacks in Paris linked to the Algerian war.

Of course there were even more punishments next day, even more pointless hard labour, but that was not what mattered.

Some time around the end of December 1960, Captain Hamdi couldn't help but notice that his regime of torture and humiliation was getting him nowhere. He was left with a choice between murder or toleration. He was not allowed to murder his prisoners, so he decided to tolerate their apparently harmless eccentricities, never realizing that he had suffered a severe setback.

201. The Rift

At the end of January the first rumours of the imminent collapse of the union with Egypt reached the camp. A considerable amount of discontent against their Egyptian superiors had built up among the Syrian army officers. The prisoners laughed out loud when they heard the report on Captain Hamdi broadcast by Radio Earth Closet; Hamdi, it said, had only just noticed that his bosses in Damascus were Egyptians to a man.

But by now Hamdi had far more to worry about than the prisoners guessed. For the first time he was asking himself what would happen later. His prisoners included not only many scholars and influential civilians, but more than fifty army officers from all parts of the country, including two generals. These were men who had been discharged for sympathizing with the communists or the Muslim Brotherhood, and had ended up in Gahan.

He decided to use torture only in extreme cases in future, and gave his men a vague explanation to account for this sudden change of policy. By the middle of February torture had been practically discontinued at Gahan. Even Abu Satur wasn't allowed to whip prisoners any more, and he went around the camp looking dazed. He asked for a transfer, but Captain Hamdi pretended not to hear him, and consoled him by saying that they'd have to wait and see.

As time went on Abu Satur turned yellow in the face. He was said to have hepatitis, and soon after that he disappeared.

Rumours were rife: it was said that there had been a severe crisis in Damascus, with the dismissal of increasing numbers of high-ranking Syrian politicians from their posts. The prisoners celebrated such rumours as a victory over Hamdi, and threw themselves into yet more cultural activities. A number of the criminal fraternity began learning to write.

In the middle of all this good news, however, came one report that struck Farid to the heart. A government newspaper of early December, stolen from the captain's office, said on the front page that President Satlan had praised the USSR for saying nothing in condemnation of the wave of arrests which was systematically destroying the Communist Parties of Egypt and Syria. For the first time in weeks, there was disagreement among the camp inmates again. Three high-up Communist Party functionaries tried to explain away the silence from Russia as a wise move; everyone else deplored it. The three talked wordily on about tactics that were necessary if socialism was to continue its victorious progress around the world.

Farid couldn't get his head around that. He lay awake at night, wondering what kind of socialism it was whose superpower knuckled under to a small-time dictator, leaving its own supporters to fend for themselves. Did it really want to change the world for the better?

202. The False Martyr

A report in an anti-Satlan Lebanese newspaper set off the next quarrel in the camp. It had been smuggled in from Beirut in mid-January, and described an international campaign for the freedom of Basil Omani, who was said to be mortally sick.

Basil Osmani was the highest communist functionary ever to fall into the net of the Syrian secret service. The first General Secretary of the Party, Khalid Malis, had escaped the police and was now in Moscow, where he had to keep his mouth shut, since the Russians were linked to Satlan by the arms trade, the building of the Aswan Dam, and other major but secret projects which they didn't want spoiled by an asylum seeker.

The second in command, Basil Osmani, had been in Hut 7 of the Gahan prison camp. He was treated with special courtesy by the camp commandant, Captain Hamdi, out of fear rather than respect, for his prisoner was one of the Osmani clan, which owned great tracts of land and whole villages on the Euphrates. Hamdi himself came from one of those villages, and his ancestors had always been serfs of the Osmanis. After forty years, his father had risen to the point where he could lease a small farm from the clan. Hamdi was absolutely convinced that the Arab clans would survive all political parties and all states, so he considered himself the sheikh of the camp and treated Basil Osmani as a sheikh of equally high birth who just happened to be visiting him.

Farid had disliked Osmani from the first. The functionary had been jovial when they met, like a sheikh to his children, authoritarian and arrogant – a patriarch from the country facing a self-confident young man from the city.

His family had more or less openly sent Osmani plenty of money in the camp, and he used it to bribe the guards and soldiers and to lavish presents on Commandant Hamdi. The other inmates of his hut, which the prisoners nicknamed "The Euphrates", did not go short of food, cigarettes, and medicaments.

But now this Lebanese newspaper had come to light, saying that the whole world was demanding the immediate liberation of Basil

Osmani, who was being held in the camp at Tad and severely mis-treated. He had a weak heart, said the paper, and doctors said that Osmani was on the point of death.

Not a word about the murders that really had been committed in the camps. Nothing about the beatings given to the prisoners by the guards when they arrived, and certainly nothing about torture and inhuman degradations. The great pro-Osmani campaign was taken up in Western Europe. Churches, trade unions, political parties and intellectuals from Paris to London were firmly backing the cause of the Syrian functionary who was said to be mortally sick. But he was not in the death camp of Tad, he was in Gahan, enjoying the best of health, although he had put on rather too much weight for lack of exercise.

This news report with all its false claims hurt, and when Farid cau-tiously asked Osmani how such lies had arisen, he laughed smugly. "Young Comrade, our class enemy tells lies all the time. We have to pick up their weapons and turn those weapons against them ourselves."

Farid felt like throwing up. When Radio Earth Closet courteously corrected the newspaper report that evening, congratulating the functionary on his present state of good health, Osmani was furious. Immediately after that, it was clear that the witty radio reporter was being ostracized by the communist faithful in the camp. One man whispered to Farid, "I'd advise you to keep away from that viper. He's a Trotskyite." Such an accusation amounted to a death sentence in the Communist Party.

"And I would advise you," replied Farid, "to use your brain and not your backside when you have something to say."

Next day Farid himself was taken away and put in solitary confine-ment for two weeks. It may be mere coincidence, he thought, but if so then it was mere coincidence that he hated Basil Osmani.

203. The Chemistry of Isolation

Solitary confinement wore you down. The commandant had his most unpleasant soldiers and guards keeping watch on you. To overcome the absence of sound, which filled his brain with a strange void, Farid began constructing chemical reactions in his head. He carried out processes synthesizing simple elements into complex compounds, and once he had achieved a substance he gave it a name and then, three days later, tried dismantling it again step by step, until he was back with the simple elements.

The bucket for faeces and urine sometimes wasn't taken away for days, on purpose, and then the isolation cell stank horribly. And in the midst of this wretchedness, Farid's body asserted itself. When he closed his eyes he had erotic dreams. He wondered where his mind found these fantasies.

In the camp all days were alike, in solitary confinement even the time of day was lost in everlasting darkness, but it must have been mid-April when a soldier – a Damascene, judging by his accent – said that Farid's friends (he meant the Russians) had sent a man called Gagarin flying around the earth. Farid didn't understand. But the soldier was talkative that day, and told him about a party to which Osmani had invited all the officers, guards, and soldiers. They had enjoyed a great many delicacies from Damascus in his hut: roast meat, pistachios, fruit. But the soldier, he said, had drunk too much, and his head was still spinning. "Gagarin went around the world in a rocket, I do it with alcohol," he said, laughing at his own joke.

❧

When Farid was let out of solitary confinement again, the radio presenter had disappeared.

"He was deported to Tad after a quarrel with a guard," old Said told him.

At that, and in front of all his fellow prisoners, Farid accused Osmani of being behind both his own solitary confinement and the radio presenter's deportation. "A man who does a thing like that can never be a communist. You're still the descendant of a feudal tribe. You don't understand anything, you're just playing the same old egotistic game as your father."

Osmani reacted indignantly, but there was nothing he dared do. His comrades warned him that strong anti-communist feeling was abroad in the camp. Two days earlier there had been a brawl between Ba'athists and communists. Osmani knew it had been a mistake for the soldiers to join in and hit out only at the Ba'athists, on Captain Hamid's instructions. The camp was split more deeply by this partisanship than it had ever been by torture or the work of informers.

For suddenly, in the eyes of many prisoners, the Ba'athists figured as martyrs and the communists as their persecutors. So Osmani held his tongue, even though Farid had spoken out so clearly.

204. Salto Vitale

By now relations between the Syrians and the Egyptians were soured beyond redemption. President Satlan reacted to the crisis with yet more dismissals of Syrians from all political and strategic posts in the Union, by arresting yet more opponents of the regime, and by strengthening the powers of the secret service. He appointed the head of the secret service, Abdulhamid Sarrag, to the post of vice-president and supreme administrator of the province of Syria.

That was the most stupid move the Egyptian could have made. The Syrian army carried out a coup on 28 September 1961 and declared union with Egypt at an end. People danced in the streets for joy, and sang songs against Satlan and his Syrian vice-president. Popular rejoicing lasted for days. The Syrians were glad to regain their independence, and did not guess that they were witnessing the burial of the dream of a united Arabia. They danced as if they were at a wedding instead.

All the Egyptians, now humiliated by Syria, were sent home, and many Syrian secret service men fled to Cairo to go underground there.

As for Elias Mushtak, he did as he had promised and lit thirty large candles to the Virgin Mary. All his life, he firmly believed that his prayers to Our Lady had been answered.

On 4 October, Farid and a thousand other political prisoners were freed. Buses took them to Hidjas rail station. Each of them was given a hundred lira for the journey, and a packet of bread, fruit, and three cans of meat and two of sardines as a gift. Farid gave his packet to an old beggar he didn't know. The man had been sitting outside the station there for years.

Then he boarded the Number 5 bus to go home. Suddenly, when he got out at the stop near his street, the moment of his arrest came vividly back to him. Overcome by the memory, he stopped and looked around. All at once he saw Lilo standing at the door of his barber's shop as he had been then. At the same moment Lilo saw him. The barber looked closely once again, to make sure, and then ran with outstretched arms to the neighbour who had been missing for so long.

Farid hugged him. When he let go of the man again, he realized that the barber was making throaty sounds of joy, but could utter no words. With difficulty, he read from his lips that Lilo had lost his voice soon after Farid's arrest, and had been having treatment for it ever since.

Claire almost collapsed with joy and relief when Farid arrived home. She kept kissing and embracing him. Elias was still at the confectioner's shop, and would be back later.

She wanted to tell the whole world that Farid was free at last, but just now Farid himself had only one wish: for a bath. He ran hot water into the big tub and lay in it. Gradually he felt the dirt of the camp coming off him. The water turned grey, and stank of mould and rust, oil and sweat. He let it run out and refilled the bathtub. This time he added some orange-blossom essence to the water. Only now did he begin to feel really all right again.

Josef was the first visitor. He rushed right into the bathroom, where Farid had just begun to dress, flung his arms around his friend, and kissed his eyes. When Farid freed himself from Josef's embrace, he saw Matta standing in the doorway. "My brother," he cried. "Thank

God. Faride and I have been praying for you." Farid embraced Matta, and then gently impelled both him and Josef out of the bathroom. "If you don't leave me alone for a moment I'll be standing here in my underwear until midnight," he said, and saw Matta's fiancée and his mother laughing in the inner courtyard.

Laila was very soon there too. Immediately after Claire called she had taken a taxi, urging the driver to hurry so much that he wished he had a siren and a flashing blue light. The moment she arrived she hugged Farid for a long time and kissed him without restraint. But she had to leave again almost at once, for she had a wedding dress to deliver that day. As she said goodbye, she whispered into Farid's ear, "As soon as you can get your breath back, you must come and see me." He nodded without a word.

Although the telephone was ringing almost without a break, Farid waited in vain all evening for one particular call, but it was always someone else on the line. Hadn't Rana heard that he was free? Once, when the company were talking about amazing natural phenomena, Claire had mentioned the milk teeth that Rana's grandmother grew before her death. She had died just before Christmas, said Claire, who in spite of the hostility between the two families had gone to the funeral. Farid was amazed to think of his mother going there on her own, and he knew she had done it only for Rana's sake. But where was Rana now?

All the neighbours and relations came, but something strange oppressed Farid's heart: they were all acting as if he had merely been away on a journey. At first he couldn't understand it, but gradually he realized they didn't want to acknowledge where he had been since April of last year, they didn't want to know that he had raised his voice against Satlan in spite of them and their silence, and had gone to prison for it. Worst of all, he thought, was his father, who when he came in late that evening was almost embarrassed when he embraced him, and could think of nothing better to say than, "I hope that'll teach you that politics are not for us Christians. You'd better leave them alone!"

Farid was determined to do the exact opposite.

But he heard the worst news only just before midnight, when

Matta, the last guest, had left the house. Claire took his hands, kissed him on the eyes, and shed tears. Then he knew that something bad had happened to Rana.

BOOK OF LOVE VI

Love lives only in the memory but it needs oblivion too.

༈

DAMASCUS, APRIL 1960–OCTOBER 1961

205. A Bus Ride

Rana had chosen a window seat. The bus was almost empty when she boarded it, and filled up only as it came closer and closer to the Old Town. She suddenly noticed a man molesting a woman from behind in the crush of passengers. The woman turned around and asked him to keep his distance. The man acted as if he didn't understand, but Rana saw the bulge in his trousers. She turned away, disgusted, and looked out of the window.

The bus had just reached the Al Buzuriye spice market. Memories surfaced in her mind. Memories of the year 1960, when she was still studying literature at the university, and taking lessons in painting and drawing from a well-known woman artist at the same time. She had wanted to be an artist herself, but she knew that she couldn't earn a living that way. Literature had been her second passion, and with a degree in it she could at least survive by teaching.

Back then, she too had been standing in a crowded bus, and suddenly felt a man very close to her back. His hot breath burned her neck. A cloud of sweat and a smell like a brimming ashtray enveloped her. She felt sick. The man kept pressing against her. Then she felt his hard member between her buttocks. She turned angrily, and was surprised to see how inoffensive the man looked. He had a small beard, and wore glasses. Rana asked him to keep his distance. He smiled and went on pushing and waggling himself about, as if to get through his trousers, her dress, and two sets of underwear. She asked him a second time, but that just encouraged him to take even more liberties. "Don't be like that, admit it, you're enjoying it," he whispered, holding her hip firmly in one hand.

At that she slapped him in the face so hard that he lost his balance and fell on another man's lap. Rana had expected all the passengers to turn on him and support her. But it was exactly the opposite. Apart from one young woman, they had all been against her and took the shameless man under their protection. One man was particularly indignant. "There's no decency or morals these days," he cried. "To think I'd live to see the day when a woman hits a man."

"She's no woman," the man whose face she had slapped replied. "I swear she's a man." Rana got out at the next stop and took a taxi home.

This time she heard the woman quietly begging her molester to stop, and then, after three or four stops, saw her escaping to the safety of a seat that had just been vacated. The importunate man, now standing behind a farmer, cursed his bad luck in clearly audible tones.

When the bus reached Saitun Alley, Rana glanced at Farid's house. A burning pain stabbed her breast, and she began to cry. A woman near her asked if there was anything she could do. Rana shook her head. "Thank you, no, it's just a sad memory," she whispered.

A few days after her last meeting with Farid, she had longed for a word from him. Never guessing what had happened, she called him at home. Claire answered the phone, and after a few words her voice failed her. Rana's heart was racing anxiously. Gradually, she learned that Farid had been arrested. It was as much as Claire could do to tell her. She ended by saying there was nothing anyone could do for him.

Rana felt desolate as she had never in her life felt before. She hung up, ran out, took a taxi and went to Farid's mother. That had been about midday, and Claire was alone. She embraced the girl, and they both wept. Farid's mother had aged by years within a few days. You could see grey hairs on her head for the first time. Rana stayed for several hours.

"You can come here whenever you feel like it," said Claire, hugging her as she said goodbye. "Farid loves you very much."

"I love him too," said Rana, hurrying out. At that time his mother didn't even know if he was still alive. No lawyers could be hired by a prisoner's family, no questions officially asked. It was only by roundabout ways and with many bribes that she and Elias discovered he was being held in Gahan. However, they couldn't visit him or write him letters. Even the powerful Catholic patriarch made only one remark, which soon became habitual in his mouth: "If it were murder, robbery, or hashish, I would have spoken up for him, but he's a political."

When Rana came home she stuck Farid's photograph into the last page of her Bible. Jack was always snooping, and even searched her chest of drawers, but he didn't touch religious books.

A week later her mother heard of Farid's arrest, and gave her spite free rein. All her hatred of the Mushtaks surfaced, and even Rana's father was glad that their arch-enemy's son had fallen into the hands of the police. "The Mushtaks are great tacticians, but they have no backbone. They'll join any party. They've already had Hablanists, Dartanists and Shaklanists among them. Today they're Satlanists, Ba'athists, Syrian Nationalists and communists. There's always one of them supporting the party in power and another in prison. That way they can be rulers and martyrs at the same time. I'm sure that if the Muslim Brotherhood came to power a Mushtak would convert to Islam like a shot. Subtle, that's what they are, subtle," he said in tones of abhorrence.

All these memories were now passing through Rana's mind on the bus ride. It was at the next stop that she had dismounted when she last saw Farid in his dead grandmother's house. After a few steps she had reached al-Kassabah Alley and then turned into Misq Alley. He had been waiting for her. His silent grief, his presentiments were as fresh in her mind now as then, when she was lying in bed with him. The room had been overheated, but he was freezing cold.

Now the bus was going through the eastern gate. Then it turned left, and followed the wall of the Old Town before it drove towards the stadium and Abbasid Square.

Rana still could hardly grasp how events in her life had come so thick and fast after that last day with Farid, and she hated herself for being so naïve at the time. She shook her head.

Rami had always been her favourite cousin. Unlike his brothers, he seemed neither particularly religious nor extremely conservative, and he didn't covet cars and money. His father, Sami Kudsi, was the poorest member of his family, and at the age of thirty had lost his inheritance in bad speculations, but he claimed to be a survival artist, and kept his wife and five children on the little deals he did. As a bankrupt, he wasn't officially allowed to own anything. His wife said he was a broker, but no one believed that. More likely, it was rumoured, he was a receiver of stolen goods. Somehow he had managed to get his boys a free education in a good Orthodox school, where the five brothers studied and took their final exams one after another.

In retrospect, Rana blamed herself bitterly for having felt so safe with Rami. It was just that he had always understood her, and fanaticism of any kind was not in his nature. So she had told him about the approaches made by his youngest brother Kafi, and both had laughed until the tears came at the shock she had given that religious fanatic.

Of course she didn't dare tell him about Farid, but at least here was someone she could talk to. The fact that he liked her had not escaped her notice. But Rami had been so pleasant and unassuming. He had just been promoted to first lieutenant, and was having further training at the military academy in economics and logistics. "That means I won't rise fast in the army, but I won't fall either. Someone has to look after the practical side," he said wryly. He had no ambition at all, and devoted his mind to the purchases made by the army, from bootlaces to complete winter equipment. He didn't like wearing uniform, and did not even carry a gun.

Rami was also the only man who invited her to the cinema or to eat an ice cream without any ulterior motives. Or so she had thought, because that was how she remembered him from their childhood. Why had she been so naïve? Why had she never noticed that she was a woman now, and the way her cousin looked at her had changed?

After Farid's arrest, when she felt she was stifling in the malicious atmosphere of her parents' house, she had phoned Rami and asked if he would like to go to the cinema with her. Her mother and brother had no objection to her going out with him – he was the only man they didn't object to – even if she happened to come home late.

And then the catastrophe happened.

Rami had come to lunch that Sunday. He liked the kebbeh that his aunt baked. Jack was there too. Only her father was away for a week; he had flown to New York to attend a lawyers' conference.

Rana's mother had been unusually pleasant to her daughter, and she made the best meat pasty imaginable that day. Kebbeh was the usual Sunday lunch of prosperous Christians, and she had been lavish with spices and roasted pine nuts. She had served Lebanese red wine with the meal. "Wine sensitizes the palate, and my kebbeh is at its best with red wine," she claimed. At first Rana said she didn't want any, but then she drank a glass for the sake of politeness, although diluted with cold water and ice.

They laughed a lot. She had seldom seen her mother so relaxed and easy-going. Finally Jack went off to his room, and they could hear his favourite record down in the drawing room, songs performed by the Egyptian singer Abdulhalim, whom Rana liked too.

Then her mother also left the drawing room, saying she would make coffee. Rana laughed with Rami at the ear-splitting sound of the music, and Rami kept refilling their wine glasses. Her head was beginning to feel heavy, but she enjoyed Rami's company and his jokes.

Suddenly he put his arm around her neck. "Oh, how happy it makes me to hear you laugh," he said. At first she thought nothing of it, but when he kissed her throat she froze, abruptly stood up and said she was going to ask her brother to turn his music down. But she had taken only one step towards the door when Rami became a wall barring her way. He didn't do it quickly, but at his leisure. His footsteps were perfectly steady, his outstretched arms did not tremble.

He seized her like someone claiming his own property. At that moment she understood it all. She saw not only the trap and her own stupidity in ever sitting alone in a room with this man, she also understood her family's plotting, and the misery suffered by women for thousands of years, and she struggled with all her might, but like a trained karate fighter Rami threw her to the floor. It happened very fast. She lay there on the heavy Persian rug, and he lay on top of her, still beaming. "I really, really like your laugh, do you know?" he babbled. His weight immobilized her. Rana felt dazed. "Please," she begged him. "Rami, please let me get up." But he became deaf, a deaf brute, kissing her and trying to push his tongue inside her mouth.

"No," screamed Rana, kicking and turning her head aside so that Rami couldn't get at her lips. He grinned, and did not become frantic or nervous, but acted as if he had all the time in the world. Gradually he was pressing ever more heavily down on her body, and then she felt his right hand reaching for her panties. She screamed and begged at the same time, but no one heard her.

The pain was like fiery pincers stabbing her. She wept and hit him, but he forced his way further in until she felt dizzy.

When her mother came back after an eternity, she pretended to be surprised, threw herself theatrically on the sofa, and wept. But Rana saw the hypocrisy in her eyes. Jack came running in too, in pretended horror, but instead of being angry he consoled her by saying she had a very good bargain in Rami, he was more than she deserved.

A few days later her father came home. He spoke to his wife first and then to Rami, not to her. After three days he finally came to her room, not to comfort her but to tell her it was her own fault, and she must either die or marry Rami, who had said he was ready to atone for his wrongdoing by taking her as his wife.

Rana cried and screamed, but she had no chance. She felt sick and ran a temperature, but three days later she was dragged into the drawing room, where a priest, who knew the whole story, swiftly performed the marriage ceremony and signed the register. When he asked Rana if she took Rami as her husband, she replied loud and clear, "No," but her denial was drowned out by a chorus of "Yes" from everyone else present. Rana thought she had gone out of her mind.

She wouldn't sign the register herself, so her father took her hand and signed for her, while her brother held her other hand in a steely grip. Rana was crying, but no one took any notice.

At that moment she had a vision. For a second she was dead, and when she opened her eyes again a second life began. She felt her heart turning into a cactus.

There was no point drowning in her own tears. Her enemies

outnumbered her. They're rejoicing at your unhappiness, an inner voice told her. You must follow your heart and be a cactus, one that will survive this man who has brought you such misfortune. Your revenge is your memory which will never let you forgive, and when the moment comes you must close your eyes again, die for a second, and then come back to life as Rana once more. And when that happens, the cactus will flower and die.

When she had reached this point in her memories, the bus was just coming to the large Square of Seven Fountains. Rana stood up and went slowly to the door.

The next stop was hers.

206. Josef's Promise

Claire thought she would not survive Farid's arrest. Damascus was a desert without him. When the news came, Elias had left the confectioner's shop at once and gone to see his friends and acquaintances. Many of them were in the highest political positions, but they offered only sympathy and regret. Claire tried at least to find out, through her former school friends, if Farid was still alive and where he was being held. But not until early in the afternoon of the day he disappeared did a distant cousin of Madeleine's tell her that her son was held prisoner in the secret service building. This cousin was married to one of the Interior Minister's bodyguards, but even she could do nothing for Farid because he was "a political".

At first Claire felt relieved. She knew now that her son was not dead. She phoned Elias at once, and on hearing her news he looked around for help all the more urgently. Late that afternoon he came home as pale as a dying man.

"What are friends for?" he asked bitterly, and didn't wait for her to answer. "To tell you how sorry they are. And is that all? What cowardly times we live in! The boy's taken a wrong turning and they inflate it into an affair of state. As if my son Farid were any danger to President Satlan!"

At that moment Claire felt boundless love for her husband Elias, whose concern for his only son had suddenly made him forget everything else. She embraced him and kissed him on the lips.

"That's how it is," said Elias. "Anyone would think he'd been smuggling the year's entire harvest abroad, or stealing cars and jewellery in broad daylight, or dumping tons of hashish in police headquarters on the sly. If there's one thing I wish on those who govern us, it's for this filthy union to break up, and on the day it does I'll light thirty candles to Our Lady."

Claire was laughing and crying at the same time. She kept hugging him. Suddenly he was the young Elias again, the man she had loved so much over twenty years ago. "Hush, or they'll take you away too, and I'll be left all alone. And who will I have to hug then?"

Elias kissed her. "I'll never forgive Satlan and his henchmen, if only for making you sad," he replied, holding Claire close, for he sensed her despair.

The neighbours visited. They sat with Farid's parents, all of them downcast, praising the boy who had always been so charming and helpful. The house was full of guests. Even two of Farid's teachers were brave enough to come; the rest feared that Elias and Claire were under observation, and they would lose their jobs.

Late that afternoon Josef arrived. He whispered to Claire that she must come with him at once. Claire excused herself to her other guests and followed him. "It's something I promised Farid," he explained as they came out into the street, and he went ahead of her. She didn't understand. Josef went upstairs to the flat roof of his house, which had a fence around it. The sun was just sinking, turning large and red.

Two chairs stood in one corner. Josef pulled one out for her. "You sit here," he told her, and sat opposite her on the other chair himself.

"I promised Farid," he said at last in a low, husky voice, "that if anything happened to him I'd go to you and bring you here, where he always liked to sit with me. And then we'd both think hard about him, and that would help him."

Claire sat with her face to the sun. She closed her eyes, and wished she were dead, but a voice inside her said, "Think of the happy times with him. He needs you." Then she smiled through her tears, and for the first time that day she felt something like hope revive.

207. Dunia and the Bedroom Woman

Rana came to see Claire and told her the whole story of Rami. But Claire was so full of grief herself that she had no room for more sorrow. She soothed Rana, and said Farid wouldn't love her any the less because she'd been forced into marriage. But first he must survive the prison camp, and apparently President Satlan had said that as long as he was in power, his enemies would stay in jail.

Unlike Claire, Laila had changed towards Rana. She spoke without reserve, criticizing her severely. In her place, said Laila, she would never have married Rami, not even after a rape. It was like a slap in the face to Rana.

A few days later, however, Laila phoned, apologized for her fierce accusations, and invited Rana for a coffee. Rana hoped they could come together again. She had plenty of time on her hands, for Rami was more than occupied with his work. So she went to see Laila, and was surprised to find her house full of women visiting her. At least a dozen of them, all laughing and talking together, had assembled. Farid's cousin walked around like a queen, with everyone adoring her. One of those present gave a short talk about Arab women in the pre-Islamic period. The speaker's voice was indistinct, and much of what she said was very disconnected, but Rana at least caught the gist of it: women in the desert before the coming of Islam had chosen their own partners. And they had sat with men, it was the natural thing to do, they joined in conversations with them, and wore no veils. Names were determined by the mother, not the father. The Prophet Muhammad himself was usually addressed by reference to his mother's name, not his father's, and was known as Muhammad bin Amina. The man always moved in with his woman partner, not vice versa. The woman could separate from him at any time. It was quite simple, being achieved just by changing the alignment of the tent entrance.

And another thing: a woman could marry up to ten husbands. It was known as communal marriage.

A discussion followed the talk, and seemed likely to go on for ever. Rana was bored. After a while she rose to her feet and left. Three weeks later, when Laila asked her to come again, she declined, saying she couldn't concentrate enough at the moment. She didn't like to tell the truth, which was that she didn't think much of these women's daydreams.

Dunia, on the other hand, was refreshing. Her friend liked to laugh and seemed to rise above everything. She had done as her mother wished and married a rich carpet dealer. Not that she had loved the man; Dunia loved no one but her little dog Fifi, but she knew how to adapt to her husband, and there was a sober and expedient kind of affection in their marriage.

But at Dunia's wedding everything nearly went wrong. When she talked about that disaster, she made her audience laugh. Two weeks before her wedding, Dunia had suffered an accident while she was exercising. She bled heavily, and the doctor said she had torn her hymen. Her father, who was just back from Saudi Arabia, was horrified when the doctor told him. "If only she'd broken an arm or a leg! But she has to go and break her own hymen! I'm ruined," wailed the Saudi king's adviser. He was at a loss. "What will happen now?" he asked the doctor, who was an old family friend.

"Better ask her fiancé to come and see me. I'll explain for you," said the doctor.

"You don't know him. He's conservative and suspicious. He'll accuse you of being in league with us," replied Dunia's father, and he left the consulting rooms with his daughter. For the first time, Dunia noticed that her father stooped as he walked.

He knew that at the time, and for large sums of money, you could have a girl's hymen repaired in Paris. Many daughters of the *nouveaux riches* Gulf families flew to France, pretending that the trip was a vacation, stayed for a couple of weeks and came back virgins, rather like the houris, the eternal virgins of Paradise whose hymens are renewed after every act of love. But there wasn't time for that. Dunia's fiancé would have seen through the reason for her sudden visit to

Paris. Looking decades older, her father sat in the drawing room of his house, waiting for the return of his wife, who had just gone away for a couple of days to visit relations in the country and invite them all to the wedding.

Although it was summer, he was freezing cold. For years he had been kowtowing in the Saudi royal palace, grimly fighting to defend his position against all who envied him, in the middle of the desert and far from his beloved Damascus – and now this had to happen. If he lost face now, he might as well blow his brains out at once.

"Dear God, I'm finished. Help me, and I'll sacrifice forty sheep to you in Mecca," Dunia heard her father whisper to himself. Not until her mother came home and took matters in hand did he calm down a little.

She took her daughter to the Old Town to see a strong and sturdy elderly lady who described herself as a "bedroom woman". Dunia was surprised, for in Arabic this word sounded very like the word for a hairdresser. No doubt the chamber woman did depilate the bride when necessary, in those places where the bridegroom would rather not encounter hair. But her main task was different. On the way to her Dunia's mother explained it to her daughter, and Rana now discovered for the first time that the profession of bedroom woman had existed in Damascus for centuries.

The bedroom woman attended the wedding at the invitation of the bride's parents, and while the guests were celebrating she was ready on call. If the bride was frightened and reluctant when evening came, she would slip into the conjugal bedroom and help the bridegroom to "take" his wife. She reassured the newly married girl, caressed her, and if necessary even held her legs apart and cursed and slapped her to make her docile, so that the bridegroom could penetrate her unopposed. She also knew all kinds of tricks to arouse men who couldn't get an erection. Her good offices made her welcome to the bridegroom's parents too.

"But what does that have to do with me?" Dunia asked her mother just as they were reaching the house of the bedroom woman, who heard Dunia's anxious question, and smiled. "Give your husband enough liquor, and when he wants to take you to bed say you're scared and you're going to scream. Get him to call for me, and then you must calm down and show willing. That's all you have to do," she firmly told Dunia.

Dunia herself was surprised by her mother's confidence and composure as the wedding night came. Her father, on the other hand, was pale as a corpse. He looked so sad that her brother Kamal said, jokingly, someone ought to tell the old man he wasn't at a funeral. Of course Kamal hadn't been allowed to know the tale of Dunia's hymen, and nor had anyone else.

When the bridegroom entered the bedroom he was swaying from all the liquor that had gone to his head. He was surprised by his bride's excessive timidity when she asked him not to come any closer or she'd scream. Allowing her the favour she asked, he sent for the bedroom woman. He had been told by his own mother, only a little while before, that he should ask for the woman's services so that the party could go on, undisturbed by excessive screaming.

The bedroom woman arrived, whispered something to the bridegroom, and he began to undress. Then she assured Dunia that it wouldn't hurt at all, and would very soon be over.

"It was very funny," said Dunia, "there was my husband, dead drunk, dancing around in circles and undressing. He looked much more handsome naked than with his suit on, and I wanted him – he smelled so good, too – but the woman stood between us, held my legs apart as if she were going to look inside me, and took hold of my husband's thing. He was enormously amused by that, he kept laughing all the time, and he didn't see what she was doing. I felt him come inside me, but it didn't hurt. Before I could come to a climax, however, the chamber woman cried out, "Congratulations, O lion among men, on this pearl of virginity!" And she began ululating at the top of her voice, and uttering cries of joy and good wishes. While we were washing, she took the sheet with a big bloodstain in the middle of it out to the guests, and they all danced and sang with joy over my clear demonstration of virginity.

Where the bedroom woman came by all that blood was her own secret. But anyway, my husband, my parents and his, and all our friends and relations were pleased. That night my father took my mother's arm with tears in his eyes and told her, "I'll never forget what you did. You have saved me." And next morning he flew back to his king in Saudi Arabia, a happy man."

208. Late Enlightenment

Josef's studies did not demand much of him. He had to be present only in geography classes, because there was practical work to be done there. He knew more about history, on the other hand, than his professors did, so instead of attending lectures he was often to be found in the Café Havana on Port Said Street, where journalists and politicians met. Anyone who ever wanted to engage in these professions had to graduate in the "Havana Academy". Since Josef's heart beat for politics, the café gave him far more interesting contacts than any lecture.

He liked the street, where there were many other restaurants as well as his favourite haunt, besides cinemas, stores selling Indian goods, and coffee bars. The Café Brazil was a meeting place for men of letters. You could also choose from several famous confectioners' shops, and most of the newspapers published in Damascus had their offices here. But he particularly liked the Librairie Universelle, a bookshop that had imported excellent literature from all over the world ever since the days of the French occupation. The owner knew him well, and would even get him banned titles. Conveniently, the shop was just opposite the Café Havana.

One fine day in autumn Josef was just coming out of the café, and was about to cross the broad street with its many traffic lanes, when he saw his father getting out of a tram and making purposefully for a nearby building. By now his father was almost blind. He rang the doorbell, and soon disappeared into the house. Josef stopped in surprise in the middle of the street. A bus driver had to brake sharply, and swore. Josef, startled, waved an apology. He went up to the unobtrusive door between two large display windows. The ancient copper plate on it said, in almost illegible lettering, "Khuri". The name meant nothing to him.

When he came home, he asked his mother if she knew a family called Khuri. Madeleine looked up in surprise.

"Why do you ask?"

"Because my father went into a house with that nameplate, and I've never heard of the family before."

Madeleine laughed. "Think nothing of it. He's only visiting his lover."

Josef felt anger rise in him. "Do I ever dismiss any of your questions like that, Mother?" he replied, and was about to walk out of the room in a huff, but Madeleine took her son's arm and said, "Don't be so prim and proper. I'm telling you the truth. Rimon has loved Marta since childhood. She was a beauty, and she thought your father was a wonderful boxer. Her husband Sarkis Khuri, one of a noble family, controlled all the cocoa imports, and he was the biggest chocolate manufacturer in Damascus too. He spent some of his money on sponsoring Rimon, because he believed in your father's strength, and in all his interviews your father had to mention that he drank cocoa every morning.

"Marta fell madly in love with your father. But Rimon wasn't planning to sleep with a woman whose husband was his sponsor. The three of them met every week, and Rimon adored Marta and Marta adored him, but in thirty years it never came to any more. Then her husband fell sick, and he lost his money at exactly the time when your father was building huge palaces and earning large sums. Suddenly Mr. Khuri was dependent on Rimon's help, which your father gave generously, and he also made sure that the childless couple received a small pension from the Catholic community. But there's nothing worse than an impoverished nobleman. Khuri wasn't a bit grateful to your father, but saw him as an enemy. And he was always making snide remarks and saying he was sure that Marta and Rimon were deceiving him. However, the two of them just went on sitting next to each other, and even in *forty* years they never touched.

"But your father inherited poor eyesight from his mother, who went blind at the age of forty. He was terribly short-sighted when he was thirty, and from then on his eyes got worse and worse. Perhaps you remember that about ten years ago, when he could hardly see at all and kept on stumbling over things, I begged him to go and see an oculist. After a few days he came home with a pair of glasses, and he was very pleased, because not only could he see where he was going better, he could see the dice when he played backgammon too. He went about as proud as a child with its first pair of patent leather shoes.

"But three days later he came home without his glasses. He didn't tell you children why, but he's never kept anything from me. He'd been horrified when he was suddenly able to see his beloved Marta so clearly. As I told you, she'd been a beauty once, but she hadn't aged well. She had growths on her nose, her hair was thin, and her hands had warts all over them. Rimon had never noticed that over the years. So that day he threw the glasses under a tram."

209. Spring in Autumn

Rana heard the news that Farid was free from Laila, the morning after his return. She phoned his house at nine. Claire laughed. "You're faster than a gazelle," she joked, and felt life flowing through her veins again.

Farid had just woken up. His first night in freedom had been a short one. Matta and his fiancée Faride had been the last guests to leave, at about one in the morning. They wanted Farid to be witness at their wedding, and had been waiting for him all these months. Farid was deeply moved. He laid a hand on Matta's head. "Of course I will," he said. "You only have to name the day."

"We already have. Matta has been fixing a new day with the priest every three months, hoping for your release. Last time the priest advised us to ask a different witness," said Faride. "Thank God I was there too, or Matta would just about have murdered him. He told the priest never to make such a suggestion again, but to pray for his brother Farid to be set free. Now we've picked the first Sunday in December, and if that date suits you we'll get married at last." All the time Faride was talking, Matta looked at her lovingly, and now he nodded happily.

"Then that's agreed," said Farid, and he got to his feet and marked Sunday, 3 December with a large cross.

He had been tired when he went to bed, but his feelings were in such turmoil that he could hardly sleep. He was smiling at the scene with the priest as Faride described it, imagining Matta's fury and the cleric's pale face. What a loyal, staunch friend Matta was! Then, at the end of the evening, came the news of Rana's forced marriage. And the place was so noisy! Damascus at night pulsated with an incredible volume of sound for someone who had spent over a year out in the desert. All Farid had heard in the prison camp were the screams of the prisoners and the cry of jackals. The desert swallowed up everything else. But here the city never seemed to sleep, and finally, when there was no one left in the streets calling out or hooting car horns, the muezzin began calling the faithful to prayer.

Farid woke up, and went into the courtyard barefoot. Claire was sitting by the fountain. He asked quietly who it was on the phone. She spoke into the receiver. "He must have picked up your scent, he's just asking who you are. Shall I tell him?"

Rana laughed.

"Hello, dear heart." Farid greeted her, in the words he had been repeating over and over for months on end.

"Hello. Do you still want to see me in spite of everything that's happened?" she asked shyly.

"Every day," he said. "Your marriage means nothing to me, and if it doesn't mean anything to you either then let's see each other." Those were the very words that Rana had been hoping for months to hear.

She told him the way to where she lived.

The city was in a bustling mood, it was beautiful, picturesque October weather, and the Damascenes felt something like liberty again for the first time in years. Farid didn't think that General Amilan, who had sent Satlan packing, was any better than his predecessor, but the people's hopes of democracy were almost tangible, and the release of all political prisoners made an encouraging start. The old Syrian political parties and the newspapers banned by Satlan emerged into the light of day again.

Damascus is at its loveliest in autumn, thought Farid. The cries of street sellers and the swallows in the sky sounded like melancholy songs of farewell.

The university was to open its doors again in two weeks' time. What a pity, Farid thought, that all his dreams of going through his studies there with Rana close to him had been dashed by her forced marriage.

Some things had changed since his disappearance. Josef had told him, in rapid staccato telegraphese, that the Interior Minister of the time had closed the club after Gibran did something stupid. Now they were trying to get permission to reopen it. Gibran had been arrested, and after a short while was handed over to the al-Asfuriye mental hospital, where he was still a patient.

"What about Karime?"

"She doesn't want to hear any more about Gibran. She had to bear a good deal of humiliation because of him, and now she just wants to be left alone."

Late that night Amin had phoned. He was in Aleppo in the north of the country, he said, and wanted to congratulate Farid on his release and remind him that, now everything was out in the open again, it was time for him to take up the battle once more. Amin told him that he and four other communists had managed to escape from the much-feared prison camp in Tad. He had found shelter with a family in Aleppo who were nothing to do with politics, but had guts. Then he said that he had fallen in love with Salime, the eldest daughter of the family, and they had married three months ago. He would very much like to see Farid, he added, but it was better for him to stay in Aleppo, where he had a lot of work laying tiles.

"I'll miss you very much," said Farid.

"I'll miss you too," replied Amin. "I've heard good things about the way you stood up to Osmani. I can't stand the man. I'm …" and here Amin hesitated for a moment, "I'm very proud of you," he went on at last, and Farid said nothing, wondering how such news could make its way to Aleppo from a camp in the desert.

৵

Rana had been living in her new house since last summer. It was a present from her father to the newly married couple, and stood in Fardus Street opposite the cinema, which also bore the name of the street, in the middle of the vibrant business quarter of the New Town. The building had been constructed in the 1930s in the European style, of white stone.

The first floor was rented out to a large Air France branch office and a fashion boutique. Rana and her husband lived in the two floors above those premises. The flat roof, which had a tall screen all around it, was Rana's domain. Orange trees, oleanders, roses, and jasmine grew there in large containers. She had turned what was once a maid's bedroom on the roof into a little studio, where she often sat painting.

Rami never came up to the roof. As he saw it, a rooftop was the place to hang out washing, and the laundry was women's business. He regarded painting as an occupation for women too, and perhaps for men who weren't quite right in the head.

Rana marvelled at Farid's lack of scars. She had had nightmares in which he was badly disfigured by torture and abuse. But here he was before her, more handsome than ever, somehow more virile, wittier. As soon as he saw her he had run to her, took her in his strong arms, and cried, "Where shall I take you, princess?" Then he kissed her on the mouth.

"Oh, put me down, I'm heavy! We must go two floors up," she whispered in his ear.

A steep staircase led up past those two floors to the flat roof. Once there, he could enjoy the sight of the plants and the attractively furnished studio.

Rana was paler than she used to be, but she smelled even more fragrant than before. He kissed her, and soon after that laid her down on the big old couch in her studio as naturally as if they hadn't been parted for a second. Close to her, Farid once again had the feeling he had known ever since they were together in Beirut. As soon as he kissed her she seemed to surround him like the world itself. She sank into him through every pore, and he and she were one.

Farid told her about his imprisonment, and then heard the story of the worst day in her life, her defeat as Rami and her family practised their deception on her. And she told him that she had resolved to live like a cactus until they could leave the country together, for no kind of life was possible for them here.

She took his head in both hands and kissed his eyes. "I'll pray for you, my heart," she said, kissing him again, "I'll pray that nothing happens to you while you're underground liberating humanity." And then she could no longer restrain her laughter. They rolled on the floor, play-fighting.

They couldn't have said, later, how often they made love that day. In the afternoon, a sparrow flew down from the orange tree and looked into the studio. It chirruped and flew away, only to come back with another sparrow. Now they were both looking at Rana and Farid.

"That's his girlfriend," said Farid. "He's showing her how to enjoy forbidden love."

Rana smiled. "No, I've been feeding the first one for weeks. He's probably jealous. The other one isn't a girl, it's another male and his friend. I expect they're challenging you to fight."

When Farid sat up, the sparrows flew away. Rana looked at her naked lover. Behind him, she saw the jasmine in all the glory of its white flowers, and for a moment she thought it was spring.

BOOK OF GROWTH III

Courage kills and so does cowardice.

ॐ

DAMASCUS, 1961–1965

210. Josef's Injury

The university was a surprise to Farid in every respect. The natural sciences department did have super-modern buildings and the most modern of laboratories, but the course of studies itself was extremely outmoded, and relied heavily on learning by heart. The standard in the first year was well below what it had been in his elite school. Two years earlier a number of scientists had left the country, since professors could earn ten times as much in Kuwait and Saudi Arabia as in Damascus. They were replaced by young, inexperienced lecturers. Sometimes the new professors didn't even have doctoral degrees.

Even at the start of his university course, Farid realized that after studying natural sciences for four years he would come away with nothing but a handsome diploma in fine calligraphy, adorned with arabesques. It was absurd even to think of research and development.

But if he was honest with himself, he didn't mind that too much. He could perfectly well imagine a life full of more interesting things than chemical formulae: there was Rana, whom he would see often now, there was his work in the underground, there were all the novels he was reading, and the club with its motley collection of members.

The club got its license back two weeks after the coup, and a week later it reopened with a big party. Amin came specially from Aleppo for the occasion, with his pale, quiet wife Salime. Farid thought his friend was much more amusing and relaxed than before. His arch-enemy Michel showed the little tiler respect too.

The whole neighbourhood celebrated, and there were some thirty dishes to choose from, as well as plenty of different drinks. Even the bishop came, and delivered a gentle warning against making jokes about the government. "I could tell jokes too, my children, and His Holiness John XXIII is a kindly man and likes cheerfulness, but I refrain from telling them all the same."

"What a shame!" someone cried. The assembled guests tried every way they could to spur him on to tell those jokes. He shook with laughter, and those sitting near him crowed with glee to see the red wine dripping to the floor. Taufik hurried up with a dishcloth to dry the bishop's hand.

"No, no, I'm not telling you," he said. "A man has two ears but only one mouth, and that illustrates the divine wisdom of telling only half of what you hear."

Some looked embarrassed, for Gibran was still having psychiatric treatment, but rumour had it he was soon to be released.

There was someone else missing too, although few noticed. "Suleiman's been arrested," Josef whispered to Farid. "The new regime has an account to settle with all secret service men."

"But Suleiman was only a little fish," said Farid in surprise.

"I know, but they're after the little fish and the big fish alike. Sarrag the criminal secret police chief is in jail too."

"Criminal, did you say? It was your revered Satlan who promoted him to the job."

"I believed in Satlan, yes, but I never claimed he was infallible," said Josef dryly. "That criminal Sarrag was one of his biggest mistakes."

"What about Suleiman's parents?" asked Farid, trying to change the subject.

"They're allowed to visit him. They say it was all a misunderstanding."

"What else would they say?" replied Farid. "That he handed me and Gibran over to the secret service?"

"They certainly ought to admit it," said Josef, "after going about telling everyone I gave Gibran away. Just because I thought his jokes about Satlan were in poor taste, and I said so openly. Taufik almost murdered me, and saw sense only at the last minute. The neighbours spat when I passed by and insulted my mother and my sisters with their accusations."

"Oh, come on, it's all over now. Don't bear a grudge," said Farid. But when he turned around, he was horrified to see that Josef had tears in his eyes.

211. Gibran's Return

Farid was woken by the stormy ringing of the doorbell. The university was closed on Fridays, and as he had been at a meeting of his Party cell until late at night he wanted to sleep late. His mother opened the door. He sat up in bed, and heard Josef in the inner courtyard, telling Claire, "No, he'll have to get up. Gibran's free."

"I'm awake," groaned Farid. When he came down into the court-yard, Josef and his mother had already drunk their coffee.

"How about me?" he protested.

"They're expecting you at the club. We've laid on a big breakfast for Gibran, and they sent me to fetch you at once. There's tea and coffee flowing like water there, don't worry," Josef said, hauling Farid to the door. He just had time to drop a kiss on Claire's cheek, and then he willingly followed his friend. She smiled. In some ways they were still little boys.

About two in the afternoon Farid had to leave the celebrations to go to the cinema. He wanted to be there as early as possible to keep a seat for Rana, who was going to be a little late. When she did arrive she would join him in the third row to the right, apparently by chance but knowing just where she was going.

In the bus he kept thinking of Gibran. Two shiny patches disfig-ured his temples, just like Matta's. "The male nurse and the doctor were in a temper. It burned like hell, but the medication had left me delirious, and it was days before I realized what they'd been doing to me. But never mind, that was what I wanted."

Gibran had risked a great deal, and when he was arrested he staked everything on a single throw: he pretended to be crazy. That trick had saved his life once before, in Indonesia. "That's when I realized the power of madness. I was waiting to be executed – and that's another story, but it was all to do with arms smuggling and a lot of money, and my partner wanted to be rid of me. I'll tell you about it some other time, but there in Indonesia I found that madness was my guardian angel, and I knew I must keep it up or I'd be a dead man. So I stood outside myself, checking that I wasn't acting normally for a single second. The Indonesians tried everything they could to make me sane again, but I just went crazier and crazier, running around the jail stark naked, shitting everywhere, almost scratching people's eyes out, laughing like a hyena. They beat me until I fainted, and as soon as I came back to my senses I started again. It's easy to act crazy for a short while. Any child can do it perfectly in front of the mirror – but if you want to keep it going, you have to strain yourself to the limit.

For brief moments I really was crazy now and then. The mask stuck to my face, and I said confused things even when I was on my own. And at such times a cold hand clutched my heart. Gibran, I told myself, you're not just acting crazy, you *are* crazy. The Indonesians tormented me for six months, and only then did they believe I was deranged and threw me out. I had to leave the country on the next ship. Its captain was an old friend of mine. He was horrified at the sight of me, but once we'd put to sea I showered and shaved, and we ended up laughing a lot and drinking together."

It had not been a difficult decision for him to opt for mental disturbance again in Damascus, for otherwise they would certainly have beaten him to death. He was maltreated by secret service men in jail for two weeks, and then they were convinced that he really wasn't pretending. However, in the psychiatric hospital he discovered that the secret service had its eyes and ears there too, so he had to go on pretending to be crazy, and only when the coup brought Satlan's regime down was Gibran cured overnight, along with twenty other inmates.

But Karime would have nothing more to do with him. Gibran went to see her. He wanted to tell her how he had longed for her, and ask why she never visited him, but she wouldn't even open her door. That was two weeks after his discharge from hospital, and Gibran came to the club looking grey and stooped, as if he had aged ten years. Yet he remembered Karime to the last day of his life, and he was always returning to the house of memory, which never sent him away.

212. Matta's Wedding

Farid would never have expected Matta to have such a big wedding. His aunt's house was crammed to the roof with guests. Claire and Elias had generously provided all the drinks. Josef came with his whole family. Even Matta's parents were invited, although they had no say in the arrangements; that was his aunt's business alone. This was the first time Farid had seen Matta's whole family: the nine brightly dressed peasant boys who were his brothers, and his father, whose name was Tamer and who seemed far too old. And then there was his mother Nasibe, whose beauty did not escape Farid. Nor did her bad temper. She seemed withdrawn all evening.

"As if she'd come to a funeral," he said quietly to his mother.

"Nasibe is a bad loser, but that's a long story. Celebrate your friend's wedding and take no notice of her," Claire whispered back.

The bride's family was a noisy, colourful clan from the mountains. They sang and danced, to the disapproval of Matta's devout parents, but they had to put up with it or their son would have turned them out.

Matta and Faride were very lucky. The first week of December was almost like summer, with temperatures up to 25 °C by day. Even the nights were mild and summery. Gibran enlivened the evening in his own way, standing by the balustrade on the second floor and turning to the inner courtyard to tell amusing stories. The guests were delighted, and Taufik and his helpers served the drinks.

Matta's aunt was very happy. She had never had so many guests in her house before. They filled the rooms of the first floor and second floor, they were thronging the corridors too, they even went up to the flat roof to celebrate.

Faride's relations entertained the wedding guests better than any theatrical company. They spent all evening leaping about with great verve. As soon as a moment's silence came, a couple of women would begin trilling or dancing, and then others would join them and sing along too. When the men hopped and stamped the ground shook. Elias and Claire were enjoying themselves too, singing and dancing together for the first time since the days when they were so deeply in love.

"Matta's found himself just the right family," said Josef, and Farid looked at the bridal couple with satisfaction. Memories rose in him, taking him far back into the past. He had always liked Matta from the first day when he met him in the village square in Mala. Farid hadn't even been ten at the time, and Matta was a couple of years older.

He would have been spared so much if he'd been allowed to live with his cousin Aida. As a shepherd, Matta would happily have roamed the steppes, mountains, and forests; it was the life he had been born for.

But even before his time at the monastery he had sometimes acted strangely. When the boys were sitting together he would often freeze as if he were a statue, only to explode suddenly like a firework display. He had always talked to himself, too, and when Farid asked what the matter was he would answer in an incoherent way, or laugh until the tears came for no reason at all.

Some of the Fathers in the monastery had thought he was possessed by evil spirits. Father Istfan, who censored the students' letters, had in all seriousness tried to exorcize them, laying hands on Matta and adjuring the spirits to leave the boy. Matta had laughed at the priest, which only confirmed Istfan in his assumption that the devil in person was laughing at him from inside the novice. But with astonishing courage, the boy had told him to his face that it was he, Father Istfan, who had the Devil in his own heart, for Matta, like everyone else, could smell the odor of decaying bodies and sulphur emanating from his mouth. That went home. Father Istfan struck poor Matta in the face and sent him packing.

And then Matta had run away, and when he was taken to the doctor later he no longer knew who he was. He had told confused tales, saying they put something in his tea in the monastery, and that was why he couldn't remember anything.

But today this same Matta was celebrating his wedding to the woman who, as Claire said, gave him all that he lacked.

213. Hegel in Damascus

Two municipal measures changed the face of the city in 1962. The last tram rails were torn up, and the river Barada was covered over.

General Amilan went back to his barracks, as he had promised, handing power over to a civilian government which was a coalition of conservative parties. There was an amnesty for all prisoners but Sarrag, formerly chief of the secret police. He managed to escape and join his old boss Satlan in Egypt, where he was welcomed as a hero, but that wasn't until early May.

At the beginning of March, Farid was asked by the Central Committee of his Party whether he would take over as head of the new editorial team for the underground magazine *Youth*, and expand its scope. The offer was delivered by the comrade in charge of coordination for the city of Damascus. Farid was already running the youth and culture sections of the organization in Damascus, another comrade called Salih looked after finance and the archives, and a third, a gloomy and silent comrade called Taher, was responsible for running the network of cells. The idea was to work more effectively in the underground through these links. The head of the coordination office, a son-in-law of the General Secretary of the Party, congratulated Farid on the offer, which was an honour, but he asked for time to think whether he was up to the job. He always felt curiously shy about expressing his opinion openly in front of Party comrades whom he didn't know, so he did not tell this man that his memories of editorial meetings were not particularly happy. He went home and thought and thought, but still he couldn't make up his mind. Only the

Party's political training course in early April tipped the scales, and he accepted the editorship.

At this meeting, Farid and another twenty comrades did their best to follow the boring utterances of an elderly man who spoke in a nasal voice. He called himself Comrade Gaber, and talked about Hegel. It was spring, and Farid felt terribly weary as the man droned on in his monotonous voice about thesis, antithesis, and synthesis. He had hard work keeping his eyes open, particularly as one comrade sitting near him was already snoring. He sat up straight and glanced through a crack in the curtains over the window. The large apartment where the meeting took place was in a modern building in the New Town. There was vibrant life down in the street under the beautiful blue sky. People were going about in short-sleeved shirts, happily enjoying the fresh breeze that blew through Damascus at this time of year, scented with apricot and almond blossom, while the mists of Hegelian concepts grew ever more opaque around him.

Suddenly Farid knew that Laila was right. He couldn't change anything here, because the Party consisted of old, rotten wood. The Communist Party, she had said, would at the most share an administration but wouldn't overthrow one, for in any such political upheaval it would go down itself. Somehow, he thought, Hegel just doesn't suit Damascus.

When the comrade finally reached the eagerly awaited end of his speech, they all enjoyed the coffee break.

Next another and rather livelier comrade from the Central Committee spoke on plans for the leadership to listen more to the grassroots in future, thus improving the work of the Party.

Encouraged by these remarks, a comrade stood up and asked, in a southern accent, whether the leadership was thinking of holding a Party Congress at long last, after more than twenty years, and before the General Secretary died of old age and power passed to his wife or his son. Perhaps Comrade Secretary General had forgotten how a Communist Party works.

This sounded almost like a contribution to the satirical magazine *al-Mudhik al-Mubki*, "What Makes Us Laugh and Cry", which had recently begun publishing again. It was popular and it was feared, with the result that dictators regularly banned it.

No one dared to laugh. The face of the envoy from the Central Committee twitched in a peculiar way, and he noted something down. "Any other questions?" he asked at last, icily. Farid would have liked to know a few things about the unpleasant Comrade Osmani, who was back in the leadership again, but he dared not speak. He felt unwell. Ever since the first question, the atmosphere had been curiously ominous, as if before a thunderstorm. At such moments he felt more fear than during police interrogations.

Another comrade rose, reeled off thanks to the Party leadership, and asked in a subservient tone whether the Party had any rules or guidelines for the protection of those working underground. "Everyone improvises," the man went on bitterly, "and we none of us know how to guard against informers. I've fallen into a secret service trap three times already."

The Central Committee envoy nodded, impressed. He wrote all that down. "I will put your important idea to the politburo of the Committee. Very good, very good," he praised the man. The comrade proudly sat down again.

Then a thin student rose to his feet. Farid had been joking with him at the coffee break. His name was Nagib, and he was studying Arabic literature at Damascus University. "And I'd like to ask," he began, "why the comrades don't write about love in our magazines, instead of printing long hymns of praise to the agriculture of the Soviet Union? No one reads them, least of all the Russians. Our journals are illegal, so how am I supposed to persuade a student to read them and risk being thrown out of the university if all they print is eulogies of Soviet achievements, and never a word about love? You can discuss love with anyone. And then everyone would read the magazine."

Laughter rippled round the room.

"Write about what? Write about what?" the envoy was heard to ask.

"Love," explained one of the older comrades, spluttering with laughter.

"I mean," continued Nagib, undaunted, "I'm working with over ten students who sympathize with our Party, and all their heads are full of any number of questions about love. It seems to me we'd be much better motivated to throw off the fetters of society if we tackled that subject."

"The subject of screwing!" cried one man with assumed indignation. The comrades laughed heartily, and Nagib went red in the face.

"If the Party would address that question it would have a much firmer footing among the young," he said, fighting for his idea one last time, but then his words were drowned out by loud and confused voices. There were cries for everyone to keep an eye on the time and not fritter away the meeting with useless chatter.

The comrade from the Central Committee who wanted to listen to the grassroots didn't write anything in his notebook this time. "The comrade is still young, we must be patient with him," he said sarcastically.

Nagib stood up and left the room. Malicious laughter rang out when one of the comrades cried, "He's off to the brothel to take a course on love."

What peasants they are, thought Farid, but he dared not protest. As time went by he realized more and more clearly that discussions in the Party didn't revolve around the best way for the country to go. They talked, asked questions, and provoked comment just to please those present. Anyone who gave his frank opinion was in danger, because his words showed what he thought, whereas those who said nothing were flexible and could adapt to the majority. So most people said nothing, or at least didn't say what they really thought.

The representative of the leadership turned to the platform. "I would like to request that at the next meeting for training purposes we should make sure the participants are more mature."

Many people laughed and clapped, and Farid hated his own cowardice. On the way home that night, he decided to overcome his fears, and as a first step he set himself the task of editing the journal *Youth*. He didn't guess what a risk he was talking. Later, he would even claim that he had fallen into a trap set by Osmani that night, but that was exaggerating.

When he reached the door of his house he saw Claire sitting by the fountain. She looked careworn, and he knew at once that something had happened. "However late you came home, Josef wanted you go to straight to him. Rasuk has had an accident," she said, shaking her head. "Poor boy – he'd only done a week of his army service."

Rasuk had died when a military transport vehicle collided with a bulldozer. Ten soldiers were killed, ten more badly injured.

Josef said that Rasuk's coffin had been brought home in the afternoon. He had been to see the family just after that. Azar, who was now running a little vegetable store near Bab Tuma, went with him. And Suleiman had offered to run errands for the family, but Rasuk's parents sent him away. Apparently they had found out that under Satlan, Suleiman had informed not only against Gibran and Farid but against Rasuk's girlfriend Elizabeth too. The police had expelled the Englishwoman from Syria. "His father is crying like an abandoned child, and he's been trying to wake his son up as if he were only asleep," Josef said.

214. Coincidence

It really was coincidence, although Josef wouldn't believe him either then or ten years later. Farid had fixed to walk from the university with him through the Suk al Hamidye and so to the Ummayad Mosque. Josef wanted to enjoy the atmosphere there. "Unlike a Christian church," he said, "a mosque has a lot of life and not too much sanctity about it. You feel at ease there." And he joked that it would do a Young Communist like Farid good to experience the sensuality behind the façade, and see more in life than materialism and the economy. So around midday, after lectures, they set off. They stopped on the way at a snack bar, drank juice, ate a falafel each, and then sat for a while with a boy who was selling cactus figs chilled on a block of ice. They tasted best in the autumn.

It was indeed more comfortable in the mosque than in a church. The floor itself, covered with beautiful carpets, looked far more welcoming than the hard pews in church. A church had always been a place for prayer, while mosques were meeting places. The carpets invited you to linger. Several men were asleep, lying by the walls, others were reading or walking quietly around, deep in thought. A number of believers had gathered around the tomb of John the

Baptist. They were quietly murmuring requests and prayers, touching the walls, columns, and grille of the tomb, and transferring the blessing of the touch to their faces. In one corner, a scholar was delivering a lecture to a small audience as he sat on the floor, leaning back against a column. There was a sense of deep peace. No one asked Josef and Farid what they wanted here, or whether they were Muslims. It was taken for granted that anyone could sit in the mosque.

"If all of Islam were like this mosque," whispered Josef, "I'd convert today, but then I'd find myself in cahoots with oil sheikhs and members of the Muslim Brotherhood. So I'd rather stay a Christian."

"Which means you find yourself in cahoots with all the dictatorships of Latin America, and those wonderful Christian colonialists, Fascists, and Falangists. No, I don't really want to be their brother. You'd better join us or you'll miss the new dawn," said Farid. Josef choked with laughter.

"Nicely put, little Stalinist, but I don't see any dawn coming with your bunch. More like dusk." Suddenly someone dug him in the ribs. An old man was reproving the two of them with a look of displeasure.

As they left, Farid decided he would like an ice in the famous Bakdash ice cream parlour near the mosque. At first Josef didn't want to join him, but then he let himself be persuaded. As they entered the ice cream parlour they saw Rana, sitting at a table with Dunia, and quite by chance there were two more seats free there.

"Very cleverly contrived," muttered Josef, unable even to manage a weary grin. He greeted the girls dryly and sat down opposite Dunia, whom he knew only from a visit to her brother Kamal and from Farid's many stories.

"So what do they call you and me?" he boldly asked. Dunia didn't understand his question. "I mean, are we go-betweens or extras? Is it a marriage or a movie being made?"

Dunia laughed at the ugly young man's irony. She didn't remember anything at all about him.

When Farid took Rana's hand, Josef called, "Lights, camera, take 376, Romeo and Juliet eating ices."

Farid was furious, but when Rana smiled at him and whispered, "A Mushtak thundercloud," he quickly suppressed the volcano inside him, although it went on seething deep down. Rana had often told him that he was getting more and more like his father, who sometimes lost his temper for moments on end. Claire called those moments "Mushtak thunderclouds". Farid had the same fits of temper. But Rana, unlike his mother, didn't know how to deal with them, and hated them. She herself, like Claire, had an equable nature.

Josef was unbearable that day, making snide and venomous remarks the whole time, so that Farid wondered why the two young women didn't just get up and walk out.

Dunia told them that after the family's former textiles factory had been denationalized again, her brother Kamal had tried to increase his own share in it by selling stock. Dunia didn't think this was a good idea, because you could never rely on governments, but Kamal had been very sure of himself. He wanted to be an industrialist, of course in the family business. The country grew its own cotton, but instead of selling it as a raw material he was going to have it made into fine textiles and then export it. Dunia smiled at her brother's dreams.

On the way home through the spice market and down Straight Street, Farid and Josef were silent. Then Josef suddenly said, "I'd never have thought that spoiled idiot Kamal could think on such a scale. Good for him."

When they reached the Kishle intersection, they saw an ambulance standing at the turning into Abbara Alley. It was too wide to get right into the alley itself. The blue light was flashing all the time. A large and pale-faced crowd surrounded the vehicle.

"Rasuk's father went crazy," said Sadik the vegetable dealer, when Josef asked what had happened. And out came the paramedics already, pushing the stretcher to the ambulance. Rasuk's father lay strapped to it under a blanket, unconscious. His black-clad wife was running after the men, wearing a single slipper – she had lost the other on the way – weeping and striking herself in the face.

"I thought she'd go crazy," said Sadik, "but it was his father."

"He's been so fond of his son ever since he was born," whispered Josef. Farid had already heard at the club that he'd been going to the cemetery at night, barefoot, taking his son his favourite food: sheep's cheese with olive oil wrapped in a thin flatbread.

And Rasuk's father had taken to going up to the flat roof of his house more and more often, waiting there for his son with a quilt and a pullover. He had been sure that Rasuk would come back to him by parachute.

When the ambulance raced away, his wife could no longer stand upright. She fell to her knees. Josef and Farid ran to her, took her under her arms, and helped her home. A pale girl followed them with the lost slipper.

215. One Of Us

Josef had an incredible story to tell. Suleiman's father Abdallah, that quiet, unobtrusive man, he said, had almost stabbed a Muslim with a pair of scissors. The man was taken to hospital just in time for them to save his life. "It's not the stabbing itself that surprised me, it's how the tailor found out he was a Franco supporter," he added.

It was well known in the quarter not only that Suleiman's father was under his wife's thumb, but also that he was a fervent supporter of the Spanish General Franco, whose picture hung in the family's sitting room next to the Virgin Mary. It was years before the neighbours realised how deep Abdallah's veneration of Franco went. They thought it was mere opportunism, and the Spanish consul's chauffeur was making himself out to be more Spanish than the consul himself. But Farid also knew that the man hated Muslims and dreamed of Syria's return to the pre-Islamic period. A mistake, but he and several thousand Syrians firmly believed it would be a good thing.

That day, so Josef learned a week later, Suleiman's father had been on the way home when he saw a Muslim outside the tailor's shop calling another man a "Christian swine" and an "idol-worshipper". He didn't know either of them. All the same, he went straight into the tailor's workshop, picked up a pair of scissors, and stabbed the Muslim twice in the back with them. The wounded man fell to the ground and his Christian rival fled, for fear that he would be accused of the assault. Suleiman's father put the scissors in a bag, left the man lying on the ground, and went calmly home.

A day later he brought the scissors back to Khuri the tailor, who had told the police that yes, the attack had taken place just outside his shop, but he hadn't witnessed it himself because he was standing with his back to the door at the time, listening to songs by Um Kulthum on the radio while he pressed a suit. The radio was turned up very loud today too. Suleiman's father could hardly hear what the young tailor was saying.

Josef was bewildered. Khuri was an ardent pro-Satlan man, like himself, and a radical socialist. As they were friends, he went on asking questions until Khuri admitted that yes, he had in fact seen it all, and the weapon hadn't been a knife but scissors. Finally he found them and showed them to Josef.

"So why did you lie about it?"

"I can't get one of us into trouble," said Khuri, and Josef was just about to correct him, saying that Suleiman's father had never supported Satlan, when he understood. By "us" the socialist Khuri did not mean adherents of Satlan, but the Christian community.

Two days later the army carried out its coup. General Mutamiran announced that Syria was now free, and nothing stood in the way of the liberation of Palestine any longer. It was 8 March 1963.

216. "Youth"

Drinking coffee with Claire by the fountain in the morning was a special pleasure to Farid. He always gave himself an hour for it, and then the rest of the day could follow. He would hear news from her about the seething life of the quarter, and the rumours going around the Old Town, rumours that the students did not pick up.

But Claire was also a good listener. She always seemed to know his timetable, and asked sensible, interested questions about exams and practical work, his lectures and his grades. However, she never asked questions about his political activities, but waited for him to tell her of his own accord. His father took no interest in him. When he heard from Claire in 1965 that she was giving a small party to celebrate Farid's diploma in natural sciences, Elias was amazed by the speed with which his son had completed his studies, even after losing two years during his time in the prison camp.

Every day Farid was deep in a book as he travelled to the university. The bus ride was a good time to read. He always had a novel and a book of poetry with him, and every time the bus was about to pass the street where Rana lived he raised his hand, glanced quickly at the last house on the right, and murmured a soft greeting.

ഐ

One day in May he got out at the university bus stop, breathing in the scent of flowers in the nearby museum garden. He still had the taste of the cardamom which his mother added to coffee in his mouth. Then he saw skinny young Comrade Nagib who'd been snubbed at the Communist Party training course. He was already halfway up the steep path between the bus stop and the university gates. Farid quickened his pace to catch up with him, and as if Nagib had felt his eyes on his back he turned and stopped, suddenly recognizing his comrade.

"Hello, how are you?" asked Farid, out of breath.

"Fine. You're studying here too?" asked Nagib.

"Yes," he said. "I was going to get in touch with you through the Party, because I've decided to take on *Youth*. What you said that day at the meeting fascinated me, but I was too much of a coward to say so."

"Who isn't?" said Nagib quietly. "But are you sure you want to edit *Youth*?"

"No, I'm not sure, but I'll give it a go anyway. The Party leadership claims that the magazine is free, and produced by young people for young people. So I can always use that rope to hang the censors."

"Good heavens, and you call yourself a coward? God save us, or rather Lenin save us from your sort of courage," he said. "By the way, in real life my name is Isa." He offered his thin hand, which seemed to consist only of skin and bone. "I know you're Farid. I've heard a lot about you," he said, surprising his comrade.

From then on they met in the cafeteria twice a week, and then went on long walks. Isa was a voracious reader and a sceptic.

Farid's official appointment by the Central Committee was some time coming. In the interim, he and Isa designed a complete issue of *Youth*. It was to have sixteen pages containing news, jokes, puzzles, accounts of historical events and contributions on sexuality, love, and other subjects. The second issue was almost ready too when Farid finally got the job. His request to have Isa on the editorial team was granted, but the committee rejected the idea of conscripting a woman comrade to write on women's questions. Isa and Farid therefore thought up a way to get around the committee's refusal. They would ask women friends of theirs to write on the subject, and then publish them under the pseudonym Farisa.

The first issue came out in October 1963. Over five thousand copies were distributed, and requests for more came in from all over the country. For the first time in the history of the Syrian Communist Party, its secret press had to do a second print run. And for the first time the official Syrian organs of the press mentioned the illegal communist journal. The state cultural magazine printed a long quotation from a forceful article on the poor state of the Arab film industry, written by Farid after intensive discussion with Josef. "How is an Arab film ever to work up any credible tension," he had said, "if every film has to satisfy all Sunni, Shi'ite, Druse, Jewish, and Christian censors from Morocco to Saudi Arabia? Never a word of criticism of Islam, no scene showing a Christian quarreling with a Muslim, no scene in which a Jew is right about something, none in which a woman invites a man to come to bed with her. No film dares to caricature a dictator, no film may show that its heroes can drink wine without actually being criminals. No film ever shows that a child can be right and its parents wrong. What's left but a heap of garbage? And there's really no need for Zionism to condemn that – which is the favourite explanation our directors give for their failure – or for imperialists to condemn it either, the favourite explanation given by our Minister of Culture. Such films fail entirely on their own demerits. Not just abroad, but here in our own country too."

Readers' letters were encouraging, and contained a great many unsolicited contributions. Isa and Farid were delighted, and included two excellent pieces from women living in the north of the country in the second number, one about forced marriage and the other about the role of sexuality in women's liberation.

It was a great surprise to Farid that while Rana refused to write for *Youth*, Laila was keen to do so. And Josef took enormous pleasure in providing a contribution. "I'm almost beginning to think of joining the Communist Party," he said, "but I think I'll wait, because after producing such a good journal you won't grow old in the Party yourself." And he laughed as he always did, not knowing that those were prophetic words. The Central Committee let only two more issues appear, and then came down heavily on *Youth*.

The first trouble was over a joke that the Central Committee misunderstood. It was in the answer to a riddle in the first issue. The riddle was: how do you make four evangelists into three musketeers? The answer, allegedly sent in by a reader in Damascus with the very common woman's name Farisa, was, you cut out Stalin. The merging of the names Farid and Isa was an easy conundrum for the Committee to crack. Farid was made to feel the disapproval of those in high places at a short meeting with a member of the Central Committee, but he also saw how cowardly the man was; he didn't dare to say he was angry because, as a Stalinist, the answer to the riddle insulted him. Farid told Isa about it, but instead of being pleased his co-editor suddenly turned pale.

Years later, when he thought back to this period, Farid was still wondering whether the Central Committee had been asleep, or whether it let those three issues come out uncensored on purpose to get rid of him for good.

In the second issue, Isa published his first translation from the works of Wilhelm Reich. And Farid brought up the question of the principles of civil disobedience as he had put them together from his wide reading. Laila's short but extremely radical discussion of marriage and oppression found a place in it, as well as the urging of the Marxist philosopher Ismail Hadi to find Arab roots for justice and democracy instead of coming out with bad imitations of European theories. But Farid couldn't accept Josef's essay on myths about the penis in the minds of Arab men. "The title on its own," he told his friend, "could get me a life sentence: *You Can Find a Homeland*

Anywhere But Not A Penis." Farid laughed, and Josef swallowed his disappointment. "It's just that the time's not right yet," he muttered quietly.

The new issue aroused lively interest again. The Central Committee remained silent. That troubled Isa, although Farid saw it as no reason for anxiety. Six months later he was to discover his mistake.

217. Love of the Eunuchs

One fine spring day General Mutamiran made a speech promising to liberate Palestine and build up Arab socialism. As the first step towards this goal, all seventeen national newspapers and eleven journals were banned. Elias was cross at supper because now he wouldn't be able to read his favourite paper *al-Ayam* any more. Only the papers of the Ba'ath Party were still available. Elias glanced at them twice, and after that he stopped buying newspapers at all. This was in the summer of 1963, and from then on he listened to BBC London instead. Claire couldn't have her magazine *Dunia*, which told her so much of what was going on in the world, and Farid and Josef missed the satirical magazine *al-Mudhik al-Mubki*.

There were two failed coups that summer, and General Mutamiran showed no mercy. All involved were executed.

Farid and Isa spent three nights discussing love as the next main subject for *Youth*.

"It will be difficult to get that through," said Isa despairingly, when he realized how determined Farid was. "Our Party has deep-rooted inhibitions about sex. They don't just derive from Stalin and Lenin, they go right back to Marx himself."

Farid knew that Isa was right. All meetings were attended by men sitting together, and they seemed to him like the members of a club of eunuchs. Even at parties they acted in a pious, asexual way. No one brought a wife or even mentioned her in conversation. "Yet they're all thinking of women the whole time," said Isa sadly.

Even Amin, when Farid asked him why the Party didn't take up the cause of women, said there were more important things to do. First communism must be strengthened, the workers and Palestine must be liberated, and the Arab countries united under communist leadership. After that they could talk about the emancipation of women, if their problems hadn't been solved anyway when the revolution was ushered in.

Somehow work on the magazine had opened Farid's eyes to a number of contradictions. He kept seeing a certain image in his mind's eye: the Communist Party sitting in smoke-filled rooms with the curtains drawn, talking about Hegel, while life outside kept on changing. He couldn't help thinking of the sad cardinals of Constantinople debating how many angels could dance on the head of a pin as the Ottomans captured the city.

Just before Christmas there was a party at the club. Farid invited not just Isa but the comrades from his Party cell and the co-ordinating centre. All six men came, but three of them sat on their chairs all night as stiff as plaster statues. They were horrified by the behaviour of the club members and the people who lived in the street, always hugging each other and talking at their ease and without inhibition. Isa laughed at the three of them. "They look as if they were in Siberia. These are the people you want to liberate, gentlemen," he said quietly.

Isa liked Josef from the first. They sat together all evening. At a late hour, when old Gibran was in the table tennis room telling an erotic story of an experience that he said he once had in Havana, the seated comrades rose and warned Farid, as they left, to beware of this anti-communist, anti-Cuban propaganda. He was horrified by their narrow minds.

"Those aren't Communist Party members, anyone would think they had *no* members," snapped Josef, laughing. Isa thought this an excellent joke, and laughed too. Before Farid said goodbye to Josef that evening, his friend told him that Isa had persuaded him to write an article on the problems of the streets of Damascus for the fourth issue of the magazine.

Farid was speechless with delight. But Number 4 was never published.

218. An Icy Spring

Society was becoming militarized. Within nine months, General Mutamiran forced school students to wear uniforms, and no one who had passed his final examination could claim his high school diploma without doing a month's course in a military camp first. Isa told Farid it was all humbug, and a nauseating spectacle. The magazine *Youth* undertook not just to write about love and sexuality, but to ask questions about the purpose of this imposition of military discipline on schools.

Issue 3 came out at the end of March 1964. The front page showed a child holding a white dove. The dove seemed to be asleep with an olive branch in its beak, as if it had reached its journey's end and felt safe in those small hands. The subject of the article was less peaceful than the picture suggested: it was a study of children and war, a plea against the arming of young people. But that wasn't all; there was also a long translation from Wilhelm Reich about power and the suppression of sexuality. In addition, there were caricatures from all over the world opposing military dictatorship and exploitation.

Two days after the journal came out, Farid and Isa were invited to a special meeting, which soon turned out not to be a meeting at all, but a lawcourt with eleven prosecutors led by a furious judge. Comrade Jakub came from the Euphrates region, and was responsible for culture in the Party. He was also Osmani's right-hand man.

Farid was alarmed. He had never dreamed that his efforts to change society would bring him before such a ruthless committee of his own Party, obliged to listen to accusations against himself. He and Isa were naïve, they were unwittingly serving imperialism by weakening the revolutionary Communist Party. Because of their journal, Comrade Secretary General Khalid Malis had been summoned before President Mutamiran, and had to apologize for a communist magazine that was putting out propaganda on behalf of a Jew by the name of Wilhelm Reich, was questioning the army, and calling for disobedience – and all this at a time when General Mutamiran was trying to come closer to the Communist Party and the Soviet Union, and had offered the communists two ministerial posts in his Popular Front coalition.

Jakub spoke for half an hour without pausing for breath. Isa was slumped in his seat, looking miserably at the floor. It took Farid some time to turn from fury to contempt, but then he looked closely at the men's faces. The three comrades who had sat through the club's cheerful party with gloomy expressions on their faces looked perfectly relaxed here and were smiling all the time, nodding agreement, and reinforcing the accusations against the magazine by interpolating comments.

Farid, who had now been a Party member for nearly eight years, knew almost all those present. They were the most pitiful figures ever to have been set up by a political party for such a purpose. Who else would agree to act as an Inquisition without any sense of shame? One of them said, during a tea break, "Better stay in the Party and go wrong with it than be outside the Party and be right."

Farid said not a word of apology during this hearing. Instead, he accused Jakub of grovelling, for as a young man he himself had published poems on Stalin, praising the occupation by the French as an act of civilization. Farid defended the magazine, line by line, and declined to discuss what the dictator had said, offered, or whispered to the Secretary General. The point that mattered was whether the magazine enlightened young people in this country. "And listen to this, Comrade Jakub," he cried, raising his voice now, "I'll still be in favour of enlightenment in ten years' time, unlike you – or are you going to reissue your hymns of praise to General Weygand and the heroic Stalin?"

A grey, veiled look came over Jakub's face. Farid was sweating in his excitement.

"Why would we want to go into delicate matters back in the past when you were still in nappies?" An older comrade came to Jakub's aid. Such a reply was not the kind of thing you found in any of the Russian, Chinese, or Cuban novels about social intercourse among comrades.

The man who had spoken was a textiles worker and had spent many years in prison for the Party, but even prison, Farid thought whenever he met him, is no cure for stupidity.

"We're here to discuss your abuse of the Central Committee's confidence in you, and we must tackle the subject of the consequences."

At that moment Farid realized that the verdict on him had already been learned by heart, for these last words were not those of a textiles worker, but of a bureaucrat of Osmani's kind.

Isa too understood what the remark disguised. He rose, trembling, and apologized volubly and submissively. As he did so, he died to Farid. The litany of self-accusation was demeaning.

Three years passed before Farid saw Isa again, by chance, in a cinema. Isa smiled at him, but the smile aroused only revulsion in Farid, who turned away.

The leadership was in a hurry in that spring of 1964. A week later, Farid was removed from all his posts in the Party. Even his member-ship was frozen for six months, the next harshest penalty to expulsion. And this penalty in itself showed that Osmani was behind the whole thing. He didn't want to make a martyr of Farid, which was what would have happened if he had been expelled immediately. Osmani was relying on his tried and trusted methods: humiliation first, then keeping his victim on tenterhooks until, driven by his own injured ambition, he left the Party of his own accord. That was Osmani's aim.

If there was ever a figure of authority who knew the way mean tricks would work, he was the man. Just under a year later, Farid left the Party when it was next shaken by disputes. This was early in January 1965, when the armed Palestinian resistance movement erupted under Arafat's leadership. The Communist Party had instruc-tions from Moscow to be suspicious of armed conflict, and it ignored these events. Arafat was a member of the Muslim Brotherhood and a Saudi agent, whispered the communists, like old washerwomen gos-siping. Officially, they said nothing. At the end of January hundreds of young members left the Party. Farid justified the termination of his membership in a furious letter that no one ever read.

However, it was a step into the void. Low as the Communist Party had sunk, it was a community offering mutual protection, a club of like-minded people. Now he had to endure the feeling that he belonged nowhere. He roamed the city alone, with a record playing in his head and stuck in a groove: nine years for nothing, and all you get is failure.

He felt deeply ashamed. He dared not phone Amin, but he

immediately told Rana what had happened. She was glad that now he would have more time for her and their love, and he could finish his studies as soon as possible.

But the sense of being thrown off track accompanied him like a shadow. Curiously, he was ashamed to tell Josef about it. For six months, he never mentioned that he had left the Party. When he finally did pluck up the courage to do it, he was grateful for his friend's understanding. Josef never even hinted that he could have told him so.

219. The Fair

Rana called early, and Claire joked with her for a long time. Farid came into the inner courtyard barefoot, guessing who his mother was talking to. "And here comes a beggar," said Claire, "unwashed, unshaven, barefoot. You can see how much he loves you. He wouldn't have jumped out of bed so quickly for anyone else, even me." Then she handed him the receiver. She was happy; his girlfriend had just told her that Farid had left the Communist Party, and from now on she would be able to sleep easily again.

Rana was in cheerful mood. The International Autumn Fair in Damascus opened its gates in a few days' time. Farid didn't understand why she was so pleased by the prospect of the exhibition, which bored him with all its stands of industrial exhibits. When he said so, she laughed. "Industrial exhibits? Stands? My love, who do you think I am, the Minister of Trade? No, they give the best concerts in the world at the Fair. Last year I saw Feiruz. I'd like to go to something like that with you this year. You can hear great international figures, people such as Duke Ellington, Miriam Makeba, famous Cuban and Hungarian groups."

"Who's Duke Ellington?" he cautiously asked.

"Don't say you've never heard of him! He's one of the greatest jazz musicians in the world. But perhaps he was taboo for you – after all, he's an American imperialist. Last September people were dancing in the auditorium, and they wouldn't let him leave the stage until he'd given them a tenth encore. That's why he likes coming to Damascus so much."

Farid suddenly felt how much there was in the world for him yet to discover. And once again it was Rana who opened the door to life for him. She had already bought tickets for Feiruz. Her husband Rami often had to be abroad with delegations of some kind, why she wasn't allowed to know. She supposed he was buying weapons for the army.

Josef knew Duke Ellington's music. He had been at that legendary first appearance of the musician in the city in 1963, and Laila wanted to go as well. Through her husband, she bought seats in one of the front rows, at a discount too. The three of them went. Laila got on well with Josef at once, and soon they were joking together with as much easy familiarity as if they had been friends for ever. On the way back she even linked arms with him. Finally she invited him and Farid in for a glass of tea, and they stayed until midnight and then took a taxi home.

"How about doing a deal?" said Josef as they parted, and before Farid could ask what he meant he went on, "Your cousin for my entire tribe. What a wonderful woman!" And he laughed at his surprised friend.

Duke Ellington played wonderfully well. And Feiruz, the best of all Lebanese women singers, who had fallen in love with Damascus and appeared in the city every autumn, was fantastic. The Damascenes were at her feet. She sang softly, stood still, almost motionless, without any mime or gestures. He songs had great lyrics and catchy tunes. Unlike Um Kulthum, who sang of the tragedy of abandonment, of loneliness, and of unrequited love, Feiruz sang songs full of confidence, even cheerfulness, usually to a dance rhythm that had her audience tapping their feet. They roared with enthusiasm, perhaps partly because Feiruz was a strong woman, and in the middle of Arabia at that! Rana adored the singer. She held Farid's hand and kissed it fleetingly now and then. He could smell her intoxicating fragrance.

After the concert she asked him home with her. They went up to her little studio on the roof and made love until they were exhausted. The night filled them with peace and confidence. But when Farid dressed again, Rana suddenly began shedding tears. He looked at her in concern.

"Don't worry, I'm only crying because this is such a beautiful moment. I'm crying because I can never manage to hold such moments and keep them."

Threads of light were beginning to weave the day. He held her close once more. "I want to live with you and no one else," he said.

220. Treasure Hunting

A new craze had broken out in Damascus in the early sixties: searching for hidden or buried precious metals. Treasure hunting was strictly forbidden, since the government regarded any finds as state property, and private appropriation of them counted as theft.

But people still went out at night searching, some of them with beeping devices, many with magic spells and mysterious cards. They tapped walls and floors everywhere, trying to find any hollow spaces. When they did turn up, however, they were seldom evidence of a lucky find, and generally just showed that repairs were urgently needed.

Josef laughed at his aunts, tapping their way around the house. His father threatened, in desperation, that if they broke so much as one of his expensive tiles he'd make them sell their own gold bangles to pay for the damage. After that his aunts did their tapping with a rubber hammer.

"People want to get their hands on money quickly, and do you know why?" asked Josef, as so often not waiting for an answer. "The emigrants have turned their heads. My cousin Nicolas goes about in midsummer looking like a really big shot, all dandified in a suit. He drives the fifty metres from his house to the vegetable store in his Mercedes, parks it in the middle of the street, and no police officer dares take his number down. Then he stands there, shouting his order for vegetables over the heads of the people waiting in line, and the vegetable seller doesn't even object to such discourtesy, he leaves all his other loyal customers to serve Nicolas. And do you know why?

Because Nicolas will tip him a whole lira. The neighbours have never done any such thing. I mean, imagine tipping a vegetable seller. And would you like to know what Nicolas did before he emigrated?" asked Josef bitterly.

Farid nodded.

"He was breaking stones for my father at three lira an hour. Two days ago he invited my parents around to his place and showed them his gold bath taps. Madeleine hated it, but you should have seen the wonder and amazement in the eyes of my father and my aunts – they were bowled right over."

❧

At the end of November Kamal came to drink tea with Farid. He was devastated; he had lost his entire fortune overnight. The government had nationalized his factory again, leaving him with nothing but his debts. The whole thing was like some English comedy, but Kamal didn't feel like laughing.

Soon after that he went to join his father in Saudi Arabia, and came back ten years later a multi-millionaire. But he wanted no more to do with textiles, and instead opened new casinos everywhere in partnership with the new President of Syria's cousin.

BOOK OF LAUGHTER III

Both chemical factories and dictators contaminate their surroundings.

❧

DAMASCUS, 1961–1965

221. Fasting in Space

Josef said that a good friend had given him two tickets to an interesting event being held by the Muslim Brotherhood, and asked Farid if he would like to go along. "Space From the Viewpoint of the Muslim Brotherhood" was the title of the event.

"And here you see again how backward our church is," he said, with a trace of envy in his voice.

"Aren't you afraid?" asked Farid, who couldn't stand the extremely conservative Muslim Brotherhood. They were financed by Saudi Arabia, and were the most brutal of anti-communists and misogynists.

"Afraid? What would I be afraid of? That they'll persuade me to convert? I don't even believe in my own religion, why would I believe in theirs? Or do you think I ought to fear they'll beat me up for being a Christian? First, I'm not a communist; second, I'm not a woman; and third, even the government courts their favour these days. They've turned moderate and socially acceptable. They probably want to prove that we were in space long before the Russians and Americans." Josef laughed. "You know how Orientals have been in space for thousands of years. Way back we had that old Syrian liar Lucian, who said he flew through space. Remember Sindbad's flying carpet, and how the Prophet Elijah went up to heaven in his fiery chariot, remember the ascension of Christ and the Virgin Mary, and Mi'raj, Muhammad's ride to heaven. A Muslim Brother told me the other day, in all seriousness, the French were calling their most powerful warplanes the Mirage after it."

But no one talked about any of that in the lecture hall of the chemistry faculty. Farid was annoyed. The Muslim Brothers always got the best hall in the university for their events so that they could make propaganda out of it. It was said that over half the university authorities sympathized with them.

When the bearded speaker entered the hall the audience rose and said a short prayer. Then they sat down again. After a brief introduction about modern times the scholar, who held two doctorates, came quickly to his subject. He put the central points of his lecture in the form of questions and answers. "Where does a Muslim direct his prayers when he is in space? How can he locate Mecca when he is in space? How will he fast in space? How often should he pray when his rocket orbits the earth ten times, how often if he flies twice as fast? And may a Muslim astronaut marry a being from another planet?"

Josef looked in astonishment at Farid, who had a hand over his mouth to keep from bursting into laughter.

The scholar provided all these questions with answers that appeared in all seriousness to be giving religion a modern face and yet keep it Islamic, but there was no way of sitting through too much of this. After quarter of an hour, the two friends quietly left the hall.

222. Munir's Father

If you didn't know Munir well you would have thought he was a Swede or a Dane, for he was blond and blue-eyed. But he was born in a village on the Euphrates, a long way from Europe.

His parents, however, had been living in Damascus for over twenty years, not far from the French hospital. They owned the biggest bakery in the Christian quarter. Munir was studying mathematics. He was far too down to earth and rational to be religious, but in the Middle East religion is more than just your faith, it is a part of your cultural identity. The overwhelming majority of students of the natural sciences were Muslims. When Munir found out that Farid came from Mala he was pleased to know another member of the Christian minority, and from the first called him "my cousin".

One day he came into the cafeteria when their fellow students happened to be telling jokes about their parents' generation, which still wasn't politicized in spite of the turmoil in the Middle East. Munir didn't like that.

"It wouldn't be exaggerating to describe my father as the best-read baker in Damascus," he said. "Bakers have a tough life. They wake up when everyone else is still fast asleep, and then they have to go to bed just as the evening's getting interesting. Day in, day out, seven days a week. But my father wasn't going to give up reading every evening, writing down wise things, putting them in order, and he was proud that he could recite them without making any mistakes.

"Three of his customers in particular noticed: a communist lawyer, a nationalist teacher, and a third man called Khalid, who worked in a bank. Khalid's political affiliation? Well, for the sake of simplicity let's say it was liberal.

"The three of them admired my father and listened to him when he spoke of the mood among the people. His bakery was large, and made two tons of flour into bread every day. Anyone who serves so many customers, day after day, can tell exactly how people are feeling.

"Of the three men, the communist was the cleverest, the nationalist the hardest. What about the liberal? For the sake of simplicity, let's say he was the most astute.

"My father liked the lawyer best. As a communist from a distinguished family, he often visited my father, a baker from a rich family of bakers, and they always argued about the role of property. My mother liked the lawyer, but she didn't believe a word he said.

"My paternal grandmother couldn't stand the lawyer, and tried to warn my father of the dangers of communism, but he soothed her, saying that the lawyer, who was among the leaders of his Party, had assured him that under communism the property of bakers wouldn't be touched.

"When the communists were persecuted, Father was asked to hide some important documents, Party papers, and a number of red flags with the hammer and sickle on them. The lawyer disappeared. He wouldn't hide with us, presumably for fear of my grandmother.

'But I am always with you in spirit, fighting with you against dictatorship,' Father read out from his friend's letter to us all. 'A communist is the first to set to work and to be martyred, the last to sit down and eat.'

"Tears rose to my father's eyes at these words, and his mother had to bite her tongue to keep from making sharp remarks about communists. She knew her son, who wouldn't hurt a fly except when he turned sentimental, and then he was unpredictable and everyone took care not to cross him.

"A week later, to his horror, my father heard the lawyer's voice on the radio. In trying to tune into the BBC station broadcasting in Arabic from London – he always liked to listen to the news on it, to find out what was going on in Damascus – he had chanced upon the Voice of Moscow wavelength. We were sitting at supper, and my father, stunned, let his bread drop on his plate. It wasn't words his friend was spewing out, it was revolutionary lava. He was calling – from Moscow! – for the people of Damascus to rise and rebel.

"My grandmother's hour had come. She cursed the traitor and his roots in an Orthodox family that not only fought bitterly against our Catholic Church, but had also produced such a vile man, one who could think of nothing better to do than urge people to commit suicide while he sat safely in Russia. Grandmother emphasized the word 'Russia' with all the hatred of a fanatical Catholic for the Russian Orthodox Church, which to her was the incarnation of all evil. My grandmother never recognized the existence of the Soviet Union.

"Soon Moscow was exerting pressure on Damascus, and the persecution of communists began. Khalid Malis, the Secretary General of the Party, and his leadership came back from Moscow and – no doubt for tactical reasons – praised the same government for whose overthrow they had been calling a couple of days ago.

"The lawyer came back to our bakery, and tried explaining to my father, with many clever words, how his flight, his talk on the radio, and his return were to be understood.

"Father's face was grey as ashes. 'But I, unfortunately, can't get out of the country with my bakery, my wife, my six children and my mother.' From that day on Father never read another word written by a communist."

If anyone else had told this story Farid would have been indignant, but he believed it when it came from Munir.

"My father's friendship with the nationalist teacher," Munir continued his story, "didn't last long. Father admired the man's courage and energy, but as we're Assyrians a time soon came when he could no longer bear the rise of Arab nationalism, which was getting stronger and stronger and had the teacher too under its spell. The radio spouted nationalist stuff, nationalist slogans screamed from the walls, and great banners waved in the sky praising the Fatherland in giant letters.

"When the teacher tried convincing my father that all Syrian citizens were Arabs even if they didn't know it or didn't want it, he exploded. 'The caliphs, a thousand years ago, had a better idea of it than you. They didn't force the Aramaians or the Jews or the Persians to be Arabs, or the Spanish or the Kurds.'

"The man rose, looking injured, and left. After that day he bought his bread from our rivals, and my father ignored all five nationalist parties.

"His third friend, Safi Khalid, worked in a bank, as I was saying, and described himself as liberal. He often visited, and my grandmother liked him because he was so courteous. My mother, on the other hand, couldn't stand him. 'A chameleon,' she would say quietly when he arrived. My father didn't let her dislike influence him. 'Your mother and mine have made a secret pact never to agree with each other,' he said, winking at me.

"When Safi was persecuted for his politics he took shelter with us. We gave him food, and I was supposed to go and buy him the newspaper every day. But as my family had never before bought a daily paper the informer in our street would have noticed, so I had to go a long way to a news stand to buy the paper, and smuggle it home in a bag.

'When I'm a minister, which I hope will be soon, I'll never forget your sacrifices for me,' Safi told my father one evening, and once again my grandmother was moved to tears.

"Father acted very noble. 'There's no need to reward me. My bakery gives me enough, but I'd be grateful if you still share my opinion on the human situation then.'

'You can be sure I will, every day. It's your voice that I'll always want to hear.'

'And how is he going to get in touch with you when you're a minister?' asked my mother suspiciously. The liberal knew as well as she did that our ministers are surrounded by secret service men and bodyguards, and no one can get at them for purposes either good or bad.

'You're right,' he said, confirming her doubts. 'You'd better stand outside your bakery, my friend, and when I drive past I'll stop, embrace you in front of everyone, drink tea with you and listen to what you have to say in praise or blame of the regime.'

"My mother had to own herself defeated, and put up with her mother-in-law's triumph.

"After the next coup, Safi was promoted straight from his hiding place with us to a ministerial post. So from now on my father placed an apprentice on watch at our door, and when the lad saw the motorized police on the third day he shouted, 'Here he comes, here he comes!'

"That was the sign. My father and his employees dropped everything and ran out, waving to the minister, but the black limousine drove on. My mother's triumph knew no bounds.

"Times were troubled then. The minister fell from favour after only three months, and was immediately declared an enemy of the people. 'Why didn't you wave?' asked the surprised liberal when my father accused him of breaking his word. And he asked my father to wave harder if he, Safi, ever got to be minister again soon. Meanwhile he hid with us once more, and we had to feed him for three months. My father had an arch of little coloured lights put up around the display window, and a red arrow of neon lighting hanging in the middle of the street showed clearly where the bakery was. So when the once-toppled liberal was able to take his place at the magnificent ministerial desk again, my father and all his staff stood outside the door in white coats waving and waving to the minister as he drove by in his limousine. Even the little lights seemed to be winking too. But Safi appeared to have gone blind.

"When my father told this story at home my mother was furious, and swore to leave the house once and for all if that ungrateful, slimy slug was ever welcomed to it as a guest again, if only for a second. My father waved at the black limousine for twenty-two days on end. Without success. Then, an embittered man, he had the coloured lights and the neon arrow taken down. He aged by years that day.

"Soon after that, the liberal lost his job again, let's say for the sake of simplicity it was for crooked arms dealing. Two days later he appeared at the bakery, all muffled up, said there was a big conspiracy behind it, he'd soon be rehabilitated, for a very short time he just needed... My father looked right through him. 'Next, please,' he said, and turned to his customers.

"Since that day my father hasn't wanted to know any more about any political parties."

223. Paradise

General Kabdan, who overthrew President Mutamiran at the end of 1964, hated the fundamentalists and had them tortured and killed. Murtada, a nineteen-year-old Islamist, lobbed a hand grenade at General Kabdan, but it went off only after some delay. The President was already at a safe distance when it exploded, so the detonation threw him to the ground, but apart from the weight of his muscular bodyguard on top of him he suffered no harm. The would-be assassin, however, was hit by a splinter in his forehead and fell unconscious. When he returned to his senses he was lying in a white bed and four women, also in white, were looking at him. He thought he was in Paradise and the women were the houris, the promised nymphs with their immortal charms whom, so his sheikh had told him, he could deflower daily, and as soon as his prick came out of them their virginity would be restored.

"You made it, Murtada," he told himself loudly, because his hearing was still affected by the detonation. "It was all true." And just to increase his happiness yet more he asked if the women would take him out and show him the rivers flowing with milk and honey, because all these years, somehow, it hadn't been quite clear to him exactly how honey could flow like water, or why the milk didn't turn sour in the sun. The houris looked at each other and chuckled. Their laughter sounded like Paradise too.

"What milk?" asked the eldest nymph. "What honey?" She wasn't twenty-five yet, and she had sensuous lips and full breasts. Murtada longed to lay his head between them.

"There's a stream somewhere around here," she said, "but it's dried up now in summer, and the garbage in it stinks to high heaven." That sounded to him very earthly.

"You're in Mazzeh military hospital," said the second nymph. He suddenly noticed the iron bars over the window. And for the first time Murtada understood that there are worse things in life than death.

BOOK OF GROWTH IV

A dictator lives not on earth but in his head.

᠄

DAMASCUS, 1965–1968

224. The Problem of Brothers

In the middle of July 1965, a month after General Baidan's perfidious coup against his own party comrade President Kabdan, Josef and Farid received the diplomas qualifying them to work as teachers. They had both had to wait two years longer than their former fellow students, Farid because of his imprisonment, Josef simply because he was in no hurry to qualify. He was busy with a thousand other activities, was better known in the university than many of the lecturers, and spent more time in the cafeteria than the lecture hall. He could afford this delay because, like Farid, he hadn't had to do two years' military service; a man who was an only child wasn't drafted into the army, and instead his family just had to pay a fee amounting to a private soldier's pay for two years' service, which didn't come to much. In making this regulation the state had acknowledged the wish of clans to protect their sons and heirs. As women, Josef's sisters didn't count, because once they married they would be contributing only to their husbands' bloodlines.

A little while before receiving his diploma, Josef had met a woman who interested him. It was the first time he had felt any such attraction in the five years since the sad story of Fatima. Nadia Markos was fascinated by him, for he had something to say on any subject, and what he said was often very cogent.

Her parents were from an old family of Damascene craftsmen who set great store by tradition. That irritated Josef, but Nadia thought the world of her mother and father. And before a month was up she told him they'd like him to be engaged to her, or he couldn't meet her any more. Josef laughed at that, since he could move about the university as he liked with Nadia every day, and he called this threat a paper tiger.

But two weeks later Nadia told him the bad news: three rich cousins had asked for her hand in marriage. She'd close her eyes to their limousines and their villas, but Josef must act fast and get engaged to her, or she wouldn't be able to give her parents any reason for turning her cousins down. And from now on, she said, she wouldn't be allowed to go to the university except in her youngest brother's company.

He half-heartedly agreed, and soon he was engaged. But he had insisted that they didn't want a big party. They'd keep it to the two families and Farid, whom he described as "my brother by other parents".

Farid himself thought the Markos family tedious, but it was a good party. The only person who seemed out of place was Josef. He somehow looked all wrong in his new suit, and he was so agitated that he couldn't even propose a toast well. However, his parents felt emotional, and they liked his fiancée.

Nadia had four older brothers and one younger brother, whose name was Girgi. Girgi was just fifteen and dreamed of nothing but driving a Mercedes by the time he was twenty. That was the one idea in his head. "His mouth is a car exhaust," said Josef of his future brother-in-law, and he wasn't exaggerating. Girgi's world was as simple and neatly arranged as his interests. Those who liked cars were his friends, those who did not were his enemies.

Since Josef hated cars, Girgi was bent on finding an opportunity to show his parents that this fiancé of Nadia's was bad news in more ways than just his unprepossessing outward appearance. At the time engaged couples were never allowed out unsupervised, and this tradition gave him more power than his head could cope with. Since

Nadia's elder brothers were already married and fully occupied with their own affairs, only the youngest, who was also his mother's favourite, was available for supervision duty, and he took advantage of it. Farid's advice to Josef to use presents and invitations to get around this guardian of virtue, or persuade him to turn a blind eye, would have worked in ninety-nine percent of such cases. Girgi was the hundredth.

Josef desperately tried to shake off the shadow sticking to him all the time, but in the end it was Nadia who showed him the only way to do it. "I'm afraid there's nothing for it," she sighed, when Girgi had kept them from exchanging a kiss yet again. "We'll have to get married."

Next day Josef called Farid. "I need you," was all he said, in a voice that cracked. When his friend rang the doorbell a little later, Madeleine let him in with visible relief. "You're a loyal soul, like your mother. Josef is being impossible, shouting at everyone, even me. I don't know what's the matter with him. Please tell him he'll never find another such well-bred, intelligent wife," she said, patting his cheek and going to the kitchen. Soon she brought them coffee.

Josef was ranting, and Farid listened. Arab society, he raged, hadn't moved on since the time of the Mongol hordes. Not only had it been mummifying its ancient customs for generations, it taught you to lie and deceive as well. Just as if cities had never been built but we were still living in the desert, the clan was everything and the individual nothing.

"But not an endless nothing," Farid said, trying to make his friend laugh. It didn't work. Josef was head over heels in love with Nadia, but he hardly knew her, and their engagement had taken her further from him rather than bringing them closer. More and more often, she struck him as a split personality. With her family she was conformist and docile, at the university she was an enlightened, lively woman.

And now he was to marry in haste just to get rid of her pest of a brother Girgi. "In Europe a couple can be happy or not, live together or part from each other, just as love dictates. Here you get married or divorced for hundreds of different reasons, and none of them has anything to do with love."

The trouble was he couldn't decide what to do, and that put him in a bad temper.

"Come on, let's go to the cinema. They're showing *West Side Story*. You asked me to tell you when they were screening it again …"

"Exactly, that's what I need now," Josef interrupted his friend. "A film to make me forget this ghastly society of ours for a couple of hours."

The film was moving. It wasn't just that it was yet another version of the Romeo and Juliet story, this time set in the slums of New York. They were both fascinated by the dancing of the young cast and Leonard Bernstein's music. When they came out of the cinema Josef was in a much better temper, and invited his friend to the Havana for a coffee, hoping to pick up some unofficial news there.

But before they had finished their coffee, a man of dwarfish stature climbed on a table in the middle of the room and tapped his empty glass with a knife. The place fell silent. "I have to announce, gentlemen," he cried in emotional tones, "that the Damascus brothel is closing its doors for ever at eight sharp tomorrow morning."

Expressions of outrage were heard.

"You omen of bad luck!" said the café owner angrily, for within a few minutes the men were rushing out.

"How much money do you have with you?" asked Josef.

"Twenty lira."

"That ought to be enough." He paid for their coffee and left the café with Farid. They were the last to go. The proprietor just shook his head.

225. Goodbye

There was chaos in the brothel that last evening. Farid had never been there before. Josef had gone three or four times, he couldn't remember the exact number. Farid's own ideas of a brothel were abruptly terminated that evening. He had always imagined such a place as something like a palace out of the *Thousand and One Nights*.

You went in, you were bathed in scented water and massaged with aromatic oils. You were dressed in magnificently coloured flowing robes, led to a room where semi-veiled women awaited their suitors, you inspected them and chose one, then you plunged into an erotic orgy, surfacing only occasionally to bathe and recover your strength. In Farid's imagination, there were also naked dancing girls whirling about.

None of this bore the slightest resemblance to what he saw in the Damascus brothel. The plain yellow building, not far from the university campus, was surrounded by a high wall, impossible to scale, against which all and sundry had pissed. There was a small shelter for a doorman at the entrance. Two police officers usually stood at the gate to check that no men under twenty came in.

That last night, however, both officers were drunk, staggering about the small inner courtyard, so there was no one on the gate. Young men and ragged children were running about the corridors open-mouthed, trying to catch a last glimpse of the women's naked bodies. The place did brisk business that night. Men stood in line outside the doors of the whores on offer for five, ten, or twenty lira. Only on the top floor did peace and calm prevail. A few customers waited here in comfortable armchairs, and the women cost between fifty and a hundred lira.

Josef borrowed ten lira from his friend and waited in line for his favourite whore, a dark-skinned Egyptian girl. Farid saw her as she glanced briefly out of the door and shouted for a matron called Badria.

Next moment he heard the woman Badria's deep, masculine voice reply. She exceeded all notions of obesity as she came rolling along, hung about with massive, tasteless gold jewellery.

Farid didn't feel attracted to any of the whores. Some of them were really pretty, but the idea of man after man emptying himself into a woman at ten minute intervals made him feel nauseated rather than sexually aroused. However, he was glad to have satisfied his curiosity. He had never thought he would ever walk about a brothel so freely.

Josef thought he would have to wait at least two hours, so they agreed to meet in the café on the top floor.

Farid sat down at a small bistro table. A man in his fifties was amusing himself with a young whore at the next table, drinking a bottle of red wine with her. He seemed to have known her for a long time, spoke to her in friendly tones, and didn't keep touching her like all the other men, who missed no opportunity to paw a passing prostitute.

Suddenly another girl stormed into the café, brought a bouquet of red roses down on a young man's head, and pursued him to the bar, where she flung the now battered bouquet in his face, shouting, "I never want to see you again, never, understand?"

The man protested pitifully, but the whore, a small, wiry girl, turned and marched out.

"The coward," said the young whore at the table next to Farid. "He only wants Fatima here in the brothel. First he says he loves her, and when she finally believes him, he won't even take her to the cinema in case someone sees them together. I've seen enough of his sort."

A little later, the young whore suddenly laughed out loud and pointed to a thin man just coming into the café, who went to the bar and ordered a coffee. This gentleman, who was extremely elegant but had a rather dusty look about him, seemed deeply offended by the idea that the President was going to close the brothel down.

"Do I interfere with his politics? Do I tell him not to take money from Saudi Arabia? Of course not. So why does he want to deprive me of my only pleasure?"

"That's Hassan Sabbat, notary, multi-millionaire, and lover of our matron Badria," said the young whore, giggling.

"You can't be serious! Badria? Surely he couldn't even offer himself as a wick to light her fire!" said the man with her. The whore giggled. "Very true, but love is blind."

Here in the café, Farid learned how mistaken were all the myths in Arab novels and films about honest girls turning whore in desperation. My father raped me, they said, and forced me into prostitution. Or my wonderful husband, my mother, my sister fell ill, so I just had to sell myself to get money for medicine and doctors. These ridiculous moral tales ended with some old actor regretfully telling the fallen woman, "My child, a woman's honour is a match that will burn once only." And at almost all screenings of such films young men would call out, in the dark auditorium, "But a lighter will burn thousands of times."

The young whore at the next table had already packed her bag, she said. She was moving to Beirut, to work in an establishment in Mutanabi Street. Sad as her fate might be, she sounded more self-assured than most of the married women in Damascus.

When Josef came up to the café it was after midnight, and they were just in time to catch the last bus to Bab Sharki.

"I'm going to marry Nadia, but I won't celebrate the wedding with any of those bastards in her family. And I want you to be my witness," he said. Farid must have been looking at him with such a baffled expression that Josef asked, quite concerned, "Did something upset you here among the whores?"

⁂

A day after the brothel was closed down, Matta came to see Farid, his chest swelling proudly. "My brother," he said, "you must come for a ride with me."

"A ride? On your bike?" asked Farid, whose imagination stretched no further.

"Oh no," laughed Matta. "I've bought myself a Suzuki. Brand new! A superbike."

Sure enough, outside the door stood one of the motorized three-wheeled scooters that were buzzing about the Old Town like wasps, making a terrible noise and stink, but very useful. They could get down any narrow alley, delivering goods to the most remote back door. Italians and Japanese were competing for this lucrative market, but independently of the manufacturer these little vehicles were all called Suzukis.

The Syrians welded a kind of mini-seat on the Suzukis, next to the rider's saddle. Farid sat on this, and Matta rode up and down Saitun Alley, grinning proudly.

"My wife sold her jewellery so that I'd never have to push a hand-cart again," he said, and there was a happy gleam in his eyes.

226. Beginnings

Through Nadia's eldest brother, Josef had soon found a job as a teacher in Rauda Street, a high-class part of Damascus. The brother had been a member of the Ba'ath Party since his youth, and was now high up in the Foreign Trade department. He had a good friend in the Ministry of Culture. He also liked Josef and Nadia and wanted to see them properly provided for.

Farid, on the other hand, got a post allotted at random in the pool of hundreds of available candidates that late summer of 1965, people who had no government contacts who didn't want to bribe anyone. His contract was for two years as a probationary teacher in a school south of Damascus, not forty kilometres away. He could go home in the evenings either in a shared taxi or by bus.

Katana was an ugly garrison town; take away the barracks and you were left with a large, dusty village with dirty streets and rusty snack bars. But the school building was new. Farid began teaching there in October with enthusiasm. He taught the seventh, eighth, and ninth grades. The pupils were strictly brought up, and thought it a heaven-sent miracle that the new teacher didn't hit them.

It was time to leave his parents' house, and with Josef's help, he found a tiny apartment. It was dark, consisting only of one room, a kitchen alcove, and a lavatory, but it wasn't far from where Rana lived. Claire was sad, but she knew her son must lead his own life now. Within a week he had furnished the new apartment, and he enjoyed a long afternoon there with Rana. They cooked together, made love, and were as happy as two children keeping a secret.

"Let's run away," she said quietly, before she said goodbye.

In mid-March, three weeks after a coup by the leftist General Taisan had overthrown his conservative colleague Baidan, Farid unexpectedly suffered a harsh setback. It came after his quarrel in February with the school principal, a sadist and bootlicker who had come into the classroom during physics and hit out, sputtering with fury, at one of the pupils. Apparently the boy, whose name was Ismail, had insulted the Syrian flag at break.

Farid swallowed hard, and after school he brushed up his

knowledge of the new legislation on schools. It gave the teacher and no one else authority to discipline his own pupils. An older colleague told him that the principal always tried to intimidate new teachers, laying claim to the grades they taught as his own preserve. "Of course a principal has the right to summon any pupil to his office, but turning up unannounced during lessons to humiliate a child is just malice," he said.

Less than a week later, the principal appeared again. This time he wanted to punish a boy called Jusuf. During the patriotic slogan that the Ba'ath Party required all schoolchildren to recite in the morning, he was said to have insulted the Arab nation. Instead of calling out, "Nation with an eternal mission!" Jusuf had apparently called, "Nation with a flatulent mission!" The principal flourished his bamboo cane. Jusuf turned pale. Farid knew that the boy had a heart defect, and he knew that the principal knew it too.

"I'm sorry, but you can't do that in my classroom. First, beating pupils has been forbidden for two years, and second, you're disturbing lessons over an unproven accusation. Jusuf," he asked, turning to the boy, "did you say what the principal says you called out?"

Jusuf leaped to his feet. "No, sir. I never insulted our Fatherland. But Yunus from Grade Eight said if I didn't give him ten marbles as protection money he'd tell the principal I did."

"That will do, Jusuf, you can sit down," said Farid, turning to his boss, who was rooted to the spot. "As you see, my pupil is not guilty of anything. It's the tale-bearer who ought to be asked why such notions of the Fatherland enter his head. And if you don't mind, I have very little time for teaching even without interruptions, so please let me go on."

The principal left the room without a word, and never came back again. Jusuf's statement turned out to be correct, but the principal never said another word about that either. In the middle of March, however, Farid was transferred for disciplinary reasons to a village on the southern border with Israel. Among themselves, the teachers called it Syrian Siberia.

Farid was furious. The reprimands were down in writing, and thus official, but no one had given him a hearing, and it made no difference to the young head of the education department in the Ministry of Culture whether the rest of the teachers and the pupils contested them or not. He, Farid, was accused of having incited and encouraged school students to make fun of the Ba'ath Party and the principal. Probationary teachers had almost no rights at all.

His request to be allowed to stay until the end of the school year met with a curt refusal. He was to report to the middle school in the village of Shaga within a week, or he would be summarily dismissed.

The Grade Seven pupils wept when he said goodbye, and Jusuf, the boy with the heart defect, came up and offered him his hand, with two hardboiled eggs in it. "Something for the journey, from my grandmother," he said. Farid could no longer hold back his tears.

Shaga was 200 kilometres from Damascus, and almost half the way to the village was through impassable country. Going there and back every day would be impossible. He had to change buses twice and then go in a shared taxi for some distance to get back to Damascus from the village, and the journey took four hours.

Rana was very sad. "I want you to know," she said, "that even if I have to wait all my life to live free with you for a single day, I won't regret it."

With a heavy heart, Farid gave up his rented apartment and packed his things. Josef and Nadia came to see him off in the bus, and Matta insisted on taking him and his case to the bus stop himself. He wept as he said goodbye, and then rattled away fast on his Suzuki.

"It won't be long before they transfer you back to Damascus for disciplinary reasons instead," said Josef, watching Matta go. "Hell's here, not down south where they regard teachers as demigods. Here they think they're crap. They know a teacher doesn't even earn as much as their family chauffeur, so how would they respect him? Knowledge doesn't count for as much as the make of car you drive. And I don't even ride a bike. Sometimes my pupils see me get out of a crowded bus and shake their heads as they sit in their Mercedes. And you always have some of the sons of the top brass to teach here, so too bad if you provoke one of those uneducated apes. Punish him and you're attacking the Foreign Minister, or even worse the head of the secret police. The kids are always showing you they know it, too."

"You know how Josef is!" Nadia intervened. "Never happy. I keep telling him he ought to be giving private tuition to one boy at a time instead of educating these hordes, and he'd earn twice as much, but he won't listen to me."

Josef laughed. "Nadia doesn't want me to die of a heart attack, she'd rather I died of a stroke. Those kids and private tuition! They just don't want to learn anything. They've already been to Venice and New York, London and Paris, they're burned out at the age of fourteen. And you think they'd want to learn geography?"

"Calm down," said Farid. "I don't know if they need teachers or tractors more down in the south, but I'd have liked to stay here," he added, and boarded the bus, because the driver was already starting the engine.

He looked gloomily out of the window, envying everyone who could stay in Damascus. He had no idea that one of the most exciting periods of his life was just beginning.

227. First Signs

Dunia was the first to notice that Rana wasn't well. Four weeks after Farid had left, she visited her friend without phoning first, and was alarmed. Rana seemed desperate, and was letting herself go. She said she hurt all over, but the doctors hadn't found anything, and her husband was always cross with her. He said she was plain lazy and addicted to reading books. Rami had locked the books away, and he locked her studio on the flat roof too. She wasn't even allowed to read newspapers and magazines. Instead, she had to learn crochet and knitting from his cousin Majda, and his sister was supposed to teach her to bake cookies and iron properly.

Rana showed Dunia her efforts. They were very clumsy. "An elephant could knit better than me." She laughed and cried by turns.

Dunia was bewildered, but she knew Rana couldn't stand that stolid housewife Majda.

Finally she encouraged her friend to get up, wash, and smarten herself up, and by the time Rana was ready Dunia had brought some kind of order into the apartment and cleared up the garbage lying around everywhere. Rana seemed to have lost all her *joie de vivre*, as if she had given up entirely.

They went to Sibki Park. "You ought to go on vacation with Rami," said Dunia. "You need a little fresh air, that's all, you want to get out of your own four walls."

"Rami can't take a vacation. He has to stay here and make sure he keeps his job."

"But you're not yourself at all," Dunia told her forcefully. "Why don't I talk to him?"

Dunia knew that discussing his wife's psychological condition with a Syrian was like trying to square the circle. Psychological sickness was regarded as a disgrace to the whole family, in particular a woman's husband. So all psychological problems were denied, only total derangement was recognized – and for that there was the al-Asfuriye mental hospital. All the same, she was prepared to speak to Rami. Rana shook her head. She felt guilty because she couldn't love him but was just a burden.

"Are you sure?" Dunia pressed her.

"Yes, thank you, I must deal with this by myself. First I have to get his cousin off my back. I have to or I'll kill myself with one of those knitting needles."

Dunia began phoning her friend every day. After some time she thought Rana seemed better, and invited her to come around to her place when several other young women were visiting.

When she arrived five or six of Dunia's neighbours were sitting around her new record player, drinking coffee and talking. Rana didn't know any of them. Dunia put a new Beatles record on and invited her friends to dance. She'd been to London with her husband, she told them, and she learned the new dances there. The women were delighted, and once their hostess had cleared away all the vases and little tables she showed them the latest steps. Rana smiled wearily, but didn't feel like joining in. Even when the women, led by Dunia, tied scarves around their hips and began swaying in an oriental dance, she stayed where she was. "I have to think," she said.

"Music and thinking don't go together. Music wants to get into your body, make your nerves swing and your heart beat like a drum," said Dunia, who danced with wonderful eroticism. But Rana was not to be persuaded.

Later, the women all prepared a refreshing tabbouleh salad, the dish for which Damascus is famous, but she had no appetite. She just sat there trying to be polite, but the women's cheerfulness got on her nerves. After a while she asked her friend to drive her home. Dunia was one of the first women in Damascus to hold a driving licence.

"I long so much for Farid," said Rana when they stopped outside her house. "I haven't seen him since he went to the south. Somehow he's going further and further away from me. I feel so lost. And then there's my husband demanding his rights as if I were his slave."

Dunia tried to soothe her friend, helped her to undress, and was about to leave when Rami came in. He was surprised to find her visiting, but was charming and polite. Finally he accompanied her to the door and offered her his hand.

"Rana needs a doctor, urgently. She's sick," said Dunia quietly.

Rami withdrew his hand. "She has everything she could wish for. She's just bored," he replied, narrow-lipped, and all trace of friendliness vanished from his face. Dunia was afraid that if she said any more he might take it out on Rana for letting him down in front of other people. She swallowed. Rami looked at her, incensed, and closed the door after her without another word.

228. Radicals

Farid was glad to get out of the bus intact when it arrived in Daraa. The driver had been overtired. He had a night shift behind him, and then had to go on driving without a break because his colleague was sick. Farid, sitting to his right, had noticed how he kept nodding off at the wheel, so he talked steadily to him for two hours.

The dusty town of Daraa was the last stop of any size in the dry Hauran plain. From here, the road wound up towards the Golan Heights. The landscape became more precipitous, but also more colourful because of all the little rivers. The uniform brown of the steppes disappeared as soon as they were past the first bend in the road. Not only was the land fertile in the triangle between Jordan, Israel, and Syria, smuggling flourished more than any other trade. But like the wretched town of Daraa, the shabby villages along the way were evidence not so much of poverty as of the absence of any pleasure in life. Despite the fertility of the region, the houses were dilapidated, the roads neglected. Children ran barefoot after the bus, throwing stones. The peasants' children had no underwear at all, those of the Palestinian refugees wore whatever their mothers had made from the white cotton sacks which contained the flour and rice donated to them. The coloured emblems of the donors stamped on the sacks lasted for ever: the famous American hand-print, the Australian hopping kangaroo, the Canadian maple leaf.

The little bus had been cobbled together, with much Syrian ingenuity, from parts of at least fifteen brands of vehicle. Amazingly, this technical marvel stayed in one piece as it groaned its alarming way up the mountains, and jolted like a rock falling unpredictably down to the valleys again. After exactly two hours the bus had reached the village of Shaga. The passengers applauded enthusiastically.

It was Friday and the school was closed. Farid was to start teaching on Saturday. There was no hotel or boarding house in the village, and only a few buildings had electricity. Strangers spent the night with the village elder, so Farid asked the way to his house. The bus driver told him to get in again and drove him to the door. It turned out that the village elder was a generous host, who offered to let the new teacher stay with him for free, but Farid thanked him and declined.

In the spring of 1965, the village was still twenty kilometres from the Israeli border. The area was under strict military control; the bus had been stopped three times, while soldiers carefully checked the passengers' papers and asked where they were going. The peasants knew just what to expect, and no one was travelling without ID. Shaga had both an elementary school and a large new middle school, the only one in the whole region. Many of the pupils had to cross valleys and climb mountains on their way to school early in the morning, and arrived for lessons exhausted.

Farid didn't have to explain that he had been transferred for disciplinary reasons, for it appeared that no teacher ever came willingly to Shaga. All twelve of the staff were exiles, and they all said they had been unfairly banished.

Husni the principal, a gentle-natured man of gloomy appearance, gave him a sobering account of the situation. It was downright impossible to teach properly in Shaga, he said. The other teachers nodded, with wry smiles. The pupils had no money for books, and those sent by the Ministry of Culture for this poverty-stricken region had been lost somewhere on the way. Moreover, there couldn't be anything like a normal school day when operations by Palestinian guerrillas on the border, followed by punitive Israeli actions and manoeuvres by the Syrian armed forces, turned the area into a battlefield every other week. In addition most of the children had to help their parents by night, smuggling arms, hashish, and cigarettes. He could only ask their new colleague not to pitch his expectations too high, said Husni, but at least to teach the poor devils the bare essentials.

The principal talked non-stop, but humorously, and since he mentioned Allah and his Prophet more often than necessary Farid guessed he was a Muslim Brother, and that was why he had been sent here.

The other teachers listened, looking relaxed, and drank the dark, sweet tea brought by the janitor. "Einstein himself," said Husni, in conclusion, "would have grown up to be nothing but a smuggler or the member of a Palestinian commando group if he'd lived here."

It was just before nine when the teachers went to their pupils, who had been waiting for an hour. On the way they introduced themselves by their names, subjects, and the reasons why they had been sent here. Farid was to teach chemistry, physics, and mathematics to the seventh, eighth, and ninth grades, thirty-two hours in all over six days. He soon realized that so far as the students' achievements were concerned, they were hopelessly backward, but their curiosity was great, and in practical matters they were equal to any young Damascene of eighteen.

"Children here grow up very quickly. They don't just live every day, they have to survive it. That's sad, but it matures them quickly. If you see death before your eyes all the time you want to taste life as soon as possible," said Adib, a pleasant man who taught Arabic. He had been moved here from Daraa after calling for an uprising against the corrupt governor of the southern province. First he spent a year in prison, then he was banished from Daraa for five years.

Farid tried to teach his pupils the essentials, and was amazed to see how fast they picked things up. At the end of every lesson he gave them ten minutes to ask questions and look for answers with him. He tried to satisfy their curiosity about natural phenomena, which made him realize how slight his own knowledge was.

They asked how rainbows were made, and why water in the sea looks blue although it is has no colour. They wanted to know why Eskimos went on living in the biting cold instead of moving to warmer climates, or why the Bedouin almost died of thirst in the desert, yet still stayed there. They asked where the wind comes from, and why we don't all fall over when the earth turns. They wanted to know how and why the borders of countries were drawn, and who had taught bees all over the world to build hexagonal honeycombs. Soon Farid's pupils were ready to give up their break period to go on talking in the classroom, and he felt that he was really teaching for the first time in his life.

But he also realized that their questions were stretching him to his limits, and he saw all that Damascus University had failed to do in educating him. He had followed the equations of Einstein, Planck, Rutherford, and Schrödinger, he had passed tests and written essays on them. But what use was that in Grade Seven of this God-forsaken school, a place with no proper chalk, a place where the pupils had to manage without textbooks and exercise books, but all the same wanted to know why the sun goes on burning and never gets any smaller?

He went wearily back to his modest furnished room, lit by a sooty oil lamp that smelled of kerosene. But he was glad of his friendly land-lady, an old widow who often went to Daraa to see her married sons and daughters there. Then the house with its little inner courtyard was all his. He liked to sit in the shady corner under a vine, looking at the old apple tree and the poor flower pots.

Claire and Rana complained that he hardly came to Damascus at all, but his only day off was Friday, and ten hours of travelling there and back were too much of a strain for him to get through the whole week after it, teaching three classes with forty pupils in each. So he usually stayed in Shaga, exploring its surroundings so far as the army would allow. Most of his colleagues did the same; only the principal and two other teachers came from Daraa, and went back to their families at the weekend.

Since Shaga was a very boring little place, with no café or restaurant or cinema, the teachers met almost every evening in someone's room. Their antipathy to the government was a link that held them together despite their very different views. They played cards or backgammon, and when they had played games long enough they drank tea and told jokes, or confided their sorrows to one another.

Farid soon became particularly close to three young teachers: Adib taught Arabic, Salman taught history and geography, and Fadi was the art and sports teacher.

Outside school he discussed politics, morality, and violence with them. One day Adib cautiously asked him if he'd like to read the Radical movement's newspaper. Farid couldn't believe his eyes. It was called *Now*, and it was the logical and indeed the radical continuation of his own ideas as expressed in *Youth*. The paper was poorly printed, but the articles were full of wit, and frankly criticized conditions in the Middle East. The newspaper deliberately leaned on the Qarmates who had founded a Soviet-style republic in Arabia in the tenth century.

After reading it carefully, Farid decided that the ideas of the Radicals were somewhere between Russian anarchism and Cuban armed conflict. They wanted to make Syria a country without exploitation, without an army, and without privileges. Men and women were to be given absolute equality in all their rights and duties, particularly in the right to divorce. Religion was to be separate from the state, and declared the private business of every individual. Marriage would be performed by the state independent of any religious affiliation. People were to live and love freely, without fear and without war, they were to be able to say what they thought openly, and determine everything themselves through direct democracy, rather than being ruled by parties or clans. Farid had dreamed of just this for a long time. Now he suddenly saw young people with weapons in their hands trying to put his ideas into practice.

229. A Meeting

"If you really love Rana, then either run away with her or make a clean break," said Dunia vehemently. She had found out that he was in Damascus, called him, and now they were sitting in a café near the parliament building. Dunia had grown very plump, and only her face still reminded him of her former beauty. "Her love for you is making her sick. She's reached the point where she thinks of living with her husband as unfaithfulness to you, and it makes her suffer. Every time she meets you she feels hopeful, but then you disappear again. I don't need particularly sharp eyes to know when you've been with her. Do you think this is any way to behave?"

"What are you trying to say? We have to be patient until we can find a way to be together. Rana didn't want to give me up, and I've stayed unmarried for her sake myself."

"Yes, but you go out, you have work, you're politically active, and she's a prisoner here within her own four walls. It's unjust. And that's not all. There's also the fact that she can't come to terms with the situation. Here's my husband on one side, she says, there's my lover on the other. She's living on a high springboard, and every time it sways she feels sick. I've tried and failed to get her to go easy, take life as it comes. She's waiting with her bags packed, but you never bring the air tickets to set her free."

"And now you blame it all on me instead of her husband, who won't let her study or paint! As if love and not the idiocy of men who beat and imprison their wives were a sin," said Farid indignantly.

"No, I'm not blaming anyone. I'm only desperately trying to find some way out of this for my dearest friend, because I can see she's getting more and more desperate. And I think you're the only one who can save her, but you must act fast. Yes, perhaps I *am* blaming you for something, your cruel inactivity. What are you waiting for? In your place and hers I'd have been off and away long ago."

"But you're not in my place and hers. We ran away once and failed, that's why I'm trying to change the dreadful conditions that destroy us all," said Farid. However, he didn't sound very convincing.

"You don't mean that seriously, do you? Have you just swallowed Mao's Little Red Book, or what? We're in the heart of Arabia here, not China or Cuba. Nothing ever changes here. If you really want to save this wonderful love of yours for Rana, you'd better hurry up before it's too late."

"So what makes the Chinese any better than us? What do they have that we don't? A third leg?" Farid's voice was sharp, but he spoke quietly, because the café was full.

"Perhaps, perhaps," said Dunia sadly, for she could see that she was getting nowhere. She said no more for a moment, and then, lowering her voice, went on. "I have about ten thousand dollars in a special account. If you two need it to run away, it'll be my wedding present to you."

"That's sweet of you, and we'll certainly ask you for help when the moment comes. But tell me, how are you yourself?" he said, changing the subject, feeling bad about speaking so angrily to Rana's faithful friend.

"Oh, I'm fine. I've adjusted to life, and my husband does a lot to keep me in good humour. Successfully, as you can see."

Farid left the café knowing that Rana's friend was more human and approachable than he had ever thought. Dunia watched him go until the crowd swallowed him up. She marvelled at her clever friend Rana, who could love such an apathetic man so passionately.

230. Song of the Cicadas

Farid was still in the school building late in the evening. He was planning to correct Grade 8's chemistry test and then look in on Adib for a game of cards. He had a solid table to work at here in the school, and electric light; his lodgings had neither. Husni appeared in the doorway saying he was going to make fresh tea in half an hour's time.

When he came back, he sat down, stared at his tea glass, and said more to himself than Farid, "They sent us here to be rid of us. Either you give notice after a year of this hell, or the Israelis give you the *coup de grace*."

Husni was certainly not a kindred spirit. He was conservative and strictly Muslim, but he was kind to the children and sorry for them. Every week lessons were interrupted for hours, if not days, because the Israelis or Palestinians were involved in some operation. For many children their way to school was dangerous, potentially fatal. A secret war was being waged in a strip of land twenty kilometres wide on both sides of the border, and as if by mutual consent Damascus and Tel Aviv never mentioned it. Before Farid's arrival the pupils and their teachers had dug a trench where they sheltered during attacks. They had learned to run for it fast and crouch there close together. The sight moved Farid to tears. They kept their hands over their ears for fear that an exploding bomb might deafen them. Farid and two other teachers went into the trench with them every time; the others drank tea with the principal.

Once an Israeli helicopter hovered over the trench, and a soldier waved when Farid looked up. The helicopter was less than five metres above the ground, and made you feel as if a whirlwind might suck you up. Farid was furious, because the children were screaming in terror. He shook his fist at the pilot and yelled at him for God's sake to go away, but his voice was lost in the infernal din. The Israeli showed his own middle finger, and finally turned away.

In the village they told fantastic tales of special bombs that "pupped" and bore other bombs, and a cream that made you invisible. They said the Israeli soldiers rubbed it over themselves so that they could track down armed Palestinians in the villages and shoot them.

There were several camps of Palestinians around the village. The farmers disliked these irregulars because they trampled over their fields and held target practice among the fruit trees. To make matters worse, the Israelis moved into the area around Shaga after every Palestinian operation, pursuing their enemies all the way to the valley beyond the village, and the Syrians never fired a shot at the Israelis. Intent on striking at the irregulars, the Israelis dropped incendiary bombs into the fields where they suspected they might be lurking, and destroyed the harvest. The local crops were tomatoes grown for the canning factories in Damascus, wheat, tobacco, and fruit of particularly fine quality.

No one paid the farmers for the loss of their harvest, so many became smugglers and left their orchards and fields to the Palestinians and Israelis.

The principal poured tea. It was already after six in the evening.

"Aren't you going home today?" asked Farid.

"I keep a thin mattress here, that's all I need in summer. I have to write my reports for the Ministry, and I'll never get it done at home. That's why I'm working a night shift," he explained, sipping the strong, sweet tea.

"What reports?" asked Farid, surprised.

"Oh, it's a ridiculous business. I'm transferred here for disciplinary reasons myself, but I have to write a report on every single one of you others. I mustn't be too positive, or they won't trust me, or they'll say I give a good report to anyone close to the Muslim Brotherhood. They know I'm supposed to belong to them, just because I'm a believer. I hate doing these reports, so I keep postponing them, but I've just had the second reminder. The third would mean my salary was docked."

Now Farid knew why the principal had invited him to drink tea. "You want to know what to write about me."

The principal didn't look at him. "The others have already written everything down for me, and I hardly know you, so I didn't want to be unfair to you."

Farid laughed. There was something tragi-comic about the situation. The same neglectful government that left the village children without school books would send three reminders that an informer's report was due, as if the future of Syrian culture depended on it.

"Oh, just go ahead and be negative about me!" he said. "Tell them I don't like the place and I keep complaining of the injustice suffered by all the farmers here. Say I keep complaining of the bad roads, and I …"

"That won't interest anyone, my dear colleague," Husni interrupted him. "In Damascus they want to know what you're doing here, what you talk about, and how I assess your political affiliations. So?"

This was an interrogation, and for a moment Farid thought the principal was a genuine informer. The secret service often blackmailed members of the opposition and made compliant informants of them. But at least this man was talking about it openly.

"Well, write that I'm a converted communist. I mean someone who wants socialism, but neither the Russian nor the Chinese kind."

"What kind, then? An Arab kind?"

"A Farid Mushtak kind," he said, forcing himself to laugh. "But don't ever say that I try unloading my views on the children, because I'd consider that educationally wrong. You can say that you're the only one who knows my political opinions, and that was only in private conversation."

They went on talking for half an hour, and Farid had a queasy feeling when he left the principal, who had taken it all down in shorthand on a sheet of paper. When he told the other teachers about it, they reassured him. Husni was okay, they said, and a victim of informers himself.

Only two years later he was to discover that his colleagues had been wrong. Husni's hatred of communists outweighed his personal misfortunes. He had accused his new teacher of subversion and sophisticated manipulation of the children, encouraging them to be materialists who no longer saw anything divine in natural phenomena. His was a Cuban kind of communism, Husni claimed.

Next morning Farid woke with a start. Salvoes of gunfire followed the sound of bombs going off, and again and again the noise of a jet fighter rent the sky. The widow in whose house he was lodging was already in the inner courtyard. She was pale, and pointed south.

"They've been fighting for an hour. Do you think they'll come to our village?"

"No idea," he replied. He quickly dressed and ran out into the road. Screams and the hollow sound of bombs dropping came from the southern part of the village. Black smoke was rising. An ambulance raced past him.

It was a hot June day. The seasonal workers, mainly Bedouin or poor peasants from neighbouring villages, came to meet him. "It's hell there, hell!" shouted one of the reapers. "They're dropping incendiary bombs and surrounding the camp down by the spring, but the Palestinians are fighting like the devil." Then he ran on.

Farid went in the direction from which he heard screaming. A farm had been hit. The farmer, a man in his fifties, was sitting on the ground weeping. The house was in flames. Farid joined the other people handing on a chain of buckets full of water. It took them two hours to put the fire out.

"What am I to do now? Where do I start?" asked the farmer, and he and his wife and four sons looked in horror at the smoking remains of their house. The neighbours tried to console him by pointing out that neither the family nor his barn with the harvest in it had been hit. The house itself was mud brick.

Gradually the southern end of the village quietened down. No one ever found out what the Israeli and Palestinian losses were, and once again grisly rumours were told and passed on everywhere.

When the fire was out, and Farid realized that he felt like a stranger among all these people who knew each other, he went out into the fields. Leaden silence weighed down, and the whole world seemed hollow. Suddenly he heard the song of a cicada. For a while it fiddled away alone, then an answer came from the shady place under the pomegranate tree, and a little later it was a concert performance with many orchestral parts, as if the first cicada had given the signal that the danger was over and life had returned to normal.

Moved by the song of the cicadas, Farid set off for home. Not far from the burned-out house several peasants accosted him and, in ornate Arabic, requested him to do them the honour of drinking tea with them. He accepted the invitation, particularly as he didn't know what else to do that day. The peasants took him to a large farm where ten of them, young and old, were sitting around a small fire. They all rose and welcomed him warmly. "You're not a city dweller," said one toothless old farmer, clapping him on the shoulder.

"Yes, I am, I'm a genuine Damascene," he replied, smiling awkwardly.

"Oh no, they're all bastards. Different blood flows in your veins. You're from the mountains," said the farmer. Farid preferred to stay loyal to his city of Damascus, and wasn't going to claim Mala as his native place.

"I really am from Damascus, but we're not all bastards. And I can hardly run away from here, because I was never a good sportsman," he joked.

A young farmer told the toothless man to mind his manners. His son was one of Farid's pupils and spoke warmly of him. When he mentioned the boy's name, Farid was astonished. He was one of the most troublesome boys, and he often had to speak sternly to him.

The men told him jokes about the teacher from Damascus who had preceded him, but disappeared after three weeks. He was particularly amused when the young farmer told him about a theatrical group from Damascus which toured the front line to encourage the people there. They called themselves the Standing Firm Company. But before any of the actors had delivered so much as a single line on stage they took to their heels and ran for it, involuntarily providing the audience with a perfect comedy. They left half their props behind. There had been fighting between the Israelis and Palestinians south of Shaga that evening.

When Farid went on his way again it was already noon. He was hungry. In the village he saw hundreds of seasonal workers lining the streets. Suffering from the intolerable heat, they were leaning against the walls of buildings and trying to retreat into what little shade there was.

The house where he himself lived was providing shade for three people in the street, two men and a woman. Farid greeted them and asked if they would like a drink of water. All three gratefully said yes. The door of the house was locked, for the widow had gone away, but luckily he had the key on him. He unlocked the door, went in, and filled a large jug with cool water. When he was taking it out again he found the woman waiting in the doorway to spare him the trouble. Farid stopped dead at the sight of her. He had never in his life seen such a beauty.

"Thank you very much," she said, smiling. As if dazed, he gave her the jug. She poured water from its spout into her mouth in a curving jet, stood there squarely before him, left hand on her hip, and drank and drank.

"Hey, daughter of the devil, leave a drop for us!" joked one of the men. The woman laughed, and spilled some of the water over her shirt, but it was welcome refreshment to her. She handed the jug on and looked with amusement at Farid, who was still standing motionless in the doorway.

"Perhaps Mr. Teacher doesn't like our manners," she said flirtatiously. She was about twenty, but with her mischievous smile she seemed as playful and carefree as a girl of ten.

Farid smiled too. The peasants here called any idiot in European clothes "Mr. Teacher".

Very soon the jug was empty. He filled it again, and was going to take the water out, but when he turned away from the tap the young woman was standing in the middle of the courtyard, with both hands on her hips now, smiling radiantly at him. She was shabbily dressed, in a yellow man's shirt with a red shawl over a mended skirt, and with her feet in clumping men's sandals, but she could have worn anything and still looked good.

"I thought I'd save Mr. Teacher the trouble," she said.

"What's your name?" he asked almost inaudibly.

"Sharifa bint Abdulrahman bin Salih bin Gawash bin Saqir, of the Gasalah tribe," she replied.

"And is it okay for people to call you just Sharifa if they're in a hurry?"

She looked amused. "What is Mr. Teacher's name?"

"Farid without any bint or bin."

"Just Farid, plain as dry bread."

"If you're hungry, I have bread, olives, cheese, canned tuna and a few tomatoes here," he offered, hoping she would stay.

"I'll be back once I've shaken off those two vultures," she agreed, as carefree as a child fixing to come and play with another.

Two hours later she was back.

231. Sharifa

She ate like a lioness, laughed like a little girl, and was as lovely as a Greek statue. Farid couldn't take his eyes off her, and had hardly any appetite. They sat in the courtyard under the vine, where his landlady had placed an old wooden table, Sharifa on a wooden bench, he in a wicker armchair opposite her. As they ate, he listened to her story.

Her Bedouin tribe was one of the poorest of all, and lived in the steppes between Jordan and Syria. She had been lucky enough to marry the man she loved, but he soon went off to Damascus looking for work, and after a while he sent her letters from Kuwait. He had planned to spend only two years working there, and then come back as soon as possible, but he'd been away for six years now. He had left her behind with her parents, for his contract didn't allow him to take his wife with him. But there was nothing for her to share at home but hunger. So she had to work as a picker during the tomato harvest, ten piastres for each ten-kilo crate, and by the time you'd earned a whole lira you had no back and no hands left. The sun burned pitilessly down, and the supervisors were shouting at the pickers all the time because they didn't want to keep the trucks waiting long.

She slept out of doors, and men pestered her every night, but the twenty women pickers had formed an alliance and slept close together to protect themselves. Now, however, work was interrupted every other day, and then she didn't get any money, so she was planning to go to Damascus tomorrow, hoping to work in peace and earn something there. All her worldly goods were in a poor little bundle that she had put down behind an oleander in the courtyard, feeling ashamed of it.

"May I stay the night here somewhere?" she asked, as darkness fell.

"Of course. I'll bring you a mattress and sheet, and you can sleep here, but only for tonight, because my landlady will probably be back tomorrow."

Farid made her a bed in the open air, and showed her where she could wash. Then he went to bed too. He saw her washing thoroughly and singing softly as she did so, and then she slipped under her own covers. He felt a great desire to hold her close and kiss her lips, but next moment he felt ashamed of himself. After a while he fell asleep.

It was pitch dark when he felt her hand on his cheek. He didn't know how long he had been sleeping.

"Do you want me?"

She was naked, and without waiting for an answer she slipped into bed with him. He lit the oil lamp. She smiled shyly and hid her face under the covers, baring her perfect back. Farid lay back on his pillows, feeling wretched.

"You're in love with a woman. I noticed right away. Other men try to grab me before they've said three words together, but you're already spoken for," she said, laughing. She kissed his nose and nestled close to his chest. Soon after that she fell asleep. She lay there before him like a beautiful child, and he stayed awake for a long time. Only as day began to dawn did he sleep too.

When he woke she was already gone. So were his wristwatch, his stocks of sugar, flour, and oil, and all his underwear except what he had been wearing the day before. The mattress and sheet had gone with her too. She had left him only twenty lira in his wallet.

"Generous!" he said, and smiled.

232. Illusion

5 June 1967 was a perfectly ordinary Monday. Farid was going to discuss the main points of the physics test that he had given his three grades the previous Thursday, and had now corrected. Considering the situation, his students were doing well. They had stopped just learning by heart, and were genuinely trying to understand what he told them. Their average marks were generally satisfactory.

The humid heat made him get up early, and a strange restlessness drove him out of doors. As he walked through the fields, he was thinking of Rana and Claire. When his mother said goodbye to him on Friday two weeks ago, she had been crying. "You go further and further away. I hardly ever see you, I feel I'm chained to the spot here. I wish I could go with you, cook for you, take ten novels with me and tell Elias I won't be back until I've read them all. And then I'd read more slowly than a short-sighted turtle."

But Farid didn't want her here. It was dangerous. Only two weeks ago, a cannon ball had hit a bus during a Syrian army manoeuvre. Luckily the bus was empty, and its driver had come off with no worse than a fright.

Around seven o'clock Farid entered the schoolhouse. Husni was just rolling up his thin mattress and putting it away in a cupboard. He looked like a ghost in his washed-out pyjamas.

Farid went into the Grade 8 classroom. He was to give the first two lessons here, and he liked to be first so that he could welcome the children himself.

Lessons for all the grades began with extraordinary punctuality that morning. Hardly anyone was absent. But just after eight-thirty, MIG 23 jet fighters thundered over the school. Soon after that the janitor looked in at the door and shouted, "War's broken out!" Farid froze. For weeks before both sides, Arabs and Israelis alike, had been clamouring for war, and now it had come. All the same, for a moment he felt almost surprised, as if no one had believed that this war could really begin.

Husni and two teachers standing close to him were praying in the yard, looking up at the sky. Later, they said they had been shouting the *kursi* verse from the Koran after the jet fighters so that God would protect the planes.

In less than an hour the children had left. The radio in the principal's office was broadcasting songs, communiqués, and pro-war speeches. It was clear that the region would soon be declared a restricted military area, so Husni recommended all the teachers to go home at once themselves.

Salman gathered Fadi, Adib, and Farid around him. "Let's go a little way together," he whispered. Farid felt that this boded no good. His heart was thudding wildly. Almost two years ago he had joined the Radicals group, gone to training camps run by the Palestinians in the summer vacation, even fought in a nocturnal operation against Israeli positions in the summer of 1966. Salman was head of the Radical teachers in Shaga, and he was a tough character.

"We must go to our bases along the border. Our liberated territories and the farmers will be delivered up helpless to the Israelis there," he said quietly but firmly.

"Of course. Let's go," replied Fadi. "Now." He seemed amused to realize that he had just involuntarily quoted the name of their organization's journal.

"Our comrades think the situation is very critical. If a Syrian government shows its famous cowardice once more, all we can rely on is a popular uprising, and we must stand shoulder to shoulder with the peasants. After that no one in Damascus will be able to govern without us. But the peasants are unprepared, and our men and women don't get more than four hours' sleep a day. There are far too few of us."

Farid had never before heard a more comprehensive and credible analysis of a situation delivered within five minutes.

"Then we must do it, come what may. The peasants deserved our support against the Israelis," said Adib, but his voice and his hesitant manner reflected his inner turmoil.

"I think it's a bad idea. I'm not going along with it," said Farid, feeling as forlorn as if he were falling into a deep hole. "I'm not questioning your courage and bravery, but I'm afraid. I'm just plain afraid, and not ashamed of it, because my doubts are based on the superior forces of the enemy. Haven't we spent hours discussing what a guerrilla ought to do in his moment of weakness? Who says we have to die for a state that's repellent to us?"

"We'll die for our principles and the word we gave the peasants," said Salman brusquely.

Farid wanted to reply that the peasants would probably have a better chance of survival if they refrained from joining such a hopelessly ill-armed resistance group, but he dared not.

"You know that cowards risk expulsion, comrade, fond as we are of you," said Salman, trying to prevent him from backing out. Farid felt deeply injured. No one had ever accused him of cowardice before.

"Then expel me. I'll have to live with it." And he left without a word of goodbye.

The principal and the other teachers had all gone some time ago. He waited outside the school for the next bus, and saw his three friends walking away southward. Adib turned briefly once and waved. Farid waved back, biting his lip, for now he must admit to cowardice.

An hour later he was in the bus on the way to Daraa. Tanks and trucks were rolling towards them on the other side of the road, and the sky was full of Syrian fighter bombers and helicopters. The bus driver turned up the radio so loud that Farid's ears hurt. It wasn't only in the bus that voices were droning from transistor radios, it was the same at the central station in Daraa, where after a short wait he boarded a shared taxi going to Damascus. War bulletins and singers bawling out bellicose verses quickly cobbled together were coming from all the stores, cafés, and houses. They spoke of blood and the Fatherland, and above all the certainty of victory over "the bandits' mini-state", meaning Israel. On the Egyptian "Voice of the Arabs" station, the shrill-voiced Egyptian broadcaster Ahmad Said was congratulating himself and the nation warmly on their chance to witness this historic moment, "when the Arabs will throw the Israelis into the sea."

Around five in the afternoon, Farid left the taxi at the junction with Saitun Alley. When he opened the front door Claire leaped up from her chair by the fountain. "Our Lady has heard my prayer!" she cried, hurrying to embrace her only child. Elias Mushtak smiled; even he could no longer conceal his relief behind the mask of indifference. "Your mother has been worried sick about you," he said in a voice that shook.

"A hundred and fifty million Arabs against three million Israelis, that's not really fair," remarked Claire over coffee.

Elias grinned. "Subtract a hundred and forty-nine million who are glued to the radio, and half of the remaining million Arabs aren't fit for service."

"And another thing," Farid put in, "the Israelis know what they're fighting for and what they're defending. Do the Arabs?"

After coffee, Elias went to the bedroom, and soon Claire and Farid heard the calm voice of a newsreader and knew that he was listening to his favourite BBC London station.

The telephone rang. "That will be Rana," said Claire.

❧

The club was like NATO headquarters that evening. A large map was pinned to the wall in the table tennis room, with strong lights from standard lamps turned on it. Josef stood in front of the map with a long, thin, bamboo cane, with men in densely packed rows facing him. They were following news of the battles as it came over the radio, picking out the places mentioned with the help of the pointing bamboo cane in the hands of an expert on geography. When Farid appeared in the doorway, Josef broke off his presentation of the front line, leaned the cane against the wall, and hurried towards his friend.

"I've been terrified you'd be caught there on the front," he said, hugging him warmly. Matta had appeared behind Josef. "Brother," he said, kissing his eyes.

"Someone with sense at last in this bunch of lunatics," said Gibran, who was sitting some way off, as if physically emphasizing his distance from the assembled company.

"He's had a bad day," whispered Josef.

"Where's Nadia?" asked Farid, looking around. There were only four women from their street there, among about forty men.

"With her parents," Josef replied. Farid shook hands with everyone, took Gibran's arm, and sat down with him and the others.

"Strike, brother, strike! Oh, Arab brothers from the Gulf to the Atlantic, strike now!" roared Ahmad Said hoarsely from the radio placed below the map.

Gibran began to laugh. "That bastard! How does he expect an oil sheikh or a poor Moroccan to strike? And strike where exactly?"

"Quiet!" Josef shouted at him. "This is no time for jokes!"

"... your hour has come, brother! Hear the Israeli fighters shot down from the sky like flies by our modern Egyptian anti-aircraft defence ... I'm just getting news of the first train full of Israeli

687

prisoners coming towards Cairo. The prisoners are glad to have it all over and done with," Ahmad Said continued.

Gibran looked at the windows of the nearby houses. Everyone was sitting by the radio this summer evening, rejoicing at the news of that first trainload of Israeli prisoners.

"I can't stand this," said Gibran, and he rose and went out. But after a short walk down the street he turned, came back, sat down in a distant corner, looking concerned, and demonstratively put his hands over his ears. Taufik led him into the café and gave him a tea. "I'm surrounded by idiots," Gibran whispered. "There's no helping them."

Josef was expecting the defeat of the Israeli air force at around ten in the evening. The Israelis had over four hundred fighter planes, it couldn't be much longer than that. All of a sudden joiners became anti-aircraft experts and tilers were rocket specialists. Names like Rommel, Montgomery, and Saladin flew around the room like table tennis balls in any lull between the reports of more victories coming over the radio.

"The news will come any moment now," said Josef.

"What news?" asked Farid.

"News of the liberation of Tel Aviv. The Palestinian flag will be flying over the city."

Gibran stepped out of the café, and laughed and laughed. They all knew he was crazy, but they still couldn't make out what had amused him so mightily. The old sailor pointed alternately to two women hanging up white sheets with clothes pegs on the rooftops of their houses. Still no one understood what was so funny about it. But when more women appeared on the roofs of another four houses, also pegging sheets to their washing lines, Josef turned thoughtful.

"Why are they all doing their laundry like that in the middle of the night? Let's hear BBC London," he said, and there was uncertainty in his voice.

A heavy silence fell over the place.

233. Women's Views

Rana couldn't bear to listen to the radio any more. As if everyone had gone crazy, they were all singing for the war. She didn't know whether the planes thundering low over the city were Israeli or Syrian jet fighters, but she felt almost dead with fear. Her neighbour Saliha asked if she would like to come over. Saliha's house, unlike her own, had a cellar that would do duty as an air raid shelter, and her husband suspected that the Israelis would leave Damascus in rubble and ashes. Rana took nothing with her, she just hurried over. The cellar was full of people. Saliha's husband was sitting in his wheelchair, telling the assembled pale-faced neighbouring women about his own wartime experiences. He had once been a military officer, but a splinter from a hand grenade had caught him in the back during an exercise. Since then he had been paralysed, and a thorn in the flesh of Saliha, who prayed every evening before she went to sleep that the Prophet Muhammad would soon take her husband to him, so that she could have a few years of peaceful life. "But the Prophet is a man of good taste, why would he want that bore's company?" she had once said to Rana.

Another woman, whose husband was also an officer, was begging God to save him. Even if he came home without arms and legs, she'd a hundred times rather that than be left a widow. Saliha looked at Rana and rolled her eyes.

"You said it, dear neighbour, you said it," remarked Saliha's husband, Captain Mahmud al Samawi (retired), encouraging the desperate woman. Rana drank a glass of fragrant tea, and felt safer under the solid vaulted roof of the cellar. You could hardly hear the airplanes here. Mahmud was sure the Arabs would win. "It's just a case of a couple of days, and then the Arab colossus will be washing his feet in the sea off Tel Aviv."

The retired captain's voice drowned out the radio in the corner. As every news item came through he felt further confirmed in his beliefs, and lectured the women. Sometimes he corrected the newsreader.

The howl of sirens made its way down into the cellar. "There, hear that? Now the anti-aircraft defence is answering back," he cried.

Drops of his saliva landed on the face of the woman next to him. Disgusted, she wiped her cheek. "We're already in the firing line," she finally remarked.

"No, no. Those are ground-to-air rockets and high velocity four-bore guns sifting their way through the aircraft, ratatatam … ratatatam …" explained the captain, spraying the woman again with each "ratatatam", until she moved elsewhere.

"Are you worried?" asked Saliha quietly.

"Yes," said Rana. She was thinking of Farid. She had called his mother three times. Claire had been very nice to her, but was in dreadful anxiety herself. Her boy still hadn't phoned, she had said despairingly last time.

"I know, if my husband went away I'm sure I'd worry too, but then he never does," said Saliha, who always had a feeling that Rana and Rami were not happy together.

Through the cellar window, they saw people hurrying by outside. Jubilant shouting was heard. If they had caught the gist of it properly, a hit had just been scored on an Israeli fighter. A nearby explosion shattered the building. Rana was grateful for Saliha for letting her sit here among the other women instead of having to stay in her house alone. Her mother had called that afternoon, asking if she would like to go to her brother Jack's place. Her parents had already gone there, after swiftly hanging up white sheets on their rooftop, as the Israeli radio station was advising the Damascenes to do. Of course no one in the capital would admit it, but it was a remarkable fact that hundreds of thousands of people thought of nothing but whiter than white laundry in these days of the war. Her parents were going to stay with Jack "until things clear up," as her mother always put it when she was at a loss. Rana's brother had made a lot of money with shady import deals, and at the age of twenty-five, three months before the war, he had bought a villa in a village near Damascus. Rana never visited him.

An hour later Saliha exchanged glances with Rana. "We're going to fetch bread and cheese and a few olives. We'll be right back," she called out. Rana rose to go with her just as a jet fighter was breaking the sound barrier above the buildings.

What would life be worth without Farid? Rana asked herself hopelessly as they went upstairs. It was almost two in the afternoon by now. "May I make a quick phone call?"

"Of course, the phone's in the drawing room. I'll be in the kitchen having a cigarette."

Farid still hadn't come home. Her fear grew. She felt ridiculous as she hung up. It was childish to try to reassure Claire by saying nothing could happen to Farid because they both loved him.

Saliha carried the large tray with sheep's milk cheese, olives, preserved eggplant, tomatoes, and curd cheese, Rana the smaller one with the teapot and tea glasses rinsed with hot water. The women were delighted. Saliha's husband ate nothing, just drank tea.

Time crawled by, and the retired captain became more and more intolerable. He kept talking about his own heroic deeds. Rana noticed that Saliha seized every opportunity to go up into the house and smoke a cigarette. Around six in the evening they both went up again to prepare supper. Rana breathed a sigh of relief, for she couldn't rest down in the cellar. She asked Saliha if she could phone again, and shed tears when she heard Farid's voice at last.

She ran happily into the kitchen.

"Everything all right?"

"Everything all right," she said. And while the homely lentil dish mujadara was cooking, Saliha took her up to the second floor to show her pictures of her childhood. Rana pretended to be interested, but her thoughts were far away. Gradually darkness fell over Damascus. The sky was quiet now. From where they stood they could see into a nightclub with its windows open because of the heat. An Oriental dancer was moving between the tables, all of them occupied. Early as it was in the evening, the men seemed to be drunk already.

"That's Rihane. My husband sits here for nights on end. That window is his television," said Saliha.

"How does he get up to this floor?"

"He had a special elevator from France built in. That way he can follow me right up to the third floor."

Rihane was still looking across at Saliha's house, as if she missed her audience there. She didn't seem to be moving her feet but hovering between the tables, and she elegantly avoided the many hands trying to grab parts of her body.

"Disgusting, isn't it?" said Rana on the way to the kitchen.

234. Sobering Up

The Arab media kept the lie going for another whole day before it collapsed like a house of cards. The defeat had been devastating. Within six hours, Israel had destroyed all the airfields and air forces of Egypt, Syria, and Jordan without meeting any resistance worth the name.

Ahmad Said had fallen silent. On the radio they began preparing the population to face the worst disgrace in its history. Josef had his most severe crisis yet. His beloved Satlan turned out to be a fool, the man mainly responsible for this defeat. Josef didn't want to see anyone. Even Farid couldn't get through to him. Nadia said on the phone he needed peace and quiet.

On the third day Rana called Farid. Surprisingly, Rami had come home. He was hiding away in the bedroom, crying like a little boy who has lost his toys.

જ

All the members of the government had fled from Damascus. They were hiding in Aleppo, or according to many news reports even in Baghdad. On the third day of the war, when the first Israelis reached the Suez Canal, the Egyptian government had asked for a ceasefire. Thereupon the Israelis attacked Syria and Jordan. Within two days they took the West Bank and the Golan Heights. They were less than a kilometre from the village square and the school in Shaga. Not a single high-ranking Syrian army officer was to be seen anywhere along the whole front.

White bedlinen fluttered on all the rooftops of Damascus. But the Israelis didn't arrive. They had conquered three times the area of their own country, and long-term occupation of great cities like Cairo and

Damascus could have devastating consequences, so they refrained. Farid walked the streets, observing the people of the city. They were depressed and ashamed. He couldn't make up his mind where to go, he drank a coffee here, a tea there, and listened to conversations. Then he phoned his cousin Laila, who was delighted to hear that he wanted to come and see her.

SO

Later, he wandered with Laila through the houses of the quarter where the rich lived. She had the keys of her customers who had fled from Damascus and asked her to water their flowers. None of them had forgotten to leave white sheets fluttering from their balconies or rooftops, as the Israeli radio station had advised.

"I'm their night watchman and housekeeper at the moment, but normally they're my customers."

Those were wonderful hours with Laila. Her husband Simon was recording in Athens, and would be there all June. After doing her rounds, Laila suggested spending the night in a rich architect's magnificent villa. They bathed together, slipped into white towelling robes, made themselves an excellent supper, drank a bottle of champagne, and sat in the drawing room like a couple of housebreakers.

She comforted him when he told her about his cowardice in not taking up arms with the Radicals. Laila said his decision was very sensible. "And good sense," she added, "is the sister of cowardice." Sensible people were out of place at the front in wartime. "I despise heroes who paralyse others by speaking for them and saying they'll accept death, instead of cooperating with them to make death impossible."

Farid breathed freely again for the first time in days.

"Why should you die when a whole army that we've been feeding since Independence runs away in time of need? How would you win a victory with officers who aren't even allowed to choose the woman they'll love and marry? Their clans marry them off instead. Our officers have never practised conquering or liberating a village, they've just learned to strike out at their own people, and everyone knows how easy that is. And now we discover that the government in Egypt

knew about the planned attack ahead of time, through Russian espionage, even knew just when it would come. But did Satlan negotiate?
Not he, he relied on what his field marshal Abdulhakim Kahban said."

"Poor Josef." The words escaped Farid as Laila was lighting a
hashish cigarette.

"Would you like one of these, former comrade?" she asked with a
seductive smile.

Farid didn't answer, but took the cigarette and drew deeply on it
twice.

235. Laila's Night

Laila fetched a second bottle, and they put out the many wall and
ceiling lights. It wasn't quite dark, all the same. A little light fell
through the open doorway into the drawing room, where she and
Farid were sitting on an enormous couch, nibbling salted pistachios
and drinking chilled champagne.

"My wages as housekeeper," she said cheerfully, leaning against
him. She stroked his head and clinked glasses. As usual, he was fascinated by her and wanted to kiss her forehead, but his lips suddenly
fixed on her mouth.

Her saliva tasted sweet. She held Farid very close. Her fragrance
intoxicated him, and he kissed her again. Laila embraced him and
slid underneath him. Their robes fell to the floor of their own accord.
His hands sought something to hold and found the soft skin of her
thighs.

When he was finally lying beside her on the carpet, exhausted, he
wasn't sure why he had suddenly wanted so much to make love to
Laila. It was a new, strange sense of closeness that he didn't know even
with Rana.

"You sang as beautifully as a dolphin when you came," he said,
looking at the ceiling.

"I love dolphins," she replied, kissing him tenderly.

"Do you regret this?"

"No, comrade. There are many things that Moon Women regret, but never love. Particularly not love with the lost halves of themselves."

Laila uttered a peal of clear laughter, tickled him, and when he was about to get up and sit on the couch again she flung herself on him and forced his shoulders back on the carpet with all her might. They scuffled like two children. He sensed her excitement from her goosebumps. His lips wandered like a butterfly thirsty for dew, and closed around one nipple. Laila quivered and uttered an ecstatic cry.

Later they lay still. His head was resting on Laila's belly, he breathed in her sweat. A sense of happiness came over him, but at the same time he felt profoundly sad. Then he suddenly saw the half-moon. It lay there blue before him, as if it had just risen, embedded in the soft skin beneath Laila's left breast. Farid sat up and kissed the place.

"Hello, moon," he whispered.

"Do you know when you first sucked at my breast?" she asked, crossing her arms behind her head.

He thought the question was a joke. "Sixty-five minutes and thirty seconds ago," he said, laughing.

"Wrong. The first time was twenty-six years ago." Farid looked at her disbelievingly. "You were one year old when your mother brought you to Beirut. My mother had invited her to stay with us and convalesce by the sea. I think Claire was going through a crisis at the time and urgently needed rest."

"Yes, she's told me about it. Elias had a mistress. Some parliamentarian's stupid wife."

"Well, however it was, you two were staying with us, and because I'd loved you from the first, and you'd keep quiet for me, they left you with me when they went out of the house. I was seven, and a very independent child. One day I was sitting on the balcony of my room with you. You were on my lap, looking at you with your big eyes. I was madly in love with you. It sounds crazy, but that's how it was. I told you stories for hours, and I was convinced you understood everything. Suddenly you started sucking my forefinger, and as if I were playing with dolls I said: there, there, baby, you can have some milk. I was wearing a summer dress that unbuttoned down the front. And suddenly you had my breast in your mouth and you were sucking at it like a hungry puppy, and I was in the seventh heaven. My breasts have been very sensitive ever since that day."

236. Drinking the Rainbow

Rami never took any leave. He was married not so much to Rana as to the army logistics corps. He was in charge of transportation, purchases, and new ways to make the army more effective and faster. The defeat by Israel, he claimed, was mainly because the enemy had organized everything very rationally and had moved extremely fast.

He had been out and about all the time since the end of the war. Sometimes he didn't come home for weeks. Rana was allowed to know only how long he would be away, never where he was going and why. Now and then he let slip that he had been on the border, or in East Berlin, Prague, or Moscow. But she wasn't much interested in what he was planning, buying, or negotiating.

That summer of 1967 was unbearably hot. Rana slept badly and kept waking from nightmares in which Farid, his face bleeding, was crying out for help. She prayed for him. Her husband, if he was there, slept on beside her undisturbed.

At the end of August she had her fourth abortion. She knew the midwife by now. Rana did not want to bear Rami a child; she'd sooner die. The abortions weren't as bad as she had feared, and every time she was able to leave her bed a week later.

She felt constantly depressed. Sadness was her prison. Not that anything much had happened, far from it. Nothing at all had happened, except that she had lost seven or eight years of her life. She looked at her goldfish in its round bowl, and whispered, "Hello, sister."

When she sought comfort in the novels she had once loved so much, the lines blurred. She asked herself whether the life she lived now was worth living. Dunia said she ought to eat more yoghurt and take valerian to relax her. As if she needed to feel even wearier than she did already.

She kept wondering what way out there still was for her. Sometimes her thoughts were like a carousel, and she couldn't get off.

"You ought to use a depilatory," said Rami when he stroked her legs. She laughed to herself. Those aren't hairs, those were my prickles he felt. The desert spread all around her, and the silence was suffocating. Dunia had once been like an oasis, but now that friendship was fading, and the closer Dunia came to her the more it dissolved. Like a mirage.

☙

Over the years, Rana had made the flat roof around her small studio into a flowering oasis. One morning early in September she heard someone calling out for water in her sleep. She woke up, and knew at once that her plants were thirsty.

She ran barefoot upstairs in her thin nightdress. The September sky was as clear as in summer, radiant with the most beautiful Damascene blue. The leaves and thin stems of the plants were drooping.

"Oh, God," whispered Rana. She picked up the hose, turned the tap on, and began sprinkling the large containers. She heard the roots rousing themselves beneath the dry soil and whispering thanks. The plants seemed to raise their leaves and stems, gradually reaching towards the sky.

"That's better," she told them encouragingly. They had almost all been presents from friends and relations. She thought she could hear a gurgle of laughter.

Suddenly she lost herself in thought. "Back then my decision to live as a cactus just came to me, but being a cactus isn't easy," she said quietly, remember how she had been naïve enough to think that she had a right to love and happiness. A right to love, perhaps, but happiness? She smiled. "I even began furnishing a house in my head for Farid and me. I knew all about it, even the colour of the curtains," she went on out loud, watering the oleander. She shook her head. "So stupid, planning a life that we'll never have, not a second of it. A virus, a car, a war, can end everything. And all the while we dream of our future, time is quietly running away like sand through our fingers.

The little heap of it left on the palm of the hand is only the memory of life."

Now she heard the leaves of the little orange tree that Dunia had given her crying out for a shower. She let a curving jet of water fall on the tree and its few little fruits.

"Years ago, before she was entirely drained away inside, Dunia told me she had to be ready for her husband at any time, like his shoehorn, with the difference that he didn't take his shoehorn to bed with him. But that's just what he does with her, every evening. He wanted her to be always available to him, and after a year she was worn out. Today Dunia acts as if someone else had said that, not herself ..."

She listened to the flowers.

"Oh, you want some too? I thought you were a sister of the desert," she said, turning the jet of water on the fanned leaves of the palm tree that her cousin Marie had brought her from Iraq. Marie was married to a rich businessman who moved between Baghdad and Damascus. She would have liked to stay in Damascus, but she couldn't, and since then she had never felt at home anywhere. Her three children suffered from it, but she acted the part of a happy wife.

The palm made a rustling sound of pleasure.

"I'm related to you, not Marie. I bear no fruit either," Rana went on. "I don't want to exert myself to pretend I'm happily married. Marie has denied all her dreams and plans, ideas and feelings for fear of her husband. She fills her inner void with submissive obedience. So now she's not afraid of him any more, quite the opposite, she enjoys her submissiveness on the evenings when he wants to take her to bed, because that's the only place where he's kind to her. She told me so herself. And then Marie is avenged on that despot. She makes him kiss her feet and her backside, she enjoys it when he goes on his knees and begs. At such moments she imagines that she's the one who gives orders."

Rana watered all the flowers and little trees, and finally sat on a stool and decided to make a rainbow with the jet of water and the sunlight.

"Do you want to drink the rainbow?" she asked, and chuckled at her own idea. She saw the plants dancing happily by way of answer in the light September breeze. After several attempts she managed to catch the light just as she was watering the little olive tree that her Aunt Soraya had brought her back from Jerusalem.

"When you've become as empty as Aunt Soraya," she said, "when you have nothing more inside you to offer, you have to look after the outer husk. What else is there to do?"

"Nothing," she heard her own answer. "Just look at Aunt Soraya," she went on, examining a red rose. "She plucks some of her hair, colours the rest, wears seductive lingerie like a whore under the plain clothes her jealous husband insists on." Aunt Soraya had married a pilot who travelled the world, getting more stupid all the time. He had been very outgoing and liberal as a young man, but now – although he was a Christian – he acted like a Muslim Brother.

"Roses love the rainbow," said Rana, as she reached the large terracotta pot where a bushy Damascus rose grew. Her school friend Nadjla had given it to her two years ago. As the only girl among seven brothers, Nadjla had been lost in her family. No one took any notice of her, and at seventeen she was married off to her cousin. After that she had to serve his old parents and four brothers, who were all bachelors. She was docile, and followed her husband like a hound following its master. Nadjla read his wishes in his eyes and acted as if she had made the suggestion herself. Her husband rewarded her for it. "Good dog, that's right, good dog," whispered Rana, laughing.

She sprayed a sparrow that was watching curiously from the fence around the roof. It quickly flew away.

"And then there's my mother. Only now," she called after the sparrow, "does she discover that my father doesn't love her. And he's right. Who loves a shiny pot that clatters only because it's empty? Sometimes I don't even feel like an empty pot. I'm my husband's waste bin."

She giggled, and tried to make the rainbow again. After several attempts, it arched above the jasmine at the edge of the roof garden. She didn't notice the water raining down on the street below.

"But at least I know that I don't love my husband. Dunia irritates me with her show of affection for hers. She said she sacrifices herself for him. And when I ask her what exactly she's sacrificing she sounds vague, the only clear thing is that she's a mixture of good housewife and cheap whore."

She shook her head, remembering their quarrel. It had been one Sunday four or five weeks ago. "So let's not call it love or affection, exploitation is more like it," Rana had said. Dunia had been furious and shouted at her, "You're letting your lover's left-wing views send you crazy. Those and all your books about women who hate their husbands."

Rana was as ungrateful and vindictive as a camel, said Dunia. Yes, so Rami had taken her by force, but he was a nice man all the same, an attractive man who lavished presents on her and even bore her rejection of him patiently. Any other woman would be happy to live with him. But Rana was living for an illusion – her love for an anarchist with a death-wish.

Angry words had been spoken that Sunday afternoon. She had retorted that Dunia didn't even look in the mirror any more, so as not to see what six or seven years had made of her: a fat, frustrated matron. Dunia shouted back that she'd rather be a matron than deranged, and Rana would soon end up in the al-Asfuriye mental hospital. She really said it: al-Asfuriye.

Dunia gave up arguing. She was a thinking woman now, she said, and she was free. You had to train men like wild animals. Then, as time went on, they learned to come home and be faithful.

Remembering this made Rana laugh. "A fine picture of wretchedness Dunia drew me. That's not love, that's animal-taming. When love is the real thing it asks no sacrifice and it doesn't exploit you." She was sure she wouldn't for a moment sacrifice herself for Farid because she loved him. Her heart was a cactus. She was patient, she kept quiet. But she didn't confuse that with love, and she would leave Rami as soon as it was possible for Farid to live with her.

However, a cactus has a hard life. A week before her quarrel with Dunia she felt like exploding. Rami came home unexpectedly with two high-ranking officers, woke her and asked her to serve them some small nibbles. All three of them were drunk and noisy. She gave Rami everything she could find in the kitchen, putting it on two trays, and went back to bed. But she couldn't sleep.

It was late when he came to her, stinking of cigars and liquor. And when she refused to sleep with him he hit her. Rami raped her, and she cried. As he forced his way inside her he said he was ashamed of her. His colleagues' wives would make up their faces and entertain guests at any time, even late at night. She should be glad he was a good Christian, because a Muslim would have thrown a woman like her out long ago and married a second wife. After a while he stopped shouting and hitting her, and fell into a deep sleep.

Next day her family visited, and Rami repeated all his accusations. He told them about his superior officers' visit last night, called it "tedious but a duty", and condemned Rana's behaviour. He didn't mention that he had hit her repeatedly. Her mother and brother thought he was quite right. Her father, distressed, said nothing, but his look spoke volumes.

Rana wondered what chance she had with a husband like that. There was only one solution: to play dead. It's difficult only at first. Then you learn to go far away in your mind, to some high and distant place, and from there you watch what your husband is doing in bed with a corpse and you feel nothing, no disgust, no anger, nothing.

With time she had learned not to feel anything in certain parts of her body. She felt neither pain nor pleasure in her lips, her breasts, her earlobes. She was like the Indian fakir she had seen on a newsreel in the cinema. He had walked, smiling, over broken glass and red-hot coals. But when Farid touched her she was all aflame.

✺

Rana didn't notice how time was passing. Suddenly the rainbow was gone, and her husband, in his uniform, was there on the roof in front of her. Repelled, he cast a glance at her, turned, and went back into the apartment.

Quarter of an hour later her family were all there. Her brother Jack was looking at her angrily. Her mother was crying, and her father spent a long time on the telephone.

Rana was shivering with cold in her wet nightdress.

237. The Mental Hospital

When she woke up again she was in a white bed. The walls and the ceiling were white too. She heard screams like the cries of a frightened animal, and there was a strong smell of camphor. Her back hurt, her tongue was dry. She was freezing. Her head felt heavy as lead, but gradually she managed to turn it to one side. There was another woman in the bare room with her, fastened down to her bed with three straps. She looked as thin and her skin as greyish brown and wrinkled as if she were the naked mummy Rana had once seen in the Egyptian Museum. The woman lay still. Rana thought she must be dead, and a strange anxiety took hold of her. Where was she? Why was she lying in this store-room with a dead woman? Did they think she was dead too? When the woman turned her head aside, Rana breathed a sigh of relief. The woman's thin, weathered face expressed suffering, like someone in a painting of the tormented souls lining Christ's path.

"They're trying to poison me," said the woman hoarsely. "They've injected poison into me so that I'll die slowly and they can inherit my house." The woman breathed in with a whistling sound and looked at the ceiling. "Who brought you here? Are they trying to poison you too?" Rana shook her head. She wanted to say she didn't know, but she was sure no one was trying to poison her.

Looking down at her body, Rana saw that she herself was not strapped down. She sat up, but the chill in the room threw her back on the white sheet.

She thought of the rainbow, and was surprised to find that she wasn't wet any more, nor was she wearing her own clothes, only this white garment.

"You have to trick them," whispered the woman. "If you want to survive here you mustn't be honest with anyone. Be absent, play dead," she added, barely audibly.

How had she come here? Rana wondered. Her parents had been holding on to her. Then what? Where had her husband been? What had he done?

"Fly through the air like me, sail through the storms, see beaches and palaces, play with children and sleep with handsome men. I go walking through Damascus, I eat ices in the Suk al Hamidiye, while that fool of a doctor asks my dead body questions here in the madhouse, stuffs it with bitter pills, listens to it, measures it, takes photographs. But since I'm not answering his questions, no, I'm talking to the woman at my table in the ice cream parlour instead, he doesn't understand me, he thinks I'm crazy. I let him think so. Here in al-Asfuriye, the House of Sparrows, I'm safe from poisoning until my son comes from America to take me away."

The woman was talking incoherently, and Rana cautiously returned to the point in time that was becoming clearer in her memory now. Her husband had gone to the door, and at that moment she realized that he had called a doctor. What for? She felt well. Rather sad, yes, but why would she need a doctor?

She had tried to get up from the couch and follow her husband to the door to tell him he could send the doctor away, she was perfectly all right again. Then her mother had taken her by the right arm, snapping at her father, who was hesitating, telling him not to stand around going to sleep on his feet but to help her. Rana had tried to tear herself free.

"Leave me alone and go home," she had begged her parents, but they didn't seem to understand what she was saying. They pushed her down on the couch again with iron force. She had screamed with fear because she thought they had gone out of their minds. Then she felt the needle go in.

Rana spent two weeks in the psychiatric hospital. Then, at her family's wish, Dr. Huss the deputy medical director discharged her. Rana went home. She seemed to be better. On her first day back, she threw her pills in the waste bin.

238. Sabri and Rachel

"A woman once loved a man with a large wart on his nose," said Gibran. "She thought him the most handsome man in the world.

Years later, however, she noticed the wart one morning. 'How long have you had that wart on your nose?' she asked. 'Ever since you stopped loving me,' said the man sadly."

Gibran slurped his tea noisily and nodded, as if he were thinking of Karime.

"Come along, old friend," said Michel the joiner, rousing him from his thoughts. "Can't you tell us a love story with a happy ending for a change?"

Gibran laughed. "Yes, indeed." And he drank some more tea before he began his story. "Sabri was a handsome young man, brave and rather dashing. He was younger than me, but very tall and strong, so people took him for my elder brother. When I was out and about with him, no one dared to insult me – I'd always been small and emaciated.

"Well, one day Sabri fell in love with Rachel, a Jewish girl from nearby Jews' Alley. It was all a little crazy. Sabri and Rachel were the talk of the Christian and Jewish quarters alike. The brothers of both lovers beat them, but they always found their way back together.

"Only Sabri's parents were happy about Rachel, because in marrying her their son would be converting a Jew. His father was on the committee of the Catholic Church. He thought of Jews as poor blind folk who couldn't see that the Son of God had come long ago. So he encouraged Sabri to open Rachel's eyes.

"However, all that came to a sudden end when the state of Israel was proclaimed two months later. The Jews of Damascus were happy, but they couldn't say so openly. People eyed them with suspicion wherever they went. Sabri's father was the first to take fright. He was a minor civil servant in the Interior Ministry, where he had done well under the French and stayed on after Independence, simply changing the flag on the wall.

'You're crazy,' his father angrily told him. 'What will people say if my son marries an Israeli girl?' But he had met his match in Sabri, who was hard as granite.

'They'll say Sabri has married a Syrian Jew,' the young man replied. Sabri's father knew how obstinate his taciturn son could be.

"From then on the whole family, as if by mutual consent, set about running Rachel down. She had bad teeth, they said, her legs were much too short, and her nose was too long. Furthermore, she was always breaking into unseemly laughter, and she wouldn't inherit anything.

"Sabri walked out on his family in the middle of their tirades and went to see his Rachel, after his daily fight with one of her many brothers, who all wanted to forbid him even to walk past their house.

"One day Sabri disappeared for two whole weeks. When he came back it was arm in arm with Rachel. He had no idea that while he was marrying her in a small town in the north, his family's malicious tongues had turned his wife into an Israeli spy who, apparently, had abducted the naïve Sabri.

"Sabri's family now disowned him as a traitor. His father announced it officially, so that his departmental head would be truly convinced of his employee's patriotism. Rachel's family wore mourning. Her father disowned and disinherited his daughter.

"Sabri wasn't bothered what they thought in either the Jewish or the Christian quarter. I often visited him in Saliye. He and Rachel loved each other, and were happy to be left in peace in the New Town, far from Damascus, where they lived anonymously.

"But they didn't live there long. When the first military confrontation between Israel and Syria came, someone or other accused the couple of using a device to show the Israeli bombers where to drop their bombs.

"This was nonsense, but Sabri and Rachel were interrogated and tortured, and no one would protect them, neither bishop nor rabbi, let alone their own families.

"It was a week in hell, and when they came out again, they were changed. Their laughter had died.

"Before a month was up the two of them had disappeared. It's almost twenty years ago now. The rumours about them were vicious and unfounded. Six months later I had a letter in which they told me they were living happily in New York. Sabri went on writing for years. His children, he told me, were Jews by Jewish law, Christian Arabs by Arab law, and US citizens by American law. That was his contribution to world peace.

"Sabri was always slightly crazy," Gibran concluded his story. Matta laughed. "Like me, like me," he cried.

Taufik, who had been standing in the doorway of the hall all this time, watching the faces of Gibran's audience in the table tennis room, whispered something to Gibran at the end of the evening. Late that night the seaman was seen staying on to help Taufik clear up. That same night, Gibran's rented room was raided by five men from the special units. "They wore camouflage gear, the whole works," one of his neighbours said, "as if they were off to liberate Palestine."

Gibran disappeared for ever, and only one man would smile mysteriously and look pleased about it. That was Taufik. A month later the club was closed down.

239. Despair

When the school re-opened in early October the village of Shaga had changed entirely. It was on the front line now, and there were more soldiers than farmers in it.

Of the three Radicals, only Adib had survived. However, he had spent two months wandering in the wilderness to avoid falling into the hands of Israelis, Jordanians, or Syrians. His expression had turned distrustful. He said little, and never mingled with his colleagues in the evenings again.

In school and in the village the talk was all of the heroic Radicals. Any village that had hoisted their flag had been taken by the Israeli army only after a long, bitter battle for every alley and every house. The number of women who died carrying arms was astonishingly high.

All the locals discussed it as much and as proudly as if they themselves had been among the banned Radicals. On the other hand, it was whispered that the surviving fighters from that group had been shot by the Jordanian or Syrian security forces, for they were more of a danger to those in power in both countries than the Israelis.

Farid was in despair, so upset that he could hardly sleep. There was no prospect of any imminent change. But he also lay awake at night because he no longer had the strength to teach. He wanted to run away with Rana at long last and begin a new life, but he didn't know how.

In the autumn of 1967, the Syrian government under General Taisan was morally finished. Captain Amran saw that this was the moment for a bloodless coup, and he carried one out with his brothers Shaftan and Badran and his two cousins. Not a shot was fired. The Syrians had long ago stopped mourning any ruler who was overthrown or greeting a new one with joy.

Farid watched the janitor taking down the pictures of President Taisan in all the classrooms, tearing up the photographs, and leaning the empty picture frames against the wall in his own little room.

"The kids will be glad they don't have to look at President Taisan's ugly mug any more. Let's hope the new man's better-looking," he said, grinning like all the Syrians, who by now had taken to indulging in a special kind of disrespect during the period between the fall of one ruler and the establishment of the next in power. They called it their interim freedom.

"Well, he won't look like Omar Sharif, that's for sure," replied Farid.

A week later the photographs of the new President arrived. He looked sombre.

"Those poor kids," said the janitor, and he began hanging up the pictures.

240. In Flight

Since Christmas, Farid had thought of nothing but his plan for himself and Rana to disappear. Only Claire was to know where they were hiding, no one else. The best thing would be to get away to France, study there, and then emigrate to Canada, a country that had already taken in many Christians from their part of the world. Getting Canadian citizenship was never a problem for academics. Daily violence and the rise of the fundamentalists were leading to a drastic reduction in the number of Christians in the Middle East.

Claire was all in favour of this plan, and promised Farid fifty thousand dollars that she had put aside for him. "I want you to get out of this political inferno and know something other than hatred and fighting," she said firmly.

Rana wept tears of joy. She herself had saved almost ten thousand dollars for their flight since her marriage.

From now on, Farid used every spare moment getting hold of documents that would allow him to study in France. Rana had phoned a girlfriend in Paris who was married to an influential surgeon and could get her a place at the university. After that she would automatically be granted a visa to enter the country.

Soon Farid had handed in his papers, and now he had only to face an interview at the French Embassy, where the cultural attaché would decide whether or not he could apply to Paris. But whatever happened he mustn't let anyone at the school in Shaga know of his plans. One report to the authorities would be enough to get him banned from travelling.

On Saturday 9 March he asked the principal for permission to go to Damascus, saying that he was having severe headaches. In a private conversation, he told Husni that he had a long history of epilepsy, although he had concealed it when he applied for teaching posts so as to be accepted because he loved teaching so much. However, he said, he always had problems in spring and autumn, when the weather changed, and he had to take strong drugs then under medical supervision. Farid had no pangs of conscience over pretending sickness. He knew that the principal had a substitute for him; Husni's best friend was a retired mathematician who would be happy to earn a few lira on the side.

Next Monday Farid got a medical certificate in Damascus saying he was unfit to work for a week. On Wednesday, punctually at ten in the morning, he was in the waiting room at the French Embassy, elegantly dressed, on Claire's advice. The cultural attaché was fascinated by his French, and when Farid explained that he had spent three years with the Jesuits the man laughed. "Then I can call you *mon frère*. I spent four years with the order too, though not in a boarding school. My father hated the Church itself, but he thought highly of the training and discipline in Jesuit schools."

"The very part of it that gets on their pupils' nerves," replied Farid frankly, and the attaché nodded. At the end of the interview he shook hands with the young Syrian in a friendly way. "I'll do all I can to see that you get a place to study in Paris," he said, and he sounded as if he meant it. "You ought to receive notice of permission within two weeks."

Elated by his success, Farid wanted to share his pleasure with someone. Josef was away with his pupils on a four-day school trip to Palmyra, so he called Laila and invited her to lunch.

"Let's meet at the Ali Baba in an hour's time," she said.

"Fine, so long as you'll let me pay. I have plenty of money and something happy to celebrate," he told her.

"Wonderful. I can do with celebrating something happy," replied Laila, sighing.

She entered the restaurant at the appointed time and smiled at Farid. She was more beautiful than ever, but sad. For months she had been at odds with her husband, who had come back from Athens last summer a changed man, but wouldn't talk about it.

Farid told her only that he would be leaving the service of the state at the end of the year. "The Mushtaks don't make good civil servants," said Laila. "My sister Barbara is sick of it too. She'd like to leave her job, but her husband won't hear of it."

Laila let her cousin's good mood infect her, and forgot her own troubles over the delicious meal, which lasted more than three hours.

As the bus home was approaching the stop near his street, Farid took a quick look down Saitun Alley, and then stayed sitting where he was. Three cars were always parked next to his parents' house; they had now been joined by two more. One was in the middle of the road, right opposite the entrance to the building. Only secret service men parked like that. And there was a Landrover at the turning into the street, although parking there was strictly forbidden. Now Farid saw two men in it. They were extremely poorly disguised.

He did not get out until the next stop, after the eastern gate, strolled inconspicuously back and looked at the cross-country vehicle again. Yes, no doubt about it: the secret service.

So he turned down Ananias Alley. His mind was in turmoil. What had happened? Only recently a small rising had easily been nipped in the bud, so Amran was firmly in the saddle. Then why more arrests, after that insignificant shoot-out in a barracks? Two officers, allegedly financed by Iraq to lead a coup against Amran, had been arrested in mid-February by the President's brother and his special units, and were annihilated along with their supporters.

Since his expulsion from the Radicals last summer, Farid had avoided all political activities. He wanted no more to do with any of it. Nationalists, communists, fundamentalists, Radicals, adherents of the Iraqi regime had all been arrested on a grand scale. Even Palestinians ended up in jail the moment they disregarded Amran's orders not to encourage any anti-Israel operations on Syrian soil. Some called the dictator a coward, but he didn't want anyone or anything endangering his power. So in those early years, he avoided any confrontation with Israel, and the Palestinians had to keep their heads down and stay quiet.

But why was the secret service on Farid's trail? Had old communist or Radical documents fallen into the hands of the police during one of their many raids, and had his name featured there? Or had someone informed on him? He was sure he hadn't committed any crime, but how was he to explain that to the men who were after him?

A thousand questions were racing through Farid's mind when he unexpectedly found himself standing at Matta's door. His friend had just been making tea.

"Brother, how pale you are! Come in. Faride and I will be happy to drink tea with you – come in!" Matta said in friendly tones.

"They want to arrest me again," said Farid, and he didn't know why his tears were falling.

"You can stay here, brother, and anyone who touches you had better watch out," replied Matta.

"No, that won't do me any good, or you and Faride either. They know that we're friends and come from the same village. But you could do me a favour. Can you go to our place on the quiet and see if my suspicions are correct? Here's a hundred lira, buy two sacks of potatoes and one of onions at a vegetable dealer, phone Claire and tell her you've bought what she wanted. Just to be on the safe side, so that she won't show any agitation while the secret service men are in the house. Our own Fiat is parked outside it, Dr. Rahbani's Ford, and the pharmacist Sadek's new Renault. Do you know him?"

"Yes, of course. His beautiful wife Hanan is a good customer of mine," said Matta proudly.

"Good. And right now there are two strange cars there too, not by chance, I'm sure. I'd like you to look at them carefully, but be sure not to say anything. They're not fools."

"Don't worry, brother," said Matta, and he turned to Faride. "And you look after my dear brother, little pigeon, and calm his fears."

She kissed him on the forehead. "Look after yourself, dear heart. I'm very proud of you," she told him.

Matta came back two hours later. The secret service men weren't in the house but sitting in their cars. They had searched him and tried to intimidate him with trick questions, but Matta had acted dumb. Finally he was allowed to take the potatoes and onions into the house, but not to speak to Claire. When he insisted that he wanted to be paid, and started shouting, the men allowed her to give him the money under their supervision.

Farid kissed him and Faride as he left, and went to Straight Street, where he took a taxi and gave the driver an address in the Midan quarter.

He was a hunted animal now. And the hunters after him were invisible; any civilian, including the taxi driver, could be one of them.

Why had everything gone wrong? Who was pursuing him?

"Hotel al-Nasim," said the driver, rousing him from his thoughts.

The hotel belonged to a distant cousin of Josef's. He was discreet. When he saw Farid he understood without any need for words, and made no difficulties.

Farid had ten such addresses stored in his memory. People who could be relied on, who hated dictatorship, and who weren't directly connected to him in any way. But he couldn't stay anywhere for long. His best camouflage was to keep moving. Only the time between one and five in the morning was peaceful, and he would lie down to sleep exhausted, desperate, and often hungry.

He fled through Damascus, a hunted man. The secret service had men checking all the ways out of the city. Farid soon forgot to think about his bad luck. He didn't think of Rana or Claire either, he thought of nothing at all, as if he had lost every idea except one: survival.

On the run, he came to know all the streets very well. Damascus, that beautiful, light, and spacious city had become an overpopulated village. Hundreds of thousands of peasants had fled to the metropolis. The men who had seized power were peasants like them, and that attracted people. Tenement buildings were going up everywhere, and the government turned not just one but two blind eyes to illegal construction work in the slums on the outskirts of the city.

Again and again Farid found friends who would quietly take him in, and in time he found that he could spot the secret service men sitting in cafés, pretending to read the paper. Reading the paper in a café is an art, and Farid could tell whether a man was doing it for pleasure or in the line of duty.

His money was beginning to run low, and after three days without food he called Laila from a café. It was a risk, of course, in spite of all his precautions. Who could tell whether informers didn't know everyone's secret signals by now?

She had told him a way to ask her for help in case of need, without saying a single give-away word: he was to let her phone ring three times, hang up, then let it ring five times, and finally three times again. That meant they were to meet at the Café Fredy near the Central Bank in an hour's time.

Laila appeared punctually at the appointed place, and inconspicuously approached his table. She was as pale as on the day of her father's death, and kissed Farid on the cheek.

"I've missed you," she said. "How are you?" Then she felt ashamed of herself for asking such a question.

"Wretched. I have to find some way out of this," he said. "I have three or four problems to solve at the same time. I must leave the country, and I want to get away to France with Rana as soon as possible. Claire has given me enough money for that." Farid hesitated. "You might be able to help me by reassuring her, bringing me my papers from the embassy, and getting a good forger to make me a passport. Josef knows a brilliant man. He's expensive but he does good work. When I have all those things I must get across the mountains to Beirut somehow. Once I'm over the border and I have my papers for the university, I can get a visa in the French Embassy there."

"That wouldn't be difficult to start with, since no one's after me. The only thing is that as soon as I set foot in your house I'll be kept under observation, though surely not for long. When they see it was just a family visit and I'm going home again like a good girl, not acting as a courier, they'll leave me alone again. But you'll have to be patient. I won't get back to you until I've rustled up all the things you need. Meanwhile you can lie low in an apartment belonging to one of my best friends. She's in the US on a lecture tour at the moment, she won't be back for three months. Change your appearance, grow a moustache, let your hair grow longer than usual. And mingle with people. No one will recognise you. Go shopping, get some good clothes, cook yourself something nice, and relax. It will be all right.

And by the way, the neighbours above you are rich students from Saudi Arabia. They're not interested in anyone else in the building, and they don't know any of the others there. The neighbours below you are old and hard of hearing, but I'll drop in today and let them know a cousin of my friend is staying in her apartment for a few weeks, and he needs to be left in peace because he's writing a book."

Laila looked into Farid's eyes. She did not, as usual, feel his erotic attraction. He was a helpless child now, her child, and she would protect him as she had in the past when she first held him in her arms.

A flicker of hope flared up in him when he entered his new hiding place, and after a hot shower he slept soundly again for the first time in weeks. But two days later that hope was destroyed. By chance, a woman in the building next door saw someone slipping into the apartment by night. She took Farid for a burglar and alerted the police. The young CID officer who made the arrest, First Lieutenant Sidki, was astonished when a Major Mahdi Said of the secret service phoned later to congratulate him. "You have taken a dangerous terrorist out of circulation."

241. Lonely Night

Rana had heard only briefly from Laila, and suddenly she was alone with her horror. There was no one she could talk to. Dunia was away, Claire was too desperate herself for Rana to hope for any comfort from her, and Laila wasn't answering the phone or opening her door. Claire explained that she felt guilty about Farid's arrest. She ought to have warned him about the over-zealous neighbour.

Night lay heavy on Rana. She couldn't sleep. What are they doing to him now, she wondered? The Radicals are in a worse position than anyone because they took up arms against the regime, like the Muslim Brotherhood. They'll torture him, and here I am lying in a soft bed next to a spineless army officer who'll do anything not to rub the authorities up the wrong way.

Her head felt as if it would explode. She got out of bed. I ought to have hidden Farid here, she told herself. No one would have thought of that, and if they did I'd have been arrested too, and my misery would have come to a fitting end. She drew aside the curtains over the bedroom window. The neon lights over the cinema sign were turned off, but she could clearly make out the striking face of Anthony Quinn as Zorba the Greek.

Barefoot, she left the bedroom, quietly opened the door leading up to the top floor, and stopped for a moment. A fresh breeze drew her on and up. On the roof, she breathed more easily. A few cars were driving by down below, nearly all of them taxis picking up drunks from the nightclubs and taking them home at this time of night. Farid would certainly be in the camp for "dangerous elements", as the government and her husband described their political opponents – somewhere far away in the desert. He might be asleep at this hour, but did he think of her when he was awake? She listened for his voice calling inside her, but she couldn't hear anything.

Someone in the building next door was trying to find a broadcasting station. His radio babbled a symphony of many different sounds. When it stopped abruptly, an alarming silence filled the sky. Rana closed her eyes, and imagined Farid lying on the couch in her studio.

Two cats were hissing at each other on a nearby roof. Then the darkness swallowed them up. "Where are you, my darling?" she whispered. An airplane rent the silence. The windows of her studio vibrated. She wanted to take only one plane flight, with Farid out of this country, never mind where so long as she was with him. But his feet dragged so heavily. He clung to Damascus. The city was a part of his soul, though to her it was a cage. She saw the world outside, but couldn't get out through the strong mesh of the wire netting.

She went to the edge of the roof and looked through a gap in the wooden fence. All windows were shut now. People were sleeping behind them, with their daytime masks and their false teeth lying on their bedside tables. She had a mask too. She wasn't wearing it now, but it was always ready to hand, and she put it on whenever her husband or anyone else came near her.

"Farid," she whispered, "can you hear me? You must stop wanting to change things! Listen to me. Let people live the lives of their own time, and let us save our love."

Rain began to fall. She sat down on a chair; she wasn't cold. Over the last few years he hadn't been able to leave the rest of the world behind as he once did. He suffered when he was enjoying her company because the outside world was suffering. He wore a mask too, but he thought it was his real face, and that saddened her. When day dawned she began to freeze. Only now did she notice that she was wet to the skin.

"Come, my child," said her father, taking her hand. She was happy, smiled at him, and went downstairs almost hovering, she felt so light. If her mother and Rami hadn't been standing there she would have thought she was in a dream.

"The doctor will be here soon," said her husband, and for a moment she thought someone must have had an accident.

BOOK OF LAUGHTER IV

He who sows suspicion reaps traitors.

ঌ

DAMASCUS, 1965–1968

242. Poetry

When Josef's favourite poet, Nuri Hakim, was arrested, the intellectuals in the Café Havana said Hakim was lucky, for President Baidan, after all, was more humane than his predecessor, and hadn't had the poet's wife arrested too, or his three children, or his father.

Many of the guests in the Café Baladi didn't know who Hakim was, but they knew he was accused of blasphemy. He could consider himself lucky, for Al-Hallaj had been crucified for making similar remarks, and Hakim was still alive.

The intellectuals in the Café Kanyamakan, who sympathized with the Muslim Brotherhood, denounced President Baidan as weak, and suspected that he hadn't flung the poet into prison at all, but hidden him away in a villa with a bodyguard to protect him from the anger of the faithful.

The intellectuals in the Café Journal suspected provocation instigated by the Israelis. At a time when Damascus, under the courageous President Baidan, was challenging imperialism, along comes someone publishing a poem in a state newspaper full of linguistic errors, stylistic howlers, and injuries to the religious feelings of mankind, and getting it past the censor.

Josef mourned at length for the frail little poet, and pinned the poem to the wall beside his bed. Religions were works of art, and should not be practised but admired in museums, Nuri Hakim had written. He was condemned to fifteen years in jail.

243. Adding Up the Truth

Munir was a born mathematician. He shone in his department at the university, and if his professors respected anyone, they respected him.

He was always coming into the cafeteria telling people things he had found out, and Farid had discovered then, for the first time, that maths was not a dry subject. When Munir proved mathematically why something in politics or the economy didn't work, you were soon in fits of laughter.

One day he came in with a thick exercise book, looking as if he hadn't had much sleep.

"Look at this," he said. "I've just been working it out: our country loses as many working days a year because of Ramadan alone as Britain has lost in all its strikes since the Second World War."

No one could believe that, but Munir set out all his statistics and calculations. It was obvious that during Ramadan the entire country was operating on the back burner. A Muslim Brother waxed indignant and attacked Munir, but they confined themselves to verbal fencing, to the amusement of the students in the cafeteria.

But one day Munir had worse on his mind. He used to listen to the news every morning before coming to the university, and one day he began meticulously writing down the losses allegedly suffered by Israel in its military confrontations with the Arab countries or the thirteen groups of Palestinian freedom fighters. Since January 1965 the Palestinians had been plastering the walls of the city of Damascus with reports of their huge successes, never guessing that Munir was carefully writing it all down.

One April morning in 1967 he came into the cafeteria, climbed on a chair and asked for silence. Because it was Munir the students did fall silent at once, although they wouldn't usually even in the lecture hall.

"Dear friends and comrades," he began, almost inaudibly.

"Louder!" shouted his fellow students at the back of the big room. Munir cleared his throat. "Dear friends and comrades!" he repeated. "It is my privilege to announce that Israel has finally been defeated. According to the casualty figures of the dead on all fronts, there isn't a single Israeli left capable of bearing arms. Any survivors are severely injured and lying in the ruins of bridges, buildings, and the burning remains of their military vehicles, helicopters, and tanks, all destroyed by our brave men, so now we must allow humanitarian aid to get through to those poor wounded Israelis, as we've been in duty bound to do ever since Saladin's time."

A day later he disappeared. His father made valiant efforts on his behalf, and was even willing to sign a statement saying that his son had been crazy from childhood on. He thought it would be only a formality enabling the state to save face if it let Munir go after accusing him of disseminating pro-Israeli propaganda.

But his father was wrong. Munir really had gone crazy.

BOOK OF HELL II

Those who come to Tad are lost.
Those who leave Tad are reborn.

જ

TAD, 200 KM NORTH-EAST OF DAMASCUS, APRIL 1968–APRIL 1969

244. The Way to Golgotha

From Damascus they drove along the main road as it wound north through the bleak landscape like a black snake in flight. After about twenty kilometres the column of trucks turned off along into the road going east. When the camp of Gahan was left behind, they all knew their destination: Tad.

Night fell like a heavy cloak on the earth, and the trucks jolted over potholes and rocks. The light of the headlamps danced wildly across the plain.

They were a hundred and fifty prisoners in four trucks, accompanied by several small transporter vans each carrying ten armed soldiers.

Farid crouched on the floor of the truck with his eyes closed. Those terrible days passed through his mind again: the shock as he sat in the kitchen reading the newspaper, and suddenly heard the noise of the police wrenching the front door of the apartment off its hinges. Then being handed over to the secret service next evening, an elaborately staged performance. They acted as if he were an Israeli general. He sat at the back of the police car with his hands and feet bound, with an officer on each side of him.

Through the windshield he had seen people bound for home, laden with shopping bags, laughing and gesticulating. It was still chilly outside, but you could already feel that spring was coming. People walked with a livelier step, took their time, strolled for pleasure.

"See that, you bastard?" asked the officer to his right, in a strong southern accent. "Any of them interested in you? You want to liberate those donkeys? They'd sell their country and their honour for a bag of candies."

"And their mothers into the bargain," agreed the man on Farid's other side. He had a scarred, fleshy face, like a crook in a bad caricature. The driver cast a nasty glance at the pair of them in the rear-view mirror.

"Yes, right," said the first secret service man, returning to the subject. "And back home they'll get under the shower, stuff their bellies, goggle at a crime movie on TV, and screw all night. And you'll be executed before you've had any fun out of life at all."

Farid felt desperate. He longed for Rana, and was ashamed of himself for not listening to her in time.

After torture and interrogation, he was finally tried by a military tribunal in the cellar of the secret service building, and was condemned to life imprisonment in a labour camp. His crime was described as conspiracy against the Fatherland. He had not been allowed a defence lawyer.

When he woke up again on the flatbed of the truck, day was beginning to dawn. It was cold. The trucks were still driving with their headlamps on. They were just coming to a hilly region, and they stopped briefly at a barrier. Brakes squealed. Beyond the rusty barrier the road ran on through the endless sand like a dark and broken thread.

Most of the detainees had been woken by the squealing brakes, and thought they had arrived, but a little later the column continued on its way. After a while they drove past a double fence. The camp was visible now and then through the sand dunes. Farid saw two large rows of huts with metal roofs. Finally the road described a sharp right bend, and the trucks stopped. A cloud of very fine sand trickled down on the prisoners.

"We're there," someone said softly.

The camp was in a hollow. No one driving a car on the main traffic routes through the desert to Palmyra, Homs, or Iraq would see that a prison with over two thousand inmates and guards was hidden here.

245. Reception

It was just after seven when Farid jumped down from the truck. He saw a horrific panorama before him. How could such a huge camp exist in this wilderness of sand and stones?

From the square where the trucks and vans had stopped, he could see both gates. The main gate faced north, the other gate east to a low-lying stone quarry that yawned open like a black muzzle. The rock here was basalt. Farid's eyes went in alarm to the double fence of dense barbed wire, with a death zone several metres wide in the middle.

Armed soldiers stood behind weather-beaten windows in the tall watch towers at the four corners of the camp. Each of them had a platform with movable searchlights on it.

Beyond the large main gate there was a low, two-storey, grey concrete building on the right. Farid counted sixteen large huts in two rows behind it. The two palm trees on the exercise ground were a strange sight; their leaves were the only green thing as far as the eye could see.

The camp commandant, Captain Garasi, received them at the gate. He was surrounded by officers, soldiers, and civilians, and he had a face like a bulldog's. Later, Farid found this first impression of his confirmed; he was known as Bulldog to the inmates who had been here for some time.

The captain's bearing was stiff, as if he were under the influence of drugs. His grey hair together with his low officer's rank showed that he had joined the army as a private soldier and worked his way up. Anyone who joined with a high school diploma was a captain by the age of twenty-eight at the latest. The Bulldog must be in his late fifties.

For some reason the officers kept the new prisoners waiting a long time. Farid was freezing in the cold dusk of dawn, and felt how empty his stomach was.

"It is my duty," the camp commandant began after an eternity, "in the name of His Excellency President Amran, to drain the poison with which you injure the Fatherland and its people, you ... you damn mangy dogs."

They could hear how difficult he found speaking publicly, how bad his articulation was, and how stiff the sentences he had learned by heart sounded. Only the abuse, uttered in a southern accent, carried complete conviction.

"If one of my officers, soldiers, or guards gives you an order I expect unconditional obedience, or you'll rue the day your mothers bore you a thousand times over. His Excellency has given me a free hand to do anything I like with you."

As if at a word of command the guards, who until now had been looking bored, made for the prisoners. Soon after that the air was full of dust and screams.

Farid particularly noticed one of the guards, an old man of about seventy. He had been standing close to the commandant all the time, leaning on a stick. Farid had taken him for a medical orderly or the captain's factotum. But the old man was the first to attack the prisoners, hitting out mercilessly and with sadistic delight. Whenever Farid raised his head he caught sight of him again. A time came when he himself was in the terrible old man's reach, and could see him salivating and whinny with pleasure as every blow went home.

Bleeding, and with the last of his strength, Farid reached the hut allotted to him. It was Number 5, in the front row of huts and level with the palm trees. He had a place near the east-facing entrance. The huts had only metal gratings over them at both ends, so that the inmates could be checked any time.

From his place, he could see the east gate leading to the basalt quarry, the soldiers' barracks, and the kitchen directly opposite the administration building, as well as part of the monastery ruins. Apparently the solitary confinement cells were in their cellars. Close to the ruins stood another small, grey building. That, Farid soon found out, was the former death row, where condemned men used to spend their last night of life. But after a prison riot in 1960, executions at Tad had been banned. The building contained six large cells, the only ones to contain two comfortable plank beds each. Farid was told by Ali Abusaid, a Satlan supporter who had been in Tad for four years, that Garasi put his favourites in there, so the inmates called the place Garasi's Hotel.

Farid's eyes wandered to the hospital. "How many doctors work there?" he asked, leaning on the grating.

Ali Abusaid laughed. "One. Dr. Josef Maqdisi."

"Only one doctor for two thousand people?" Farid was indignant.

"If only he really were," replied Abusaid. "He's a swine, not a doctor. But the hospital's another story. I'll tell you later."

Farid was glad to have a place to sleep in the fresh air, for many of the new arrivals were accommodated at the other end of the hut, where there were two earth closets and a large washbasin with three faucets. But he felt less happy about it when every gust of wind blew sand into his face and he was freezing cold at night.

"And who's that crazy old man who was beating us so hard?" Farid asked.

The man was a fossil. No one in the camp knew what his real name was, but they called him Istanbuli, because he larded his speech with so many Turkish words. At the age of twelve he had been a kitchen boy in the barracks under the Ottoman occupation, and he had gone on to serve every new master of the camp. He had never risen beyond the rank of a private soldier. Wherever the camp commandant went, Istanbuli followed like his shadow. And when Garasi gave the order to beat the prisoners, Istanbuli was first in line.

He had been retired in 1962, but after a week he was back asking to be reinstated. He couldn't cope with the chaos of modern life outside the camp. Captain Garasi liked the old man. He backed his request and was allowed to give him his job back, although now Istanbuli was paid only his pension instead of normal wages. But that made no difference to him. He lived very well on the bribes he got, which amounted to more than a general's official salary.

⁊&

A bell rang at six in the evening.

Two officers and several NCOs stood beside the palm trees. The guards walked past the huts and called out numbers, upon which the prisoner inside whose number it was would reply "One hundred and ten, sir!" or whatever his number happened to be, without looking up. The NCOs noted the numbers down.

At seven prisoners carried large pans out to the huts. They contained a nauseating soup made with beans and pieces of potato mixed with lentils. Countless dead beetles floated on top. But Farid's hunger was tearing at his stomach, so he fell on the food, shovelling the hot soup into his mouth and swallowing it without chewing, to avoid biting into one of the beetles.

He was sweating after getting it down in such a hurry, but he enjoyed the piece of bread he was given. It tasted fresh and smelled of sourdough.

Later, some of the inmates of the hut took tea and sugar out of a hiding place. A primitive boiler was also produced. It ran on heating oil abstracted by prisoners from the kitchen, and the tea was made in an old tin can.

Farid had a single sip from the mug being handed around. The tea tasted sweet and bitter, and smelled of diesel oil, but it was his first illicit drink here, and the fact filled him with a strange kind of pleasure.

Lights went out at eight. Farid wearily lay down on his mat, but he couldn't sleep. The darkness was a hole, and he was falling deeper and deeper into it. The world was alien and far away. Who was he? What was he doing here? This was Tad prison camp, and he hadn't been brought here by colonialists or such people, but by his own countrymen, men who called themselves socialists too, who even included communists faithful to Moscow in the government, although the Communist Party had to remain illegal. This state of affairs was known as "doing the Syrian splits". Amran maintained excellent relations with all the socialist countries, so no one at all was going to ask questions about a prisoner. Farid was abandoned to his misery.

That night Rana faded to a memory, and his mother appeared before his mind's eye only briefly, then sinking back into the darkness again. At last sleep came.

For the first few days sheer chaos ruled in the camp, for an unprecedented wave of arrests was sweeping across the country. The huts were suffocatingly overcrowded. They stank of shit and decomposition, sweat and ammonia. Then, after a while, the days lost their distinguishing marks and names. Time merged into a shapeless chain of boredom, loneliness, and pain.

246. Nagi

Tad held not only dangerous political prisoners of all parties, but also the worst kinds of criminals: pitiless murderers, pimps, rapists, and dangerous youths who had been practicing butchery at the age of fourteen and were ready to kill anyone. Human life meant nothing to them.

Conscientious objectors and deserters suffered worst of all. They were mercilessly tortured, first when arrested, then during interrogation, and finally in the camp. Every one of them was to be made an example. They were regarded as dangerous because they were hostile not only to the government but also to the army.

It was in Tad that Farid saw the first conscientious objector of his life. The young man wasn't twenty yet, but you could tell what he had been through just by looking at him. Garasi hated him and called him a pansy and a cowardly traitor. His name was Nagi Salam, and he had been condemned to twenty years in the labour camp, followed by five years of military service at the front. If he refused to serve at the front, which, being Nagi, he obviously would, he would then get life imprisonment. The state didn't want to kill him, just to torment him all his life.

The political prisoners avoided the boy, because for all their ideological differences they were united on one point: they advocated violence, and to many of them, Radicals, communists, and Muslim Brothers alike, armed struggle seemed the only possible way.

Garasi put Nagi in Hut 12 with the worst criminals, who tormented and pestered him without mercy. He bore it all in silence, and didn't defend himself even when a criminal of small and weedy build slapped his face. A time came when the criminals themselves found it no fun any more to tyrannize over him, because a tormentor needs some kind of reaction from his victim. You get no kick out of torturing a stone.

247. Garasi

Captain Garasi was absolute lord and master over this island of men deprived of their rights in the middle of a desert of sand and oblivion. Compared to him, a government minister was no more than a factotum. He was God in person, deciding on the life or death, happiness or misery, hunger, pain, and loneliness of every single prisoner. He was a dangerous mixture of ignorance and arrogant self-confidence. Garasi felt no particular hatred for Muslim Brothers, communists, or Radicals. He wasn't capable of it; he neither hated nor loved anyone at all.

At twenty he had married a woman, given her three children, and took no further notice of her. When his wife fell sick with a strange fever, he never visited her for fear of infection. At a safe distance away in the camp, he waited for her to die.

There were rumours that he smoked large quantities of hashish in secret, and sometimes wept all night in his Spartan apartment over the interrogation cells and the offices. Garasi didn't like the soldiers, and he was too rigid and hard-hearted for their taste. Unlike the prison guards, the soldiers were not in this camp of lost souls by their own choice. Many of them suffered even more than the prisoners from the captain's harsh punishments. Garasi reacted with a sense of injury to every lapse of discipline, as if it threatened him personally with failure, and responded with corresponding brutality.

He thought little of his military rank; only his social task mattered to him. His idea of the world since childhood had comprised only shepherds and sheep. "Like the President of the Republic, I'm a shepherd," he would say, "except that his flock is larger."

Garasi was proud of having so many intellectuals and educated men in his flock. He, who had had reading and writing literally beaten into him in the army, now determined the fate of twenty professors, twenty-five doctors of medicine, ten architects, thirty-five lawyers, a hundred and thirty journalists including five editors-in-chief, over thirty writers, and forty engineers, chemists, and teachers. Not the finest quarter in all Damascus, Cairo, or Beirut could boast so many men with university degrees.

He called those who obeyed him, "my boy, my son." Those who would not accept this humiliation were physically punished, and Garasi helped out with the torturing himself, not for pleasure but out of a feeling that, as a shepherd, he had to care for his sheep. And apart from a few rich and privileged political prisoners, and the criminal gang leaders whom he spared, there was not a single camp inmate who hadn't been beaten by Garasi in person at some time. Worst was the rage that made him blind, for then he struck out like a brute beast. Sometimes he actually injured himself in the process, staggering about and smashing everything around him. Farid once saw Garasi whipping four prisoners with his own hands, until he was in such a rage that he turned the whip on the soldiers and NCOs around him too. The officers, standing a little further off, sent for Istanbuli, who was in the kitchen at this time of day. He seized the commandant from behind, picked him up, and whirled him around fast in a circle until the captain dropped his whip and hung there in the old soldier's arms like a limp sack.

248. Loyalty and Recantation

Since Farid hadn't yet discovered the true reason for his arrest, he thought his really bad luck was that he was regarded not as a former communist but as a Radical. Muslim Brothers, nationalists, and communists hated each other like poison, but they were united on one point: if they fell into the hands of the government they would never sign a declaration saying they recanted. That was considered cowardly treachery. Farid would have signed anything to get out of this place, but no one was asking him to. The secret service knew that the wily Radicals allowed their members to sign anything, just so long as they were freed to carry on with the armed struggle underground. Radicals regarded dictators and their adherents as criminals, and considered any statement made to criminals invalid.

Farid remembered communists who had committed suicide after they had been freed, unable to bear the scorn of their own comrades. The Communist Party no longer offered aid to a prisoner who had broken under torture; it became a second punitive authority. Only your own failure was still your loyal companion.

But Farid would have been prepared to accept any humiliation. He knew that political prisoners who recanted were brought out for the media. Former high-up functionaries had to declare their shame and remorse on television, rather less important men on the radio, and third-class politicals in one of the governmental newspapers, all vowing allegiance to the Fatherland and its President.

Much worse than this dreadful media show was humiliation in front of your friends and family. By signing you admitted that your entire career up to this point had been a failure.

Amran's government needed repentant sinners, you could sense that in Tad. Prisoners weren't asked about what they had done any more, they were tortured at once *en masse* to get recantations.

The Interior Minister was putting pressure on Garasi. The captain stepped up the tortures and made the already near-inedible food even worse, but only very few abandoned their resistance and signed. Gradually, Garasi came to realize that he was dealing with a particularly tough, battle-hardened generation. He had never before had so many prisoners who still defied him, some of them even after years, and refused to be his flock. He was often near tears in his fury to find that some bleeding, trembling thing lying on the floor was still morally superior to him and the state.

249. At Night

Night hung like a black cloak over him, and the moon was the slit cut by a sharp knife in that garment. Farid stood at the grating for a long time, listening to the silence. At last he lay down on his mat and fell asleep.

In the middle of the night he was woken by a kick. "Get up, you bastards!" two guards were shouting. The light was glaring. Farid saw the others already standing with their faces to the wall, and he turned to it too. A whiplash intended for his neighbour struck his own back as well, burning like fire. The guard shouted, "Hold your tongue!" Evidently the man next to him had said something before Farid himself woke up. Within minutes all the prisoners in Hut 5 were on their feet.

Now Garasi appeared in full uniform. Out of the corner of his eye, Farid could see him striding past. "No heroes are going to survive here, only sensible men," roared the captain. "I warned you, and now what do I hear? One of you has smuggled in a newspaper."

Four guards and three soldiers spent a long time searching for the alleged newspaper. Finally they found it underneath the straw mat where a man called Marwan slept. He was well known as one of the Muslim Brotherhood. Garasi was fuming with anger. He hit, kicked, and shouted abuse at the prisoner, who just kept repeating, "God's punishment of the unrighteous will be great!"

By now the captain was in such a rage that as he swung his foot back to deliver a kick, he slipped and fell right beside his victim. Marwan saw this as aid from heaven, summoned up all his strength, shouted, "Allahu Akbar!" and spat his own blood into Garasi's face. Farid saw some of the inmates laughing soundlessly as they faced the wall.

The commandant swiftly got to his feet and left the hut, his face smeared. His soldiers followed him with his victim, and did not allow the other prisoners to stand easy, as they usually did after such nocturnal raids. But as soon as the last guard had left, they burst out laughing. Everyone claimed to have seen yet another detail of Garasi's humiliation.

Marwan didn't come back for two weeks, and then he was only a pale shadow of himself, encrusted with filth. He could hardly keep on his feet, and he stank horribly. A week later he had to be taken to the military hospital in Damascus, and never came back. Contradictory rumours were in circulation, varying between a heroic death and freedom dearly bought.

250. The Quarry

The guards came at six in the morning. Huts 4, 5, and 6 were due for punishment. Some three hundred prisoners were made to run in circles, calling out, "Left, right, long live the Fatherland! Left, right, unity, liberty and socialism! Left, right, long live the Arab nation! Left, right, we are a nation with an eternal mission!"

About twenty guards were lined up, and the column of prisoners had to run the gauntlet past them. They made very sure that everyone was shouting at the top of his voice. Farid was running in silence when a guard's whip suddenly caught his ear. After that the man fell out of line with the other guards, caught up with Farid, and kept whipping him until he finally heard this stubborn prisoner shouting. As a punishment, all the prisoners had to run five more rounds that morning. Farid realized that it was best to go along with orders from the first, to spare yourself and the others pain.

After that the three hundred prisoners had half an hour to go and use the earth closets. Only now came their real punishment: they were to work in the basalt quarry. The reason for their punishment remained Garasi's secret. In double quick time, they went through the east gate, where they were handed hammers, shovels, and iron bars. A broad path with barbed wire on both sides led to the quarry. Once there it narrowed and wound its way down into the depths, which resembled a landscape from old science fiction movies, with bizarre, sharp fractures in the rock. The prisoners had a steep downward climb of twenty metres. Slowly, the yellow of the desert gave way to a greyish black colour, darker the further down they went, until they were surrounded by a ghostly nocturnal black at the bottom of the quarry. Now Farid knew the source of the dark gravel covering all the roads around the camp a metre deep: it was the volcanic basalt from the quarry.

The prisoners had hardly arrived before armed soldiers followed and took up their position at the top of the ravine. The NCOs sat under large sun umbrellas and kept watch from that vantage point. Down in the basalt ravine there were three umbrellas for the guards too.

As soon as the sun was out the black rock quickly warmed up, and the higher it rose the more unbearable the heat became. "No one's ever managed to escape from here," whispered one of the prisoners when he saw Farid's questioning glance.

Large pieces of rock had to be broken out with hammers and iron bars, then reduced to gravel, and pushed all the way up again in rusty wheelbarrows. It was dangerous work, for the fractures in the basalt were as sharp as razor blades. Splinters stuck up everywhere, piercing the prisoners' bad footwear. By midday the entire place was a huge oven, and the air flickered with heat. The guards kept whipping the prisoners for no reason. It was hell on earth. Everything blurred before Farid's eyes, and his movements were purely mechanical.

At some point they could break for half an hour, but they got nothing to eat. The guards just distributed water, half a litre for everyone. The water tasted of rubber, but it quenched the fire in Farid's throat.

His hands hurt. As the day wore on he couldn't feel his feet any more. He was feverish that night. One of the prisoners gave him a bitter-tasting pill that he had taken from a hiding place. It was supposed to bring his temperature down, but after an hour he felt so bad that his neighbours called the guards. They just grinned derisively. "If he snuffs it we'll save on his food. But rats don't die that easily."

Farid threw up several times. His temples were thudding and there was a roaring in his ears. Only at dawn, exhausted, did he fall asleep. When he woke up he was alone in the hut. He heard someone weeping, and another man comforting him.

Farid was sweating. He felt cold inside, and he had stomach cramps. He threw up again; his fellow prisoners had left a bucket beside him. All he vomited was yellow, bitter fluid.

Garasi stopped briefly by the entrance to the hut. "That dog will die soon. He has sunstroke, he's spitting blood," said the man with the commandant.

"Oh, they don't die. The Devil himself got their mothers pregnant. I'll bet you this one's only playing sick. If he's not in the quarry tomorrow bring him to me, and I'll soon get him on his feet again."

"Yes, sir," replied the other man. Farid lay motionless under his blanket. Had he really been spitting blood? He began to feel his life would end here in this camp, and he longed so much for Rana. He began shedding tears under the blanket.

Around midday, in his sleep, he heard a quiet knock. He woke up. There was a man behind the grating. He wore a soldier's uniform, but no cap. The man beckoned him over and pushed a can through the grating. "Here, this is for you. Eat it and then put the can down close inside the grating," he said briefly, and went away.

The soldier's face was scarred, but even the scars couldn't hide its kindness. Farid picked up the can. The hot soup tasted good. It was made of carrots and potatoes.

He ate quickly, wrapped in his blanket, and then put the can down beside the grating. When he woke up again hours later, it had gone.

In the evening the others came back, worn and weary, but as soon as they were sitting down they began to laugh and crack jokes about Garasi the bulldog. When Farid told the old communist Zachariah about the soldier and the soup, he smiled. "That's not a soldier, that's our guardian angel Salih. He's been in here forever. He killed seven men in a single evening," he added, passing the side of his hand across his throat to show how.

251. Dawn

Next morning Farid woke just as dawn was approaching. He felt weak. In the past, early morning had his favourite time of day. He liked to be alone with the silence, and hadn't slept more than six hours a night since he was ten. Sometimes he was up at four, listening to the world as it woke. He had discovered that of all times of day, early morning dawn retained its innocence best. It was as still as it had been ten thousand years ago: the moment of calm before the storm.

Ever since he fell in love with Rana, his first thought in the morning had been for her. It was a time when he could talk to her, even though, as she admitted with some shame, she was still fast asleep then.

Early morning in the camp was grey and mute, stinking of sewers and tasting bitter like rotten teeth. It was the end of rest and the beginning of torment. Water was laid on in the huts for only an hour in the early morning, and without previous warning. So as not to lose a drop, the prisoners always stood three large plastic buckets under the taps in the washbasin the evening before. All other available buckets, bowls, and mugs stood very close, for the water flowed at a different pressure every day, and sometimes the guards forgot to turn it off again. On such days the prisoners drank all they wanted and rejoiced, splashing each other like children and fooling around.

Farid sat up and drew his blanket around his shoulders. He still felt shaky on his legs, but he wasn't so dizzy now. He felt hungry, always a sign that he was getting better.

He tried to stand up, but then he felt sick again and dropped back on his mat. He didn't wake again until midday. The camp was empty; Garasi seemed to have forgotten him. He left Farid alone for the next three or four weeks. During that time he was trying hard to catch some very big fish from the ranks of the communists and the Muslim Brotherhood in his net. And his brutality and the hopelessness of life in the huts soon brought him success. At the end of September about ten Muslim Brothers and as many communists broke, signed their recantations, sang hymns of praise to the government, and were released. Garasi was in an excellent temper for a few days, for the Interior Minister had praised him.

252. Milhelm

The criminal fraternity formed a state of their own in the camp, with rulers, servants, an upper class and a lower class, winners and losers. There were about three hundred of them, including over sixty young offenders.

They ran a market that functioned by the same laws of supply and demand as markets in the outside world. Anything could be ordered, from food and clothing to medicaments, hashish, and liquor. Services of all kinds were on offer too, from working in the basalt quarry in another prisoner's place to administering physical punishment, strictly observing those humiliations, injuries, and broken bones that had been ordered. Everything had its exact price.

The criminal state worked efficiently and without any bureaucracy. Orders were taken and carried out with few words; accounts were paid without a murmur. Bargains were sealed with your word of honour, and breaking your word was harshly punished. The overlord of this state was a long-stay resident in the hospital, which was known to the prisoners as the Mafia Lodgings. His name was Milhelm Badri, and he was very tall. He seldom spoke; words emerged from his mouth with difficulty, every one of them a forceps delivery. His eyes were always clouded, looking past his interlocutors into space. They reminded Farid of the eyes of dead fish.

Milhelm's world was not our five continents but this specially subdivided camp, and he had been in it for a very long time. Other groups of prisoners formed the neighbouring states of his domain. He called communists Russians, the Muslim Brothers Saudis, the radicals Cubans, the Satlanists Egyptians, but the criminals were "my men".

He paid wages and gave presents to his supporters on religious festivals. Sometimes it was only a packet of bad cigarettes, but for his subjects they meant a great deal, particularly as other prisoners got nothing at all.

Garasi harassed all the other prisoners without distinction, but he spared the criminals. As he saw it, they were already well-disciplined members of his flock, and he had regarded Milhelm as a trusty sheepdog for twenty years. The fact that he in turn often obeyed Mil-helm's orders was in the nature of the relationship between a dog and his master.

253. Darwish

Farid was on the way to the kitchen when two notorious thugs jostled him. They were crooks ready to beat up anyone for a cigarette. Farid ran to safety in the kitchen as fast as he could, but he knew they were waiting outside. It seemed like someone's order.

And he had been looking forward to today. He liked being on kitchen duty, where the agreeable Samih was responsible for everything. Samih sensed Farid's nervousness when it was time for him to carry the food out. At first Farid hesitated, then he told him about the two thugs outside the door.

"We'll see about that," said Samih calmly, and shouted through the door between the kitchen and the bakery for someone called Darwish. In came a hulk of a man with a bare, hairy torso. His chest was sprinkled with tattoos and scars, and several chunks of silver hung from a heavy chain around his neck, clashing noisily as they moved. A powerful colossus. Samih explained about the two characters lying in wait.

"So who's this laddie?" asked Darwish, without deigning even to look at Farid. His voice conveyed morose displeasure, as if he had been interrupted in important work for no good reason.

"A decent man," said Samih briefly.

"Then let's take a look," grunted the hulk, and watched Farid picking up two of the thirty-two buckets of soup that he would have to carry to the huts. He hadn't gone three paces before the two thugs emerged from the shadows. He knew they couldn't have been standing so close to the kitchen for a second unnoticed by the guards. You were severely punished for being outside the huts without permission. The two thugs grinned at him, and Farid saw the glint of something that might be a knife or a screwdriver in one man's hand.

"Stop!" That was Darwish, or more accurately it was a thunderbolt that could speak Arabic. Farid stopped dead. So did the two thugs.

"Keep on walking, what's this to do with you? The soup will be getting cold," Darwish told Farid, passing him and seizing the two thugs, who suddenly looked pitifully weedy. When Farid put the buckets down beside the guard in Hut 1 and turned back, the thugs were lying on the ground.

He picked up the next two buckets in the kitchen, and as he set off again he saw Darwish knocking the two men's heads together. There was a frightful sound as they crashed together. Farid handed over the buckets and went back. Now they were on their knees, begging for mercy.

"Take a good look at my friend here," said Darwish. "And whenever you set eyes on him, think of yours truly. Do we understand each other?"

When Farid was on his way with the buckets for the third time, the hulking figure stopped him and put out his hand. It was holding a cobbler's knife. "Here," he said, "one of those guys was very keen to give you this. It could be useful, but hide it well." Then he set off back to the bakery. Farid delivered all the other buckets of soup. Then he had to wheel a handcart of bread from the bakery to the huts. Meanwhile, Darwish was silently drinking his tea. When Farid was through with the buckets, he sat down on a stool in the bakery. His shift left him on duty until midnight.

Darwish pushed a glass over to him. "So what did you do to them, laddie?" he asked quietly. "Those are dangerous bastards."

"Nothing. I guess someone was paying them," Farid replied. However, he couldn't think who might be behind it.

Darwish, so Farid learned that night, was a pimp and a multiple murderer thirty-three times over. He had killed an entire criminal clan in a single day, overpowering his enemies at a wedding. The prisoners called him "Darwish with the brand". He had a triangular mark on his forehead, with two lines roughly suggesting an X in the middle of it. As a twelve-year-old in Jordan, he had been arrested for burglary and thrown out of the country, and the police had branded him on the forehead with a red-hot iron so that he couldn't hide anywhere.

"Those Jordanians were prophets. They knew back then what a crook you'd turn out to be," said Farid, joking with the kindly giant.

"They're assholes. They knew damn all! But what else can a man be with this mark on his face? An imam, a teacher, principal of a girls' school, eh? No, he can only be a pimp, and then no one will look at him because all that interests them is his girls' bums and breasts. That's what those assholes made me with that stamp of theirs, my boy!"

254. Solitary Confinement

The chink of keys woke him early in the morning. He sat up, but a kick in the chest sent him flying back again.

Two guards were standing over him. He recognized the one who had kicked him, a thin little man whose skin was sprinkled with warts and wrinkles, and who was notorious for his brutality, which he used to compensate for his small stature. He was nicknamed "Crocodile", and he liked the name. The second man was tall and even-tempered.

"Get up, son of a whore, you're to be interrogated," shouted Crocodile. The tall guard was going to handcuff him, but the ugly gnome waved the cuffs aside. "Where's he going to run? Into the barbed wire?" He laughed. Farid staggered out of the hut. The sun outside was dazzling. He saw the prisoners staring at him, and hated this humiliation. When the occupants of Hut 3 gave him a cheerful greeting he realized that they were trying to encourage him, and waved back.

"Traitor to the Fatherland!" shouted Crocodile behind him, hitting Farid's neck with the flat of his hand so hard that he tumbled forward. He scrambled up again as fast as he could and did what he had repeatedly trained to do with the Radicals: he kicked the gnome in the balls. It all happened very fast, and before the tall guard walking ahead realized what was up Farid had punched Crocodile in the face as well. The small man doubled up with pain, holding his hands in front of his genitals.

"I'm no traitor, you son of a pimp," cried Farid, before everything went dark before his eyes.

As he slowly regained consciousness he heard whispering in the darkness. He was lying on the floor trussed up like a chicken. His punishment, fifty lashes and two months' solitary confinement, was for resisting guards.

The heroic conduct that Farid had intended to show was gone at the first lash. In the brief moment before the second came, all he could do was writhe in fear. The second lash confirmed his fears: it hurt even more than the first. Farid wanted to stay strong, but the pain consumed all his strength, and he heard himself screaming. A time came when he felt nothing any more. When he came back to his senses he was lying in complete darkness, and his body, woken by the pain, was returning to life.

He realized that he was in one of the solitary confinement cells. The floor was concrete, the walls massive stone. He didn't know whether it was day or night, for the cell was pitch dark. No light came through the spyhole in the door, and when he heard cicadas in the distance he assumed that it was night and went to sleep.

For the first time in his life he felt that light was magic. A ray of sun forced itself through an opening in his pitch dark cell and danced over the wall. Slowly, the light moved through the cell, filling it with a muted radiance that filled Farid's heart with longing. He felt unutterably lonely, and began to weep.

"You only get to eat every other day in here, and it's always at noon," said the guard who pushed a large, battered tin bowl in the cell. A lump of mashed potato filled half the bowl, and there was a flatbread on top of it. The potato tasted of rancid fat, but the bread was good.

For the first few days in solitary confinement, Farid felt it was almost pleasantly restful. The cell was small, but clean and dry. The hut had to be shared with a hundred and twenty other prisoners, and it always smelled of dirt and decay and was horribly noisy.

But after a few days Farid noticed lethargy affecting his thoughts. He began asking himself questions to occupy his mind. First he enumerated everything that he missed. In the process, he realized that in the camp he had lost those small moments of pleasure in daily life that had once seemed so natural: light, movement, warmth, open doors, going for a walk, shaving, drinking a glass of tea, singing when he felt like it.

The darkness was oppressive today; the air seemed to be boiling. Not a breath of wind came through the crack under the iron door of his cell. It must be cloudy outside, or else a sandstorm had covered the sun, and no ray of light penetrated the cellars. Farid's thoughts lapsed into apathy once more. He tried singing again, and three times the songs died away after a few pitiful verses. He switched from the melancholy ballads of Um Kulthum to the cheerful dance rhythms of his favourite singer Feiruz, but his singing was still no good.

Was it night outside? He listened, but he couldn't hear any cicadas. When the guard brought his food he added two large, crisp rolls to the bowl of beans. "From Darwish," he vouchsafed dryly.

So it was only midday. Farid had been thinking it was night. A few hours later he felt fresh air coming in under the door. Gradually the cell grew cooler, and he could sleep.

Darkness swallowed up his thoughts, erased them. He couldn't think any idea out to its logical conclusion. At some point he always lost the thread. He wondered what he could do about it, and thought the best thing would be to wake his brain up by walking while he thought. He went up and down in his cell, brushing the palm of his hand over the stone masonry, doing ten or twenty push-ups, and repeating this exercise several times a day.

It was only gradually that he understood the full cruelty of solitary confinement. Time was the worst of it. Time didn't seem to pass at all. If you didn't defeat it first it would break you, that was to say if you stopped thinking, if you stopped expressing what you had thought.

"They shut us up crowded close together," he said to himself in an undertone, taking care to pronounce the words clearly, "until we don't just *feel* like sheep in a shed, we really *are* sheep. Ali Abusaid told me that one of Garasi's officers hit him and kept saying, 'Go on, admit it, you're a sheep!' And he went on hitting Ali with a stick until he bleated, and then the officer laughed and left him in peace."

Farid took a deep breath. "Left him in peace," he repeated out loud, because for a moment he didn't know how to go on, but then his thoughts continued to flow. "On that point," he said, laughing at the idea, "Garasi and the Communist Party leadership are very like each other. The Party leaders too treat their members like castrated sheep.

They have to obey and be shorn, milked, and slaughtered, but they must never want anything for themselves. That's not what matters to Garasi. He doesn't care a bit what his tortured sheep and wethers want, just so long as they behave like part of his flock."

He concentrated on following this train of thought to its end, and before he spoke the next words out loud he suddenly saw the patch of sunlight fall on the wall. With it, a cool breeze blew into his cell. Farid sat on the floor, delighted by his victory over the darkness.

255. Time Drags By

"Rana," said his lips, although he wasn't thinking of Rana. The heart is related to the tongue, he'd read that years ago somewhere, they have the same muscular structure. "Rana," he whispered again. It was like a prayer. He was close to her now. When he arrived in Tad, one of the old prisoners had told him that if he wanted to survive he must leave all the people he had loved outside and forget them instantly, for they would only be a burden to him here. But whenever Farid realized that he was in danger of becoming an animal, and his thoughts were beginning to revolve around nothing but naked survival, he clung to Rana, and in his imagination he built a future full of warmth, love, books, and music with her.

"Rana," he whispered again, "if you only knew what they do to us here." He was fighting back his tears when he heard a soft, barely audible knock on the door.

"Some bread for you."

It was unmistakably Samih's voice. He pushed a flat package under the door into the cell, and left his fingers there for a moment. Farid stroked their tips.

"Thank you," he whispered.

The bag of bread contained a scrap of paper too. Farid held it in the ray of sunlight. There wasn't much written on it, just, "We're thinking of you. Be brave. We love you." And there were several signatures underneath. He folded the paper into a tiny square and hid it in the lining of his trousers. The bread tasted wonderful. Darwish had painted it with olive oil and thyme before he baked it.

Farid felt better once he had eaten it. His thoughts went back to his comparison of the leadership of the Communist Party with Captain Garasi. "Yes, and when it comes to sexuality," he went on out loud, "Garasi's purely animal nature makes him better than the communist leaders. They've domesticated the brute beast in themselves."

As he spoke the word "sexuality", which in Arabic is *gins*, Farid realized that he could make it into two anagrams: *sign*, meaning "prison", and *ngis*, meaning "impure". He tried forming variants of both those words, but it didn't help for long.

ॐ

He felt more desperate every day, for it wasn't just his attempt to conquer isolation by speaking his thoughts out loud that failed. Whatever he tried to think about was defeated by the darkness. He tried mind games, he tried imaginary love-talk with Rana, arguments with Laila, complex experiments in the natural sciences – all of it just flared briefly like a firework, and then the darkness swallowed it up.

He missed human company, and longed for it. By now he would rather have even the unbearable smell of the camp inmates than this room, which felt like a casket. For the first time in his life he recognized how precious human voices were.

"Rana," he whispered, stretching his arms out in the darkness like a drowning man. He concentrated his mind on his lover, remembering her special fragrance, her soft skin. Soon he felt her closeness and warmth flowing through his body. He thought of her beautiful face and her neck, the neck he had always loved to kiss lingeringly when he lay close to her back. She was so sensitive just there … Farid smiled, and fell asleep.

256. Alphabet of Humanity

When he came out of solitary confinement after two months, he had aged by years. He washed several times, the other prisoners found him clean clothing, and everyday life in the camp went on again.

A week later a chance incident split the camp, bringing out the prisoners' differences. A minor quarrel between Muslim Brothers and the communists developed into a bitter fight, with injured men on both sides. Garasi was delighted.

Ali Abusaid's spontaneous idea of founding a reconciliation group developed into the proposal of electing a secret "committee" of the prisoners to settle quarrels, or if possible prevent them in the first place, but most of all to foster the cohesion of all the political prisoners. However, the election of the ten-man committee was a setback for the communists; only one of their number was chosen. Farid represented the independent Left.

The committee worked hard on projects for restoring to the prisoners what Garasi and the camp administration had taken from them: their human dignity. After some weeks, the committee put forward a plan, although its success was limited. Any contacts with the outside world, any attempts to get hold information and materials, were possible only through the soldiers who were forced to do their military service in the camp. A number of them did make tentative approaches to the prisoners at first, but then they took fright, or were transferred, for Garasi had his eyes and ears everywhere. A dense network of informers among the prisoners meant that any planned operation was like walking through a minefield. And hostility between the different political parties got in the way of any sensible resistance project even more than the informers. Farid lay awake for nights on end. He debated with the others, sought solutions, tried to bribe soldiers to procure medicaments and reading matter in Damascus. But most of the soldiers were afraid.

Reconciliation itself was difficult. The prisoners lay side by side in the huts, crammed together like sheep in a shed. Insect pests and lack of sleep turned them into bad-tempered beasts of prey who would attack each other for the least little thing, inflicting mental and physical pain, as if Garasi's tortures weren't enough. In despair, the committee recognized the limits of its moral authority. Yet it had achieved something: all the prisoners respected the tireless commitment of its members, who remained largely anonymous. That respect was the first common ground between all the camp inmates. It was a tiny seed, but it fell on fertile ground.

257. Autumn

The first harbingers of autumn came from the north; the sun no longer blazed so pitilessly down.

Garasi and his guards showed some restraint for several days. The food suddenly improved. The prisoners had real pieces of meat in their soup for the first time, and grapes for dessert. There was a rumour among the inmates that the grapes were poisoned, but no one could resist them all the same.

"There's going to be an important visitor soon," said the prisoners who had been in Tad for over ten years.

One afternoon they learned from the soldiers that the new head of the secret service, Colonel Badran, was coming. A troop of prisoners, under the supervision of armed soldiers, was sent out to the camp forecourt where the buses had brought them on their arrival. They were to whitewash everything. Flower pots were put outside the entrance, and a second troop of prisoners had to spruce up the inner courtyard. The guards who had so much enjoyed bringing their whips down on the prisoners' backs suddenly acted quite peaceably.

"Hey, my skin's just itching for the touch of your whip," one of the criminals called out to a guard. "Are you all sick, or have you turned hippy? Make love, not war," he chanted, hands to his balls. The guard was seething with rage, but he turned his back on the prisoners.

The huts and the earth closets were cleaned up too. A special squad of prisoners was told off to clean the administration building, and the soldiers had to attend to their own barracks. Tons of garbage were thrown on three trucks standing ready and dumped somewhere in the desert. A day later the camp looked neat as a new pin: that made it a truly repellent sight.

The visitor was late. Garasi told the prisoners to shave, wash, and behave well, because the new head of the secret service was an educated man who liked order and discipline. Badran was President Amran's youngest brother, he added, and had played a considerable part in the latest coup.

Next morning the prisoners were summoned from their huts and lined up in the yard. A table laid with a white cloth, with a jug of water and a bunch of flowers on it, stood under the palm trees. There were two chairs behind the table.

Rumour went that Badran had been in the office for two hours already, examining the files, and that he was not pleased with Garasi's chaotic approach. The camp commandant was said to be very upset, because he had thought his work was exemplary. And as if to confirm all this, the prisoners suddenly heard Garasi's voice through the open window. "Why would we want to keep records of the interrogations? Isn't it my job to help these poor devils return to the bosom of the Fatherland?"

Whereupon Badran was heard laughing heartily, and asking whether Garasi was a survivor of Noah's Ark.

When they finally appeared in the yard, the commandant looked old and depressed beside the athletic young officer, whose bearing showed that he was full of energy. He wore a casual summer uniform emphasizing his muscular build but no cap, unlike Garasi.

The colonel sat down on one of the chairs. Garasi remained on his feet, inspecting the prisoners. The front row was only about five metres from the table. Soldiers with machine guns and expressionless faces were stationed to right and left of the table, with orders to shoot anyone who came closer to it than two metres; Garasi didn't want to run any risks. Plenty of members of the Muslim Brotherhood were capable of an attempted suicide assassination.

Garasi addressed the prisoners stiffly, his voice hoarse with agitation. Perhaps it was his nervousness, or perhaps his brain was eaten away by drugs, but anyway he delivered a speech that unintentionally tipped over into comedy. The prisoners forgot the reward they had been promised and began first to chuckle, then to laugh louder and

louder, until at last their mirth was unbridled. Garasi, utterly confused, was put off his stride so badly that all he could do was abuse
the prisoners, flinging the worst insults he knew at them. They went
on roaring with laughter, and Garasi was at a loss. He gasped for air,
while the prisoners' laughter rolled across the yard like a stormy sea.

Colonel Badran rose to his feet and left the camp without a word.

258. Development Aid

Towards the end of September, three officers of the State Security
Service of the Democratic Republic of Germany arrived: blond men
who always wore sunglasses. Intrigued, the prisoners wondered why
the Germans had been brought to the camp. As observers? As experts
on torture? The three of them were generally known only as "the East
Germans".

It was common knowledge that consultants from several Eastern
European countries had been training the Syrian secret service in
Damascus over the last year. The word was that, since 1960 at the
latest, former Nazis had also been active in Egypt as armaments
experts. A Palestinian who had already been in a Jordanian prison
told Farid that the secret service there had tortured him under the
direct instructions of Englishmen, and the British were angry because
the Jordanians couldn't keep their violence within bounds. You had
to preserve your distance and keep cool during interrogations and
torture, they said.

One of the East Germans was astonished to find such modern
instruments of torture in the middle of the desert. Tad even had its
own generator. Garasi grinned. "We're independent here. Even if the
lights go out all over the country we can make our own electricity," he
explained. He had no idea that these foreign guests were soon to be
his instructors. Their broken Arabic led him to underestimate them.

"I suppose we can't afford better Germans," he said to his adjutant
regretfully, but there was a note of deep scorn in his voice.

On the fourth day, and to the surprise of their host, the foreigners brought six large German shepherd dogs with them as a gift for the guards. With the help of these well-trained animals, the camp could be cut off entirely from the outside world. They even built a dog run for them.

Soon the Germans, like all the officers in the camp, had been given nicknames by the detainees: they were Sausage, Potato, and Shanklish. Sausage was a tall, thin officer; Potato was short and fat; and Shanklish stank to high heaven. His name came from the only Syrian cheese that smells unpleasant. Shanklish was also the dog trainer. Out in the yard, he fed the animals with top-quality meat before the eyes of the hungry prisoners, and gave them clean water to drink. From then on the dogs prowled around loose all night, and now no one dared ignore the ban on leaving the huts.

The soldiers were reluctant to mix with the East Germans. They didn't like the three blond men, considering them both mean and over-zealous, two mortal sins in the eyes of any Syrian.

Even at seven in the morning the three men were in Garasi's office, shaved and in freshly ironed uniforms. At first Garasi himself didn't stumble out of his service apartment until around nine, but when Colonel Badran, to whom the Germans had apparently reported this, phoned and spoke to him angrily, the captain told off two soldiers to be his alarm call. After that he was always in his office at six in the morning, and when the foreigners turned up he would pay them out by looking pointedly at his watch.

Garasi hated them, for suddenly he wasn't sole lord and master of the camp any more. The prisoners became aware of that too. Garasi had to interrogate a prisoner in the presence of the Germans. The three of them might not be able to speak very good Arabic – they were always mixing up words of the masculine and feminine genders – but they understood everything. In silence, they noted down all that was said. Then, when Garasi had sent the prisoner away again, they taught him how to conduct a more productive interrogation. But the captain was as stubborn as a donkey, and didn't learn fast.

The three Germans were polite and correct, and within a very short time they had more or less deprived Garasi of power. Their wishes were always backed up by phone calls from secret service headquarters. For the first time, the captain felt he had been hung out to dry. He was on the point of exploding daily, but at the last moment he controlled himself for fear of his superior Colonel Badran. He could rely only on his soldiers and officers, who confirmed him in his dislike of the Germans. To ensure the support of those who ranked below him, he slackened the leash slightly.

The prisoners and their committee took note of all this, and with the help of some of the more willing soldiers who were open to bribery they began bringing in news from outside, as well as more medicinal drugs, paper, ink, and pens. Towards the end of October the first camera was smuggled into the camp.

At the end of November Lebanese newspapers reported that East Germans in the service of Syria were torturing prisoners, but the general public couldn't believe it. Surely men from the Eastern bloc wouldn't do such things. In the camp, however, the situation of the socialists and communists became worse than ever. Jakob Daro, leader of the communist group, could find no answer to the growing contempt of the other parties.

"Those are your comrades!" the prisoners told him, and some even spat at him. Daro was an experienced polemicist, but words were no help to him now.

259. Helplessness

After only a week, the methods of the East Germans were showing results. In spite of all the efforts of their resistance committee, prisoners were changing their minds by the dozen and signing recantations. Some gave up because of injured pride, after suffering torture at the hands of foreigners. But Farid would never have expected such a tough character as Faleh to weaken. He was one of the boldest of the Muslim Brotherhood.

First Faleh was interrogated at length by Garasi, who asked questions that he had answered several times before. So he repeated those answers, and the Germans wrote down what he said.

Then the captain rose and left the room. The Germans stayed behind. Suddenly Faleh's wife and three small children were led in. They were crying, and begged him to give in because they missed him and needed him. Faleh couldn't withstand this pressure, and he signed his recantation. The administration gave him clean clothes and a little money, and took him and his family to Damascus in a Landrover.

The prisoners in Tad had not been prepared for this kind of thing. The innovation of the German experts was to use a man's own family to prolong his torture. For many of the prisoners, the tears of their children, wives, or mothers struck more sharply than any whip.

Garasi's fury at the East Germans and their methods knew no bounds. He swore, and drank more heavily than ever.

"Assholes! I treat the prisoners like my own children, but they all have to play the hero. And then along come these European weaklings, these half-men, no moustaches, not even any hair on their chests, and they manage to soften up the traitors," a soldier heard him wailing.

It wasn't until early November that the prisoners found out how to stand firm. One of the Muslim Brothers shouted at his wife and children that they should be ashamed of themselves, and they'd better clear out. He threatened his wife that if she wrote him another letter or came to visit him, she could consider herself divorced.

A week later it was known all over the country that East Germans were abusing the men's love for their families.

Garasi heaved a sign of relief.

260. Silence

15 November 1968 was a warm day, almost like summer. Farid woke early. He had just been dreaming of Rana and the way she kissed his nipples. It had tickled, and he woke up.

He never celebrated his own birthday, but she always wanted to spend hers with him, and now it was November the 15th. He took a little candle out of its hiding place and lit it.

"Happy birthday, dear heart," he whispered, smiling. He knew that wherever Rana was, she would be thinking of him today.

There wasn't a soul in the courtyard. The German shepherd dogs were doing their rounds, and always glanced briefly at Farid as they passed his hut. "Rana," he whispered.

At that moment he felt sure that he would live with his lover some day, and for a little while he was at peace with the world.

જ

That same day, the committee had intended to discuss what the prisoners could do about the threat of those three blond men. They assumed that Garasi would have no objection to a rising against the Germans, but how could it be staged without offering provocation to the captain himself?

Farid was going to suggest a hunger strike, with the departure of the Germans as their sole demand for ending it. That way Garasi would realize that despite his own torture methods, the prisoners would accept him but never the foreigners.

Shortly before the planned discussion, however, two guards came to Hut 5 and took Farid away to be interrogated. They were civil enough, and Farid cursed his bad luck. He passed Hut 4, and exchanged glances with another committee member, who looked back at him with concern.

"Routine questioning," whispered Farid.

"Shut your mouth," shouted one of the guards. Farid walked on.

"Ah, good to see you. This is our strategist, the man who thinks himself Che Guevara leading an armed struggle," Garasi greeted him. Farid glanced at the corner of the room, where the three blond men were sitting.

"What are these pimps doing here?" he asked the captain, who raised his eyebrows over the rim of his sunglasses.

"There now, our young friend shows no respect! These are experts helping me out."

"And I'm not saying a word as long as those bastards sit there. Captain, we are citizens of a free country, and no foreigner may interrogate me in my own land."

"Calm down, young man. I'm asking the questions around here, and you will answer them if you don't want me to lose my temper. So let's begin. We can always torture you, but we don't want to do that." Garasi spoke as calmly as if he were under the influence of drugs. Although Farid kept his eyes fixed on the captain, he noticed Sausage, the tall German, nodding with satisfaction. And as if that had been Garasi's reward, the commandant now stepped up his friendliness. "Farid Mushtak, you're trained in chemistry, your country needs you more urgently than ever. Let's forget our differences. You are a decent man, you've fought for the people and made mistakes. Come, give me your hand and leave this place to continue the struggle and build the country up again."

Farid did not reply. So this is how they're doing it now, he thought.

Garasi went on speaking forcefully. "Farid, you are a member of the prisoners' secret committee. Tell me the names of the others, and no lies, please. Tell me and you're free."

"Oh, come on, captain! You won't get any names from me. You have enough informers. As you know, I don't belong to any political party. I'm always ready to make a public statement of remorse and loyalty."

"A clever fellow. But you're not tricking Garasi that way. Your Radicals couldn't care less about remorse ..."

"I was expelled from their group because I wouldn't take up arms," Farid interrupted.

"Hold your tongue!" shouted the captain, and Farid saw Sausage, in the distance, signing to him to play it down. Garasi immediately spoke more calmly. "We're not interested in your signature. Tell us three names of your secret committee and you're free. How's that for an offer?" Farid saw Sausage and Potato turning their thumbs up approvingly. Shanklish remained deep in thought.

So that was it. He was to be destroyed piecemeal. Nausea rose in him. "Right, here's my plain answer," he said calmly. "I will never give you names, not if it costs me my life."

The commandant beckoned to two guards who were sure to be standing somewhere behind Farid. He mustn't turn around, he had quickly learned that, for he did he would be hit in the face.

The guards put leather straps around Farid's arms and legs and tied him to a chair. Then they applied metal clamps to his fingers.

"I'm still listening. Isn't there anything you'd like to say to me?" asked Garasi. Farid just looked at him steadily. What an asshole, he thought. If stupidity could make a man sick he'd be dead by now. The captain gave a signal for the torture by electric shock to begin. A young officer pushed a button on a console. At the first shock Farid felt as if his soul had left his body. He tried to scream and opened his mouth, but his voice failed him. He felt as if he had exploded and fallen apart, but he was still strapped tight to the chair, writhing in pain.

The electric shock had dried up Farid's tongue, lips, and gums. They were all as dry and rough as wood. The electricity jolted through his body again.

"Farid, you can talk and then we'll stop."

Burning thirst tormented him. Shanklish, the German with the terrible body odor, rose to his feet and poured water from an earthenware jug into a glass with ice cubes in it. The sound of the ice cubes clinking made Farid's eyes pop out of his head. "Talk, and you can drink all you like," said Garasi.

Farid's refusal made the captain even angrier. It was obvious how hard he was having to work to control himself. He signalled to the guard again.

"Open your mouth," said the man, and when Farid did not react he took his jaw in his powerful hand. Terrible pain caught Farid's face, as if it were wedged in a vice. He was afraid his lower jaw would break. Resistance was useless. The guard put a piece of bare wire in his mouth, and the officer at the console started the device. Farid felt the strength of the current increase, and his throat, jaws, face muscles, and eyelids all twitched in painful spasms.

"Let go of the wire," said Garasi, "it will hold of itself now." And indeed, Farid's upper and lower jaws were numbed by the current, biting down on the piece of copper wire. He wanted to spit the diabolical thing out, but his jaws would not obey him.

The burning elm danced in the firelight, crackling as it sent out sparks that painted dazzling geometrical patterns in the air. Jagged green lightning kept emerging from the darkness and striking his eyes.

To end his torments, and with a huge effort of will, Farid threw himself backward with all his might. His head hit the floor, and he immediately felt relief as consciousness left him.

261. The Guardian Angel

When he came back to his senses he was still strapped to the chair in front of Garasi's desk. The room was empty. His mouth and the back of his head hurt. He tasted blood; the bare wire had cut his gums as he fell.

There was complete silence, as if the entire camp had been abandoned. To his surprise, the clock on the wall showed that it was one in the afternoon. Had the torture lasted that long, or had he been lying unconscious all those hours?

He heard the door opening, but he did not turn. His heart was thudding. Then he felt a hand on his head.

"What have those bastards done to you?" whispered Samih, moving in front of Farid so that they could see each other. He was carrying an earthenware water jug. Farid sucked from the spout. The water sizzled in his hot, dehydrated body. He drank and drank, feeling Samih's cool hand on his forehead, and as if the water were running over, tears came to his eyes.

"Darwish sends you greetings. And I'm to tell you, laddie, Darwish admires you!"

Farid smiled and moved his head away from the jug. Without any word of goodbye, swift and soundless as a cat, Samih disappeared again.

Farid wondered why he never thought of death under torture: not of dying and going to Paradise, like the Muslim Brothers, nor of a heroic death for the communist cause. Many prisoners sang the Internationale or recited from the Koran while they were being tortured. He felt almost ashamed of it, but under torture he always thought of

Rana's beautiful hands, and how she laid them on his forehead when he was sad. He longed for those hands now.

⁂

He heard steps in the stairwell. Garasi, followed by the Germans, entered the room. "Take him away and fetch me Muhsin Abu Khal from Hut 9," he said, sitting down at his desk.

"And as for you," he told Farid as the guards undid the straps, "I'm going to crush you like a cockroach, and no Guevara or Castro will be able to save you."

262. The Rising

January 1969 was icy cold. Snow had fallen all over the country for the first time in forty years. The prisoners were freezing in their unheated, open huts.

At the end of January Hamid Tabet, a teacher with heart disease who was one of the Muslim Brotherhood, died under torture. During a raid the evening before, the guards had found the unfortunate man's secret diary in which he had been carefully recording life in the camp in detail. Captain Garasi regarded the mere possession of paper and pencil as an unforgivable personal attack on him. A knife, and even a pistol and a kilo of hashish were discovered in the same raid, but the owners of these items got off lightly, just a few punches in the camp commandant's office. But the diary infuriated the captain, and when the timid teacher, with unexpected courage, called Garasi an enemy of Islam and a lackey of the unbelievers, the commandant's rage knew no bounds.

Beside himself with anger, he went over to the young officer operating the electric shock button, pushed him abruptly aside, cursed the prisoner, and turned the current up to maximum. No one stopped him. One of the Germans had leaped to his feet, and tried to revive the teacher, but Hamid Tabet was no longer reacting. The Germans went straight off to Damascus and didn't come back until next day, after the corpse had been smuggled into the hospital there. The camp commandant received a medical certificate stating that Hamid Tabet had died in the military hospital after a long-standing history of heart disease.

Such a false certificate was nothing new either to Captain Garasi or the doctors. A routine case, but just as no one life is like any other, so no death resembles another. Hamid Tabet had not, perhaps, been a charismatic and eloquent leader, but his friends loved him for what he was.

He died at a time when the prisoners needed little more to overcome their fears at last. Hamid did more by his death than he had ever done in life. He gave the others the final incentive to free themselves from the pit. There was no going back now. And Captain Garasi, with his bulldog's nose, soon scented it.

He panicked, for he had much at stake. His promotion to the rank of major was to be the culmination and end of his military career, and at the same time the basis for his pension. Nothing else must happen in his camp until he got that promotion. So he set his informers to work, and talked to some of the prisoners himself, deploring the unfortunate slip-up. He tried to pacify the communists and Satlanists with the argument that the dead man had been only an insignificant Muslim Brother. Garasi also put a stop to the torture, and even the food was slightly better again. But the prisoners' committee saw their one and only chance, and undeterred they called for a hunger strike. That was on 14 February 1969.

The camp commandant didn't understand the reports of his informers in Huts 1 and 3, who went to see him early in the morning and told him about the hunger strike. "Then let them starve!" But his smile died away when the guards said that not just one or two but all sixteen huts were refusing food.

Around ten o'clock, one of the officers came and put a sheet of paper in front of Garasi. The prisoners' missive addressed neither him nor the Syrian government, but world opinion. And in succinct, but clear language, they demanded:

1. The immediate removal of the East German torture experts.
2. The cessation of all torture and degradation of prisoners held at Tad.
3. The cessation of slave labour in the basalt quarry.
4. A public inquiry into the wrongs that have already been suffered.
5. The free choice of a legal representative.
6. Better provision of food and medicaments.
7. The release of all young offenders under twenty.
8. More freedom to exercise in the yard.
9. Weekly visits from family members.
10. Medical treatment of the sick by doctors whom the prisoners trust.

Garasi grinned. "Where do they think we are, Switzerland?" But his voice sounded uncertain.

At midday all the officers met in his office. Even the three Germans looked paler than they were anyway. Such an oppressive silence had never lain over the camp before. Over one and a half thousand prisoners had united to make demands in language that sounded as determined as if they hadn't had enough of a taste of hell yet. For the first time in their lives, the officers felt curiously afraid. One false step, and they knew there would be no stopping a catastrophe.

Garasi sought a solution similar to the one the Interior Minister had once explained to him. "Our policy is to kill the Muslim Brothers, the Satlanists, and the communists, while at the same time staying friends with Saudi Arabia, Satlan of Egypt, and the Soviet Union."

After some thought, he announced a three-point plan. "First we keep quiet and cut off all information going out of the camp. Second, we arrest the leaders of the strike and put them in solitary confinement until they die. Third, we tempt the prisoners with better food and at the same time show them, quite calmly, that we're not impressed by their strike, they're only risking their own lives, and they can't overcome the state with such silly tricks anyway."

The officers nodded. Even the Germans suddenly seemed to respect the old commandant.

263. The End of the Tunnel

Garasi had declined to enter into any kind of negotiation with the prisoners, but when the hunger strike had gone on for two weeks he was baffled. The officers advised him to make concessions, and he gave way.

That step put the prisoners' committee in a very dangerous situation. Up to this point, only Farid was known to the informers as a member of it. If the members of a whole delegation now revealed their identities, it could mean death for them all. So they decided to send only three men. The seven others would stay under cover so that they could continue the struggle if all three delegates were killed. Salman the Muslim Brother and the journalist Ali Abusaid volunteered to accompany Farid.

The camp commandant, gracious as a pasha, offered them tea. The prisoners politely declined. Farid could not say for certain whether hunger had sharpened his senses, but he suddenly smelled the captain's fear. Garasi had his mind on just one thing, getting his major's pension. And that in itself made him vulnerable.

"Listen, Captain," Farid opened the conversation, turning on the camp commandant the eyes of a hungry panther sure of its prey. "You and the Germans between you killed Hamid Tabet, and you will have to answer for it. The Germans can disappear again without trace, but you're in a trap."

In the following five seconds it became clear to him that he had won the battle. He didn't yet know whether he would survive the victory himself, but he saw that Hamid Tabet's murderer was paralysed by fear. Garasi knew that if he didn't nip that accusation in the bud here in the camp, by going along with the prisoners' demands, he could expect assassination by one of the Muslim Brotherhood any time after the first day of his retirement. The captain's face fell. Panic seized hold of him. He did not reply coherently, just stuttered, "What? Tabet? What Tabet?" only to fall prey to even worse panic next minute. He didn't hit out, but he shouted, like a man demented, that the state would rather see dead men than renegades. Suddenly he fell silent. He was obviously trying to smile. Then he spoke quietly, adopting a paternal manner. He would go to meet them and reward them for keeping quiet. He was not a monster. They could talk to him.

Work in the quarry, interrogations, freedom to exercise, those were all matters in which he had some influence. The food would be better in future too, and a doctor whom they trusted would treat the sick prisoners every day. However, he would have to discuss all the other demands with the Ministry. The presence of the Germans was a delicate strategic matter, and only the Ministry could permit family visits. But he, Commandant Garasi, swore by his military honour to do what he could for the prisoners' demands. But first they must restore order and end the hunger strike.

"The Germans must go at once, don't you understand yet?" cried Salman the Muslim Brother, standing up. The others followed suit.

"It's now or never!" said Ali Abusaid the journalist. For it was clear to them all that even the criminal fraternity among them – and so far it had been difficult to persuade those men to do anything – would react if they discovered that they had been sent to a special camp designed for studies in interrogation. So the committee let it be known that the secret service HQ was holding on to the Germans because they were carrying out long-term experiments. All the detainees at Tad would die, because the authorities were interested only in experimenting with their lives in every imaginable way. In other words: the prisoners were raw material for the testing of new torture methods, and President Amran was the first in Arabia to be introducing such methods and recording their effects.

The prisoners' committee exaggerated, but there was no other way of convincing the criminals. Now they too joined the political prisoners in insisting that the Germans must go unconditionally, and at once. They wouldn't go along with the other demands, but agreement on this one point was a breakthrough, and meant the end of total isolation. It was the criminals who sent the first secret message through to Damascus with news from Tad. How they did it they weren't saying.

"We have our own pigeon post," said one of the big gangland bosses when Farid tried questioning him.

264. Last Attempt

Garasi was no longer in control of the camp, and that evening the officers knew it. An anxious first lieutenant broke his word and phoned Colonel Badran. Low-voiced, he told him about the mood among the soldiers. The colonel listened quietly, so quietly that the young officer asked from time to time, "Are you still there?"

Unlike the European and American newspapers, it took the Arab press a long time to react to the hunger strike at Tad. The Lebanese were first to report it, then the Jordanians and Iraqis, who traditionally did not have good relations with Damascus.

On 1 March the Syrian government newspaper also published a short report of certain differences of opinion at Tad. Half-heartedly, it called for explanations and the punishment of those responsible. However, the place was still described as a prison for serious criminal offenders and terrorists.

Garasi was cracking up. He set his guards on the prisoners, and ordered raid after raid. But neither the "Tad Printing Press", with its logo of a pencil and three pieces of barbed wire, nor the camera which had taken the pictures of all parts of the camp could be found.

Colonel Badran was extremely displeased. What annoyed him most was the steady trickle of news and photographs getting out of the country. He summoned Garasi.

On his return, the commandant told his officers that it had felt like an interrogation. The cold demeanour of young Colonel Badran, who hadn't even returned his military salute, had been alarming. He had wordlessly slammed a French newspaper down on his desk in front of Garasi. "How did *Le Monde* get to know these criminals were in your camp? I've checked the list. It's correct in every particular, and it must have been smuggled out only a few days ago. Don't you see what's going on? The Jews will finish us off. First they occupy the Golan Heights, now they're spreading lies about human rights in Syria. What are cameras doing in a camp? Captain Garasi, you are treating those prisoners as if they were on vacation at Tad. When are you going to wake up?"

The colonel had laid particular emphasis on the word "captain".

Badran had been an army captain himself before the coup. He was seething, for France was demanding an official explanation from the Syrian government: was it true that torture camps existed, and were Germans and Russians working there? Development aid and negotiations on arms deals had been put on ice.

Colonel Badran demanded a firmer hand with the prisoners and no leave for anyone working at the camp until the leak had been tracked down.

"You want a firmer hand with the prisoners, but suppose there are deaths?" asked Garasi.

"Then come to me. I'll shoulder the responsibility."

This was something new to Garasi. He had never heard anything like it in thirty years. "Can I tell you something in confidence?" he pleaded.

Badran sensed that this experienced officer was carrying another secret around with him. "Go ahead."

"The Germans imposed on us," said Garasi in a hoarse tone, "have offended the national sensibilities of the prisoners. It was the only thing that let the politicals build a bridge with the criminal fraternity. All of a sudden the Muslim Brothers and the pimps are united against us. There's never been any such thing before."

Colonel Badran was thoughtful, and remained silent. Garasi secretly smiled behind his smooth mask of concern.

"I'll have to speak to the President about it. This is a tricky business. The Germans stay for now. We can't have criminals and terrorists dictating what's good for the Fatherland and what isn't. You must keep your camp cut off from the outside world. It wasn't the Germans who sent those lies abroad, it was Syrians," announced the colonel, standing up.

265. Victory

Garasi decided to act with the utmost severity. At the beginning of June 1969, only one more year would stand between him and retirement. So he must make just one more little effort, and then he would have reached safety.

"Only a firm hand will keep that devil's spawn down," he shouted hysterically when his officers told him that yet again none of the prisoners had touched food all day.

Two days later the first two men, a criminal and a Satlanist, died of inanition.

The prisoners' committee asked for an hour's commemoration to be observed that night. They sensed the discouraging effect of death.

Next morning Garasi had five doctors brought in from Damascus. They went from hut to hut, examining the prisoners. Three were so weak that they had to go to hospital at once.

However, the detainees were afraid the sick men would be mistreated in Damascus. They were reassured only when the doctors solemnly swore to take care nothing happened to them.

Around midday, Garasi sent the cook out into the yard to grill deliciously seasoned kebabs, bake fresh bread, and offer mixed salads. It immeasurably increased the prisoners' torment. More than ten men were unable to hold out any longer, and ate so much and so greedily that they had terrible stomach pains. Next day, however, they were back on hunger strike.

Finally President Amran intervened. He fired his Interior Minister. A day later Garasi sent for Farid, Salman, and Ali Abusaid. Seated at his desk, he looked thin and debilitated. "We'll come to terms with you. The Germans flew home to their own country last night. Work in the quarry has been stopped, and anyone who doesn't commit a punishable offence will not be touched, as before. Food will improve, you can have longer to exercise in the yard, and from now on two doctors will be on duty for six hours a day in the camp. Visits from family are permitted once a month, and young offenders under twenty will be taken to a new re-education centre. In return we expect you to behave well and observe discipline, cleanliness, and patriotism." Garasi's voice was shaky, although he was trying hard to say those last words in a peremptory tone. There was nothing of his former bearing left. Anyone could see he was afraid.

Farid, Salman, and Ali Abusaid ran down the staircase three steps at a time, and out in the yard they began rejoicing and dancing. "We did it! We won! Cheer up, we won!"

The guards watched them. Farid was turning somersaults and rolling along the ground, only to leap up again next minute whooping like a lunatic, uttering noises that made all the others laugh. Ali Abusaid performed several perfect cartwheels. Criminals, Muslim Brothers, nationalists, Radicals, and communists alike fell into each other's arms to celebrate the end of the hunger strike.

Word was sent to the kitchen and the bakery. Before long there was vegetable soup and crisp flatbread. Darwish came to Hut 5. Its doors, like those of all the other huts, stood open. He greeted everyone, handed out cigarettes, and congratulated them on their victory. Then he went over to Farid, who was sitting on the floor spooning up his soup, bent down, picked him up like a baby, and kissed him on the cheek.

"You deserve it, laddie!" he cried. Many of the prisoners were laughing and weeping at the same time. "We'll soon be home," they rejoiced, and when the guards came and kept assuring them that they'd all make a new start now and forget the past the prisoners applauded. Farid winked at Ali Abusaid, who was sitting opposite him enjoying a cigarette. "They live on forgetfulness, like chickens," said the journalist, resigned.

"And we live on memory, like camels," replied Farid.

It was 12 March 1969.

266. The End of Garasi

Garasi stood beside the truck that was taking his household goods from his service apartment in the camp back to his home village of Daraia near the capital city Damascus. "Look at me," he told his officers. "This is my reward: I've sacrificed myself for the Fatherland for thirty-three years, and now I'm discharged from the army because some criminal goes and dies. Because that's the reason, even if no one says so. They'd rather claim I was involved in a conspiracy." All of a sudden his voice had a defiant edge. "Why don't they put their cards on the table? Then I'd have something to say myself about those bastard experts I had foisted on me – oh yes, they left the sinking ship as soon as things got too hot. Off and away they went. But the powers that be don't want to hear about such things. It all has to be my fault."

Then, as if regretting this outburst against his superiors, he changed tack and was all humility. "I told the Interior Minister, please, even if he didn't have any sympathy for me he might at least think of my children … how will they … at school …" And Garasi, whose eyes were usually hard as marble, was weeping and sobbing. His words drowned in his tears; no one could make out what he was saying any more.

Then the gate opened, and he stopped short in surprise. A Landrover drove up to him and ostentatiously stopped only a metre or so away. A man in civilian clothes beckoned the startled captain over to him. Garasi went. Little could be heard, but the commandant's stooping posture showed that the civilian was more powerful than he was. What he was saying seemed to confuse Garasi. The captain pointed despairingly but energetically at the truck, but the civilian in the car moved not a muscle. He just stared wordlessly into the distance. Through the open gate, the assembled officers, NCOs, and soldiers now saw two jeeps and a small van, the kind used for transporting prisoners. Garasi was pleading with the civilian, but the silence choked his words. And the captain who had so recently been lord over the lives of thousands, collapsed. His arms, which he had always used to emphasize what he said, dangled helplessly as he went towards the small van. A powerful man was holding the back hatch open. And when Garasi stood hesitating by the vehicle, the secret service man gave him a firm and disrespectful push that sent him flying inside it. Then the man bolted the hatch and got into the front seat next to the driver.

Without giving the officers, NCOs, and soldiers standing around so much as a glance, the man in civilian clothes made a slight gesture, indicating his wishes to the driver of the Landrover, and the vehicle raced out of the gate, churning up a great deal of sand and dust. After a while it disappeared from sight in the endless desert.

The truck containing Garasi's household goods was looted that same night. When a phone call came from secret service HQ days later, saying that the former commandant's belongings were to be sent to his children in Daraia, the man on duty was rather confused, not just because the truck was now empty, but also because the caller spoke of the convicted officer Garasi.

267. Nabil

The worst of it for the officers, NCOs, and soldiers in the camp was the embargo on contact with the outside world imposed on all of them by the secret service HQ. Their telephone lines were tapped, and the connection was broken at any hint of ambiguity. A motorized unit formed an impenetrable ring surrounding the camp. Large notices in English, French, and Arabic now stood for a radius of ten kilometres around it, declaring the terrain a military restricted area and forbidding intrusion on pain of death. No journalist ventured to come anywhere near the camp.

Inside it, cheerful chaos prevailed after Garasi's departure. Secret service HQ, which had power over the camp "for dangerous elements", was taking its time. And as if all the prisoners had lost their memories in the elation of victory, they were mingling on friendly terms with the soldiers, officers, and guards. They ate, smoked, played cards, and joked together, and discussed what the future would bring. Suddenly hearty, childlike laughter found its way into the camp.

It was at this time that Farid got to know a young soldier called Nabil. Aged twenty, Nabil had had bad luck. Two days after arriving at his barracks north of Damascus, he had had an angry exchange of words with an NCO, who saw to it that the young man was transferred to duty at Tad. But Nabil assured Farid, in confidence, that the real reason for his disciplinary transfer was the NCO's hatred of all townies and Christians. Nabil was both. His parents came from Bab Tuma in Damascus, where his father ran a small food store selling preserved delicacies. Like many young people, Nabil knew the famous confectioner's shop belonging to Farid's father, and told him that he sometimes used to spend all his weekend pocket money there on his favourite sweetmeat, a confection known as nightingale nests.

He had fallen unhappily in love with a rich young woman, but soon she decided to marry a wealthy neighbour, and he had to bury his love deep in his heart. Six months ago, however, she got in touch with him again; it seemed that her marriage had disappointed her, and she wanted to run away with Nabil.

Farid listened to the young soldier's tale of woe for nights on end. He soon realized that just having someone listening to him acted on Nabil like a magnet. He sought Farid out as often as he could to tell him more about his sorrows and his perplexity.

For a long time Farid had thought listening an art mastered better by women than men. Claire said that in that case, he himself had very feminine ears. He knew that listening makes you wise, but he had no idea that in his own case his ability to listen would actually save his life.

268. The Cold Voice

The elm was burning. The fire played around its stout, split trunk and licked up to the tree's low crown, a blazing pyramid spraying sparks into the dark sky with all its might, as if they were those long-lost glow-worms that can hide away for decades, emerging at last in their search for love.

The strong wind sang its loud song through the flames. It sounded like screams of pain in chorus. The sparks went out in mid-flight, but many splinters of the tree were strong enough to withstand the cold air above and fall back to the ground, still glowing. The dry grass and bushes caught fire. The air smelled of burning wood and thyme. A spark suddenly dug into his right cheek. Farid started up, his heart racing, and struck the burning splinter of wood away. Everything immediately dissolved into darkness.

It was some time before his eyes, dazzled by the fire, could see the sleeping men around him in the large, dark hut. His vision clouded over again, but he didn't feel like lying down any more. Sitting on the floor, he held his head in both hands. His temples were throbbing with pain, and sparks flashed in a dark firmament behind his closed eyelids. He helplessly rubbed the root of his nose, which was supposed to help when you felt dazed.

The yard was dark, and the faint light of the lantern made it seem even darker. A blackbird was singing. Farid's eyes wandered from the place where he sat, looking through the grating and across the yard with the two palms at its centre. The sky was growing brighter only slowly, but now Farid could see the blackbird on top of the right-hand palm. As if it felt reassured now that it could see the sun from its high perch, it sang one last time and flew away.

Farid was freezing to the core. He had a numb sensation in his limbs, but his head was clear; the dazed sensation had gone away. Very slowly he rose to his feet to go to the grating and get more fresh air. After a while he heard moans in the far corner of the hut, where Basil was penetrating his lover Fahmi's backside. As usual, Fahmi was begging his passionate lover to be quiet and not pinch him so hard.

Farid closed his eyes. The cold breeze felt pleasantly cool on his hot face. He breathed in and out deeply, as the doctor had once recommended, because at such moments the brain needs plenty of oxygen. In the middle of his third or fourth breath he heard the voice again. Ever since childhood, he had experienced it after every fit of unconsciousness: a clear, cold voice speaking to him. As a child he had thought he was hearing a real person, but as the years passed he knew that the voice was inside him.

A successor to the dismissed commandant would be coming today and would destroy the camp, said the voice. Trembling all over, Farid decided to say nothing to the other prisoners. He didn't want to crush their reviving hopes.

For the first time in over a decade, he thought back to his years at the monastery of St. Sebastian. Above all, he thought of Brother Gabriel, who like Farid himself had suffered from epilepsy, and after an epileptic fit had prophetic knowledge of events that sometimes didn't come true until several years later.

"Epilepsy," Brother Gabriel had said at the time, "cleanses the mind of all the layers of civilization that have accumulated over it for ten thousand years. For a few seconds the brain is naked and innocent as a newborn child. In those seconds it is at one with God, and that's where the knowledge come from. It's a kind of knowledge that animals and babies have too, and we can't explain it. But neither the babies nor the animals can tell us what they've experienced. If an adult ever comes by that knowledge again he's a prophet. And all prophets have been epileptics."

269. Mahdi's Arrival

Shortly after the midday meal on that same day, the new camp commandant arrived. A bus drove up to the camp gates behind his inconspicuous Landrover. There were ten officers and about twenty NCOs in the bus, and another was following with civilian staff. Only the Landrover drove in through the gates; the other vehicles parked outside.

The new commandant was not a tall man, but the way he walked showed that he was athletic. He couldn't be older than forty. His head was handsome, although he had a bald patch, and his eyes were hidden behind reflecting sunglasses.

He stationed himself in front of the palm on the left, just where the previous commandant always liked to stand, but unlike Garasi the new man wore civilian clothes. He was talking almost cheerfully to three civilians who seemed to be his subordinates. His voice was quiet, so quiet that even though the prisoners kept absolutely still they could hardly make anything out.

The soldiers quickly formed up under the orders of the new officers. Soon after that some of them stormed into the administration building and the barracks. The rest of them surrounded the camp.

Apparently the men had precise instructions, for a little later screams were heard, and the prisoners, eyes wide with shock, saw the former officers and NCOs being driven out of various buildings under the blows of their own men.

After that the entire Mafia leadership, including Dr. Maqdisi, was brought out of the hospital, bamboo canes wielded by the secret service men whipped down on them, and they were sent to join the disgraced officers and NCOs. Over eighty men now stood there, paralysed, held at bay in the yard by only ten civilians.

They were wailing like bereaved widows. What a humiliation, in front of all the soldiers and prisoners! Finally one of the civilians raised his hand, and the wailing stopped. There was deathly silence.

"The convicted prisoner Abdulhamid Garasi," began the new camp commandant in a calm voice, "made a confession in front of a military tribunal to the effect that all of you, officers, NCOs, and criminals, rendered services to the dangerous elements in this camp, smuggling information, drugs, arms and books, even radio sets and cameras in for them. You have done the Fatherland more harm than the Israelis did in twenty years. All the accused army men, consequently, are discharged with immediate effect. They have quarter of an hour to pack their things and go to the gates. From there they will be taken to a prison until judgement is passed on them. The criminals will go to a special prison where they will keep quiet for ever."

Farid heard not a trace of anger or vengefulness in that voice as it announced the destruction of so many lives. His legs felt weak, because the commandant was doing exactly what the cold voice had prophesied to him. He sank to the ground, but held the bars of the grating with both hands.

"Mother, oh, my dear Mother," he heard himself whispering. He looked at the figures who had been acting so big only recently, and who now stood there small and bowed. Some fell on their knees. "Sir, have mercy on my children! I'm guilty, but they – they can't help it," cried an NCO. He had been one of the few kindly ones among the brutes. His tears infected the others, and many of them began to weep, including Milhelm, the gangland big boss.

The old guard Istanbuli pleaded hoarsely that he had nothing to do with any of it. He was here as a volunteer and hadn't taken a lira for anything at all. He begged to be allowed to go home. He was an old man, he said.

"An old man, yes," replied the commandant, "but Garasi

incriminated you in particular. You were the courier between Milhelm and the journalists, he said. The enemies of the Fatherland had only to take their lies to Milhelm, that scum of humanity, and you passed the reports and photos on. Congratulations! A well-organized gang. Istanbuli, the old fool whom the army has fed for forty years, collected from both Milhelm and the journalists and put those lying reports into circulation. The *New York Times, Le Monde, Der Spiegel* – they all printed the stories to destroy Syria's reputation. It so happens that all those newspapers and magazines are owned by Jews. You might not believe it, Istanbuli, but we already have your contact man the journalist Hadi Almasri behind bars, and he's told us to the dollar what sums you had from him. Think of that! And where, then, is the money?" asked the commandant, in venomously dulcet tones. "Your wife has now found the box for us. Five thousand three hundred and seventy dollars. Every dollar earned by treachery. A nice trade! Do you know what the penalty for treachery is? For proven activity as an agent for an enemy power? Do you happen to know, little uncle? No? The death penalty," said the new commandant, not even sternly but more as if it were a joke, yet death could be tasted in his words.

Three of the civilians kicked one of the most objectionable and hard-hearted NCOs as he crawled to the new commandant on his knees. "Sir, let me kiss your hand. I beg you for mercy, my wife is very sick, I needed money. Garasi blinded me! What poor devil can refuse a commandant who wants to share his loot?" But the new commandant remained unmoved. Only the corners of his mouth twitched with revulsion. His smooth, dark-skinned face gave nothing away.

Farid felt pity stir in him, and hated himself for it. Pity for the officers and guards who had tormented him. He was ashamed of himself. But when he saw his two guardian angels Darwish and Samih standing casually in the kitchen doorway, watching the spectacle, his peace of mind returned.

Oddly enough, none of the common soldiers were punished. Far from it; the new officers and NCOs spoke to them in very friendly tones. Suddenly Farid saw the soldier Nabil whom he liked. He was on guard at the entrance gate, and when Farid waved to him he smiled and gave a little nod.

The new team got down to work, and it was clear that they served their commandant with liking and great respect. The higher-ranking officers of the new regime sat in a semi-circle around the commandant in his civilian clothes, on chairs that had speedily been brought out and in the shade of the two palm trees.

Half an hour later the detainees learned the commandant's name: Major Mahdi Said.

270. At Close Quarters

Next morning the guards and soldiers told the detainees in the eight front huts to pick up their two thin blankets and straw mats and move into the other eight huts. It was hell. The huts were over-full anyway. Fights broke out, the smell of other men's sweat was a torment. Farid noticed something in him changing. He turned angry and aggressive in defence of his straw mat and his food ration. Hunger, overcrowding, and weariness robbed the detainees of respect, friendship, and personal affection. To his horror, Farid found that Sami Beirumi, a journalist whom he had always liked, proved to be quarrelsome and sly now that they were crammed into the same hut together, and didn't even shrink from stealing the bread of a fellow prisoner lying in a fever. He ate it before the sick man woke up.

No one knew why they had all been crowded in together at such close quarters, but soon they heard hammers, saws, and drills at work in the vacated huts. Six days later all the prisoners were moved to the front rows of huts again, and the back rows became the building site. They had spent only a few hours in their new quarters when one of the detainees spotted microphones in the ceiling.

"Those are the visible ones, but they wouldn't have needed all that time to install them. So what else have they hidden away?" he asked out loud in Hut 4, when other men found places on the floor and in the walls that looked freshly plastered. Several beams in the ceiling had odd little holes in them, conspicuous because of their symmetrical arrangement.

Farid was sure now that the new camp commandant was about to conduct another stage of the experiment, for if the assumptions of a detainee who was a professor of physics were correct, the huts were now under surveillance all around the clock. There was talk of new, sensitive microphones from Russia, so small that you couldn't see them at all with the naked eye. The prisoners were helpless, every one of them exposed to the guards like an open book.

Next day, when one of the prisoners tried scratching at the new plaster, he was taken away within minutes, and brought back an hour later with his fingers broken. That proved it to everyone: they could keep nothing secret any more. Fear paralysed them. Even in the darkest times, the huts had always been a place of refuge, with a certain protective intimacy about them. Of course they had also been subject to nocturnal raids, but those were regarded as attacks, intrusions into the detainees' personal area. The new commandant, however, had simply done away with all intimacy.

Only the solitary confinement cells in the cellars of the monastery ruins at the east gate of the camp had been spared the technicians' attentions.

≫

Mahdi Said was an important man. He was regularly flown by helicopter to the Interior Ministry, and came back only a few days later. He seldom spent the night in the camp commandant's service apartment. Even if it was late, his chauffeur usually drove him to Damascus and brought him back next morning.

Yet Mahdi Said – unlike Garasi – seemed to have a perfect team. Not only was the atmosphere among the officers quiet and amicable, but all went to plan even when the commandant wasn't there.

271. The Cold Hand of Fear

It was two weeks before the first prisoners were fetched for interrogation. They were two men from Hut 5. Three hours later only one of them was brought back, a Muslim Brother called Sabah Kasem. What happened to the other man no one knew. He never reappeared. The commandant, unlike his predecessor, was a devout Muslim, but rejected the ideas of the Muslim Brotherhood. Intellectually he was of a completely different calibre from that brutal drunk Garasi. "He knew my life from the records as well as if he'd grown up with me," said the interrogated prisoner. But he also said that Mahdi Said had presented him with the choice between a slow death and re-education to make him a good citizen. He wouldn't have to reject his faith or sign some theatrical piece of paper, just show that he wanted to be a patriot. The first step in re-education, said the commandant, was total obedience. It was up to the detainees to cooperate, and when Sabah refused to cooperate in any way with the camp authorities the new commandant hadn't even seemed angry, just told him to go away and think about it. "But," added Sabah, "there was more of a threat in those words than in all Garasi's hysterics. That's why I'm contemplating giving up and going back to real life, martyr or not. A hot shower, a water-pipe to smoke in my courtyard at home, sitting with my children among my pots of basil and rose trees – that's my idea of Paradise." But his voice betrayed great fear as well as this modest hope. The detainees tried to soothe him, but that fear already had his heart in its cold hand.

Next day Sabah called for one of the guards and asked him to tell the commandant he wanted to be a good citizen. Soon after that he was taken away and disappeared for ever. The Muslim Brothers in the camp cursed him.

About ten prisoners had to go for interrogation every day. Some were treated gently, others brutally tortured. The torture victims spoke of a cold-blooded Mahdi Said who always stayed in the background and, unlike Garasi, didn't get his own hands dirty. He strolled back and forth between the rooms where the prisoners were being interrogated and tortured, gave orders in a whisper, and then went away again. He himself interrogated only the most important detainees.

Farid found it hard to come to terms with all this. The defeat of the prisoners was absolute. The world had forgotten them again, and the regime didn't mind about its poor reputation. The government in Damascus was even proud of it, saying it showed how revolutionary it was, and sure enough, the media of the socialist countries repeated this nonsense as if paid to do so by the state.

Microphones and presumably tiny cameras were installed everywhere, robbing the detainees of their courage. One day a new rumour went around: Mahdi Said personally lent his torturers a hand in only one thing, giving injections. No one knew the details. Some said that prisoners were injected with a truth serum, others mentioned pentothal, barbiturates, and other psychotropic drugs. Colonel Badran, they claimed, had ordered these things from East Berlin.

✢

It was 17 April, Syrian Independence Day. The loudspeakers in the courtyard blared out the national anthem and Austrian marching music. Now and then telegrams from all over the world to President Amran were read out. But unlike his predecessor, Mahdi Said did not make the prisoners sing songs of praise to the President. He wasn't celebrating; even on Independence Day he came back from Damascus by helicopter early in the morning and went through his daily quota of ten prisoners. The journalist Ali Abusaid, who with Farid had carried through the strikers' demands, whispered to his partner of the time that many detainees were being "turned" during interrogation and then sent back to the huts. As good citizens of new standing they had to show their loyalty by spreading false information, recruiting more men to collaborate with the secret service, and sniffing out troublemakers.

And Ali Abusaid had another tale to tell. He had recognized one of the new guards as his youngest cousin, a nasty piece of work. His cousin had told him in a place behind Hut 1, the only square metre where anyone could go more or less unobserved, that several prisoners had now told Mahdi Said the names of all the leaders of the strike, the men who had won the battle against his predecessor. And almost with relish, his cousin finally added, "And he doesn't want remorse and loyalty from you and your friends. He wants to crush you."

The injection most often mentioned by the detainees, said the frightened journalist, was one of the new commandant's most diabolical methods. It contained a mixture of several psychotropic drugs, and depending on the strength of the dose it made people talkative, docile, or feeble-minded. If it was given in too high a concentration, or to someone with a nervous disability, it could be fatal.

A day later Bishara came back from exercise in the yard, beaming. "Mahdi is one of us," he whispered. Farid froze.

"What do you mean?" he quietly asked Bishara, looking up at the holes in the beams. He knew he was overheard.

"He's a Christian." And as if it were a state secret, Bishara added quietly, "And he's wily. He converted to Islam only to get promotion, had himself circumcized, said *Ashhadu anna la Illaha illa Allah* once ... and the fools believed he was a Muslim now. But blood's thicker than water. He's one of us, and he's particularly courteous to the Christians. A very educated man. He speaks four languages."

"And who put this nonsense into your head?" asked Farid, irritated by such naivety in an old communist suddenly keen to lay claim to his Christian faith. "From all I've heard Mahdi is a fanatical Muslim, close to the Muslim Brotherhood, and all he has against them is that they want to topple his government." But Farid's anger with Bishara, who was desperately clutching at straws to give himself some hope in the ocean of his fears, gradually turned to pity.

It wasn't long before reality caught up with Bishara. A Christian detainee had been tortured until he went out of his mind. When Bishara heard of that he began to sob despairingly.

After a while the prisoners heard about the building of a camp for those who had been "saved". It was between Damascus and Tad, in the middle of a green oasis with sports fields, an artificial lake, and clean little apartments. "They prepare people for a positive return to society there," said Salih, one of the Palestinian prisoners, not without enthusiasm.

Farid was listening with only half an ear. He was stunned by another piece of news: the miserable death of the conscientious objector Nagi

Salam, whom he had liked. He had not come back after interrogation. It was said he had been taken away, supported by two soldiers, and was later found unconscious in Damascus, in the stairwell of the building where his parents lived. The doctor they called had been unable to do anything for him.

In fact the ring of silence around the camp was complete. The prisoners knew nothing of the outside world if the commandant did not allow it. So Mahdi Said obviously *wanted* them to hear the news of Nagi's death. No one knew why.

272. The Injection

Mahdi Said interrogated the most important prisoners by night, and on those occasions he did not, unusually for him, go back to Damascus. Night was the worst time for interrogations; it made you feel small, lonely, and weak. The day had drained the prisoners of all their strength, while Mahdi Said had enjoyed a siesta of two or three hours. If questioning went on until dawn it was sheer hell for the exhausted detainees. After two endless nocturnal interrogations, Ali Abusaid left the camp where he had buried five years of his life in the sand. Farid was in despair, for with Ali's departure he had lost a valuable support.

It was after midnight when two soldiers appeared in Hut 5 and told Farid to come for questioning. He felt the same unspeakable fear as he had felt in his boyhood at the monastery gate. A fear of what was about to happen, and infinite loneliness. "Mother, oh Mother, where are you?" he heard himself whisper in the voice of a thirteen-year-old boy.

"Get moving, son of a whore," barked the smaller guard. He was obviously uneasy. "Your mother would have done better to bring a dog into the world!" Farid could feel no strength in his legs. His temples were throbbing, his heart was ramming his ribcage as if to escape from it.

Outside, the sky was clear and cicadas were chirping. For a moment

Farid thought of Rana. She loved nothing so much as the music of the cicadas by night.

"I hear you're a dangerous fellow. To me you're a cockroach! A rent boy. A queer. I could tell right away from your face!" said the guard as they went along, his voice hoarse with agitation.

"Let him alone, calm down," the other guard intervened. When they arrived he sent away the smaller man, who was snorting with rage, and escorted Farid up the stairs by himself.

"Here," he said quietly outside the camp commandant's office. When the door opened, Farid shot across the room. A blow had caught him in the middle of the face. He staggered around in a circle and saw the two guards who must have been waiting for him. A radio was playing in the office. The folk singer Lamia Haufik was singing a song about Arab honour and generosity to strangers. As Farid lay on the floor his fear receded for a moment. He thought of the rather plump singer, whom he had always regarded as terrible – vulgar and dull – and he had a feeling that these thugs were peasants avenging themselves on any city dweller for the ignominy the cities had inflicted on them over the centuries, doing so even without the urging of their superior officers and for no reward, just as a kind of lynch justice supervised by the state while they wore its uniform.

Mahdi came in through a side door and sat down at his desk. One of the guards switched off the radio. "That'll do, boys, you'll get plenty of chance to play with him," said the major, casting a final glance at the file before him and closing it. Farid was still lying on the floor, pressed up against the drawers of a second desk. "So you're Farid Mushtak, the dangerous underground military expert and true leader of the strike. Congratulations!" Mahdi gestured to the men to pick him up and seat him on a chair. It was only a small wave of his hand, but as precise and effective as a traditional temple ritual of long standing. The men dragged Farid over the floor, put him on the chair in front of the camp commandant's large walnut desk, tied his hands behind the chair back, and retreated into the background.

"Would you like a cigarette?" asked Mahdi Said, offering him a French pack. Farid was surprised by the sound of Mahdi's voice. It seemed familiar to him, but he didn't know who it reminded him of.

"No," he replied.

"And are you really called Farid Mushtak, or is that one of your many cover names?"

"It's my real name."

"But you're also called Salih, Ali, George, Samer, Shams, the Palestinians even called you Omar in their training camp, is that right?"

"Yes, that's right," said Farid, trying to keep calm. He stared at a curious metal box on the desk in front of him.

"I don't care for people who tell me lies, so I'll ask you again: is Farid Mushtak your real name?"

"Yes," said Farid, rather surprised.

"And were you in the monastery of St. Sebastian, as your file says?"

"Yes. I said so when I was first questioned, and that's correct," said Farid, trying to lighten the atmosphere slightly so as to shed some of his fear, which had been heightened by the commandant's suspicions.

"When were you there?"

"From the summer of 1953 to the summer of 1956," replied Farid. "I was only a boy, and my father made me go into the monastery."

"Ah yes, your father," repeated Mahdi Said, standing up. "Let me tell you something," he went on in a different, almost agitated voice, which suddenly sounded much higher. "I don't believe a word of it. You weren't in the monastery, you were in the partisan training camp run by those two bastards Tanios and Salman who ruled the mountains between 1953 and 1956. Do those names mean anything to you? Don't give me that stupid look. I just want to find out why Mr. Farid Mushtak always happened to be at the centre of rebellions. For instance, he just happened to be photographed with George Habash in Jordan in 1965, and two years later, in Lebanon in the summer of 1967, with Nayef Hawatmen, George Hawi, and other notable Christian and communist figures, isn't that so?"

The major took out an old photo that Farid immediately recognized. It had been taken at a farewell dinner in Beirut.

"And furthermore," said Mahdi, putting the photo back in the folder, "is it true that you were able to accompany the Popular Front's first operation in Israel as an observer?"

"Yes, that's so, but it was …" stammered Farid, astonished by the extent of the Syrian secret service's information.

"What an honour!" continued Mahdi. "And is it a fact that, quite by chance, you found yourself at the Israeli front and equally by chance joined the Radicals there?"

"Yes, I've said all that before. And the Radicals threw me out because I refused to bear arms."

"So they did," agreed Mahdi, laughing. "When it came to fighting Israel you played the angel of peace, but you had no scruples about our President Amran. The kind of revolutionary I really like. But let's get to the heart of the matter: I want to know what threads have been interwoven for twenty years to create unrest in Arabia and prevent our nation from taking its rightful place in the sun. You must tell me all about it, calmly and objectively. I believe you to be a very danger-ous man, not even a communist, but a man commissioned to commit yet greater crimes. You must help me or I'll be disappointed, and my boys here will be upset, and that will be really uncomfortable for you. So let's begin with that monastery. What was your task there?"

"None at all. I didn't know about the rebels at the time, I was only a naïve child. I didn't want to go into the monastery. It was my father's decision …" replied Farid quietly.

"If you'll allow me, sir," one of the thugs interrupted in the accent of the Mediterranean coast, "if you'll allow me I'll get him to spit out everything you want to hear, along with his teeth." And both guards laughed. But Mahdi Said waved the offer away. "No, no, this is not what you coastal folk would call a little anchovy, this is a shark whose teeth and everything else will grow again. But I know his kind. Never fear, when I need someone I'll send for you two," he said, opening the metal box. Farid saw the syringe and two ampoules as well as a small flask containing some kind of powder. He heard the two thugs leaving the room. And the clerk who had been sitting in a corner almost motionless all this time, taking down every word of the interrogation in shorthand, closed his notebook and went out of the room without a sound as well. There were to be no witnesses, so other prisoners who were given injections had said. Farid felt paralysed by his fear. It was so overwhelming that for a moment he had no voice left, and his tongue was so dry that it stuck to his palate.

In panic, he saw death grinning at him from the syringe.

"I can't tolerate injections, and a high dose of truth serum could kill me. Major, you know I haven't been a member of any political party since I parted with the Radicals in the summer of 1967. I'll sign whatever you like. I'm completely insignificant, I'll never mingle with politics again."

"Oh," said Mahdi, "and who led the famous strike that's ruined our reputation abroad for years, eh? Do you know that our beloved country is mentioned in the same breath as South Africa, South Vietnam, Persia, and Saudi Arabia? Israel would have paid millions to distract the world's attention from the Golan Heights. Now the Zionists have what they wanted for free, and it's your responsibility."

Mahdi adjusted the reflective sunglasses that he always wore during interrogations. Many suspected it was his way of unsettling the men being questioned. Worst of all for Farid was that he could see himself reflected in both lenses and disappearing into the distance, as if his own reflection were distancing itself from him.

"It really was the first non-political strike of my life," he repeated, "and it was done out of despair, because Abdulhamid Garasi treated us worse than animals. Under the supervision of the East Germans too. That was degrading. It really was the first non-political strike of my life. That's why we were all united, even the young offenders and the criminals. The strike became political only because the camp leadership was corrupt and didn't take us seriously. You know all that," replied Fari, in fear, because he had scented death in the major's words. But he still noticed his tone of voice turn submissive and pleading.

Mahdi was standing before him now. He perched on the edge of the desk and smiled at him, then he stood up once more and slowly walked past him. Farid did not turn around.

"Please, sir," he whispered, as he felt Mahdi unbuttoning the cuff of his right sleeve and slowly rolling it up, "I have epilepsy because I had meningitis as a boy in the monastery, and it was left untreated for a long time, so my meninges are delicate, like … like Nagi's. An injection could kill me. I beg you ... please no injection. I'll tell you everything." His voice was barely audible now.

"Never fear, my boy," said Major Mahdi in a loud and triumphant voice, as if to let the whole world know that within a few weeks he had cracked Farid Mushtak, the hardest case in the camp. "Never fear. I won't hurt you if you're a good lad," he assured his victim.

Farid felt Mahdi's cold hand stroking his bare arm. It was a slow movement of the fingers, as if they were carefully groping into a dark tunnel under his skin. Then the needle burned deep into his arm.

Complete darkness.

BOOK OF LAUGHTER V

Laughter breaks and enters, opening mouths, hearts, and wounds.

ॐ

TAD, MARCH 1969–APRIL 1969

273. My Mother Says

When Farid thought back to it, the time between the victory over Captain Garasi in mid-March and the arrival of Mahdi Said in the first week of April had been the craziest period of his life. Hungry as the prisoners were for laughter, their lived unfolded and flowered. They hardly slept. Every evening there were stories, dramatic performances, accounts of films they had seen. Most vividly of all Farid remembered a biting monologue delivered in Hut 5 by the young actor and conscientious objector Hassan Bakkali. It had been received with boundless mirth.

"Reporting for duty, Captain Bulldog!" cried the actor, standing in the middle of the hut and exaggeratedly staring, as if under the influence of drugs.

"Captain, sir, why are we at war with Israel? She has nothing against it, my mother says, and I'm not asking because I'm scared, we'd just like to know why we have to die. If the Israelis are stronger than us then they'll slaughter us. Is it any fun, starting a war against an enemy with superior forces when you're weak and stupid yourself? No, my mother says!

"Our people live in a Paradise of freedom and democracy. Well, it says so in all the school textbooks, and we hear it day after day on the radio too, so even the illiterate know. The British, Americans, Germans, Swedes, and most of all the Swiss really envy us our democracy. They come here pretending to be tourists, to learn how real democracy works and see what the Syrians are doing with all their freedom. Only my mother won't believe it. She's always saying: if problems were dogs, you'd have to buy pebbles from the jeweller's. But she learned that saying about the pebbles from our neighbour Mustafa. You see, captain, sir, Mustafa was a good traffic cop. His wife Sahra was the most beautiful woman in our quarter. And one day, when he stopped the Interior Minister's son for doing a mere hundred and twenty kilometres an hour in the city traffic and asked for his driver's licence, he was beaten up by the seventeen-year-old lad and fired by his father next day. So now there's the pair of them, Mustafa and Sahra, left without any money, and so angry that they keep fighting each other. One day, when the man noticed how beautiful his wife was, he had an idea: he'd stop beating her, make up her face, and offer her to a few rich men. She was happy to go along with this plan, just to be rid of her husband for a few hours and stuff herself with the kind of sweetmeats she'd only ever seen in the display windows of confectioners and delicatessen stores.

"From now on they lived a peaceful life, because Sahra brought home more money than thirteen policemen earn, and Mustafa kept house very well and played backgammon with pensioners. People said he wore the horns, but to be honest, he didn't mind that. He and his wife laughed at their neighbours. And it was when someone said the two of them were a problem to the whole quarter that Mustafa said that about the dogs and the pebbles.

"But I've strayed away from the subject. I was going to talk about Israel. Well, the Israelis are supposed to be weaker than we are – and oh yes, you bet they are, because we're a hundred and twenty million courageous Arabs with a heroic history. And how many Israelis are there? Three or four million, so let's suppose that's fifty Arabs attacking one Israeli. My God, people would be standing in line like they were buying butter! Is that honourable for an Arab? Is it manly, fifty to one? Certainly not, my mother says. A victory like that doesn't even gladden the heart of the dead.

"Arabs give refuge to the weak, so if they aren't exactly weak then let's give the poor Israelis some of the mighty land of Arabia. They're a small and ancient people, and we'll be praised for treating them so well.

"My mother never thinks about religion when she's judging what someone is like. For instance, she always called the olive oil dealer Samman an arsehole without ever asking about his religious beliefs. He gives his best oil to light the lamps in church, and sells us the low-quality blends.

"His father was just the same, a devout robber. He robbed the rich of their money, he spent half of it on drink and whores, and gave the other half to the poor to pray for the salvation of his soul. So he thought God would weigh his sins against one rich man that he'd robbed in the balance against the prayers of five hundred poor.

"But forgive me, I've strayed off the subject again. That hashish cigarette was too strong. My mother loves our President. Didn't he say he'd even attack America if the crunch came? My mother says a war against the Americans would be a really good idea. If they defeat us, they'll rebuild our land again better than ever, the way they did in Germany and Japan. It's an old American custom: they flatten countries and then rebuild them. And if we beat them, then we can finally emigrate to America without needing a visa."

BOOK OF GROWTH V

Presidents come and go, but the records on file remain.

✥

274. Bulos

When Farid came back to his senses he was lying on a plank bed, with a bright neon light shining down from the ceiling. There was no window in the room, and no light switch. A chair and a small table stood by the wall. The cell was clean, with a concrete floor and whitewashed walls. But the iron door was rusty and reminded him of the doors of other solitary confinement cells. So here he was in the Presidential Suite, as the prisoners called this particularly large one.

There was a curiously bitter taste in his mouth. He remembered the injection and looked at his arm. The place where the needle had gone in had a reddish rim.

Had he fainted, or had he told Mahdi all he wanted to hear in his delirium? He tried to reach the door, but had to cling to the wall because his legs were too weak. Farid closed his eyes and breathed deeply. Then he put his ear to the cold door. The soldiers on guard were telling each other jokes about the Bedouin and their women. He knocked at the door, waited, and then heard footsteps.

"What do you want?"

"What day is it today?" asked Farid.

"Somewhere between Monday and Sunday," replied a deep voice. Another man uttered a high laugh.

"Can I have a little water, please?" asked Farid.

"With ice and soda or neat?" asked yet another man in an artificial falsetto, like a barmaid, and snorted with laughter.

A day later he was given water and allowed to use the lavatory. When he came back Mahdi was sitting on the chair, grinning at him. The soldiers chained Farid's hands and feet, and fastened the ends of the chains to iron rings welded to the head and foot of the plank bed. Farid remembered the camel he had seen as a child.

Mahdi slowly took off his sunglasses. At that moment Farid recognized him, and at last he was able to identify the voice that had seemed familiar to him all this time.

"Bulos," he whispered, near tears.

"So we meet again, but in the right circumstances," retorted Bulos, grinning. Paralysing fear took hold of Farid.

"Bulos," he whispered again. "It's you."

"Yes, indeed, Mr. Mushtak, it's me. Your clan murdered my father, you betrayed and almost destroyed me. Now I'm about to pay you and your clan back."

"What do you mean, murdered? Who murdered whom?" asked Farid with the last of his strength. He was utterly baffled.

"Your uncle Hasib shot my father just for a moment's joking with Hasib's wife, an American whore. Don't you know about that? My father was unarmed. Never heard of it?"

Farid shook his head.

"I actually believe you. Yes, how would you know? My father was Musa Shahin from Mala, Jusuf Shahin's fifth son. Does that mean anything to you?"

Farid was knocked backward by the shock. He nodded, as if dazed. Of course. Rana's Uncle Musa had been shot dead that Easter Sunday in 1941 when the bishops were trying to reconcile the two clan leaders.

"And then my mother, my sister Mona, and I were plunged into misery. I was five. As a widow, my mother had to go back to her skinflint of a father, who humiliated her and us day and night, until she married that monster who forced us to turn Catholic. It was misery of the genuine Mushtak kind, my mother always said. All those nights when I was tormented, all the tears my mother shed, all the wretchedness I had to bear – I swore I'd pay a Mushtak out for it some day, and what do you think? When I was almost on the point of forgetting, following the way of Jesus Christ and loving my enemies, up popped a Mushtak who betrayed me. You did all you could to ruin me, but you were out of luck. I bore the torture and the questioning, I hated you every second of it, as much as I'd loved you every second before that. There's nothing worse on earth than discovering that you love a traitor." Mahdi's face was dark and pale at the same time.

"I never betrayed you. You wouldn't stop to hear that neither Gabriel nor anyone else ever learned a word about you from me. Stupid coincidences must have confirmed your ideas all that time, they fed your suspicions of me, but I suffered badly enough myself. In the end I left the monastery in a much worse state than you," said Farid.

But his hopes of explaining, or at least arousing a little pity, disappeared when Bulos merely grinned unpleasantly and shook his head. "So there you are. My mother was right when she said the Mushtaks were master liars and slippery as vipers, but it does me good to listen to you now, seeing you chained up like a dog. It was a lot of work getting you taken to Tad. You won't escape me now. No one can hear you. This is the only place where no microphones or cameras keep watch. You're going to live for a long time here, suffering so much that you'll wish for death ten times a day."

He stood up, knocked twice on the door, and then calmly sat down again. Two large guards came in and hit Farid until he lost consciousness.

Farid went through hell for four days. And every day he hoped to reach Bulos's heart and arouse some pity in him, but his archenemy came back again and again only to tell him about the torments inflicted on him, Bulos, by the Mushtaks. Sometimes he talked about his stepfather, and the merciless revenge he himself had taken on the man later, when he was an old, broken failure. Humiliated by Mahdi, he had hanged himself in the cellar of his factory after it was closed down.

One morning Farid heard a soft knocking. He listened. "Farid," said a familiar voice, but he couldn't quite identify it.

"Farid, it's me, Nabil. Can you hear me, Farid?"

"Nabil, my friend, what are you doing here?"

"I'm on duty as a substitute here for half a day. My comrade's okay, he's keeping a lookout for me."

"Nabil, please help me. I'm dying."

"How can I help you? We don't even have a key to your cells, and this one has the stoutest door of all, you can't even push a piece of paper under it."

"Listen carefully, Nabil. You can save my life. Is there any way you can get to Damascus in the near future?"

"Yes, I have three days off, starting tomorrow, because I spent a week outside working on the camp fortifications."

"Listen: go to my mother. We live opposite the Catholic patriarchal residence in Saitun Alley, near the east gate. My mother's name is Claire. Tell her they must do everything they can to get me out of here, because a son of the Shahins is trying to kill me."

"Whose son?"

"The Shahins. They're my family's sworn enemies, and it's their son who has power here. And he wants to kill me. Did you get all that?"

"Of course. Let's hope I don't find your mother at home, because then I can go to your father at the confectioner's shop, and while he's listening to me I can eat half of what's in his window. Did I tell you that as a child I sometimes spent all my pocket money on a nightingale nest?"

"You did, yes," replied Farid, smiling faintly, and then he sank to the floor by the door and listened to the young soldier's confidences as he talked of his wish for a swift end to his military service.

Finally Farid asked the soldier to repeat everything he was to tell Claire, and Nabil did not disappoint him.

275. Metamorphosis

Two days later Farid was running a high temperature. He heard a
knock at the door, but he couldn't get up. One of the soldiers on guard
came in and gave him water. Farid was so weak that he couldn't even
talk. "Poor devil," said the soldier, trickling something liquid into his
mouth. "My God, what are they doing to you? And you think you can
destroy the state with those shaking hands, you idiot? You're only a
poor lost child." He leaned Farid up against the wall, went out and
called to his colleague. "Do you have a painkiller tablet? If not, go and
find one." The other man whispered something. "Yes, you'll get your
bloody cigarette! Hurry up, will you, the man's dying," shouted the
soldier by way of reply.

Mahdi didn't show up for three days. When he came back, Farid
had to some extent recovered his strength.

He was surprised by Mahdi's detailed knowledge. The commandant seemed to have found out about everything he did in his entire
life. He could repeat, word for word, many of Farid's letters and many
conversations with his Party comrades. But he obviously didn't know
about Rana.

Mahdi seemed to enjoy telling Farid about his own career, and
how cleverly he had jumped all the dangerous hurdles and cleared
his enemies out of his way. After that final examination for his high
school diploma he had gone home. By then his mother and sister had
moved to Safita, a pretty little town where his stepfather was unsuc-
cessfully trying to start an arrack distillery. Mahdi was to study chemistry and help to make arrack later. But his heart was set on studying
law. He had dreamed of being a just and good judge, and he went to
Damascus to get a place at the university there. Just before his examinations he fell passionately in love, but his stepfather was on his heels
and turned his inamorata's parents against his own stepson. A little
later the young woman broke off her relationship with Mahdi.

He put the woman out of his mind, and registered to train at the
police academy. From there he was detailed for duty with the secret
service, and as his logical and ruthless mind was outstanding his
boss sent him to Moscow for further training with the KGB. In fact

Mahdi's crafty superior officer, who hated communism, wanted to discover just what the KGB was up to among the young Syrian officers. Mahdi was duly recruited by the KGB, and told everything to his boss in Damascus, a cousin of his present superior officer Badran.

"But why did you convert to Islam? Badran and the rest of the government aren't notably Muslim," said Farid, still hoping these conversations might bring his torments to an end.

"Because religion has never mattered to me at all, or at least not since the monastery – but no, it never really did. I happened to be born into the Orthodox community and then I was forced to turn Catholic. I had all the qualifications to take a hand in the running of the country, a little Islamic phrase and my foreskin were the only obstacles, but not for me. Snip, snip, I was circumcized within five minutes, I recited the phrase, so Bulos became Mahdi, and I can only say that in point of fact all reasonable people from Badran to Shaftan and even President Amran, devoutly as they pray for the cameras, couldn't care less about any kind of religion. They get tanked up, they fuck any orifice they can find. Religion is a good way of controlling fools," he said forcefully, and then he grinned and stood up. He knocked at the door, and the gates of hell opened for Farid. He begged Mahdi to spare him that day because he felt so wretched. He kissed his hands and boots, as ordered by one of the guards, but Mahdi only laughed. Another guard struck Farid in the face and ordered him to bark. Farid barked and wept until the guard hauled him along by the ear and said, "Not like a dog, like a donkey." The man stank of alcohol.

Farid imitated a donkey, and had to keep it up for half an hour until he was lying on the floor exhausted. Then came absolute darkness, in which he once again saw the camel with fear in its eyes as it stood tethered in the courtyard of the caravanserai. When he came back to his senses he was alone. It was an eerie feeling. For the first time he doubted his own perception, for he had not seen or heard Mahdi and the two guards leave the cell. Farid looked at his arm. He saw the mark of a second needle, red and itching, on his right wrist, but when had they given him the injection?

276. The Ransom

When Claire had heard what the soldier had to say she thanked him with a gift of fifty lira, twice his monthly wages, and urged him to tell Farid she wouldn't rest until he was free. The soldier went straight to Bab Tuma and spent ten lira on nightingale nests from Elias's confectionery shop.

Claire went to her husband immediately and told him everything. Elias froze. "Those bastards the Shahins," he said. The message was clear to him. A member of that family who was either a high-ranking officer or a depraved criminal must have found his way to Tad and was trying to kill Farid.

Claire had never seen her husband so angry before. "I'm going to the Patriarch, and even if it costs me all I have those Shahins won't murder my son," he cried in his distress. At that moment Claire admired her husband, who was small of stature but could become a lion within seconds.

Elias immediately phoned the Catholic Patriarch. There was desperation and fury in his voice. The experienced old churchman knew that he must help his friend, and asked him to come and see him at once. He listened to what Elias told him, and spoke reassuringly. Then he telephoned George Salamoni, one of the richest and most audacious Christians in Damascus. Half an hour later that smooth-spoken whisky importer arrived in person. The Patriarch explained, and asked for his assistance, since Elias gave so much support to the Catholic Church.

Salamoni thought for a moment. "There's only one person who can help, but he'll be very expensive," he said calmly.

"There's no price I wouldn't pay to save my son," replied Elias.

"Come with me, then," said the whisky merchant, and took his leave of the Patriarch. His black Mercedes was parked outside in the yard.

"The President's brother Shaftan is the most corrupt man in the world, but he does what he says he'll do," said Salamoni, driving off. "We'll go straight to him. Fundamentally, he's the secret ruler of this country."

Elias knew that Shaftan was the head of the special unit that had built the ring of defences around Damascus, but he would never have expected to meet the President's brother where Salamoni was taking him.

Salamoni wanted to know all about Farid. If what Elias said wasn't true, he added, he couldn't guarantee anything. Elias briefly told him what Claire had said. Salamoni nodded thoughtfully.

"I thought Shaftan was outside Damascus with the troops," said Elias, as Salamoni reached the Abu Rumanna quarter. There were no barracks here, only the villas of the richest Damascenes and the foreign consulates. Salamoni laughed. "He's been here for a month in a palace that he bought for ten lira from Bardana, a rich textiles dealer."

"Ten lira? You must be joking," said Elias.

"I seldom joke," replied Salamoni, "but you'd sell your house for a single lira if a cold-blooded man put his pistol to your temple, and you knew he was brutal enough to sit his ten-year-old son on his lap to watch the executions of his enemies, just to toughen the boy up."

"And he lives here?" asked Elias.

"No one knows where he lives, but he has his secretariat here, and if you state your request and the matter's important enough you can see him in person. If not, his employees deal with it."

The house was impressive, and two helicopters stood on the lawn of the large garden. At the entrance Salamoni gave the soldiers in their combat uniforms his name, and a few minutes later a young lieutenant came running down the steps.

"Monsieur Salamoni," he said breathlessly, "forgive me for keeping you waiting, but all hell's let loose today." He greeted Salamoni, and shook Elias's hand without interest.

The steps up from the entrance led to a large hall with a reception desk. Two women kept picking up phones, saying something, laughing, hanging up again and making notes. There were tastefully arranged seating areas among the tall marble columns, as if the place were a luxury hotel. Several men were waiting there patiently, motionless as waxworks. The lieutenant led Salamoni and Elias past the groups of chairs to a broad and majestic marble staircase, and went ahead of them. On the second floor, he opened a door and showed his guests into a spacious room. The furniture, walls, and ceiling dated from the nineteenth century. The only jarring note was represented by a green office desk and a beige swivel chair behind it.

At the lieutenant's civil request, Salamoni told him about Farid's fate, stressing the fact that Elias's only son now belonged to no political party at all. He had been very sick with meningitis as a child and still suffered from the consequences. The lieutenant noted it all down, ordered tea over the phone for himself and his guests, and then turned to Elias. "Mr. Mushtak, if Monsieur Salamoni asks me to do something then I do it, but I want to be sure what I'm letting myself in for before I go to Comrade Shaftan. Is it true about the meningitis, or does your son just have migraines?"

Elias felt a lump in his throat. "Sir, he was in an intensive care ward when he was twelve. They didn't know how to cure meningitis properly at the time, so to this day he still has epileptic fits and falls unconscious. I can show you the diagnosis of three specialists," he replied.

"No, no, that won't be necessary," said the officer, and then fell silent. The only sound in the room came from the clock on the wall.

"Was your son armed when he was arrested?" the lieutenant went on at last. Elias thought it a strange question. "No, sir, my son had no weapon with him. He was afraid, and was hiding with his cousin."

Once again the lieutenant preserved a long silence. Salamoni was used to it, and relaxed, but Elias felt his heart thudding. What would the young man ask next? He breathed a sigh of relief when the officer took a sheet of paper out of a drawer and looked at him in a friendly way. "I can't promise anything, but I'll do my best. However, the decision is for Comrade Shaftan to make."

The lieutenant went on to ask Elias for Farid's personal details, and carefully wrote them down. A woman came in with a tray, handed Salamoni a glass of tea and then went over to Elias. He took a glass and placed it beside the officer, as a sign of his own humble status, before taking the third glass himself. The officer took no notice of this courtesy.

When the woman left, Salamoni whispered to the lieutenant, "The matter is quite urgent. The young man really is very sick, and I owe Monsieur Mushtak a great deal."

"I'll be off at once," said the officer, "but you owe no one anything, monsieur, for you lavish generous gifts on us with no thought for yourself. That's what fascinates me so much in you." And he was already rising, took the sheets of paper he had written, and hurried out of the door.

"He forgot his tea," said Elias.

Salamoni made a sign indicating that they were being overheard. "Yes, that's the way he always is. Lieutenant Butros is a true humanitarian. He helps whenever he can," he replied.

It was an hour before Lieutenant Butros came back, beaming. "Comrade Shaftan listened to me. Farid will be free as soon as possible, and from today he will be under Comrade Shaftan's protection. It will cost a hundred," said the officer to Salamoni, as if he were the one who was Farid's father. Salamoni glanced at Elias. Elias nodded. He had understood: a hundred thousand dollars. Shaftan took only dollars; Syrian lira were no use to him.

"We'll pay," said Salamoni.

"Then let's go to the boss. He'd like to meet you personally," said Lieutenant Butros, going ahead to the next staircase.

The third floor was even more magnificent than the second. The outer office was furnished in burgundy red. A pretty secretary briefly looked up from her typewriter, smiled at the lieutenant, and bent over her work again.

Two young men in black uniforms stood to attention. Machine guns gleamed in front of their chests. The man on the right stood at ease again, opened a handsome wooden door, forcefully pulled open a second door made of thick steel, and then pressed down the handle of another wooden door in the depths of the thick wall. Arab music met their ears. Elias saw a huge hall before him. There was a gigantic desk in the middle of the room, with five or six telephones on it. The walls were adorned with shining golden daggers and swords. A large window offered a fine panoramic view of the city of Damascus; outside, a new steel fire escape was being fitted.

Elias gave a start when he suddenly saw the mighty Shaftan, who came to meet them when he had switched off the radio. He wore a green military uniform much too large for him, intended to emphasize his strength and virility, but he looked more like a three-dimensional caricature. Shaftan took Salamoni's hand in both his own, as an expression of particular warmth. "I wanted to thank you in person for that excellent Scotch. Lieutenant Butros brought me the case two months ago. I can only say I've drunk no other whisky since. I'm afraid you've spoiled me," he said, smiling, and then turned to Elias, speaking in a soft voice. "You can rest assured that from now on no one will touch your only son. However, my brother Amran must approve his actual release."

"My dear sir, we know that you are as one with our President," Salamoni insisted, to get a binding statement out of him.

"Ah, you all consider my humble self so important," countered Shaftan hypocritically, "but for good citizens of course one is ready do everything. Is there any other way I can help you?"

"Your kindness puts me to shame," said Salamoni gallantly.

"And you," said Shaftan, turning to the faithful Butros, "will go to Badran at once and tell him that Farid Mushtak is under my direct protection until our leader returns from Moscow. No one is to touch him. He is to be transferred immediately to the hospital and kept well protected so that no son of a whore does anything to him until His Excellency has made his decision. Take Badran the cinecamera I brought him back from Paris. I'm sure he'll be pleased. And tell him the young man's mother may visit him once a week," he added. Lieutenant Butros saluted and left the room.

"My brother's crazy about movies. He'd have been a brilliant film maker himself if he hadn't gone into the army. And I've brought him the latest thing from Paris: a Super-Eight camera. You can shoot real feature films with it," he told Salamoni, and then turned back to Elias. "You and your wife may rest assured that nothing will happen to your son, but I hope he will always bear this incident in mind," he concluded, and offered his hand.

Elias could no longer conceal his relief. "God protect you and your children," he said almost inaudibly. Shaftan took a long and warm farewell of Salamoni, and accompanied him to the door.

When Elias was back in the outer office the secretary, to his surprise, handed him an envelope. "The address," she said. He didn't understand, but took the envelope from her. He was still in a very emotional state.

"How can I thank you?" he asked Salamoni in the car. Salamoni laughed. "Don't bother. I like to help a decent man like you. Did you know that your father once helped mine out of a fix? But that's a long time ago. In our family George Mushtak always stood for ideas of salvation and selfless Christian loving kindness, and now I can be proud to say that I have helped a Mushtak. I consider prisons terrible places. No cultivated human being should languish in them."

"But you'll have had costs. Shaftan will want more of that expensive Scotch whisky," said Elias, much moved.

"Ah, who cares?" laughed Salamoni. "That's nothing. Once we used to pay taxes to the excise office, now that peasants rule us I pay in kind. Peasants like that. And I get what I want considerably cheaper." His voice dripped contempt.

"So what about this address?" asked Elias, without opening the envelope.

"Oh, that's his eldest son Lahfan's office. Your name is down there now, and it won't be crossed off until you've paid the money. They keep everything very correct," said Salamoni, laughing at the absurdity of it.

Elias looked at the address. It was an export-import agency. "It must be near the Central Bank," he surmised. Salamoni nodded. "And more payments go into it than into the Bank. You may have to stand in line."

When Elias got out of the car at Saitun Alley, he clasped his rescuer's hand firmly. "But I need your address too, because you must try my new chocolate creations. Such delicacies come only from Elias Mushtak."

Salamoni laughed. He gave Elias a visiting card out of a little silver box hanging from the dashboard. "My wife will be delighted. She thinks very highly of your confectionery," he said, and the car raced away.

277. Cold Sharper Than a Razorblade

Mahdi ranted and raged over the telephone, feeling deeply humiliated. But Badran was not to be moved. The prisoner Farid Mushtak was no longer Mahdi Said's business. Dangerous or not, he was under the protection of Badran's brother. "And his mother is coming to see him every week until the President decides. If Shaftan hears from her that her son is being badly treated, I can't keep you on any more, understand?"

"Yes." Mahdi's voice was barely audible, as if he were down in a deep pit. He hadn't felt so small since those days in the monastery. That bastard of a prisoner from the bloody Mushtak clan was more important to Badran now than he was! As if they hadn't been friends for a decade, as if they hadn't faced many moments of mortal danger together. Shaftan, Shaftan! The hell with Badran and his brother. Mahdi was sure that Shaftan had been cashing in again.

He did a lot of thinking that day, and now he understood why several high-ranking officers were beginning to murmur discontentedly. One general had hinted to him that the army wasn't happy about President Amran's clan. Amran had handed the country over to the Russians, he said, and any common cowherd from his tribe mattered more to the President than an experienced, patriotic general. Mahdi had cautiously contradicted this, but when the general said there were some patriots who would like to get to know him, because they admired his loyalty, his Syrian pride, and his determination, he had agreed to think about it. After his humiliating conversation with Badran he reached for the telephone three times, but kept hanging up again. Badran had all his employees' phones tapped. Mahdi knew the general's private address. He'd just drop in and see him some time in the next few weeks, in a casual kind of way.

He got into his jeep and drove to the ruins of Palmyra. His adjutant, First Lieutenant Saadi, was astonished when Mahdi told him, as he left, to have Farid Mushtak transferred to the hospital. From today he was to be nursed and well looked after. "Orders from the very top," added Mahdi gloomily, and he raced away in his jeep. He didn't return until late, when he was told by his adjutant that Badran had called him three times and left a message for him to call back.

"Where were you?" Badran's voice sounded as carefree on the line as if nothing had happened.

"I drove out to the ruins. I've always wanted to see them at my leisure," replied Mahdi,

"Did I annoy you?"

"No, but I can't understand why a terrorist with a past a mile long should be put up in ..." and here Mahdi laughed derisively, "... in a luxury hotel just to please his mama."

"Yes, I thought my good friend Mahdi hadn't understood the whole story. I'm not interested in that whore, but Shaftan is as clever as they come – he'll know why he's making this move. Perhaps he wants something from the Catholic Patriarch. They say the Patriarch intervened on behalf of that bastard Farid Mushtak. No one's really supposed to know, but I'd rather tell you as my best friend than anger you. My friend is a deep well – his name is Mahdi and still he isn't happy."

Mahdi laughed. A wily character, Badran, he thought, that's what makes him capable of heading a hydra like the secret service.

"Do you know what news I'm reading just now?" But before Mahdi could reply, Badran was continuing. "It seems the Pope has come to a secret agreement with the Italian communists. He won't oppose them in Italy any more, and in return they'll go along with him in his drive to save Church treasures in the communist countries, from China to Russia. Wasn't it Jesus who said, render unto Caesar that which is Caesar's, and unto God the things that are God's?"

"That's right."

"Then do me a favour and treat that son of a whore well until he's free. That will satisfy God, and he'll have kept his word to the Patriarch. But we haven't been forbidden to arrest our fine gentleman again in, say, three months' time, have we?"

It took Mahdi's breath away. The chill in Badran's voice was as sharp as a razor blade. When would he himself learn to master such coldness?

"Are you still there, Caesar?"

"Yes, sure. You're right. That's what we'll do. I don't want that criminal Mushtak to misinterpret your brother's kindness of heart and his amnesty and go underground again."

"No, you're there to prevent that very thing," said Badran, laughing.

When Mahdi hung up, he was glad to think that Badran cared whether or not he was happy. So he wasn't quite so unimportant after all. None the less, he decided to go and see the general. Having finally come to this decision, he smiled. He felt that he too was capable of icy, cutting cold.

278. The Visit

Claire shed tears of joy. Farid took her in his arms and kissed her eyes again and again. "I can always rely on you," he whispered. A soldier was sitting in the corner, observing them both closely.

"How did you get here?" he asked in some surprise.

"My driver dropped everything to bring me. Now he's waiting patiently outside the door for a couple of hours," she said, wiping away her tears with a handkerchief.

"What – my father's outside?" asked Farid in surprise.

"Yes, but the camp commandant wouldn't let him see you. The permission was only for me," she said.

When Claire had to leave the camp at about one in the afternoon, Elias was standing in the narrow area of shade provided by a wall. The sun was blazing mercilessly down, and there wasn't a tree in sight. Claire kissed him and walked quickly to the car. She didn't say a word until they had reached the main road.

"The camp commandant is Musa Shahin's son. Musa who was shot by your brother Hasib in 1941. Do you remember the little boy?"

In sombre mood, Elias shook his head.

"His mother came from the north, and as a widow she went back to her parents. He's been calling himself Mahdi Said since he converted to Islam."

"One of those despicable Shahins," retorted Elias, and spat scornfully out of the window.

"Yes," said Claire, and she took two folded notes out of her pocket. She had felt Farid swiftly slipping them in as she said goodbye. The soldier had been busy at the door for a moment, impatiently complaining that he wanted to go for his lunch break.

Both notes were for her. In the first he asked her to tell Rana that he would soon be out of Tad, and then he wanted to be with her for ever. In the second, he wanted her to let Matta know that Mahdi Said was none other than the monastery pupil Bulos, and he was now living in the Christian quarter of Damascus, although no more could be found out in the camp.

Claire wondered what the meaning of this second note might be, but Matta beamed. "Yes, we were inseparable, and Farid knows that Bulos would never turn down any request of mine."

"Perhaps Farid's afraid that bastard will do something else to hurt him before he's released," Elias surmised. "But how can we find out exactly where the man lives?"

"Never fear, Matta will do it," said that faithful friend. And within three days Matta had indeed found out where Mahdi Said lived.

BOOK OF LONELINESS II

Love is the only sickness whose victims don't want a cure.

᠌ঌ৹

THE AL-ASFURIYE PSYCHIATRIC HOSPITAL, 15 KM NORTH OF
DAMASCUS, SPRING 1968–SUMMER 1969

279. In the House of Sparrows

Dr. Edward Salam, a small, frail, elderly figure, was waiting at the
entrance to the psychiatric hospital. The only thing about him that
shone perfectly was his bald patch. He was there to receive Rana personally. It was a sign of special cordiality, and he wanted his staff to
notice it.

Rana's mother and brother seemed to be in a hurry. As soon as the
medical director had greeted his patient they drove away. Dr. Salam
thought Rana was as pretty as a picture. Her pallor gave her face an
almost angelic look.

The friendship between Rana's father, that well-known lawyer
Basil Shahin, and Dr. Salam was of long standing. They had both been
members of the Rotary Club until it was banned in 1965. His friend
had often spoken enthusiastically to Dr. Salam of his daughter's clever
mind, so he had expected that his patient would seem rather severe
and mannish. All the clever women he had met during his studies
and his practice of psychiatry had lacked feminine beauty.

"A room in my own department," he quietly told a male nurse who briefly met him outside his office. "We'll drink a coffee, and then Rana can rest for a while," he added, opening the door.

Rana entered a spacious office with pot plants in it. The cardamom-flavored coffee that the red-haired head nurse brought them tasted really good for a hospital.

What a difference from her first stay in this place ten months ago, when she had been treated like an animal!

"Would you like something to read?" asked Dr. Salam.

"No thank you. I feel so tired," replied Rana almost inaudibly.

She closed her eyes for a moment. Where's Farid? she wondered. What are they doing to him? She felt a small hand on her shoulder. Dr. Salam was smiling at her. Had she dropped off to sleep?

"You can rest now. We'll talk a little tomorrow," he told her kindly.

Her room was small, clean, and bright: a bed, a narrow table, a shower and a separate lavatory. The barred window faced south. Outside, a gardener was pruning a wild oleander bush.

She lay down on the bed. Someone had scratched the outline of a sailing boat on the wall. It could be made out only indistinctly. Two letters mysteriously adorned the sail: A.L.

She sat up and looked at her trembling hands. A male nurse knocked, came in, and gave her a mug of steaming tea and a tiny dish with two tablets in it. The tea tasted horrible, the tablets bitter. She looked out of the window. Where's Farid now? she asked herself again, and lay down. She glanced at her watch, the watch she had worn ever since her elopement to Beirut with Farid fifteen years ago. He had bought it for her with his first wages. Whenever she looked at the watch she felt a pleasant little tickle in her right ear. Back then, Farid had kissed her ear as she put the watch on.

A leaden weariness overcame her, probably induced by the tablets. She didn't want to sleep, and tried to raise herself from the pillow. But then later she heard another knock and woke up. The red-haired nurse was standing in the doorway. Rana turned her face to the window. It was full daylight. How long had she been asleep?

"Dr. Salam would like to speak to you," said the woman, tight-lipped.

When she entered his room, he came out in front of his desk and offered her his hand. A scent of rosewater preceded him.

"I don't like this woman. She doesn't mean well," said Rana, but he didn't seem to have heard her.

"Come along, let's sit down," he said. "Kadira, could you bring us a pot of coffee?" And as soon as the nurse had left the room, he said, "I'd like to listen to anything you have to say at your leisure, so that I can understand you and help you." He led her to the comfortable chair where she was to sit opposite him. Evidently she wasn't expected to lie on a couch, as she had with the psychiatrist last year.

Looking at her with his clever little eyes, he smiled. Two lines at the corners of his mouth emphasized his friendliness.

"I'm thinking of a woman who was once a neighbour of mine," Rana began, hesitantly and quietly. "You remind me of her. She had a kind face like yours, and she was delicately built too." Dr. Salam smiled. "She sang me the only song I knew as a small child. My mother never sang to me. But one day my parents wanted to go out with friends to celebrate something in a restaurant, and they asked our neighbour to come and look after me and Jack. Jack was three then and I was five. He went to sleep at once, but I was too excited. I watched the old woman and her kind face, feeling curious about her. Then she began to sing. She sang a song that made me laugh, and after that ..." Rana stopped, and began crying. Dr. Salam took the coffee pot that was brought in and poured two cups. Then he leaned over the little table with the tray where the full coffee cups stood with steam rising from them. Rana took one, thanked him quietly, and wiped away her tears.

"You'll know the song. 'Sleep, baby, sleep, I'll cook you a dove, my dear. Little dove, never fear, never fear, I'm lying to make my child sleep.' Pretty, isn't it?'

Dr. Salam nodded, smiling.

"I held the woman's hand and she told me about her life, and then she kissed me and said she wished I were her daughter. Then she wept. She didn't say why, she just wept. Years later I discovered that she had lost a daughter of my age. But from the day when she sang me that song, I used to visit her and she spoiled me like a princess. My mother realized how fond I was of our neighbour, and after a while she wouldn't let me go to see her any more. I never understood why."

She lost track of the time she spent talking to Dr. Salam. In the evening she was told she could go to the common room. A young nurse went with her. There was a comedy show on television, but all the women patients there sat absorbed in their own worlds. They called out, sang, shouted and cried, and the television was on at full volume the whole time. No one paid it any attention. One woman sat with her back to the screen, pulling faces. The women's voices died away, leaving no trace in Rana's mind. The air was heavy; she could hardly breathe. After a short time she rose to her feet and left the room. The nurse went with her.

Two dogs were barking outside in the darkness. She saw her face reflected in the window, pale and lost as it looked back at her. She stood by the window in silence. Down in the dark garden a cigarette glowed, and for a moment she saw a man's face. She undressed and stood at the window naked. Perhaps Farid was seeing her now in his dreams. She didn't hear the door open. The red-haired nurse came in and shook her head with pretended compassion. Then she handed Rana some tablets, put her long nightdress on her, and helped her into bed.

Al-Asfuriye, the House of Sparrows – that was the name of the psychiatric hospital. She suddenly remembered a language teacher who had once told her that in Arabic the words for "insanity", "ghosts", and "Paradise" were closely related. They all had to do with hiding away.

280. First Report

Dr. Salam, chief medical director. Reception report, Monday 15 April 1968, 16.00 hours.
Hospitalization: patient brought in by mother and brother three days ago, seems willing to be here, perhaps even relieved. Was here for three weeks in summer last year (I was in Paris at the time, 8th Psychiatric Congress. Little useful information from my deputy, Dr. Huss).

According to mother, has always given family cause for concern, "difficult". Has been increasingly unwell for last two or three months, withdrawn, hardly eating, has not seemed normal. Keeps going up on the roof to spray water over neighbours and passers by. Not much further background to be gleaned from the family

Psychostatus: Young, pretty, obviously intelligent woman, father is a well-known attorney. On admission clearly aware, generally well-orientated, but expression hypotonic, physical movement restricted, body language conveys desperation, anxious, suggestion of Veraguth's eyelid folds. Speech monotonous, monosyllabic, thought processes slowed down and inhibited, but no formal thought disturbances present. Mood despondent, possible lack of affective control. Speech reserved, confined to a few subjects: feels she can't go on, she is a burden to everyone else, can no longer perform her domestic duties (also marital duties?), despairing. Strong feelings of guilt.

Also sense of failure regarding parents, especially father. Poor relationship with mother. Suicidal feelings allegedly present, but nothing concrete. No delusions or hallucinatory experiences. General loss of interest, weak drives, abulia. Sleep disturbances, difficulty in falling asleep, insomnia. No deep morning sleep.

Somatic condition (pending examination by Dr. Balkani): good general condition, slightly undernourished. Says she has lost 4 kilos in recent weeks.

Anamnesis: no serious anamnesic disturbances.

Heredity: great-uncle on mother's side apparently suffered from depression. Mother also takes anti-depressants. Patient grew up in comfortable circumstances in Damascus, younger brother. No developmental problems can be traced, very good school student with excellent high school diploma (father publicly boasts of it). Had planned to study at university, but married in 1961 to cousin on her mother's side (Rami Kudsi now a colonel). Seems to have been psychologically well balanced until her marriage. No indication of earlier depressive or manic phases.

Traditional moral upbringing, can be assumed that father especially was strict and not communicative. Mother disappointed that Rana was not a boy (obsessed with securing family bloodline). Mother/daughter relationship poor from the first.

All this in some contradiction to the mental independence

evidenced by educational achievements and aspirations. Denies conflicts with her father, although I would not be surprised to find that they exist. Appears very conformist, husband certainly matches parents' wishes. No children. Cautiously approached on subject of her marriage, she reacts with anxious uneasiness, becomes reserved, suspicious. Feels guilty towards husband but will not say why. Unclear whether reserve is to be attributed only to depression, or whether it is particularly difficult for her to speak to me, because I am a friend of her father's. Dr. Bishara would be helpful here.

Diagnosis: initial phrase of a probably exogenous depression, with an element of anxiety. No indications of cyclothymia.

Procedure: admission to quiet room in acute ward for women. Begin with bed rest, exercise only in company of staff. Watch for suicidal signs. No visitors at first; patient to feel distanced from her family and safe.

Medication: begin with imipramine and low dosage of levomepromazine. Chloral to help her sleep. If effects insufficient, perhaps chlorpromazine.

In view of the presumably neurotic factors, Dr. Bishara to have regular conversations with her on the ward. Patient to come to my office once a week.

281. On a Distant Island

Farid was laughing at her. And as if he were an appetizing dish to eat, she found her mouth watering. When she woke up, the sky was looking in through her window. It was very early, the garden still lay in shadow, and a rooster was crowing far away. She felt strong, and opened the window. The air smelled of jasmine and orange blossom. She held the bars and breathed deeply with relief. She was free. She was feeling better every day now that she was here.

Over the last few days she had felt a curious sense of peace. Questions surfaced, could not be answered, and left her in melancholy mood. Why had Jack always been preferred to her? He had been allowed to go out into the street any time, visit his friends, go to the cinema. But every outing she wanted to make had to be carefully checked first. And when she and Jack made the same mistakes, she had always been punished more severely, on the grounds that mistakes do girls more damage than boys. And then everyone was so serious. She had always liked laughter, and as a child she loved anyone who smiled at her.

She liked the peace and quiet of this institution, so she refused to see any of her family. Dr. Salam understood, and went along with her wishes without any ifs or buts. He had even spoken angrily to her mother when she pestered him, and sent her off home. Dr. Salam said nothing about this little altercation, which had been conducted in his office. Rana heard of it only from Adnan, the nice male nurse with the glass eye. When her mother left, Dr. Salam had told Adnan that they would have to keep her in the closed ward for a couple of years.

Adnan was a joker who kept taking his glass eye out, hiding it in his mouth behind closed lips, and then putting on sunglasses. When he met anyone he laughed, and his eye would peep out of his mouth.

She didn't want anyone to know that she had begun to feel better here after only a few days. Not even Dr. Salam the medical director. It wasn't difficult for her to feel unwell; she just had to think of the day when her cousin had raped her in her family's drawing room.

She didn't have to split into two people here. For years she had been able to endure life with Rami only by leaving herself as soon as he touched her. He had her body captive, she put her mind to one side and watched, or walked through the house and quite often outside it too. And she didn't come back until she heard him groaning in orgasm. He used to bellow and snore at the same time; he sounded like a bull. She wasn't used to that from Farid. Farid made sounds like a little puppy yelping when he reached his climax.

She remembered one icy cold winter. She was lying in bed, running a high temperature. A cold followed by flu had left her very weak, but her husband wouldn't take a single day off work to look after her. The President trusted him, he said, and he wasn't about to disappoint the President just because she had a sniffle. She exploded, calling him and the President names, saying the President had enslaved him. He turned pale and went into the kitchen. An hour later he came back, drunk, and shouted at her never to say such things about the President again. Then he beat her as she lay in bed. She was afraid he was going to kill her. Finally he left her alone, and disappeared for a week. At the end of that time he came back, beaming as if nothing had happened, and called her "little pigeon" again, because he wanted to sleep with her.

282. Hanna Bishara

When Dr. Bishara came into the consultation room on Monday morning after two weeks of vacation, the staff were discussing the new admissions: one was a case of emotional menopausal depression in a recently divorced woman patient of fifty-two, with abuse of medicaments and suicidal tendencies. The second case was one of acute recidivism of chronic schizophrenia with delusions, patient not responsive at present.

Hanna Bishara was not asked to take on either of these two new patients that morning. Nor did she offer to; she was thinking of her old patient in the closed women's ward who had jumped out of a window two days earlier, breaking a leg and three ribs.

After a short discussion, her colleagues left the room. Dr. Salam beckoned to Hanna Bishara to follow him into his office.

"Young woman, late twenties, married, no children, chronic depression and severe lack of appetite, borderline anorexic with a weight of forty-three kilos and height of one metre sixty, high degree of anxiety," explained Dr. Salam, glancing several times at the papers in front of him. He seemed very glad to have this particular patient here. A slight smile showed on his face. "Rana Shahin is my patient. You'll need to go particularly carefully with her. Her father – an excellent lawyer – is a good friend of mine, her husband a high-ranking army officer. Would you please get to know the young woman? And tell me how you're doing with her now and then," he said in an unusually gentle tone, making preparations for his daily rounds.

Dr. Bishara knew that Edward Salam had a particularly soft spot for young women patients, whom he treated with paternal care. He had always wished he had a daughter, but his wife gave him four sons, and he didn't get on well with any of them. However, that wasn't the only reason for Rana's preferential treatment. The medical director needed her and other patients with relatively slight mental disturbances to raise the reputation of his psychiatric hospital and rescue it from the derogatory associations of a "nuthouse" – not altogether easy in view of the condition of the majority of patients, about whom no one asked any more.

Hanna Bishara, a specialist in neurology, also saw a good opportunity for herself in these endeavors of the medical director. She had spent years doing further training in psychoanalysis and psychotherapy, and Salam had made her his closest confidant, in preference to five older doctors. And she would get no chance at all outside this hospital. There wasn't a single private psychiatric practice in the whole of Damascus.

283. Mother

When Hanna Bishara entered the room she saw a deeply disturbed young woman: the curtains over the window were drawn, leaving only a tiny gap between them, and Rana was sitting in a corner in the semi-darkness. When the doctor came in she visibly took fright, but immediately tried to recover her self-control and sit up straight in the chair at the small desk. At the same time, however, she turned away and said nothing, so there was no eye contact between them, and no conversation. Dr. Bishara was clearly surprised by the sight of the fragile, delicate figure, sensed her great fear of all intruders, and sat down at a suitable distance. After a while she broke the silence and spoke gently: she'd like to get to know Rana, she said, so that she could form a picture of her life and the time before her admission, and then perhaps she could help her to understand the inner reasons for her own suffering better. Rana stood up as if she felt pressure being put on her, and took refuge on her bed, where she sat wrapped in a blanket to protect herself from further questions. The doctor said quietly that she respected Rana's reserve, and then rose, adding as she left the room that she would look in again that afternoon.

But she had no luck that afternoon either. I'm getting nowhere at all, thought Hanna Bishara in the evening, feeling disappointment and perplexity. A beautiful young woman from the best circles of society, practically without a care in the world – and now this happens to her. What could have caused it? In the corridor she met her older colleague Hisham.

"Well, how are you doing?" he greeted her, as usual.

"It'd be easier opening an oyster with your bare hands," she said, quoting his own dictum about mute patients. He smiled. "Just as I always say. I've come from a similar case. Two hours, and it's not just my tongue that's all furred up."

Hanna Bishara went to the ward office to take a closer look at Rana's case notes and the medical director's admission report on her. But they were not much help either over the next few days. Dr. Bishara felt Rana's distrust as a personal failure, particularly as the young woman reacted to the medical director himself in a remarkably positive, almost confidential way. Hanna Bishara began to suspect that on a deeper plane Rana's distrust of her related to her mother.

This idea was fully confirmed in their next session. The doctor very cautiously broached the subject of Rana's childhood and her relationship with her mother. At first the young woman just shook her head with a wry twist of her mouth, but then, after a silence, she began to talk after all, and at the end of their hour together she found relief in a fit of tears.

"I suspect your mother felt so hurt that her first child was 'only' a girl that she never forgave you, and was always taking her disappointment out on you," said Hanna Bishara.

Rana looked up. She felt that the doctor was not just quoting from medical textbooks but speaking from her own experience. She smiled at her.

When Hanna Bishara came next afternoon, everything seemed

just the same as at their first meeting – except for her patient's shy, questioning look, as if the young woman had been waiting for her.

Hanna Bishara recollected that, in passing, Rana had told her how as far back as she could remember her mother had never let her have anything she said she wished for. So she began by asking if there was anything that Rana would like just now. After a short pause the answer came in a soft but very clear voice, "Could someone tell Dunia I'd like to see her?" Dr. Bishara learned that Dunia was a very good friend whom Rana had known since childhood. The doctor promised that she would see about it. "But perhaps we ought to discuss your medicaments first, and work out a plan together to improve your appetite," she said, and was astonished when Rana quietly but audibly agreed with her.

Unfortunately the experienced Dr. Salam was right when he said he doubted whether Rana's friend would comply with her wish. Dr. Bishara had been more optimistic, but her phone call to Dunia was a disappointment. Dunia wasn't going to visit a psychiatric hospital; like many Arabs she seemed to be afraid of them, although she didn't say so. But still, she was ready to talk to her friend on the phone.

Rana smiled quietly when the doctor said that, sad to say, Dunia couldn't visit her. "I ought to have known it," she murmured, "but I was being silly."

284. Liking

"Would you like to go into the garden?" she asked. Rana looked up, and was surprised to find the doctor reading her own thoughts. A little later she was walking in the garden with Dr. Bishara, shyly exchanging greetings with the other patients.

No, she had certainly not been a highly gifted girl, Rana thought, before carefully answering that question from the doctor out loud. She'd just worked hard, that was why she had done well in school and passed all her examinations without much difficulty.

Had she been popular, Dr. Bishara asked? No, she replied. The doctor did not press her further. That was kind of her, but the way Rana had answered at once, as if "no" were the answer only to be expected, alarmed them both.

Rana fell silent. The doctor felt as if she were standing in a dark wood, and must grope her way out of it laboriously. Her questions were probing fingers. Rana replied briefly, with long silences in which she often seemed to have entirely forgotten both the doctor and herself.

But then a moment came when their conversation reverted to mothers. Rana remembered moments in her childhood when she had felt something like affection for hers.

"Did your mother kiss you often?"

"Kiss me?" Rana actually laughed for the first time. "My mother's mouth isn't made for kissing. She could never bring herself to do it." She felt silent again and ignored all further questions. The doctor sensed deep sadness behind her withdrawal.

Hanna Bishara, said the male nurse Adnan, was Dr. Salaam's right hand. She came from a rich Christian family, and was the first woman doctor to work in this mental hospital. He liked her. Head Nurse Kadira did not. That was another reason to like Hanna Bishara, though Rana. She herself disliked Kadira and her cold manner.

Head Nurse Kadira was not tall, but she was strong, with masculine features and fiery red hair. She wore shoes with crescent-shaped iron reinforcements at their toes and heels, so that as she walked down the corridor she sounded like a soldier on the march, but with a curiously teetering step. She said little, and her eyes were windows with no curtains over them; you looked straight into a void.

There was a lot of talk about the head nurse. People said she was wedded to the hospital, and crazy herself. One woman patient told Rana that she had seen Kadira urinating, and she was a man below the waist, female only from the waist up.

285. An Outing

Had Rana been particularly afraid of being with boys, the doctor wanted to know. Hesitantly, she said no, and then preserved a long silence. Thinking about it, she decided her answer was not quite right. Then she remembered the incident in the summer of 1954, when she was fourteen. There was to be a family outing, with a picnic on the river, one Sunday in July. At first it seemed a delightful idea, but then she found out that Jack had been allowed to ask two friends, the Interior Minister's twin sons. Rana suspected that her mother was trying to ingratiate herself with their powerful family by inviting the boys. Or perhaps she only wanted to be able to mention at her coffee mornings what good friends her son was with the Minister's twins. Rana would have preferred to stay at home. Then she could have phoned Farid, or gone to the cinema with Dunia, but neither her mother nor her father would allow it. Her father waxed enthusiastic about the beautiful river that flowed into a lake. "Water as clear as glass, just the thing for a little fish like you." He knew that Rana loved to swim.

But during the outing something happened that she couldn't forget. The twin brothers were nice boys, but they kept looking at Rana in an odd way. The day was hot. Her father invited her and the others to swim, and soon she had left everyone else behind. The lake was deep, and her father had been right: the water was clear as glass and refreshing. Her mother was already setting out the picnic in the shade of a tall oak tree.

When her father was tired of swimming he climbed out of the water and told the boys to keep an eye on Rana. All three of them laughed, and soon they were playing catch and diving under the water. They formed into two groups, Rana and Jack against the twins, but before five minutes were up all three boys were chasing her. She was surprised, furious with her brother, and tried to get away. But Jack held her firmly by one hand, and one twin by the other. Suddenly she felt the third boy's fingers under her swimsuit. He was grinning at her. Rana saw in his face that he knew exactly what he was doing. He boldly squeezed her nipples. Rana couldn't defend herself. Pleading, she turned to her brother. "Let go of me!" she cried. But Jack pretended not to hear her. The boy's hand was now sliding down over her stomach to her vagina. "No!" cried Rana, kicking out at both her brother and the other twin, and finally she managed to free herself. She dived down, swam through the waterweeds in the depths of the lake, swallowed water, and came up again a long way from the other three, coughing and crying.

The boys went on playing. They laughed. But Rana swam far out, to keep a safe distance away from them. When she finally came out of the water, they were already sitting by the camp fire lit for the picnic, laughing. None of them took any notice of Rana.

That was over fourteen years ago, but suddenly it seemed like yesterday. Her throat felt tight. She said goodbye to the doctor, who had borne her silence patiently.

286. Brightly Coloured Birds

Of all the patients in the hospital, Sami was the strangest. He kept raising his hands and announcing his name and job to some invisible inspector. Then he would assure his unseen interlocutor that he was innocent, and wasn't a bird. But he was a completely different person when someone in a white coat appeared, even if it was only the porter. Then he spoke thoughtfully and reasonably, and you might have thought him completely sane. Sometimes his "reasonable" manner intrigued strangers, who took him for one of the staff until he began telling them about the experiments being made underground here to turn human beings into birds and fish. He had told Rana in confidence that Dr. Salam was giving him pills so that in due course he would be able to fly like a bird. It was being done for the benefit of the air force. But he only pretended to take the pills, said Sami. As soon as the doctor turned his back, he spat them out again. "And one day the pill hit a worm, and what do you think? It sprouted wings and flew away."

But Rana found it difficult to draw the line between being crazy and acting crazy in other patients as well as Sami, and sometimes even in herself. It was a balancing act. At least, she reassured herself, the part of her brain where Farid lived was still sane, and that was a large part. She checked every day when she got up to see whether she could recall every detail of a given meeting with Farid, and always felt better when she found that it worked.

And in some ways she felt that the world of this hospital was more honest than the sane world outside. Rana thought of the women in her neighbourhood who gave up all their own desires out of fear, and just did what other people expected them to do.

'I'd rather be with these brightly coloured birds here,' she whispered, and smiled at the gardener, who was doing a little dance with his rake.

287. Second Report

Dr. Salam, chief medical director, 3 July 1968, 17.00 hours.
Patient to some extent responding to medication, shows more energy, thinks and speaks with less inhibition. However, mood still very despondent. Feelings of guilt and failure, in particular lacks any idea of future prospects. Affect clearly less labile, but still potentially suicidal. Seems to have settled down well, helps the staff where she can, is solicitous of weaker women patients. Nursing staff say that a kind of friendship has developed between patient and male nurse, Adnan. According to Sister Sahida, is now also sleeping through the night without chloral.

Imipramine can be increased by 50 mg, for the time being continue levomepromazine at the same dosage. May be permitted to go for walks alone now, only for an hour at a time to start with.

Dr. Bishara satisfied. Two months after their first meeting, patient laughed for the first time, a few days ago began painting (watercolours). On warm summer days spends more time outside than in her room. Patient does not seem very anxious for her family to visit her. Keeps her distance from husband in particular. Ward nurse says he has visited only twice. Conversations with Dr. Bishara seem to mean a good deal to her, she tells me they talk about her childhood most of the time. Dr. B. has learned that patient's mother also had phases of severe depression.

288. Opening Up

Psychiatry was his domain. No medical director in the Republic had such a high reputation as Dr. Salam, but only within the walls of his own hospital. Hanna Bishara had a free hand there. It was she who had arranged for soft classical music by Bach or Mozart, to be played in all the wards.

Hanna Bishara always gave a straight answer when Rana asked her a question. Dr. Salam phrased his answers so carefully that sometimes Rana wasn't sure whether he meant yes or no.

"Why do many of the patients here have burn marks on their temples?" Rana asked. Hanna Bishara told her about the electric shocks that such patients needed to cure them.

Dr. Bishara was a happy woman, but in general she didn't mention her private life much. However, when Rana asked to see photographs of her husband and her children, she brought some next day. They talked about the wedding night, and the doctor asked if Rana had been prepared for that first time with her husband. She didn't feel like telling the doctor yet that he had raped her, but confined herself to a "no". "My mother can't talk about either love or sex," she added. The doctor nodded, and wrote it down in her little notebook.

When Hanna Bishara left that afternoon, Rana watched her go, and felt that it wasn't fair for her to leave this woman in the dark. A woman who helped her, who didn't ask insistent questions, and she, Rana, was leaving her to puzzle over the reason for her sadness. A little later she got to her feet and ran after her, but the doctor was not in the ward any more. The nurse on duty tried to reach her by phone, and was in luck.

"There's something important I'd like to tell you. When will you have time?"

"Any time, for you," replied the doctor. She sensed that the gate which had been closed to her so long had just opened at least a crack, and hurried back to the ward.

Then Rana told her the whole story of herself and Farid, and Hanna Bishara listened for four hours. She made not a single note, but every word was imprinted on her mind.

289. Two Doctors and One Patient

December 1968 brought more rain than the country had seen all year. A strong wind whipped heavy raindrops against the window. Dr. Salam was watching one of the male patients who had been dancing in the garden, and was now being led back indoors by two male nurses.

"Go on. I'm listening," he prompted Dr. Bishara, who had briefly paused in the middle of reading her report.

"After a difficult start, a definitely productive mental process has now developed, one in which Rana can admit to her grief over her forbidden love for Farid, her fears and uncertainty since his arrest, and can carry on without falling into despair. She also feels able to stand up to her conflicts with her own family, in particular her mother, who offered her neither protection nor emotional warmth. Equally positive has been her overcoming of her anorexic tendencies, with slow but steady weight gain, and she is becoming physically stronger. So we are reaching a phase of stabilization which makes it seem appropriate to prepare her for discharge in the near future ..."

"But that would require her to make a personal decision to go back to her husband," Dr. Salam interrupted, turning slowly back to his desk. Dr. Bishara gave him her case notes, with a question in her eyes. The medical director shook his head. "She ought to stay here a little longer. It's still too soon!"

Why, Hanna Bishara wondered that evening on her way home, is he so set on postponing Rana's return home? Does he suspect that she never *will* want to go back to her husband? But what chance does she stand if she leaves him now – a woman on her own, without a profession, here in Damascus? Or is that itself his reason: to keep her here until she knows her own mind?

Hanna Bishara could find no answer. By now she had come to realize that sometimes there *is* no clear answer.

290. Third Report

Dr. Salam, chief medical director, 22 March 1969, 15.00hrs.
Patient surprised to find that I know about relationship with Farid M., yet do not condemn her for it. Does not seem to have expected understanding. Obviously entertains great hostility towards mother and brother on this subject. Disappointed rather than hostile towards father for ranging himself on mother's side. Clearly feels very much alone. Will allow her to get in touch with Farid's mother by telephone. Once a month, from my office. Farid M. obviously still detained, but patient wept for joy on learning that he is still alive. She should talk to Dr. Bishara about it, but discretion is key. For now she seems to feel safe and protected in the hospital.

Continue imipramine and levomepromazine until further notice. Can go for walks alone as long as she likes, but not in the evening.

Still no special wish for family visits. According to Head Nurse Kadira, husband is very cold towards her. Comes once a month and talks to patient, who never answers.

291. Kisses

When Farid kissed her, his kiss was like a pebble and she like a lake rippling all the way from her mouth to her toes.

She had never been kissed by her parents, only by other relations, but she shrank from those kisses. Uncle Bulos, who always smelled of sour milk, had been particularly nauseating. He used to hold her so tight that she could scarcely breathe, and the dense stubble on his chin was scratchy. Kisses from Aunt Basma, her mother's sister, were even nastier; her mouth had smelled of decay. When Rana was little, her father once whispered to her, "Aunt Basma died ages ago."

And her father had laughed. Aunt Basma reminded Rana of the dead mouse that her father had found behind the couch years ago, after a long search. The drawing room stank of it for days.

Aunt Basma had died on a Sunday in May 1945. Rana remembered precisely. It had been a beautiful spring day. She was playing indoors when the first French bombs dropped on the city. Her parents were still at the funeral, and Rana and her brother had gone to the neighbours. Suddenly her father arrived. He took her hand and ran ahead with her, while her mother hurried along behind with Jack in her arms. The French bombers and heavy artillery were aiming at targets in Damascus. One of them was the parliament building, very close to her parents' house. It seemed to take the four of them forever to reach Bab Tuma, and then they had to spend a week staying with George Abiad, a lawyer who was a friend of her father's, in a large house with lemon trees and in the company of his horrible children, until at last the fighting stopped.

The French withdrew from Damascus, leaving six hundred Syrian dead and three thousand wounded. Many houses were destroyed.

Her parents were glad to get home and find their house still standing. "Our Lady protected it," said her mother. But Rana felt sure it was the evil spirit under the stairs who – even though he was evil – needed a place to live too. She was glad, all the same. Riad and Fuad, George Abiad's children, had been spiteful, calling Rana and her brother refugees and hitting them when the grown-ups weren't looking. The two boys were big and strong, particularly Riad, who was a colossus, and liked to sit on Rana's stomach saying he wouldn't get off until she kissed him on the mouth, and she'd better not tell tales, because if she did he'd put a rat in her bed one night, and rats liked to eat little girls' ears. After that Rana often woke up in the night and felt her ears. But she'd had to kiss Riad three times because he was pressing all the breath out of her.

Here in the psychiatric hospital, over twenty-three years later, she saw him in a dream with a rat in his hand, and she ran down a little flight of stairs to the courtyard where her parents were sitting. She screamed, but no one heard her, and whenever she reached the last step the stairs grew longer. Riad came no closer to her, but the flight of stairs still never seemed to end.

292. Fourth Report

Dr. Salam, chief medical director, 15 May 1969, 11.00hrs.
Psychopathologically, distinct improvement and stabilisation in patient. Drive and sleep patterns normalised, psychomotor functions also normal, affectively adequate to the situation and responding to it, no more indications of suicidal moods. In conversation in the last few weeks very frank, affectively modulated, able to empathize. Still sees her future as very dark, in particular cannot imagine returning to husband, but seems to know of no alternative. Cannot count on support of her parents. Medication: 150 mg imipramine, was able to discontinue levomepromazine over last two weeks.

Popular in the ward, feels safe and sheltered. Does not want to be discharged yet, but must begin facing reality. She rejects my suggestion of a stay with relatives or abroad, for which her husband's consent could be obtained with a little pressure. Cannot yet make up her mind what to do. In view of difficult family situation and the anhedonia still present, inability to make decisions and tendency to brood still part of the picture for the time being. I prescribe an active life with plenty of exercise. Possibility that therapeutic conversations may merely increase brooding tendency? Dr. Bishara rejects this, strongly wishes to continue therapy. Once a week will be enough.

ॐ

In early June, Rana heard from Claire that Farid was soon to be granted an amnesty, and she, as his mother, was able to see him once a week. He was well, said Claire, and longing for Rana.

Three days later she asked the medical director to be discharged. She knew how she was going to live now, she said.

When her husband arrived with flowers she said a warm goodbye to Hanna Bishara, and hugged Edward Salam. "You've helped me so much. Thank you!" she whispered to him, kissing his right cheek. There were tears in the doctor's eyes. A daughter was leaving him, and he knew it was for ever.

BOOK OF BUTTERFLIES

When a butterfly first sees the light it forgets everything
except that it can fly.

֍

DAMASCUS, BEIRUT, SUMMER 1969–SEPTEMBER 1969

293. Suspicion

Matta was standing at the door, looking pale. Claire made him sit down by the fountain and brewed him a strong mocha. He was nervously cracking his finger joints. When she came back she also brought a plate of sablés, Matta's favourite cookies.

"Bulos lied to me," he said after a while. Claire sat very still. "He swore by our sacred vow of brotherhood that he'd never seen Farid since the monastery, and then he wanted to know who gave me that information. It's terrible, just think of it! I risked my life for Bulos, and then I ask him a favour for my brother Farid, and ..." Matta fell silent.

The doorbell rang. It was a neighbouring woman bringing a domestic still around for Claire. When she came back to Matta she saw that he was weeping.

"What's the matter?"

"I risked my life for him, and now he lies to me. Who knows, perhaps he was always lying to me," he said, standing up. "I just wanted him to spare Farid. That's all. But I'll go to him again. Perhaps I'll take my wife, she can soften a heart of stone when she cries." He smiled shyly.

Farid should be proud that there are people who love him so much, thought Claire. At the door she hugged Matta more tenderly than ever before. He was sobbing like a child. "Farid is my brother. Matta will see to it," he whispered defiantly, and went out. Suddenly a strange feeling came over Claire. When he sat there like that, lost in thought, his features were very like Elias's. She too had heard the rumours that Nasibe, the young widow who was passionately in love with Elias long ago, had become pregnant by him and married the poor shepherd in a hurry to avoid scandal. Elias denied it all. Nasibe had had a thousand and one relationships with men, he always said. But Matta's aunt said that when her deranged nephew came back from the mental hospital, he was sure of only one thing: Farid was his brother.

294. Out of the Cocoon

President Amran returned from Moscow in a good mood, and next day pardoned seven hundred political prisoners, a hundred and eleven of them held in Tad. Two large buses took the freed men to Damascus. First they just sat deep in thought, looking almost sad. It was not easy to say goodbye to their companions in misfortune. Many wept, but when they understood that they were really free they almost all went crazy. They jumped up from their seats, sang in strange languages that no one could understand, danced in the central aisle, fell into each other's arms, clapped one another on the back and the shoulder and exchanged happy kisses.

"If you carry on like that the police will send us straight to the nuthouse. Calm down, we're in the suburbs of Damascus already," begged the bus driver. The freed prisoners sat down again, looked out of the window at beautiful women, whistled, played at hiding, laughed like little schoolboys.

Farid reached his house around midday, and wanted to storm in through the front door, dance around the fountain with Claire, and shout for joy, but the door was locked. He rang the bell, and Claire came to answer it in her cooking apron. "Holy Virgin!" she cried. Farid hugged her and carried her to the fountain. She was laughing.

"Since when have you been locking the front door?"

"Since the city filled up with so many anonymous strangers. They flock in and take anything that isn't nailed down. And others come along and involve you in shady business that could put you behind bars for ten years. Someone left a kilo of hashish in a flower pot at Suleiman's cousin Faris's house. He doesn't smoke and he despises drugs, but that didn't help him with the police. A number of people have had locks fitted to their doors since his arrest."

Farid wanted to have a bath, but Claire said that first, as when he came home from Gahan, he must go and see his father, who was waiting impatiently for his arrival. And indeed, on this second occasion Elias was in transports of joy. He laughed and wept and kept stroking his son's face. Almost awkwardly, he offered him sweetmeats.

"Those bastards tortured him, although he isn't in any political party," he told his old neighbour Nuri, who ran the flower shop and could make the most beautiful bouquets, even though he was drunk all day.

"That's what happens when peasants get power," said Nuri scornfully. "My father always told me: if you have just two piastres, then spend one on a piece of bread and the other on a fragrant rose. But fewer and fewer of us do that kind of thing now. I've noticed it for years, people only want flowers for funerals. Peasants don't think flowers are necessary. They won't pay good money for such things. Last week one of them was telling me how many kilos of wheat he could buy for a bouquet like this. I told him he'd better give his wife not flowers but a bagful of wheat. And do you know what he said? That was a good tip, he told me."

✺

It was about three when Farid reached Rana on the telephone. She was at home alone, and he told her the plan he had been working out for months.

"Wonderful," said Rana, feeling that she was near the gates of heaven. "There's only one thing I want to ask you: let's not leave before September the 6th."

"Why not?"

"Because my husband is flying to Moscow for two weeks on the 5th. I shall need a day's rest before we finally leave."

"Right, but by then you must have your passport and all your documents translated into German by a sworn interpreter."

"I already have my passport, but why German? I thought we were flying to Paris."

"Officially we still are. I'll tell you all the rest of it once we're in safety," said Farid.

る

It was easier than Farid expected to get hold of two skilfully forged passports. Josef didn't ask why he needed them. "Muhsin will do them for you, they'll look more genuine than the real thing," he joked, "but he's expensive." Farid didn't mind about the price.

The forger did not have a sophisticated workshop, but was the possessor of a brilliant mind and felt no respect at all for his employer. He was a hard-working civil servant with the registration and passports office, and had a taste for overtime unusual in such jobs.

Muhsin Sharara was a Muslim, but as he was a bookworm he happened to have read the Gospels, where he found the story of the raising of Lazarus. That had been in the early sixties, when President Satlan began on his great wave of arrests. People would pay a thousand dollars – a fortune then – for a "good" passport. He listed all registrations of the deaths of children, and began selling passports. Only two things weren't quite right about them: the passport photo and the fact that the real bearer of the holder's name had died decades ago. Muhsin had erased the entry of his or her date of death from the register with an ink remover that was little known at the time. Everything else in his passports, including the rubber stamp and the signature of the head of the passport office, was genuine.

So at the end of August Farid was in possession of four passports: two real ones and two forged ones in the names of Sarkis and Georgina

Shammas, a married couple. The two real passports contained visas to go and study in Germany.

295. The Wound and the Trap

Farid soon settled in again. The voice of Feiruz on the radio was part of every morning, like the first coffee with Claire and the cry of the muezzin from the nearby mosque. But he noticed that the Damascenes had withdrawn into a cocoon of silence, because they were afraid. They talked a lot and were always cracking jokes, but only to cover up for that silence.

One hot August day Farid didn't feel like doing anything much. He was standing in the doorway of the house, watching two dogs scuffle for a bone in the shade. Suddenly Matta came running down the street, stopped in front of him, and told him, still breathless, that he knew for sure now that Bulos had betrayed him in the monastery.

"Let's not talk about it. It's over," said Farid, for Matta had already spent the whole of the last few days searching like a man possessed for the proof of Bulos's treachery. Only Bulos could have given him up to the police when he ran away from the monastery that second time. Matta's tone was not heated. His voice was cold, and he set out his evidence meticulously.

"The police must have known. They were waiting for me at the last barrier before the main road. And I can do my sums well enough to be sure that only two people knew I was running away: you and Bulos," Matta ended his argument, and nodded thoughtfully. "Why does he want to destroy us? Why? What have we ever done to him?"

"Perhaps because in his own way he loved us and couldn't hold us. He didn't want you to leave. You were his greatest support, and he loved you. At first he liked me too, but he got on my nerves, and then he found out that I'm a Mushtak, while he was and is a Shahin."

"My dear brother, what on earth do all those books of yours teach you? Bulos loved no one, not even himself. He abused my trust, and I was a fool," said Matta bitterly.

But he had a touch of the wily fox about him now. Mahdi discovered nothing of what he was thinking, but Matta had acquired Bulos's wife as a customer, ran errands and carried purchases for her, asking little money. Since then she had taken to telling him about her husband's loveless ways and her own loneliness.

જી

"Would you like to help me?" asked Farid at the end of August.

"Of course. What do you want me to do?" replied Matta.

"Look closely at this ticket," said Farid, showing him an air ticket made out by the French airline.

"So?"

"That's my flight for 14 September. I'm flying with Air France at twenty hours exactly on that day. Can you remember that? Sunday, 14 September."

"Of course I can remember it. That's the Feast of the Holy Cross in Mala, but I haven't been there for years," said Matta.

"And you won't be able to go this year either, because you and Faride must come to the airport to see us off."

"Of course we'll come, but what does that have to do with the air ticket? Why did you show it to me?"

"I want you to be sure to let Bulos know I'm flying with Air France that day," said Farid.

Matta's face showed anger. "Brother, what do you take me for?"

"My most loyal friend. If you tell Bulos that, you'll be doing me and yourself a favour. You'll have nothing to fear. He can't touch me now. Believe me, this will just make him drop his mask and show his ugly face, but he won't get his hands on me again. You'll be helping me enormously by pretending to be so naïve that you give him that news without stopping to think about it. It will keep him concentrating on the airport and not even thinking about any other route. Okay?"

"And you're sure I'll be helping you by letting that traitor know exactly when you plan to fly?"

"Yes, absolutely. You'll save me by fooling him."

"You're also sure that at this moment you're in full possession of your wits?"

"As sure as I'm certain that your name is Matta and you're as loyal to me as a brother. But you mustn't give Bulos the information too obviously. He's more suspicious than a rat. You must be cunning as a fox yourself, and then just go to the airport with Claire on 14 September."

"Swear to me that you'll be in safety then. Swear by the health of your mother."

"Why my mother?"

"Because as a communist you could put your hand on the Bible and swear to any lie."

"I swear by the health of my mother, by the light of my eyes, and by Rana's life that you will be helping me greatly by letting Bulos know, as soon as possible, that I'm leaving the country on 14 September."

"I'll do it," said Matta, and there was a curious gleam in his eyes.

An opportunity came along ten days before that. He had delivered an order to Bulos's wife, who was laying in large stocks of provisions from the spice market: herbs, grain, oils, and olive oil soap. She asked him when he would be able to bring her the twenty kilos of small pickling aubergines she had ordered from the village of Qabun, and Matta replied that he'd do it this week if she liked, because he would be busy from Monday to Saturday next week working for the Mushtaks. "They're giving a farewell party on the Saturday for their son Farid, and I'll be transporting all they need for it with my Suzuki."

Bulos, hovering in the background, was attentively following this conversation. "Oh, is Farid going away?" he suddenly asked, with no idea that at that moment he was taking his first step into the fox's trap.

"Yes, he's flying to Paris on Sunday, to study there," said Matta, and waited for Bulos to ask him about the airline and the time of day. But Bulos just smiled and went back to his newspaper.

Matta thought he had failed, but he was wrong. On Thursday 11 September, from his office, Mahdi called a colleague at the airport, and received confirmation that Farid Mushtak had booked on an Air France flight that day. Mahdi hung up and immediately rang his friend Badran.

"Yes, good, pick him up then," said Badran, noticing only when he had put the receiver down again that he had spoken to Mahdi Said much as he spoke to his German shepherd dog.

296. Rana's Revenge

Rana had a long search before she found a second-hand dealer who would take her house contents complete. All the others wanted to buy only selected items of household goods, but after a brief look, and at the low price she was asking, Abdullah al Asmar found it an offer he couldn't refuse. The young widow wanted to get rid of everything, even the family photographs, her late husband's letters, his underwear, suits, uniforms, three fine pistols, and all the books. She told him the sight of these things grieved her. The second-hand dealer, a man well used to house clearances, put on a show of sympathetic understanding. "You're telling me nothing new, madame. I lost my own first wife when I was your age. I felt I wanted to die too," he said in a faltering voice.

"But I want to live, you see. I want to start again, and all this junk is like lead weighing me down," she replied, and the second-hand dealer almost laughed. Junk, she called it! Three Rolexes, two gold Omega watches, a collection of gold coins, a stamp collection, walnut-wood cupboards, damask curtains, paintings, records, four radios and three television sets, two of them still in their original packaging. They agreed on twenty thousand dollars, and the dealer was sure he had struck the bargain of his life. The showcase that contained hunting rifles from all over the world would fetch over ten thousand alone.

A day later, on Saturday 13 September, his men cleared the house from attic to cellar. Down in the cellar there were countless jars of preserved and bottled fruit. Rana gave those away to the men. When they had finished, the dealer handed the young widow the sum on which they had agreed, and made off in a hurry.

Rana walked around the empty house. Her footsteps echoed back from the walls. When she reached the middle of the drawing room, now illuminated like a theatrical stage by the sun, she stopped. She took the wedding photo from her purse, slowly tore it in two, and placed the half with the picture of her smiling husband in the middle of the room. She stuffed the other half back in her purse.

Then she closed her eyes. A cactus came into bloom in her heart, and for a second she felt its spines. She had goosebumps, and was briefly dazed. When she came back to reality she heaved a sigh of relief.

She went to the Hotel Samiramis in the city centre and took a room there. Later she called down to reception and ordered a light supper from room service. She stood at the window for a while, with her eyes wandering over several building sites. Then she looked down at the street. Damascus has become a large village, she thought. She had never before seen so many passers by in peasant garments.

And then, as they had agreed, she rang Farid.

297. The Flight of the Butterflies

He sat quietly in his parents' bedroom. Outside, this September Sunday was as bright as summer, but the curtains dimmed the light. Farid was watching his father, who had fallen asleep. He looked shrunken, very small as he lay there, breathing peacefully.

Suddenly, as if waking abruptly from a nightmare, he sat up. "Farid," he said, seeing his son.

"Yes, it's me, Father."

"Have I been asleep for long?"

"Mother says you need to get plenty of sleep because the medicaments make you tired," he said. Elias folded his hands in his lap and lowered his gaze.

"So you're flying today?" he asked.

"Officially, yes, but for you and Mama I'm really flying tomorrow at thirteen hours from Beirut."

"And you have someone to get you over the border?"

"Don't worry about that," replied Farid, glancing at his watch. It was just before three in the afternoon. "I must be off," he said, standing up.

"God bless you wherever you go. I may never see you again," said Elias, fighting back tears.

"Yes, you will, Papa. I won't be far away. A three-hour flight and you'll be with me. Our world is so small now, but that man Shahin would never leave me in peace here," he replied, hugging his father.

Years later, he was still asking himself why he hadn't kissed Elias then. He couldn't find the answer.

Outside the courtyard Laila, Josef, Matta and his wife Faride were sitting with Claire, who was trying to smile through her tears.

Farid embraced his mother. "You and your Elias must come and see me soon. It would be a good trip for lovers to make."

"I'll be there very soon," everyone heard Elias call. Claire laughed. Farid kissed her, and shed tears himself.

"We'll give you a hug at the airport," said Josef. "I'll be driving straight there from home, with my wife."

"Let me embrace you now. Who knows, we may not have time there," replied Farid, holding him close. Josef laughed to hide his awkwardness.

Laila sniffed tearfully. "I'll think of you even at the last moment of my life," she whispered in his ear, and kissed him on the lips.

"Leave a little of him for Rana," joked Claire.

Faride too had tears in her eyes. "May God punish those who tormented you and are forcing you to leave now. I know it's wrong, but I'm going to light a candle to Our Lady every day and ask her to make your enemy's hands fall off." Hatred and grief were at odds in her voice.

The doorbell rang. The taxi was there.

"Goodbye," said Farid. At the door, Matta hugged him.

"Watch out for yourself. That traitor knows now."

"Don't worry. But whatever happens at the airport, stay with Claire," said Farid, embracing his mother once again, and then he got into the taxi. Claire, Josef, Faride and Matta waved. At the corner of Straight Street, Farid waved back one last time.

"The Hotel Samiramis," he told the driver.

298. The Reckoning

Claire, Laila, Matta and his wife reached the airport around seven in the evening. Josef was already there. He looked anxious. "Not a sign of Farid anywhere, but secret service men all over the place, a blind man could spot that," he said. Claire smiled.

At seven-thirty Mahdi Said, accompanied by two burly men, entered the departures hall. Matta could hardly restrain his fury. "That traitor," he said viciously.

At a quarter to eight, Farid Mushtak was twice called to board the plane. Bulos, alias Mahdi, was standing at the Air France desk. He signalled to two secret service men in civilian clothes. Next moment they were racing down the gangway leading to the plane. Ten minutes later they came back, and even from a distance could be seen shaking their heads.

Suddenly Mahdi Said caught sight of Claire and Matta. He immediately sent one of his men over to them.

"Major Mahdi would like to speak to you," said the man. For a moment Matta felt his heart stop.

"Tell the major that I, however, would not like to speak to him," said Claire, "and the bird he hopes to catch here is sitting in a different aircraft on its way to Paris. It must be flying over Greece around now." And she laughed.

"So that was it!" cried Josef, striking his brow with the flat of his hand. Displeased, the man went back to his superior officer, who next moment called his team together and marched to the exit with them. Farid was called three more times before the Air France plane rolled on to the runway.

"That traitor really did mean to kill Farid. And I'm absolutely sure now that he was the one who gave me away. Damn him," swore Matta on the way back in the taxi. His little three-wheeled Suzuki scooter was still parked outside Farid's house. It was just after nine when Claire, Matta, and Faride got out. Claire paid the driver, thanked Matta and his wife for coming with her, and waved as they rode away on Matta's Suzuki. It was only a short ride.

"But where are you going at this time of night?" asked Faride, when she noticed that Matta was not dismounting from the scooter. She herself was exhausted.

"I need a little fresh air to get over Farid leaving. Don't wait up for me. I'll be very quiet and take care not to wake you when I come in."

Slowly, he rode down the alleys, and then came to broad Bab Tuma Street. Less than ten minutes later he reached Marcel Karameh Street. He stopped outside Number 31, switched the engine off, and sat there for a while.

The sultry September night lay heavy over the city. People were sleeping with their windows and balcony doors open. Matta knew that Bulos spent the night in the attic storey, apart from his wife. There was still a light on up there.

Just before midnight it went out. Matta waited for another fifteen minutes, and then looked at the time once more. He was sure that Farid was well over the border into Lebanon by now. He quietly got out of his three-wheeled scooter and tied a large jute sack around his waist. Then, soundless as a panther, he began climbing the old ivy.

BOOK OF LOVE VII

Those who are loved do not die.

⁑

299. Arrival

Sarkis and Georgina Shammas, man and wife, entered the lobby of the Hotel Paris in East Beirut. The man at the reception desk inspected them suspiciously.

"Do you have a double room for the night?" asked the husband.

"Yes, sir, and all rooms have a direct view of the sea. Fifty lira a day, breakfast included," replied the receptionist automatically.

"*D'accord.*" Sarkis Shammas looked at his wife, and nodded.

"May I see your passports, please? You'll be aware that since the civil war in Jordan and the mass exodus of Palestinians we have to register our guests' passports. I know it's a nuisance, but ..."

"Here you are," replied the guest, putting two Syrian passports down on the counter. When the hotel clerk read the names he gave them a friendly smile. "Right, I won't be needing those any more," he said, handing the documents back. "You're one of us. You know – well, I can speak frankly now. It's not just Palestinians, it's all kinds of Muslims coming here: hungry Pakistanis, Afghans, Indonesians, God knows who else. They marry some Lebanese Muslim woman or other, and that makes them Lebanese. Then they breed like rabbits, and we Christians, the real Lebanese, get the blame for it in our own country. You're welcome here, sir, very welcome," reiterated the man behind the desk in friendly tones. "My cousin lives in Bab Tuma. Do you know him? François Frangi, that's his name, are you acquainted with him?"

"No." The stranger's voice sounded brittle and nipped all curiosity in the bud.

The hotel bellboy, a thin Sudanese in a bright red uniform, came hurrying up. The two cases were heavy, and he hauled them into the first-floor room groaning quietly. When he came back downstairs he was beaming all over his face.

"Real gentlefolks," he said, lighting a cigarette.

"You mean more than a lira tip?" asked the clerk at reception. "Let me guess – two lira?"

The bellboy grinned. "More than that."

So my nose didn't let me down, thought the receptionist. Prosperous Christians on honeymoon, most likely. No, he must correct that assessment, *very* prosperous Christians. They didn't even haggle. He would have let them have the room half-price in this slack season. And now they tipped the bellboy more than two lira. Only the super-rich Saudis handed out more.

"Three?"

"That's right," replied the Sudanese, his eyebrows shooting up as he grinned with delight.

300. The Answer

As soon as Georgina and Sarkis Shammas had closed the door of their room behind the bellboy, they fell on the big bed, almost fainting with desire.

They kissed, laughed, wept for joy, and undressed each other. The woman pressed close to the man and sucked his lower lip, while he caressed her and kissed her right leg, which she had flung over his shoulder.

And when he could delay his climax no longer, he told her he loved her. The woman felt as if liquid fire were running through her veins. "I love you too, Farid," she said.

When they had quenched their thirst for the first time, they lay side by side, and he licked her perspiring face.

"I find it so hard to call you Sarkis," she said. "Why was it so easy for you to say Georgina to me? Have you ever had a relationship with a Georgina?" And she affectionately pulled his earlobe.

"No, nothing like that, but in the underground you get used to new names quickly."

"Farid and Rana are right for a love story, but Sarkis and Georgina sound to me more like saints' names. *Kyrie eleison.*"

Farid laughed. "I'm afraid I couldn't pick and choose. As I understand it, the forger used the names of children who died in our own birth years. The only thing that mattered was for the passports to get us over the Syrian border safe and sound. I'm sure Mahdi was quick to pass my name on to all the border checkpoints. We fly at thirteen hours tomorrow. When we leave the hotel after breakfast I'll destroy the forged passports on the way to the airport, and then we'll be Rana and Farid again – for ever."

"Are we really safe at last? And now can you tell me why we're flying to Germany and not France?"

"Yes, dear heart, we have two places to study at Heidelberg. I'll continue my researches into chemistry, and you can study philosophy if you want to. Claire's cousin got us accepted. He's a well-known Orientalist at the university. And no one will find us there. Mahdi and his secret service have known we were planning to go to France for some time. So I confirmed them in that belief, and even organized the flight. Claire gave me the money for an air ticket with Air France, and I let Mahdi know, through a good friend, when I'd be flying. The bastard will certainly have found out details from the airline, and if I know him he was at the airport in person to see me humiliated. The plane was due to take off just as we arrived in Beirut."

"Are you sure?"

"That we've shaken him off? As good as certain. I'll get in touch with Claire from Germany once we have nothing more to fear, and then we'll find out all about it."

"My compliments! What a good thing my lover knows his way about the underground," said Rana, embracing him. He smelled particularly delicious today. Soon she fell asleep.

When she woke up it was already day outside. Light filtered through the slats of the shutters. Farid was breathing peacefully. He looked more handsome than ever in the dim light, and she tenderly nibbled his throat. He woke up and kissed her.

"Am I dreaming, or is it all true?" he asked, tickling her. Only when she laughed out loud and almost fell off the bed did he stop.

"It's a strange thing, but I long for you even though you're here sleeping with me," he whispered, bending over her.

"You're beside me, but not at this precise moment sleeping *with* me," she said mischievously. Burning with desire, she sat astride his thighs and pressed him gently down on the bed. Then she made ardent love to him, and thought of their first meeting at the Sabunis' house. It was his first touch that had gone to her heart. Here in this comfortable bed, Rana felt it again. Every touch of his hands set off electric currents under her skin. She felt it tickling so that she was always on the point of laughter.

Outside, the gulls swooped and cried, and a fire flared up in her, streaming through her veins. Farid trembled, and held her close.

Rana slid off the bed, slipped her shirt on and went to the window. The clock on the tower of a nearby church struck ten. Rana flung the double window open and saw the wind crinkling the surface of the sea. The waves foamed on the stones of the breakwater. A young mother and her son were feeding the gulls with stale bread, and the birds were screaming as they fought for it. When the two sides of the window struck the wall, two pigeons flew up in alarm.

A passenger plane was cutting through the sky at a great height, leaving a white trail behind it. It looked like the first line of chalk that Rana used to draw on the asphalt as a child to mark out the spaces of her favourite hopscotch game, "Heaven and Hell".

She closed her eyes and breathed in the fresh breeze caressing her face. Then, at the top of her voice, she cried out, "Yes!"

Farid, still lying in bed exhausted with his eyes closed, and enjoying the pleasure of drowsing briefly off, woke with a start. Rana turned and looked at him. He gazed back at her, surprised.

How was he to know that her "Yes!" was an answer to the question he had asked her nine and a half years before?

BOOK OF DEATH II

Truth is a jewel whose owner is rich and lives dangerously.

و

ٮ

DAMASCUS, MEDITERRANEAN COAST, SPRING–AUTUMN 1970

301. Rumours

Colonel Badran was a passionate movie buff, and loved thrillers. He had written three screenplays himself, but they were now gathering dust in a drawer. Today he was wearing civilian clothes and sunglasses as he walked beside the widow Said, following her murdered husband's coffin and filming the whole occasion with his new Super-Eight camera.

When the little party of mourners left the widow Said's apartment later, the colonel stayed on. He confided to her that her husband's ambition had led him to join a conspiracy. Several high-ranking officers, he said, had been planning a coup, and they had promised Mahdi the job of Interior Minister. At first her husband had gone along with them, but then he had scruples, and tried to back out.

The widow couldn't help giggling. "Scruples!" she said, spluttering with laughter. "Mahdi and scruples? You must be joking!" The colonel hesitated, but when the widow fell backward on the couch because she was laughing so hard, it was too much for him. He sat down beside her and laid a hand on the knee she had bared. It was as soft as if she had no bones. She didn't flinch away. He pressed harder, and the widow lay still, closed her eyes, and opened her legs.

Badran caressed her tenderly and carefully, and was surprised to find what sexy lingerie she was wearing under her mourning. She was willing and ardent. Badran enjoyed their love-play on the couch, and when the widow was almost beside herself in her longing for the release of orgasm, he carried her into the bedroom, where he laid her carefully on the bed and made passionate love to her. When they had finished, the widow felt happy for the first time in what seemed an eternity.

Badran lay in her arms, laughing and shaking his head.

"What is it?"

"I don't even know your first name, madame, and I've already slept with you!"

She smiled. "I'm Balkis, and I don't want to be called anything else." And then she told him how cold Mahdi Said had been. "Just the opposite of you, brutal with his hands, but he was useless further down."

Their relationship didn't remain a secret for long, and soon there was an ugly rumour going around that Mahdi had to die because the colonel was having an affair with his wife, and the two of them had strangled him for fear of scandal.

302. Persistence

Commissioner Barudi didn't believe that Badran had anything to do with the murder. The man had too many mistresses in Damascus for that. Barudi had tracked down four of them.

For a long time he thought it possible that there was a political motive for Mahdi's death, but the evidence of the fingerprints failed to reinforce his suspicion. Paper is one of the few materials from which fingerprints do not disappear. So he had prints lifted from the note found with the murdered major, and in secret he also obtained the prints of the condemned officers from the army files. None of them resembled those on the scrap of wrapping paper at all.

Was Badran covering up for something? And if so, why?

After a few days the widow could be disregarded as a source of information, because she was the colonel's lover. Commissioner Barudi put all his information into a folder and carefully kept it with him.

Old Adjutant Mansur, who shared the room with him, noticed that the commissioner had a secret, but he was unable to find out what it was. Since the "Mahdi" case, the young first lieutenant was no longer as hard-working as before. He arrived late for work, and often didn't seem to have his mind on it.

"You wait, you peasant fool, Mansur will get the better of you yet," whispered the adjutant, with a smile playing around his mouth.

In summer Barudi launched out on a new line of research. He decided to discover where the paper found in the murdered man's pocket came from. The answer was easy. Five souvenir shops in the Christian quarter used the pale grey paper in question, another ten used a yellowish wrapping paper. He wrote down the names of the owners and their staff, but this track led nowhere.

At the end of August Barudi took two weeks' vacation, for he noticed how the murder was obsessing him so much that it kept him from working on other cases. He wanted to find out exactly what had happened once and for all, and either chalk up a huge success or forget the entire thing for ever.

Who was this man Mahdi Said?

All Barudi knew was that he came from the small town of Safita in the north of the country, and had originally been a Christian by the name of Said Bustani.

Was it, he wondered as he boarded the bus to Safita, a case of revenge by some religious Christian group?

He arrived in Safita four hours later. The town was beautiful, which made him feel optimistic, and suddenly he felt he was very close to his goal. After two hours his presentiments were confirmed. The Bustani family was well known in town. The murdered man's mother, Rihane Bustani, was a severe elderly widow who bore the marks of her hard life. She was withdrawn, and wouldn't say a word to the commissioner, but suddenly her daughter Mona appeared in the doorway and invited the commissioner to her house. She thought well of his efforts, because he didn't seemed impressed by the idea that her brother was supposed to have taken part in the political plot.

"I'm here in a private capacity; I just want to know the truth," said the commissioner, suddenly feeling ravenous. "You don't have to answer any of my questions." For he realized that he had no means of making her.

"Wait a moment, and I'll be right back," said the woman, going back into her mother's house. Barudi put her age at twenty-five. Later he found out that Mona was thirty-six, one year older than her murdered brother.

She was of rather sturdy build, but had a smooth, broad face with plenty of room on it for her smile. "Come along," she told him, when she came out again. "I'm sure you must be hungry. Didn't you say you'd come all the way from Damascus?"

Mona and her husband Faruk, who joined them later, were kindness and hospitality itself. They entertained Barudi to a delicious meal, and gave him all the information he needed about the murdered major. And when evening drew on, they insisted that he must spend the night with them.

Barudi had really meant to go on to the monastery of St. Sebastian, but no bus went up into the mountains by night. He slept restlessly, constantly switching on the little bedside lamp and writing down everything that occurred to him. Next morning, after a hearty breakfast, he took his leave. Mona's husband waved goodbye one last time from the bus station, and then disappeared in a dense black cloud.

Barudi took out the little notebook containing his new discoveries. He underlined the following entries: the murdered man was known as Bulos in the monastery. His name as a child had been Said Bustani. Later, he converted to Islam in order to further his career, which grieved his sister. From then on he was called Mahdi Said.

He transferred the latest facts he had gleaned, written on several scraps of paper, to the notebook, taking care to write neatly.

Mona's mother Rihane came from Latakia. She fell in love with the rich and dashing son of a farmer in the south, a man called Musa Shahin, married him, and moved to his village of Mala, never guessing that her husband's family and another clan, the Mushtaks, were involved in a blood feud with each other. In the village, one Hasib Mushtak shot Mona's father when the little girl was seven. She remembers her father, who liked to laugh and sing and was a handsome man. The widow moved back with Mona and her brother Said to their grandparents' home in Latakia, where she met Karim Bustani, then the manager of the Latakia arrack distillery. He married her, and made her convert from the Orthodox to the Catholic faith. She and her children took the name of Bustani. But the children's stepfather disliked Said from the first, and sent him off to the monastery. In the same year Karim Bustani moved with his family to Safita, where he tried to open a small arrack distillery of his own. He failed miserably, because he was harsh and unfriendly by nature.

Barudi received a cool reception at the monastery, but one of the Fathers did remember that about fifteen years before there had been a considerable problem in which Bulos Bustani was involved. Barudi had spent five days at the monastery's guesthouse before a workman there told him about the three friends Bulos, Barnaba, and Matta. He, the workman, had been a pupil at the monastery himself at the time, and for a while he belonged to the secret society calling itself the Syrian Brothers that Bulos had founded. He also knew about the hostility that had suddenly sprung up between Bulos and the aforesaid Barnaba, and how after that Matta went crazy.

Barudi packed his case and went home. He had three names on his list: Bulos (Said) Bustani, Barnaba (Farid) Mushtak, and Matta (Matta) Blota.

He was delighted. At last he was tying up the loose ends. So it was all to do with a blood feud. One of the couple, either Matta or Farid, must be the murderer, he told himself on the way back to Damascus. But which? Next day he went to Mala, where he heard from a loquacious barber that Matta was in fact a half-brother of Farid Mushtak. "His father Elias Mushtak made Matta's mother Nasibe pregnant, and a poor shepherd married her, but he never would accept her firstborn son, he always just called him 'Mushtak's filth.'"

With that the investigation came full circle. Barudi spent a night writing the case up in his room, putting everything in order, rephrasing sentences. He knew his boss would immediately refuse to reopen the case if the least little thing didn't add up.

He slept uneasily. When he woke, he washed and shaved with great care. He was expecting difficulties, although he didn't anticipate the problems that were actually ahead of him.

303. An Undignified Departure

Barudi had been expecting almost anything when he entered the CID building, but not the new notice on his own office door. It said Commissioner Mahmud Sultani. Barudi stopped just for a moment, and then went on. He knew that his boss set great store by the formalities, and would sulk like an injured child if you didn't come straight to see him on your return from vacation and shake his hand deferentially. He knocked on the secretary's door. Mrs. Sukari gave him a pale smile, returned his "Good morning", and appeared to be very busy. "You can go in to the boss," she said. "He's expecting you."

"Ah, so here's our Sherlock Holmes," Colonel Kuga greeted him venomously, shaking his head as Barudi came in. He offered a limp hand, and pointed to an old chair in front of his desk. Barudi sat down and placed his report on the desk.

"You ought to be glad Adjutant Mansur has a kind heart and doesn't tell tales," Kuga began his speech. "Who do you think you are, First Lieutenant Barudi? I myself was keen to find out the truth as a young officer, but I never went behind my boss's back. Do you know what will happen to you if I hand the papers that you secretly collected over to Colonel Badran? Well, do you? Do you know that Mansur could have claimed a reward if he'd passed on all the stuff you spied out to Badran instead of me? Mansur found it in a folder underneath your desk. If you're going to make yourself out incorruptible, then please don't be sloppy about it. All that folder shows is that you're useless as a criminal investigator. It's only out of friendship for your former boss Colonel Kalagi that I am now going to destroy the folder before your eyes, and then forget that you ever put the documents in it together behind my back."

The colonel rose, went to a safe, and took out Barudi's folder. He pressed the button of some new-fangled machine and threw the folder in it. A noise like the sound of an electric mill grinding was heard, and then thin snippets of paper no more than a millimetre wide fell out. Barudi could barely keep back his tears. All his work was destroyed.

"Your transfer to the Jordanian border came through yesterday," said Colonel Kuga finally, in a rather calmer voice. "You're to start in charge of the little border checkpoint there in three days' time. It's a quiet posting," he said, offering his hand in goodbye, as if to express the fact that he wanted no more talk about it.

Barudi dragged himself out. His feet were heavy. As he closed the door quietly behind him and went into the secretary's office, Mrs. Sukari briefly looked up. "Your personal possessions are in a carton in your old office," she said dryly, and went on noisily typing.

He didn't take a deep breath until he was out in the corridor. This was the worst day of his life. He had been betrayed by Mansur's intrigues and fired from his job – downgraded to the border police.

Barudi opened the door of his former office. A portly young commissioner sat there playing cards with Mansur, who pretended to be sympathetic, but Barudi couldn't help seeing his triumphant smile.

"You didn't find my folder just by chance, you took it from its hiding place and gave me away," he growled, feeling that he could sink no lower now.

"Your turn," Mansur told the young commissioner at the table. The commissioner put down the jack of hearts.

Barudi took the carton containing his comb, the two ties he kept in the office for urgent official occasions, his nameplate, which he had had made of walnut wood, and a few journals and textbooks that he used to keep in his desk drawers. Then he left without saying goodbye.

A small hope died in a distant corner of his heart.

BOOK OF COLOUR

The loveliest of all colours is the secret colour of words.

ॐ

304. The Last Piece in the Mosaic

In 1962 a young Muslim woman was murdered before my eyes and those of all our neighbours, because she had crossed the religious divide and loved a Christian man. The sad thing was that the man wasn't worth it. He was a gigolo.

I thought at the time, as a sixteen-year-old who saw the world as a never-ending chain of stories, that someone ought to write a novel about all the varieties of forbidden love to be found in Arabia, and I longed to do just that with all the naivety of a lover. But my armoury of narrative tools was not well enough developed yet for me to turn such an idea into a story. I made my first attempts from 1965 to 1967. They failed miserably.

In the years that followed, I completed my university studies of chemistry, physics and mathematics. But censorship and political dictatorship showed me that my plans to live in Syria as a teacher and writer were not going to work out. A despotic regime leaves no room for any in-between shades; those who are not for it are against it.

I felt close to suffocation when I left my family and my city of Damascus at the end of 1970. I had written off to several foreign universities applying for a further course of study there, and they still had not replied. But now that my university studies in Damascus were over, and my postponement of military service had thus run out, the authorities could draft me into the army any day. I had to get out of Syria fast and hope to be accepted by a university in another country.

I went to Beirut, where I had friends and relations, which was lucky for me. Three days later my draft card arrived. If I had stayed in Damascus I would have had to report to one of the assembly centres for recruits within forty-eight hours. My name would have been given to all the border posts, and legal emigration would have been impossible. When it comes to subjugating human beings, the most dilatory of Third World bureaucrats are transformed into fast-moving and highly effective servants of the state. I would not have survived my three years of military service.

At the time Beirut was teeming with political groups from all the Arab countries, which made that beautiful city on the Mediterranean a base for the overthrow of their terrible regimes, not infrequently with financial backing from another and yet worse regime. Consequently, the city was also a happy hunting ground for all the secret services in the world. Persecution mania was more infectious than the common cold. Anyone who hoped to survive in that jungle must be constantly on his guard and avoid all unnecessary contacts. Every day I read news in the paper of Arabs in exile who had disappeared or had been abducted or murdered.

I had to wait three months before hearing that Heidelberg University would accept me. During that time I lived very quietly and inconspicuously in Beirut with my friend Samir, a fellow pupil at our elite Catholic school in Damascus from the first year to our final exams. His apartment was large and well furnished. I began on my novel again, but once more I failed. Beirut was full of unrest; the harbingers of the civil war were knocking at the city gates with bloodstained hands. Suddenly my story turned into a sentimental civil war romance, with a happy ending in which society was liberated.

My host, Samir, was from a prosperous Christian family of goldsmiths. After his school studies he had gone to Beirut to build up a business of his own there. He had bought a large apartment for himself and the wife his father had chosen for him, a rich jeweller's daughter. But a month before the wedding day the bride eloped with a young doctor. Samir was not upset. He hadn't been in love with his fiancée anyway, he simply meant to marry her. At the time he was in love with a young prostitute and visited her almost every night. Then, a year later, he married a wife chosen by his mother, and this time it worked. But by then I was in Germany.

When I arrived in Beirut, Samir was busy transferring his business as inconspicuously as possible to the USA, because he suspected that there would soon be civil war in the Middle East. There was a sum of over a million dollars to be moved, and he wanted to get it past the excise and revenue authorities as elegantly as possible. In two years, he succeeded. The civil war broke out after another two years.

So Samir was more than busy with transferring his money, conducting his daily business and visiting his girlfriend. I saw him every day, but there was no time for more than a coffee or a brief chat. I had seldom known such intense peace in my life. I was free all day, I lived with my fictional characters, I enjoyed the quiet life by the sea, yet I longed to emigrate. I had nightmares in which I was abducted and taken to a Damascus barracks. Captivity is never worse than when you must suffer it after learning to breathe the air of freedom.

But at last my acceptance from Heidelberg arrived, and a week later I had my visa. Just before I flew out my parents came to say goodbye to me. They stayed with my uncle Elias, my father's youngest brother, and we spent some emotional days together.

My father liked talking to his brother, whom he seldom saw, although he was very fond of him. They played backgammon or visited mutual friends. I invited my mother out for coffee on the beach or in town, and we walked for hours. One morning we were sitting in a café down by the harbour. It was stormy out at sea, with waves breaking against the harbour wall, tossing and roaring. Their foam was blown inland and sprayed the windows of the café where we sat safely in the warm, enjoying our mocha spiced with stories. I thought briefly that if we were in a film now, Anthony Quinn would surely come in, just the way he walks into the steamed-up café in

Zorba the Greek. However, this was real life, and all kinds of people came through the door, but no Anthony Quinn.

"You like stories," said my mother, looking out at the gulls struggling against the stormy wind. I nodded.

So she began on hers. "No one would believe a woman could be so strong." She knew Farid's family only slightly, although they lived not far from our house. But in their inner courtyards and hammams all the women of the quarter were whispering about the elopement of the lovers Rana and Farid, and Rana's revenge when she sold the entire contents of her and her husband's apartment to a second-hand dealer. The core of my mother's story was clear, but there were gaps in the tale before that act of revenge. It drew its narrative power from the fascinating subject of a woman who had dared to play the part of a cactus, survive the desert, and then blossom. In Arabic the word for "patience" suggests courage and endurance rather than toleration. *Sabr* means both "patience" and "cactus".

My mother described every moment as meticulously as a detective reconstructing a case from clues. But no CID officer in the world could have given such an exact idea of the look on the husband's face when he came back to his apartment to find it cleared right out. My mother described it with as much relish as if the revenge had been her own. She laughed till the tears came at the thought of the army officer going to the door of his apartment again, just to make sure he was in the right one, and then, still unable to work it out, seeing the torn wedding photograph on the floor.

She talked for over three hours. And before I went to sleep that night, I filled a small notebook with the plot of a story. I was wondering what course it must take to reach its end, the elopement that was recorded fact. Around three in the morning I had it all down, and I was absolutely sure that this was just the story I was looking for. I swore that as soon as I had reached Germany, unpacked my case, and put the contents away, I would begin writing my novel. But that was the plan of a naïve young man who had never lived in exile before. I had read a number of books on the subject, but you can't learn life in exile like mathematics. It is always an individual's story, and as unique as the exile's own fingerprints.

It was not until the early 1980s, one rainy April evening in Heidelberg, that I picked up that little notebook again and read through the
sketch of my novel. The idea of a story about forbidden love that had
come to me when I was sixteen lived on inside it like the pupa in its
cocoon, neither a caterpillar nor a butterfly.

I badly needed information about the two feuding clans. As I
couldn't go to Damascus myself, Salim Blota, a distant cousin from
Mala, did some thorough research on the background of the story
for me. After a year he sent me a thick book of notes. Much of the
information in it couldn't be used in my novel, but it also contained
a treasure: three detailed family trees, of the Mushtaks, the Shahins,
and the Sururs, Farid's family on his mother's side.

I guessed now that the novel would take time as well as peace and
quiet, and I began thinking of it as a secret project. I spent about
four years writing the first draft. I finished that version in the autumn
of 1986. But the story contained too much about the Crusades, and
featured a deranged narrator who was seven hundred years old and
couldn't die until he reached the end of his story. However, the story
never did end, but always went back to the beginning again. Only
traces of that narrator remain in the present version, in the person of
the eccentric and loquacious seaman Gibran.

After a tour in autumn 1987, during which I told variants of the
story and read extracts from it in over seventy towns and cities, I still
wasn't ready to offer the novel for publication, although it had gone
down well with my audiences. It wasn't quite right yet. Something was
troubling me, but what? It was some time before I pinpointed the difficulty. In short, although I had studied Arab society closely, I still wasn't
well enough informed about the way power functions in Arab clans,
and still less did I understand how strong its supremacy is. I discovered that I had read mountains of politically motivated simplifications
of history, which whether well-intentioned or not ultimately offered
misinformation. Again and again I had been led astray by colonial-
ist ideas of us, assuming that they were fact. So I had to go back and
cleanse my brain by making a thorough study of the origins of Arab
society. It was my good fortune that from the mid-1960s such studies
and a number of bold critical analyses had been written, and more

were always being published, usually outside the field of university research. Let me mention five authors here as representative of many: Nawal Sa'dawi, who has written on the role of Arab women; Hussein Muruwa and Mehdi Amel (both of Lebanon); Hadi al Alawi (Iraq), who undertook a critical examination of the independent contribution of the Arabs to civilization; and Sadel Jalal al Azm (Syria), who has written soundly based criticism of contemporary Arab society.

Although most of my characters are Christians, like myself, our culture is Arabic and Islamic. An understanding of that fact in all its aspects is essential for the credibility of my story, above all for the way in which the characters naturally act. A faithful portrait cannot be painted in the dark.

I also realized that I still had not found the right voice for the narrator. On my reading tour in 1987 it had struck me that in view of the thorny subject of "love and death", the voice I had chosen was much too naïve and light. A naïve voice, smoothing everything over by cheerfully omitting the painful passages, was not what I needed.

I am no friend of what is called the political novel, but a character cannot live under one of the worst of Middle Eastern despotisms and be entirely untouched by it, which in this context would mean telling a story as if no abductions or wars ever happened, and there were no prison camps in which human beings are degraded. I wanted to tell a story of love in difficult circumstances. In the novel, politics and real history serve as the stage setting and props for a novel about forbidden love in the conditions prevalent in Damascus. As far as the props are concerned, I have taken the liberty of turning towns and villages upside down, lengthening streets and converting houses. Dictators interest me as a universal manifestation, and I introduce its Arab variant here in fictional terms. Similarities with living dictators were unavoidable, but they are of secondary importance. What mattered to me was to show how dictators interfere with the life of the individual. And as I am not describing reality but telling a fictional story, I have allowed myself to extend or curtail the lives of dictators as the story required.

Several experiments with a different narrative voice failed. I soon found myself preaching and moralizing, since the plot of the novel led me into taking sides with the weak and oppressed. My search for the right voice was to take me a whole decade. It is odd, but I never had this difficulty in my earlier books.

The blue folder containing the chapters I had already written, with the plan of the book, was on the bookshelf in front of me. I wanted to see it every morning, so that I wouldn't forget how important this love story was to me. I looked at it for years.

Before I came to Germany I had not known that in exile you think of your own city every morning. For over thirty-four years, whenever I open my eyes I have thought of Damascus, the most beautiful city in the world, and since 1987 I have also thought every day of the love story I wanted to write.

I looked for ways to solve my problems, and researched details for every chapter. This research was so productive, thanks to help from many people, that I soon had a small library devoted entirely to the novel: about two hundred books, and a large archive containing photocopies of old texts and photographs of people, streets, houses, clothes and places, maps, and city plans of Damascus over the years. I gave this part of my library the title "Forbidden Love".

In 1991 I offered a summary and two samples from the completed "Book of Loneliness I" (the monastery section: Ch. 114, *The Journey*, and Ch. 121, *Joan of Arc*) to the German Literary Fund, and was granted a stipend for April 1992 to March 1993. I was and am grateful. These samples have gone into the novel without major alterations.

But many more versions failed before I hit upon the final form of the story, which also determined its narrative voice. Some of those versions cost me only time, others were interesting experiences.

On 14 August 1995 I had a dream that influenced me a great deal. If you are to understand it, I must explain that I spent three summers in Damascus learning calligraphy from an old master of that art. This master also had another passion: he was an artist in mosaic, and created large works for mosques and rich Arabs. He collected brightly coloured leftover pieces of tiles from marble and tile factories, broke them up into tiny parts with incredible patience, and finally sorted them into different bowls by colour and veining. He had about a hundred such bowls containing all shades of colour.

He began by designing every mosaic in pencil on paper, and then laid out his picture on the sheet of paper with the mosaic pieces. With each piece, colour and life came into the pattern he had drawn. I was not allowed to touch anything, only watch. He did not glue the piece into place, as was usual at the time; that would have fixed the form of the mosaic far too soon for his liking. When the picture was complete it was time for tiny corrections, and he worked on them for weeks and months. To avoid any danger of disturbing them, he wrote a serial number on the underside of each piece. Number one was the first piece at the top right of the design, and from there on he filled in the picture, piece by piece and row by row, until the last one was placed at the bottom left-hand corner.

The structure of my novel resembled this process more than anything else. In my dream, my master was the spectator, and I was the mosaic artist.

"But I see only writing on the pieces," he said, a little bewildered. "Where are the colours?"

"Each of these pieces tells a story, and when you have read them they show you their own secret colours. And as soon as you have read all the stories you will see the picture," I replied proudly, and woke up with a happy laugh

Mosaic is the form for a story like this, I thought, a story with a thousand and one pieces in it, doing justice to life in Arabia with all its flaws. And like a mosaic, the further from the observer the picture appears, the smoother and more harmonious it will be.

I began setting out the stories, piece by piece, and as I was telling the first story I suddenly had my narrative voice. After that my work on the novel was not a problem any more, and called only for time.

In all these years I have been able to publish separate stories from the periphery of the book, so long as they did not give away the main action of the novel. "The Colour of Words" is the title of a volume in which Root Leeb painted watercolours illustrating a selection from my works. Some of the texts included there are Ch. 96, *The Scooter*, Ch. 104, *Grandfather's Glasses*, and Ch. 113, *Grandfather's Salt*, in the "Book of Laughter I".

In the long gestation of this novel, I have had support from many people. They helped me in a number of different ways with the extensive work that had to be done. They provided me with materials, banned reports and tapes from inside prisons, they smuggled books and interviews out of Syria, they got access to archives for me, gave me detailed information about the army, history, religions, language, the work of the secret service, and psychiatry.

They and I sometimes faced unfortunate reversals of fortune. One incident will serve to illustrate those setbacks. Early in the 1990s I had commissioned a good friend to go to the archives of a certain Arab journal and copy me its issues of the fifties and sixties. I needed exact pictures of the everyday life of that period. At the time this was the only way to do such research, since the Internet in its present form was not yet up and running.

I paid a lot of money, and was put off with promises for four years. But at last, one cold February evening in 1996, I went to Frankfurt airport to collect three large cartons – and discovered on opening them that instead of the archive copies, I had been sent the waste from a printing press, all completely worthless, even including oil-stained paper that had been used to clean the presses. Today I can laugh about it, since by tortuous ways I did at last get access to the extensive archives of a journal, but that night I was close to exploding with rage.

Despite such setbacks, I may say now that during my life I have been fortunate enough to meet many people who gave me selfless support. Without their help this novel would have been impossible. If I were to mention them all I would need a long appendix, and individuals would be lost in the proliferation of names. So I will forbear to enumerate them, but I salute them all gratefully for the support they gave me. I hope very much that I have made the best I could out of the information they provided.

One more thing: the event that shook me so much in 1962 and acted as catalyst to my story for so many years dwindled as the novel took shape more clearly. In the present version the story occupies only a single page, Ch. 13, *Scruples*, in the "Book of Love II".

ᴈᴑ

And now I write the sentence towards which I have been working for decades.

This is the last piece in the mosaic of my story. It is at the bottom left-hand corner of the design, and is numbered 304.

So now I am going to go and drink an espresso in celebration of the day. From tomorrow, I will think only of Damascus when I wake up in the morning.

Rafik Schami